THE EMPYREAN AGE

THE EMPYREAN AGE

TONY
GONZALES

A TOM DOHERTY ASSOCIATES BOOK
NEW YORK

This is a work of fiction. All of the characters, organizations, and events portrayed in this novel are either products of the author's imagination or are used fictitiously.

EVE: THE EMPYREAN AGE

Originally published in Great Britain in 2008 by Gollancz, an imprint of the Orion Publishing Group.

A Tor Book
Published by Tom Doherty Associates, LLC
175 Fifth Avenue
New York, NY 10010

Tor® is a registered trademark of Tom Doherty Associates, LLC.

ISBN-13: 978-1-61523-480-6

Printed in the United States of America

For CCP
May you always create and inspire

ACKNOWLEDGMENTS

Without knowing the personal experiences of other authors, all I can say is that writing a novel—at least on your first try—is a long journey, and ultimately the end result of a collaborative effort involving many people who helped me to stay on the path.

Before I begin thanking those who have helped me directly, let me first say that I can take no credit whatsoever for the deep, immersive background history for *EVE*. That achievement belongs to an immensely creative gentleman named Keli Óskarsson, and the original band of CCP founders who made the dream of EVE Online come alive. Many of their names are listed below, and if there are any that I missed, know that this work is as much to their credit as it is my own. Anything that I've accomplished with this book is because I've stood squarely on their shoulders and contributed to a vision that was their creation first.

So with several very dear exceptions that I've saved for last, the following is an attempt to thank those who have helped me, in the approximate order in which this very unusual journey took place for me.

To Torfi Ólafsson, the gateway through which my connection to the entire nation of Iceland and CCP was made possible, I'll be in your debt forever; to Börkur Eiríksson, your paintings bring to life what no words can describe; to Hilmar Pétursson, you may be an engineer by training, but you were born a natural leader; to Jon Hallur, your music was with me on every page I wrote; to Nathan Richardsson, I will never forget our walk back from Loftkastalinn, when you told me the news that would change my life forever; to Greg Kruk, my good friend, we followed our bliss all the way to Iceland, and your creative vision has inspired me and thousands of others; to Jói Jónsson, may every other graphic designer on planet Earth learn from your example; to Tom Edwards, you have such a gentle soul, you've only just started to spread your wings, and like Torfi, I owe you a debt I can never repay; to Dan Speed, your intellect and your honesty are invaluable to me; to Noah Ward, your creative talents and leadership will guide *EVE* to heights that no other MMO can reach; to Helgi Mar, you are the most reliable man I've ever met; to Lisa Wagnes, your patience and guidance carried me through a world of doubt; to Mike Wagnes, you encouraged me to take a risk, and for the second time, I listened.

Special thanks are in order for Orion Books, especially Malcolm Edwards, Simon Spanton, and Gillian Redfearn, who not only gave an unpublished author a chance, but did so with endless optimism and grace.

Super special thanks go to Matt Woodward, Hjalti Daníelsson, Ian "Ginger" Bishop, Kristján Blöndal, Willem van Biljon, Svanur Björnsson, the Mercury vols, the EVE Game Design Team, and the marketing crew for making this story come to life in the EVE Online universe.

This book is for all of CCP, but I have special memories from writing it that include all of you for playing a role in making this happen: Charles D., Reynir H., Ívar K., Elísabet and Jonas, Hófí, Anna Katrin, Lilja, Beta and Jon, Kári, Vincent B., Kristinn S., Mark H., Ari E., Rabbi, Ingo, Villi, Magnus B., Moussa, Carl, Colin, Chantal, Matti and Maria, Pete T., Pétur O., Arend, Unnar, Kjartan E., Ívar E., Húni, Anna Rut, Pat, Stuart, Gauti, Lína, Ben B., Ásgeir, James

W., Mike R., Valery M., Arnar V., Dave D., Thor G., Ryan D., Tobias N., Winterblink, Urban Mongral, MMM Publishing, and the EVE TV Crew.

To the wonderful fans of EVE Online, the wind beneath our wings all this time, and especially to GrumpE and Infantry Blue, who helped me find my way through this amazing virtual universe.

To the best damn friends in the world, where would I be without you: Brian Keating, Keith and Laura Williamson, Mark and Natalia Williamson, Will and Amy Doll, Ron Scotto, and Ken Caffrey.

To the real *Retford* crew, may this book be sufficient evidence that I am not, in fact, in the witness protection program: Dan and Patti Moroses, Joe and Chrissa Stulpin, Billy and Michelle Mack, Dino DiFabio, and Diana Short.

To Alainna, Alissa, Joe and Denise, Lou and Sue, Joe Jr., Billy, and Michele Malone, for making me feel like I was part of the family.

To Cathy and George Malone, for your generosity, guidance, and precious friendship.

To Mom and Dad, for your timeless support, encouragement, and optimism for everything that I pursue in life, I love you both.

And last, but most precious of all, to my beloved wife, Andrea, who has put up with my anxieties and stress, trials and tribulations, car crashes, editing requests, and bouts of giddy lunacy with the patience of a saint for the past five years. From the bottom of my heart, thank you.

PART I

The Birth of Legends

I

The first experience of life was a bright point of light followed by the sound of distant, muted whispers. A flood of sensory information registered self-awareness, when just before there was only a sea of blackness. A new mind took inventory of the world surrounding him: his chest, rising and falling with the sensation of air rushing into his lungs; the taste of saliva and the contraction of throat muscles as he swallowed; hands that opened and closed into fists as he commanded; all virgin experiences, so it seemed, for a man who was just born inside a coffin.

Lying supine, he blinked several times, struggling to make sense of his narrow confines. A glass shield was just inches from his face, where he gazed with frustrating uncertainty upon a reflection that was his own. An older man, with creases stretched across a high forehead and steel-gray eyes set upon severe cheekbones, returned the bewildered stare.

Who am I? this lost soul asked, struggling to reach backward in time for a memory or reference, anything to place this surreal state of being into context. But there was nothing there, and the sea of blackness prevailed.

As he tried to lift his shoulders, a medical device

descended from inside the chamber and passed a bluish light over the entire length of his body. It was then that he realized the base of his skull was fastened to the bed's surface, and that the connection was through a metallic socket implanted directly into the bone.

I am a capsuleer, he realized, peering through the glass at a ceiling high above. *One of the immortals, but . . . what happened to me?* The devicc hovered over his squinting eyes before an artificial voice spoke softly:

'Good morning. Your vital signs are excellent. Try to relax while I assess the rebuilding progress of your temporal lobe. Scanning . . .'

With the center light focusing on his eyes, additional beams were projected onto his face. Then he felt a tingling sensation in the back of his head.

'I'm going to ask you several questions,' the voice continued. He found her voice soothing, despite its artificial tone. 'Do you know what today's date is?'

'No,' he answered. 'Where am I?'

The voice remained impassive, but gentle. 'Do you know what your name is?'

He was about to answer 'No' in desperation again when a bright flash illuminated the room beyond the glass, followed by a loud muffled *thud* that shook the chamber. He felt his pulse accelerate as his instincts registered danger for the first time.

'Good morning. Your vital signs are excellent,' the automated voice repeated. 'Try to relax while I . . . Good morning. Your vital signs are . . .'

The device hovering above him flickered once, and then retracted back into its lair. He realized that a new face was staring at him through the glass, and that the predatory look in this stranger's eyes was reason enough to be very afraid.

EVE: THE EMPYREAN AGE

With a series of mechanical clicks and hisses, the chamber's lid began to open.

HIDDEN ABOVE THE chamber was a camera lens, one of hundreds located throughout the starship. Optical data was routed directly into a cybernetic implant which, like the man inside the chamber, was embedded within the skull of the ship's pilot. Using onboard processors and the raw computing power of his cerebral cortex, telemetry was converted into ocular images that he could therefore 'see', despite being hundreds of meters away from the chamber itself.

Terrifying events were unfolding before him: an assassin had infiltrated the ship, sealed himself in the cargo bay, activated the CRU (Clone Reanimation Unit) prematurely, and was now moments away from murdering the most important figure in Theology Council history.

The same cybernetic implant feeding data to the pilot's brain made his ship a natural extension of his own physical self. All he needed was to *will* his starship into action, and his biochemical signals were translated into digital instructions that were executed immediately by automated systems or the hundreds of crew members onboard. Because of this union between man and machine, the ship could react as quickly as its pilot could think – but only if he knew how to act. Dealing with onboard saboteurs was a situation that had, until now, been unthinkable.

Opening a command channel through the cruiser's subspace communication arrays, the pilot watched helplessly as the assassin stood over the CRU and began taunting the vulnerable clone of Falek Grange.

'Lord Victor, we have an emergency,' the pilot said.

'Lieutenant Thornsson,' the stern voice replied from dozens of light years away. 'Go ahead.'

'We escaped from Karsoth's forces and survived a Covenant ambush,' the pilot replied. 'But there's an assassin onboard and—'

The pilot lost his concentration as the attacker's clenched, metal-plated fist crashed down upon Falek Grange's face, spraying droplets of blood across the room.

DESPITE THE PHYSICAL appearance of an older man, this incarnation of Falek Grange was less than five minutes old. Every cell in his body was an exact replica of the original man, who by now had been dead for almost forty minutes. Although the brain of this clone contained elemental knowledge artificially distilled from simulated life experiences that an older man *should* have, in this case the core attributes of Falek's original personality and personal memories were absent. A person awakening in this state has knowledge, but lacks the understanding of *why* he knows what he does.

To call this condition 'amnesia' would be inaccurate, for the term implies that there was once a memory to lose. This was far worse. For Falek Grange, there were no memories. Every experience from now on would seem both new and distantly familiar all at once.

But there was nothing familiar about the horrid violence that Falek was enduring now. With each blow, Falek could feel both skin and bone breaking beneath the assailant's mailed fists. Every strike was perfectly placed to inflict maximum pain; just when Falek thought he would lose consciousness, the assassin instructed the CRU to inject him with enough adrenaline to keep him awake. With his head still attached to the neural interface and his hands clamped to the chamber walls, Falek was helpless to defend himself.

When the sparks of pain and numbing disorientation parted for just a moment, he gurgled out a single, pleading question:

'Why . . . ?'

The assassin – a much younger man, with features similar to Falek's – removed his gauntlets, unveiling thick, calloused hands. As if in prayer, he murmured a series of phrases in a foreign language, closing his eyes while speaking.

Then he pressed both his hands into the deep, symmetric lacerations on Falek's eye sockets and jawbone.

'*UNHOLY BEAST!*' THORNSSON raged as he watched Falek scream. 'The assassin is Covenant!'

'You have to seal him inside the CRU,' Victor answered. 'Force it shut if you have to—'

'I can't! He disabled the hatch – my crew can't get inside!'

The assassin raised both blood-soaked hands upward as if to make an offering, and then lowered them to allow droplets of the crimson fluid to fall into his mouth.

'There's nothing they can do at all?' Victor pleaded.

'They're trying everything to break in,' the pilot replied. 'We don't stow any explosives onboard to blast through . . .'

He thought about that for a moment, and then added:

'Unless . . .'

'A PITY THAT you'll never know your crimes,' the assassin said, manipulating the bloody controls of the CRU. 'They are too numerous to mention in the time we have left.'

Falek Grange would have sobbed if he could; his eyes were swollen shut as his body rushed fluids to the trauma sites on his face. But the physical pain was no less excruciating than the mental anguish of not knowing if this cruel fate was deserved.

A shudder wracked his aching body as the locking shunt connecting his implant to the CRU withdrew from his skull.

'My master has passed judgment on you,' the assassin continued, placing one hand over Falek's disfigured face and running it slowly toward his neck. 'It is my devoted honor to serve him.'

Using his free hand, the assassin brandished a small scepter. As Falek felt the grip around his neck tighten, he wished for the nothingness that was before the whispers brought him to life.

'This will purge New Eden of your curse once and for all.'

'YOUR CLONES HAVE been destroyed, as all of ours have,' Victor warned. 'You know what that means!'

'I believe in *her*, my lord,' Thornsson said, swallowing hard as the assassin forcibly yanked Falek upright by his neck and positioned the scepter beneath his head. 'And she believed in *him*.'

With a single thought, Lieutenant Thornsson armed the self-destruct sequence for his ship.

'This is all I can do to save him,' he said, just as the assassin thrust the back of Falek's exposed skull downward. 'Tell her that I did this for her glory . . .'

'She already knows, my friend,' Victor replied.

FALEK HAD LITTLE time to scream as the electrically charged scepter made brief contact with the implant's socket, producing a sickening flash of white and red. As the surrounding tissue vaporized along with metal, the lid of the CRU forcibly closed down, knocking the scepter loose and forcing the assassin to release his choking grip. Falek collapsed, unconscious, onto his back within the chamber as the lid shut completely and formed an airtight seal. The last thing the enraged assassin would ever see was a reinforced blast shield rise from the floor and enclose the CRU, where his prey continued to breathe.

Powered by an aneutronic fusion reactor, the Prophecy-class battle-cruiser piloted by Lieutenant Thornsson relied on magnetic containment fields to regulate the flow of plasma used for propulsion. If these fields collapsed, the plasma would scatter internally and destroy the surrounding structure.

They also served as the primary self-destruct mechanism for the ship.

Lieutenant Thornsson was sacrificing himself and his crew in a desperate attempt to save the life of Falek Grange. Normally occurring after a sixty-second countdown, the fail-safes regulating the fields were instructed to switch off earlier, making it impossible for anyone onboard to escape. In the exact instant when the blast shield locked into place over the CRU, the containment fields ceased, and the engine room's plasma began incinerating everything in its path, eating its way back into the fusion reactor within seconds.

Expanding outward in every direction, the resulting explosion tore the ship in two, obliterating the decks leading up to the forward superstructure. Fragments of superheated debris travelling at immense speeds perforated every remaining section of the ship. For the crew closest to the engine room at the time of the blast, death came as quickly as a thought. For those in the forward compartments, there may have been just enough time to grasp the severity of what was happening, but not much more.

For Falek Grange, the experience was the same as the blackness from which he had emerged. Protected by the blast shield, the CRU continued to function, keeping him alive for the time being. Suspended inside the chamber, he floated among the ruins of a shattered starship, unwillingly clinging to an existence whose single memory was of being tortured and beaten to within an inch of his life.

2

Delve Region – 05K-Y6 Constellation
System 1B-VKF

'How many times does that kid have to screw up,' Vince started, holding the two charred electrical couplings up for emphasis, 'before you realize he just can't handle this yet?'

Téa remained defiant. 'You ever think that the problem is how you're teaching him? He's a lot smarter than you give him credit for.'

Vince gritted his teeth. 'Look, I'm serious here, someone is going to get hurt if this keeps up—'

A blaring intercom interrupted the two squabbling siblings. 'Did you find the problem?'

'A capacitor rig was installed wrong, courtesy of the boy genius,' Vince answered. 'I have to replace a bunch of cable, and we're out of spare caps.'

'Oh, that's real big of you, blaming him like that,' Téa protested. 'You're unbelievable sometimes!'

'Téa, enough,' the voice interrupted. 'I need you in front with me. Put the kid on the winch controls before you head up.'

She glared at Vince, fuming.

'You heard the captain,' he said, smirking. 'Go someplace where you can be useful for a change.'

'Vince, forget the cap, just replace cables,' the intercom continued. 'Get into a survival suit when you're done. A battlecruiser blew up out here, and if there's salvage, we need it. You've got about five minutes.'

'*Yes, sir,*' Vince mocked, setting down on a knee and ripping access panels off the bulkhead. They fell with a crash as he reached for a soldering torch.

Téa stormed past. 'Just one fucking shred of compassion for *once.*'

He lowered a welding mask over his face. 'Don't hate me because I'm right,' he muttered, as sparks showered onto the metal grating.

TÉA WAS ACCUSTOMED to the putrid concoction of odors aboard the *Retford.* The recycled air was ripe with the heavy stench of mildew, sweat, and mechanical lubricants. Flickering lamps illuminated the pipes and bulkhead fittings that snaked along the ceilings as she navigated the ship's narrow corridors, which she could probably manage while blindfolded. Like the rest of the small crew, these metal catacombs had been her home for years, replacing a life in Caldari society that was only slightly worse than this.

'Gear?' she asked, ascending a small ladder.

Scanning the confined galley, she already knew that the boy was here. Apart from the bridge, there were no other rooms with a view outside. This was the only place on the *Retford* where one could find some peace, if just for a short time.

The tip of a tiny shoe was protruding from the galley's single table. Téa squatted to look below. 'Hey,' she said. 'Whatcha' doin' down here?'

Gear sat with his hands clasped around his knees, his hazel eyes full of dejection. Lowering herself beneath the table, she took a seat on the floor beside him.

'Sometimes, learning isn't easy,' she said softly.

The child looked up, gesturing with his hands: *I did it the way he told me to!*

'Oh, I believe you!' she said, her heart wrenching with sympathy. 'Vince is careless at times. He isn't the best teacher . . .'

Gear's hands motioned in a flurry. *He's a big jerk! And he told Captain Jonas about my mistake!*

'Captain Jonas isn't mad at you,' she said, leaning forward to place a gentle hand on his cheek. Her pale skin contrasted sharply with his olive tone. 'In fact, he needs your help with the winch again.'

All I ever do around here is work the winch, Gear motioned. *Vince won't let me do anything else.*

'You'll get your chance,' she said, brushing aside the thick locks of hair from his forehead. 'Everyone does. But you're the best winch operator on the ship – even better than Captain Jonas.'

Gear shrugged. *It's easy, once you get used to it.*

'You know, the captain thinks that a battlecruiser blew up out here . . .'

Really? His eyes lit up. *A battlecruiser?*

'Yes,' she smiled. 'There's only one way to find out for sure!'

The boy scampered out from beneath the table and disappeared down the ladder.

THREE YEARS OF this, Jonas thought. *And I'm no closer to getting rich than when I was planetside.* He rubbed his temples, staring at all the yellow markers in the schematic display before him. Each was an indicator of a component that was either malfunctioning or in danger of ceasing completely. The *Retford* was a sick starship, urgently in need of an overhaul. *But with what money?* Jonas thought, annoyed that it was taking Téa so long to reach the 'bridge', which in this frigate was little more than a cramped room with a forward view and two uncomfortable seats. *This flying shitcan represents my entire net worth, and it's crewed by two goddamn fugitives and a ten-year-old kid who can't talk.* Disgusted, he shut down the schematic and switched to the scanner. A flashing marker indicated the approximate location where the battlecruiser explosion was detected. *At least I have my health,* he thought, just as the door behind him opened. *For now, anyway.*

'What took you so long?' he muttered.

'I was trying to fix the damage that my asshole brother did,' Téa answered, settling into the seat beside him. 'Gear's just a child, for God's sake, and Vince needn't be so hard on him.'

'You're only half right,' Jonas said, powering down the ship's noncritical functions to conserve energy for the warp drives. 'Gear's just a kid, but Vince is the only one fixing damage around here, which happens to be to *my* ship.'

Téa's hands were moving furiously over the controls. 'Your explosion triangulates to a position approximately seven AUs from here,' she said, her face reddening. 'And we can resolve all possible wreckage tracks with ninety-nine percent confidence.'

'Ninety-nine? Are you sure you're doing the math right?'

She sat upright and took a deep breath. 'Jonas, I want to ask that we use the next salvage proceeds to get him the surgery he needs to restore his voice. Now, before you get all angry, let me explain—'

'Téa, what you do with your cut is your own business, but I really don't advise you telling anyone else how to spend theirs.'

'But he has so much potential! Think of how much more he could help us if only he could—'

'He is a liability until he either proves otherwise or I can drop him off someplace where I don't think he'll get killed, period. Now, are these coordinates accurate or not?'

'You men are all just assholes, the whole lot—'

'*Téa!*'

'Yes.' She was on the verge of tears. 'We're at ninety-nine because there's no redshift in the playback.'

'So what does that mean?'

She turned her deep green eyes toward him and glared. There was just enough light inside the bridge to accent the deep scar along her right eye socket.

'It means your prize was sitting perfectly still when it exploded, *Captain*.'

OVER THE COURSE of a typical career, salvaging offered the least favorable risk/reward ratio compared with other space professions. Its sole advantage was that it was the cheapest to maintain, requiring only a functional spacecraft and a cutting winch array, which in the case of the *Retford* cost more than the ship itself. However, insofar as success was concerned, a profitable expedition to retrieve intact items from a starship explosion was the statistical equivalent of predicting when and where lightning will strike.

First, a ship had to be within sensor range to detect the explosion. Next, the speeding fragments had to be located and intercepted without placing the salvager in the direct path of the debris. Then there was the recovery phase, which required cutting into the scrap with the ship's winch crane, or worse, venturing directly inside the wreckage with a survival suit and a cutting laser. And finally, there was the challenge of completing the salvage without being spotted by the 'competition', as Jonas referred to any hostile ship that chanced upon their operation.

All this risk-taking was for the slim chance of recovering something – legal or otherwise – that could be resold. Starships were very expensive commodities, were often used to transport very expensive things, and were attacked and destroyed with enough frequency to make salvaging a viable, if hazardous, profession. Exactly how viable was a matter of pure luck, which Jonas hoped would continue to stay 'good' as the *Retford* cautiously approached the tumbling, charred remnants of a shattered Amarrian battlecruiser.

The wreckage before their eyes was more than double the size of the *Retford;* Téa shuddered as the icy tomb filled the canopy. Great composite alloy beams that once supported thick armor plates, now twisted and ruined, rolled past the view as the *Retford* slowed to a full stop. It was difficult to fathom how this gutted, metal carcass was once a powerful warship; even more unthinkable was the kind of force required to rip it apart.

'Gear, slow that thing down, would you please?' Vince said, depressurizing the airlock as he waited. A greenish-white tractor beam extended from the winch and impacted against the spinning hulk, gradually slowing it down until it was stationary.

'There isn't much left here,' Téa muttered. 'Looks like the forward superstructure of a Prophecy-class variant . . . but those hull breaches were all caused from the inside.'

Jonas maneuvered the *Retford* even closer, expertly nestling the small frigate within the shredded confines of the wreck. The cutting equipment and scanners were now in range. 'Whenever you're ready, Gear.'

From his vantage inside the airlock, Vince could see mechanical arms extend from the winch and probe the mangled hull. A preliminary list of salvageable parts began to scroll across the display in his helmet as Gear worked the controls.

'Pretty shitty pickings for a battlecruiser,' he muttered. 'Where's all the good stuff?'

A warning appeared on the main display. 'Whoa!' Jonas exclaimed. 'Something's still airtight in there. Gear, move that dorsal scanner back a few meters!'

The wire-frame image in front of Jonas panned back. There was a large container embedded in the wreckage. 'Vince, can you get in there?'

'Yeah, but I need a little help . . .'

Before he could finish, Gear was already using the cutting lasers to detach a segment of wreckage big enough for the mysterious container to fit through. Vince checked the fuel gauge on his thruster pack one last time as the mechanical arms peeled away the remnants of hull plating.

'I'm opening the outer doors,' Jonas said. 'It's your show now.'

As the cargo doors slid apart, Vince stepped outside of the airlock into the exposed bay. Before him was the wreckage, surrounded by pitch-black space. Floodlights were trained on the gaping hole cut open by the winch, and immediately Vince could recognize the charred remnants of a single corpse floating inside. *Poor bastard*, he thought. *But better him than me.* The container was still anchored to what had been the floor grating of a compartment onboard the cruiser.

Using the thrusters on his suit, Vince propelled himself across the small chasm separating the edge of the cargo bay from the wreckage. Despite hundreds of space walks, he still experienced a brief moment of disorientation as the

surface beneath him gave way to an eternity of nothingness. Careful to avoid the edges of the makeshift entrance,
Vince pulled himself into the cavity and over the container.
He was drawn to a small transparent pane on its surface
immediately, and drifted closer to see what was inside.

'What the . . . ?' Vince started, pressing his mask right
against it. 'Is that . . . ?'

The reddish-purple form turned and coughed up blood
globules that floated to the underside of the glass. Vince
flinched, sending his cutting laser equipment spiralling
across the compartment.

'Holy *fuck*! There's something alive in here!'

Jonas blinked. 'Are you kidding?'

'No! Hell no, I'm not!'

As the mass stopped moving, the deformed silhouette of
a man's head finally became recognizable. 'Oh, man,' Vince
gasped. 'There is one seriously fucked-up human being inside this thing!'

'Can you cut the container away from its mooring?' Téa
asked.

'No,' Vince said, allowing himself to drift backward
to examine the base of the structure. 'But the winch lasers
can. If Gear makes a good cut, we can fit the entire section
inside.'

'All right, get out of there,' Jonas said. 'Gear, you think
you can handle this?'

Clicking the microphone twice, Gear positioned the
winch across the open cavity while Vince drifted back
across the void to safety. Within minutes, the entire container and a section of the surrounding floor plates were
secured inside the cargo bay. As soon as the outer doors
closed and the area re-pressurized, Jonas and Téa rushed
inside.

'How do you open this thing?' Jonas muttered, running

his hands along the container edges. Gear ran into the bay hauling a bag filled with medical equipment.

'Wait a minute,' Téa said, kneeling alongside the container. 'I've seen these before . . .'

Vince stripped off his helmet. 'For his sake, you'd better open it quick.'

'Lai Dai used to make them,' she said, typing into an instrument panel built into the side of the container. 'It's an automated intensive care unit, typically used near battlefields to treat injured soldiers, but this one's been modified . . .'

Téa stopped in midsentence, and her eyes opened wide in horror.

'What?' Jonas asked.

Nervously, she looked over her shoulder at Gear, 'Sweetheart, stand back a little, okay? You shouldn't see this.'

The boy gave her a disapproving look as Jonas took the first aid equipment from him. Vince understood the cue from his sister. 'You heard her, little man. Outside.'

Gear slinked back into the shadows, toward the cargo bay's exit.

'Thank you,' she said quietly. 'The victim . . . he's definitely Amarrian.'

'How can you tell from looking at *that*,' Vince asked. 'Are you sure?'

'*Yes,*' she breathed. 'If Gear finds out that we have an Amarrian onboard, he'll never forgive me.'

'Well,' Vince replied, looking toward the exit. 'You know that's not going to stay a secret for long, right?'

Jonas became impatient. 'Téa, can you open the thing or—'

Everyone startled as the container clicked and hissed, its lid opening slowly. A naked, older Amarrian male lay inside, and his face was barely recognizable. A pool of blood coated the surface beneath him.

'Fuck,' Vince said, looking away. 'He looks better with the lid closed.'

'Very weak pulse,' Téa said, placing her fingers on the victim's neck. 'Massive head trauma . . . there has to be hemorrhaging inside his skull.'

'There isn't much we can do for him here,' Jonas said, glancing at a console on the bay wall. 'Where's all this blood coming from?'

'The back of his head . . . we have to turn him onto his side to look,' she said, gently placing both hands along the victim's ears. 'Vince, hold right here . . .'

The three adults positioned their hands. 'On three,' Jonas said. 'Keep his head steady now . . . one . . . two . . . *three*!'

3

Delve Region – YX-LYK Constellation
System MJXW-P: The Matriarch Citadel

Her footsteps made no sound as she entered the room; her magnificent visage glided forward silently, as though carried by an invisible force that controlled every movement with unnatural precision and grace. A veiled robe adorned with the royal insignia of House Sarum flowed over tightly fitted garments, concealing the powerful, athletic figure beneath. But Lord Victor Eliade, alone in the private antechamber, could sense the urgency in her presence and gathered his thoughts carefully. It was essential to convey resolute strength and composure during this dark hour.

'Your Majesty,' he said, kneeling before the former Amarr heiress.

'Arise,' she commanded, standing over the much older man and extending her hand. 'Tell me the fate of Lord Falek.'

Victor composed himself and looked upward. As always, her young beauty stunned him momentarily. He took her hand gently and stood, careful to hold her gaze.

'With a very heavy heart, I must report that he is missing,' he started, mentally bracing himself. 'Dozens of his supporters on the Theology Council have disappeared as well.'

'I was told that he was safely aboard one of our ships!' she breathed, her expression changing for the worse. 'How could this happen?'

'The ship you speak of was infiltrated by a Blood Raider assassin,' he said. 'Its pilot, a devoted servant to you, saw the intruder's intentions and self-destructed. He did this knowing there would be no clone for him to awaken in; he sacrificed his own life for the chance to save Lord Falek.'

Jamyl Sarum faltered, taking a step backward, one hand reaching over her heart.

'Your Majesty, we have been compromised,' Victor continued. 'They destroyed our clone banks, and then they ambushed and murdered our fleeing pilots in space. Whoever did this knew *everything:* where to find us, how to kill us, and how to make sure we never rose again!'

Her back was against the wall. 'How is this possible . . . ?'

Victor deliberately pressed the truth even harder. 'Lord Falek's clone was the only specimen to survive the attacks on our facilities, and even then, they knew *exactly* how to find him afterward.'

He could see that she was breathing faster, and just when she was on the verge of speaking again, he delivered the crushing blow:

'I fear that Lord Falek may be dead, Your Majesty.'

'*No,*' she exclaimed forcibly, but not in desperation. With her head bowed, the muscles in her body contracted, forcing her posture upright while her hands rolled into tight fists that hung poised like war clubs. Victor had seen this transformation many times before, and quickly dropped to a knee.

'Falek Grange is alive, Lord Victor,' Jamyl announced, her voice much more authoritative and composed. 'I *know* it.'

'I have faith, my queen.' Victor kept his eyes closed, trying to shut every thought out of his mind. But he knew such was a futile effort.

'You are a practical man; your doubts are understandable,' she said, lifting his chin with an outstretched finger.

Victor allowed himself to behold her. 'Forgive me . . .'

Her expression radiated kindness, and her emerald green eyes seemed to glow. 'Falek trusted you above all others, as I did in him. Now *you*, Lord Victor, will be my captain of captains.'

A powerful rush of inspiration nearly overtook him. He rose slowly to his feet. 'I will give everything that I am to your service, my queen.'

There was absolute authority in her voice. 'You will search the wreckage site where Lieutenant Thornsson self-destructed,' she said, turning away and walking slowly toward the room's window. The system's orange sun was just starting to break the plane of the moon outside. 'The remnants of Lord Falek's CRU will be among the debris.'

It was likely vaporized during the explosion, Victor

thought, damning himself for allowing doubt to enter his mind again.

Her hands clasped firmly behind her back. 'The CRU was stowed and anchored forward, inside a reinforced structure. If any part of that ship survived the explosion intact,' she said, turning around slowly. Her majestic figure occluded the sunlight pouring into the room. 'Then you will find evidence to disprove your faithless assumptions.'

'It will be as you say, my queen,' he said, squinting. 'I shall ready my ship immediately.'

'Faith makes us all stronger, my captain.' She had become a dark silhouette, as rays of blinding light streamed past her. 'Go *now*, Lord Victor, and see for yourself.'

NOBODY NOTICED THAT Gear had slipped back into the cargo bay; the three adults were all too distracted by the horribly disfigured man in their arms. The gruesome sight was too much for him, and he ran from the scene, retching onto the deck as he went. Startled at the interruption, Téa nearly went after him, then thought better of it. She knew the boy's delicate character was already hurt, and that he must have seen that the ethnicity of the victim was Amarrian.

But neither Vince nor Jonas cared where the child had gone. Instead, they were transfixed by the cauterized metallic cavity in the base of the man's skull.

'A capsuleer,' Vince breathed. 'He's a goddamn capsuleer!'

'We can't help him,' Téa blurted, nearly panicking. 'We should just replenish the medical unit with whatever we can and leave him adrift in the wreckage!'

'That's *not* an option,' Jonas said. 'Do what you can to stabilize him, and—'

'No, Jonas, you're not thinking it through,' Vince warned, backing away from the container. Blood was smeared along his hands and forearms, which he was now desperate to clean off. 'He's an *immortal*, okay? Someone is going to come looking for him—'

'Which is exactly why we're going to keep him, Vince,' Jonas said. 'Dead or alive, that "someone" is going to pay a lot of money to get him back, and we *need* that money.'

Téa was turning pale. 'You can't be serious . . . you know how powerful these people are!'

'And yet there's one lying helpless right there in your arms,' Jonas retorted, wiping his hands down with a cloth. 'He doesn't look like he's going to be immortal for much longer, so why don't you be your usual humanitarian self—'

'He's not human!' Vince shouted. 'These freaks don't give a goddamn how many people they kill because they don't fear death! There are no consequences to anything they do! What fucking part of that don't you understand? Other capsuleers will come looking for him, and when they do—'

'Vince, I think you should shut up and do what you're told,' Jonas growled, fingering the sidearm on his waist. 'Here's a little refresher: This is my ship. You can leave whenever you like. But if you stay, you have to do what I tell you to. Got it? And right now, I want you to go to the galley, fix yourself something to drink, and relax.'

'Please,' Téa begged. 'What about Gear? For his sake, you know the boy is terrified of Amarrians, and for good reason!'

Jonas tossed his hands up in exasperation.

'Hey, if you two want to dodge bounty hunters and death squads planetside, you can get off at the next stop. *Have fun!* I mean, *fuck!* Have you two already forgotten why you're here? Is that scar on your face all healed up finally?'

'That's enough, Jonas!' Vince snapped, taking a large stride toward him. He was met with a gun barrel pointed between his eyes. Vince stopped in his tracks, his face as red as a sunset. Téa looked away as tears streamed down her cheek.

'You're so afraid to die,' Jonas snarled. 'But do you call *this* living? That man right there could potentially be worth *millions.* Maybe even a hundred million. You don't get these chances working for state corporations, remember? This is why we got into this business in the first place! That *man* right there is your ticket to a *real* life, a chance to get off this bucket and do whatever the hell you want. And *you*, Téa, are you really looking out for the kid's best interests by passing up on this? Eh? *Look at me!*'

Téa turned to face her captain. 'Goddamn you, Jonas . . .'

'Tell me honestly that you'd pass up on a real shot at the money you need for the kid's surgery.'

'We can accomplish that without resorting to this,' she answered.

Jonas looked as if he was disgusted with her answer. 'I guess I'll have to keep looking out for everyone's best interests here then,' he said, holstering the weapon. 'Now, *we* are going to Lorado Station, where we will get John Doe here some medical attention and, if possible, beg and or steal some spare parts. We're so broke right now that I'm not above doing either. And while I'm doing that, I suggest that the both of you get out and find some "entertainment", because you need it.'

He gave them a furious look. 'Do what you can to keep him alive. Prep his rig for transport and strap yourselves in for hyperspace.'

Jonas stormed out, leaving the two siblings standing there with 'John Doe' lying unconscious inside his tomb.

'I'd kill him if I could fly the ship,' Vince said, trembling as he spoke. 'I swear, I'd break his goddamn neck.'

Téa looked over John Doe, noting that she couldn't feel any pity for him despite his grotesque misfortune. *A cruel, wicked heart beats beneath that chest*, she thought, checking his vital signs one last time before allowing the lid to close. *I've betrayed a child because of this madness.*

'No more killing,' she mumbled. 'For all the good it's done for us.'

4

Delve Region – D5-S0W Constellation
System T-IPZB: Lorado Station

Sometime during the numbing fog of a violent dream, the universe shuddered as the *Retford*'s warp drive shut down. Jonas awoke with a start, spilling the water in his mug between his legs. Instead of cursing as he usually would, he dropped the rest onto the floor and stared, drooling, at the tiny puddles on the grating below as the mug skidded to a halt. It was silly, he knew, to be so fascinated by so simple a thing, and that allowing the spectacle to corrupt his attention for much longer could prove deadly.

'Wake up, shithead,' the intercom blurted. 'Send the ID!'

A warning tone blared throughout the bridge as a sentry gun locked onto the *Retford*. The danger finally registered, snatching him out of the fog.

'Umm . . . Harbor Control, this is the civilian transport *Retford*, IDENT number three—'

Téa hollered at him again through the intercom. 'Electronically, you imbecile! Snap out of it!'

Fighting through the dizzying haze of jump sickness, Jonas fumbled over the bridge panel to broadcast the *Retford*'s electronic ID to the harbor control system of Lorado Station. If the authentication process took too long, the station's defenses would assume the ship was hostile, and open fire with the heavy-caliber sentry guns floating nearby.

A bit of overkill, Jonas thought, relieved to see that his ship was awarded permission to approach the station. *Considering that those guns are designed to punch holes through battleships.*

Blinking a few times to clear his vision, Jonas made some adjustments to the ship's thrusters, easing her toward the docking bay. The station was twenty kilometers ahead, its metallic towers rising from the dark surface of a forbidding asteroid. Abandoned mining structures and equipment littered the surrounding space, trapped in the gravitational tug of the mountain-sized rock and its sister asteroids nearby. An industrial cargo ship was being towed into the hangar bay, with several escort frigates orbiting nearby. All of them were Amarrian.

Business as usual, he thought. *Smugglers hauling everything from drugs to slaves to firearms and everything else you could think of, provided that it was illegal. And speaking of slaves . . .*

He toggled the intercom. 'Téa, the kid has to stay onboard.'

There was a pause. 'You think?'

Jonas ignored the sarcasm. 'How's our patient doing?'

Another pause. 'Oh, he's talking now. He said he'd like for you to go fuck yourself.'

Morale has reached an all-time low around here, Jonas thought.

'Leave him in the bay and stay out of sight. We're docking in two minutes. Vince?'

'What.'

They'll thank me when we're swimming in money. 'Check back in an hour. Not a word about our cargo to anyone, right?'

'Whatever.'

'The girls and booze are on me, but you're on your own if you want to gamble.'

'Fine.'

You're welcome, Jonas thought, turning the intercom off. The bridge view was filled with the station hangar, a massive array of composite alloys designed to withstand the harsh environment of space and the massive bulk of starships. Jonas throttled back the thrusters as towing drones took position on either side of the *Retford*, gently nudging her toward a docking collar. He noted that there were many empty slips in the hangar, and that the local time was around 03:00. *Good*, he thought. *The less people around, the better.*

Located in the Delve Region, Lorado Station was a trading outpost far from the major shipping lanes, and an ideal haven for all travellers of ill repute. Besides the smugglers, there were various criminals, fugitives, and pirates who used the station to conduct the illicit business of their trades. Although the dominant ethnicity in the region was Amarrian, the outpost drew an eclectic mix of races who all shared two things in common: a mandate to stay as far away from Empire authorities as possible, and that someone, somewhere, was willing to pay a hefty sum of money in exchange for their severed head.

Filthy rich or dirt poor, everyone here is running from something, Jonas thought, removing the Gistii-I0 from his holster and locking it in a cabinet. Among other security measures designed to keep Lorado Station a 'civilized business establishment', the station's airlock wouldn't open to allow him inside if he was armed. Vince had already gone through, disappearing in one of the station's shuttles. *Which probably whisked him someplace where he could drink and feel sorry for himself*, he thought, stepping inside.

When the door in front of him slid open, he walked through, feeling very alone without the Gistii at his side. *Death-dealing is an art form*, he mused, approaching a station directory. *People find creative ways to kill each other all the time.*

THE PURIFIER-CLASS BOMBER responded to his thoughts with a series of barrel rolls as it streaked toward the IP6V-X stargate. Despite the radical danger to himself, Victor could barely keep focused on the task at hand. Deep within territory regularly patrolled by the Blood Raider Covenant, he was making his way toward the last position reported by Lieutenant Thornsson. Travelling to the wreckage site so soon after the apparent slaughter of all the men loyal to Falek Grange was tantamount to suicide, for it seemed probable that the assassins would return to rule out the impossibly slim chance that he had somehow survived.

And what if he did survive? he thought, willing his ship to activate the stargate. In an instant, he was transported dozens of light years away. There were no other spacecraft nearby, at least for now. *Such a bittersweet prospect, finding the man whose shadow has been cast over me for so long, and so soon after reaching the pinnacle of glory!*

As the warp drive catapulted the powerful warship to faster-than-light speeds, he cursed himself again, convulsing in the neuro-embryonic containment fluid surrounding him inside the bomber's capsule.

Focus! She can hear my mind, but . . .

Victor concentrated on the starmap, retracing his route across the cosmos. He had already jumped across seven systems, and was literally dozens of light years from the Matriarch Citadel. *When she is close, I can feel her probing my mind, but out here . . .*

He let his mind relax, allowing the subconscious to fly the ship . . .

I wonder if her powers are limited by distance.

As the warp drive shut down and the quantum glow of the lB-VKF stargate emerged into view, the reality dawned on him:

Yet another secret about her that old Falek may have taken to his death.

'GABLE, IT'S ME. Jonas.'

A long, raspy yawn was heard on the audio, and the video was blocked from the other side. 'What do you want now, Joney . . .'

His loins stirred at the sound of her half-asleep voice. 'Something different for a change.'

'It's the middle of the night, and you're not welcome here anymore, remember?'

'I need your help. Please.'

'Ooo, *Captain* Joney-boy needs *my* help? What do you need now, more money? A quick fix? Sorry, the bar's closed, and so are my legs. Have a nice life.'

'Don't hang up,' he pleaded, looking around to make sure no one was nearby. 'I have someone onboard who's seriously hurt. I'm asking you to have a look at him.'

'What happened to Vince?'

'It's not Vince, it's someone we picked up on the last trip. Can you come down here please?'

'Who the hell do you think I am? Send him to sick bay and I'll *consider* looking at him after you pay up some of the money you owe me.'

'Gable, this is serious. I don't trust the medic drones here, and he'll die if he doesn't get help. You're the only one that can help him.'

She exhaled a long sigh. 'If this is more of your bull-shit . . .'

'No bull, Gable. This is the real deal. Dock 7B.'

There was a pause. 'Fine.'

THE SIGHT OF the wreckage made his stomach turn several times, once for each possibility that the dreadful scene implied. Gently, he eased the 2,800 ton warship to within meters of the ravaged hulk. The imagery passing through the lenses of camera drones orbiting outside was almost too surreal to believe.

Somebody was already here!

Unmistakable evidence of cutting equipment was everywhere he looked; shorn metal with perfect edges that no explosion could create were evident along the largest recognizable section of wreckage. Then the camera drones, responding to anxious recognition from Victor, zoomed into the exposed cross-section. The sight of a rectangular cut in the floor grating jolted his soul.

How could Sarum have possibly known that this happened?

'HAVE YOU LOST your fucking mind?' Gable nearly screamed. 'Do you realize what you've done by bringing him here?'

Jonas remained passive. 'Can you help him or not?'

Her short, petite figure was trembling with anger. 'Other capsuleers will come looking for him! Don't you understand that?'

'So what if they do,' he said, his mind drifting toward the last time he shared a bed with her. 'He's probably worth a fortune, you know.'

'You selfish, *stupid* bastard!' Her expression was incredulous, as if she couldn't believe he was capable of such a lethal blunder. 'You have absolutely no idea what you're dealing with, do you?'

'Stop being so dramatic,' he scoffed. 'We picked him up in the middle of nowhere, there weren't any witnesses, and most importantly, no one knows he's here but us. Relax!'

She looked down at the mangled capsuleer, holding a hand to her forehead. 'You've killed us all—'

'Oh, please,' he said, rolling his eyes. 'You know, that surprises me, coming from a tough gal like yourself. I thought doctors were supposed to be pragmatic.'

She shook her head. 'I think we're through here,' she said, hurriedly walking toward the airlock. But Jonas grabbed her arm as she walked past.

'Look,' he said, gripping tightly and staring intently at her. 'There's a man dying over there. A *man*, who bleeds just like you and I do. Capsuleer or not, he's going to die if you don't help him. Now I know you're a capable doc, and I'll overlook the fact that just a few Caldari corporations are willing to pay a lot of money for information on your whereabouts . . .'

Her face turned bright red. 'Fuck you! Let go of me, you—'

Jonas was too strong for her, and just gripped even tighter. 'You know how this works, Gable. I don't like holding your past over you, but in this case, it's worth it. And if I'm right, it'll be worth it for *both* of us. All I ask is that you try – for once in your life – to do the right thing.'

He let go finally, and she stood there glaring at him with bitter contempt.

'I'm going to do this,' she said. 'But not because of anything you've said or threatened me with.'

'Oh yeah?' Jonas said, crossing his arms.

Gable pressed a button on the console, and a slab detached from the open chamber and pulled away. It hovered one meter above the floor, with the battered capsuleer lying unconscious on top.

She started pushing the stretcher toward the airlock. 'I'll do it in the hope that whoever comes for him considers my efforts to save his life before killing me.'

THE PURIFIER WAS more than 100 kilometers from the wreckage and cloaked, completely invisible to the squadron of Blood Raider interceptors that had just arrived. Victor watched as the ships inspected the wreckage, much the same as he had just a few minutes ago, and then as they disappeared into hyperspace. They had undoubtedly reached the same conclusion that he did:

That the question of Falek Grange's survival still cannot be answered, and the race was on to find him.

'Did they see you?' Jamyl asked.

'No, Your Majesty,' he said. 'But they saw the wreckage.'

'Falek left instructions for his Council allies in the event of his demise . . . a plan he called *Revelations*.'

'I know it well,' he said.

'The survivors who knew of that plan are en route to their destinations now,' she said. 'Whoever took him is *not* a capsuleer, and likely brought him someplace close to where you are.'

It was pointless to try and hide his thoughts from her, and so he asked plainly. 'My queen, you can see into the minds of anyone you choose, and Falek was your champion . . .'

'He is no longer the man that he was, Lord Victor,' she answered sharply, sending a nervous pang through Victor's stomach. 'He is now a stranger to me, and to himself.'

Victor remembered what Thornsson had told him, that Falek's clone was activated before his saved persona could be restored.

So there must be boundaries, he thought. *Limits to what she can see and hear –*

'Don't *test* me, Victor,' she growled. 'Position yourself within proximity of the outposts nearby. The Blood Raiders will find him for us, and you must be ready to act swiftly when they do.'

Victor was astonished. *She is truly divine.*

'As you wish, my queen.'

5

Jamyl Sarum and two of her servants walked quietly along the corridor circling the cathedral tower, a vast crystalline structure with tall windows that revealed a breathtaking view of the Great Baromir Nebula. A million stars and countless worlds coalesced in that swirling dust cloud thousands of light years across, hopelessly beyond the reach of the civilizations in New Eden. The human race, orphaned here since the cataclysmic collapse of the EVE gate tens of millennia earlier, had little more than 5,000 stars to claim as home. For all its presumed power and technological prowess, much of the universe still remained an inaccessible mystery to humanity.

A tragic constant throughout the ages, the greatest enemy of humanity was *always* humanity. The passage of time and the wonders of space exploration did little to cool the glowing embers within the soul of man, which were always ready to flare into a searing, destructive heat with the slightest provocation. Trillions of people called the systems of New Eden home, and their diversity necessitated the creation of borders that often crashed against each other with devastating result. Equilibrium between the four dominant races was a noble concept practical in theory and little else, as political boundaries proved only as strong as the will of those consigned to protect them. The only balance that ever existed in New Eden's history was the constant struggle between two factions among man: those who crave absolute power, and those determined to resist oppression no matter what the cost.

The Amarr Empire is the oldest and largest civilization in the recorded history since the collapse of EVE. The first to rediscover warp technology, they expanded their empire as far and as fast as their starships would allow, subjugating the inhabitants of dozens of worlds during their conquests. Interpreting their success as undisputed proof of God's alliance with their race and cause, the Amarrian religion spread with a fervor that proved more powerful than their weapons – if you happen to be born a 'True Amarr.' As for the rest of mankind, the appearance of gold-tinted warships descending from the skies was condemnation to either death, or a lifetime of servitude to Amarrian masters.

A pureblood descendant from one of five ancient royal families, the Amarr emperor is the most powerful ruler in all of New Eden. In recent history, the most notable was Emperor Heideran, whose reign lasted for more than

500 years. Kept alive with the aid of cybernetic implants throughout the centuries, it was during Heideran's rule that the rest of New Eden finally caught up with Amarr's technology and began to push back against the borders imposed on them. The definitive end to the Empire's expansion was the infamous 'Battle of Vak'Atioth', named after the system where Jovian forces decimated the Imperial Navy, thus opening the floodgates for a mass rebellion among Amarr's vast slave population, and ultimately leading to the creation of the Minmatar Republic.

Heideran's death years later created a power vacuum at a time when Amarr appeared more vulnerable than ever before. Tradition demanded that the new emperor be decided by Succession Trials, an elaborate ritual in which the best ship captains representing each of the five Royal Houses competed against each other in ship-to-ship combat. In the Amarrian religion, the emperor's ascendancy to power is the will of God, and thus the winning champion was a divine endorsement of the throne for the heir that he or she represented. The remaining, defeated heirs were required, by holy edict, to commit suicide – an honorable fate, and a sanctioned journey to the blessed afterlife that awaited all those who died in service to God.

But these trials would be the first in which the gladiators – and the heirs they represented – were capsuleers. At no other time in history did such a powerful caste rise to prominence so quickly, and their potential to tip the balance of power among the nation states of New Eden was imminent. Nowhere was this more evident than their participation in the ancient traditions, none of which had accounted for the entrance of immortals to the realm of the living politic. Jamyl Sarum, along with the other heirs, were trained capsuleers. And when the champion representing the Doriam Kor-Azor won the Succession Trials to determine who would be crowned next, the heirs *all* followed through with the suicide ritual before a broadcast audience of trillions.

Self-destructing their ships one by one, the grim site of the heir's corpses floating in space was evidence enough of their devoted compliance with tradition. But when the battleship commanded by Jamyl Sarum exploded, there was no corpse to be found. Only its shattered hulk remained, leaving many to wonder if they had witnessed a miracle, or if she had defiled the holiest of rituals by allowing herself to be cloned. That day was more than four years ago, and New Eden had changed a great deal since.

'Faith reveals all the mysteries of the universe,' Jamyl said aloud, stopping abruptly to gaze at the great nebula. The two Ammatar servants following in her wake paused, bowing their cloaked heads in approval.

'I know who is responsible for the murder of my followers . . .'

The servants hoped that she wasn't speaking to them.

'When the Council session convened, the conspirators sat before them, concealing their true intent . . .'

Sensing danger, the servants cautiously backed away from her, never once daring to raise their heads.

'They waited, like animals, for Lord Falek and his followers to board their ships and depart . . .'

Her slender hands rolled into tight fists, and she kept her gaze fixed on the view outside.

'Betrayed by Amarr's own priests, ambushed in space by Amarr's own admirals, sabotaged by Amarr's own scientists, murdered in clone stasis by Amarr's own . . .'

She turned toward the two bowed, cowering servants.

'. . . assassins? Or shall I say, traitors?'

One of the servants began to shiver.

'Perhaps we have an infidel among us,' she said, slowly approaching them. 'Who could know all these secrets? Coordinate so precisely with Falek's enemies, conspire with the unholy Covenant, and kill members of the Council out in the open?'

Looking down at the servants, she placed a hand on each of their heads and slowly, almost sensuously, ran them down the sides of their faces toward the small of their necks. 'Who among mortal men wields such power?'

The two remained silent, making every effort not to make a sound.

Jamyl closed her eyes.

'You are so afraid . . .'

Her hands suddenly tightened around both servants' tunics, and with unnatural strength, she lifted the two from their kneeling positions off the ground with startling ease. They hung from each of her outstretched arms, shaking uncontrollably.

'Mercy . . . !' one of them whimpered.

'You fear me because you *know* my power,' she said, her eyes still closed. '*He* fears me because he fears to *lose* power.'

The slaves were desperate. 'Merciful grace,' one pleaded. 'We are loyal to you alone! We cannot betray you—'

'The false keeper of my empire knows that I live,' she growled, as her own arms began to shake – not from fatigue, but from anger. 'He knows that I have returned to restore Amarr to the glory she was meant to be! That I alone hold that right!'

'Your Majesty, *please* . . .'

'What evil is this that inhabits my kingdom? Who dares to rob Amarr of her destiny!'

'*Please! No!*'

Her furious rage could be heard throughout the cathedral.

'So great will Karsoth's suffering be! He shall wish he was never born!'

And suddenly she collapsed, unconscious, and the two servants tumbled to the ground – terrified, but unharmed. They hurried to her, gently lifting her head off the ground and brushing the hair away from her forehead, now drenched with perspiration.

'Wake up, Your Majesty,' one of them said, as the sound of running boots and the shouts of men echoed from beyond. 'You've had another spell!'

She awoke with a gasp, breathing heavily. Armed Paladins approached cautiously, careful not to get any closer than just a few meters – a lesson they once learned the hard way.

Jamyl Sarum lifted her head up from the lap of her servant and blinked. An expression of complete bewilderment and fear was apparent on her face.

'How did I get here?' she asked, sounding like a lost child. 'Where is Lord Falek?'

6

Lonetrek Region – Minnen Constellation
The Piak System, Planet III
Sovereignty of the Caldari State

Currents of black water were starting to run down the gulleys along both sides of the street, washing away the accumulated soot deposited there by the factory looming in the distance. The mist-like rain, produced in part by terraformers half a continent away, was scheduled to last for weeks longer. Heavy smog hung just over the heads of workers marching through the muck, alongside the tracks of a decrepit transportation system that was falling into ruin.

They emerged from metallic housing structures that provided shelter, warmth, and little else. There were rows upon rows of these spartan living spaces filling a rock basin dozens of kilometers across, at the center of which stood the Caldari Constructions Armor Forge, one of several industrial mega complexes owned and operated by the corporation. Here at this factory, the composite alloys used to build everything from micro-tools to the heavy plating of capital ship armor were manufactured, often under perilous conditions for the workers who manned the equipment inside.

On a clear day, the corporation's space elevator complex was visible high atop the ridge encircling the basin. Giant cargo containers descended gently from the clouds, supported by carbon nanotube cables extending all the way up into space and ending at an orbital dockyard, where starships offloaded raw ore mined from asteroids and took on finished products. There were ten cables in all, moving heavy materials up and down from the sky all day, every day, with the methodical timing of a corporation striving to meet demanding production schedules.

Opposite the elevators, on the far side of the basin, were the corporate overseers of this vast machine. Luxurious domed housing structures, filled with exotic plants and stocked with every conceivable amenity associated with comfort and pleasure, contrasted sharply with the dirty shanties far below. This was where the corporate executives made their residence, the managers and foremen of the mechanical symphony playing below. They travelled to work in hovercars, their boots never once touching the filthy ground during their quick journeys to the Armor Forge. Drawing the occasional glance from a weary worker, they sped past the crowds of people drudging on to another day's toil in return for a meager wage.

The streets were quickly filling as the morning shift moved past the returning night crews. Most of the men and women walked with their shoulders hunched against the cold, the rain, and their bone-numbing fatigue. But today there was something different about the crowd. Some of the denizens marched with straight backs and deadpan resolve, as if they knew that this day would stand apart from all the others.

One man walked among them with a heavy limp, and his name was Tibus Heth.

THE HOVERCAR SLIPPED around boulders and ravines with effortless grace, zipping down the steep rock face of the basin and levelling off over the harsh terrain below.

What a grim day, Altug thought to himself, slowing the vehicle down. The rain was steady now, leaving dark streaks on the windshield as droplets rolled down the glass. Sensors probing ahead of the vehicle found the western edge of the 'Shallows', the nickname of the vast housing complex the corporation provided for its Armor Forge workers. The long avenues carving through it led to the western gate, about five kilometers ahead. The vehicle gently came to a hover about a meter above the ground and started down the road, travelling slowly due to the reduced visibility.

Altug could see some of the workers returning to the tiny shelters, some of which were right next to a derelict rail station. *Poor bastards*, he thought. *It's a shame we had to cut funding for transportation, but the margins aren't as thick as they used to be.* As the hovercar approached the gate, the smog cleared enough to catch sight of the two sentry towers facing the west. *Those will be the next cuts*, he thought, distracted by the pronounced limp of one of the workers as the car passed by. *No need to pay guards to just sit up there all day doing nothing when—*

A loud *thud* startled him as the windshield's view was suddenly obscured with a worker lying horizontally across it. Panicking, he squeezed the brakes, forcing the hovercar to a sudden stop; the victim was thrown, rolling twice in the mud before coming to rest. Altug was shocked, and instinctively glanced up toward the towers. Both were obscured from view by the smog again. Cursing to himself, he unlocked the doors to step outside. But as they slid open, he felt several sets of hands force him back into the vehicle. Then the hovercar's doors were forced shut.

'Good morning,' a voice said, startling him again. A man was now sitting right beside him. 'Altug Borascus, yes?'

'What the hell are you doing in my—'

The man jabbed something into his side, sending a wave

of paralyzing, excruciating pain throughout his limbs. As soon as he removed it, the pain stopped.

'I don't like repeating myself,' the intruder said, politely. 'Are you Altug—'

'Yes!' he said. 'What do you want?'

'A ride to work,' the man said. He appeared to be in his mid-forties, but with white hair and harsh features. Scars ran along both of his cheeks, and his eyes were intense. 'Drive to the security checkpoint, let them do the retina scan, and tell them I'm your guest.'

Altug noticed that the man's hands were thick and strong, like a steel worker's. One of them held a pistol. 'Who are you?'

'My name is Tibus Heth,' the man smiled. 'An employee of this corporation and fellow Caldari kinsman.' Leaning toward Altug, the smile disappeared. 'You aren't my enemy, *friend*. If you cooperate, you'll be rewarded.'

Something about the way he said '*friend*' sent a chill down Altug's spine. Looking at the road ahead, the victim he collided with was nowhere to be found. Then something jabbed into his side again, delivering a second bolt of searing pain.

'*Drive*,' Tibus ordered. 'We have a lot to do.'

THE GUARDS IN the sentry towers, also under the employ of the Caldari Constructions, never noticed the 'accident' between Altug Borascus's hovercar and the factory worker who intentionally threw himself in its path, nor did they notice the men who stopped him from getting out as a white-haired cripple slipped into the passenger-side seat. In fact, the corporation-issued night-vision equipment needed to see through the inclement weather and choking smog was inoperable, since the funds for replacement batteries were long since depleted.

Not that functional security equipment would have made any difference. On the western and northern gates, the guards posted inside the sentry towers were all disarmed, handcuffed, and gagged long before Altug's hovercar ever reached the security checkpoint. The men carrying out the assaults – also employees of the corporation and ethnic Caldari citizens – were careful not to kill anyone, or cause irreparable physical harm to their victims. They boldly assumed the posts of the fallen guards, some even using their radios to make innocuously sounding comments about the weather to give an appearance of normality, while small groups of men and women made their purposeful way through the oblivious crowd, moving as fast as they could *without running* to get inside the factory.

'GOOD MORNING, MR. BORASCUS,' the guard said, before the door opened fully. 'Who's your guest?'

Altug emerged slowly from the elevator with Tibus close behind him. They were standing on a catwalk overlooking an assembly hangar, a vast indoor structure where molten alloys were poured into the required molds for this production line. Today, the line was casting armor plate sections for Hawk-class assault frigates; men operating robot-like MTACs (Mechanized Torso-Actuated Chassis) moved about the assembly floor three storeys below their feet, lifting the cooling plates from the assembly line and placing them on racks for transport to the space elevators.

Altug spoke without a trace of emotion. 'Mr. Heth has expressed an interest in factory management,' he answered, as deliberately as he could. 'We're going to speak in my office about its various . . . nuances.'

The guard eyed Tibus suspiciously, who returned the scrutiny with a wink.

'Fortune's been good to me for a change, soldier,' Tibus said. 'Today's my lucky break.'

'What's your regular assignment?'

Tibus chuckled. 'Usually I'm marching around in one of those MTACs down there,' he said. 'Always wondered what the view was like from up top.'

'Alright,' the guard said, standing aside to make room on the narrow grating for them to pass. 'Have a good day, sir.'

Altug said nothing, silently fuming at the man for failing to recognize that he was a hostage. He made a mental note of the guard's name, and would have employment termination orders prepared for him the moment this crisis ended. Then he cringed as the door behind him closed.

'Sit down at your terminal,' Tibus commanded. He could feel the pain device pressed into the small of his back, and did as he was told.

'Now set off the contamination alarms in the west and north wings,' he growled. 'Quickly.'

Altug twitched involuntarily. 'You can't be serious—'

A searing jolt of pain made him shriek. Tibus started laughing maniacally, slapping Altug on the back and pointing at the screen. The guard turned to peer into the office.

'*Laugh*,' Tibus ordered.

Another quick jolt of pain invoked a shriek, which Altug contorted into a hoarse, fake laugh. The guard gave them a quizzical look.

'Good,' Tibus said, keeping the device pressed against Altug's spine. 'Keep your eyes on the screen. Play along, friend. This will be over soon.'

Altug was on the verge of tears. *Why is this happening to me? Who is this raving madman, and why aren't the guards in here shooting him dead?*

'Turn your head and look at me,' Tibus said. 'Nice and easy. Try to look relaxed.'

Altug turned, quivering, and stared into the dark eyes of his captor.

'I made you a promise,' Tibus said, looking thoughtful as he spoke, motioning with one free hand as though trying to explain something. 'Do as I say, and you'll be rewarded. But if you delay me one more time—'

Tibus pressed the gun in his other hand, concealed behind the terminal, into Altug's crotch.

He smiled, as he might when greeting an old friend.

'Set off the fucking contamination alarms in the west and north wings, Mr. Borascus.'

I can't believe I'm doing this, Altug thought, turning toward the screen and tapping the keys lightly with his weak, trembling, manicured fingers.

THE DISTANCE ACROSS the Armor Forge factory, from the western gates to its eastern counterpart, was approximately eight kilometers. A ten-terawatt reactor sat squarely in between them, supplying power to everything in the facility, including the space elevators and housing complexes surrounding the basin. Short of an orbital bombardment, a containment breach was the direst emergency possible, endangering everyone and everything within a sixty-kilometer radius of ground zero.

As the alarms bellowed throughout the complex, workers and managers alike stopped what they were doing and launched into a mass exodus toward the exits. Hovercars and people running on foot emerged from the facility like swarms of insects, as a countdown sounded for the massive lead doors that were about to seal the northern and western sections off from the rest of the base. In just a few moments, it would be impossible for anyone to enter the facility from those two entrances, and anyone trapped inside would remain there until the emergency subsided, or they succumbed to whatever nuclear catastrophe was imminent.

While many guards abandoned their responsibilities and fled with the rest of the crowd, some chose to stay behind, trying to ensure everyone within their assigned areas got out safely. One such guard was the same one posted at the office of Altug Borascus, who dutifully barged inside to escort its occupants out of the facility. But he stumbled to a halt, not expecting to see Altug handcuffed to the wall railing, and certainly not expecting the powerful punch thrown from his blind side by Tibus Heth.

Unconscious before hitting the floor, the guard collapsed and was quickly descended upon by the surprisingly agile Tibus, who had him bound in seconds. The staccato thunder of gunfire and exploding charges shattered the glass of the office, and Altug screamed as the muzzle flash of a plasma rifle illuminated the room with an eerie green strobe. Another guard was trading gunfire with unseen attackers further down the catwalk, entirely unaware of the people inside the office as he tried to close in for a better shot.

The moment his rifle barrel broke the plane of the office door, Tibus swung his hand up beneath it and knocked the guard's aim to vertical. Vulnerable for that split second, Tibus followed up with an elbow to the man's ribs and quickly extended his fist upward, connecting with the bridge of his nose. Stunned, the guard staggered back and lost his balance, tumbling over the railing. In the blink of an eye, Tibus had dived forward with outstretched arms. His hands found the falling guard's utility belt and gripped it tightly. The sudden weight transfer dragged

Tibus forward across the floor grating and toward the edge, and with an agonizing scream, he kicked out with his good leg, trying to wedge it against a vertical support in the railing.

His leg slammed hard into the pole but held fast, the guard dangling upside down within his grip. Both men were screaming; one from the sheer terror of being dropped from three storeys up, the other from the physical agony of supporting the dead weight of a man with his forearms. Altug, amazed at this feat of athletic heroism, heard footsteps running down the catwalk. A group of workers appeared and grabbed the flailing legs of the guard, pulled him over the railing to safety and immediately restrained him.

Tibus brushed away the hands of the workers trying to help him stand back up. 'How much do we control?' he asked.

'Half,' one of the larger men said. 'The northern and western sections are locked down, and the teams are flushing out stragglers.'

'Hostages?'

'A good mix, lots of different professions. Plenty of managers,' he said with a smile. 'We can shut down anything you want.'

'Casualties?'

'A few broken bones here and there, but no deaths.'

'Well done,' Tibus commended, hobbling toward the guard whose life he had just saved. 'Anything you want to say to me?'

The man's nose was shattered. As blood poured freely from both nostrils, he stared blankly at the space before him. 'Get him cleaned up,' Tibus ordered, patting him on the shoulder. 'You'll thank me later.'

As the workers dragged the guard away, Tibus turned back to Altug.

'Mr. Borascus, do you ever watch the news?' he asked, limping closer.

'Yes,' Altug answered cautiously.

'Good, because we're about to make some of our own,' he announced, removing the handcuffs from Altug. 'The space elevators. Shut them down. *Now.*'

7

Steeped in martial tradition, the Caldari State is a veritable fortress of corporate dominance, immersed in a culture governed by the laws of competition. From early childhood, the Caldari are taught to embrace conflict, a spartan philosophy which they hold responsible for the survival of their race in the post-EVE collapse era. A testament to natural selection, their behavior descends from the fortitude of ancestors who inhabited some of the harshest worlds of New Eden.

The spirit of competition eventually spawned powerful corporations that turned the gears of a mighty capitalistic economy. Power in the Caldari State was consolidated into the hands of eight mega-corporations that controlled every aspect of life in their society. From the provision of housing, health care and employment; to the establishment of independent police forces; and the joint funding of a national military capable of mobilizing on a moment's notice, the corporations became the very identity of the Caldari State. Every man, woman and child eligible for citizenship was by definition directly affiliated with a corporation, to which each was assigned a role commensurate with his or her natural abilities. Those who failed to live up to the expectations of that role were ostracized, and became outcasts regulated to the basement of a society that had little compassion or tolerance for misfortune.

But the success of the early days began to change once the boundaries of New Eden opened to reveal other civilizations who had also survived the dark ages, and none was as influential or damning as the Gallenteans. Initially a welcome ally of the Caldari State, the two civilizations merged and collaborated on the development of space exploration technology, thus creating mutual opportunities for expanding deeper into the largely untapped systems of New Eden. But the Gallenteans were passionate liberals and eager traders; the Caldari, on the other hand, were loath to create opportunities for any race other than themselves. The former's insistence of access to markets that had been controlled by mega-corporations for centuries clashed with the regimented Caldari, igniting a contest that quickly transformed into rampant nationalism.

The birthplace of Caldari civilization was the planet Caldari Prime, which fate cruelly placed in the same Gallentean home system of Luminaire. As free-spirited Gallentean influence continued to grate against militaristic Caldari culture, the patience of resident nationalists evaporated, ultimately leading to acts of terrorism by Caldari radicals. The flashpoint that would lead to open conflict was the sabotage of a retaining dome protecting the underwater Gallentean city of Nouvelle Rouvenor, a barbarous act which claimed the lives of more than half a million people.

In the war that followed, the Caldari were driven from Caldari Prime by the much more powerful Gallenteans, who would have fought a decisive victory if not for the advent of capsuleer technology, which forced the conflict to a stalemate years later. And while the economies of both nations eventually recovered from the massive resource drain of the war machine, the Caldari economic expansion was short-lived, due in part to the increased determination of its own mega-corporations to retain control of inter-state markets and shutting out foreign competition from the other three major civilizations. Keeping the peace in a society where corporations are responsible for the welfare of its citizens while simultaneously relying on them to be consumers within the markets that they control proved to be a myopic strategy at best. The gap between those with, and without, wealth was insurmountable, and at long last, trouble had finally arrived.

Caldari Constructions, while undeserving of mega-corporate status, was still a cog in the ailing economic machine of the Caldari State, and was the beneficiary of contracts awarded by both corporations and independently wealthy individuals for general metallurgy and component fabrication services. There were rival corporations who had offered the same services for less, both inside and out of the Caldari State, but Constructions was the 'ethnically sound choice', in addition to offering the largest bribes and the most decadent of 'perks' to sweeten the deal, all behind the tightly closed doors of boardrooms, executive clubs, and private estates.

High above the Armor Forge on Piak III, where Tibus Heth and his band of rebellious Caldari brothers and sisters were mopping up the remnants of corporate security inside the facility, an industrial freighter owned by the Kaalakiota Corporation – the largest and most powerful of all the mega-corporations – was approaching the Constructions space elevator dockyard, precisely on time as dictated by the tight production schedules of its starship manufacturing division. Its mission docket was typical: offload thousands of tons of raw material, and pick up a designated cargo of assorted starship armor plating for transport back to Kaalakiota shipyards.

The captain of that freighter, preoccupied with the delicate task of docking a starship more than 800 meters in length, failed to notice that the containers suspended on the elevator cables weren't moving.

THEIR MOANS AND purrs were professionally timed to coincide with the frantic thrusts of his pelvis, maximizing the erotic high of his experience and the sensuous services they were hired to provide. 'Satelles Girls', named after the business enterprise with the same name, were the best 'escorts' that money could buy, and a popular favorite in the 'relationship management' business of Caldari executives. These three voluptuous specimens were all of Gallentean ethnicity, a personal – if unpatriotic – choice of Caldari Constructions CEO Torkebaira Shutsu, who always chose to surround himself with symbols of absolute wealth and affluence no matter what the occasion.

Today's occasion was a self-imposed challenge to the effect of attempting to please three Satelles girls simultaneously, a feat that had already proved unsuccessful twice thus far, and was close to a third disappointment when the intercom in his personal suite interrupted the event.

'Sir, pick up the line,' the voice said, with a tone that suggested familiarity with the shrieks inside. 'This is urgent.'

But the urgency was lost in the heat of the moment, as an encouraging crescendo of moans from the ladies of Satelles hinted that a successful resolution to Mr. Shutsu's challenge was imminent.

'The space elevators have been shut down,' the voice continued. 'And we've lost control of more than half of the Armor Forge complex.'

The thrusting ceased, and the reddish face of Mr. Shutsu transformed into crisp paleness.

'Oh,' one of the women said disappointedly, noting the sudden absence of firmness inside of her. 'What happened?'

'HARBOR CONTROL, THIS is the Kaalakiota freighter *Ulysses,*' the irritated captain said. 'I've been here for almost ten minutes. What's the problem?'

'We apologize for the delay,' announced a voice that was synthetically apologetic. 'We are experiencing technical difficulties and ask for your patience while we work to resolve the issue.'

Cursing, the captain leaned forward to peer through the bridge windows at the dockyard, glistening against the murky atmosphere of Piak III beyond. The giant cargo gantries were all motionless, and there were no MTACs marching along the loading ramps, both signs that it was anything but business as usual at this facility.

The voice of another freighter captain broke the silence. 'Kaal captain, this is the Lai Dai freighter *Caputon* parked opposite of you in two-bravo. Do you have any idea what's going on?'

'No,' the *Ulysses* captain answered. 'And I'm sitting on a huge collateral payment for the freight I'm supposed to pick up here.'

'Then you're just as screwed as I am,' the intercom replied. 'I just heard there's trouble on the ground down there, something about a factory riot. I was hoping you'd heard differently.'

'A riot? You kidding me?'

'Nope. Including you and me, freighters from four mega-corps are sitting around waiting for paid cargo that's never going to get here. You know what? Fuck it, I'm leaving. I've absolutely had it with these Constructions idiots.'

'Roger that,' the *Ulysses* captain replied. 'I'm going to pass this along to my dispatch . . .'

Lonetrek Region – Minnen Constellation
The Piak System – Planet III, Moon 5
Caldari Constructions Headquarters

'People,' Mr. Shutsu started. 'Explain to me – carefully – what's happening with the Armor Forge.'

The meeting room design, while still adhering to Caldari minimalism, was constructed with precious metals and sensitive nanotech alloys that reacted to temperature – a feature originally conceived by artists but often deployed by executives seeking to gauge the emotional state of their employees. Seated around a table lined with platinum trim were each of the Constructions top level executives and managers. Their reflections were slightly blushed, as the heat from each set of hands resting on the polished surface spread in ripples that bounced gently against the table borders like waves in a pool.

'The northern and western sections of the complex were commandeered by coordinated teams of low-grade employees,' said Hannaken Shonen, the Production Director. 'Then a manager on the western assembly floor set off a bogus contamination alarm, forcing the lockdown of those sections and sealing the attackers inside. The same manager then used his clearance to shut down the space elevators, and within minutes the production lines were stopped as well.'

'This is going to cost us billions,' blurted Tamo Heinu-liala, the Constructions Chief Financial Officer. 'Forget about the capital costs, that's nothing compared to the public relations nightmare we'll have with clients—'

'*Shut up*,' Mr. Shutsu growled. A collective pulse of red smeared across the table, where it was brightest beneath Tamo's hands. 'Tell me about this manager, Hannaken.'

The Production Director cleared his throat. 'His name is Altug Borascus, a high-grade employee with dual backgrounds in computer science and manufacturing optimization. He was on track for—'

'Is he complicit in this . . . disturbance?' Mr. Shutsu asked.

'We don't know,' Hannaken answered. 'We know nothing, except that it was his ID that authenticated the alarm.'

'And we can't override it because . . .'

'The comm towers are in the northern wing, which they now control.'

Mr. Shutsu straightened his posture and clasped his hands behind his back. 'Has any one of these . . . saboteurs . . . made any demands?'

'None that we're aware of,' answered Nilen Koina, the Constructions CMO. 'Without those towers, we can't know how many of our security personnel are left, or if they've managed to secure the remaining wings.'

The table was a uniform reddish-orange now, intensifying as Mr. Shutsu alternated his glare between executives. 'Tamo, how many merchandise transfers are scheduled right now?'

'Four,' the man answered nervously. 'The recipients are all mega-corps.'

Mr. Shutsu turned his chin upward, clenching his teeth. 'Which ones?'

'Lai Dai, Wiyrkomi, Hyasyoda, and—'

A crisp, jovial female voice interrupted Tamo. 'Sir, Ms. Oiritsuu of Kaalakiota is requesting an immediate conference. Shall I put her through?'

Mr. Shutsu locked eyes with Tamo, who appeared uncomfortable. A slight, almost imperceptible nod confirmed the identity of the fourth mega-corporation.

'We'll take the call.'

A full-size apparition of Haatakan Oiritsuu, the CEO of the Caldari State's largest and most powerful mega-corporation, materialized in the room alongside of Mr. Shutsu. A tall, slender woman with a fair complexion, high cheekbones, and shoulder-length light-brown hair, she was wearing a form-fitting business suit that began at the top of her neck and tapered downward as if it were a single piece. She stood with perfect posture, and looked more like a military officer than a business executive.

'Good morning, Mr. Shutsu,' she said. 'I don't normally intervene in situations such as this, but these are unique circumstances.'

Mr. Shutsu turned to face the image, bending forward slightly with a customary bow. 'We are honored to have you with us. How can we be of service?'

'Actually sir, I came to inquire on how *we* may be of service to *you*. Specifically, I'm offering assistance in the recovery of the nearly six billion credits' worth of Kaalakiota merchandise currently suspended on the space elevators of your Armor Forge complex.'

'The delay in shipping is regrettable, but I assure you, we have the situation under control,' Mr. Shutsu replied, straightening up a bit. A sudden blitz of messenger device activity nearly distracted him. 'While your offer is most gracious, I don't believe it will be necessary.'

'Far be it from me to disagree before your associates,' she said, her expression now deadly serious. 'But I would hardly call the loss of three factories *controlling* the situation.'

The conference table was now a full collage of pulsing, reddish hues. 'I'm sorry, Ms. Oiritsuu, but we've merely lost contact with *one* facility—'

'Don't you ever watch the *news*, Mr. Shutsu?' Her eyes narrowed, and it was apparent that she was about to lose her patience.

Sensing the dread in the room, he glanced at his board members, all of whom were just as pale as Tamo. Nilen was pointing toward the datapad in her hand.

Mr. Shutsu exhaled a nervous laugh while moving toward the table. 'The news, of course. Please allow me a moment to catch up on things.'

Nilen slid the device across, leaving a crimson wake on the table. Mr. Shutsu snatched it up and began reading:

To: Nilen Koina
From: Tobas Marchin
Date: 108.03.31 07:40 Piak Local

Nilen, this just came off the newswires:

—Forwarded from CC Security—

108.03.31 07:39 PIAK LOCAL
*** BREAKING NEWS ***
STATEWIDE HAS LEARNED THAT THREE CALDARI CONSTRUCTIONS FACTORIES IN THE PIAK, AIKANTOH, AND LITIURA SYSTEMS HAVE BEEN SEIZED BY RIOTING WORKERS. REPORTS OF HALTED PRODUCTION AND SHIPPING SCHEDULES FROM EACH OF THESE SITES HAVE BEEN VERIFIED BY ON-SCENE NEWS AGENTS. WE ARE FOLLOWING THIS STORY CLOSELY AND WILL CONTINUE TO PROVIDE COVERAGE AS IT BECOMES AVAILABLE.

This is confirmed ... the plants are all offline, and we can't reach anyone at any of the sites. What the hell is happening?

Tobas Marchin, Director
Caldari Constructions Security

'Things aren't as orderly as you think, Mr. Shutsu,' she said, folding her arms and studying him like a lab experiment. 'Now, you were just discussing the use of force to regain control of your facilities, correct?'

The man was ashen, complementing a boardroom full of executives who were incapacitated with shock. When he opened his mouth to speak, she waved him off.

'A Home Guard police carrier is en route to Piak III, where it will send dropships with mechanized infantry to assist in the recovery of our merchandise. In exchange for my word to make every effort to minimize casualties to your employees, you will give Home Guard full tactical command of the Armor Forge operation. Do we have a deal?'

Mr. Shutsu nodded in bewildered agreement.

'Once I have my merchandise back, we'll negotiate the fee for assisting in the recovery of your other facilities. My delayed shipping compensation demands will be along momentarily.'

Tamo suddenly began to choke, his eyes bulging at the new figure on his datapad. 'Eight billion! That's worth more than the value of the merchandise!'

'Mr. Heinulaila, my clients are capsuleers,' the holograph said, turning to face the dishevelled Caldari Constructions CFO. 'They aren't nearly as patient as I am.'

8

For those who have acted out of passion, whether self-induced or compelled by circumstance, there is a defining moment when the realization of consequence sets in with brutal clarity. Throughout the Armor Forge, fleeing residents were collectively becoming aware that their mass panic to escape a contamination alarm was a hoax, clearly intended to distract them from more significant events happening inside the complex. There was not a single resident who was asleep; thousands of people were out on the streets, indifferent to the worsening weather and carrying what little they could through the sludge. Stirred by anger and led by curiosity, they abandoned their evacuation plans and began to follow the convoys of armed security vehicles snaking their way toward the western and northern gates.

As the rain intensified, so too did the tempers of those residents demanding an explanation for what had happened, many of whom feared losing their wages for what should have been another day's work in the factory. Others noted the seized space elevators on the ridgeline, gasping at the giant cargo containers suspended in midair between breaks in the smog overhead. As rumors of a revolt spread among the populace, the tempers of guards began to wear as they found themselves face to face with belligerent workers.

Of all the different versions of the truth circulating among the drenched crowd, one name was common to them all: Tibus Heth.

'I CAN'T BELIEVE it,' Heidan said, shaking his head. The plasma rifle in his hands, taken moments earlier from the

Constructions guard now lying unconscious on the assembly line floor, was rattling from adrenaline tremors. 'I can't believe we actually pulled it off.'

'You hit him with that rifle stock like he was Gallentean,' Janus muttered, carefully removing the guard's helmet and inspecting the injury to his skull. 'He needs a medic *now.*'

Heidan grimaced, reaching for the commlink on the guard's shoulder and removing it. Rows of cargo MTACs from the nightshift towered over them, standing side by side in designated spots like giant statues.

'Alpha command, Thunder-five. Southeast MTAC hangar secure. Requesting medics for a head trauma injury, over.'

'Thunder-five, copy. Stay put, medics en route.'

'Roger, command. Standing by.'

Heiden stared at the injured guard, suddenly overwhelmed with sorrow. 'Why couldn't you just freeze when I told you to . . . ?'

Janus was kneeling in front of the guard's head, gently checking his breathing and monitoring his pulse.

'He did what he was supposed to. Besides,' he said, looking up and flashing a reassuring grin, 'what self-respecting Caldarian gives up without a fight?'

'That's why I feel so bad,' Heidan said, also kneeling down. 'He's one of our own, just . . . didn't know we're trying to help him.'

'He'll know when he wakes up,' Janus said, peering down the hangar for signs of the medic squad. 'A little pain now and then is a healthy thing.'

'If he even wakes up,' Heidan muttered, looking panicked. 'Fuck, what are we doing here, anyway? Do you realize what we just did?'

'Now, take it easy, Heid—'

'Take a look around! See all those lights? You hear those sirens? We're enemies of the State now, and there's going to be hell to pay for it!'

'Hell is slaving every day for a State that's indifferent to your existence,' a heavy, familiar voice interrupted. It was coming from the guard's commlink, which to the horror of both men had been left on ever since Heidan's check-in. 'Have courage, man. You're not alone in this.'

The entrance to the hangar opened, revealing the medic team. They immediately began sprinting across, pushing a hover stretcher in front of them.

The voice of Tibus Heth continued on the commlink. 'Escort your brothers to the infirmary, then report directly to me for assignment.'

Shaking, Heidan replied, 'Yes, sir.'

THE CONSTRUCTIONS GUARDS positioned outside the gates reacted as if they couldn't believe what they were hearing, demanding confirmation and giving each other incredulous looks. Then a commander shouted orders, and the guards reluctantly raised their weapons and began firing over the crowd, sending them into a panic. Heavy caliber turrets on nearby armored personnel carriers opened up next, firing bright plasma charges that illuminated the landscape in fiery strobes. The guards advanced behind the fleeing workers, retaking the ground where they once stood. Moving quickly, they erected electrical barriers 200 meters from the gate, creating a charged perimeter that would render anyone who tried to pass unconscious with a powerful jolt.

While some workers tended to those who were trampled during the frenzy, others turned to throw anything they could find at the guards. Warnings broadcast for them

EVE: THE EMPYREAN AGE61

to return to their homes went unheeded, and just enraged the crowd even more.

But then the anger subsided, replaced temporarily by awe and curiosity, as piercing bright lights shone down through the hanging smog and a deafening roar engulfed the basin. A Home Guard dropship descended from the sky, landing in between the Constructions perimeter and the fortified entrance to the western gate.

Curiosity gave way to fear as the dropship's ramp lowered. Two combat MTACs marched out, with heavily armed infantry following close behind.

'HOME GUARD!' TIBUS scoffed. 'I'm insulted they didn't send the Navy.'

Chuckles rang out in the office of Altug Borascus, which was now serving as Heth's personal command center. Workers had been arriving in pairs, giving terse reports and scurrying back out, returning to set up equipment, and then leaving again to fulfill other assignments. It was happening at a dizzying pace, each person acting with methodical efficiency, as if this event had been years in the planning.

'Sir, we're on the news networks,' one of the women in the office said, pointing at the screen in front of her. 'Revolts are underway at the other complexes!'

The wave of cheers that followed was too much for Altug.

'You *stupid* fools! You're going to get us all killed!'

Save for the faint din of machines, the room went completely silent. Altug wasn't finished yet.

'You're all going to burn for this. Do you understand me? You have no idea what you're up against!'

He was struggling against the restraints clamping his

hands behind the chair, defiantly ranting as though impervious to the hostility surrounding him.

'Tibus, do you think you're just going to walk out of here? You and your, your . . . *minions*, whoever these thugs are . . . Do you really think they're going to put you in a jail for this you *fucking* idiot? *They're not!* They're going to kill every fucking one of you!'

Several workers got up from their seats and took long strides toward Altug with clenched fists.

'Stop,' Tibus ordered them, glaring at Altug. 'Leave me with him.'

The workers hesitated, then moved toward the exit. 'Wait for Kaalakiota to initiate first contact,' Tibus continued, hobbling slowly toward the desk. 'I'll be monitoring the situation from here.'

And then the door closed, leaving the two men alone.

'So what are you going to do, beat me up?' Altug demanded. 'I'm not afraid of you—'

'I'm going to ask your advice,' Tibus said without a trace of anger. 'What would you do if you were in my position?'

Altug was unprepared for the question. 'I'd . . . turn myself in and end this, of course!'

Tibus turned to face him. 'Hmm . . . but you just said they're going to kill me anyway, right?'

'You'll be justly held accountable for your crimes against this corporation and the Caldari State!'

'I've gone to great lengths to avoid hurting anyone, Altug,' he said, limping toward the desk. 'I never shied away from my responsibilities in this.'

'*Responsibilities?*' Altug asked incredulously. 'You've cost this corporation millions in lost productivity, perhaps more, and selfishly convinced these workers to throw themselves into the fire along with you! Responsibility . . . please! Only a fool would say something like that!'

Tibus smiled, looking downward. 'Do you think you know yourself?'

'What?'

'I said, do you think you *know* yourself.' His teeth were clenched.

'What kind of ridiculous question is that?'

'These workers – your *countrymen* – thought they knew themselves and their nation when they agreed to work for Constructions . . . bought into the company party line about reaping the benefits of corporate earnings, doing their part for the betterment of the State. So here we are, working fourteen-hour shifts, popping protein supplements and organic mush for meals while *the leadership* feasts on imported roes and spirits, spending company money on pill parties and orgies, growing fatter and weaker by the moment under the despicable illusion of status and power—'

'You're serious? That's what this is all about?' Altug asked mockingly. 'A cry for attention from the unheralded, under-compensated, *unwanted* laborer—'

Tibus limped forward, grabbed Altug with both hands, and lifted him and the chair he was bound to off the floor.

'This is about the strength of our State,' Tibus growled, inches from Altug's face. 'Thanks to *your* leadership, the so-called Caldari elite, the Gallentean economy has grown tenfold since the end of the war, while ours – the one *you* were responsible for – shrivelled into impotence.'

Spittle was flying off of Tibus's mouth as he spoke. 'Want to talk about attention? Let's bring some attention to the fact you've made us the weakest state in New Eden, when it's *us* who should be ruling it!'

Altug hit the floor with a crash, forcing the air out his lungs.

'Your counterparts on the other side of the line are superior to you in every way,' Tibus snarled, standing over him like a predator. 'It's *your* actions that are unacceptable. My crimes today are nothing compared to your own.'

Tibus reached down and yanked the chair upright again.

'You're right, Altug. I don't plan on leaving this place alive, and neither does anyone else who *volunteered* to be here. They'd rather burn than work one more day for *you*, you pathetic weakling, and spend the last moments of their lives standing up for something besides corporate greed.'

Tibus threw open the door to the office, waving in the men waiting outside.

'You think you know what's going on here? You think you know who we are? You have *no* idea.'

9

As much as the Caldari State tried to control the information that travelled across its borders, events on the scale of what was happening on Piak III were impossible to contain. In recent years, incidents of civil unrest anywhere in New Eden were relatively infrequent, but rumors of open revolts – especially on Caldari worlds, of all places – were almost impossible to believe. But the news of Kaalikiota's direct intervention, complete with footage of angry mobs and Home Guard infantry outside of the Armor Forge gates, dispelled any lingering doubt. The only question now was just how widespread the consequences would be.

Capital markets, in particular the Concord Securities Exchange (CSE), were reacting to the news in predictable fashion: Caldari Constructions stock was plummeting, and institutions with holdings in the corporation were taking financial punishment more or less commensurate with the size of their investment. To make matters worse, these markets – moved just as much by gossip as by corporate announcements – were displaying warning signs of instability along all sectors related to Caldari State industries.

For years, analysts from banking institutions across New Eden were quietly expressing concern about the decaying strength of the Caldari economy, some even speculating that a collapse – while unthinkable just a decade ago – was now a real possibility. They argued that if not for the capsuleer-driven starship technology market – and the resulting heavy demand for ship components that factories like the Armor Forge produced – the collapse might have already happened.

While publicly dismissing alarmist's concerns, there were those among the mega-corporate elite who understood that the Caldari State was not impervious to economic realities, and took secret measures to not only hedge against their own downfall, but to profit from it as well. The resulting selloff in Caldari assets, accelerated by massive institutional orders to flood the markets with shares of Constructions stock, set off every single technical analysis warning in the financial empire. The 'Constructions Revolt', as the newswires were calling the event, was now everyone's problem.

'THE NAME WE keep hearing is "Tibus Heth",' Nilen said, sounding annoyed. 'He's a low-grade MTAC operator assigned to the western assembly array. But I told you already, it's just comm chatter the guards are hearing from the mobs outside the gate. We still don't know who's in charge on the inside, *sir.*'

'Mind your tone, Nilen,' Mr. Shutsu warned. 'Remember, I still control what happens to whom in *here.*'

'We've lost over thirty percent of our market value in under an hour,' Tamo croaked. He was soaked in perspiration. 'And the broader indices are all following suit, like as if they *want* us to fail.'

'They have the advantage only for as long as it takes for me to get a name,' Mr. Shutsu said. 'Once I have it, this stops being a "worker revolt", and the person responsible becomes a monster before the eyes of the State.'

'How?' asked Tamo.

Mr. Shutsu straightened his posture, but appeared calm. 'The people responsible for these acts are *terrorists.* They have broken the trust that we afforded them, spit in the face of the charity that we provide, and deprived their countrymen of the wages earned in return for their loyalty to *us.*'

'Yes,' Nilen said, who was thinking now. 'They're sealed inside, we can spin this any way that we want—'

'A hostage scenario,' Hannaken blurted. 'Cutthroat criminals blackmailing for money at the expense of hard-working Constructions employees—'

'Prepare a statement to that effect,' Mr. Shutsu ordered. 'Acknowledge our failure to maintain security, but make sure the language clearly states infiltration by terrorists.'

The receptionist interrupted: 'Sir, there's an incoming comm request from Mr. Altug Borascus. Shall I patch it—'

'*Yes,*' Mr. Shutsu said. 'The rest of you, stay quiet!'

A giant pair of dark, intense eyes materialized, nearly filling the entire width of the room. A pulse of bright red waves raced across the conference room table, betraying the fear felt by the Constructions executives. Mr. Shutsu did not appear fazed, turning to face the holograph with composure and strength.

'You aren't Altug Borascus,' he said, clasping his hands behind him.

'No,' the apparition said. The creases between his eyes were severe, and the corneas radiated unremitting anger. 'My name is Tibus Heth.'

'You have my attention, Mr. Heth,' Mr. Shutsu answered. 'What can I do for you?'

'The first thing you should know is that I don't want to hurt anyone,' the eyes said. 'I've gone to great lengths—'

Weakness, Mr. Shutsu immediately thought. 'Did you not understand the question . . . Mr. Heth?'

The giant eyes blinked, clearly surprised.

'I said, what can I do for you?' Mr. Shutsu repeated, glaring toward the image and waiting impatiently for an answer.

'Tell the Home Guard MTACs to back off,' the eyes growled.

'Oh, I'm afraid I can't do that,' Mr. Shutsu replied. 'They've taken control of the military operation underway to retrieve what you've stolen from them.'

'And I'll destroy it all if they come any closer,' the eyes said. 'Tell them to back off, *now.*'

'Mr. Heth,' the CEO snapped, as if speaking to one of his own board members. 'We have exactly one thing in common, and that is the fact that we are both powerless to impose authority on Home Guard. A word of advice: if you destroy their property, you'll only bring about your own death much faster, and you'll have accomplished nothing.'

'Don't test me, Shutsu—'

'You've already taken away everything that I could have offered,' he said. 'Your coup has succeeded! All of New Eden is watching, and I am helpless to do anything but watch along with them. It's not me you should be speaking with at all.'

The eyes were reddening before everyone in the room. 'I'm warning you, get me someone in Kaalakiota, or else—'

Desperate and weak, the CEO thought. *Perfect*. 'Mr. Heth, I'm not the enemy,' he continued, striding closer to the image. 'We can help each other. What you've done now, it doesn't have to end in death.'

'I'm not afraid of death!'

Give him sympathy. 'But imagine the tragedy of dying before your message can be heard!' Mr. Shutsu pleaded. 'You've made it this far; for the sake of everyone with you, let's work together to make sure it doesn't end *here*. I can offer you nothing, except for myself. And so I will meet you, alone, to discuss how we can work through this *together*.'

The expression in the eyes changed, and for the first time, Tibus was silent.

Mr. Shutsu took another step forward, while the rest of the room held their breath. 'Man to man, Tibus.'

'If you try anything . . .'

'You have the advantage. I am beaten.'

There was a moment before the eyes answered. 'The western gates will open exactly twenty minutes from now. Move inside the perimeter and wait there for the inner shielding doors to open. I'll come out to meet you myself, unarmed, except for the detonators—' The eyes narrowed. 'They'll set off the cable charges if I go horizontal for any reason, so make sure you pass that along to Home Guard's snipers.'

As naive as a child. 'I understand,' Mr. Shutsu said. 'Then we have a deal?'

'Well find out in twenty minutes,' the eyes answered. 'If you don't show, I'll blow the cables to hell anyway.'

And with that, the eyes vanished.

Mr. Shutsu whirled around to face his impressed executive team. 'Hannaken, you have twenty minutes to prepare that statement. Receptionist! Get me Home Guard!'

'Are you really going to follow him inside?' Nilen asked.

'Of course not,' Mr. Shutsu scoffed. 'More importantly, he's lying. This Tibus fool underestimates me. There aren't any charges beneath those cables.'

'How do you know?' Tamo asked.

Mr. Shutsu stormed toward the exits.

'You don't reach my level without knowing a lie when you hear one,' he said.

'EXCELLENT WORK, HEIDAN,' Tibus commended, switching the terminal off and removing his headset. 'I think our deceptive display of incompetence was convincing enough.'

The younger man, clearly rattled from the ordeal, moved away from Altug's desk as the greenish hue of the twin cameras pointing at him diminished. 'I have to go out there now, don't I?'

'Yes,' Tibus answered. 'But you're not alone. If anything happens, we'll be right behind you.'

A worker entered the room, carrying the body armor effects of a Constructions guard, the same one who nearly fell to his death outside the office. Tibus took the chest protector from her and tapped it with his fist.

'Military grade composite,' he said. 'It'll stop everything out there but the heavy caliber rounds, which they won't use with Shutsu standing in the way.'

Heidan took the gear from him, looking it over carefully.

He took a deep breath, exhaling slowly. 'It's an honor to be going first, sir.'

Tibus limped forward and grabbed the man by his shoulders.

'The honor is mine,' he said. Then he turned to face the rest of group.

'You know what you have to do. Let's move.'

'VERY IMPRESSIVE,' HAATAKAN Oiritsuu sneered. 'Desperation yields such bravery in men.'

'Thank you, madam,' Mr. Shutsu said, bowing before the holographic image. 'Again, I'll make full restitution if any merchandise is lost. Otherwise—'

'Restitution is mine regardless,' the Kaalakiota CEO hissed. 'Now I want to make one thing absolutely certain, and you'd best think it through carefully before answering: you are authorizing Home Guard to use lethal force against the employees of your corporation, correct?'

'That is precisely correct,' Mr. Shutsu said, without hesitation. 'But only after I confirm that the man who meets me at the gates is Tibus Heth.'

'And this press statement you're issuing—'

'—will provide official confirmation that we have a hostage situation and that known terrorist elements are responsible.'

'Then it's time you boarded a dropship, Mr. Shutsu,' she said, folding her arms. 'This is the only chance you'll ever have to redeem yourself.'

10

With his heart racing and beads of sweat dripping from his brow, young Heidan marched forward, clad head to feet in body armor that was the property of Caldari Constructions. Unarmed, he stood before the thick lead doors, while behind him dozens of fellow workers hurried to move the last of several makeshift barriers into place. Using the MTACs, they were hauling starship armor plates forward from the assembly floor and placing them in staggered 'kill zone' formations at the entrance. Men and women armed with weapons taken from the Constructions armory were moving into firing positions behind them. If any Home Guard soldiers attempted to raid the complex once the shield doors opened, they would be subject to a bloodbath first. The plan was simply to keep intruders out, taking full advantage of the fact that Tibus and his followers had no intention of ever leaving.

A voice spoke inside Heidan's helmet: 'Ninety seconds.'

The young man remembered how close he had come to ending his own life, when he decided he couldn't stand to work one more day in the complex. Tibus had found him inside his assigned habitat module, sobbing like a child and gripping the sharpened edge of a sliver of scrap metal, moments away from plunging the crude blade into his wrists.

So many others had chosen this way out. There was nothing to live for, he explained, except another day's toil for an indifferent corporation, earning wages that could buy him nothing beyond the borders of company property. No amount of work would free him from this perpetual bondage. And for whose benefit? The corporate elite? Where was the greatness that was supposed to accompany State citizenship? What pride was there in being Caldari?

To which Heth stood before him and answered:

Greatness is compelled by the pursuit of noble ideals.

Those words marked the beginning of Heidan's rebirth, and his resolute devotion to a cause more fulfilling to his soul than anything a corporation could offer. It was a simple matter of ego, of the basic necessity of any man to be able to provide for his family, and of the satisfaction in knowing that a day's work was contributing to a greater purpose. Only now the Caldari elite, grown fat with the opulence of their stature, had become oblivious to those elemental needs, and in their profound greed failed to recognize the grave danger in depriving men of those very things.

'Sixty seconds.'

They couldn't change the Caldari State, Tibus told him. But they could draw attention to its deficiencies here, at this very place, revealing to the universe that the elite are not as powerful as they think, and that their civilization was in peril of collapsing from the weight of their gluttony. *This was a noble idea worth living for*, he remembered Tibus saying with clenched fists, *and with it great moments worth dying for.* The longer they held their ground here, the more people around the State would become empowered, reminded of the spirit of their race, the one that had survived the perils of New Eden despite facing unspeakable odds.

To take this path, Heidan knew well, was certain death. But there was nothing to lose; no one would mourn him or anyone else with the courage to take up Heth's charge. Whether they died in a few moments or in a few decades, there would be no memory of their existence if they did nothing. This time, right now, would define them. And if it made even the slightest difference to the fate of his countrymen, it would be worth the memories of a thousand lifetimes.

'Thirty seconds,' Tibus said, taking over the countdown. 'How do you feel?'

'I'm ready,' Heidan said nervously.

'Every man must learn to face himself. The fear is your own doing, and it can be beaten.'

Heidan, gulped, shaking his head. 'I'm not scared any-more, sir. This . . . is an honor. I want to do this.'

'I know you do,' Tibus said, taking a stern tone. 'Remem-ber the mission. Just walk him back here. Do *not* make physical contact – he has to enter under his own power. Un-derstood?'

Heidan focused, forcing the fear from his mind. 'Yes, sir.'

A deep, tumbling mechanical drone broke the silence as the shield doors slowly began to open. Water from the driving rain outside began pouring in at his feet, illumi-nated by hundreds of floodlights shining down to capture the event.

'We are with you,' Tibus said, as the door cleared over him. 'Seize this moment.'

THE SHEER INDIGNITY of this disgusts me, Mr. Shutsu thought, stepping off the dropship's ramp into the mud and shielding his eyes from the blaze of spotlights. Imme-diately, the growing mob of onlookers began jeering at him. *We employ, feed, and clothe these pissants, and yet here I am, subjecting myself to their humiliating scrutiny.* He could feel the gaze of a million stares upon him, both here in person and watching from all over the State as camera drones swooped in to capture the spectacle. Far ahead in the distance, the great shield doors beyond the sentry towers were opening to allow a tiny, insignificant speck to emerge. If it was Tibus Heth, then it would be the last journey of his pathetic life, as the penalty for these outrageous crimes would be nothing less than death.

Roaring in unison, the crowd erupted into a chant: 'Heth! Heth! Heth!', fuelling the rage that Mr. Shutsu was now struggling to control. *Ungrateful bastards*, he thought, pausing besides the two formations of Home

Guard soldiers. *We'll see how they feel about their hero once he's dead.* The rain, pouring down in sheets, was cascading over the hulk of a towering combat MTAC. Glancing upward, he could see the visored face of its pilot staring down at him.

The Home Guard field commander approached him. 'Sir, the snipers are watching for your signal,' he said. 'Heth will probably make you take off that earpiece before he says anything. Comply with him – if you raise both hands over your head, we'll know to open fire. Understand?'

Mr. Shutsu nodded, taking his first steps toward the dark figure ahead.

'Remember, you're perfectly safe out there,' the commander reassured. 'Once we take him down, we'll secure your safety and then storm the complex. Good luck.'

THERE GOES MY *sacrificial offering*, Tibus marvelled, watching Heidan approach the Constructions CEO from the relative safety of the armor fortifications. *This young, pure Caldari soul, whom I place upon the altar of change.* It would be disappointing if they failed to kill him on the spot, as Tibus well expected them to do. *Our race needs to see spilt blood to understand what's at stake, to understand that we are great no more.* Now was the time, after countless sleepless nights, training and retraining these beleaguered workers underneath the very noses of their corporate masters, convincing them that this coup could work, and that they could taste what power *really* was, instead of reeling in oppressive dread of it. Tibus paused to consider if he should regret the bloodshed that was about to ensue, questioning for a moment if this display of defiance was worth the heavy price about to be paid.

This is the way of things, he remembered being taught,

as the two men approached each other in the open. *To kill in the name of survival is merely the guiding hand of nature herself.*

MR. SHUTSU APPROACHED THE shadowy figure, now just several meters away.

'Mr. Heth, I presume?' he called out.

'That's right,' a voice called. 'Let's take this indoors.'

The faintest beginnings of recognition began to take shape in Mr. Shutsu's brain. *Just a little bit closer*, he thought. *All I need is a good look at his eyes . . .*

Growing louder by the moment, the crowd's frenzied chanting of 'Heth! Heth!' overtook the sound of driving rain.

And then the moment of clarity arrived, as he recognized before him the same eyes that appeared in the boardroom. This was his man, and as would a god, he would strike him down in a vengeful fury.

IT WAS HIS hands that marked the beginning of the end, the way the Constructions CEO suddenly raised both of them over his head and jumped away from where he was standing. Puzzled momentarily, there was a flash from the direction of the Home Guard dropship, and then an abrupt view of the dark, roiling clouds above. Barely aware of the gurgling, sucking noise coming from his chest, Heidan's view of the world began to fade away.

The reddish-white mist hung in the saturated air for what seemed like an eternity, captured by dozens of cameras nearby. To the millions of people watching, there was no question of what had just happened.

For an instant, the grounds surrounding the western gates of the Constructions Armor Forge went silent. It was the final calm before the storm of the century was unleashed.

HEIDAN'S BODY HAD barely touched the ground when the Home Guard infantry units, flanked on either side with combat MTACs, began charging toward the gate. But the enraged mob, now numbering in the thousands, began selflessly throwing themselves into the electrical barrier erected by the Constructions guards.

'Sir, should we close the doors?' shouted a worker. Eyeing the soldiers charging toward his position, Tibus was suddenly overwhelmed with a sense of duty, and of a compelling obligation to rescue the man whom he had wilfully sacrificed.

'No!' he shouted, hobbling to a nearby cargo MTAC. 'You! Get out of there and grab a rifle!'

'Yes, sir!' the stunned operator responded, leaping down from the machine. Tibus pulled himself inside and strapped into the controls.

'One hundred and fifty meters!' another worker yelled, just as the first plasma rounds began hitting the barriers. 'Permission to return fire, sir?'

'As soon as I get clear!' Tibus shouted before closing the hatch. Then he used the MTAC's mechanical arms to hoist up a section of starship armor plating, holding it in front of the vehicle's torso like a shield.

'What the hell is he doing?' someone demanded, ducking behind the barrier as more charges screamed overhead.

Tibus couldn't hear him, as he urged the mechanical beast to advance as fast as it could go in the direction of Heidan's dying body, rotating the armor plating toward the advancing infantry and using it to fend off a barrage of small arms fire.

* * *

'FINISH HIM!' MR. SHUTSU shouted, looking over his shoulder at the lone MTAC charging toward the felled bastard he had left behind. 'Kill the both of them!'

The Home Guard infantry units running alongside of him ignored his request. 'Keep moving forward, sir, we have to get you to safety!'

An eruption of squawking radios suddenly broadcast a dire warning:

'They're through! Home Guard, we need help! The barriers are down, we can't hold back all these people—'

The Constructions guard never finished his sentence, and Mr. Shutsu saw a flood of rabid workers pour through the barriers and begin a frenzied charge toward them.

THE MUDDY SURFACE was as much a blessing as it was a curse, slowing everyone down but also making everything an easier target to hit. The cargo MTAC piloted by Tibus, never designed to operate in these terrain conditions, was laboring as each leg sank into the muck by as much as a meter per step. Hazardous as that was, the lack of mobility was the least of his problems. Without an electronic sensor system to provide him with a tactical view of the battlefield, he was blind to the shifting dangers beyond the armor plating extended to his left side.

When he was just a dozen meters from reaching Heidan, a volley of rockets fired from a Home Guard MTAC struck the armor plating. The series of powerful explosions, timed just milliseconds apart, knocked the cargo MTAC onto its side in a violent crash. Though shielded from the searing heat of the blasts, the concussive effects were not entirely absorbed by the plating or the minimal protection offered by the cockpit. Stunned and temporarily deafened, Tibus released his safety harness and pulled himself out of the vehicle, staggering toward Heidan.

In a surreal moment destined to become the birth of legends, Tibus knelt down in the mud and hoisted the mortally wounded man onto his shoulders. Battered and bleeding, he began to limp back toward the shielding doors of the complex as quickly as he could.

THE HOME GUARD field commander, perched in the cockpit of his combat MTAC, recognized the deteriorating situation and reassigned priorities, ignoring the smoking ruins of the toppled machine and focusing on the problem of riot control. The combat MTACs were equipped with acoustic beam projectors, which emitted non-lethal but powerful blasts of high-pitched sound waves guaranteed to repel and disorient anyone with unprotected ears within range.

Calling off the infantry attack on the complex, the MTACs activated the projectors, arcing them across the advancing mobs and herding them back toward the breaches in the fencing. Impervious to the noise, the soldiers assigned to Mr. Shutsu tried in vain to protect the man's ears, but to no avail. He writhed and screamed, as did every other unprotected person within range of the device, desperate to do anything possible to escape from the maddening shrill.

Seizing the opportunity, Tibus Heth's compatriots emerged from their barriers in MTACs and on foot, meeting up with the maimed duo out in the open and hurriedly transporting them back to safety. As the shielding doors began to close, Home Guard soldiers assisted the remaining Constructions guards with repairing the fence and retaking ground lost to the rioting workers.

Silently, the Home Guard field commander acknowledged that they had failed in their mission. There would be dire consequences, but he was still relieved with this outcome. In his entire career as a soldier, he never imagined a day when he would be ordered to slaughter Caldari citizens.

HEIDAN WAS RUSHED to the infirmary inside the complex. In the presence of captured Constructions guards recovering from the initial assault, medics tried desperately to revive the young worker. But life had long since departed his shattered body. They had just closed the man's eyelids when Tibus entered the room. His expression, hopeful at first, quickly changed to sternness as he observed the medics.

The body armor worn by Heidan was discarded on the floor alongside his gurney. Tibus lifted the bloody remnants up and hobbled toward the Constructions guards, waving it as he spoke.

'Corp-issued nanofibre composite, correct?'

The guard, handcuffed to his own gurney, nodded.

'All of you have been wearing this,' Tibus growled, holding it up. A gaping hole was evident in the front and back of the vest. 'Nanofibre composite can stop a high-powered sniper round. This vest didn't. Do you know why?'

The guard shook his head.

Tibus tossed the tattered remnants onto his lap. 'Because it's not what you think it is. Or rather, not what you were *told* it was.'

Using his free hand, the guard inspected the armor. His face was ashen pale, and Tibus wouldn't take his stare off of him.

'You want to share your thoughts with us?' he asked.

Running his hand along the inside of the vest, the guard spoke. 'They told us these had trauma membrane linings on the inside,' he said. 'Adrenaline, universal blood coagulants, bio-nano sealants . . . stuff that might have saved Heidan's life. This was filled with something else.'

'You were always a dead man walking,' Tibus muttered. The blood dripping from cuts on his face and scalp made him look like a ferocious warrior. 'All of us were.'

'Not anymore,' the guard answered, meeting Tibus's stare. 'Not if my allegiance is to you, sir.'

11

The downward spiral of Constructions stock resumed the moment the shield doors at the Armor Forge closed. Following behind it were the broader indices composed of mega-corporations, which joined in the selling frenzy with reckless abandon. But just as quickly, money poured into more secure investments – mostly Gallentean assets – causing a wild spike in broader CSE market volatility. As various financial analysts voiced concern about the lack of closure to the crisis, speculation began on just how much lower Caldari funds could go without triggering an economic catastrophe in the State.

But then something unusual started to happen: huge individual purchase orders for Constructions stock, literally tens of thousands of them, originating from multiple constellations throughout the Caldari State and beyond, began flooding the CSE. Expecting to find banks and other financial institutions behind the activity, SCC (Secure Commerce Commission) officials instead found private retail accounts generating the transactions, many of which had been dormant for years.

For the first time since the universe learned about what

was happening at the Armor Forge, Caldari Constructions stock stabilized for a moment, and then began rocketing upward. Wary of interfering with what appeared to be a godsend for those investors desperately trying to unload their positions, the SCC allowed the transactions to continue, unwittingly participating in one of the boldest corporate takeovers in history.

MR. SHUTSU SAT INSIDE the cabin of his personal dropship, soaked and filthy from the harrowing ordeal, contemplating his public failure in silence. Camera drones might have followed him inside if not for the swift riflestock strikes of his Home Guard escorts, who felled several of the pestering machines before the craft's boarding ramp finally closed.

From his window view, he could see a triage center established just inside the perimeter fencing, where the lives of some rioters were close to ending. Death had already claimed dozens of Constructions workers this day. The first to throw themselves against the fencing were electrocuted and burned beyond recognition; others had been trampled by the flood of workers who stumbled through the breaches; some even drowned in mud, pinned facedown during the mad rush.

Animals, he cursed. *They brought this upon themselves, and deserve to suffer for it.*

The voice of the dropship pilot sounded on the intercom. 'Sir, three messages for you, liftoff in sixty seconds. Destination?'

Mr. Shutsu scanned the data queue. One was the Kaalakiota CEO, which he promptly ignored. *She knows I'm ruined; there's no need to hear her say it,* he thought, moving on to the next message. It was from the office of Altug Borascus:

All of New Eden knows it was your cowardice that
killed those people. — Tibus Heth

Denied the satisfaction of knowing for certain that Heth
was dead, anger turned the blood in Mr. Shutsu's veins to
acid. But that wasn't even the worst of it. The parting shot
of his adversary was lost to the text of the next message:

The listed shares of Caldari Constructions stock have
been purchased by a single investor. My client needs
your private holdings to complete his takeover. I'll contact you shortly. If you want the attached photo kept
away from the media, you'll take my call. — The Broker.

The photo revealed – with vivid clarity – his naked self
with the three Gallentean prostitutes from Satelles, taken
earlier today.

'Sir, we're ready to leave,' the pilot interrupted again.
'Do you have a destination?'

'HQ,' Mr. Shutsu growled. 'As fast as you can.'

As the dropship's engines roared to life, the reality of
the day's worsening events crushed the CEO's spirits. *The
'Broker'*, he agonized. *Who the fuck is he?* Perhaps for the
last time, Mr. Shutsu admired the Armor Forge – the majestic production facility that had made him a billionaire
several times over – until it disappeared from view as the
craft ascended through the atmosphere and into the blackness of space.

A LONE FIGURE walked briskly along the main road
leading to the western gate, wearing the traditional uniform of a Constructions worker beneath a cloak and hood
that protected him from the rain. His face had the features

of a middle-aged man, with gray stubble coating a sharp jawbone, and deep creases beneath and to the sides of his emerald-colored eyes. A person studying him closely might have noticed his unusually soft, almost baby-like skin; a highly suspicious attribute given the rest of his tough demeanor, but no one would make that distinction now.

The rolling thunder of a dropship's engines drew the man's attention. Looking upward, he saw the fiery blast of the craft's exhaust as it lifted off and vanished into the clouds. A small band of workers was running in his direction, away from the commotion up ahead. Tuning out the sound of the downpour, the man focused on their conversation as they hurried past.

'Shutsu *ran*, that fucking coward!'

'And Heth survived! I still can't believe they took a shot at him!'

'We're not gonna get paid today, are we—'

'Fuck the paycheck, it's not worth anything!'

'I'm followin' Heth now, that guy's a hero, man.'

'We should find some weapons and go after those Home Guard guys!'

'Yeah, we wouldn't last five seconds against them—'

'Who cares? Anything's better than living like this!'

The man smiled, sidestepping other bands of roving workers, amused with their rebellious spirit and even more delighted with their willingness to do great harm to themselves. The crowd thickened as the guard towers of the western gate finally appeared through the smog. Stepping off the main road, he turned toward an alley lined with habitat-modules and produced a datapad. With a few taps on the screen, thousands of new Caldari Constructions shareholder accounts transferred their holdings to a single account under the name of Mr. Xavier Black. Satisfied that the transactions were completed, the man slipped on an earpiece. It was time to make a call to Mr. Shutsu.

'SIR, HAATAKAN OIRITSUU has been trying to reach you for—'

'I *know*,' Mr. Shutsu hissed back at his CFO, leaving mud stains on the floor of the boardroom as he marched toward the head of the table. 'I'm intentionally holding her off until we've worked out matters here first. What's the price of our stock?'

'Fifteen,' Tamo answered. 'Up from a low of eight and screaming higher. We're the only Caldari asset that's rebounding in this market.'

So then it's true about this 'Broker.' 'What about the reaction to our press release?'

'No one's buying it,' Nilen said, slamming her datapad onto the table. 'Whatever credibility we had was lost when we shot that worker – which, in case you didn't already know, wasn't Tibus Heth. They're showing pictures of the real Tibus carrying the one *we* killed all over the networks. We've turned him into a goddamn hero.'

'Then it's time to start planning an early retirement,' Mr. Shutsu confessed. 'Oiritsuu will launch a decisive raid on the complex to settle this matter for good, and when she does, it's over for us.'

'It's over now,' an unannounced voice boomed from the boardroom speakers. 'Once you agree to my terms.'

A series of quizzical looks flashed across each of the executives – except for Mr. Shutsu.

'The Broker, I presume,' he said calmly, motioning for the others to remain quiet.

A cloaked figure materialized at the head of the room, off to Mr. Shutsu's right. 'Ninety percent of Caldari Constructions' listed stock belongs to a single shareholder named Xavier Black, who is my client. You have five seconds to verify the account, which is registered with the SCC as a prime credit investor.'

Tamo was already typing furiously into his datapad, and the drop of his jaw confirmed the Broker's statement.

'Allow me to be the first to thank Mr. Black for investing in us,' Mr. Shutsu said. 'How can we be of service to your client?'

'Mr. Black wants control of the company,' the Broker said. 'You, and the executives present, will each sell me your company shares at the strike price of your employee options.'

Tamo broke out into a delirious laugh. 'Our options are priced at *one*, that's a ludicrous bid—'

'*Tamo, quiet!*' Mr. Shutsu shouted. But it was too late. The Broker's image turned slowly to face the portly CFO, intentionally allowing the uncomfortable moment to hang in the air.

'Tamo Heinulaila,' the Broker started, speaking as though reading from a dossier. 'Caldari Male Deteis, age fifty-five, unmarried, originally from the Akkilen System, appointed Chief Financial Officer of Caldari Constructions seven years ago—'

'Oh, so *what*,' Tamo interrupted, as pulses of red spread across the conference room table from his hands. 'You've done a little reading on me—'

'*Tamo!*' Mr. Shutsu screamed.

The Broker continued. 'Residences in the Forge, Citadel, and Lonetrek regions, all under several different aliases, one of which was investigated by Home Guard Security and led to your subsequent arrest. Do you remember the charges?'

The CFO suddenly began to sweat.

'Sexual deviance,' the Broker said. 'Multiple counts of

it, including solicitation of sex from children on numerous occasions. The rest of you haven't heard about this because it was conveniently stricken from the public archives, well before charges could be formally presented. Bribes, paid to certain, *influential* Home Guard personnel, came directly out of Constructions accounts. Copies of those transactions, selected voice recordings, and a list of those aliases, are available *here.*'

Before the quivering Tamo could speak, lists of information scrolled before the room, readily accessible to each of the datapads present at the table.

'You'll think twice about interrupting me again,' the Broker warned. 'The other part of the plea bargain stipulated that Tamo serve as a mole within the company, with special focus on the behavior of its executives. Sister companies though you may be, Kaalakiota's policy has always been to keep a very close eye on its investments, which includes your personal lives. And my, they *are* personal, aren't they? Who knows how many other pedophiles are in the room.'

Mr. Shutsu himself was now struggling to maintain his composure, glaring at Tamo with eyes that could burn holes through steel.

'None of you has any secrets,' the Broker said. 'Those all belong to me now. So I'll be perfectly clear: I didn't come here to destroy you. But I won't take "no" for an answer, either.'

The air reeked of ruinous closure for the careers in the room, as it was apparent that this monster held all the cards, and with them, absolute control.

'With all due respect, Kaalakiota owns sixty-five percent of the company,' Mr. Shutsu said, still focusing his glare on Tamo. 'Even with all of our shares, you can't claim acting ownership unless—'

'—Kaalakiota sells me their stake in Constructions, yes,' the Broker interrupted, turning to face the doomed CEO. 'If you'd bothered to answer Ms. Oiritsuu's call, you might have learned about our deal sooner.'

'Deal?' Mr. Shutsu swallowed, at last becoming unravelled. 'You've already settled?'

'No,' the Broker answered. 'My deal with her is contingent upon your acceptance of my offer to buy *you* out. Given the day's events and the exposure her corporation faces with the capsuleers, she is *very* eager to distance herself from you.'

It's over, Mr. Shutsu realized, his expression drifting off into a dreamy, defeated state.

'Yes, it is,' the Broker said, reading the CEO's expression. 'But I left you one option: refuse my bid for your shares, and you can derail my deal with Kaalakiota. Of course, your secrets will then become public knowledge, and you'll incur the wrath of the most powerful CEO in the Caldari State, who has the means to find you wherever you are—'

'Enough,' Mr. Shutsu said, pulling a gun from his jacket. 'All of you, transfer your shares. *Now.*'

Tamo began to whimper, and the enraged CEO strode toward him. 'I said transfer the fucking shares!' he demanded, pistol-whipping the man and opening a gash in his head. He shrieked in agony for only a moment, as the gun's barrel was pressed firmly into the side of his neck.

'Don't make me say it again,' Mr. Shutsu breathed.

Trembling, the man's fingers manipulated the datapad and signed away his fortune, while the Broker's grainy image looked on.

'I can't believe this is happening,' Nilen said, also on the verge of tears. 'This isn't happening to me, it just can't be—'

'Shut your mouth!' the deranged Mr. Shutsu said, swinging the gun toward her. 'Transfer the shares now! All of you!'

One by one, the executives' fortunes were transferred to the account of Mr. Xavier Black. There was a stench of urine in the air, and the sound of stifled sobs as Tamo wept openly.

The Broker turned to face the CEO. 'Only your shares remain,' he said, without emotion.

'Yes,' Mr. Shutsu replied, slumping into his chair and deliberately tapping the keys of his datapad with exaggerated, single-handed movements. 'Here, take them. Take them all.'

A final press of the keypad completed the deal.

'You made the right choice,' the Broker said.

'I did, didn't I?' the CEO sneered, eyeing the ruined members of his executive team.

His face suddenly contorted. After taking a few deep breaths, he placed the gun under his chin and squeezed the trigger.

'SIR, ALTUG JUST received a personal message,' one of the workers announced. 'I think someone else is trying to reach us.'

Tibus, wiping down the wounds on his head, threw the bloody rag onto the floor. 'Oh, yeah?'

Hobbling over to where Altug was seated, Tibus leaned down and yanked the man upright by his collar, and then threw him into the personal seat of his own office. The worker monitoring the terminal barely had time to move out of the way before Altug crashed down into it.

'Read it,' Tibus growled. 'Loud enough so that all of us can hear.'

Flushed with anger, Altug leaned forward to allow the retina authentication to complete. Both he and the worker blinked several times after reading the message in its entirety.

'Well?' Tibus asked.

'It's addressed to you personally, sir,' the worker muttered.

'Read the goddamn thing!' Tibus shouted.

Altug cleared his throat. 'It says, "To Mr. Tibus Heth; Caldari Constructions was just purchased by a private investor named Xavier Black, who has designated himself acting Chief Executive Officer until a suitable replacement can be found. As Mr. Black's representative, I have been instructed to meet with you personally, within the confines of the Armor Forge, to discuss the matter in private."'

The scowl on Tibus's face transformed to amusement. 'Well that's a good one, isn't it?'

The worker continued where Altug left off. 'Altug Borascus, the owner of this comm account, can verify the transfer of shares and ownership with his credentials.'

'Okay, Altug,' Tibus laughed. 'Verify this nonsense for mc, please. And then I'll kill you just for going along with it.'

Altug had already lost the color in his face, thanks to the manipulation of screens by the worker, whose expression was also bewildered.

'Sir, this is real.'

Tibus turned deadly serious. 'Stop fucking around, I'm not in the—'

'It's real,' Altug mumbled, resigned to defeat. 'These transactions can't be forged. Every member of the executive team, from Shutsu all the way down, just transferred all of their holdings to an account held by someone named Xavier Black.'

'Get out of my way, both of you,' Tibus muttered, limping over and shoving both of them aside to see for himself. In truth, he understood little of what the display indicated, except for the zeroes next to each executive's name, and the very large number besides the name Xavier Black.

'How the fuck is this possible?' he breathed.

'You made it possible,' the worker replied, unable to keep the smile from taking shape on his face. 'There's more to the message . . . keep reading.'

WITH RAISED FISTS and pointed fingers, the workers closest to the fencing perimeter were shouting threats at the soldiers on the other side, who stood by impassively, waiting for orders from the Home Guard field commander. With the gates at their back, they stood a few meters apart from each other along the entire length of the line, observing the belligerent crowd, watching for signs of another possible rush to get through.

One man, whose face was partially obscured with a hood, forced his way to the front, stopping beside a pack of especially furious workers. He stood perfectly still, seemingly impervious to the madness around him, and as such drew the attention of the two soldiers closest to him.

His silence, the soldiers realized, was telling them something. No sooner had their suspicions been raised when the field commander issued a new order to be on the lookout for a man identifying himself as Xavier Black. Once located, they were to let him pass through the barrier and approach the gates unescorted.

The two soldiers glanced at each other for a moment, then fixed upon the man with the hood, who casually crossed both his forearms into an 'X', and pulled his black cloak around in front of him.

Camera drones, catching the silent communication, focused on the area as more soldiers approached and formed a semicircle in front of the mysterious man. When they opened the fence to let him through, every spotlight in the area trained on him, and followed his solitary path right up to the great shielding doors, which opened just enough to allow him inside.

12

As the rumbling doors locked shut behind him, the Broker surveyed the scene. The staggered-formations of starship armor plating, each about three meters high, bore blackened scars from the barrage of fire that poured in during the Home Guard assault. Built to withstand much more powerful forces, the integrity of each plate was intact, and none had been penetrated. Constructions workers were everywhere, including the catwalk gantries high above, each pointing a rifle directly at him.

'Keep your hands where I can see them,' a voice warned, as two men approached him cautiously. 'No sudden movements.'

The Broker smiled, raising both of his arms to his sides and with his palms facing upward. 'The legendary Tibus Heth,' he proclaimed, ignoring the workers as they removed the earpiece and datapad from his pockets. 'Caldari patriot, champion of the proletariat. What a great honor to meet you!'

'Flattery got a lot of people killed today,' Tibus muttered, inspecting the devices handed to him. 'Take off your hood and cloak, slowly.'

'Of course,' the Broker said. His hands removed the cloth from his head, revealing a metallic socket at the base of his skull. It shined brilliantly in the glare of floodlights above, invoking a series of gasps and murmurs from the workers inside.

Tibus was unimpressed. 'You may be a capsuleer,' he growled, approaching the Broker. 'But to me you're just another man.'

'Spoken like a true leader of men,' the Broker laughed. 'You've had time to verify my claims. Why so defensive? I've come to you as an ally.'

'You've seen what happens when I let my guard down,' Tibus said, motioning toward the assembly lines far down the array. 'Let's go for a walk.'

GIVEN THE FRENZIED attempts by the media, State officials, and the corporate empire to get information about the Armor Forge, the absolute worst scenario that could transpire would be a communications blackout. But that was precisely what was transpiring, and the uncertainty was causing more damage than the actual news. *Something more drastic than what we've seen has already happened* was the sensation among the general populace and financial markets. And while the hostage situation – or revolt, depending on who you asked – still appeared unresolved, rumors began circulating that the guards stationed at the Forge's sister facilities in Aikantoh and Litiura had abandoned their posts, effectively leaving the workers to their own devices. Efforts to reach Constructions officials went unanswered, and Kaalakiota had yet to issue a statement about the botched assault and tragic riot afterward.

With the flood of bad news and uncertainty, trading in

Constructions stock was finally halted – but only after reaching an all-time high.

'TELL ME, TIBUS,' the Broker asked. 'What is it that drives you? Is it hatred, or a kind of . . . *civic* responsibility?'

'Right now? Anger,' Tibus answered, looking at the man as they walked along the assembly line. Workers in the gantry high above were shadowing them.

'You found a way to exploit the desperation around you,' the Broker said. 'You transformed despair into hope; found among the ruins of your life a faith worth dying for.'

Tibus stopped in his tracks. 'With all due respect, I don't know who you are,' he snapped. 'You said in your message that you represented Xavier Black—'

'An alias,' the Broker interrupted. 'One of thousands that I use, but I assure you, the money in that account is very real.'

'Then who the hell are you?' Tibus demanded, fingering the holster on his hip.

The man smiled, then continued his stroll. 'The name I'm known best for is the "Broker", and thanks to you, I now own this corporation. But I'm still looking for a good man to run it.'

'Bullshit,' Tibus growled, unholstering the pistol and pointing it at him.

'I saw you sacrifice a man today,' the Broker said, unfazed. 'The one named Heidan. It was brilliant.'

'That's not true—'

'Great leaders never hesitate to make difficult choices. You're a hero to your countrymen because of it. And his death – or should I say *murder* – brought you more power than you think.'

'I didn't come here for power, I came here to—'

'—die a soldier's death? To avenge that injury of yours, the one that makes you limp like an invalid—'

'I'm going to kill you right here if you don't leave,' Tibus growled, thrusting the gun into the Broker's face.

The man didn't even blink. 'Neither of us fears death, Tibus. Both of us are prepared to make the hard choices. And we both share a bitter contempt of the people who did this to you.'

'You don't know anything about what happened to me.'

'I know you better than you know yourself. You came here to seize power for a short while; I've come here to make it permanent. Give me my datapad, and I'll give you ownership of Caldari Constructions, control over the fates of millions – and, if you rule wisely, the means to deal with the Gallenteans however you see fit.'

Lowering his weapon slightly, Tibus was struggling to understand. 'What's in this for you?'

The Broker looked grave as he spoke. 'A war is coming,' he said. 'And it will bring the darkest days that man has ever known. It is why we exist, us capsuleers; this war is the very reason why we were created. It will not be a battle of nation states, Tibus. This war will decide the survival of some races, and the extermination of others.'

Tibus couldn't believe what he was hearing.

'The Caldari are an endangered species,' the Broker continued. 'Economically incompetent, politically fragmented . . . what cause will the people of this State rally to when the war begins? Money? Starvation?'

Tibus leaned against the railing on the assembly line, stunned that this immortal capsuleer saw the universe in the same light as he.

'The people of this State need a leader,' the Broker continued, taking a step toward him. 'Someone to guide them through the dangers ahead as *one, united nation*, and not the disjointed self-interests of stumbling corporations.'

Tibus reached into his pocket, pulling the Broker's datapad from his satchel.

'You asked how I stand to gain from this,' the Broker said. 'And the answer is that *my* survival depends on the survival of *this State*. What I do now, I do for us both.'

The Broker gently took the datapad and tapped in a few keystrokes. 'You are now a king,' he beamed. 'See for yourself.'

Leaning forward to read the device, Tibus's instincts were screaming that this moment couldn't possibly be real. The mind of a martyr disconnects when the reward of death is denied, and like every other worker who joined his cause, he fully expected that the Armor Forge would be his grave.

'Janus,' Tibus muttered in his radio. 'Have Altug reconfirm the new owner of Constructions.'

'It's already confirmed,' the worker breathed. 'We listened to the whole thing, saw the money transfer as it happened . . .'

The Broker extended his hand. 'To a new alliance.'

Tibus stared at the man's open palm as a whirlwind of emotions assaulted him. But before realizing that he had even done so, he found himself shaking the Broker's hand.

'To a new beginning,' Tibus said. 'Thank you.'

Staring at him with his unnaturally green eyes, the Broker held his grip for a moment. 'This path is your choice, Tibus. But listen closely – you need to understand something about this partnership: I am immortal, and I am invisible. I can be anyone, anywhere, at any time. Do not ever, under any circumstances, attempt to interfere with my death.'

Tibus let go of his grip.

'You'll never see this face again,' the Broker continued, stepping away from him. 'Don't lose the earpiece you took from me – I'll contact you through it in a few moments.'

Before Tibus could answer, the Broker jumped back and pulled himself on top of the assembly line. Moving quickly, he darted in between the half-constructed armor components and cast molds, working his way toward the alloy smelters.

Dozens of workers herded toward the assembly line and strained over each other to watch as the Broker climbed to the maintenance platform, emerging just below the sixth smelter in the line. To everyone's surprise, he activated the release vent. As molten alloy poured into the mold casing below, the Broker stepped off the platform. He vaporized in a fiery flash of orange steam, all but disappearing from existence as the vat of liquid metal consumed him.

Tibus Heth, too stunned to speak, stared at his right hand – the one he had used to make his pact with the Broker. His heart nearly stopped when the earpiece in his satchel began to ring.

13

Genesis Region – Sanctum Constellation
The Yulai System, Planet IX
CONCORD Bureau Station

Far from the Armor Forge and the Caldari territories, at the political junction of New Eden, the newly appointed Minmatar ambassador, Keitan Yun, took a moment to review his notes before approaching the podium. The CONCORD Assembly, long the bastion of international diplomacy and protectorate of interstellar travel, was about to convene for a general session. Ambassadors representing each nation state took their designated seats within a vast, spherical amphitheater suspended inside the main hub of the station, an architectural masterpiece symbolic of diplomacy's place at the center of all civil affairs. From the massive, glimmering central sphere spread the five major arms of the station, four of which were designated to the Gallente Federation, Caldari State, Minmatar Republic, and the Amarr Empire. The last arm, extending apart from all the others, belonged to the Jove Empire, which had not sent a representative to an Assembly session in decades.

Behind each ambassador were thousands of seats, but today a much smaller contingent of spectators was present. Regional governors, corporate executives, union officials, and others with a vested interest in international affairs chatted with each other in hushed tones, taking care to not let their voices carry across to political enemies inside. Glancing upward, Keitan took note of the Amarrian ambassador,

Larik Saal, who appeared wholly disinterested and indifferent to his surroundings. *Typical arrogance*, Keitan thought. *So many others have failed to convince them. Why should my attempt be any different?*

'Session will now commence,' announced the CONCORD session moderator. 'Ambassador Yun, you may begin your introductory address before we proceed with the day's agenda. Congratulations on your appointment.'

Rising to his feet amidst polite applause that came primarily from the Minmatar and Gallentean sections of the audience, Keitan cleared his throat.

'Thank you, Your Honor. It is a privilege and a lifelong dream of mine to be speaking here, at the cornerstone of our civilization, and on behalf of my beloved Republic, to whom I owe my origins, and my soul.'

All of the Assembly members nodded approvingly, except for Ambassador Saal.

'During my tenure as a professor, I found that the study of history compels a thorough examination of humanity itself. To gain an understanding of our past we must first understand ourselves, and the relationship we share with our fellow man. As an academic, I always emphasized parity in the telling of our history. As diplomats, we have a responsibility to our children to be objective when we record events as they take place today. Only then can we navigate through the challenges ahead, and forge a better future for us all.'

Keitan paused for a mild burst of applause, while the Amarrian ambassador stifled a yawn.

'As the technology of our civilization advances, so too does our responsibility to promote its application toward the advancement of peace. With the union of man and machine, we have taken our first small steps into an age of post-humanism, in which science has liberated mankind from the chains of mortality. The capsuleers are the empyreans of our age; they are our shepherds to the stars; and these times will undoubtedly be recorded as being among the most pivotal in the history of man.

'The awesome responsibilities that come with these advancements have brought with them great challenges. I am certain we will meet some of these with success. But my experience tells me that others, tragically, will remain unconquered, impeding the progress of our humanity and sheltering us from a great enlightenment. I say this because, time and time again within these hallowed Assembly grounds, our efforts to rise and conquer the fundamental challenges of universal equality and human rights have *failed*.'

The CONCORD moderator frowned as his colleagues looked on impassively.

'I have always found it astonishing that we have the will and the means to achieve the seemingly impossible, like building titans, or creating oceans on dead planets, and yet here we cannot agree on the fundamental tenets of human decency. The silence in this hall right now, as I speak these words, tells me that the *means* are here, but it is the *will* that we are lacking. I stand before you as the ambassador of an enslaved race, speaking to an audience within which the enslavers are listening, and ask myself: How have we survived, we of New Eden, when the definition of humanity remains so elusive, so *transparent*, to so many?'

A disapproving shout rang out from the Amarrian section, followed closely by bellows of support from the Gallentean and Minmatar stands.

'For years I studied the history made within this Assembly, and I am convinced that history will judge our generation by the achievements we have *not* made here. So many times, goodwill has been a disguise for indifference; men have stood on this very spot and insulted my

Republic with their empty promises, ignoring the pleas of ambassadors like myself begging for them to see reason instead of selfishly running from it.'

Murmurs rang out from the Amarrian contingency seated behind Ambassador Saal, who was now smirking.

'My nation holds a seat at this Assembly, and yet the overlords who spit on our freedom are permitted to share this honor as well. Is there any greater insult than this? Here, they can legislate policies for the alleged betterment of New Eden, when the plight of *billions* cry out from within their own borders. Why is such blatant hypocrisy allowed to persist? What justification can we give, as an Assembly, to allow in our presence a brutal empire that embraces slavery, peddles the women and children of my nation like cattle across its borders, drugs them into obedience, and then dares to appear in this sacred hall under the pretense of diplomacy and goodwill?'

Ambassador Saal leapt out of his seat. 'I've heard enough!' he shouted, as the audience erupted into discord. 'I've not travelled all this way to be insulted by a novice. How *dare* you!'

After demanding order, the CONCORD moderator turned a fierce gaze at Keitan. 'Ambassador Yun, you will end your introductory remarks *now.* Please take your seat.'

Keitan, encouraged with his reception, obliged. The Gallentean audience was on its feet, but surprisingly, many of the Minmatars were still seated.

'Ambassador Saal,' the moderator continued. 'I'll allow you a brief response.'

'Response?' the Amarrian said, storming up to the podium. 'A response to a man who views me, the father of two beautiful, young daughters, as a monster incapable of understanding humanity? I have dedicated myself to God, to peace, and to bridging the gap between our nations, as our beloved, departed emperors asked us to!'

The audience's polarity had reversed, with the Amarrians now shouting their approval and the Gallenteans hissing their displeasure.

'I pity you, Ambassador Yun,' he roared, turning to face Keitan. 'I pity your beleaguered nation, and the bitter past that our peoples share. But those "cries" you hear come from within your own borders, not mine! You accuse us of embracing slavery, yet it is *your* nation which has torn itself to pieces. Amarr is *one* nation, united under God. You Minmatar are nothing but scattered gangs and tribes, *still* fighting each other for land and greed after thousands of years, and still committing unspeakable acts of savagery that could never exist in our kingdom!

'Don't you *dare* lecture me on humanity, Ambassador Yun, when it is your people who are unable to feed themselves! In Amarr no one is denied the just rewards of a full day's work. There is abundant food on the tables of every man, woman, and child within our borders! We provide spiritual fulfillment and strengthen family bonds, regardless of social status! It is a sad facet of life, Ambassador, that not all men can become kings. Some of us must toil in fields while others rise to become capsuleers. We recognize that God created us all with different strengths, and so help me, that does *not* make us enslavers!'

Cheers erupted from the Amarrian section while Keitan shook his head in disgust.

'The truth, Ambassador Yun, is that *we* are the model society for New Eden, and that the so-called *Republic* of Minmatar would not have survived this long without our help, beginning with Emperor Heideran's reforms, Emperor Kor-Azor's advocacy for peace, and now Chamberlain

Karsoth, who has – in his boundless generosity – *increased* the benefit programs established by *both* emperors for your nation. God knows we have offered our compassion and done our best to aid the poor souls of Minmatar. And we have done so whilst battling the *real* overlords of your land: the corrupt, spineless leadership of your Republic! And this . . . *this* is the gratitude you have to show us?'

Ambassador Saal turned to face the CONCORD moderator. 'Your Honor,' he asked. 'How much longer must I tolerate this vilification and disrespect before the members of this session?'

The moderator looked apologetic. 'On behalf of the CONCORD Assembly, please accept our sincerest regrets,' he said, his face then darkening with anger. 'Ambassador Yun, your conduct and accusations are completely unacceptable. We expect a man of your stature and reputation to exercise better judgment, especially during your first address as a member of this Assembly!'

'Your Honor, I request the chance to present a counterargument—'

'Denied, Ambassador!' the moderator fumed. 'This was neither the time nor the place for combative discourse, and I won't tolerate another outburst! We are now behind with our agenda thanks to your selfish remarks, and you are hereby *dismissed* for the remainder of this session.'

'What?' Keitan said, stunned. 'How can you—'

'You'll stop right there, Ambassador, or your dismissal shall be made *permanent*! The Assembly will recess for ten minutes. We apologize for this unexpected delay!'

The lights illuminating the CONCORD Assembly members darkened, and the audience broke into shouts and heated discussion. Camera drones floating inside the amphitheater followed Keitan as he made his way to the exit, recording the unmistakable humiliation on his face. The realization that he had naively attempted too much in this political forum, whatever the validity of his claims, took the breath from his lungs. He would have much to answer for, both here, and in his beloved Republic.

14

Staring at the star field outside, Keitan sat in numbed silence, mentally replaying his debacle at the CONCORD Assembly over and over. Of the numerous personal blunders in his forty-two years, there were none that he wished he could take back more than this.

How could I have been so foolish? he wondered, squinting as the shuttle passed through a stargate. *I should know better by now than to speak my passion to anyone, let alone the Assembly.* Glancing around the cabin, he was grateful that no other passengers were onboard. The added scrutiny would be unbearable, and besides, he preferred the solitude to prepare for his meeting with the prime minister. *To whom I shall admit my failure in person*, he resolved, *and concede that her reservations about my appointment were well founded.*

Another bright flash, followed by the pilot's announcement that they were less than two minutes away from docking, brought home the chilling reality that they had arrived in the Illuin System. Keitan's hands tightened around the seat railing as the shuttle accelerated into warp. Between the dread of inevitable reprimands and his profound hatred of space travel, Keitan began to worry if his stomach was capable of holding its contents long enough to retain what little dignity he had left.

Metropolis Region – Gedur Constellation
The Illuin System – Planet III
Republic Parliament Bureau Station

'That went well,' Prime Minister Karin Midular muttered, rubbing her temples as the news networks replayed the Assembly meeting. 'I suppose getting thrown out of session isn't the *most* embarrassing thing that could have happened.'

'The man has courage,' countered Parliament Head Maleatu Shakor. 'He spoke what we all feel, or at least ought to.'

'Opting for courage when common sense should prevail is idiocy,' Karin retorted. 'This is a political nightmare, an absolute catastrophe—'

'Oh, you and your politics,' Maleatu scoffed, feeling his way to a bench at the side of the room. 'The Assembly has always been a circus for us, and if you had any common sense at all, you'd have abandoned it years ago.'

'That "circus" is the only viable means we have to get more of our people out of Amarr,' Karin growled. 'I *need* to show the populace some good news, anything to bolster support for my domestic initiatives!'

'Still think this is about you, eh?' Maleatu sneered, staring impassively across the room. 'I thought I was the only blind person in the room.'

Keitan's diminutive frame appeared in the doorway. 'Am I interrupting?'

'Ah,' the old Brutor smiled, turning an ear toward the sound of his voice. 'Welcome, *novice*.'

'Shush, you!' Karin scolded. 'Keitan, have a seat.'

'I'm just joking,' Maleatu laughed. 'Truth be told, you're the first man to really speak for Minmatar in that forum for some time.'

Karin focused intensely on the thin Sebiestor tribesman. 'What do you have to say for yourself?'

Unable to meet her piercing glare, Keitan fumbled to find the words, his heart palpitating with the fear of stuttering before her. 'I thought . . . thought I could strengthen your bargaining position for . . . for the goodwill release initiative, Prime Min—'

'By insulting them?' Karin demanded, leaning forward. 'Have you completely lost your mind?'

Keitan felt as though the ground was crumbling beneath his feet. 'It would have . . . have placed more international pressure on them to . . . to acquiesce, but not enough Minmatars . . .'

Karin buried her head in her hands.

'. . . they all just . . . just *sat* there,' Keitan said, his bony shoulders slumping in shame. 'I . . . I didn't count on them being silent.'

'Don't worry, Karin,' Maleatu grumbled. 'The Amarrians will happily release us their old and crippled slaves. It frees up room in their trash freighters.'

An aide appeared in the doorway. 'Prime Minister, the Gallentean economic advisers are here.'

Karin shot an angry glance at Maleatu as she rose from her desk. 'I'll be right out,' she said, dismissing the visitor. 'Keitan, what am I supposed to do with you? The Amarrians would be well within their rights to demand your removal, and I'd be hard pressed to disagree.'

The ambassador nodded, hanging his head. 'Would you like my resignation?'

Exhaling deeply, she walked over and paused, studying

him for a moment. 'I don't want that, no. But let's see how Karsoth reacts before making any final decisions.'

As she left the office, Maleatu rose from the bench and turned toward the door, using his cane to follow the edges of objects to guide his path.

'You do realize you were going to fail no matter what you said out there.'

Keitan looked up at the blind man. 'What do you mean?'

'Half of that session audience was controlled by Amarr,' Maleatu said. 'Those that they can't bribe, they threaten. These days, most Minmatars are vulnerable to both. Saal was right: the Republic really *is* failing.'

'I never thought I'd hear you say that,' Keitan said, suddenly defiant. 'You've been a pillar of strength in Parliament, the people rally to—'

'To what? Independence? The fighting spirit? Let's forget for a moment that a third of our population is enslaved. The rest will leave the Republic as soon as they can! Every Minmatar's dream of a better life is anywhere but here. Those that remain seek work with cartels and mobs instead of honest trades. We're like a pack of starving dogs – we've turned against each other just to survive. We were seven great tribes once. Now, you and me, Brutor and Sebiestor, we may as well be two different races entirely. In this new world, we have no history to share. And *CONCORD*,' he said with disdain, moving toward the door. 'They may as well be Amarrians themselves.'

'Listen to you!' Keitan stammered. 'You're a capsuleer! You've been the symbol of Minmatar patriotism and defiance for years! Don't give up hope for Minmatar, these people need you more than—'

'Karin Midular's politics can't fix this, and neither can diplomacy,' Maleatu said, stopping to place a heavy hand on the ambassador's frail shoulder. 'Whether you believe it or not, you have courage, Keitan. It moves me, and it won't be forgotten.'

THE STATION'S CAVERNOUS main level concourse was teeming with people, mostly Republic fleet ship crews and supporting personnel returning from extended deployments in space. Many were actively negotiating with capsuleer representatives for new ship assignments; others were on shore leave, passing the time trading with Gallentean vendors and seeking various forms of real and virtual entertainment. A mountain-sized section of the main hangar was visible on one side of the great hall, extending more than a kilometer above and below, where dozens of starship docking gantries were visible. Shaken from the day's events, Keitan wandered aimlessly through the crowd, hoping to remain invisible and wishing he had chosen to remain at Republic University teaching history instead of foolishly deciding to become part of it.

Pausing to admire the arrival of a Tempest-class battleship, Keitan wondered if it was worth the energy to fret over public recognition. *Who among these people even cares about what happens at the Assembly*, he thought, *let alone my pathetic attempt to inspire them—*

'"So many times, goodwill has been a disguise for indifference . . ."'

The female voice, spoken from within a meter of where he was standing, made Keitan jump. When he turned, his gaze was greeted by a stunningly attractive woman; she was an exotic combination of Minmatar skin and facial structure mixed with the sensuous, disarming eyes and lips of a Gallentean.

'Hello, Ambassador Yun,' she said, fixing her hazel eyes on his own. 'I admired your Assembly speech today.'

Keitan realized that the woman was at least ten centimeters taller than he was, and, judging from the form-fitted white business suit that she was wearing, physically powerful. Fully intimidated by her presence and fearful of how the words would come out of his mouth, the Sebiestor attempted to speak.

'Thank . . . thank you,' he stammered, silently cursing his stutter. 'But . . . but it really did . . . didn't—'

' "How have we survived, we of New Eden, when the definition of humanity remains so elusive, so *transparent*, to so many",' she purred, quoting another line from his address verbatim, the words sounding like music to Keitan's mortified ears. She extended a hand toward him. 'I've often wondered the same. My name is Ameline, and it is a pleasure to meet you.'

Keitan reached forward to take her hand. 'And you as well, but – *oww!*'

The moment their hands touched, Ameline had Keitan's arm twisted and immobilized behind his back. She pivoted gracefully alongside him, keeping his arm locked while embracing him with her own. Her face was inches away from his, and if not for his wild-eyed, frightful expression, the two might have been mistaken for lovers.

'Shhhh,' she whispered into his ear. 'You've drawn the attention of powerful people, and I've come to bring you to them.'

Making a feeble attempt to break free of her grip, Keitan was only met with more shooting pain as she twisted his hand a little bit harder.

' "Karin Midular's politics can't fix this, and neither can diplomacy," ' she said. Keitan froze. *How could she know my conversation with Shakor? Should I scream for help?*

'You won't be harmed if you cooperate,' she said, guiding them forward through the crowd. 'You would be honored if you knew who I was taking you to see.'

Keitan was terrified to the point of quivering, even more so when she kissed him gently on the cheek. 'I don't want to hurt you, Ambassador. Let's walk together, as partners would. There's a ship waiting for us here, and we're getting on it whether you want to or not.'

15

Pitted directly across from his luminescent captor, Keitan found himself struggling mightily to avoid losing consciousness as he battled the physical side effects of jump sickness. Trapped within the passenger cabin of a Republic Wolf-class assault frigate, Ameline sat comfortably near the room's only exit, a veritable barrier beyond which he could never pass. She stared at him coldly, inured or immune to the hardships of prolonged interstellar travel. Almost two hours had passed since the two boarded the capsuleer-piloted craft, and they had yet to exchange words.

But Keitan had long since lost count of the jumps endured during this journey, and was now so overwhelmed with physical discomfort that he could no longer stand to remain silent.

'You must be enjoying this,' he stammered. 'Saves you the trouble of torturing me yourself.'

'I recall offering you sedatives several times,' she answered. 'Your suffering is your own choice.'

'My being here is *not*,' he answered, losing his temper. 'You're a criminal no matter who you report to.'

'Only in the jurisdiction of empire systems,' she said. 'The last of which we left behind twenty jumps ago.'

A wave of dizziness ravaged him, forcing him to clutch at the seat handles. 'So what are you, some kind of pirate? The Republic would never pay a bribe for my release—'

'Quiet,' she said sternly. 'Look forward and tell me what you see.'

Keitan turned his bloodshot eyes on the cabin viewport. An acceleration gate loomed in the distance, its symmetric blue-white navigation lights shimmering against the blackness of space along the entire length of its metallic structure. Dozens of warships were patrolling around it, several of which altered course to move toward them.

'We're in the Great Wildlands Region,' Ameline said. 'Do you recognize those ships?'

An icy lead ball formed in the pit of Keitan's stomach. '*Thukkers*,' he breathed, turning to follow the renegade tribal markings painted on the underside of an interceptor as it coasted past them. 'They'll attack us if we don't leave!'

'Under normal circumstances, yes,' Ameline said, remaining stoic. 'But they take orders from the same people I'm taking you to see. We won't be harmed.'

'For now,' Keitan muttered, clutching his stomach as the ship approached the acceleration gate. 'So are you one of them? Is that why we've been spared?'

Ameline remained silent. The broadside of a Thukker battleship, bristling with weaponry that should have reduced their ship to dust, angled and dropped from view as the Wolf oriented itself with the center of the gate. Keitan reeled away from the viewport as arcing bolts of electrostatic charges engulfed the ship.

'This will be the most unpleasant part of our journey,' Ameline warned, getting up from her seat. 'Don't look forward or else you'll—'

It was too late. Keitan, nearly incapacitated with vertigo symptoms, was finally overtaken as the gate's metallic rungs hurled past the ship. His last conscious thought was being fearful of landing on the hard, cold floor as he slumped over the side of his seat into oblivion.

LIGHT BEGAN TO pierce through the darkness, and the visage of Ameline's angelic beauty emerged into view. It was a bittersweet reception, and difficult for him to accept that a face so mesmerizing could be the mask of such a vicious outlaw.

'You were only out for a minute or so,' she said, wrapping her arm around his shoulder, helping him to sit up. 'Look at the view outside now.'

Keitan stubbornly attempted to refuse her assistance, only to find himself heaved to his feet with a forceful thrust from Ameline's strong legs.

'Is it possible for you to keep your hands off of me—'

She placed her index finger over his mouth. 'Look. Outside.'

Angrily turning away from her, Keitan looked through the viewport and was met with a surreal vision; a breathtaking spectacle of paradoxical purpose; a scene so diabolically magnificent that Keitan Yun, never without words, was literally shocked into silence. Before him amidst the swirling cosmic background of an ancient nebula was an armada so vast that its numbers were impossible to count; an epic megascape of shipyards and stations surrounded by a lattice of Minmatar warships, each beset by swarms of maintenance drones and manned construction vehicles.

Overlooking the rows of perfectly aligned battleships and heavy assault cruisers was a line of capital ships, each capable of unleashing apocalyptic destructive power, positioned throughout like monolithic guardians. Twelve dreadnoughts, each more than three kilometers in height alone,

were positioned around the centerpiece queen of this starship hive: a Ragnorak-class Minmatar titan in its final stages
of construction, awash in the reddish glimmer of countless
beacons and lights, itself so massive that the mighty dreadnoughts seemed insignificant by comparison.

Keitan, his mouth agape, could muster but a single word:
'How?'

'The market value of what you see here is worth more
than the entire Republic economy,' Ameline said, also fixated upon the view. The pilot of the Wolf was flying slowly
past the formations of ships, deliberately providing a close
view of the epic display. 'This is just one of three hidden
staging areas, all hosted and protected by the Thukker
tribe.'

'One of *three*?' Keitan gasped, watching as a team of
MTACs welded armor plates onto the exposed rib structure of a carrier. 'Where could the money for all this possibly come from?'

'The money trail goes back hundreds of years,' she said,
turning to face him. 'To the first hours of the fledgling
Minmatar Republic, when Gallentean aid was all that supported us . . .'

'That can't be!' Keitan stammered. 'Federation assistance was intended for reconstruction after the Rebellion,
not an arms buildup!'

'So it says in your history texts,' Ameline said. 'Which
should also state that the Federation Senate opted to fi-
nance the aid as a percentage of the *total* fiscal budget,
as an allocation that would scale in perpetuity with economic performance. Now tell me . . . which nation state
has seen the strongest growth since the inception of the
Republic?'

Impossible, Keitan thought, as his mind raced through
the history of Minmatar-Gallentean relations. *The size of*

the Federation budget has grown a thousand times over since then! The amount of money pouring into this hidden war chest for the better part of two centuries must have been staggering, entirely too large for the Senate not to notice – or have they been intentionally looking away? *And what thievery*, he thought angrily. *Where would the Republic be today if that money had been used the way it was intended?*

'Who's responsible for this?' he breathed. 'How could they convince the Thukkers to cooperate?'

Rolling into view was the gaping entrance of the titan's hangar, currently a patchwork of unpainted metal sections crawling with drones, shimmering with the intermittent strobes and sparks of countless welding torches. Growing larger and larger, the sheer size of the structure gave Keitan the sensation that they were descending toward the surface of a planet, and not a man-made machine.

'The Elders are responsible,' Ameline said. 'They are the reason why you're here.'

'The Elders aren't real,' Keitan whispered, backing away from the viewport. 'Ancient mythology can't be the explanation for this . . .'

Again, she remained silent.

WHEN THE WOLF's airlock doors opened, Keitan found himself standing before a long, narrow overpass, barely wide enough for two people to stand on side by side, stretching far across to a distant platform.

'Step forward,' Ameline ordered.

Reluctantly, he stepped through the doors, and would have collapsed if not for Ameline's strong arms darting forward to support him. The walkway bridged across a great chasm, perhaps the unfinished hangar of the titan, and above him was a height at least as great as the depths below.

'Keep going,' she said, pulling him forward by the arm.

Bewildered, he walked on, trying to stay focused on the narrow surface beneath his feet. Looking over his shoulder, he noticed that the same pathway leading away from the Wolf's docking collar was retracting, its edge following them as they walked. When they were barely twenty meters away from the doors, the lights inside the hangar began to dim.

'This is far enough,' she said, stopping.

'Enough for what?' he asked, fearing the immense dimensions around him. 'Why are we stopping here?'

'Don't move,' she warned as the Wolf disappeared completely. Total darkness had engulfed them. 'I'll be right beside you.'

Keitan tried to compose himself, terrified at the sound of his own breathing. The blackness was so absolute that he had lost all sense of direction. He felt Ameline tighten her grip on his arm slightly, and for the first time found her touch reassuring.

Seven white figures emerged from the darkness, at first just tiny spots of light, but then transforming into apparitions that were several meters taller than he was. Their faces were indiscernible, nor was there shape to their limbs, but they appeared to be human. Despite the radiant light, Keitan was still unable to see anything, not even his hands before his face. It was as if the ghosts were all that existed in the universe.

'We Elders are no myth, Sebiestor,' an older voice spoke. 'Do you know why we brought you here?'

Racing through his memory, he summoned all he could remember of this lost, ancient history. The legendary Elders, the mythological incarnation of the seven Minmatar tribes, were selected men and women from every generation dating back to antiquity, each charged with the responsibility of absorbing the accumulated knowledge of the ages and using it to guide their journey toward the future. Although human, they were treated with the reverence of gods and hidden from public view to keep their identities secret. They were believed to have been murdered by the Amarrians during the occupation of the Minmatar home worlds, and many in the present-day Republic doubted they ever existed at all. Yet here they were, standing before him, and given the surreal circumstances of everything he had witnessed already, there was no reason to believe that these beings were anything other than what they claimed to be.

'My fail . . . failure at the Assembly . . .' he stuttered.

'To Republic politicians perhaps,' a female voice said. 'But not to us. You spoke truthfully about the indignation of Minmatar and the hypocrisy of governance among the empires. Your actions today were anything but a failure. They were bold.'

Keitan attempted to kneel, but Ameline stopped him.

'We are not gods,' another voice said. Each of the Elders was taking turns speaking. 'It is only our years and wisdom which earn your respect, nothing more.'

'Thank . . . thank you,' Keitan said. 'Forgive me . . . but what is this place?'

'A sanctuary for our race; a sacred home to recover from the wounds inflicted by Amarr. In the centuries that have passed, much of our strength has been restored.'

Keitan thought twice about what he was going to ask next, but succumbed to curiosity. 'With . . . with all due respect, what of the Republic?'

'Your love of the Republic is well documented. But it is Minmatar that you hold closest to your heart, and therein makes all the difference. The two are not the same.'

'The Republic is all we have holding us together,' Keitan

said, becoming emboldened with political charge. 'The cost of all these . . . these *war* machines could have made such a difference in the way—'

'The Republic will fail because its leaders have tried to reinvent Minmatar in the likeness of the nations that nearly destroyed it. We will never regain what was taken from us this way.'

'So all of this is just to take back the worlds we lost?' Keitan demanded. 'A quest for retribution and vengeance? Haven't we shed enough blood already?' Ameline tightened her grip forcefully this time.

The seven apparitions held steady. 'Such would be a fool's obsession; land means nothing when we can roam the heavens at will. It is primitive of you, and indeed all of the empires, to think of the universe we share as a collection of territories. We are unbound, Keitan, free to travel wherever our ships can take us. But the use of force is necessary to take *ourselves* back, including those tribes living *freely* under Amarr rule.'

Keitan realized the implied meaning. 'The Nefantars . . .'

'Yes. The betrayers of our race, co-conspirators with the conquering Amarrians, vengefully turned upon by the other tribes and hunted with merciless wrath everywhere they travel. But all is not how it seems, Keitan. This outcome was the price the Nefantars willingly paid for their *sacrifice.*'

'Sacrifice?' Keitan scoffed. 'To what, the Amarrian God? Those traitors helped paladins to hunt down and butcher us like animals!'

'A desperate, horrific diversion to shelter those whom they were trying to protect: the last survivors of a tribe whom you believe are no longer with us . . .'

Keitan's jaw dropped. *'The Starkmanir!'* he gasped, clutching his mouth. 'Impossible! They were exterminated first, right at the start of the invasion!'

'You need only gaze upon the guardian at your side to see that they still live.'

A soft beam of light fell on Ameline, still standing perfectly straight with his arm in her hand, like an angel warrior. *Absolutely stunning*, he thought, marvelling at her exotic facial features, understanding now why he was unable to place her origins before. She was a living reminder of the horrors suffered by the Minmatar; the passing of an entire civilization seemed to flash before his eyes as he studied her, bringing to life the forgotten relics of an ancient past to which he now felt a powerful bond.

'Descendants of the original purebloods all live on Ammatar worlds, under the supervision and protection of Nefantar overlords, toiling alongside other Minmatar slaves, as oblivious to their own origins as the Paladins are about their survival.'

'You're going after them, aren't you . . .' His voice trailed off as he considered the staggering force these Elders could bring to bear against any foe that stood before them.

'The Starkmanir bloodline will be restored, the Nefantar will be realigned, and here in the Sanctuaries, Minmatar will be made whole once again.'

'But what of those who live in the Republic?' Keitan asked, trembling as a rush of emotions assaulted him.

'Your government is saturated with corruption, and Prime Minister Midular has failed to accomplish the one objective she could have controlled: promoting unity among the remnants of the tribes. Her policy of appeasement with Amarr has only deepened the rifts between them. But we will do this much for the Republic: when the evil among her ranks least expects it, we will purge her government of Amarrian influence once and for all.'

The evil among her ranks, Keitan thought, flashing back to the Minmatars who remained silent at the Assembly. *My god, it can't be them all!*

'No outsider has ever seen these grounds and returned to empire space. As *our* ambassador, you will be the first. You will be our voice, to both your government, and to the Assembly powers. You will continue to speak your passion, for the worthy people of your Republic need inspiration and hope now more than ever before. Tell them *only* that they will be judged by their actions, but say nothing of our existence. We have sacrificed and lost too much, and we will stop at nothing to retake the destiny that was stolen from us by Amarr.'

The apparitions began to fade, and the lighting inside the hangar began to return.

'Ameline will be your connection to us; she will never leave your side. She is your guardian and your guide. Her words are our own – heed them well.'

The Starkmanir released her grip on Keitan's arm, but stayed close.

'Go, Sebiestor,' the voice said. 'Return to your beloved Republic, but keep Minmatar close to your heart.'

They were gone, and the lighting was fully restored. He looked at his guardian, but she avoided his stare, staying focused only on the open airlock doors of the Wolf as the pathway extended again. Keitan took his first steps toward it, lost in thoughts of salvation and hope, war and despair. His universe had just changed forever, and his speech at the Assembly today seemed a distant, insignificant memory.

'We'll stop when we reach the Skarkon System,' she called out. 'You can rest there before we continue on to Illuin.'

Whether he was willing or not, Keitan Yun was now New Eden's ambassador to an uncertain, tumultuous future.

16

Molden Heath Region – Eoldulf Constellation
The Skarkon System – Secret Deadspace Naval
Training Grounds
Sovereignty of the Minmatar Republic

Shimmering in the radiance of the local sun, brilliant waves of orange and red diffracted around the tunnel-shaped warp core, bathing the planets and moons of the Skarkon System in ghostly beams as they hurled past the forward view. Panning the camera drone to his left, Lieutenant Korvin Lears admired the perfect formation of Taranis-class interceptors flying beside his own, watching the light dance off their curved, reflective armor surfaces. Physically united with his ship, he considered for a moment that he was barely able to feel the neuro-embryonic fluid caressing every inch of his skin, marvelling that its unique quantum properties were protecting him from the physical effects of hyperspace travel.

This will always be exhilarating for me, the capsuleer

thought, *being able to pilot a starship, the thrill of hyper-space jumps, the privilege of flying for the Navy, all of it.* The mere sight of the Federation interceptors, staggered two hundred meters off each other's wingtips and basking in the bluish-white glow of their engines, was pure inspiration for him. Willing the camera drones to pan to his right, his mental imagery focused on the contrastingly loose formation of Republic Fleet warships on the other side. The brownish-orange-colored hulls of the Jaguar-class assault frigates made for a menacing appearance; their symmetrical twin-keel design cut through space like the blades of spears. *I hope they're ready for this*, Korvin thought as the warp core began to destabilize around them. *These guys need something positive to build on . . .*

'Knights, get ready,' the Federation squadron commander warned, just as the celestial objects outside slowed to a halt. Immediately, the Taranis's targeting system detected multiple hostile drone targets: Three enemy battleships, surrounded by five sentry guns spaced across an engagement sphere 100 kilometers in diameter. Korvin recognized the tactical situation immediately.

'Knight squadron, engage those battleships, designate Able, Bravo, and Charlie; Talon squadron will provide cover; gunship support in two,' the commander ordered.

'Copy, engaging,' Korvin replied, pointing the nose of his interceptor toward the battleship group and igniting the microwarp drive. Within seconds, his ship was catapulted to speeds exceeding two kilometers per second. The warfare tactic was straightforward. Battleships were armed with large bore, slow-tracking turret weapons that were ineffective against smaller, speedier targets. By closing the distance between them quickly, the interceptors could outrun the turning radius of the turrets, and could use their stasis webs and warp scramblers to cripple the lumbering targets long enough for heavier reinforcements to arrive.

A heavy salvo fired from one of the sentry guns slammed into Korvin's ship, knocking it off course. *Goddamnit*, he cursed, realigning his vector and praying that his shields could withstand another hit. *What the hell are those Talons doing?* Panning the camera out, he could see the other interceptors also taking fire from the deadly-accurate sentries, which had the most superior range and tracking speed of any other weapons platform in the engagement. Talon squadron's only objective was to take down those guns before they could damage or destroy the interceptors.

But instead of concentrating the entire group's firepower on individual guns, the Talon commander had assigned one assault frigate per sentry. It was a costly mistake: a second volley slammed into Korvin's ship, vaporizing the remnants of the interceptor's shields and cutting into the armor plating beneath.

The cold, automated voice of the combat moderator's voice announced his simulated death: 'Knight Five, destroyed.'

Fuck, Korvin muttered, steering his ship away from the fight. *Exactly what we didn't need to happen.* The drone-operated sentry gun that had been pounding his ship moved on to the next interceptor in his wing, and within seconds, the rest of Knight squadron was 'destroyed' as well. None of them had even come close to reaching the battleships.

'Mission *failed*,' the Federation commander announced. 'No fault of your own, Knights, but keep that to yourselves. You should hear the shouting on the Republic channel right now. Report back to Skarkon-Three station for debriefing. Out.'

So much for unity and morale building, Korvin mused,

willing his Taranis to set course for the base. *Better hit the lounge early tonight, before the fistfights get out of hand.*

JOINT MILITARY OPERATIONS between the Federation and Republic had been a cornerstone of the relationship between the two nations for the past two hundred years. The Gallenteans, eager to coach the Minmatars without treading on their pride, offered the exercises as a means of building confidence and self-sufficiency for the Republic. In recent years, it was hoped that the prestige of capsuleers, coupled with a strong navy, could unite a fragmented nation and bolster the strength of its government against the gangs and cartels threatening to wrestle control from Midular's government. But no one had foreseen the socio-economic climate of the Republic deteriorating so quickly, and now even military cohesiveness was beginning to crumble.

An avid student of history, Korvin reflected on the state of the Republic as he showered off remnants of pod fluid. *It's a national identity crisis*, he thought, drying before a full-length mirror and taking care to pad down the implant socket at the base of his neck. *They just don't know who they are anymore.* Running a hand over his rugged chin and jawbone, he decided against a shave before setting out to prowl the station's nightlife. The stubble gave him a tougher look, and the dress code was certainly less strict here than in Gallentean facilities. *Four tribes left, a third of them enslaved, and no one gives a damn except for us*, he mused, slipping into his dress-down Navy uniform, all but ensuring that a woman would be sharing his bed this evening.

Maybe democracy wasn't the best answer for Minmatar, he thought, stepping outside of his quarters. *They won't ac-*

cept centralized command, and they refuse to cooperate with each other, even when facing adversity. Korvin caught some young, attractive teenagers – Vherokior tribeswomen by the looks of it – whispering about him as the doors to the elevator closed. *It's a leadership problem; Midular is too weak to earn the respect of the tribes, and too contemporary for all the tradition in that race. The people want a fighter, not an appeaser. They want to see some strength, something bold; something to make them proud instead of humbled over and over.*

Noticing a reflection of himself inside the elevator, he straightened out his mane of blond hair, still damp from the shower. *Little things would help. Like jobs. A place to live. Pretty much everything that the Republic can't offer right now, certainly not to the people who need it most.*

The doors opened to reveal the main concourse, still packed with people despite the late hour. Taking his time, Korvin strolled through the crowd, pausing to admire the spectacular ship hangar view before moving on to the lounges. He could sense people noticing him, admiring his good looks, gawking at the socket in his neck. Being a celebrity had its bad moments for certain, but tonight he didn't mind. It was good to enjoy the benefits of genetic luck and years of hard work from time to time after all—

Catching his eye from thirty meters away was a gorgeous woman dressed completely in white. It wasn't often that a man like Korvin Lears was dumbstruck by good looks, but these features were unlike any he'd ever seen. Their eyes met for a fleeting moment; and without even realizing it, he began to move toward her, driven by lust and an overpowering eagerness to make her acquaintance. Closing to within ten meters, he was met with disappointment, seeing that she had a companion – a small, feeble

Sebiestor tribesman, much shorter than she was, and clearly not her type at all.

It would be rude to interrupt them, he knew – but he was a capsuleer. She would *want* to meet him, and that would just have to be accepted by her man.

'Excuse me, lady in white?' he called out loudly, readying his arsenal of pickup lines. 'Aren't you someone I know?'

The couple stopped and turned. She was a much more intimidating woman than he expected, but the shorter man was someone very familiar to him indeed.

'Professor Yun!' Korvin exclaimed, genuinely excited, his primordial instincts vaporized for now. 'How are you doing?'

The man looked exhausted, sickly even, but then his expression changed: 'Korvin Lears, is that you?'

'Ha, it sure is! How long has it been?'

Keitan shook his head, squinting to identify the insignia on his uniform.

'Much longer than the time it's taken you to earn those bars, Lieutenant. I see you've lived up to the expectations of your family – congratulations on becoming a capsuleer, Korvin.'

Truly excited to see his old friend, Korvin went to take the older man's extended hand, but the attractive female thrust herself in between.

'Hi,' she said. 'I'm with Keitan. Who are you?'

'Whoa, Professor!' Korvin smiled, then stopped as he noticed the grave, almost dire expression on Keitan's face. The woman was studying him; he was certain that she was sizing him up, and not in a good way.

'I'm sorry, my name is Lieutenant Korvin Lears of the Federation Navy. I used to travel all the way from Hulm to

Luminaire just to hear his lectures at Republic University. I'm a history enthusiast, and Professor Yun has this absolutely *enthralling* way of presenting—'

'Well that's very nice,' she dismissed. 'Good to meet you, and my, would you look at the hour, honey?' she said, turning seductively toward Keitan. 'You promised me some . . . together time, remember?'

Korvin's jaw dropped halfway to his shoes, while Keitan glared at her. Everything about their relationship was awkward, and it was blatantly obvious to the Gallentean that this was an act. The professor stepped past her, even as she intensified her stare.

'Korvin,' he said, taking the taller man by the arm. 'The Navy is an excellent fit for you. Your family raised you with good values – you have a good heart. But take some advice: forget everything that you've ever learned from me.'

'What?'

Keitan shook his head emphatically. 'Throw it away, discard it, cast it from your thoughts – permanently.'

The Gallentean pilot was stunned. 'Professor, what's wrong?'

'I've lost all my faith in the democratic institutions of the Republic. It's all been a sham, a lie, a waste . . . I feel like a fool for having believed so much in it all these years.'

'You can't be serious . . .'

'I've never been more serious in all my life. I'm a changed, bitter man now. I don't blame you for being an idealist, I don't . . . In fact, I used to be one myself. But not anymore. If you listen to one thing that I say, take one bit of advice to hold dear to, let it be this: drastic changes are imminent, and you would do well to trust your instincts and get out of harm's way.'

'Ahem,' Ameline said, playfully taking Keitan by the waist. 'Baby, we have to be going now.'

The professor's expression never changed, while Korvin's bewilderment only deepened.

'Take care of yourself, Lieutenant,' Keitan said, as the two moved into an elevator. 'It was good to see you.'

'Wait!' Korvin pleaded. 'What do you mean?'

As the doors closed, a drunken Brutor tribesman boasted a hearty laugh.

'She likes *men*, not Gallenteans!'

'Fuck off,' Korvin muttered, marching away from the scene. His evening ruined, Keitan's words weighed heavily on his mind as he sought the nearest lounge. After taking a seat and ordering a drink, a news broadcast on one of the concourse's giant holovids caught his attention.

It had something to do with the Caldari State, specifically the Caldari Constructions Corporation, and of its newly appointed CEO, a former company MTAC operator named Tibus Heth.

PART II

—

The Death of Innocence

17

Delve Region – D5-S0W Constellation
System T-IPZB: Lorado Station

The mind of Falek Grange was marred with violence, flash-backs to scenes of familiar places, and faces that whispered of a past he could not possibly know:

Mercy, there were faces once, calling out a name . . . my name! There's a young woman, a leader, desperate to find me . . . angry, dangerous, this person . . . a despot, evil, sinister, capable of doing great harm . . . Who is she? Who am I? These images are so gruesome, so raw and disturbing, contaminated with filth and despair, and pain . . . so much pain! The agony, the sound of it, the breaking of my bones, the consumption of my flesh. Why? What have I done? What was I before this? No, not that light again . . . there is danger beyond that light! Don't go to it! Stay in the shadows, you cannot imagine the horrors beyond that light! No! Somebody help me, please! Can anyone hear me? Please, someone . . . help!

'Settle down,' a woman's voice said. 'I'm bringing you back to consciousness.'

Falek felt the sting of bright light pouring into his eyes.

'Who are you?' he gasped. 'Don't hurt me anymore . . .
please . . .'

'No one's hurting you,' the woman grumbled, sounding
annoyed. 'I'm treating your injuries.'

'Where am I?' he asked. Throbbing soreness wracked
every inch of his body. The back of his head felt the worst,
as visions of the assassin and his wicked scepter returned.
'Why did that man try to kill me?'

'I don't know anything about it,' she snapped. 'I'm going to test your nervous system. Tell me where you feel
pain.'

'Who am I?' Falek asked. 'Do I have a name?'

'You're John friggin' Doe,' she snapped, just as needle
points punctured both of his feet. 'Feel anything?'

'Yes! My feet!'

'Both of them?'

'. . . Yes!'

He felt a pin plunge into his bicep.

'How about now?'

'Oww! My right arm!'

A slight pause, and then a deeper plunge. 'Anything in
your left arm?' she asked.

'No! Only the right!' Falek answered. The pain in his
bicep vanished, and once again, throbbing pulses of soreness returned to the rest of his body. His head felt as though
it were about to explode.

'Damnit,' she muttered quietly. 'What did I miss
here . . . ?'

A face appeared over him, and for the first time, he
could see the voice of the woman speaking: brown eyes;
sandy hair; and younger, perhaps in her thirties, but aged
beyond her years. *There was youth there once*, Falek
thought, robbed by ordeals and trials that betrayed what
should have been a reassuring beauty and calm. The re-

straining clips retracted from the gurney, freeing the bonds around his wrists and ankles. He saw her take his left arm, but it was sluggish, like dead weight.

There was a look of concern on her face as she took his hand. It was the first time in his short life that anyone had ever shown him kindness.

'Squeeze my fingers as hard as you can,' she said.

Falek tried, but felt a tingling, numb sensation instead.

'I have to go back in to fix this,' she said, frowning. 'I'm going to put you back under—'

'No! No more darkness,' Falek pleaded, struggling with the waves of agony pulsing over him. 'This pain is . . . unbearable . . .'

'That's something you'd better get used to,' she warned. 'Your wings are clipped, friend. Welcome back to the realm of mortals.'

'Mortals?' he breathed. 'I don't understand . . .'

Her eyes drove ice picks through his own. 'It means you're just as fucked as the rest of us.'

With all the grace of a crashing meteor, the door to Gable's operating room flew open, and Jonas stumbled through, blatantly drunk.

'Well, hello!' he announced. 'How are my two favorite people doing?'

'Get out of here, Jonas,' Gable ordered, moving toward her instrument panel. 'I'm not through with him yet.'

'He looks fine to me,' the *Retford* captain said, stumbling toward the gurney. 'How're ya feeling, champ?'

As if greeting an old friend, he playfully slapped the patient's thigh. Falek howled in agony.

'Stop it, you asshole!' Gable yelled. 'He's still in a lot of pain! Now get the fuck out of here so I can finish!'

'Baby, baby, he can wait,' Jonas mocked, brandishing a bottle of spirits and a tin filled with pills. 'How about a relaxing trip down memory lane, you and me, for old times' sake?'

'I quit using, you son of a bitch,' she growled. *'Get out of here!'*

'No one ever *really* quits the rush, sweetheart,' Jonas cooed, sliding up to her. 'Come on, let's go up to your place for a while—'

Despite his discomfort and fear, Falek was unable to restrain himself. 'Stop pushing her,' he gasped. 'Just . . . leave her be.'

The quarrelling couple stopped and stared at the battered capsuleer for a few moments. Then Jonas burst into laughter.

'You're getting better by the minute,' he said, stepping up to the gurney. 'What's your name, cappie?'

Falek focused his eyes on the man, trying to hold his composure. He still couldn't understand how this bastard 'Jonas' somehow gave him the strength to be defiant. But the way he stood over him brought back the memory of his ordeal, and of the nothingness before it.

'I . . . I don't know,' he answered.

'You don't know?' Jonas asked. 'Or you won't tell me? I could always beat it out of you—'

He raised the bottle in a threatening manner, and Falek cowered in fright. Again, Jonas laughed, delighted at his power over one of humankind's elite.

'Knock it the *fuck* off,' Gable hissed through clenched teeth. 'He has amnesia, you dickhead. *Come here*,' she growled, grabbing Jonas by the ear and dragging him to a corner. He couldn't fight her off because of the booze and drugs in either hand.

'What the hell are you doing?' he protested.

She winced from the reek of alcohol on his breath, and whispered angrily into the ear she was still gripping.

'He's a cloned capsuleer, and the CRU logs show that he was activated *before* his recorded persona could be uploaded into his cortex. Do you know what that means? He's a blank slate – a full grown adult with no name, no past, not a goddamn thing to tie him to whatever he was before you found him. And you want to know what else? He'll never fly a ship again – at least not as a capsuleer. That implant in the back of his head is destroyed, and it can't be removed or repaired without killing him. So he's mortal again. One of us.'

'Then why are you freaking out? He's completely harmless!'

She released the ear and slapped him in the temple.

'*Think!* It makes him that much more precious to whoever's looking for him! And you brought him *here!*' She started poking him in the chest for emphasis. 'Of all the places, you stupid, stupid, *stupid* imbecile, you brought him—'

Jonas grabbed her hand and thrust it into his crotch.

'—Here?' he said, laughing uproariously and then whirling around, slamming the bottle onto the floor. Falek flinched at the sound of its shattering.

'The doc says you're valuable,' Jonas proclaimed, reactivating the wrist clamps on the gurney. 'No more surgery for you today. Time to go back to sleep.'

A stream of anaesthetics poured into Falek's bloodstream, and his eyelids became impossibly heavy. He could hear more shouting and arguing as the pain began to slip away.

Why are people so cruel? he wondered, before the darkness took him again.

TÉA FOLLOWED THE sound of Gear's awkward grunts and whimpers as they bounced throughout the dark catacombs of the *Retford*. The boy could have been anywhere, in the next compartment or across the ship; the metal hull carried the slightest tone indefinitely. Hurrying past faulty fittings and blackened electronics, she rushed to him like the mother she desperately wanted to be, ignoring the list of repairs that Jonas had ordered her to do.

She found him in the recesses of the engine room, scribbling, thrashing, stroking furiously on a fresh sheet of his sketchpad – one she had paid an entire salvage share for – with his carbon pencils.

'Gear . . .' she said softly, leaning against the entrance corner.

Hunched over the pad, he continued to draw, his knees resting on the metal grating. Beside him were plasma conduits; thick, heavy pipelines that extended from the *Retford's* aneutronic fusion reactor directly beneath them. It made for a stark contrast; the delicate features of a young child against the cold, dangerous equipment surrounding him. Sensing her presence nearby, his tiny hands rushed to finish his creation.

'I am so sorry you had to see that,' she said, keeping her distance. 'We didn't know he was Amarrian until we brought him onboard . . .'

Slamming the carbon down, Gear signed angrily at her: *How come you never stand up to them? You always do everything they say, even when it's not fair!*

The unspoken words drove a stake through her heart. 'Jonas is the captain,' she said. 'We—I have to do what he says when I'm on his ship. Those are the rules.'

Jonas wants to keep him and then sell him, doesn't he? Gear motioned.

'Yes,' she answered softly. 'He thinks there's going to be a big reward, maybe enough to find a doctor who can fix your voice.'

His bottom lip quivered and the corners of his mouth

turned downward as he fought the urge to cry. Then he grabbed the carbon and resumed his frenzied drawing.

'Oh, Gear . . .' she breathed, reaching out to him. But he quickly scurried away, snatching the pad with him, as if threatened by her. She clasped her hands over her mouth, devastated that she had become so repulsive to him.

He cast a few more strokes, grunting, whimpering, until he couldn't stand it any longer and slammed the carbon, glaring at her with tear-filled eyes.

The Amarrian may be bad, he signed, as distorted grunts wheezed from his throat. *But selling him for money is wrong! You're no different from them now!*

Then he threw the sketchpad at her feet and scampered away, disappearing to another dark corner of the ship.

Téa bit hard into her knuckles, resisting the urge to scream, struggling with the weight of a bitter truth observed by a child. It was all so unfair, so wretchedly unforgiving. She hated her past, she hated the *Retford*, and above all else, she hated the power that Jonas held over her. *Why won't life let me care for anyone?* she raged. *Why did that have to be taken from me along with everything else?*

Another dagger slashed her heart when she saw Gear's creation: the sketch depicted the *Retford*'s cargo bay, as it was when the capsuleer was brought onboard, only now a ferocious monster had emerged from the salvaged container. As three adult figures cowered away from it, a young boy hung from the creature's mouth, impaled by jagged rows of teeth.

Goddamn Jonas, she thought.

Even if the symbolic representation of the picture was misunderstood, the artwork stood on its own merit as impressive to anyone: bold, strong strokes with delicate touches around the details, depicting an abstract visualization of the world through the eyes of a young Minmatar orphan. Gear was remarkably talented and bright; it was his smarts which had kept him alive long enough for the *Retford* crew to find him.

Téa was still haunted by the distress calls; desperate pleas for help from a small asteroid mining colony that had come under attack by Blood Raiders. Screams of agony filled the comm channels, followed by the sounds of gunfire, and then an eerie silence. Jonas had kept the *Retford* nearby, waiting for death to claim its last victims, and then for the pirates to leave. Heroism and ethics be damned, the single hybrid turret armament of their ship was not going to repel a Covenant attack. But more importantly, the colony's demise was a scavenging opportunity that the *Retford* could ill afford to pass up. *Psychotic Amarrians killing rich Amarrians*, Vince had said coldly. *As long as there's salvage, I could care less.*

We kept telling ourselves that, she remembered. *Until we saw the carnage inside the base.* It wasn't just Blood Raiders killing Amarrians; it was Minmatar slaves getting butchered to protect their Amarrian overlords. The masters had placed waves of slaves, drugged into senseless, euphoric obedience with Vitoc, in front of Blood Raider blades and guns, using them as human shields. But the Raiders were there for Amarrian blood, not tainted slave blood. The cult of the Covenant was a discriminating band of marauding sociopaths, taking special care to make certain that their sadistic rituals were kept pure. Those they took with them would be sacrificed. As for the rest, their lives were to be 'discarded' – by far the more humane fate of the two.

Until that day, little Gear had been subjected to every kind of abuse a Minmatar slave could be. Because of his diminutive size, they forced him into an ill-fitted survival suit and gave him a floodlight, sending him into tiny bore-holes and crevices within the asteroids. Once inside, he would prospect for signs of precious ores, setting markers for drills and mining lasers. Dangerous as the job was, the time spent in that filthy suit was preferable to time spent outside of it, where the fists of his master were often waiting to strike without reason or provocation.

Struck in his throat after complaining of thirst, Gear was left with a crushed larynx and damaged vocal cords. The event was later depicted, in disturbing detail, on a page in his sketchpad. The boy's artwork was a history of his troubled past, and an outlet for the creative talents that his time of servitude suppressed. *What despicable evil*, Téa thought, leafing through the pages. *Experiences that no human should have to endure, let alone a child.* Slavery was a damned existence, but all the more hellish in the desolate outer regions, which were visited only by prospectors, pirates, and the scavengers who stalked them both.

Gear was the only survivor of that colony. When the mayhem began, he jumped into his survival suit and did the only thing he knew how, which was to burrow into the deepest rock crevice that he could find. He would later emerge, after the Raiders left, because of his need for air. When the *Retford* arrived to ransack what was left of the facility, Gear had stumbled upon Vince and tapped him on his hip before collapsing. He was blue by the time they brought him onboard, and Téa was the one that resuscitated him.

She fell in love with him on the spot, seeing him as the son she never had but always wanted.

No one knew what his real name was, and as far as he could communicate, he didn't know if he was ever given one. Proving himself a fast learner, he picked up sign language immediately and took to drawing when Téa presented him with the sketchpad as a gift. He was fascinated with all the mechanical devices aboard the *Retford*, which earned him the nickname 'Gear.'

Page after page in that sketchpad, Gear's self-expression was evident in his art, and of the dark moments that traumatized him the most. His fear and loathing of Amarrians was as understandable as it was tragic, because the boy just wasn't truly capable of hatred in spite of everything that had happened to him. He was a good person, one of those rare anomalies in a universe that was saturated with cruelty.

Now they had taken an Amarrian onboard for the sole purpose of selling him like salvage, and Gear had called them out at their own hypocrisy. The youngest crewmember of the *Retford* embraced human decency as a matter of goodwill and obligation, despite having ample reason to doubt its existence more than anyone else on board. After all, he had been bought and sold once before.

Self-loathing was tearing through Téa's soul. But it was Jonas whom she directed blame toward more than anything else. *You just don't step in between a mother and her child*, she thought. *Someone's going to pay for this. Someone has to.*

18

A brilliant contrail of light sliced across the starfield, con-densing into the silhouette of an Amarrian Prophecy-class battlecruiser emerging from hyperspace. Trailing bluish-white plasma in its wake, starlight glanced off its mag-nificent, gold-tinted hull, accenting muscular contours blemished with the fresh wounds and burns of ship-to-ship combat. *A survivor*, Victor thought, inspecting the damaged vessel through the camera drones of his own ship. *And rel-atively unscathed.* Seven additional contacts registered on the local comms channel, and within seconds, more con-trails deposited scarred, battered Amarrian warships along-side of the Prophecy. All were Theology Council vessels, and were among the last remaining survivors of the men and women loyal to Falek Grange.

'This is Commander Aulus Gord,' the Prophecy captain announced tersely. Victor recognized the capsuleer imme-diately. '*Revelations* brings us to this checkpoint.'

'Welcome, Commander. I have control of recovery op-erations now.'

'Victor, what's happened?' Aulus demanded. 'They're trying to kill us! Why?'

'Because of our allegiance to Falek Grange,' he an-swered. 'The Chamberlain struck first to protect himself.'

'*Protect himself from what?*' Aulus shouted. 'Falek was no threat to him, and nor was the Council!'

'Not the man,' Victor replied. 'But the heiress whom the man represents.'

There was a pause. 'Sarum has been dead for *years*!'

'No, Aulus. She *lives*, and is watching us as we speak.'

The Prophecy captain was stunned. 'That's impossible!'

'Aulus, I was in her presence just hours ago – don't ask me to swear by it. Lord Falek has been presiding over her resurgence since the Amarr Succession trials. No one outside of his inner circle knows this – you are the first.'

'How did she survive? Don't tell me she was cloned!'

'She was cloned, but she's . . . different now. *Resurrected.* I've seen her power with my own eyes, Aulus. She has been . . . reborn, in the image of the divine.'

'And Karsoth knew about it? How did he suspect Falek?'

'Karsoth is a coward,' Victor hissed. 'Even the rumor of her survival is a threat to him. But it was no secret that Falek was aligned with her before the trials, and now . . . we underestimated the extent of his influence, and the lengths he would go to tighten his grip on power . . .'

'*Not the Covenant,*' Aulus snapped. 'Don't tell me that!'

'Look at the wounds on your ship,' Victor said. 'The Imperial Navy *and* the Blood Raiders put them there. Only a beast like Karsoth could find common interests between archenemies. You and I should be dead now.'

'Then there must be a traitor among us! How else could he arrange—'

'Fear compels him more than anything else,' Victor scoffed. 'If there was a traitor, Karsoth would have killed him first. No . . . we are all that remain of Falek's men, and I know in my heart that our bond is righteous. When next we enter Empire space, it will be with Sarum as our queen. But until then, we will be hunted without mercy, and our survival depends on the fate of Lord Falek!'

'Why is he so important?' Aulus demanded. 'I loved him like a brother, but the chance that he could have survived is so remote—'

'Aulus,' Victor said, his temperature rising. 'Your sword belongs to Sarum, and you must obey without question, without hesitation, and with nothing less than *absolute faith* in what you have been tasked. These orders come from Her Majesty herself: *Find him*, no matter what the cost. There is nothing else for us now, and we will not rest – not in this life or the next – until we bring Falek back to her!'

Aulus contemplated everything he had just learned. He remembered praying feverishly for her ascension to the throne, and of being devastated by her tragic death. Jamyl Sarum was the most charismatic of the heirs; her words spoke of fire and strength; of Amarrian pride and God's will. No one else could restore Amarr to her former glory, to her rightful place as the ruler of all nations; indeed, of the entire universe itself. Falek Grange was a stern, hard man, but his tireless devotion to Sarum was what earned him allies; he was in her favor, and that made him extremely powerful. Aulus followed him to hold onto what remained of his dream for an Empire ruled by Jamyl Sarum. Now Falek was feared dead, but the queen that he dreamed of was alive! It forced conflict between his spiritual need for her, versus the practical man inside which screamed that Victor's words couldn't possibly be true. But the contest was brief, for Aulus remembered his creed:

This is a test of my Faith, he thought, *and I will not fail.*

'What are your orders, my lord?'

Victor willed the starmap to display in his mind. The virtual representation of the 4O–239 system was pulsing, indicating his present location and the remnants of the Theology Council fleet. *Who would take Falek from the wreckage?* he asked himself. *Who would perform a dangerous spacewalk just to remove his CRU from the main structure . . . ? What would make that worth the risk . . . ?*

Air, he realized. *The CRU must have been airtight, or*

*there would be no reason to remove it. The Blood
Raiders . . . I saw them approach the wreckage and move
on . . . there were no capsuleers in the area . . . which leaves
rescuers or scavengers, and both would have to bring
him to the nearest base to have any chance of keeping him
alive . . .*

*. . . and it would have to be someplace that wouldn't
make a scene about his arrival.*

With a second thought, he commanded the map to display the closest known outposts, colonies, and habitable
structures, filtering out locations unequipped with pod
gantries – the specialized mechanical cranes required
to insert and retrieve capsules from starships. More than
twenty locations began flashing, all of them within three
jumps of the wreckage – and these were just the ones that
Theology Council cartographers knew about.

'How many spotters do we have in this region?' he
asked.

'Only three,' Aulus answered. 'The network for this region isn't fully developed.'

Damn, Victor thought. *Not nearly enough coverage for
them all.* The three closest bases to the wreckage site
stood out to him on the map.

'Send agents to Tripskill Ridge and Malomer Junction.
Leave the one at Lorado Station for now. Instruct them to
report on the movements of Blood Raiders, any mention
of capsuleers, salvage exploits . . . anything that could
guide us. And tell them to do it quietly, or we'll hunt *them*
down.'

He paused a moment, then added: 'We'll pay one million credits for information that leads us to him.'

'One million,' Aulus confirmed. 'It shall be done.'

Victor selected a system that was approximately equidistant from all three outposts, betting on his instincts that Falek was nearby.

'Set course for system E30I-U,' he ordered. 'We'll wait there for any news.'

May faith guide us all, he thought, just as the warp drive engaged.

Wherever you are Falek, we're coming.

19

Delve Region – D5-S0W Constellation
System T-IPZB: Lorado Station

Vince held his glass in front of him, watching the ice melt and blend into the remnants of his drink. A large, strong man, it usually took several potent concoctions to have any measurable effect on him. But tonight was different for some reason. Almost through with his first drink, he felt a warming sensation tingle his cheeks and neck, and there was a buzz behind his eyes as he motioned for a refill. *Maybe it's just age*, he told himself. *Or fatigue grinding me down, wearing away my life like some rock crumbling into dust.*

Deep in unregulated space, the closest borders to Lorado Station were Amarrian, and most of the patrons sitting inside the bar reflected that ethnicity. Pirates, smugglers, and other non-religious sorts went about their business, generally keeping to themselves, but sharing a common agreement that a pious lifestyle just wasn't suitable for their tastes. More than a few drunken toasts had been raised here to lawlessness, one of many reasons prompting the station's owner to invest heavily in weapons-screening technology. The only god that this crowd worshiped was money, and the acquisition of it by any means necessary.

Ringing the lounge area were viewports spaced a few meters apart, providing the patrons with a fine view of a corroding hangar bay and random scraps of junk caught in the gentle pull of the asteroid outside, a former mining colony long since abandoned. The owner kept the gravity inside the station slightly above standard (1.0 g), just enough to weigh down aggression somewhat and keep his patron's asses planted squarely on bar stools and the laps of strippers. Every now and then, one of the partner 'establishments' would arrive with a cargo hold full of prostitutes, attracting customers from light years away and kicking off a flurry of new business for the station. Their arrival was always a welcome change for the regulars and their usual, simulated forms of entertainment. It wasn't unheard of for an entire starship to be offered in exchange for a sexual encounter with a real human being instead of a virtual one.

But most of the time, Lorado Station was a lonely place, and being alone was exactly what Vince wanted.

The bartender, an older man of Caldari descent, kept glancing up at the holovid, which was still covering events from the Armor Forge.

'Man's a goddamn hero if you ask me,' he announced, pouring the drink. Imagery of Tibus Heth carrying an injured worker during a spectacular firefight was brightening the room. 'Wish I'd known leaders like that when I was whoring for mega-corps.'

Taking a sip, Vince listened to the raging debate about Heth's intentions, and the financial consequences of the takeover. Almost as an afterthought, the host commentator mentioned the brutal violence that had taken the lives of dozens of workers.

Financial consequences, he thought. *Things back home haven't changed a bit.*

'Which one was your pimp?'

'Lai Dai,' the bartender answered. 'Drove an indy for thirty years, took my winnings, and opened up this shit-hole of a bar as far away from my old routes as possible.'

'Rolling around in cash, are you?' Vince smiled.

'I won't exactly be a millionaire anytime soon,' he said. 'Especially since the station owner's Caldari.'

Vince gulped down half of his drink, savoring the way it burned his throat on the way down.

'No question about it then,' he croaked. 'You're completely fucked.'

Both men laughed, understanding each other. The bartender turned away, leaving Vince alone with his thoughts. Surveying the area, he noticed one patron was passed out cold; his face was lying flat on a lounge table, and an open vial of Frentix was resting in one palm. Other patrons were spread around, isolating themselves as much as possible from each other. An old frigate was approaching the docking bay, and dronc tugs were emerging to guide the vessel into an open berth. The sight made Vince's mood turn sour, and he threw back another hard gulp.

I don't know how much longer I can stand this, he thought. *I'm tired of running, and I'm tired of doing everything fucking Jonas tells me to.*

Vince set the glass down in front of him and took a deep breath, appreciating the bitter fumes of the alcohol cleansing his windpipe. *Yeah, I used to work for Lai Dai. I spent most of my life floating around a shipyard in a survival suit with a lasertorch and an armful of cable couplings, dodging mindless work drones and the random shit flying all over the place. And every single miserable step of the way, Jonas was looking over my shoulder, telling me what I should and shouldn't be doing.*

He reached out and grabbed the glass.

I should have told him 'no' when he asked me to crew for him. I should have ignored his bullshit, the 'You're my best worker, you're right at home in a survival suit, how about some adventure, a chance to get out of this corporate grind,' and all of that crap.

Vince slammed home the rest of the drink, forcefully setting the glass onto the counter and drawing the ire of the bartender.

Oh, that's right, I did say 'no' the first time. And the fucking second time he asked me.

'You want another one of those, or something to calm you down a bit?' The older man motioned to a scrolling list of drugs on display behind the counter.

'Just keep these coming,' Vince answered, holding his hands out in front of his face. 'Please.'

Because of these hands, I'd swallowed my pride and gone running to Jonas like a little girl. Not caring how strange he must have appeared to anyone looking, Vince studied the scars on his meaty knuckles. *He must have loved that, seeing how scared I was. How scared the both of us were, me and Téa. Her with her face all bludgeoned, me with a hole in my shoulder. We'd have done anything for Jonas to get us out of there. Anything. He knew that. And he's been taking advantage of it ever since.*

A full glass, with fresh ice, was placed before him.

Could I kill Jonas the way I killed Téa's asshole husband? Now there's a hell of a question. He took a sip this time, swishing it around his mouth a bit before sending it down. *Nah, it wouldn't be the same. Liberating, maybe, but not refreshing, like it was with Kavon. Some guys say they can't remember their rage, that when it's all over and they're looking at what they've done, it's as if time just skipped to the 'after' and took away the fun of it, like going to some call house and heading right to the exit without taking any of the whores for a ride. Not me. I remember everything . . . the way my fists pounded into his face, the way I'd bashed his head against the floor, the sound of his skull cracking, and that smell – man, that disgusting stink of brains. I enjoyed it so much I hadn't noticed that fucker had shot me. Didn't even feel it, not until it was over. Now that's something I'll never forget. And the thing is, it felt pretty damn good. If that makes me a monster . . . so be it.*

Another deep gulp, and rush of warmth swarmed to his temples, blurring reality into a haze.

Maybe if Jonas ever hits her, he thought. *If he hits her the way Kavon'd beaten her, the way he'd killed that baby growing inside of her, then it'd feel good to kill him. I wish I didn't need a reason, but fuck it, I'm a monster anyway, right? Even so, he's still not worth it. Not yet, anyway. Not while we're still running from three different Caldari corporate police forces. Plus whoever else is going to come after us for bringing that goddamn capsuleer on board.*

'How long are you going to ignore me?'

Looking toward his left, Vince noticed an Amarrian woman seated two stools over from him.

'I mean, a woman shows up to a dive like this, and you don't notice?'

She was wearing a mechanic's overalls with a tight-fitting sweatshirt beneath, and smelled slightly of lubricants. Her hair was dark and cut short; her face had a greasy appearance but with features that made her strangely desirable, with bottomless dark eyes that held a mysterious, sensuous appeal. But the hands on this woman struck

Vince's dulled senses as being overly powerful for her size; they were calloused and worn, with dirt buried deep beneath her fingernails.

'Guess I was too wrapped up in this drink to pay any attention,' he mumbled, placing the glass to his lips for another sip.

'I can see that,' she said. 'So, are you here for the pussy parade?'

Some of the drink went down the wrong pipe, and Vince began to choke.

'What, you think Amarrian girls don't know any dirty words?' she said. 'I could use a good lay just as much as the next gal. Or guy.'

She flashed a devious smile that revealed a beautiful set of white, straight teeth.

'You're full of surprises,' Vince croaked, composing himself. 'So, can I buy you a drink or something?'

'No,' she said. 'But I'll take your money instead.'

Vince laughed. *Something's not right here*, he thought. *But I could really use a good score.*

'What are you, some kind of deckhand or something?'

'Deckhand?' she said, raising an eyebrow. 'Try *captain*, dear.'

'*You're* a captain? Please.'

Her teeth flashed again. 'I can tell from the look on your *adorable* mug that you are *definitely* no captain yourself.'

Her words shredded Vince's pride like a scythe, but his ego was quickly defeated by lust as she stood up and moved toward the stool directly next to his. He couldn't help running his eyes over the entire length of her figure.

'It's okay,' she said, taking a seat. 'I catch everyone by surprise. It's how I survive out here. Tell me, *deckhand* . . . when'd you get here?'

Vince wasn't sure how he was feeling. It was a danger-ous combination of contempt and desire, like she was by-passing the human in him and prodding the sleeping beast beneath.

'Little while ago,' he answered. 'What are you flying?'

She rolled her eyes upward thoughtfully, as if debating whether or not to tell him the truth. 'A modified Crucifier. It's rigged for speed and a few other surprises.'

'I think I saw it getting towed in just a few minutes ago.'

'You noticed my ship, but not these curves sitting right next to you?'

She slid one of the coverall straps off her shoulders, ex-posing the firmness of a breast tucked inside.

Vince took a deep breath that sounded more like a gasp. 'Look, when you've been in space for as long as I have . . .'

'We'll get your priorities sorted, don't worry,' she said, touching his knee for a second. 'So what are *you* flying in?'

Mesmerized, Vince hesitated before answering. 'It's a Lynx-class frigate. A real shitcan.'

'Well it can't be that much of a shitcan if you're still alive. Here's something you probably already know,' she said, licking her upper lip and leaning closer. 'If you take care of her, she'll take real *good* care of you. Got it?'

Vince wondered if everyone in the bar could see the bulge in his pants.

'Yeah, I think I got it.'

'Good. It takes brawn and balls to run an old frigate like that. You've got both,' she said, glancing at his crotch. 'What's your role onboard? I'm always looking for a good crewman to hire . . . for *maintenance* responsibilities, of course.'

'I'm . . . pretty good with a torch and survival suit.'

'Ugh,' she muttered, looking disgusted suddenly. 'Please tell me you're not working on a scavenger boat.' She backed away from him, motioning for the bartender to come over.

'Why do you say it like that?' Vince asked, eager to retain her interest. 'You'd be surprised at how lucrative it is.'

'Oh?' she said, with a raised eyebrow. 'Is it lucrative right now, scavenger-boy?'

'Could very well be,' Vince said, feeding off her mannerisms. 'Our last find was pretty good . . . *real* good, as a matter of fact. In fact, you might be talking to the luckiest man in the region right now.'

She held his lustful, hopeful eyes for a moment. Then she looked toward the bartender and squinted, as if trying to see past him.

Vince took the bait and glanced in the same direction.

Lorado Station used expensive, sophisticated technology to enforce its weapons ban. But even these security measures failed to prevent the occasional maiming or death of a patron due to the resourcefulness of determined killers. In the case of this sultry woman, the available resources included her fists and legs, genetically enhanced fast-twitch muscle fibers, and extensive martial arts training, all provided by the Blood Raider Covenant, and all for the sole purpose of engineering an assassin who could still work effectively under such restrictions.

The moment that Vince looked away, she unleashed a powerful kick that exploded through a supporting leg of the barstool upon which he sat. With the chair flying out from underneath him, his full weight began to fall straight downward. Unable to brace himself, his tailbone struck the floor with his full weight on top of it, blinding his vision in a phosphene-laden flash of pain.

Hopelessly disoriented, he never saw the follow-up thrust of her knee, which crushed his face in a thunderous impact that knocked him flat onto his back.

Reacting as quickly as an older man could, the bartender lunged over the counter in a feeble attempt to restrain her. Younger, faster, and stronger in every sense of the word, she grabbed the inside of his wrist and wrenched it backward, snapping tendons and bone. While the man threw his head backward to howl in pain, her other arm darted forward, crushing the man's larynx with the web of her hand. A blurry kick flashed over the bar and connected with his sternum, sending him crashing into the rows of bottles behind.

The sound of shattering glass revived Vince from the depths of his daze. Somewhere through the numbing pain and disorientation, he could hear more thuds, cracks, and groans, but these sounds still weren't enough to pull him out of it.

Not until he heard her speak again.

'They're at Lorado Station. It was a salvage frigate . . . Falek Grange is here somewhere, I'm certain. No other ships have left since I arrived . . . As you wish, master.'

Vince was suddenly invigorated with an adrenaline-fuelled burst of self-preservation that sprang him up to his feet. Primordial instincts took control of his physical self, suppressing the pain and releasing the animal inside of him, now cornered by this assassin who had found the prey she was looking for. Multiple warnings of danger accosted his senses; in a split moment, the realization of who she was, coupled with the knowledge of what Jonas had brought to this station, triggered the realization that death – his greatest, deepest, most haunting fear – was coming for him.

That realization made Vince extremely powerful.

Surprised at his resilience, her attacks reconvened a full second later instead of a mere blink. She launched herself in the air at him, missing with several attacks but landing a flurry of punches as she touched the ground. Small as she was, her movements were fluid, precisely transferring the full weight of her mass and momentum into each strike. Vince absorbed some blows and deflected others, careful to shield the injury to his face while waiting for the right moment to launch a counterstrike.

Coming in low, he threw a weak left jab, intentionally letting his guard down to expose the swelling around his eye. She went for it immediately, snap-punching her left fist forward for a crippling shot. But Vince was already rotating his torso counterclockwise, generating momentum that was propelled into a vicious roundhouse that came up from underneath and to her left, skimming past the armpit and blasting through her chin and jaw. The blow snapped her head violently around her shoulders, overwhelming the structural resistance that even her modified muscles and bone could withstand.

Carried airborne by the brute force of his punch, her frame pirouetted almost a full 360 degrees before striking the ground, her head coming to rest in a grotesquely unnatural position. A final garble of air wheezed through her mouth as the life left her body.

'What the fuck was that all about?'

Vince whirled around with clenched fists, expecting another contest. Drawn by the commotion, a group of men wielding makeshift clubs and knives had arrived during the fray.

'Blood Raider assassin,' Vince announced. 'Check behind the bar, the old man needs help.'

His eyes were drawn to a datapad clipped to the assassin's waist. Kneeling beside her, he ripped it free, spitting out the blood flowing into his mouth from shattered sinuses.

'Is this what happens when you can't pay for tricks around here?' someone in the crowd grumbled.

'All of you need to leave *right now!*' Vince shouted, shoving the device into his pocket. 'There's a Blood Raider attack coming, everyone get the fuck *out!*'

'You're talking nonsense, matey,' another man said. 'Sounds like they're after you, not us.'

'I don't care if you believe me or not,' Vince growled. 'But you're going to die if you hang around.'

'The only one here that's got a problem is you,' he said, as two additional men joined him on each shoulder. One was wielding a heavy tool with a sharpened edge. 'I'm betting those Raiders would pay something real nice for your ass, dead or alive.'

Vince got to his feet, enraged this time instead of fearful. 'Listen to me, you little shit—'

A loud bang followed by a rumble shook the floor beneath everyone's feet, distracting everyone except Vince. Before the emergency lighting came on, he had already flattened the men threatening him. Noticing a tin of drugs on one, he reached down and grabbed it. Then he took the sharpened tool and stood over them.

'Get the fuck out of here!' he roared, watching them and everyone else scramble for the exits.

An automated warning began repeating on the station's loudspeakers: 'This is an emergency. All station personnel report to battle stations. This is not a drill. All non-station personnel, prepare for evacuation. This is an emergency . . .'

His instincts turned him back toward the assassin. *Datapads use bioencryption*, he thought. *I need to take a piece of her with me to unlock it.* He grabbed her lifeless arm and laid it out flat against the floor, then spread out the corpse's fingers as wide as they would go. Raising the weapon over his head like an executioner, he had to hack twice before one of the digits was finally severed. Then he ripped open the drug tin, emptying the caplets and placing the finger inside.

Glancing toward the bar one last time, he turned toward the exit and ran like hell.

The old bartender remained neglected on the floor behind the counter, alive but suffering extreme difficulty in breathing. Reaching for his own datapad, he keyed in a brief message with his working hand, made sure it was encrypted it, and sent it off.

Collapsing onto his back, he clutched the device in his hands, hoping to hold on just long enough to see himself turned into a millionaire by the Theology Council.

20

Delve Region – D5-S0W Constellation
System E301-U

'I will not hesitate when the test of Faith finds me . . .'

Victor recited the *Paladin's Creed* as he floated freely inside the pod of his bomber, idling in the vastness of space with seven other warships, waiting for a sign from divinity.

'. . . for only the strongest conviction will open the gates of paradise.'

They could be there for hours, perhaps even days, but their only option was to wait . . . and pray.

'My Faith in you is absolute; my sword is Yours, My God, and Your will guides me now and for all eternity.'

Observing the formation of ships surrounding him, it struck Victor that despite the tragedy and desperation of their plight that there could be such closeness in the void. Eight ships, surrounded by incomprehensible distances and wonders, seemed hopelessly insignificant against such vast dimensions. Yet here they were, united in faith, committed in purpose, and compelled by destiny to be united as holy warriors in a quest to save a brother, a fellow believer, in the name of a holy queen ordained by God.

I hope.

Detached from all physical sensations inside the pod, he nevertheless twitched in the viscous fluid, revolted at the vileness of his own doubt. Faith was supposed to be intangible, something that cannot be touched, but only believed.

Yet Jamyl Sarum shatters that notion.

Despite the fervent beliefs forged from an upbringing in a church devoted to God, he found himself woefully unprepared for a manifestation of the divine in physical form. He wanted to believe in her, but the man inside demanded proof, as if her being able to read his thoughts was insufficient evidence to convince him.

Give me a sign, he thought, directing his plea to God. *Something to make me believe.*

The divine answered immediately, in the form of a message sent by a spotter located in the T-IPZB system:

ASSASSINATION ATTEMPT AT LORADO STATION
MENTION OF SALVAGE FRIGATE, FALEK GRANGE
STATION UNDER BLOOD RAIDER ATTACK
EVACUATION UNDERWAY

Absolute fear, saturated with a fiery clarity of purpose, crawled over every inch of Victor's flesh as he shouted deployment orders to his forces.

* * *

VINCE WAS RUNNING as fast as he could, dodging station patrons too incapacitated with panic, drugs, or injuries to react to the danger. His actions were driven by primal instincts; his determination to survive required thinking only of himself, and of what was necessary to escape from the station alive.

'Jonas! Where the fuck are you?' he shouted into his datapad, rounding the corner leading to the *Retford's* berth coupling. *'Jonas, goddamnit!'*

Téa was waiting for him at the airlock, her eyes widening at the sight of her brother's appearance.

'Vince, did you hear that? I think we're under—'

'—*attack*, you genius, yes,' he growled, throwing himself down a hatch. 'Start everything up while I check the engines.'

'What the hell happened to your *face?*' she called after him.

Ignoring her, his feet hit the metal grating beneath and nearly flattened Gear, who was about to climb up.

'Kid, put yourself at the weapons station,' he ordered. 'You may get a chance to shoot at something.'

Vince ignored the boy's frantic look as he reached for his datapad again.

'Jonas! *It is time to leave!'*

Delve Region – D5-S0W Constellation
System T-IPZB: Lorado Station

The warp tunnel resembled a portal leading directly to hell. As its translucent membrane dissipated around Victor's fleet, a bright orange point blossomed into a full-blown explosion as the drives cut out. Lorado Station was under attack by a Blood Raider Covenant task force, taking punishing damage from a torrent of laser cannon fire directed by a Bhaalgorn-class battleship. A small industrial hauler attempting to exit the station's hangar was writhing in its death throes, beset by a vicious swarm of Cruor-class attack frigates. Victor counted ten enemy warships in all.

'Take the Cruors first,' he ordered, willing his bomber to cloak. 'Protect any *frigates* exiting the hangar, ignore the larger targets! Go!'

Thick beams of searing energy lanced across space, connecting with the Prophecy piloted by Aulus. The battlecruiser's hull flashed in a brilliant display of colors as its shields diffracted the blast.

'We'll draw their fire as best we can,' he said, bringing his ship to bear against the Blood Raider Ashimmu-class cruisers streaking toward them. 'Until the death, my lord!'

Victor answered with a phrase from the Scriptures: ' "*In God we shall remain brothers for all of time,*" ' he quoted, starting his invisible charge toward the goliath Bhaalgorn.

IN STARK CONTRADICTION to Vince's experience on Lorado Station, Jonas sought to quench his manly desires in the time-old fashion of simply paying a woman to 'take care of it for him.' Bloodied in the mouth after asking Gable for the same thing earlier, he'd wandered out to the concourse, selected the first female professional who would give him the time, and disappeared into a cheap hab-module to commence a session of oral stimulation and binge drinking. Upon the release of his pent-up, ship-bound desires, he'd passed out from exhaustion.

Just a few minutes into the deepest sleep he'd ever known, the datapad in his pocket began screaming for attention. Somewhere in the murky recesses of his impaired mind, he recognized that it was Vince, who was trying to warn him about something, and that it was probably important.

But then again, he reasoned, this was Vince; and nothing that Vince said was ever *that* important, especially not now, when he was so comfortable in bed.

A loud explosion shook the room, abruptly changing his rationale. His head jerked off the pillow as evacuation orders began blaring on the loudspeakers outside.

My *money*, he thought, remembering his prized cargo and bolting upright, nearly knocking the prostitute out of bed.

'I gotta get my money!' he mumbled, jumping up and leaving despite the virulent protests of his guest.

THE DOOR TO Gable's operating room flew open, and Jonas – half dressed and inebriated – stumbled to the floor as a deafening bang shook the walls. Falek, unable to see behind him while laying supine in the gurney, was trembling helplessly within his prison of medical devices.

'What's happening?' he pleaded. 'Who's attacking us?'

Jonas got to his feet and rushed to his side, ripping out cables and intravenous couplings with reckless abandon. 'You don't know?' he asked, grabbing the Amarrian by the shoulders. 'You ought to.'

Gable barged into the room, livid and desperate as the station crumbled around them. 'I should fucking kill the both of you! You've ruined everything—'

Another explosion nearly knocked the both of them off their feet. Screams and falling debris could be heard from outside the concourse, and smoke began to fill inside.

'It's time to go,' Jonas grunted, heaving the agonized

man onto his shoulders and whirling toward Gable. 'If you want out of here, now's the time!'

'They're destroying the ships trying to leave,' she yelled, delirious with anger. 'You won't make it past the—'

'*I'll take my chances,*' he shouted, brushing past her and stepping into the chaos outside. 'Anything's better than staying here!'

THE LAST CRUOR exploded in a spiralling cascade of debris and fire, hurling chunks of twisted metal through space. But within seconds, the last remaining assault frigate of Victor's group was sliced in half, a victim of the combined Blood Raider cruiser's firepower. Furious, he unleashed wave after wave of missiles, spears of fire streaking through space and opening violent gashes in the bellies of the invading warships, while still keeping part of his concentration locked on the Lorado Station hangar.

Aulus knew the battle of attrition favored the Covenant; it was just a matter of time before his own ship would wilt under the staggering firepower of the Bhaalgorn. If Falek was inside, he prayed that whoever was sheltering him could escape in time. Aulus fought until the bitter end; his turrets carved holes into the Ashimmu cruisers, venting their hulls and crews to space, reducing them to shattered, spinning hulks—

—until the Bhaalgorn's guns penetrated the last of his defenses, vaporizing entire sections of hull plating along the Prophecy's superstructure. The battlecruiser began breaking apart around Aulus; the warship's disaster management CPU barely had time to launch his pod free of the doomed ship before its reactor exploded in a brilliant flash. Helpless to do anything more while inside the capsule, he willed the tiny craft to escape, hoping he could live with himself for abandoning the brothers he left behind.

The darkest hour was upon them. Time had run out for the followers of Falek Grange.

'JONAS, ARE YOU *drunk?*' Téa exclaimed, ready at the bridge controls of the *Retford*.

'Yes,' he mumbled, hurriedly settling into his seat. A view of the hangar's exit filled the cockpit viewport, bathed in the terrifying coruscation of laser fire and explosions, casting strobes of fiery incandescence throughout. Dangerous chunks of structure debris were floating all over the bay, shaken loose from the Blood Raider bombardment outside.

'Harbor control is either dead or offline,' Téa muttered, clearly struggling to keep calm. 'You have to do this manually.'

A cruiser and two small frigates detached simultaneously from their moorings about 600 meters in front of them, nearly bumping into each other as they ignited their engines and started their escape run.

Jonas keyed the intercom. 'Vince! My engines!'

The speaker hissed back: 'You've got plasma, go!'

Working under the strict direction of harbor control guidance, the task of undocking from any station was usually managed by drones or manned tugs that guided ships into position to safely leave the hangar. Without it, undocking – particularly when there were multiple starships aligned in comparatively tight spaces – was potentially disastrous.

Jonas knew he had no drones, or vector guidance, or even permission to undock. Without thinking the situation through, he jerked the controls over before disengaging the berth couplings. The *Retford's* lateral thrusters fired, forcefully pushing the frigate away from the gantry and ripping the airlock module from its mooring. A section of its anchoring structure tore away, venting the inside of the station to the hangar's vacuum. The sound of ripping, groaning metal vibrated throughout the pressurized interior of the ship, while debris and at least two doomed souls tumbled out of the twisted gap into the open bay.

'*Jonas!*' Téa screamed.

'Shit,' he muttered, barely hearing her as he concentrated on the cluster of ships ahead of him. 'Are we breached?'

'The airlock's fucked!' Vince screamed. 'But we don't have any holes!'

Jonas wanted to exit a few seconds after the group in front of him left the hangar entrance, hoping they would distract the Blood Raiders from opening fire on the *Retford*.

'Téa, you have to get us into warp as soon as we get clear,' Jonas said, trying to blink away the drunkenness. 'Think you can handle it?'

The sparking, charred wreckage of a destroyed starship hurled across the hangar's view. The sight made Téa's stomach turn over.

'Warp?' she asked weakly. 'Warp *where?*'

'I don't care *where*,' he growled, easing the throttle forward. 'Just as long as it isn't a stargate.'

The cruiser ahead of the *Retford* emerged from the hangar and was strafed immediately by Blood Raider cannon fire.

'This is it,' Jonas warned, his brow glimmering with sweat. 'Everyone strap in! Gable! Make sure the patient is locked down!'

He didn't give her a chance to answer, because the

window of opportunity was about to close. Gunning the throttle, the *Retford* lurched forward, and the inner walls of the hangar became a solid line.

VICTOR WAS DESPERATE; his mind was mottled with doubt as his bomber unleashed salvo after salvo against the behemoth Bhaalgorn, only to watch helplessly as each missile exploded to no effect against its powerful shields. Orbiting as close as he could without colliding, he was impervious to the warship's slow, heavy weapons but powerless to inflict any real damage of his own. Of the eighteen ships that started the engagement, only he and the deadly Bhaalgorn remained.

Ignoring the orbiting bomber as if it were a gnat, the Blood Raider battleship redirected its fire at a group of ships exiting from the station hangar. Rage bubbled up within Victor; it took every ounce of restraint that he could muster to keep himself from ramming the ship. He could do nothing to prevent the massacre; he didn't even know for certain if Falek was aboard any of them, or if he would meet his death on the station, waiting for this sinister behemoth to destroy him and everything else onboard.

And then he saw it: the miracle that he had demanded from God happened again.

A tiny, helpless frigate streaked out of the hangar, brazenly flying through the engine exhaust of the cruiser fighting for its life. Victor's conscious was drawn to it like a magnet; he couldn't explain why, yet he just knew, *knew in his soul*, that the tiny ship was what he was looking for.

Demons conspiring against God betrayed the same intuition to the Bhaalgorn captain. As the warship's deadly turrets disengaged the cruiser group, Victor prayed, *prayed fervently*, for the frigate to hurry into warp. He watched as it slowed its course and turned, painfully slow, to align it-self with the warp core forming off its port side, and then in horror as bright white beams lashed out from the Bhaal-gorn, striking the vessel's midsection. The blast took the frigate's shields down completely, vaporizing chunks of armor plating and singeing the hull beneath; a second hit would destroy it for certain.

But, God be praised, the battleship's guns couldn't recharge fast enough, allowing the resilient frigate enough time to correct its course. In the blink of an eye, it vanished, leaving behind a stream of plasma contrails and smoldering debris.

Another miracle. How many more do I need?

Victor activated the warp drive of his own ship. He had the ID markings of the target vessel – its name was the *Retford*—and the divine speaking to him inside knew that Falek Grange was onboard.

21

Lonetrek Region – Sela Constellation
The Malkalen System – Planet V, Moon 1
Ishukone Corporate Headquarters

Otro Gariushi was a man accustomed to taking bold risks. The measure of a man's worth, he always thought, was his willingness to stake personal welfare on decisions affect-ing great numbers of people. He openly mocked the elit-ists and politicians who 'led by appeasement', considering it a cowardly ruse to convince fools into helping them gain what wealth could never buy. For most of his life, Otro chose to walk a dangerous path. Yet for every step of his epic – and often times, dark – journey to power, he always found allies willing to follow him, even when faced with overwhelming odds.

Leaders like Gariushi became generals, admirals, and the rulers of nations. As such, he became the CEO of the second most powerful mega-corporation in the Caldari State: Ishukone. And while not a 'head of state' in the traditional sense, by all accounts, citizens considered him to be the last great national hero, a purist who held fast to the ideals which captured the essence of being Caldari. He was loved by all who knew him, and his legend was certain to prevail for generations to come.

The tale of his rise to greatness was famed for being the most unconventional and scandalous of any corporate tycoon to date. Rumors of a personal affiliation with the Guristas pirate organization – and the sale of classified State military technology to that notorious cartel – ran unchecked in the media for years. But no one came forth to prove such claims, either for fear of retribution from the legions of people loyal to Otro, or simply because all investigative efforts proved futile, perhaps because of a lack of vigor in the first place.

Rumors were that the sale of this technology – specifically, the complete technical blueprints of the deadly Raven-class battleship – literally saved Ishukone from going into default. The windfall from that single sale, purportedly worth trillions, and subsequent copyright sales to the capsuleer population should have made Otro Gariushi the richest man in all of New Eden.

In reality, it didn't earn him a single credit.

With the help of his mysterious CFO Kinachi Hepimeki – rumored to be his sister, but again, there was no proof of this – every bit of that money was reinvested toward sustaining growth and opportunity for the employees of Ishukone. Reinforcing this strategy was his stubborn refusal to draw a salary from corporate coffers. Material wealth did little for his tastes, and more importantly, he saw the needs of his fellow compatriots as being much greater than his own. Ishukone may not have been the largest mega-corporation in the State, but it was believed to be the most financially sound during these harsh economic times.

All of this was true, except for the perception that Ishukone was financially sound.

Ishukone was victim to circumstances that not even Otro could control: national protectionism, restrictions on trade imposed by State commerce mandates, and the prevailing decline of Caldari society. The financial structure of Ishukone resembled more of a welfare state than a corporation, with Otro and his sister siphoning funds away from investments and awarding it to budgets supporting the employees under his care – all 300 million of them, and their families.

It was enough of a burden to make a man pull his hair out, if he had any, which Otro did not. A man approaching his late middle years, he still looked the part of the pirate that he used to be. Not a handsome man by any means, he had an unnaturally rough, sinister look about him that frightened children and made grown men uneasy. A skull and crossbones tattoo adorned his right cheek, sitting atop prominent bones and a crooked jaw. He used his ferocious appearance to great effect, intimidating the aristocratic boardrooms that he shared with the most powerful men and women in the Caldari State. They hated him because, rumor or not, he was a pirate, and thus should have no say in the dialogue of civilized affairs.

But as he so often enjoyed reminding them, the word 'pirate' was just a stereotype for those who refused to abide by other people's rules – in this case, mega-corporate rules. He made it perfectly clear that when matters concerned the welfare of Ishukone employees, only one set of rules would do, and those were his own. The proletariat masses who fell under the umbrella of his protection adored him all the more for it.

Ishukone avoided financial ruin twice in its history thanks to 'pipeline products', the once-in-a-lifetime kind of innovation that creates fortunes overnight. The first pipeline was pod technology, mysteriously awarded to Ishukone by the reclusive Jovians, an event which marked the dawn of the capsuleer age. The second was the Raven-class battleship, which Otro received from its disgruntled inventor on the grounds of a 'personality problem' with Ishukone's prior CEO.

The third pipeline was currently known by only two Ishukone associates: Otro Gariushi and his CFO, whose real name was Mila, and was, by virtue of being the same blood, his closest friend and adviser. This pipeline would yield the greatest of all financial windfalls, and was so secret that it was not discussed with anyone but each other:

A vaccine that could free Minmatar slaves from their dependency on Amarr's primary means of controlling them.

Vitoc is a toxic, self-mutating virus that can only be controlled through the regular administration of a temporary antidote. Known only to Imperial scientists, the properties and timing of the mutations are completely unpredictable to the scores of researchers who labored in vain to find a cure. Once infected with Vitoc, unique antidotes engineered to pacify the physical symptoms of the strain must be administered every time a mutation occurs. Without it, a death so painful awaits the infected patient that he would sooner beg for a bullet than to be left to the physical horrors caused by the virus.

By themselves, the antidotes are an extremely addictive narcotic that induces complacent euphoria. Slaves become so dependent on the antidotes that they stop at nothing to acquire it – if not for the high, then for the convenience of avoiding an excruciating demise. In this way, the Amarr Empire had an unbreakable stranglehold over its slave population, provided that knowledge of Vitoc's mutative properties were kept secret – and no means or methods were too drastic for the Empire to make sure it stayed that way.

But a cure was finally conceived: a prototype vaccine known as 'Insorum', developed by scientists who were murdered before the product could be refined. The active nanomite compounds in the vaccine were highly unstable; if it wasn't administered within just hours of synthesis, it was useless. Because of its extremely rapid decay rate, there was no way to mass produce the drug–

—until Otro Gariushi acquired a sample of the prototype, and the means to overcome both obstacles.

BORN WITH SHARP instincts bordering on precognition, Otro had a knack for sensing danger far in advance, an attribute which aided his survival during his pirating days. Today, these same intuitions served him well in his executive role. Until now, he believed that Insorum alone held the most potential to alter the balance of power in New Eden. That sentiment changed the moment Tibus Heth took control of Caldari Constructions.

Alone in his office, Otro's instincts were telling him that he had never known danger this profound in his entire life.

Three times, he had watched military drone camera footage of events at the Armor Forge, which captured scenes that the media missed. Three times, he'd screened every camera angle, searching for the best close-up shot of Tibus Heth. Finding one, he isolated and then magnified the image, moving it to one side of his display.

On the other side, he searched for a close-up of the man who was allowed through the Armor Forge perimeter and then into the complex unescorted. Again, the news drones didn't have the angle he was looking for, but the military ones did. He froze the image and magnified, then placed the two side-by-side.

The man's skin was impossibly smooth and supple, like an infant's: a telltale sign that he was a clone.

What are you up to now, you motherfucker?

Otro had never seen Tibus Heth before, which was what worried him most. Caldari Constructions was small as far as State corporations went, but this man's overnight ascension from complete obscurity to power, coupled with the circumstances under which it happened, was extremely disturbing. Without question, Tibus Heth was supported by the Broker; it couldn't have happened otherwise, and Otro needed to understand why.

The grainy images stared back as if the two men were taunting him. Otro had faced this monster known as the Broker before. He had a million personas, a million faces, and the wealth of a mega-corporation at his fingertips. Limited only by the scope of his willpower, he had the technology to clone himself into anyone, to literally put his own brain into an exact replica of another person; all he needed was a genome sequence.

But most ominously, it was believed that the Broker had the means – and the insanity – to operate multiple clones of himself at the same time.

A notorious murderer and thief, he eluded the police forces and agencies attempting to capture him with laughable ease. No one knew his real name, or what his original appearance was; none who met him ever knew what they were dealing with until after he'd already taken what he wanted and disappeared.

But above all else, he was a businessman. The Broker always made his terms and demands clear in his dealings, and he never, *ever* lost his temper. If he took any pleasure in running a blade through someone's spine to get what he wanted, it didn't show. Despite his capacity for engaging in violence, he couldn't be described as sadistic, for such would imply that he was capable of feeling emotions. The man's only concern, at all times, was business – nothing more.

As one of the most powerful men in existence, the Broker never accepted 'no' for an answer. And still, that was exactly what Otro had told him. Not once, but *twice*, he had denied the Broker's bid for Ishukone's next great pipeline. The amount of money he'd offered was staggering, enough to buy a corporation like Constructions a few times over. Still, Otro denied him.

The Broker casually asked why.

Just because Otro thought it would drive him crazy, he just smiled, shook his head, and didn't say a word.

When the Broker asked a second time, Otro just broadened his smile even more.

Expressionless, the Broker turned his back and walked away. About a dozen Ishukone Watch bodyguards asked if they should follow him. Otro told them not to bother. They could have killed him on the spot, and it wouldn't have made any difference. Hours later, a corpse was discovered in a rented hab-module. The Watch identified him as the man that Otro had met with earlier.

That encounter was two years ago. It probably passed by in the blink of an eye for the Broker.

Otro leaned back in his seat while concentrating on the images, now superimposed with financial data about the Caldari Constructions corporation.

What's in this for you? he wondered. *Why did you just give Tibus Heth an entire corporation?*

A welcome voice interrupted his concentration: 'Otro . . .'

His sister was trying to reach him on his personal data-pad. 'We've had a few developments.'

Seconds later, Mila Gariushi walked into his small, spartan office.

'They want a meeting,' she said. 'Every CEO in the State.'

'Stall them,' he grumbled, still fixated on his screens. 'Call me vindictive, but I've warned them enough times that something like this could happen.'

'Yeah,' she muttered, rubbing her eyes. 'You think they want to discuss the implications, or just want to . . . reaffirm loyalties?'

'Which do you think?' he answered, turning to face the view outside the station. 'Oh, I'm sure they'll talk about stock buybacks and security budgets. But they won't bother to try and understand *why* this happened. The thought won't even cross their minds.'

She looked out to the greenish, nebula-strewn canvas of space outside as well. 'It makes this pipeline all the more important.'

He shook his head. 'It still won't be enough.'

'You hold the key to unshackling every slave in Amarr,' she said. 'That Insorum vaccine is worth . . .'

'Blood,' he said, never taking his gaze off the view. 'Lots and lots of blood.'

'Whose?' she asked. 'Amarrian? I could live with that.'

Otro grunted. 'I could, too, if I thought it was worth it.'

'What do you mean?'

Otro took a deep breath, exhaling slowly. 'If you could save the life of someone you loved at the price of killing a complete stranger, would you do it?'

Mila didn't hesitate: 'Yes.'

'What if you couldn't be sure that killing the stranger would even save your loved one? Think you could deal with losing them both?'

'I know I couldn't bear the guilt of not trying to save the person I cared about,' she answered. 'That alone is worth the consequences.'

'What about the stranger? Any guilt at all for taking what's most precious to him?'

After a pause, she nodded. 'Maybe a little.'

'Yeah, a little . . .' Otro turned his gaze toward the display. 'I'm not sure if I could live with that anymore.'

Mila stared thoughtfully at her younger brother. They acted this way only in each other's presence, and only when they were alone. 'What's on your mind, Otro?'

He took another deliberate breath. 'You know, the Broker has a hand in this Constructions play.' With the click of a button, the view outside transformed into solid metal, and the lights dimmed. The images from the Armor Forge were transferred to a large screen directly behind him.

A lump formed in Mila's throat.

'How do you know that's him?' she asked.

'There are two middle-aged men up there, and one of them has the skin of a baby. I've seen this before.'

She studied the two images; the contrast was apparent, but it wasn't enough to convince her entirely. 'There could be any number of explanations for the skin . . .'

'Fair enough,' he said, leaning forward. 'But I never

told you that the Broker outbid Maleatu Shakor for the vaccine. By a very large sum of money.'

She blinked. 'What?'

'I turned him down. Twice.'

Mila had turned pale. 'Why the hell didn't you tell me?'

'So that when Shakor asked you if there were any other bidders, you wouldn't have to lie.'

Mila considered the merit of his answer. She had been the point of contact for secret negotiations with Shakor; it took months to persuade him that Otro could be trusted, and that what he was offering was genuine. As far as she knew, the three of them were the only ones in existence with the knowledge that Otro had acquired the precious vaccine. She refrained from asking how the Broker could have found out. There weren't many secrets that he couldn't discover – or purchase.

'Do you think he went to the Amarrians?'

'No,' Otro answered. 'If they knew I had it, we'd both be dead by now.' He shut the imagery down and reopened the view outside. 'You know what I think?'

'What?'

'I think it's obvious the Broker wants that vaccine to get something from the Amarrians. I can't even imagine what that could be, given what he was willing to pay for it. But he never, ever engages anyone unless he's already holding something over them.'

'Then what was he holding over you?' Mila asked, folding her arms.

'My patriotism.' Otro met her blue eyes with a weary look. 'I didn't know it back then, but I realize it now.'

He hung his head for a moment. 'Mila, when I give this vaccine to the Minmatars, they'll use it to break every slave's addiction to Vitoc in Amarr. Then the slaves will run riot and murder every overlord they can get their hands on. So Chamberlain Karsoth will order a crackdown, and the Imperial Navy will just crush them. You know what a mess the Republic is now; their armed forces don't stand a chance. Hell, they could end up being worse off than they are now, if you can imagine such a thing.

'This vaccine is going to start a goddamn war. I must be getting old, because that just doesn't sit well on my conscience. Meanwhile, I'll have a lot of money I can use to take care of Ishukone for a little while longer. But it won't fix the broader problems of the State. And it certainly won't change how my "executive colleagues"' – he hissed those words – 'see the universe around them.'

Otro turned to face the view of space again. 'All this sale does is put off the inevitable. The Broker's trying to accelerate things to critical mass. He wants the whole Caldari system to crash right now. That's what he's threatening me with. Constructions was his catalyst, and Tibus Heth is his detonator. And if I don't give him this vaccine, he's going to blow it all straight to hell.

'So to use the analogy, I have to kill a stranger to save the State. Whether I sell this vaccine to the Minmatars or not, a lot of people are going to die for nothing. And the fuck of it is, money isn't even the answer to our problems. We're too far past that now.'

Mila sat still, unable to move. She never imagined in her entire life that she would be at the center of such a wicked crossroad in Caldari history. All she could do was announce why she had come to Otro's office in the first place.

'I have everything that we could find on Tibus Heth here . . .'

'Leave me with it,' her brother said, leaning forward. 'Keep stalling our corporate friends. Tell them not to contact Tibus until I speak with him first. And don't mention a word about the Broker. If they find out that he's backing Heth, they'll start making him offers I *know* they'll end up regretting.'

22

Whether it was intended or not, the Constructions takeover was driving the perilous socioeconomic fissure in Caldari society even further apart.

On one side of the fissure, the corporate elite and bourgeoisie of the population reacted with outrage, condemning the takeover as the work of barbaric, ungrateful citizens. Clearly, these actions demonstrated a national urgency for stricter security and harsher punishments for civil disobedience. Whatever notion of 'patriotism' that the populace inferred from the acts of Tibus Heth was gravely mistaken for two reasons: one, it cost the fledging Constructions corporation – and all of its affiliates, up to and including the elite – their reputation. After events like this, who would risk their own business by relying on such an unstable enterprise?

Second, that same unreliable reputation was being cast as a stereotype for the entire State, especially in the eyes of the international media, and following behind it the biased scrutiny of the other nation states in New Eden. The latter was costly for everyone, rich and poor. Indeed, the fall of Caldari Constructions was a humiliating disgrace, worthy of challenging the legal merit of Heth's takeover and enacting measures to prevent debacles of this magnitude from ever happening again.

The other side of the fissure was a different story entirely.

To those inhabiting the lower tiers of Caldari society – which accounted for more than 95 percent of the population – Heth's exploits were already reaching legendary status, and with them, the seeds of a revolution were being sowed.

At its core, Heth's actions were about empowerment. In a fiercely patriotic society governed by corporate hegemony, maintaining power not only required its people's acceptance of the system, but also of accepting their role within it. There was no difference between the corporation and the ego; together they formed the identity of Caldari citizens, and the basis for which their own self-worth was judged.

Before the Armor Forge takeover, the masses blamed themselves for being unable to cross into the realm of elite status, versus the relative ease with which their rival Gallentean counterparts could do so. The Caldari never shied away from hard work; they took great pride in their devotion to industry. But opportunity eluded the vast majority of them for too long. The people were now united through their collective failures in this system. Their opinions had shifted from shame to rage, and patriotism had little to do with it. To them, the Constructions collapse demonstrated just how vulnerable they were: it proved that the promise of opportunity in exchange for corporate compliance was a lie.

Tibus Heth was not a rich man, nor was he intellectually gifted. He was unrefined and unreformed in the ways of the elite. Yet he had succeeded in capturing the conscience of a nation. The imagery of him wading through the mud, bloodied and battered, carrying a wounded comrade over his shoulders while bolts of plasma fire scorched overhead, was emblematic of Caldari hardships. It captured everything that the proletariat desired of their leaders, particularly when contrasted with the traditional images of manicured, overweight CEOs.

There was a struggle underway, and the people now believed that Tibus would carry them through it. A sense of regret emerged among the populace in that they had failed to demand such leadership sooner. But that was then. Tibus Heth was here now, and had empowered them for tomorrow. And because of him, the socioeconomic fissure in Caldari society was going to rip even further apart.

Attacks against symbols of corporate establishment, mostly in affluent locales similar to the management residences of the Armor Forge, were now dominating the news headlines. Even worse, full-blown riots between corporate police forces and citizens were erupting in the territories controlled by the Kaalakiota and Constructions corporations.

With the sole exception of Ishukone, production lines everywhere in the State were dealing with blatant recalcitrance as empowered workers openly challenged management. Inevitably, some verbal exchanges led to violence. As security forces were brought in, reports of deaths resulting from beatings and shootings began to surface; at first just a handful of eyewitness accounts, but within hours, thousands. The more rational individuals among the chaos were appalled at the savagery unleashed by both sides, but learned soon enough that demanding calm was a dangerous, futile, and ill-advised effort.

In the streets, there was also the issue of callow, impressionable youth. Unguided – and in many cases, unfed – they roamed in bands, glorifying Heth less for his financial triumph than for the fact he resembled the kind of hero that the State told them they could never become. They attacked corporate elitism with wanton regard, destroying homes, hovercars, and any symbol of wealth they could find. These youths weren't afraid to be beaten within an inch of their lives, for they had witnessed one man stand up to an army of corporate oppression, and their desire to become heroes fuelled their resolve in the face of stun batons and plasma rifles.

In the middle ranks of the corporate elite, managers scrambled to protect themselves, recalling who owed whom which favors and assessing their 'restructuring' options; most never even considered that they could become the victims of violence until it was too late. Some openly proclaimed and then recanted allegiances based on their impression of which side seemed most likely to persevere from one moment to the next. Even as fires raged, they were tormented with the question of *profit*, and were willing to align with whoever could help them retain it. In their eyes, preserving the decadent lifestyle afforded to them – and almost no one else – was paramount to their survival.

At the moment Tibus Heth wasn't even aware that plumes of smoke were rising from dozens of worlds throughout the Caldari State. He was still struggling to understand his own grip on power, and was having an extremely difficult time of it.

LEVERAGED DEBT STRUCTURES, multiple risk-adjusted discount rates, liquid-yield option notes, macroeconomic arbitrage pricing, flow-to-equity valuation considerations . . .

Tibus looked up from the financial data strewn across the desk previously occupied by Constructions CEO Torkebaira Shutsu, which still bore dark stains from his untimely demise.

'What the hell does any of this mean?' he asked.

Altug exhaled forcefully, drawing the glare of several of Heth's people in the office. 'It's a financial snapshot of the corporation you just bought. I can explain it, but that's going to take time.'

'Sigh at me one more time like that, and I'll kill you,' Tibus grumbled, knotting his enormous hands into fists. 'I'm not in the fucking mood.'

Altug straightened his posture. 'My apologies, sir. But I'm trying to help. Speaking strictly in terms of what's best for your corporation, the sooner you create a leadership structure, the better.'

'As much as I hate to admit it,' Janus said, taking a step forward, 'he's right. If we don't affirm our control, we'll lose the support of workers who are counting on us for meaningful change.'

Change? Tibus asked himself. *What change? We were never supposed to make it this far in the first place!*

'Fine,' he said. 'Congratulations, Janus: you're in charge of putting together an executive team.'

Rather than faltering like Tibus expected, Janus was emboldened.

'Altug is at your disposal. He is to do *exactly*—' he stared boreholes through the former Constructions production manager '—as you say. I won't give you a hard time if you decide to shoot him. And Janus?'

'Yes, sir?' The younger man was beaming.

'You report directly to *me*. No one else. Give yourself a title or something. Make sure you put people loyal to *me* in the right spots. I *trust* your judgment: you know who the right people are – the ones who risked their lives to stand with me. Understand?'

'Yes, sir!'

Tibus stood up and moved toward the door leading to Shutsu's personal quarters.

'Get an announcement out,' he muttered. 'Let everyone

know that it's business as usual until we put the right team together. Low-level workers don't have anything to worry about, make sure they know that . . . which reminds me. Have Altug provide you with a list of all the firm's mid-level and higher managers. Have someone else on your team check it to make sure he doesn't miss anyone.

'Then I want you to *freeze their assets*, including all their personal shit – property, assets, everything. Those fuckers are sleeping in hab-modules from now on. Do whatever's necessary to get the access you need, *but I want their money*. I don't care if you're replacing them or not – this affects everyone. Sell it all—'

Altug stifled a cough.

'—and distribute the proceeds to the low-level work-force, starting with poorest guys first. And while you're at it, figure out how much of my own stock I can sell without giving the company away. I'll use those proceeds for the same thing. If anyone bitches, tell them they'll have every opportunity to *earn* it back. If they still give you a hard time, lock 'em up in a cage and let 'em think about it for a while.

'Get it done, Janus. Get it done yesterday.'

Tibus entered the private chamber before the younger man could answer.

As THE DOOR shut behind him, Tibus was reminded of why he hated the Caldari elite.

Shutsu's personal chambers was more than 400 square meters in area – an insane amount of space even by lavish standards, given the scarcity of real estate onboard stations. The room was adorned with exotic plants, works of art, and furniture pieces constructed from the rarest materials in New Eden. A bar adjacent to the view of space was stocked with savory, hand-baked delicacies and real, organic food – not the synthesized calorie concoctions supplied to workers by the corporation.

The more he observed about the former CEO's resident living space, the darker the hate in his heart became.

Any one of the various luxuries was worth more than what a typical assembly line contractor could hope to earn in a lifetime of corporate servitude. But the centerpiece attraction – by far the most obnoxious display of opulence – was a waterfall that fell into a pool that had no physical walls. All of the water was held in place by the same graviton induction and convergence technology used in starship equipment such as tractor beams and inertia dampeners. The boundless tank rose almost three meters from the stone floor, at the convergence of seamless glass canals that encircled the entire room; thousands of vibrantly colored fish swam freely inside. Just hiring the right physicists and engineers to work out the quantum requirements of the containment field, to say nothing of the materials required to construct and supply it with power, would have cost millions of *interstellar* credits, and not the worthless local Caldari currency used in the Lonetrek region.

His seething rage nearly blinded him to the woman swimming inside the pool.

Long, wavy hair flowed over slender back muscles that merged into deliciously firm buttocks, propelled effortlessly through the water with the steady flutter kick of toned legs.

Despite the visage of a woman that would make any straight man yearn with lust, all Tibus saw was that she was Gallentean, and that made his vision turn red.

Limping across the stone tiles, he thrust his hand into the wall of water as she swam by, latching firmly onto her ankle and yanking part of her through with such violent force that she didn't have time to take a breath. Grasping her one leg outside of the pool, she was pinned beneath the surface and desperately trying to kick herself free. But Tibus was too strong, and resolutely determined to make this woman suffer for her despicable ethnicity.

She gulped in mouthfuls of water, panicking and thrashing for her life; her movements became weaker as her oxygen-starved limbs began to fail her. Only then was he satisfied with her level of suffering; he wanted to torment her to the brink of death but not beyond – not yet. With a wicked yank, he pulled her through the aquatic barrier, allowing her head to crash onto the cold floor with a sickening thud. The blow nearly knocked her unconscious, but she was no longer in control of herself as her lungs convulsed and her stomach retched out pints of water in coughs and wheezes.

Tibus grabbed her by the hair.

'Who the fuck are you?' he demanded.

In between desperate gasps, she breathed the words 'Shutsu . . . hired . . .'

'You're a *whore*?' he accused. 'Who else is in here?'

Garbled words fell from her mouth: 'Just . . . me . . .'

He dragged her damaged body back across to the door, leaving behind a wet trail stained with blood. When it opened, he threw her into the startled arms of the men – and women – working inside the office.

'*Get rid of this trash!*' he shouted. 'You'll answer to *me* if I find any more of it!'

Ignoring the stunned looks, he shut the door again before anyone could acknowledge. Only this time, convinced that he was alone, he began to hyperventilate. The mere sight and physical contact with a flesh and blood Gallentean triggered a plenary, numbing anxiety that rushed over him like the water tumbling into the pool.

What have I done? he asked aloud. *I'm supposed to be dead!*

He grabbed his head, whirling around in circles, trying to wrest an invisible foe to the ground. Vicious flashbacks of combat – of unspeakable experiences seared into his memory long before his Constructions days ever began – rushed through his psyche like a cyclone. He clutched at his white hair so hard that it began to rip out; the horrors of war, of close-quarters killing, and of comrades shred to pieces by a Gallentean enemy all but took the air out of his lungs.

I'm not supposed to be here!

He collapsed as a fusillade of reminisced plasma fire ripped holes into him. The ever-present pain in his leg suddenly exploded as if it had caught fire.

This was supposed to end at the Armor Forge . . . I was to die a hero, not live on! I don't want this! I . . .

'Tibus . . .'

The Broker's voice, speaking to him from the earpiece in his pocket, made his visions evaporate.

'I have good news, Tibus. Look.'

News feeds materialized over the bar area, showing a live Kaalakiota press conference. A police cordon was surrounding the podium as the mega-corporation's public relations specialist addressed a hostile crowd of journalists.

'They want to know why Home Guard troops were told to fire on Constructions workers,' the Broker mused.

Tibus rose to his feet, shaking off the memories and regaining his composure. 'Those orders would fly on secure military comms . . . how could the press—'

'I have a . . . *unique* . . . relationship with the media,' the Broker said. 'It seems that the monetary concerns of CEO Haatakan Oiritsuu – and her apparent disdain for the Caldari workforce, demonstrated so aptly by her authorization of force to retrieve her property – was revealed to the public as well. Your compatriots took exception to that.'

The imagery switched to scenes of burning cities and rioting youths in Caldari settlements.

'No, goddamnit!' Tibus said, horrified at what he was seeing. 'This isn't what I want!'

The Broker ignored him. 'The public backlash will eventually destroy her, Tibus. This is a great opportunity for you.'

'*I don't know what the fuck I'm doing!*' he wailed. 'All of the financial stuff is garbage to me, I can't handle it!'

'Tibus, Tibus,' the Broker said, approaching the limits of detectable sarcasm, but not crossing it enough to make him sound disingenuous. 'Leave the finances to me. Your man Janus is assembling a quality team as we speak. He'll make all the right decisions. He always has.'

The hairs on the back of Heth's neck stood straight up. 'What the hell do you mean by that?'

'*Look* at those burning Caldari cities,' the Broker said, this time with more force in his voice. 'Only you can stop it.'

Tibus stared at the images, trembling with anger, anxiety, and fear.

'*Speak to them,*' the Broker continued. 'Turn your countrymen away from each other; turn them toward your enemy instead. You have that gift. You have that passion. They need to hear your voice.'

One news feed showed a young man, probably in his twenties, getting beaten by several policemen in real time.

'All right,' Tibus breathed. 'I'll talk to them . . . tell me what I have to do!'

23

It was everything that Otro could do to shut the painful images of civil strife and violence from his mind. In the days since Tibus Heth became a household name, the properties governed by Ishukone were stable, and the Watch reported no increase in crime or incidents related to the events at the Constructions Armor Forge. It was testament to the popularity of the Gariushi legend, his years of solid leadership, and the relative contentment of those under his employ. But before he could intervene on behalf of those citizens unprotected by Ishukone, Otro had to learn as much as he could about Tibus Heth. Before reading a single word from the dossier hastily prepared for him, he already considered him an adversary.

The dossier summary confirmed his initial suspicions:

Tibus Heth, Deteis male, born 21 November 23292 AD (53 EVE Standard), in the city of Arcurio, Caldari Prime, of the Luminaire System. Under the provision of local immigration statutes, he was entitled to Caldari citizenship but only restricted worker status for the Gallente Federation. Arcurio's population was a 60–40 Caldari-Gallentean mix at the time of Heth's birth. The education system was integrated, but more competitive private schools for exclusive ethnicities were permitted by law. Parents were Caldari expatriates working in the Arcurio public transportation system, under the jurisdiction and employ of the Federation Civil Services Department. Both are now deceased; Tibus has no siblings.

Tibus was enrolled in the integrated public school system from the age of 5 through 14. He scored below-

average in placement tests for advanced academic status, and higher than average in physical fitness evaluations. Exhibited left-hemisphere dominance in natural skill set distribution. Has a high propensity for risk-taking and endurance challenges, and was subject to multiple disciplinary actions due to infractions that included physical altercations with other students.

Tibus dropped out of the public school system at the age of fifteen upon receiving official word that he would never qualify for capsuleer status due to 'insufficient discipline and cognitive abilities.' Rather than continuing with his basic education, Tibus immediately sought a career in military service. His application to join the Caldari Navy Marine Expeditionary Forces was denied on security grounds because of his birth in a non-Caldari system. He was later accepted in the Home Guard Infantry Division, which marked the beginning of his professional military career.

As a Home Guard soldier, Tibus consistently volunteered for the most dangerous assignments and longed for a full-scale conflict to prove himself in. He scored highly on 'situational awareness' combat stress tests and was an expert marksman. He was very charismatic in military settings. A natural tactician, he was quickly promoted to sergeant, but was prevented from advancing rank again due to psyche evaluations that revealed an acute inferiority complex, thus explaining his constant need to prove himself. The complications associated with this behavior are best summarized by this statement on the CNM Directorate's evaluation report: 'Such tendencies are detrimental to joint or multiple asset engagements, due to risk-taking that is unnecessary to complete the mission and potentially endangering to the soldiers under his command.'

Shortly after this report was issued, Tibus was forced into retirement for the stated reason of Home Guard military budget cuts. Subsequent applications to other corporate military arms were unanimously refused on the grounds of 'competitive suspicions.'

At this point, our investigation cannot account for a six-year gap in his biographical history. His last recorded physical appearance before this gap was his arrival at the Hyasyoda Corporation Mineral Reserve station in the Tennen System. Six years later, he applied for his current position with Caldari Constructions as an assembly line MTAC operator.

Six years, Otro thought. *That's a long time to disappear.*

He played the Armor Forge video again. The media was sensationalizing Heth's triumphs, especially his dramatic rescue of the downed worker; it had been replayed incessantly since the events first took place. One part of his instincts warned that he was wasting precious time watching the footage repeatedly, the other warned that he must have missed *something*. Watching the scene at half speed, he observed the agonizingly slow motions of Tibus as he dragged himself to the fallen man; how the image would flash and distort as bright plasma bolts lanced overhead; how he plunged both arms into the mud to lift his comrade up . . .

Something about the man's exposed forearms caught Otro's eye.

Lurching toward the console, he rewound the image to that exact frame. Even at half speed, the exposure was brief. But it was there: a grainy smudge, right in the middle of the man's wrist. Too imprecise for an implant, too detailed to be mud . . . it had to be man-made, perhaps a tattoo. Manipulating the controls, Otro cut and magnified the frame to its highest resolution. Image enhancement software sharpened the picture a bit more, but the pattern was still unrecognizable.

The Watch had data forensics experts and equipment that could tell him what it was. It would only take a minute or two.

WHILE ISHUKONE QUANTUM computers ran their comparisons and analysis against thousands of terabytes of digital image information, a computer virus – one that had been dormant for years – was awakened by the innocuous commands of a technician working for the State Media Outlet. The Outlet was the hub through which all corporate news feeds were routed, and then relayed by State-employed newscasters who selected the most relevant mega-corporate news for broadcast. Although each feed could be viewed independently, the Outlet was the only stream that had a nationwide broadcast audience, and was regularly monitored by the other empires.

The virus began manipulating the instructions controlling the subspace routing paths that Outlet stream information would be broadcast on. Instead of sending feed data from the primary news hub, it would broadcast information from a different source, one that was specified by the same technician who knew exactly how to awaken this binary monster.

This technician bore no physical resemblance to the grainy image of the man known as the Broker on Otro's screens. But for all intents and purposes, it was the same exact person.

'OH . . . NO . . .'

Otro murmured as he read the Watch data forensics

analysis. It took a few more seconds than usual to produce – an eternity by quantum standards – but the match was there.

Tibus Heth bore the insignia of the Templis Dragonaurs, which made him an international terrorist in the eyes of CONCORD and every other nation state of New Eden, including the Caldari State.

No single entity, political or otherwise, held more contempt toward the 'occupiers' of Caldari Prime than the Dragonaurs. The source of their hatred far exceeded the humiliation of being driven away from an ancestral birthplace; for this group, the mere existence of the Gallente Federation was reason enough to take up arms against them. Classified as an 'ultra-nationalist terrorist organization' by intelligence agencies, their origins dated back to the Tikiona States, which was the civilization that ultimately became what the Caldari are today. It was they who opposed Gallentean influence from their first contact more than 800 years ago; they who carried out the savage destruction of Nouvelle Rouvenor; and they who led the fiercest underground resistance campaigns after the Federation invasion of Caldari Prime.

Every terrorist organization is founded on darkness that is the light to someone; every monster could be a hero in the eyes of the desperate.

Otro shook his head, cursing himself for not seeing it sooner. Mutual cooperation in hunting and prosecuting the Templis Dragonaurs was a cornerstone agreement between the State and Federation for maintaining peace. Both nations often exchanged information to find them, especially when discovering actionable intelligence on imminent assassination attempts against Caldari peacemakers, or raids against depots in the Border Zone. Many times, the resulting battles had gone badly for both sides. Otro was certain that Tibus had been a combatant in them more than once.

Of all things, the man who had taken control of Caldari Constructions and thrust himself into the national spotlight was a terrorist. And while Otro had no love for the Gallenteans, and certainly viewed their historical context as expansionistic and cruel, he couldn't accept the extremist views that Tibus was sure to project from his new heights. Worst of all, it couldn't be proven that Tibus was a Dragonaur; aside from the markings on his wrist, the evidence against him was circumstantial. But the stakes were far too high to risk inaction. Tibus Heth had to be stopped right now.

Otro called for his sister again, as urgently as he could convey without worrying her too much. As she entered the office, her concerned expression revealed that she knew him too well.

'He's a Dragonaur,' he started. 'A Templis fucking Dragonaur.' The composite images of Heth's wrist and the Watch forensics data appeared behind him.

Staring at the data, she assimilated the implications instantly. But she didn't panic. She was too strong for that. 'You have to issue a national statement as soon as you can prepare one.'

'There isn't time to prepare one,' he muttered. 'Tell the other CEOs that I'm taking Outlet time to try and appeal for calm. Don't mention a word of *this*.' He motioned over his shoulder toward the images. 'Assuming they haven't figured it out already.'

Mila was feverishly manipulating her datapad. 'Do you think he's still with them?'

'The Dragonaurs?' His hands danced over the console as he tried to reach the Outlet. 'It doesn't matter if he is. The kind of hate you need to run with that pack is *deep*, something that's personal. You know what scares me most?'

'*What?*'

Otro blinked. 'That his message is exactly what people want to hear right now.'

'What the *hell* . . .'

'I said . . . wait, what's wrong?'

Otro's stomach turned inside out when he saw the look on his sister's face. She turned the datapad toward him.

'It's him,' she whispered. '"Subspace, 451 trans-net. Audio." That's all it says.'

Otro tried to contact the news feeds owned by Ishukone directly. But no one answered. He slammed his fists onto the console.

'You have to take it,' Mila said, sharing the frustration herself.

He keyed in the comm instructions. The voice sounded young, nasal, and unnaturally crisp.

'You don't have as much control over your people as you think,' the Broker said.

Otro was seething. 'What do you want?' he growled. 'What's your interest in Tibus Heth?'

'I have no interest in Heth. But you do. So let's make a deal . . .'

Before Otro could answer, the screen displayed the view of a stargate. It could have been any one of thousands in New Eden.

'To ship captains, this is the Perimeter Stargate in the Jita System,' the Broker continued. 'But to me, this is sub-space 451 trans-net.'

The image abruptly changed to a scene depicting a mass of electronic couplings surrounding a sphere of roiling light; intermittent jets of electrostatic charges plunged into the swirling vortex beneath it. Starships entering the portal below vanished as they passed through, instantly transported to the adjacent star system, bypassing the immense distance in between. The same gates were also used as subspace routers, transmitting packets of data across a galactic communications network, linking every system in New Eden to each other with faster-than-light communications.

'The Outlet broadcast has to pass through here to reach the rest of the Caldari State. As of now, I control exactly what goes through.'

Otro knew where this was going.

'I want that vaccine,' the Broker continued, as always, without the slightest hint of emotion. 'My terms and offer amount are unchanged.'

'You know I can't do that,' Otro said. 'The deal is off the table.'

'Be careful, Mr. Gariushi. Think it through. If you don't reconsider, you'll be forced to stand aside and let nature take its course. And you *know* what Caldari nature is capable of, don't you?'

The Ishukone CEO was fuming, unable to do anything but tremble in rage. The imagery changed back to more scenes of violence as the riots continued.

'The body count goes up by the minute,' the Broker said, sounding amused. 'How does that weigh on your conscience? Or will it only matter when the chaos kills your sister as well?'

'*Fuck you*,' Otro howled, leaping out of his seat. 'I swear on my life, I'm going find you and put a stop to this—'

'No,' the Broker cut him off. 'You already missed the chance to stop this.'

Broadcasting live on the Caldari State Media Outlet

was a close-up of Tibus Heth, who was standing behind a podium and surrounded by a group of men and women, all of whom were dressed in the plain, dark blue uniform issued to Caldari Constructions workers. Tibus, wearing a scowl on his face, drew a deep breath as he prepared to speak.

'You'll get one more chance to avoid losing everything else,' the Broker warned. 'Just one.'

24

There was a universal pause of life throughout every city on every world in the Caldari State, including those engulfed in turmoil. From city squares to the concourses of orbiting stations; from the datapads of the elite to the mess halls of factory workers, the projected image of Tibus Heth stood tall on a billion screens, transcending every layer of society in a single moment. In places where upheaval reigned, violence was halted in mid-strike. Even the financial markets paused as investors and traders gathered around terminals and data kiosks, their attention held fast by the remarkable events unfolding – for better or worse – in the Caldari State.

The man stood before this audience of almost a trillion people; his eyes carrying a distant look, his brow and forehead creased with anger and resolve; his face still scarred and bruised from his ordeal, and his mouth poised ready to speak.

'A young man died in my arms today,' he started. 'Bright, capable, brave . . . everything that we should be, he was: a true Caldari patriot.

'He was killed by a single bullet, fired from the barrel of

a mega-corporation's rifle – a bullet . . . that was intended for *me.*'

The face of Tibus Heth flushed red with anger; the slightest tremor of rage was apparent to those standing closest to him.

'The mega-corporations want me to tell you that his death was necessary; that he was guilty of committing a crime. They can go to hell, for I will *not* be compelled by *anyone* to insult that hero's memory. He spoke no last words, made no final request, cried no plea for mercy, nor whispered a prayer for forgiveness. His wound left him without the voice to speak in the final moments of his life. But I knew him well enough to know this:

'That man gave his life so that I could live. And I swear to you that I'm going to do my best to live up to his example, by any means necessary.

'His death serves warning to all those who are Caldari: the evil which took his life has killed many times before; it is piercing Caldari flesh and blood right this moment; and it will kill tomorrow and every day thereafter – unless you listen well to what I say now.

'As of 1600 hours today, I became the Chief Executive Officer and majority shareholder of Caldari Constructions. The *entire* executive team of the previous regime has been removed from power. The men and women standing behind me have already been designated to fulfill the roles of those who have departed.

'We have each sworn, on our very lives, to uphold the responsibility we have to the *Caldari State.* I don't give a *damn* about shareholders, because it's apparent that they don't give a *damn* about the workers who slave to put the fat into their bellies. In return for the life of luxury afforded to them by the proletariat armies of this State, they have returned the effort with this.'

He raised the bloodied, shattered body armor that Heidan was wearing when he was killed. Then he tossed it onto the ground before the podium.

'Look at it . . . all of you, put yourself into that armor, if you dare. What happened to us? Our wounds are self-inflicted . . . Have our leaders destroyed the Caldari soul, the Caldari conscience, the Caldari power that once was . . . and may yet still become?

'It's true that I led a coup against the masters of this corporation. I led this coup not expecting to survive, but my intent was *never* to kill my brothers. We spared the life of every guard and worker in the Armor Forge . . . you can ask them yourself . . . and I *swear* . . .'

He slammed his fist into the podium, startling some of the members behind him.

'. . . that Caldari man did *not* have to die! It was the *greed* of mega-corporations that killed him; the *greed* of sinister men that was killing Caldari Constructions. How could our leadership allow this to happen? What was it that subverted them, that turned them toward this path? Think of it . . . all of those gifted, talented individuals, the so-called *elite*, whom we charged with guiding us? From where – or from *whom* – did they learn this path?'

Leaning forward, he lowered his voice.

'It was learned from the same enemy they were supposed to protect us from . . . it was learned from the Gallenteans.'

Straightening up, he continued.

'The Caldari people are the strongest souls of New Eden; no other nation has done so much with so little. An objective look back upon our history demonstrates that the Gallenteans, from the moment they contacted us, have been the bane of our existence. They and their righteousness, they and their criticism of our way of life, they and their insistence that *their* values are appropriate for us all . . . and still . . . *still!* This goes on today, just as it did a thousand years ago!

'Is it not insulting that they can just dismiss the culture we've held dear to us for generations; to blatantly dismiss the values which have kept us alive in this cruel universe? Their self-indulgence in moral proclamations is, make no mistake about it, a superiority complex, a hateful arrogance that blinds them to the vulnerability of our human selves.

'Every ambition we have that lies beyond our borders is an act of war. Every Gallentean ambition beyond their borders is "the spread of ideals" and the "initiative for peace." We ask to shelter the livelihood of our workers by begging them for restraint in their trade policies. They accuse us of protectionism, of being enemies of free trade and free thinking. Nothing we do is acceptable to their standards, and no discourse or discussion is acceptable to their tastes.'

Again, he slammed his fist.

'I will *not* stand for this hypocrisy any longer! To the Federation, I say this: the notion that a man can be free does not exempt him from his obligations to his fellow man . . . the obligation to be decent, to be respectful of traditions that differ from your own, to acknowledge the possibility that your ideas can cause more harm than good.

'You use the rhetoric of emancipation as a guise to veil your malicious intent to seize advantage for yourself, always at the expense of other races. The very freedoms that you proclaim are exactly what divides a nation . . . and what has divided the cultural brotherhood of our own *race.*

'My promise, my solemn *oath*, is to adhere to the

values that *made us who we are*, and not to the corruption of those whom I have replaced. My responsibility is to rid the scourge of Gallentean ideals from the ranks of our corporate leaders, and I will *demand* accountability for the failure of our State. I am you, Caldari, born among these masses, and a soldier, one of millions in your ranks, and now I am accepting my responsibility to right the course of Caldari Constructions. May its example inspire the courageous Caldari spirit, and illuminate the path for all those who dare to take action in the name of saving our race.

'Effective immediately, the assets of mid-grade employees and up will be frozen and repossessed. This company will no longer reward failure. The days of entitlement strictly for caste and class merits are over. These workers will have to *earn* what they've taken from this corporation. Here, talent means nothing unless you have the willpower to exploit it fully. My measure of compensation will be based on work output, in whatever role you serve, and not the unproven potential of genetic competence.

'Personally, I will not draw one single credit from the coffers of this corporation until I've earned the right to be called its CEO.

'To those who call yourselves clients of Caldari Constructions: it is business as usual. Obligations will be met, orders will be filled, and debts will be collected. You will notice vast improvements in the production efficiency of this corporation. Understand that I am a fair man. Any attempts to subvert, deceive, or manipulate the operations of this company will be taken as a personal attack on those whom I am charged with protecting. *Do not ever cross me.* You *will* regret it.

'To the rest of my fellow compatriots, you should demand nothing less of your own leaders, who are *nothing* without you and undeserving of your allegiance until they prove otherwise. They have failed to deliver us from the humiliation of Gallentean influence. They have made us inferior to a lesser race, ignoring the threat as if the illusion of wealth and prestige somehow shelters them from the shame of national failure.

'According to the laws of the mega-corporations, I have committed crimes here today. But none . . . *none* . . . are greater than those committed by the elite, who still dare to call themselves Caldari.

'My name is Tibus Heth, and I am a Caldari patriot. The restoration of our State's dignity begins *now*.'

He held his stare at the dark lens of the camera before him. When its red light blinked off, Heth exhaled forcefully and broke into a sweat.

The Broker contacted him immediately.

'Bravo, Mr. Heth. You've done well.'

Tibus could barely keep the datapad steady against his ear.

'Do you think it worked?' he breathed, trying to conceal his voice from those standing behind him.

'I think you've turned things in the right direction,' the Broker answered. 'Power is delicious, Tibus. Watch now as they throw themselves at your feet.'

When the line went dead, Tibus turned to face his executive board – and was met with an exuberant applause led by Janus, his newly self-designated Chief Operating Officer. Half of his board was familiar faces, men who just a short while ago were confined to the lowest rungs of society, clinging for life in a corporation that was indifferent to their existence.

Familiar or not, all of them cheered, embraced, and let tears of inspiration and hope fall from their eyes.

The silence around the State was no more, as those same cheers transformed into the raucous chants 'Heth! Heth! Heth!'

Hate was awakened in the Caldari State, and the Broker was going to make sure it never slept again.

25

Metropolis Region – Gedur Constellation
The Illuin System – Republic Parliament Bureau
Station

What an absolute madman, Keitan Yun thought, turning the projection screen off. The international newsfeeds had picked up on Tibus Heth's national broadcast, which was drawing condemnation from everyone – except the majority working-class population of the Caldari State. *A raving, bigoted, deranged lunatic. Any sane leader would have made an appeal for calm. Instead, he appealed directly to their anger, stoking the flames in an attempt to do what, exactly? Keep the riots going? Shift the balance of power in the Caldari State? And for whose purpose? His own?*

The rangy Sebiestor tribesman grunted. *Heth's dramatic portrayal of the Caldari working man's struggle is insulting. We Minmatars know a thing or two about living in fear . . . Whatever his illusions of corporate oppression are, the Caldari know nothing of being held against their will as a way of life.*

Keitan allowed himself a tinge of anger. *That selfish fool,*

*vilifying the Gallenteans on a national stage . . . could the
Caldari seriously be considering any part of his ramblings?
Anything less than the absolute rejection of his ideals would
be despicable. It would speak mountains about their character and national identity . . . is Tibus Heth really the man
they want to represent it?*

He shook off the distraction, remembering his surreal
encounter with the Elders. Drawing in his cherished surroundings for inspiration, he collected himself and tried
to focus. His office seemed smaller than it really was, in
part because of his own messiness, but mostly because of
its abundance of academic artifacts. University awards,
historical Minmatar warship scale models, and framed
pictures capturing his meetings with famous international political figures were all displayed in haphazard
view.

More than anything else, his ample collection of history books – an extremely rare commodity, and an expensive indulgence that he allowed himself – dominated the
scenery. He attributed his love for books – besides the refreshing smell of printed paper, and the smooth texture of
leather binding – as part of his ego's need to hold fast to
his intellectual roots. They were a reminder of everything
he'd learned over the years; to him, they represented tan-
gible evidence that the history recorded within their pages
really happened.

Such was the motivation behind his transition from
academia to politics: to advise today's iconic figures, reminding them of how fate had judged their predecessors
under similar circumstances. History repeated itself with
disturbing recurrence throughout the ages, and from what
he could observe, it was about to repeat again, with devastating result.

Ameline stood nearby, thoughtfully paging through a

book she picked at random, ignoring the look of concerned protest from Keitan, who was not keen on sharing any of his personal belongings – let alone cherished ones – with anyone. But he had no choice in the matter. Indeed, it seemed that there were few decisions that would be his alone any longer, because of the words that the Elders had left him:

'You will be our voice, to both your government, and to the Assembly powers.'

The Starkmanir's graceful presence was a grim reminder of just how serious matters were. He was irrevocably committed; his burden was now the same as all those decision makers in his books, those whose actions definitively changed the course of human events. And like most of them, it was a burden that he wished that he didn't have to bear. The Elders' intentions were real, and his journey through the Thukker complex proved that they had the means to achieve their goals. Keitan's role was small but momentous in its significance; he was to be the emissary of last resort, the prophet through whom the last warnings of peace would ring before the strike of unprecedented calamity.

But how am I supposed to do that? he wondered. Already scorned by the Assembly, Prime Minister Karin Midular wouldn't let him near a podium any time soon. *Even if I could reach a public forum, what would I say? How do you warn a nation of danger when you're the laughingstock of international politics?*

He cursed himself aloud, rapping his small fist on the desk. *Showering New Eden's sanctioned protectorate with threats is incalculably foolish! But . . . considering the circumstances, what else remains? 'Protectorate' was never a legitimate term for describing CONCORD . . . 'Champions of the Status Quo' is more fitting, even when that status is cruel and unfair to the Minmatar Republic.*

Resting both elbows on the desk, he cupped his forehead with his hands.

I abhor violence, he thought. *Why is it always such a vital necessity for our species?*

'You look like you have the weight of a *titan* on your shoulders.'

Surprised, Keitan looked up to find Ameline escorting Maleatu Shakor, gently guiding him forward by the arm.

'For a blind man, your perception always astounds me,' Keitan answered, not wanting the company at all, and dreading the thought of having to introduce her.

'I see you've had the pleasure of meeting my new . . . assistant.'

'Oh, I know who she is,' the old man answered, feeling his way into a seat in front of Kcitan's desk. 'I also know where you've been.'

Keitan felt the top of his brow flash red. 'I was . . . I went out to recruit Ameline, because I needed . . .'

Maleatu's clouded irises glistened in the dim lighting of the office, and a wry grin spread across his face.

'The Elders didn't bring you aboard because you were a good liar.'

Keitan leaned back in his chair, suddenly feeling like there wasn't enough air in the room. Ameline took her hand off Maleatu's shoulder and stepped away, leaving the two men alone.

'How long have you known about this?'

'Known about what?' the Brutor asked, his grin broadening even more.

Keitan became incensed, lowering his voice. 'It's probably not safe to speak in here about this!'

'Are you concerned about bugs?' The old man was clearly enjoying himself. 'Well, you should be. It's been bugged ever since you got here.'

The old man burst out laughing as Keitan shifted uncomfortably in his chair.

'The expression on your face right now must be *priceless*,' Maleatu managed in between wheezes. 'We can show it to you on the playback – it's being recorded on three different cameras right now.'

'What exactly about this is funny?' Keitan fumed, looking around his office for possible places where the eavesdropping devices could be. 'And what reason would you possibly have to monitor me?'

'In hindsight, it was a waste of time,' Maleatu said. 'I mean that in the best of terms. You're the most boring person we've ever had under surveillance . . . no social life to speak of, no women in your life, no travels outside of the university lecture circuit, dead set in your routines and habits . . .'

He leaned forward, craning his neck toward Keitan. 'And nothing but genuine, loyal, selfless devotion to the Minmatar cause. That, my friend, has not gone unnoticed.'

The academic wasn't moved. 'You needed to invade my privacy to assess that?'

Maleatu turned serious. 'These dangerous times require complete assurances, Ambassador. You know what's at stake here.'

As much as he despised being the source of the statesman's jokes, he found relief that he could share his burden with someone other than Ameline.

'How many people are part of this? Where are the Elders preparing for their invasion?'

'In the Sanctuaries? Oh, I don't know exactly. Millions, at least,' he answered, stretching out his broad shoulders.

Even as an older man, he still bore the physical hulk that was characteristic of a Brutor tribesman. He was dressed in his Parliament's tunic, which was worn by most government officials.

But in his typical rebellious nature, he also wore an ancient weapon called a 'Khumaak' across his back, held in place with a leather strap that ran over his shoulder to the belt around his waist. Primitive and crude, it was a metallic disc from which seven spikes protruded, which was fixed to the end of a short mast. Blind as he was, both colleague and adversary alike took notice when he entered the room because of its menacing appearance. Replete with historical significance, the weapon had become a symbol of Minmatar resistance, and Maleatu was rarely seen in public without it.

As it was, he had to lean forward so that the weapon wouldn't scratch the chair upon which he sat.

'But in the Sanctuaries themselves, there are many, many more,' he continued. 'There are cities on moons, planets, even orbital terra-domes . . . it's the most beautiful thing I've ever seen – through the camera drones of my ship, of course.'

'How long have you known about it?' Keitan asked. The academic in him was fully engaged. 'How long has it existed?'

'I've only known about it for six years. But the Elders gave you a good idea of how old it is. Congratulations on your admission to the inner circle of these affairs.'

'I'm thankful for the opportunity, but . . . this is *theft*! They've stolen an unfathomable amount of money to build this . . . satellite civilization, or whatever you call it. How can you even hide something this big, let alone disguise its finances?'

'Physically hiding it was easy,' Maleatu answered,

straightening up. 'There are so many unsettled worlds out there, Keitan. Even the capsuleers, with their power, know little about all there is in New Eden, and just how much she has to offer.'

Maleatu unfastened the shoulder strap for the Khumaak to set the weapon aside. 'I take exception to your description of its funding as "theft." I would characterize it more as an "omission of information" from fiscal watchdogs in their Senate over the years. But you shouldn't question its merit. The money was used as it was intended: to rebuild Minmatar. The Elders are doing a better job of it than the Republic ever could.'

'Rebuilding the Minmatar *Republic* is what Federation money was intended for,' Keitan insisted. 'That means the original territories and the billions of people that still depend on it! The political process we have in place has to be given a chance to work—'

'It *was* given a chance to work,' Maleatu scoffed. 'Two hundred years later, we're only slightly better off than we were enslaved, with the exception of those fortunate enough to become capsuleers. The Amarrian ambassador pointed that out to you, remember? I don't think he was lying.'

Keitan was incensed. 'If Karin Midular ever heard you use those words—'

'Ha, Midular,' the Brutor laughed. 'Like you, her heart is in the right place, but she is *buried* politically. No one takes her seriously anymore.'

'Maleatu, there are people here who *need* the Republic, and you're not helping by being this . . . obstinate about the issue!'

'Which issue? Acting on what's best for Minmatar, or saving a dead Republic? My job was to keep the focus of affairs on the latter while the Elder staging areas were constructed. If that meant pursuing more, how should I say . . . *belligerent* political strategies, then yes, guilty as charged. But Karin made it easy by chasing nonsensical policies of appeasement with Amarr. *Appeasement*, for God's sake! What patriot could agree to such a thing?'

'You mean your *job* was to sabotage Midular's efforts to help the people who live here?' Keitan's mind was rife with anger. 'I don't suppose the Elders ever considered the possibility that democracy might prevail?'

'Keitan, was democracy going to unshackle slaves in the Throne Worlds? Will it allow us to eradicate the corruption plaguing our leadership? Will it preserve what's left of the Starkmanir, or bring the Nefantar back into our culture? We kept our dignity because people like *me* prevented *her* ideas from defeating the spirit of our race, before we could become institutionalized by the acceptance of a failed state.'

Maleatu leaned forward, gripping the Khumaak close to the blades. 'Democracy is failing because it was never suited for our way of life, the way we lived before those goddamned Amarrians destroyed everything. We've always followed the Tribes, and the Tribes have followed the Elders. We cannot abandon what we were, Keitan! The Gallenteans, bless them, are finally understanding that their ideologies are misplaced just about everywhere except for their own borders . . .'

He ran his fingers along the weapon's handle resting on his lap, thinking for a moment.

'And . . . recent *international* events suggest they're about to learn what happens when their ideals are rejected on a national scale. I hope the Elders consider just how much of a debt we owe to the Federation when the time comes. I for one would stand by their side.'

Keitan sprang out of his chair and began pacing the

area behind his desk. 'This is insanity! All right . . . fine! Let's just say for a moment that I endorse all this. How exactly am I supposed to be the Elder's "voice" to the Assembly? What the hell am I supposed to say to them, and to the Republic? Abandon all hope? Collect your things and head for cover? Anarchy will lead us to the promised land?'

'You'll know when the time comes,' Maleatu answered, re-sheathing the Khumaak and placing the strap over his shoulder. 'Oh, when the time is right, and the people know the Elders are real, they will be *inspired*. It will reinvigorate the populace. Just knowing that there's *hope* might be enough to salvage this botched experiment you call the "Republic," at least for a little while.'

As Maleatu lifted himself off the seat, Ameline appeared out of nowhere to assist him. 'But a word of advice, Keitan: there is no turning back now. The Elders have selected you to be their voice, and that decision is final. Ameline, lovely as she is, is just as capable of killing you as she is of protecting you. The Elder's secret must be kept – not for the sake of your Republic, but for the sake of your *people*.'

They both turned toward the office door.

'Don't you ever forget the difference between the two again,' Maleatu warned.

26

Karin Midular fervently believed that the survival of the Minmatar race depended on the success of the Republic. An advocate of the democratic principles utilized by the Gallente Federation, her entire political career had been devoted to the promotion of a similar, equally progressive agenda for the Minmatar government.

As the elected prime minister, she saw her responsibility as an architect of national transition; specifically, to continue the unfinished business of nation-building that started after the Rebellion hundreds of years earlier. By adapting to the modern realities of New Eden, she reasoned, the Minmatar could advance their civilization without losing their soul.

She never tolerated patriotism as a substitute for rational thinking. War, no matter how bitter the memories or potent the urge for vengeance against the Amarrians, was to be avoided at all costs. As a nation, she believed, the Republic was woefully unprepared for war. Any kind of protracted conflict meant risking hundreds of years of painstaking economic and infrastructural recovery, and she would be doing this generation of Minmatars a tragic disservice by following the lead of political warmongers down a path of destruction. But despite her efforts, this was the direction that the nation was being pulled toward anyway.

Within minutes of Maleatu Shakor's departure from the privacy of Keitan Yun's office, she received news so personally disturbing that she drove her staff away just to make time to think alone.

In a short while, the media would learn of this development as well, and its significance was sure to take the international headlines away from Tibus Heth.

LIKE THE CALDARI State, the Minmatar Republic was suffering from the consequences of an anemic economy, although for much different reasons. Their greatest impediment to prosperity was as much psychological as it was grounded in genuine faults with the political and economic system in place.

First, there was the ever-present stigma of being an enslaved race. One third of the current Minmatar population was held in bondage by the Amarr Empire; in the last 800 years, some or all of this culture was victim to slavery at some point. Today's Minmatars were just the second generation since the rebellion that spawned the creation of an independent Republic, and few realized just how fortunate they were that any part of the population had any freedom at all.

To the supreme frustration of many, those seeking retribution toward Amarr were always restrained by the laws of CONCORD. But the resulting current of resentment manifested itself more as resignation than anger. This generation of Minmatars had always known mediocrity, half freedoms, and half chances. There was more of an incentive to move on to places where the prospects for a better life existed *now*, as opposed to building the foundation for a future that was uncertain at best.

For that reason, one fifth of the Minmatar population lived in the Gallente Federation. Every day, thousands more moved there, taking with them the bright minds and skilled laborers desperately needed to build up the Republic. The hardships of life in these regions made the decision easy for those who could afford to leave, and no amount of patriotism or national pride was going to stem the exodus. Despite Midular's tireless efforts to convince them to stay, the mass emigration had increased more each year since her election to power.

The second impediment to prosperity was the Republic itself. The same institutions charged with formulating laws and policies paralyzed themselves with bureaucratic red tape. Based on the Federation jurisprudence model, the legislative process was failing because of its incompatibility with Minmatar tribal culture. Corporate legislation enacted to curb corruption made it difficult to establish businesses legitimately. Social service programs went unfunded due to an incompetent tax collection process. Criminal laws were only selectively enforced by low paid police conscripted from inner cities, all of whom were vulnerable to bribes. Every failed policy was a feedback mechanism that created more problems than they solved; the Republic government was a dangerously ineffective machine that worked just enough to avert a complete breakdown of law and order.

THE MINMATAR PLANET of Skarkon II, once a gorgeous paradise with sprawling cities and towering spires, was now a decaying quagmire, forever scarred by the violent Rebellion that had swept through there centuries earlier. Located on the fringe of Republic territory, the planet was a shadow of its former self, an altogether disconnected world strung together with bleak cities and failing industries.

From the perspective of the downtrodden, working with local crime syndicates was infinitely easier than working within the government bureaucracy. In the name of survival, the ethics of the means were unimportant. Like much of the local population, the cartels cared little about patriotism, and were generally fair in the practice of illicit trades, resorting to violence only when the intent to betray or scheme against them was clear.

On this world, organized crime was able to infiltrate and exert influence on just about everything, from surface-based industries to the space lanes above. The Archangels, part of the greater crime syndicate known as the Angel Cartel, now controlled capital assets that placed their net worth on a par with some of the largest corporations in the Republic. On the planet of Skarkon II, whether people worked in fields or offices, factories or refineries, civic or even military services, everyone was a part of the Archangel's financial network in some capacity.

This is not to say that the Archangels were the kind of savior that the population needed. As their criminal affiliation implied, they were indiscriminate in their choice of enterprises. Their business followed the daytime workforce into the flawed lifestyles they embraced afterward, supplying them with the fix for their addictions, appetites, fetishes, and lusts by luring them into the darker side of the cityscapes that they controlled exclusively. Gambling, prostitution, drugs, weapons, illicit cybernetic surgeries of all kinds, and death-match gladiatorial contests all ruled the night.

Skarkon was a cesspool of criminal activity, among the worst in New Eden, and had become emblematic of the Republic's greater issues, and of Karin Midular's ineffective government. For both political and personal reasons, she endeavored to make Skarkon the focus of an ambitious law enforcement campaign, vowing to 'rid the system of its criminal elements and to eliminate cartel influence in the region' before the end of her term in office. Amidst a barrage of politically-minded publicity and fanfare, Karin made the announcement herself just days ago, prior to Keitan Yun's debacle before the CONCORD Assembly.

Despite the enthusiastic response from officials clamoring for political visibility, the Archangels had, until now, been unusually quiet.

COMPANIONSHIP ARRIVED AND departed the life of Karin Midular with the randomness of natural disasters. Her volatile nature and innate persistence to drive to the heart of matters scared away the prospective suitors of her youth, whose numbers increased as her political strength gained. Academically brilliant, she was raised as an engineer, specializing in the starship propulsion systems used by the Republic fleet. Her foray into politics began during her brief tenure as the Chief Researcher of Core Complexion, one of the few Minmatar Republic corporations to reach international prominence. She was a natural before cameras and crowds, and never hesitated to share her personal views with audiences. Her election campaign was refreshing for the Minmatar populace, who had grown tired of the podium-smashing, vengeance-seeking war hawks, and instead favored a candidate whom they believed could lead realistic reforms that could raise the collective standard of living.

But as one policy after the next failed to get through Parliament, her political stature began to plummet, and the campaign that had promised reform brought about stagnation and decline instead. A pragmatic person by nature, her attempts to seek cordial, 'détente' relations with the Amarrians so she could focus on economic rebuilding was easily vilified by her political enemies. Dubbing her the 'Overlords' Pet', her popularity descended to the point of open, belligerent animosity during sessions.

Now she was more alone than ever before, with no one that she could turn toward for advice, which she needed because of the communiqué in her hands:

Prime Minister Midular,

Out of respect for your premiership, we have never once voiced opinions concerning your leadership, to say nothing of the fact that we, the Archangels, are more capable of providing for the welfare of this Republic than your government.

Your lack of respect is insulting. We will not be made an example of for your political gain.

At 19:00 local, the Skarkon system will be transferred

to Archangel sovereignty by right of civil petition and council approval by the planetary governors. The news will be delivered to the media at that time, accompanied with the voluntary electronic signatures of approximately ten million Skarkon residents.

All starship traffic entering the system that is not in good standing with the Angel Cartel or its affiliates will be considered hostile and fired upon.

Violence can be averted in one of two ways: by conceding the transfer of the Skarkon System to cartel sovereignty, or by issuing a public apology for your slanderous comments against the Archangels.

With Malice,
Tabe Rajus
Archangels

Karin let the paper fall from her hand. The message lights on her console were all blinking, undoubtedly bringing word that an Archangel blockade was underway in Skarkon.

In other words, she thought, *things are so bad that the Republic has more faith in the word of pirates than they do in my own leadership.*

As the comm networks overflowed with distress calls and demands for help from the Republic fleet, Karin had to command herself to stop shaking. Slowly, she arose from her seat to face the cabinet members pounding on her door outside.

27

Genesis Region – Sanctum Constellation
The Yulai System – Planet VIII
Inner Circle Tribunal Station

As the Republic government's leadership scrambled to deal with the crisis in Skarkon, the most powerful law enforcement agency in New Eden was gathering for a status review of the four Empires, and its role in maintaining the delicate peace between them. These men and women were known as the Inner Circle Tribunal, the top-level executives responsible for the strategic decisions and policy initiatives of CONCORD.

Historically, the Gallente-Caldari War marked the dawn of the Empyrean Age. The epic conflict conclusively established that a numerically inferior, pod-equipped fleet was capable of overwhelming a much larger conventional force. Overnight, the capsuleer had become one of the pivotal weapons in the history of modern warfare. The nation states, ever cognizant of their own limitations and wary of unleashing a monster they couldn't control, moved quickly to keep the strength of capsuleers in check.

From this necessity, CONCORD (Consolidated Cooperation and Relations Command) was born. While chartered for the official purpose of providing security for New Eden's spacelanes, the ulterior motive of the nation states was to prevent each other from exploiting the capsuleer's power for self-interests. The secretive Jovians, correctly anticipating the potential for dishonesty hidden within such well-intentioned measures, took an active role in defining the responsibilities of CONCORD and equipping them with the muscle required to uphold its directive.

To this day, much of the technology used in the law enforcement arm remains a closely guarded secret – a condition agreed to by the nation states only because of Jovian assurances that it could never be used except in circumstances where the laws of CONCORD were broken. The rapid-response time of CONCORD was legendary, based on the core requirement of being able to place instant, decisive firepower anywhere within Empire borders.

As far as any expert could tell – including the thousands of capsuleers who have fallen victim to their firepower – the actual weapons and ships that CONCORD used were nothing extraordinary. It was how they could move them in such overwhelming numbers so quickly that confounded would-be criminals and the government scientists who tried to duplicate the technology. No matter where an infraction took place, CONCORD could respond and deal 'justice' – loosely defined as the immediate and non-negotiable destruction of the offender's ship – at a moment's notice.

Some speculated that the secret to their power was a network of untraceable deadspace complexes hidden in Empire-controlled systems. Others argued that it was an unknown Jovian technology embedded within the stargates themselves. In any case, those secrets were known only to the Inner Circle men and women gathering now, who were charged with the vast responsibility of using it *only* against those capsuleers who broke the law.

The law, as it were, had provisions that permitted acts of aggression between capsuleers in specific conditions. As powerful as the capsuleers were, their every act was recorded in Empire space. Every starship was in constant communication with CONCORD listening posts, transmitting detailed telemetry about its location, systems, and cargo. By virtue of always knowing when a weapon was fired in space, the rules of engagement between ships could be enforced, and modified to permit sanctioned wars between capsuleer organizations. These legal war declarations kept conflicts confined to the warring parties, limiting collateral damage for non-combatants by assuring the swift destruction of those who failed to comply.

That CONCORD had killed or maimed millions of starship crewmembers while in the process of dealing justice to capsuleers was an afterthought, and testament to the deific scale of the capsuleer domain. Many considered it a natural progression of the unwritten laws which have always governed the seas and the heavens: those who boarded a ship entrusted their lives to its captain, and as such were just as deserving of punishment for whatever crime that captain committed.

This was the price for allowing a breed of immortals to rise to prominence in humanity; their eternal gift had to come at the expense of mortals. To step onto the deck of a starship was to sell your soul to a capsuleer. Because of this, they were despised and adored; feared and admired; cursed and blessed; worshiped and hunted by the vast populations of New Eden.

The only entity which was greater than their power was CONCORD, whose decisions – right or wrong – would always determine the course of events for humankind.

THE WINDOWLESS CONCORD Inner Circle Tribunal meeting room was shaped like a perfect sphere, nestled deep within an impregnable orbital fortress above the eighth planet of the Yulai System. Everything within its curved walls was a glossy, sterile white, including the circular disc which hovered at its center and the specialized chairs surrounding it. One by one, the members were seated as the chairs swung around to meet them on the access walkway, which then retracted seamlessly into the curved walls. As the lights began to dim, Inner Circle Director Irhes Angireh welcomed the other members with feigned, amicable candor.

'Good evening, people,' she said, settling into the seat, which reclined slightly. 'How are we doing?'

While she spoke, a neuro-interface probe emerged from the headrest and inserted into the socket at the base of her skull. Their cybernetic implants granted them access to the NEOCOM, the subspace datacomm network accessible to every other capsuleer in New Eden.

'Rushed,' answered Tashin Ernabaita. Like the others, he too was now interfaced with the NEOCOM. 'I have tickets to the national premier of Roxor in Luminaire, and I don't want to be late.'

'Oh, how the hell did you get tickets?' grumbled Tatoh Okkamon. 'I've been trying for months, you scoundrel.'

Grinning, the older man was about to answer when Irhes took control of the meeting.

'On to the business at hand, shall we?' A volumetric display of the Amarr Empire's national seal was rotating in the middle of the room. 'Several Theology Council members have been murdered or gone missing, most notably the esteemed Amarr Holder Falek Grange.'

As she spoke, imagery revealing everything from crime scene locations of the dead Council members to their individual profiles materialized. Her thought process was combining with raw NEOCOM data, and then transformed into projected visuals by the meeting room's technology.

'That by itself doesn't concern me,' she continued. 'What *does* concern me is that each of their clones was destroyed, in all cases by insiders who then terminated themselves before we could reach them.'

Seven different scenes all showed damaged cloning vats, with the accompanying carnage and corpses, in various stations.

'Such . . . *selfless* . . . devotion to cause implies complicity with large organizations,' she growled. '*Much* larger organizations. Although speculation is beyond the jurisdiction of this body, Chamberlain Karsoth isn't exempt from my list of suspects. But more importantly, Falek Grange's clone survived, which is to say that we can't determine its whereabouts. It was moved before the saboteurs could destroy it.

'If that clone is within Empire space, I want it found. The transportation of capsuleer clones is very much *our* business, and I want our customs officers informed – quietly – to be extra vigilant. Any pilot caught with this cargo is to be apprehended immediately, regardless of standings, and no matter what the cost.'

'Done,' Tatoh responded, as a hierarchical command tree formed above. Each node held the live picture of a CONCORD customs officer, both in space and docked. By simply thinking about it, his orders were transmitted to hundreds of law enforcement officers, all of whom acknowledged immediately. 'I believe I know the answer already, but why do you suspect Karsoth?'

'Woman's intuition,' Irhes muttered. 'The Blood Raiders claimed responsibility for Emperor Kor-Azor's assassination, leaving the heirs scared of their own shadows, and understandably so: if they can get to the emperor, they can get to anyone else. Meanwhile, Karsoth has been stalling new Succession Trials ever since, and the heirs seem content to oblige. Convenient, don't you think? I know a despot when I see one. Karsoth won't cede power that easily, and I'm certain that these Theology Council members were a threat to him somehow.'

'Grange had plenty of enemies,' Tashin commented. 'His atrocities against the Minmatar are infamous. Aside from the fact he's a butcher, there were plenty of Amarrian political adversaries who wouldn't mind his disappearance.'

'True, but he was aligned with Jamyl Sarum,' Tatoh countered. 'If I were Chamberlain Karsoth, I'd feel threatened by that as well.'

'Five years since her death, and still we speak her name,' Irhes mused. 'That woman had so much influence, even beyond Amarr's borders. Whether Karsoth is responsible for these murders or not, he won't exactly mourn the deceased. Consider it another convenience for him. Increase the number of patrols in Amarr space. Keep them visible. The capsuleers will think twice about retribution when they see the extra show of force.'

'Karsoth hasn't made any announcements yet,' Tatoh warned. 'I wonder how he'll spin it.'

'It doesn't matter,' Irhes retorted. The space above her cleared and was replaced with the Caldari State emblem. 'We'll be ready for anything. Next on the agenda: this Tibus Heth character.'

'A sensationalized press event,' quipped Esoutte Denaert. 'Nothing more.'

'I agree,' Irhes said. 'Caldari Constructions is insignificant. The capsuleers could care less about that corporation. Tibus Heth won't last one month as CEO, so we'll start preparing for his demise and a potential power vacuum later. Right now I'm more concerned about the economic fallout of Kaalakiota's bad press.'

'There won't be any,' Tatoh said, as dozens of predictive analysis charts appeared. 'At least nothing significant. Kaalakiota has thousands of capsuleers working for them, generating billions in cash flows. The CSE's market reaction was typical, but once investors gather their wits about them, it will rebound.'

'Then it's business as usual on the Caldari front,' Irhes concluded. 'Moving along to the Minmatars, so Tashin can attend his concert—' the man scoffed as the air cleared of images again. 'It seems they have some misbehaving Archcherubs in the Skarkon System. That's hardly surprising.'

'Its proximity to unregulated space worries me,' Esoutte said. 'Spillover of capsuleer conflicts from the far side of the gate could keep us very busy there.'

'Midular astonishes me,' Tashin laughed. 'How she's still in power, I'll never understand.'

'All we can do,' Irhes said pointedly, taking exception to Tashin's mocking of a female political figure, "is to make sure we stay out of engagements between the Republic and the cartel, no matter where they occur. However . . . we should also be prepared to re-task our directorate in the event that the sovereignty claim sticks. It's not impossible.'

'You really think the Assembly would allow it?' Tatoh asked.

'If the Republic petitions, yes,' Irhes said, as a flow-chart depicting the political possibilities danced overhead. 'But that would be the least of our problems then, wouldn't it?'

'Good point,' Tatoh acknowledged. 'We'll raise the readiness level and re-task response elements accordingly.'

'Excellent,' Irhes concluded, as the Federation's seal appeared overhead. 'Now, what can we say about the Gallenteans?'

'President Foiritan is still the king,' Esoutte said. 'And no one can dethrone him, which in my opinion is a good thing. That society is as close to Utopia as any we can imagine.'

'An absolute economic juggernaut,' Tatoh concurred.

'As far as his overextended tenure in office is concerned, no one cares when they're living the good life. His political enemies – all two of them – are insignificant in the polls. For us, that means no news is good news.'

'That's what I like to hear,' Tashin said, deactivating his neural interface. 'In that case, I'll be checking out now—'

'Not so fast,' Irhes said, smiling. 'We're not quite done here yet . . . we have capsuleer alliance war declarations to review – about three hundred of them.'

28

Essence Region – Vieres Constellation
The Villore System – Planet III: Moroses
Sovereignty of the Gallente Federation

Surrounded by lush gardens and gorgeous vistas of rolling wooded hills, Gallente Federation President Souro Foiritan looked on as security personnel herded the last media members and regional dignitaries toward the spaceport entrance. Housed in a reinforced hangar outside the immense biodome in which he stood, a Pegasus-class dropship was waiting to take them back to the Senate Bureau Station for transport out of the system. From where he was standing, he could see the sleek curves of the military spacecraft's engines, emblazoned with the Federation coat of arms.

Relieved to be through with the political fanfare of the

day's event, the President walked along a pathway toward a patch of flowers and trees, hands clasped behind him, with security drones following him from a short distance. The groundbreaking ceremony marked the official beginning of a herculean, Federation-funded effort to terraform the third planet of the Villore System, known as Moroses by the regional Federation government. A barren, rocky world marred with heavy tectonic activity and a thin carbon dioxide atmosphere, the planet was nevertheless a prime candidate for planetary engineering because of its gravity-friendly radius and accommodating distance from the local sun.

After years of lobbying in the Senate – and well-timed reassurances from Federation geologists that tectonic activity was decreasing to 'manageable' levels – funding was approved to begin the project, starting with the construction of a spaceport and biodome housing facility for the tens of thousands of engineers who would eventually start building the power plants, atmosphere scrubbers, space elevator complexes, mass drivers, mining complexes, and additional biodomes for the next generation of settlers laboring to create another paradise world for the Gallente Federation.

Dozens of AUs away, the construction of orbital miners was already underway at the eighth planet, a gas giant laden with hydrogen destined to be transported and injected into Moroses's atmosphere to create water vapor. Large comets and ice asteroids in the system's Oort Cloud would be fitted with engines or towed by industrial haulers for deposit onto the planet's surface. Federation purchase orders for standard and nanotech alloys, laser drills, fuel cells, aneutronic fusion reactors, and countless other manufactured goods were in the process of being filled by thousands of businesses all over New Eden, but mostly in the Gallente Federation.

It was a project that took trillions of credits just to begin, and would cost trillions more over the course of its lifetime. But that was the power of the Federation's economy, which was so robust that financing for efforts this gargantuan was easy to attain. Any Gallentean who wanted a job could have one; any who sought education or medical care was entitled to it by virtue of citizenship. The demand for labor was so great that these social privileges were extended to the growing numbers of Minmatars immigrating to the Federation, who were quick to seize the opportunities afforded to them and contribute to Gallentean society by taking their place in the workforce, providing for their own, and living a life that was an impossible dream anywhere else.

Charismatic, bold, and tireless, President Foiritan was a hugely popular man – so much so that the Federation articles of government had to be rewritten to keep him in power. Before his term, constitutional law mandated that a presidency could only last five years. Succumbing to pressure from a frothing electorate threatening to accuse incumbent Senators of nonfeasance, the law was dropped. In truth, the Senate realized that his economic policies were working so well that they welcomed his longer-term ambitions, which could only be realized by allowing him to stay the course. But most practically, there were none who could offer enticing alternatives or a brighter Federation future than Souro Foiritan, and those who aligned themselves with him benefited merely by riding his personal wave of public support.

President Foiritan gazed upward as he strolled, toward the transparent nanoalloy canopy more than a kilometer overhead, and contemplated much graver matters than the success of his presidency. Capable of almost machine-like multitasking, he had mingled with the local governors, shaken hands and smiled for publicity photos, and resolutely dodged media questions about Tibus Heth, stating only that he was 'aware' of the events in the Armor Forge.

In truth, he had read Heth's national speech a dozen times. One phrase struck the President as more ominous than any other:

'The Gallenteans, from the moment they contacted us, have been the bane of our existence . . .'

Blatant ethnic, nationalistic overtones, Foiritan thought, *from a man speaking before an international audience.* He shook his head in disbelief, considering the grim possibilities that now existed. Without so much as reading a single word about his background, he had a visceral suspicion that Tibus Heth was capable of monstrous acts. The malevolence in his words required no intuition to interpret. *This tyrant is making a statement*, Foiritan concluded, breathing the sweet smell of flowers as the biodome's atmosphere processors pushed a soft breeze over the landscape. *And as much as I would find great satisfaction in humiliating him, there are millions of Gallentean expatriates whose welfare has just been threatened.*

'Mr. President,' announced one of the drones behind him. 'The guests have all boarded. Your transport is ready for departure.'

'All right,' he answered, turning to follow his metallic companions towards the spaceport. Members of the Senate Foreign Relations Committee, the Federation Navy, and the Federation Intelligence Office were all gathering to strategize potential policy changes in response to Heth's malice.

President Foiritan was certain they weren't going to like his ideas on the subject.

'AN OLIVE BRANCH?' Federation Navy Grand Admiral Anvent Eturrer said incredulously. 'Let me make sure I understand this . . . a Caldari politician threatens us before an international audience, and you want to offer him help?'

'Why not just send him money directly,' Intelligence Chief Ariel Orviegnoure chided. 'And a case of champagne for good measure.'

'You're not thinking it through,' accused Senate Foreign Relations Committee Head Aulmont Meis. 'We have Gallenteans living in and around Caldari space, including the deep space regions. We can't just start talking tough without a plan to protect them.'

President Foiritan was frowning, slouched in his chair as he listened to them debate his proposal.

'Won't a financial aid package just insult them?' Ariel pleaded. 'Look, our entrepreneurs do well over there because Caldarians prefer our goods and services to their own. That's just honest competition.'

'I would hardly call it honest,' scoffed Wadis Chene, the Federation Economic Minister. 'The only reason they can afford our goods at all is because we subsidize our own vendors. We even cover their exchange losses versus the local Caldari currencies they trade in. If we stopped that program and passed through all transactions in interstellar credits—'

'We are not stopping the subsidy program,' Foiritan said finally. 'We're going to *increase* it. I want the float rate adjusted by product types. Keep the durable trade goods at or above equivalent Caldari products, but make sure the nondurables and commodities stay cheaper.'

Straightening up, he leaned forward. 'Then I want you to cut off Federation suppliers. From now on, all Gallentean enterprises operating in Caldari space will purchase goods and supplies *exclusively* from Caldari vendors.'

Concerned looks passed around the room as someone fumbling with a datapad dropped it onto the table.

'Mr. President,' Wadis said cautiously. 'That will run our own expatriates out of business . . .'

The president looked downward. 'No, because we're going to subsidize supplier losses as well. We'll compensate enterprises that lose business with tax breaks, or maybe even by purchasing their excess merchandise outright.'

'Like I said before,' Ariel muttered. 'Why not just send them money directly?'

More grumbles went through the room as President Foiritan shifted his deadpan gaze between each person.

'So what you're saying,' Wadis pleaded, appearing more desperate than concerned, 'is that you want to support their entire economy by fixing prices and *entirely* removing competition from their markets, effectively playing right into the same economic planning that led to their own ruin. That would completely contradict every free trade policy ever pushed in the history of the Federation.'

President Foiritan clenched his teeth. 'As you already pointed out, the "free market" rhetoric was always bullshit so long as we were subsidizing Gallentean enterprises,' he growled, letting some of his temper get the better of him. 'I can handle it politically, and the Federation can handle it economically.'

'I don't know about that,' Wadis retorted. 'This could get really expensive . . .'

'I don't *care* what it costs,' President Foiritan said

forcefully. 'I have an obligation to protect Gallentean citizens scattered across hundreds of worlds. That means I have the authority to use whatever means are at my disposal to accomplish that. This package is the best option I have. Not guns. Not tough talk. But an olive branch—' He stared at the Admiral, then moved his glare to Ariel. 'And a lot of money.'

'Mr. President, with all due respect, why are you acting so cautious?' Admiral Eturrer asked. 'I understand the value of strong economic ties, but in light of everything that's happened, is it possible that we're overreacting? Caldari Constructions isn't even a mega-corp. Why should we be so concerned about Heth?'

'It's not Heth that concerns me,' Foiritan said, standing abruptly to pace. 'Nor the entire lot of Caldari mega-corporations. It's the Caldari *people* that I'm scared of.'

'I think that's a little—' Ariel started, but President Foiritan waved her off.

'People, we've *won the war.* Whatever historians have recorded about the stalemate we fought to hundreds of years ago, the undisputed fact is that we've kicked their asses economically ever since, and it's mostly because the avarice of their own mega-corporations made it easy for us.'

The president bent forward over the table, resting his knuckles on its polished wood surface.

'But now their backs are against the wall, and you just don't know what they're capable of. Do any of you understand just how bad things are over there? How many of them are technically living in poverty? Heth is using their misery as a weapon, and I have to be honest, that scares me. A lot. Those people *want* him to have power. And he's telling them everything they want to hear. Haven't you seen all the *international* newsfeeds of him running through the mud with a shot up kid on his back?'

He raised his voice a few decibels.

'Well, they're chanting his name like he's a hero. And if I talk tough with him, it plays right into his hands. But if I send him this free lunch, it plays into *our* hands. Don't you see? This is a perception management game now. Propaganda. Public relations. Because of Heth, I can't protect my people from what Caldarians think about them. If he inspires enough hatred, if he can seriously strengthen his position by appealing directly to the neo-hardliners and blaming Gallenteans for their misery, or even *worse*, gain support from the goddamn capsuleers, then the more danger we're *all* in, not just the expats.'

The president could see that his cabinet members were considering his arguments as he continued.

'We are *scapegoats*. We're the Great Excuse. Our success is their failure. We tried to spread prosperity and failed, because the mega-corps didn't spread the wealth like we hoped. That son of a bitch Heth has a case, and a valid one at that. So now the only play we have left is to give Caldarians as little reason as possible to believe anything that comes out of that bastard's mouth.'

He folded his arms across his chest, glaring at each of them as though reprimanding a school classroom.

'The fact is, we have to protect our people. That's what matters more than anything else. And so we will take the higher ground, and if we have to swallow our pride to do that, I don't give a damn.

'Wadis, I want a draft of this package on my desk in Ladistier by tomorrow night. Admiral Eturrer, review any contingency plans for getting people out of Caldari space. I want those on my desk at the same time as this draft.

Everyone keeps quiet – there'll be hell to pay if the media gets wind of this. Meanwhile, we'll keep an eye on Heth. If he escalates matters, I want us ready to act.'

Many still wore disapproving expressions on their faces. But there would be no more debate on the matter, for the president – democratically elected or not – had final say in decisions concerning national security.

'Who will present it?' Senator Meis asked. 'And how?'

'No one in here should,' Ariel warned. 'According to Heth, we're the enemy, right?'

'This is economic aid, so it'll be presented by our Economic Minister,' President Foiritan growled, ignoring the pale look on her face as he continued. 'Congratulations, Wadis. You get the honor.'

'Then we need a pacifist to come along as well,' Wadis said. 'Someone as reasonably close to what a Caldarian might not think of as being absolutely despicable.'

'Noir,' Admiral Eturrer said immediately. 'Alexander Noir. One hundred and sixty years old and still making friends with everyone. Hell, even the Caldari Navy likes him.'

'Think he's up for it?' President Foiritan asked.

'That depends on what you're asking him to do,' the admiral answered. 'If it's just to babysit a diplomatic delegation, I think he can handle it.'

'Then the question is who's there to receive him,' Wadis added. 'Heth would eat him alive. We can't present this to him or else he'll manipulate it for his own benefit.'

'Let's wait and see what happens,' President Foiritan said. 'Maybe someone reasonable will emerge who we can actually talk to. But we're all in agreement with recruiting Noir for the job, so let's bring him up to speed with what's happening. Meeting adjourned, people. We've got work to do.'

* * *

ADMIRAL ALEXANDER NOIR, the retired Federation
Navy officer adoringly referred to as the 'Statesman of
Antiquity', was living out his golden years in the periphery of Gallentean politics. A hawk in his younger days,
he had since become the Federation's dove where it
concerned Gallente-Caldari relations, dedicating the latter part of his life to mending old war wounds and, to a
degree, achieving more in that cause than anyone else
ever had.

Content to play the role of adviser, Noir rejected numerous pleas from politicians to run for public office. Regardless, whenever he spoke, people listened. He was
even respected by the Caldari Navy; some would daresay
less as an enemy and more as a friend. Hobbling about
with the assistance of cybernetic implants and medical
drones, his frail physical appearance disguised his huge
heart and sharp mind.

When Admiral Eturrer contacted the elder statesman
to present Foiritan's plan, he accepted without hesitation,
concurring with the president's assertion that this was the
only viable political option they had. It was agreed by both
men that preparations should begin immediately, and as
quietly as possible. Noir, good man that he was, left the
conversation feeling honored that he could still contribute
to a great cause. As always, he was giddy with excitement
as he told his wife of a century what the president was asking him to do, along with the habitual disclaimer that she
was to keep these developments secret. She gave him a
kiss on the forehead and a gentle embrace, sharing his excitement and restating the endless inspiration that she de-
rived from watching his passionate pursuit of international
peace.

Once settled in the privacy of his own living quarters, where he lived alone, Admiral Anvent Eturrer prepared a message that detailed everything he could remember about the day's events. He then delivered this encrypted information to an anonymous contact who, upon its receipt, transferred a large sum of money into an alias account accessible only by him.

Admiral Anvent Eturrer had no way of knowing that his contact was the Broker, nor would he care if he did.

29

Molden Heath Region – Eoldulf Constellation
The Skarkon System – Planet III, Moon 14
Republic Parliament Bureau Station

With a primal passion, she pulled him deeper inside, wrapping her strong legs firmly around his torso. Exhaling in pleasure, Korvin used his arms to push gently off the soft ceiling, using just enough force to send them into a graceful, weightless tumble through the sweet, pure oxygen air mix of the chamber. Tightening her grip as he thrust gently, she arched back as far as her spine would allow, moaning in ecstasy. As floating globules of sweat rose from their glistening frames, his hands ran beneath the smoothness of her hips, over the firmness of her abdomen, around the silky texture of her breasts, and through the thick mane of her auburn hair.

It was almost a random fling, as they usually were whenever he prowled the night seeking release for his sexual desires. This conquest began late in the local hours of the station, where he had run into Keitan Yun. Drinking alone, absorbing the news feeds and contemplating historical implications, his ears detected the faint drum bass of music, its rhythmic tempo pulsing through the walls of the lounge in which he sat.

Half weakened by alcohol, and always half weakened by desire, he found himself irresistibly drawn to the music's source. Rivalling the wild reputation of Gallentean entertainment, Minmatar-run clubs were congregations of raw, joyous celebrations of life. Despite the throngs of people and high-energy atmosphere, they were generally peaceful affairs, despite the near unrestricted use of stims and drugs within them. Admission to these clubs was nearly as strict as gaining access to the bridge of a starship. In addition to weapon screening, those with criminal histories were denied entry; predictive brain scan technology then determined all other entrants' propensity for violence, eliminating the chance of troublemakers from entering.

Known as *Raafa-Kon* in native Matari, Minmatar nightclubs embodied the philosophy of disallowing inhibitions and equalizing all castes within its walls, a tradition that evolved from a tribal culture that demanded similar ceremonies in the worship of ancient gods. Almost all Minmatars – even those who considered each other enemies – treated these sites as if they were hallowed ground.

Passing through the elaborate security entrance manned by imposing Brutor guards, Korvin found himself staring at a cavernous, hemispherical-shaped structure that completely disoriented him for a moment. Looking straight up, he could see the 'far end' of the inverted hemisphere hundreds of meters away; the entire bowl was packed with revelers, some upside-down relative to his position even as people were dancing, grinding, and celebrating just beside him.

As strobes and volumetric displays bathed the crowd in light, he could make out the hall's gradual curve; from every single point on it, artificial gravity kept everyone's feet directly beneath them as if standing in a level room. A platform suspended in the exact center of the hall served as the conductor's lair for the event, known as the 'Raafa-Kana', or the 'ceremony leader.' The underside of the platform was packed with dozens of cameras and sensors, monitoring every inch of the hall at all times.

Korvin allowed himself to be engulfed by the crowd, unable to control his own body's response to the music. The center platform blasted harmonics that delivered targeted stimulation of the brain's superior temporal gyrus; no matter how shy or reserved the individual, the urge to dance was physically overwhelming. If anyone in the crowd noticed that he was a capsuleer, they didn't seem to care. As his lover forced another gentle aerial spin with her hips, Korvin remembered feeling thankful at the time to be unrecognized. Yet by pure coincidence, the crowd's pulsing, gyrating current had led him directly to her, still dressed in her Federation Navy flight uniform, no doubt part of the same joint-force exercise that he was, and every bit as parched for lust.

And so where he had expected to bed a Minmatar woman this evening, he instead found himself grinding with a Gallentean warrioress who was every part his equal in status and physical ability; an independent, fiercely strong individual who wanted only to have as much fun as her time aboard this station would allow. Korvin was more than eager to oblige, dancing until the ritual of seduction was complete. Hours later, they remained entombed in a weightless recreation module, immersed in physical rapture, devouring each other's flesh with carnal delight.

Opening his eyes for a moment to admire her athletic prowess in zero-g sex – which the Minmatars considered a sacred act – he caught a glimpse of his own dress uniform as it rolled past his vision, just long enough for his eyes to register the Federation coat-of-arms and the Navy flight pins above it. He abruptly remembered the words of Keitan Yun:

'Drastic changes are imminent. Trust your instincts and get out of harm's way.'

Raising both legs straight overhead like a gymnast, she positioned both calves besides each of his ears and pressed, sending both of them into a somersault. He felt himself slip even deeper inside her as she rasped a growl of encouragement. Yet for some reason the bitter words of Tibus Heth struck him:

'Gallenteans are the bane of our existence . . . Deliver us from the humiliation of their influence . . .'

Korvin slipped out of her, disrupting the passion session which had, until now, been a flawless performance. Still, it was enough to frustrate his lover.

'Oh, Lieutenant,' she growled, smacking her lips. 'So close.'

'I'm sorry . . .' he breathed, realizing that for the life of him, he couldn't remember her name.

Shit.

Sneaking a glance toward her uniform for help, he noticed for the first time the captain's rank insignia emblazoned on it.

Fucking shit.

'I was distracted by something,' he mumbled.

'What,' she said, pushing herself off in a glorious

backflip that splashed her mane of thick hair through the space in front of him, 'could possibly distract you from *this*?'

Hands raised over her head, she propped herself against the soft corner of the wall and ceiling, her full breasts elevated upward in the weightless environment. Korvin's physical reaction was immediate, but something urgent was tugging at his mind.

He suddenly became conscious of his full, naked exposure, and allowed the truth to slip. 'First I thought about how badly these joint exercises have been going. And then . . . about Tibus Heth—'

'*Heth?*' Her expression made him regret his honesty. 'You thought about Tibus Heth in the middle of all that? Well . . .' She pushed herself downward, toward the room's gravity control. 'You're not exactly helping my ego any.'

Korvin, along with everything else suspended in midair, began to descend gently toward the floor. *This one sure is confident*, he thought. *Perhaps overly so.*

'I'm sorry for killing the mood,' he answered glumly, reaching for his clothes. 'You're an amazing lover . . . Captain.'

Seated on the cushioned floor, she began pulling her uniform on. 'As long as our clothes are off, it's "Yana." And as long as we're being honest, what's bothering you so much about Tibus Heth?'

'Well, his overnight rise to power for one,' he answered, stretching to acclimate himself with gravity again. 'The nationalist overtones of his speech. And his open threats to the Federation.'

'Does that surprise you?' she asked, pulling her hair back and tying it. 'He's your typical Caldari bigot, fresh from the mega-corporate meat grinder, with a podium to shout from.'

Korvin frowned. 'Well, considering the sad state of the Caldari economy, you have a dangerous mix of circumstances that could easily escalate into . . .'

'Into what?' she demanded curtly, standing to zip up her uniform. Korvin observed that she neglected to use undergarments. 'An anti-Federation rally here or there? A resurgence of fist-waving CEOs jumping onto the ultra-nationalist bandwagon? More unemployed kids making bonfires of government monuments?'

'Well, yes,' he answered, almost shocked. 'Doesn't that worry you?'

'Not in the slightest,' she scoffed. 'You're over-thinking the situation. Anti-Gallentean sentiment has ebbed and flowed so much over the years, and it's tiring listening to it over and over. I hope they burn themselves to ashes, personally. They weren't humbled enough during the war, and I'd love the chance to serve them some humbling myself.'

Not cool, Korvin thought. 'Is that why you became a capsuleer?'

'You mean besides the prestige of becoming one of humankind's elite?' she asked. 'Or the pride of wearing a Navy uniform? Or maybe the gift of immortality?' She nodded emphatically. 'Yup. More or less.'

He studied her for a moment, focusing on the irises of her eyes. 'That's why you were assigned here then, isn't it? They want you as far away from the Caldari Border Zone as possible.'

Korvin nearly winced. *Why the hell did I just say that?*

'How did someone with your misguided instincts become a pilot in the first place, I have to wonder,' she snapped, then lowering her voice to an exaggerated whisper. 'I read your file, Korvin. I know *everything* about the pilots I fly with.'

She leaned closer to him. 'Mom and Dad were close to a certain . . . Admiral . . . Noir?'

His face flushed red, which he could tell that she enjoyed very much.

'A good word from Admiral Noir goes a long way with the Navy,' she purred. 'Maybe the capsuleer program's admission standards for *you* were a little lower than everyone else's?'

'Captain, that is *not* true,' he fumed, scrambling to get his own pants on. 'I earned my way in just like everyone else—'

'Lieutenant Lears,' she interrupted. 'We immortals are part of an exclusive club, and not without our secrets.'

She leaned toward him, and her eyes were full of fire. 'You, me, and this little fuck room *never happened.* If I hear so much as a single rumor about us and last evening, I'll have your balls in a sling so fast you'll wish you failed the admission program like you were supposed to.'

Fully dressed, her glare was unstoppable, and her posture was as rigid as the captain's rank insignia on her uniform. Somewhere in the back of his mind, he was shocked that he had gone so quickly from intimacy to flagrant hostility with this woman, and considered that her advice to forget the evening was indeed a wise idea.

But again, his mouth started moving before common sense could get the better of him.

'We may be immortal,' he said. 'But we're not invincible . . . Captain.'

Just when Korvin sensed he would regret speaking

again, Yana's datapad began to chirp. She held his glare for a few moments, allowing the shrill cry of the device to shatter the silence for a while longer before checking it.

Then Korvin's datapad began to chirp as well. As he scrambled across the floor to retrieve it, he noticed Yana's expression transform into a grimace.

'Great,' she muttered. 'Just perfect. Get dressed, Lieutenant. You've been reassigned.'

Scanning the device quickly, Korvin's eyes opened wide. 'Archangels have blockaded Skarkon?'

Keitan's words haunted him again: *I've lost all my faith in the democratic institutions of the Republic.*

'Yes, and the Federation doesn't want us to get involved,' she growled, shaking her head at the datapad. 'Apparently, Prime Minister Midular is politically inclined to demonstrate that she's capable of dealing with this herself. That means we're under strict orders to stay out of sight, and that we have to take the scenic route back to Federation territory.'

Korvin couldn't believe it. 'The scenic route' meant a long detour around Skarkon through completely lawless territory far beyond Empire borders. Any ships travelling through there were at risk from pirates, rogue drones, and crossfire from capsuleer alliance wars. But a Federation Navy starship, while untouchable in Gallentean space, was a prized target that few ships – if any at all – would ignore.

'Adding to the fun,' she continued, 'command is splitting Navy elements into teams of two to avoid attracting attention. Do you know who your wing assignment is, Lieutenant Lears?'

A quick glance at his deployment orders confirmed that it was Captain Yana Varakova.

'Lose that pathetic dress uniform and find a flight suit.

Move your ass, Lieutenant,' she barked. 'Let's hope your instincts in a starship are better than your instincts about my personal life.'

'Yes, Captain,' he said, fumbling a quick salute as he pulled a shirt on.

30

Korvin's inner eye blinked to life as camera drones fed imagery of the station's hangar bay into his visual cortex. Letting go of his corporeal self, his existence was transformed into a metaphysical union with the ship. In his mind, his arms grew into the armored transom of the Taranis; his bones morphed into its endoskeletal support beams; his blood mutated into hoards of nanites crawling beneath the ship's skin in search of damage to repair.

Alongside him was Captain Varakova's Taranis, its Federation Navy markings hastily painted over by the hangar crew. Korvin considered the irony of his danger; the woman he had just slept with was about to lead him on a trek through the most dangerous space in New Eden, without any support from the Navy or anyone else if things went wrong. But that was what capsuleers did; their immortality made them expendable, and their unique skills and abilities made them unequivocally qualified to tackle the most dangerous missions.

And our mission now, Korvin thought, *is just to survive this trip intact.*

'Standby,' the captain announced. 'An Archangel task force just jumped in.'

Working with telemetry provided by the Republic fleet, spotters were monitoring ship traffic coming through the

L4X-1V stargate, waiting for the right chance to allow the Federation ships to exit. Several pairs of Navy interceptors had left Republic space already and were deep into their flight paths. Besides this small fleet of pirate warships coming through – undoubtedly on their way to reinforce blockades at the Ennur and Mimiror gates – their journey had been uneventful.

'We're clear,' Captain Varakova announced. 'Go!'

The hangar's tunnel blurred by as powerful ion engines propelled the Taranis from the station. Protected by the inertia dampers embedded inside the hull, Korvin felt nothing as the craft accelerated instantly to a brisk 600 meters per second. Several megawatts of power transferred from the capacitor to the warp drive; after a brief journey through hyperspace, the two interceptors were directly in front of the L4X-1V stargate.

Korvin gazed at its blinking hazard lights momentarily before engaging the jump sequence. Until now, everything had been automatic, from the acceptance of his orders to the launching of his ship. But the sight of the gate wrought pure dread to his senses; a powerful sense of danger was surging through his veins, warning him not to enter.

He activated the gate with the certainty that something terrible was about to happen.

WITH THE REQUIREMENT of circumventing the most direct path back through either the Ennur and Mimiror stargates, the journey from Skarkon to Federation space required transit across more than thirty star systems – an interstellar distance equivalent to hundreds of light years. Unimpeded, the two capsuleers could make the trip in about an hour, a feat made possible by the dimension-warping phenomena of stargates and hyperspace drive technology.

No longer restricted by the relativistic confines of three-dimensional space, the discovery of additional dimensions and the means to traverse through them enabled humankind to propagate the stars and escape extinction twice – once from overpopulation and wars for scarce resources on Earth before New Eden's discovery, and after, when the EVE gate collapsed and forced humankind to rediscover the science that brought them there in the first place.

That such an epic feat could be taken for granted by capsuleers was tantamount to arrogance. Successive stargate jumps, especially when followed by hyperspace transits, was extremely taxing to human beings. Where Lieutenant Lears and Captain Varakova were concerned, the trip was tedious, even with the threat of danger lurking at every jump. But for humans, a trip requiring dozens of interstellar jumps in an hour could be lethal.

The dangers of interstellar travel – of the instantaneous transport of the physical self through higher dimensions – left the un-acclimated mind vulnerable to an ailment known as 'cynosic fibrosis.' A degenerative brain tissue condition, its symptoms ranged from mild disorientation to full-fledged psychosis if left untreated. As part of their training, starship crews were required to take daily regimens of synaptic modulators to reinforce the neurotransmissions of their brains, thus protecting themselves – to an extent – from the physical and psychological ardors of travelling instantly through space and time.

The drugs themselves had dangerous side effects for a small percentage of the population, which was enough of a deterrent to prevent casual interstellar travellers from taking them. Ship crews, and the personality types typically drawn to the profession, didn't think twice about the risks. Their life spans were likely to be cut short for more immediate reasons anyway.

Immune to such perils, Korvin was instead allowing his subconscious to monitor the ship's systems, which he had instructed to follow Yana's – *Captain Varakova's*, he corrected himself – Taranis into hyperspace as they jumped from one system to the next. With ship control as transparent as the operation of his own internal organs, his mind was free to contemplate other matters, such as the magnitude of his stupidity for sleeping with someone who outranked him. How he failed to notice her captain's rank was testament to the power of his own lust – she was, after all, irresistibly attractive – or to the primal spirituality of the Raafa-Kon; or to the audacity of failing to consider that a woman with such raw sexual appeal could possibly outrank him.

Maybe it was all of those things, he thought, suddenly having trouble remembering who had seduced whom. It had seemed so *natural* at the time; so *delicious* in the moment; he was too blinded by his urges to grasp what should have been obvious. Her raw libido – and his own – made it impossible to think about anything else.

Without even realizing it, he panned the camera over to focus on her ship, so close to his own, hurtling at superluminal speeds within the boundaries of the warp core. He wanted to be with her again, and found her abrupt hostility attractive. The fact that she was *right there*, even under these circumstances, was an unbearable tease. He wondered if she was thinking of these very things as well; if her lust for him was as genuine as it had seemed this morning; if he would be breaking the rules by checking the starmap for a system along the way which might welcome a pair of tourists visiting from the inner worlds . . .

The brilliant light streaks were visible just as the outer shell of the warp core collapsed. Several contacts registered on his sensors: One Wolf-class assault frigate, flanked on each side by Vagabond-class heavy assault cruisers. Each bore Republic Fleet markings – friendly ships – and were less than 50 kilometers from their position near the DE71–9 gate.

Because they were already six systems away from Minmatar-controlled space, this was the most improbable encounter that Korvin expected.

'Captain . . .' he started, as the images of weightless passion vanished.

'Do *not* jump through,' she ordered tersely. 'I'm going to hail them.'

'Understood, holding.'

Focusing on the Wolf, he noticed that the spacecraft looked brand new, literally as if it had been assembled within the last hour.

The same foreboding feeling as earlier descended on him like an axe. A surge of adrenaline raised his alertness to precognitive heights.

'He's not answering,' she said, breaking formation with Korvin's ship and moving toward the group. 'I'm going to approach them.'

'Captain, I don't think that's a good idea—' Korvin started.

Suddenly, the space besides the Wolf exploded in a brilliant flash of whitish-orange incandescent fireworks; bolts of supercharged plasma arcs erupted from its core and began to rotate, sustaining momentum briefly before collapsing inward, like a tunnel.

'*Cyno spike!*' Korvin shouted. 'Something's gonna come through!'

Four towering black silhouettes appeared in the cynosural field – a wormhole portal created by the jump drives of capital ships, enabling them to make interstellar crossings without stargates. Korvin recognized them immediately; they were Naglfar-class dreadnoughts. Their colossal hulks were unmistakable, and so massive that they reduced the Republic Fleet ships beside them into indiscernible specs. As the cynosural field dissipated, Korvin realized that his instruments were unable to determine if they were friendly or hostile; instead, they registered ominously as 'unknown.'

Then a fleet of Thukker warships inexplicably warped into the area, positioning their ships around the dreadnoughts in a defensive screen.

The Republic Fleet ships joined formation alongside of them.

'That's impossible,' Captain Varakova breathed. By all accounts, the Thukkers and Fleet ships should have been annihilating each other. 'What the hell are they doing . . . ?'

Threat indicators flashed across Korvin's vision as the armada of ships targeted them.

'Captain!' he shouted. The warships began closing distance on them quickly. 'Time to go!'

'Jump through! Now!' she shouted. In a flash, her ship was gone; he activated the gate just as the first volleys of autocannon fire began peppering his shields. His vision flashed white for a moment as his Taranis was transported through the DE71–9 gate—

—and again as his ship emerged directly into a Thukker ambush on the other side.

Basking in an eerie bluish-white aura, the area surrounding the gate was encased in the electromagnetic resonance of a warp disrupter. Korvin's reflexes were automatic; he willed the interceptor into a hard turn toward the nearest edge of the disrupter's range and fired his afterburners.

As his ship was locked up by Thukker warships, he panned the camera around and saw Captain Varakova's ship in the same trap. Within seconds, her interceptor was writhing in its final moments, its engines hopelessly crippled by a stasis web and getting punished by deadly cannon fire from orbiting assault frigates. Korvin's mind, assisted by the ship's computer, calculated a myriad of possibilities in a nanosecond and concluded that there was no solution, no possible way, to overcome the firepower arrayed against her.

'Save yourself!' she screamed, as fiery chunks of armor and structure were blasted off her ship. 'Go!'

Before he could respond, she vanished in a violent explosion; a searing white shockwave expanded outward from the blast, buffeting the enemy ships that killed her. A small pod, helpless and futile, struggled in the wreckage, squirming in the same deadly stasis web that crippled the Taranis.

Just when his own ship passed through the bubble's membrane into open space, Korvin heard Yana scream; a horrible, anguished, pain-ridden shrill so disturbing that his blood iced and his heart seized. The entire surface of her pod seemed to ignite in a pulse of lightning for a moment; then cannon rounds exploded through its hull, venting its neuro-embryonic fluid into space, and ejecting Yana's flash-frozen corpse into the deadly void.

Korvin's warp drive engaged; his subconscious mind was acting in self-preservation despite his conscious horror at the sight of her once divine flesh, now defiled and mutilated. Despite the cannon rounds ripping his ship apart, he was paralyzed with grief, and convinced that her immortality failed to lessen the horror of such a violent death.

His Taranis miraculously catapulted away, badly damaged but functional, leaving the angry pack of murderous Thukkers – and traitorous Republic Fleet warships – behind.

PART III

What Lies Beneath

31

Delve Region – D5-S0W Constellation
System T-IPZB

Billions of kilometers from the nearest celestial objects, the *Retford* tumbled gently through the void; errant bursts of plasma and sparks erupted through grievous wounds in the vessel's hull. Miraculously, she had survived the Blood Raider assault, but barely.

Blasted by the Bhaalgorn's powerful beam cannons, the energy stored in the *Retford*'s capacitor was lost to a potent electrical surge. The force of the strike knocked the ship and its projected warp core projection off course by several thousandths of an arc degree – a seemingly subtle amount that translated to immense distances when applied to hyperspace travel. Instead of disengaging the drive to realign with a known destination, Téa panicked, forcing the ship inside the core without knowing where in space the tunnel would deposit the *Retford* once it collapsed.

Her blunder saved their lives, for the extra few moments needed to align the ship correctly would have been enough for the Bhaalgorn to fire its cannons a second time.

* * *

SEATED IN THE gunnery area, Gear stretched out his thin limbs. He was the first *Retford* crewmember to awaken, which was to the unfamiliar sound of a man's whimpering. Stricken with terror, he realized the voice had to be the Amarrian capsuleer who Jonas brought aboard.

Shaking off the disorienting effects of cynosis, he took a few steps – carefully, to keep the soles of his boots from making any sound as he moved across the metal grating. Then a voice rang out from the passageways below:

'I can hear that you're awake . . .' the Amarrian called out. 'I have something urgent to tell you!'

Gear froze in his tracks.

'I know you're frightened,' the voice continued, taking shallow breaths between each sentence. 'I am as well . . . the ship is in danger. I can't explain how I know. But I'm certain of it.'

The former slave's conditioned instincts warned him of a very different danger than the Amarrian implied. Unanswerable questions raced through his mind:

What happened while I was asleep? Did he hurt anyone? Did he damage the ship? Is he even tied up?

His little hands darted over the gunnery instrument panel, calling for the ship's internal camera system. Téa and Jonas were slumped over in their seats on the bridge; Vince was on his back in the engine room; and the Amarrian was lying in Téa's bunk, cuffed to the railings. Opposite him was an unconscious Caldari woman who he didn't recognize.

'I don't know what I was before this,' the Amarrian pleaded. 'Nor why I'm so despised here, but . . . I swear I could never hurt anyone, let alone a child!'

Liar, Gear raged as vivid memories of beatings and torment from overlords rushed back to him. Just ten years of age, his fear and loathing of the Amarr ran as deeply as an entire lifetime's worth of cruelty.

FALEK WAS DESPERATE. Running his hand along the cold, metal bulkhead of his bunk, he could feel the *Retford*'s agony as if it was afflicting his own body.

'You don't trust me,' he said aloud. 'I understand. But what can I do to make you believe me?'

There was only silence. Judging from the lightness of the steps, he was certain this crewmember was a child. Then he had an idea.

'This ship uses a C-Type aneutronic fusion drive,' he said, closing his eyes while keeping his hand against the bulkhead. 'I know there are . . . *eight* . . . magnetic conduits running off the centerline for maneuvering thrusters . . .'

A wild-eyed woman that he had never seen before barged into the room.

'*Hey!*' Téa shouted. 'You do *not* talk to that child. *Ever.* Do you understand me?'

Falek was horrified. 'I'm just trying to warn someone that—'

'I'm *not* fucking around!' She stood over the bunk, threatening him with a pointed finger. 'I swear, I'll kill you if you say another word to him!'

'You don't understand,' he implored. 'I'm saying this to whoever will listen: the ship is badly damaged! If you try to run on impulse, you'll breach plasma internally! I swear it!'

'Oh, how the hell are you supposed to know that?' she demanded.

'Why all the yelling?' Gable groaned, slowly swinging her legs over the bunk across from Falek. 'He's a capsuleer. He probably knows more about this ship than anyone else aboard.'

'He's never been aboard!' Téa shouted, skipping the introduction of the *Retford's* newest passenger. 'Not long enough to know anything about it! And no matter what, I don't want him talking to my son!'

To Falek, the vibrations in the hull – detectable only on a quantum scale – were so powerful that he thought they would shake him off the bunk.

'The right rear dorsal containment projector is damaged,' Falek tried to say calmly. 'The next time you run plasma from the reactor, it'll burn right through the hull.'

'*Shut up!*' Téa nearly screamed. 'Our diagnostics would catch that! One more word and you're getting muzzled.'

'Let's try to calm down,' Gable intervened. 'I told you, he's a cloned capsuleer – his mind has been shaped to think like a ship. Think of it as the muscle memory of an amputee – he can intuitively *feel* what's happening even though he's not physically attached.'

'Your diagnostics are damaged,' Falek insisted. 'You can't locate the defect without a visual inspection.'

'What could cause diagnostics to miss something that important?' Gable asked calmly.

'A breach in the armor could disable it, and a power surge would almost certainly ruin it,' the Amarrian said, with urgency in his eyes. 'We took *damage* during that firefight!'

Gable stared intently at Téa.

'The containment field projector near the aft dorsal maneuvering thrusters is *destroyed*,' he repeated. 'You must believe me!'

'Can it be fixed?' Gable asked.

'Not out here,' Falek said, relieved that someone was finally taking him seriously. 'But if you can block plasma flow to the dorsal thrusters—'

He stopped in mid-sentence as a child appeared in the doorway – scared and suspicious, but also intrigued.

'—then we can safely use impulse to limp back to a shipyard,' he finished, bringing his sullen gaze on the tiny figure. 'Hello. What's your—'

'*Don't* you talk to him,' Téa warned through clenched teeth, jumping in front to block his view. But Gear pressed forward with a flurry of hand signals as Falek looked on.

She was determined to stop him from making any contact with Falek. 'Gear, maybe you should go inside—'

An angry grunt sounded from the boy's damaged larynx as he flashed an emphatic series of hand signals. Téa almost cut him off, but Gear grabbed her wrist and pointed toward Falek as if he wanted her to tell him something.

'Fine,' she said, turning toward the Amarrian. 'He wants to know how you knew there were eight thrusters.'

'Because he's a *capsuleer*,' Gable chimed again.

Falek strained as much as could to turn and face Gear. 'I can't tell you what my own name is, but I *know* starships. I was . . . born with this knowledge, this *connection* to them. I don't know anything else. But I swear, if you inspect that field projector, you'll find damage.'

Gear stared intently at him, wrestling with Falek's words. Then the intercom cackled to life.

'Téa, get up in front,' Jonas said. 'We need to stabilize this spin—'

'No!' Téa blurted. 'Don't activate thrust!'

'What are you talking about?'

'Just don't,' she blurted, throwing a glare at Falek. 'I'll come up to explain, but for God's sake, do *not* activate the thrusters!'

By the time Téa turned around, Gear had vanished.

'What's the matter with the kid's voice?' Gable asked,

peering outside of the doorway to follow his scamper down the narrow halls.

'You stay out of this,' Téa said, brushing past her as she rushed toward the bridge. 'Whoever you are.'

'WHAT'S THE PROBLEM now?' Jonas growled, rubbing his temples. His eyes, bloodshot and sunken, gave him a diabolical appearance.

Téa chose her words carefully: 'We think the containment bottles for the aft maneuvering jets are damaged.'

He gave her a disapproving look. 'And what makes you think that?'

'I don't, personally.' She struggled to say the words. 'But the capsuleer does.'

As he rolled his eyes in disgust, she followed up quickly: 'I think Gear believes him as well.'

'Oh, that makes it true, right?' he said, shaking his head. 'Fuck, Téa, give me a break already.'

She lurched forward and grabbed his hands. 'I know it sounds crazy, but can you just hold off on using thrust until we check it?'

'What the hell has gotten into you?' Flushed red, Jonas wrenched away and pointed toward the viewport. 'Look outside, genius.'

The starfield outside was spinning, and Téa could only stand the sight for a few moments before her stomach began to turn.

'We can't go anywhere until we get this under control,' Jonas said. 'Besides, the computer says containment is fine.'

'We were hit by battleship cannons,' she insisted. Jonas looked as annoyed as she could ever remember seeing him. 'I think a little caution is in order here. Did you even hear what I said?'

'Believe it or not, I did, and both me and the computer think it's bullshit,' he snapped. 'Now let me tell you about a real problem: We have a damaged capacitor, which means we can only make short jumps, and that most of us will be puking our guts up for the trip from here to . . . wherever it is we wind up.'

'Which is where, exactly?' she asked.

'I don't know, Téa,' he answered sarcastically. 'In case you forgot, Blood Raiders are hunting us and my god-damn capacitor is borked, which means I can't run any blockades unless I find a way to fix it!'

'So what are we going to do?' she asked.

'I don't fucking know, but you're not helping by asking all these stupid questions!' he hollered. 'I need time to *think*!'

Téa felt her existence begin to collapse.

'Fine, but can we just . . . hold off for a little while on the thrusters until we can prove they're not damaged?'

Jonas looked as if he might become violent when Gable's voice interrupted them on the intercom.

'Hello?' she asked. 'I think you guys better look at this.'

'Look at what?' Jonas snapped.

'The kid just went into the outer shell,' she said grimly. 'In a survival suit.'

The bottom fell out from Téa's stomach.

'Umm . . . please don't light up the engines just yet,' Gable added.

SQUIRMING AND TWISTING his way forward, Gear ma-neuvered through the ship's hull skeleton, trailing a cam-era cable line behind him. *Amarrians are all evil*, he kept telling himself. But he was puzzled by the sincerity of this capsuleer, who was treating him kindly. *Maybe because he doesn't have a choice here.* Pulling himself into an impossibly narrow chamber, he was inside the ribbed scaffolding that separated the inner hull structure from the armored plates above. Within these confines, he wasn't protected by the ship's graviton modulation system; he could feel the *Retford's* spin pulling on him, and his inner ear sensed unseen motion that would make even the strongest of adults sick to their stomachs.

But years of being forced to burrow through rumbling asteroids had prepared him for this. His young senses had adapted, and his small frame allowed him to navigate into tight areas normally reserved for drones and the robotic maintenance arrays of shipyards. Pushing himself into a T-shaped cross-sectional fitting, he recognized the plasma conduits extending from the main reactor. A sudden spike on the radiation sensors of his survival suit told him that he was close to a containment breach; he halted his advance immediately.

Forced to keep his elbows close to his body, he began pushing the cable forward using only his wrists. The aft dorsal plasma vent, and the allegedly damaged containment projector that the Amarrian capsuleer had warned him about, was just beyond another fitting that blocked his view.

Téa was utterly incoherent, crazed with Gear's dangerous venture into the *Retford's* hull, and had to be restrained from going inside after him.

'Gear, get out of there!' she kept screaming, banging on the hull with a spanner as Jonas tried to wrest it away from her.

'He can't hear you,' Gable said. 'I'm sure he's fine—'

'*Who the fuck are you?*' Téa screamed. 'Stay out of this!'

'Settle down!' Jonas shouted, gripping her from behind. 'You're out of control and it's pissing me off.'

A single blinking light appeared on the comm display next to the vault; it was originating from Gear's survival suit. Téa dropped the spanner in her struggle to wrestle free.

'Now don't panic him by acting all crazy,' Jonas warned, releasing her. She leapt at the controls, raising the audio control as high as it would go.

A rapid series of microphone clicks were immediately audible. 'What's he saying?' Jonas asked.

'He keeps saying he's all right, and to look at the camera feed assigned to this display,' Téa translated.

Crowding around the console, they squinted at the imagery. Expecting to see nothing extraordinary, Jonas instead did a double-take: a damaged containment projector, with scorch marks surrounding its dead emitters, was front and center; the spinning starfield outside the ship was barely a meter away from it, visible through a gaping hole in the armor plating.

'Holy shit,' he breathed.

Téa was about to faint.

'When a capsuleer says there's a problem . . .' Gable re marked.

'Yeah,' he muttered. 'Go check up on Vince, please.'

Elsewhere on the *Retford*, Falek switched off the intercom beside his bunk and settled beneath its covers. For the first time in his short life, he allowed himself a smile.

32

Domain Region – Throne Worlds Constellation
The Amarr System – Planet Oris
Emperor Family Academy Station: Saint Kuria the
Prophet Cathedral

Surrounded by illustrious pageantry and the regal company of Holders, Royal Paladin Guards, and Apostle's Clerics, Chamberlain Dochuta Karsoth stood before the vacant seat of the emperor, beneath the vaulted ceilings of the great cathedral. A vestment woven from gold threads and adorned with precious gemstones covered the huge girth of his fattened frame; if not for the cybernetic implants in his legs and torso, he would be unable to support the burden of his own weight. A miter emblazoned with the golden seal of Amarr rested upon his enormous head; it took two child slaves to lift it into place. His scepter, a gold-plated staff with the visage of the Holy Sign at its top, was wrapped tightly in the grip of thick fingers that bore the Ring of the Court Chamberlain – the second most powerful man in the Amarr Empire, who answered only to the emperor.

The cathedral itself, an absolute monolith of holy reverence to the Amarrian god, was epic in its proportions. Great columns of marble, emeralds, and platinum embossed with scenes from the Scriptures rose dozens of meters from the polished granite floors; great statues of the Prophets floated over the rows of pews, suspended in midair by invisible nanofiber threads. Lighting directed inside from the Amarr System's yellow sun collided with stained filters overhead, flooding the cathedral with spectacular rays of vibrant colors and hues, creating the ambience of a scene from heaven itself.

Heaven, Karsoth thought. *The most constructive farce of all time.*

A Paladin Guard captain gave a subtle nod; the cameras were now live.

The Chamberlain drew a breath to begin his latest lie to the denizens of the Amarr Empire.

'Believers of the Church, Paladins of the Righteous, oh humble among those who seek the divine, welcome!'

In perfect unison, the clergymen took seats along the altar before the throne, and the Royal Paladins split into two lines, forming a wall on either side of Karsoth, their ceremonial halberds at the ready, their curved blades glistening in perfect alignment.

'We are convened here today to discuss a matter of sinister consequence,' Karsoth began. 'A scourge has descended upon our realm; a blight which has threatened the core of our faith and the house I have sworn to protect . . .'

He leaned to his right, motioning toward the throne where Emperor Doriam Kor-Azor once sat. *May it stay vacant forever*, he thought. *This Empire belongs to me.*

'I have prayed for strength; strength to bear the burden of being the sole protectorate of this throne; for never has the Demon had so great a temptation as the void which is before us now; the void that has remained since the holy ordained was taken from us.'

He bellowed at the audience while pointing behind him.

'To covet is evil; and mark my words, there are those who covet this throne. The Demon whispers to them, testing their faith night and day, tempting them with visions of power and worldly promises of lust and greed. Take the throne, he says. No need for Succession Trials. No need for Scriptures, for the rule of God, or the laws which He hath appointed.'

Narrowing his eyes, he lowered his voice.

'It seems that we who preach these words, we who are charged with spreading the precious message of the Scriptures, are not immune to the Demon's ploy. It is with sadness, and anger, that I bring to you the news that some of us have *failed* the Test of Faith. Those who have been damned . . . those who are guilty of the most heinous crimes imaginable . . . they are none other than the corrupt souls of the Theology Council.'

Gasps rushed through the congregation; it took every ounce of self-restraint that Karsoth could muster to avoid sneering at them in triumph.

'Blessed Amarrians, it is no secret that since the death of our beloved emperor, there are those who have conspired to desecrate our Faith and defy the law of these Scriptures. These so-called Reformist heathens, motivated by political ambition, insult the sanctity of this church! They have renounced the Succession Trials; they dare to suggest that the emperor's throne can be filled by the will of man, and not by holy edict!'

Let them all cower in fear, he thought, pausing for breath. Leaning forward, he shook his fist at the audience.

'I am a servant of the Lord!' he bellowed. 'And I will not fail *my* test of faith! I am devoted to the law of Scripture, and no *man* has any right to disclaim it. If God wills a change to His law, then His word will be spoken through the next ordained Emperor of Amarr – no one else!'

He grasped the scepter with both hands, dramatically looking upward as if seeking strength from above to continue on.

'A short time ago, Paladins of the Ministry of Internal Order thwarted a plot to take my life.'

He paused for dramatic effect, savoring the murmurs among the pews and relishing the effects of his blatant lie.

'Yes, those demonic patrons saw me as an obstacle to their elaborate plans to install another heir – one held under the spell of their intent, an obedient dog who would forever be in their debt for placing him in power.'

Stamping the base of his staff against the granite floor, he imagined a clap of thunder splitting the church in half. 'But no! I stood before them with the Scriptures in my hands, with my faith in my heart, and I sent them back to hell! God revealed this plot on my life, and granteth me the sword to smite them in His name!

'Dearest servants of the Lord, we have lost one emperor too many to the hands of murderers. As Chamberlain, I am compelled to send the message of God's wrath to all those who believe the Demon's false promises; that we will no longer afford would-be assassins the privilege of a fair trial; that if they are so careless with the precious life they have been given; that if they elect to commit such acts of deviance in the name of favor from idols; then we, as True Believers, will act as God's sword and pursue these hell minions with inspired resolve.

'Humblest believers, it is thus that I inform you that the Holder Falek Grange, his loyal brigand Holder Aulus Gord, and the members of his private court on the Theology Council have each been hunted down and destroyed. We are rid of the blight they brought to that Council, whose good name was marred by the evil acts of these men; who abused their cherished privilege as capsuleers to plot, to conspire, and to betray all that we hold sacred. Their deaths, and subsequent excommunication from this Church, saved not only my life, but those of the fellow Council members who opposed their Reformist ways.

'Falek Grange was a traitor! A conspirator! And his

memory will be one of deceit and mistrust. May his death, curse his soul, serve warning to those who hear the Demon's whisper. To act on his words is to be damned for all of time!'

Pausing to admire the sound of his words as they resonated through the halls, he surveyed the crowd with fire in his eyes.

'I am steadfast in my faith; it will be stronger tomorrow and every day thereafter until my journey to the gates of heaven. Amarr will have a Succession Trial; this is my solemn mission for all of you. No man shall stand before this altar and defy the laws that have held us for millennia; the very laws which God Himself bestowed upon us.

'When the heirs are ready, when they make their peace with God and accept His divine plan, then we shall proceed with the laws of Succession. Until then,' he pointed toward the throne again. 'I will protect the sanctity of this throne with all of my might.'

Breathing deeply, he bowed his head.

'May his light guide us all in faith and reclaim, amen.'

'Amen,' the entire congregation repeated in unison.

IN THE PRIVACY of the cathedral's antechamber, Karsoth made no effort to contain his delight. *The Scriptures*, he mused, *are a tool for aspiring despots.* The texts, collected from various prophets who claimed to have received the word of God – *a god who conveniently exists only in the minds of fools* – were explicit in their instructions on how an emperor is chosen. Succession Trials were the manifestation of God's choice of emperor by using gladiators to fight on behalf of the eligible heirs. In this way, the power of birthright was limited, and the combatants – who were fighting for both their own lives and the heir they represented – were left with their skills and faith alone to decide a victor. Participants in these deadly contests were powerless to influence the outcome, let alone escape from the consequences of defeat.

Powerless indeed, Karsoth said, smiling as slaves removed the royal garments from his slovenly frame. *As the heirs should be, and as the Theology Council is now that Grange is dead, and with him, the final death of the evangelical believers of Jamyl Sarum's legend.*

He raised his arms so the slaves could remove the alb stretched over the rolls on his stomach.

Sarum . . .

Her name inspired fear – not of the divine, not of the woman, but of the threat she posed to his own plans. The mere possibility that she could still be alive was reason enough to act against Grange, whose popularity in the Council had grown more for reasons of intrigue than admiration. He was closest to Sarum when she was alive, and he was an outspoken critic of the Succession Trials when her champion lost. Because she was by far the most popular heir, especially among Amarr's armed forces, Grange took on the mystique of a prophet himself – someone who was close to divinity.

A throne was pushed beneath Karsoth, and he set the full weight of himself down. A dozen Minmatar slaves – all adolescents hopelessly addicted to Vitoc – were in the antechamber. They were each trained experts in the study of Karsoth's physical needs and desires; keen to detect and satisfy his every dark fetish without saying a word. Spreading apart his thick legs, he let them devour him; let the boys rub the muscles in his back, work the flab in his thighs, tickle the nipples of his enormous breasts with their tongues.

Grange's death puts an end to the Sarum legend, he thought, clamping his hand on the ass of a young slave and pulling him closer. *And now he will be remembered as an assassin.*

He forced the slave to take the place of the young girl going down on him, making sure he gagged and choked, while the slave he replaced found another patch of grimy skin to run her tongue over.

Sarum is dead, he reminded himself. *The heirs favor reforming the Succession Trials to save their own lives. Falek Grange's name is ruined, and the man himself is no more. I am closest to the throne . . .*

He could sense a climax approaching.

Sarum is dead.

33

Delve Region – D5-S0W Constellation
System T-IPZB

Seated cross-legged on the floor opposite Falek's bunk, Gear stared at the capsuleer with keen curiosity, eagerly awaiting an answer to his question. Téa, on the other hand, stood nearby like a guard, leaning against the doorway frame watching both of them with protective scrutiny.

'Well, it's difficult for me to describe now,' Falek continued, who was thrilled to be in the company of people who weren't openly hostile toward him. 'I haven't flown a ship since I was reborn.'

If the child hated Amarrians, he gave no hint of such resentment now. He was fascinated with Falek's answers, hanging onto every word the man said. Téa made no effort to conceal her disapproval, but she was torn between appeasing the child's natural interests and accounting for his safety. She distrusted – if not, despised – the capsuleer for who and what he was, and the fate which had befallen the *Retford* because of him.

But the more answers he gave – which all seemed genuine, honest, and candid – the more questions Gear asked. In truth, she acknowledged that the capsuleer's superhuman intuitions had saved their lives. That alone was enough to earn the boy's trust. But for her, it would take much more convincing; perhaps an act that was truly selfless, and not one driven by reasons of self-preservation.

When Gear followed up with another series of enthusiastic hand gestures, Téa – who was already tired of playing the role of translator – continued interpreting on his behalf.

'He wants to know how capsuleers can jump from one body to the next,' she grumbled.

The subconscious learning functions of Falek's advanced mind recorded each of Gear's hand signals with the accuracy of a computer.

'It's two separate technologies combined for the same purpose: cloning and subspace communications,' he answered. 'The key points for cloning are the ability to make exact replicas of the human brain and preserving its "state" – where neurons are firing and in what sequence, for example – and then being able to make changes to that state as information is passed between clones.

'Subspace communications is what allows us to transfer brain "states", which contain many petabytes of data, near instantaneously anywhere in New Eden. Well, to stations equipped to receive such volumes of information, more precisely.'

After Gear unleashed another flurry of hand signals, Téa asked: 'What happens if you're forced to jump between clones when you don't want to?'

'That's a little more complicated,' said Falek, who knew the answers to all of these questions with intimate detail, but not *how* he came to know such information. 'It's not . . . pleasant to discuss. Téa, I won't answer without your permission.'

'I appreciate that,' she answered truthfully, mindful of the imploring look from Gear. 'Just be tasteful about it.'

'All right,' he breathed. 'In combat, there isn't time for a progressive scan that can preserve state information and still keep brain tissue intact. Right before a pod capsule is breached in space, a lethal toxin is injected into the pilot that freezes all neural activity for a split second – just enough time for a snapshot of the brain to be taken. Once the data is recorded, it's transmitted via subspace to a predetermined receiving location. The entire process takes just nanoseconds to complete.'

More hand signals. 'Does it hurt? Can you remember anything afterward?'

'It is possible for the pilot to remember his death,' Falek answered. 'Memories of pain from the injection and the scan have been recorded. But most of the time, a pilot can only remember events up to the injection. That's all.'

Gear looked confused but thoughtful as he asked one more question. Téa's interest was piqued now as well.

'So, when you die the first time, you're *really* dying then, aren't you?'

Falek paused for a moment. The boy's honesty was brutal, and beautiful, all at once. 'Yes,' he answered solemnly. 'We capsuleers are all just . . . echoes of our original selves.'

'What about heaven?' Téa interpreted. 'Can you see heaven in between jumps?'

For reasons he couldn't understand, the question made it difficult for him to breathe.

'I don't know the answer to that,' he answered softly. 'I'm not sure that I could go on living if I did.'

'VINCE, WAKE UP.'

With all the crushing numbness of a shovel blade to the face, the first sensation that Vince became aware of was the deadening pain in his sinuses.

'Every time I see you, you're a mess,' Gable remarked, wincing at the dried blood all over Vince's nose and mouth. One of his eyes was swollen shut.

'Still,' she said. 'It's good to see you again.'

Blinking through pain, Vince's muscles began to tighten. A flash of pain bolted from his coccyx, forcing a grunt through teeth that he couldn't close fully. Fighting through it, he began to pull himself up.

'Easy,' she warned. 'Don't get up too fast or else—'

Blind rage – the kind of anger that detaches men from moral reasoning – was commanding Vince to rise no matter how much his body protested. As he did, the fluid build-up in his sinuses shifted, and forced its way back through the weak blood clots in his nose. It flowed like a river into his mouth, pooled along his bottom lip, and dripped off his chin in crimson globules that splattered onto the grating below.

He was hungry to taste blood that wasn't his own.

'Vince, say something,' Gable said, instantly fearful for her own safety. 'Do you remember me? It's Gable—hey!'

He brushed her aside with all the regard of a beast passing over unwanted prey, his fists knotted into balls of steel.

'HOW ARE YOU physically different from us?' Téa translated. 'Besides the socket in your neck?'

'To offload redundant processes managed by ship crews

and computers, our brains were augmented through specialized training and invasive surgery,' Falek answered. 'We use neural pathways that are dormant in human beings. The neuro-interface socket allows us to access and recall information stored on a computer as readily as data stored in our own brain tissue. We can accommodate implants that enhance our perception, intelligence, memory, willpower . . . even our own charisma. And we can learn subconsciously, as fast as it takes for the socket to safely forge neural memory pathways.'

Falek sighed. 'But besides that, we're the same as everyone else. We're not stronger, or faster than anyone. Fire doesn't shoot out of our eyeballs, nor can we flap our arms and fly . . .'

Gear let out a stifled wheeze that sounded like a giggle; a genuine smile was stretched across the freckles of his young face. The sight made the capsuleer feel refreshingly human; for him, it was the emotional equivalent of giving water to someone who had been stranded in the desert for days.

But then a much different sound followed, one that sounded like a wet, hoarse gurgle followed by loud, fast steps. Gear's face went pale, and Téa shouted a warning.

Falek felt a steel trap clamp around his neck and yank him upward. A battered man – a frothing monster – was snarling at him, inches from his face. Murder was in his eyes, just as it was with the assassin.

'You have one chance to answer me,' Vince hissed. 'Tell me who you are!'

Falek could hardly breathe. With his one good arm, he clutched frantically at the enormous hands around his throat.

'I don't know,' he squeaked.

'Bullshit!' Vince bellowed, wrenching Falek off the bunk by the neck and slamming him into the bulkhead, holding him upright so that his feet dangled over the floor.

'Stop it!' Téa screamed. 'You're going to kill him!'

Vince was oblivious to her. *'Tell me who the fuck you are!'* he bellowed, spittle and blood spraying onto Falek's face. *'Why are they after you? Why are they trying to kill us? Why?'*

His face turning red and purple, the Amarrian repeated his answer.

'He really doesn't know, Vince!' Gable hollered. 'Think! He's our only bargaining chip out of this mess!'

The monster released his grip, and Falek crashed to the floor in a heap, gasping for air. But then he was snatched by the back of his tunic and forcibly dragged outside into the corridor.

The two frantic women stayed right on his heels.

'What's it going to take to talk some sense into you?' Téa pleaded. 'She's right, he's worth more to us alive!'

'No one's alive here anymore,' Vince growled. Falek was doing nothing to resist, even as he was brutally hauled along the metallic floor.

'Vince!' Gable said, sternly. *'Vince, stop!'*

He did – so abruptly that Gable's momentum carried her into the brawn of his back. For her light frame, it may as well been a bulkhead; she fell backward, knocking Téa over with her.

The rushing sound of a hatch unsealing jolted her senses. They were at the entrance to the cargo bay, and Vince had just opened the door.

Then Jonas appeared.

'What the hell is going on?' he demanded, his eyes narrow and full of fire. 'Vince – what the *fuck* are you doing?'

With a powerful, defiant heave, Falek was thrown through the hatch and into the bay. By the time the capsuleer stopped rolling, Jonas had his gun drawn.

'Step away from there, Vince,' he snarled.

'Whoa, hey, wait a minute here,' Gable said, pulling herself off the ground cautiously. 'Everyone just take a few seconds to *breathe.*'

Téa covered her face and began to sob.

'This is serious business—' Jonas started to say. But Vince's hand slammed the hatch knob, and it crashed down and sealed with a hiss.

'*Goddamnit, Vince,*' Jonas roared, the veins in his neck bulging like iron cables. 'Get away from the fucking door!' His hands were cupped tightly around the weapon; at this range, he couldn't miss.

But Vince stared down the *Retford* captain and the barrel of his gun like he wanted to pick a fight. Amber warning lights flickered inside the cargo bay, his hand hovered over the lever that would release the outer doors and vent everything inside to space.

'You've killed us all, Jonas,' Vince growled. 'I'm glad I got to fuck you over at least once, you son of a bitch.'

'Have it your way, then,' Jonas answered, taking aim.

'Don't do it . . .' Gable pleaded, bracing herself for the worst.

Instead, Vince went perfectly rigid as 50,000 volts of electricity coursed through his frame, sapping the strength from his muscles instantly. He collapsed to the grating, convulsing and utterly incapacitated.

Looking to her right, she saw Gear standing triumphantly, holding a makeshift stun baton constructed from a coupling lance and a hydrogen battery. She never saw the staff reach past her on its way to make contact with Vince.

Jonas lowered his weapon.

'Wow,' was all he could muster, running a hand through his matted, sweat-soaked hair.

Gear dropped the equipment and ran to the hatch, jumping up to smack the knob that would open it. He scrambled to Falek's prone body and held his tiny hands out for him; the capsuleer reached out with his good arm, and the boy struggled to help him to his feet.

34

Delve Region – D5-S0W Constellation
System T-IPZB

The tip of the blade rests against our necks, Victor thought, watching a pack of Blood Raider ships swarm around the LUA5-L stargate. He envisioned legions of evil creatures inside, salivating for the chance to drink human blood once more. Eerie, coalescing bubbles of light hundreds of meters across shimmered against the blackness as the enemy activated numerous warp inhibitor fields; a blockade was already in place at the T-M0FA gate as well. The Blood Raiders were as determined to kill Falek Grange as Lord Victor was to save his life; only now, the odds favored the demons. *Have faith, Falek. We'll find you; God hasn't brought us this far just so we could fail.*

Invisible to the enemy while cloaked, Victor continued his slow orbit of the stargate, commanding himself to devise a plan to save Falek from his captors. Every gate in the system was blockaded; no ships could enter or leave without fighting their way through. The *Retford* had disappeared into hyperspace, but it was impossible for her to leave. She was hurt – probably crippled – and likely drifting somewhere here, in the deepest swaths of nothingness between the stars.

She will see us through this, he believed with all his heart, since all else was lost. The comm link opened a channel with Jamyl Sarum. *There must be a way out of this nightmare.*

Delve Region – YX-LYK Constellation
System MJXW-P: The Matriarch Citadel

Jamyl Sarum, alone in her cathedral antechamber, already knew what Victor was going to report.

'Lord Falek is aboard a salvage frigate,' he reported. 'The ship escaped from Lorado Station, but is trapped here in T-IPZB. There are Blood Raider blockades at every gate . . .'

'Yes,' Sarum replied, her eyes shut tightly. 'They will be relentless in their quest to kill him.'

'We did the best we could,' Victor continued. 'Lord Aulus and I are all that remain. He managed to escape the system before the gates were—'

'I know the fate of Lord Aulus,' Sarum interrupted. 'Your passion for battle serves you well. God has granted you the skills of a formidable warrior.'

'Thank you, Your Majesty,' he replied. 'What are your orders?'

'You asked Him for a miracle *twice*,' she threatened, her muscles tightening. 'Do you dare to challenge Him *one more time?*'

Jamyl could sense the horror in Victor; she could taste the bile back-flow into his mouth.

'Stay where you are,' she continued. 'And pray that God forgives you for being an unbeliever.'

She cut the line before he could answer.

It began like an earthquake; a torrent of rage shook her, raping her psyche with ruthless cruelty. Stumbling toward the room's only viewport, she would have gladly thrown herself through and welcomed a violent death in the void to escape from the beast inside. With clenched teeth and shaking limbs, she clutched at her head as though trying to break free of herself. The noise inside was overwhelming; a primordial scream that howled like the solar wind, buffeting her soul, trying to smash it to pieces against the walls of her own skull . . .

And then, silence.

Serenity, peaceful and pure, overwhelmed Jamyl Sarum's senses. Respite from the madness inside her slowed her breathing; the garments covering her skin soaked through instantly as a pitched fever broke. Staggering to a crystal water basin, she doused herself as if to extinguish the embers left by the monster within. Beads of sweat dripped off her cheekbones in rivers; her mouth dry as sand, she gulped water voraciously, pausing to stare at her own harried reflection.

What's happening to me? she gasped. *What have I become?*

Dozens of loyal, faithful servants stood just outside; divisions of Paladins ready to sacrifice their lives for her were inside the base; an entire armada of warships was at her command; and still she was never more alone than she was right now. The terror in the reflection confirmed everything Jamyl feared; she was an orphan to this universe, quivering at the thought of what she had become. Religion and faith be damned, the odds of survival for Falek

Grange and Victor Eliade were practically zero. After them, there would be no one alive that she could trust; no one to continue the charge to redeem the Sarum name; no one left to guard the secret of her survival since the Succession Trials; no one left within Karsoth's circle to advise on when best to renew her quest for the throne.

Her fear was the same desperation as those facing incurable diseases; those who must exist with the knowledge that what lurks inside them will one day cause their demise. It was the realization that something dark and sinister had invaded her, and that no one – not a single soul – could give her an explanation why.

Cupping mouthfuls of water, her breathing rate increased, and panic began to set in.

This isn't the way I remember myself, she thought, aware of her altered physical appearance for the first time. Stripping her soaked garments off, she was horrified – and intrigued – by what she saw. She was pure lean muscle; not with the bulk of a man but with the perfected sculpt of a woman; distinct striation was apparent in every muscle of her body.

Taking an inventory of herself, she looked over her shoulder at the v-shape of her back and the bulges in both of her calves. *This is my clone,* she realized. *Falek must have augmented it, growing the muscle tissue in preparation for my arrival . . . but why? Physical strength means nothing to me. Why would he do this? What was he preparing me for?*

'He was preparing you to rule Amarr,' a voice said. 'In His name, and not your own.'

Startled, Jamyl spun around, eyes wild with trepidation. But she was alone.

'You broke an ancient tradition for the wrong reasons,' the voice hissed, 'I intend to amend that result.'

Jamyl realized that the voice was her own, but beyond her control. Looking at her reflection again, she swore that someone else was standing there, visible only through the periphery of her vision.

I'm losing my mind, she thought. *God help me . . .*

'God *has* helped you,' the Other snapped, seamlessly continuing Jamyl's own line of thought. 'You are stronger, smarter, and have special abilities which are beyond all others. Now, embrace the *faith . . .* accept what God has given you, and stop cowering from destiny!'

Jamyl took a moment to steady herself against the basin. Whatever it was that stood beside her was alien, yet sickeningly familiar.

'Who are—' she started.

'I am you!' the Other shouted. 'Sharing the frail mind of a scared, bewildered child born to a lineage of failed rulers.'

Jamyl wanted to collapse; to die and be done with this maddening existence. Yes, the Sarum name was legendary in Amarr, but for the wrong reasons. It was true that her father had been the Grand Admiral of the Imperial Navy, that Vak'Atioth was lost to the Jovians and that the Minmatar Rebellion had taken place under his watch. She vowed to one day reclaim the greatness of her family name, but in pride only – faith would never play a role in it. Contrary to the public's belief about her, Jamyl Sarum was no believer in God or the Amarrian religion. Instead, she played the part of evangelistic crusader, vowing to one day return Amarr to greatness, while ascribing – falsely – to a divine ordainment of purpose.

Falek Grange had coached her every step of the way, molding her into the fiery leader that Amarrians wanted to believe in.

'God exists,' the Other said. 'There are trillions who

believe in our faith. Do you think that this is an accident? How can you call yourself worthy of leading an Empire of believers, when you yourself are blind to the truth? Your powers come from something divine, Jamyl Sarum. Your mastery of leadership is inspired from above; it is not a tool to be exploited by the godless rulers of this realm.'

She wanted to scream; to exorcise this demon inside her, but she knew that if she called out for help, it would only weaken her image in the eyes of those charged with her protection.

'You're not real,' Jamyl said, composing herself. 'There's an explanation for this, and I will find it, deal with it, and be rid of you.'

'Look at *you*,' the Other taunted. 'It is the weakness that I must rid you of. *That* was always Falek's plan, to build you into the proper empress. You had the potential once, until you learned that Kor-Azor would be crowned. Had you even a single shred of faith, you would be strong now, like me, instead of a cowering child. Do you know *why* it was intended for your champion to fail, Jamyl Sarum?'

Naked as the day her original self was born, Jamyl backed into the wall opposite the basin.

'What the hell are you?' she breathed.

'To test the faith of the chosen, ordained empress,' the Other hissed. 'To test the merit of she who would rule Amarr; she who should believe in the faith that she preaches! I'll tell you a secret: God knows you planned to disobey the Succession rules. He empowered you with the means to do it! He *wants* the sacred traditions rewritten, and he chose you to lead their reformation! Instead of embracing it, you denied it. You were horrified of Kor-Azor's ascension, instead of seeing it as part of His greater plan!'

Jamyl shut her eyes, and ran her shaking hands through her hair, willing herself to stay composed. *Think*, she told herself. *Think back to the Coronation, to being inside the pod of an Imperial Apocalypse battleship, of being surrounded by the other heirs and the dozens of capsuleers watching nearby . . .*

. . . I waited until my name was called, and thought of the preparations that Falek had made, to the location of where my clone was to be reanimated, to my faith that all would go according to plan . . .

. . . I triggered the self-destruct. I was about to die, but I was at peace, knowing I would reawaken, and be far away from the madness of this ancient ritual and primitive religion . . .

. . . my ship disintegrated around me. The charge in my pod detonated . . . and then . . . there was a flash. Something was there . . . I felt as if I was being watched . . . and then, blackness . . .

'Blackness?' the Other mocked. 'Open your eyes, you fool. You were touched by the hand of God while you slept.'

. . . it took three years for me to awaken. It's instantaneous for capsuleers, but for me . . . three years.

My God.

Jamyl's heart was wrenching in her chest; she could feel it trying to burst through her sternum. She missed Falek like a father, but this time, it was like desire and desperation combined. She *burned* for him now, *longed* to be with him physically as much as emotionally. He held the key to understanding her new incarnation; he knew what had happened to her, knew who she was before . . . *this . . .*

'You would rule Amarr for the purpose of revenge,' the Other said. 'You would take it to vindicate a namesake, *your* namesake, which is nothing. You seek the vindication of your father's folly, the great Mekioth Sarum, the

Grand Admiral who lost everything. Selfishness ruins empires, Jamyl. You should be offering the conquests that await you to God! That is the only acceptable crusade, and you have been chosen to lead it. I'm warning you: embrace this responsibility, or I will take it from you.'

Jamyl became angry, letting go of her fear for a moment.

'You'll take *nothing* from me,' she wailed. 'You are sick, delusional, twisted . . . I'll find a way to beat you. I want you *out*! Do you hear me? *Get out*!'

'Let yourself go,' the Other said. 'Purge yourself of weakness, and embrace the destiny of the Empress Jamyl Sarum. I have embraced Him; if only you knew what I knew, of what I am about to reveal, then perhaps your faith could be turned . . .'

Jamyl flew into a fury, a hopeless, senseless rage, wanting desperately to strike something, anything, but instead froze – and then smashed a glass statue in a loud, horrible crash.

Within seconds, Ammatar servants were at her side, with Paladin guards hovering nervously outside, careful not to look directly at her exposed flesh.

But the Jamyl Sarum of old wasn't there anymore, for she had been stashed back into the recesses of her own psyche by the Other. All the while keeping her eyes shut, she rose to her feet, gently brushing aside the servants trying to help her with unnatural strength.

They hurried to throw garments onto her, but she was indifferent to her exposed self; proud of it even, and calmly walked past them toward the commlink console.

VICTOR WAS FRANTIC. *She knows I doubted her*, he thought, on the verge of panic, physically sickened with the prospect of angering God. He reeled out another prayer, the hundredth since he was threatened by Sarum, when she called out from the void.

'Lord Victor,' she said. 'Through my mercy I am about to grant you another test of faith.'

'Your Majesty, please—' he begged. 'We have no contact with the divine, I am but human—'

'I quote to you a verse from the Scriptures,' she said, her voice as crisp as ice. '"Find the blue ring of fire, for it contains one key of revelation."'

Victor recognized it immediately. 'The Book of Trials!' he breathed. 'But is that the test?'

The line went dead, and Victor nearly wept—

—until he realized that the hull of his ship was bathing in the bluish-white brilliance of the T-IPZB system's sun: a Type OI star.

DEEP WITHIN THE Matriarch Citadel, but far from the commotion surrounding Jamyl Sarum, a scientist named Marcus Jror worked feverishly to decode the inscription on relics from a different era. One of the most talented individuals of Amarrian descent, he was pioneering archeological discoveries in New Eden that were unprecedented in historical significance – none of which would ever reach academia, the news feeds, or the eyes of anyone else.

A scientist by heart, he was also a Paladin. A meticulous, detail-oriented man, he worked in complete isolation, preferring the company of drones to humans. His loyalties were to the Sarum family first, and to Amarr second. To those who outranked him, he was crisp, direct, and respectful. To those beneath him, he was impatient, demanding, and utterly intolerable, especially to those who didn't wear a uniform bearing the insignia of Amarr.

Marcus Jror had neither time nor substance to offer companionship to anyone. And like many others who were sworn to secrecy within this hidden outpost, he respected Falek Grange less for the man, and more for Jamyl Sarum's unyielding favor toward him. For this reason alone, he shared in her extreme distress that he had disappeared – and not for fear of the divine, but for the medical implications that news of his loss could have on her.

Scientists aren't disposed to superstitious fear; and certainly not a pragmatic man such as Marcus. But unbeknownst to Jamyl, he, like Falek, had been by her side during her rebirth, and heard her speak in the tone and the tongue of someone else.

That was something he didn't understand, and because that was rare, gave him cause to fear.

A physical and mental state so wildly different from the one Falek had planned was not possible. The preparation and execution of Sarum's clone jump was flawless; multiple failsafes and layers of technical redundancy were applied at every step of the clone transfer process.

But something changed, and no theory or explanation within the known boundaries of science could explain it. The fear of Marcus Jror was not of the divine. It was of what he couldn't understand, and of the danger evident in obeying a master that was anything but herself.

Jamyl Sarum instructed him to leave for New Eden immediately, and to take his deep-space surveying and subspace tracking equipment with him. From there, he was to travel toward the EVE gate, and above all else, to stay hidden.

Marcus Jror, the scientist and Paladin, followed her orders without hesitation, no matter how fearful he was.

35

The *Retford* crew, despite their personal divisions and resentment over the plight imposed on them by their inflexible captain, were united in the cause of survival. They were absorbed in the task of repairing the ship, happily distracted by the merit of technical challenge, and thus the passing of time without fear of death bearing too heavily on their minds.

Whether too young to comprehend the danger or just brave beyond his years, it was Gear who benefited the most from these circumstances. To Téa's jealous consternation, these moments were among the happiest that she could ever remember seeing him. Of all things, he was bonding with the capsuleer, who in turn had found a friend whose time he genuinely seemed to cherish. Gear had learned more about starships – everything from their construction to how they were flown and managed – than he had during the entirety of his stay onboard the *Retford.*

Empowered with such knowledge, Gear had become a tiny foreman on the ship, advising and at times even directing which repairs should be taken and how they should be implemented. Jonas, for all his stubbornness, reluctantly accepted his advice, seeing that it originated from the capsuleer, in whom he still only saw a prize to be cashed and not the man he truly was.

Over the course of several hours with Gear, Falek had learned enough sign language to communicate effectively without Téa's assistance at all, and managed to do so with the use of only one arm. And where she had always been the center of the child's attention – and affection, at times – she suspected that Falek had already taken her place. As she labored with spanners, solderers, cables, and circuitry, she took notice of everything that Gear did – or didn't do, trying very hard not to allow herself to boil over with jealousy.

The sight of his neglected sketch pad nearby wasn't helping.

'DRINK THIS,' GABLE said, pushing a cup beneath Vince's lips. 'It'll help dissipate the lactic acid in your bloodstream.'

Every muscle in Vince's frame moaned in protest. Lying in his bunk, he flashed her a distrusting look.

'C'mon, you dumb shit, just drink it,' she said. 'You'll recover faster.'

Taking a sip, he winced in disgust, nearly spitting it out.

'No sugar onboard,' she said, following up with a dab on his mouth. 'No one seems keen on helping me find any for you after . . . whatever that was before.'

Vince downed the cup, brushing off his mouth with a meaty forearm.

'Jonas asked me to tell you that there's soldering work that needs to be done on the exterior of the ship,' she explained.

'He didn't have the balls to come down here to tell me that himself?' he muttered, straining to sit himself upright.

'Right,' Gable said, staring at him. 'I've been meaning to ask how that shoulder healed up.'

'Fine,' he grumbled. 'Just fine.'

'I have to admit, I'm surprised at you,' she said. 'I would have never thought a man with your pride would still be on this ship.'

'No one more than me,' he groaned, standing up slowly.

'Aren't you even a little bit glad to see me?' she asked.

Vince grunted. 'You probably saved my life back then,'

he said. 'I owe you a world of thanks. Look at how good life is now.'

Gable frowned. 'For someone as terrified of death as you, I expected a little more gratitude.'

'Did I miss something here?' he asked. 'You patched up a gunshot wound on me years ago . . . I thanked you, and then I left.'

'I've patched up a thousand criminals,' she answered. 'You were the only one who ever thanked me and meant it.'

'What?'

'When you're not just thinking only of yourself, you're a good man,' she said. 'Not that standing out in the crowd I'm used to exactly makes you a prize.'

Vince stretched out his limbs, grimacing from the burn in his tendons. 'Thanks.'

She stepped a little closer to him. 'We need each other, Vince.'

He raised an eyebrow. 'No, we don't.'

'More now than ever,' she said. 'To survive this, and then whatever comes after . . .'

Gable moved another step closer to him. Vince's expression changed slightly; she had to crane her neck to look up at him.

'You were always Jonas's toy,' he muttered. 'I hated that.'

'Then why didn't you tell me?' she asked.

'I felt like I shouldn't have had to,' he breathed, looking away. But she reached up and turned his jaw, glaring into his eyes.

'One word would have done it,' she whispered, closing her eyes, waiting for something. 'One . . .'

Vince suddenly stepped backward.

'Go make yourself useful somewhere else,' he growled,

brushing past her toward the doorway. 'You're just something else on this ship that belongs to Jonas, and that's gonna kill me before that capsuleer does.'

Gable flushed red. 'Fuck you, Vince!'

'You can save that for Jonas,' he said, already out in the corridor. 'You're sure as hell used to it.'

GEAR WAS ACTING unusually giddy, and asked Falek to close his eyes.

'I'm not nearly mobile enough to play any games,' Falek chuckled, pushing away the remnants of his processed nutrient mush in the galley. His appetite had caught him by surprise, and the bland meal was, for all his novel experience of living, absolutely savory.

But Gear insisted through a flurry of hand movements.

'All right,' Falek said, covering his face. 'How long do I keep them closed for?'

He felt a tap on his shoulder. When he opened up, Gear was holding an aluminium cane, complete with a three-prong support welded on the bottom for added support, and a wrist brace padded with strips of clothing.

To help you get around, Gear motioned, a smile beaming across his young face. *You'll have to use your good hand to lean on it, though. It'll get easier when we get your arm fixed.*

Falek was speechless as Gear eagerly placed it into his hands.

Try it out, he motioned. *You're too heavy for me to lug around anymore.*

The capsuleer was frozen; he was as astonished with the child's goodness as he was of the hostility expressed by everyone else. Setting the cane upright in front of him, he heaved himself up from the galley chair with unfamiliar ease. Then he slipped his arm into the cane's machine-tooled brace and took a few steps, leaning against it as he walked.

It was perfectly sized for him.

'Thank you,' he said finally.

You're welcome!

When he took a few more steps, he noticed an inscription etched into the brace's inside cover. It said:

MARIUS

'What's this?' Falek asked, turning the cane outward for him to see.

You don't have a name, so I gave you a new one, Gear motioned happily. *I think it's a good one for you. Besides, how else is anyone going to know that the cane belongs to you?*

Falek nearly gasped. 'What does it mean?'

It means 'teacher' in my old language, he signalled. *But I probably spelled it wrong. It's just how I remember it sounding. I haven't used those words in a long time.*

A grim realization dawned upon the capsuleer, tearing him down from the emotional high.

'Gear, I need to understand something,' Falek said solemnly, lowering himself back into the chair. 'We don't have the same background, do we . . . ?'

The child's expression changed to match Falek's seriousness.

'And, my kind . . . they are . . . terribly cruel to yours, aren't they?'

As Gear slowly nodded, Falek felt a wave of shame pass over him.

'No matter who or what I was before this,' Marius said,

'you and I have a friendship. And I have a debt to everyone on this ship. But to you . . . I will always do everything I can to look after you.'

Gear's expression was pure sadness now.

There isn't much you can do about that, he motioned. *The others like you, they'll hurt you for being good to people like me.*

GABLE DROPPED A bundle of cables and tools onto the metal grating besides Téa, who was on her knees and wrestling with a pair of heavy circuit boards.

'Hi,' Gable said. 'I've been told to make myself useful and give you a hand. But I'm new at this whole . . . starship repair thing.'

Téa gave her a weary look.

'You look familiar,' she grumbled. 'I meant to tell you that earlier.'

'I never had the chance to introduce myself,' Gable said with a wry smile, extending her hand. 'Gable Deitrich. I was the primary physician aboard Lorado Station . . .'

'Sorry to hear that,' she answered, returning the handshake. 'Téa Barabin. I'm Vince's sister.'

'Really!' Gable exclaimed. 'I did the surgery on him for his shoulder!'

Téa's eyes appeared to turn hollow. 'Ah yes. I remember you now.'

'Did they ever catch the bastard who shot him?'

'Yeah,' Téa muttered. It was good to have another woman onboard to talk to. 'You could say that . . .'

'IT'S THE SCANNING array,' Jonas said. 'The onboards all check out, so it has to be a physical connection issue somewhere between the hub and the hull flashing.'

He paused, waiting for an answer. The system sun

was bathing the small bridge in an eerie, bluish-tinted light.

'Plating to one side is all shot up,' Vince's voice said in the intercom. 'But the mains look all right.'

'What about the feeds?' Jonas asked, watching Vince pull himself closer to the *Retford*'s hull through a camera image. Despite the ship's slight spin, he was still outside in a survival suit working in unfathomably dangerous conditions.

'Yeah, it's cut right through,' Vince said. 'But it's a simple coupling to coupling fix. I have all the cable I need here. Should take a half-hour, tops.'

'All right,' Jonas said, marvelling at the progress his crew was making. He could see sparks shooting into space as Vince set a blowtorch to the hull. 'Be careful out there.'

Jonas knew better than to wait for a response.

'WHEN I TOLD him that I lost my baby, he just . . . snapped.'

'So Vince killed him?' Gable asked incredulously.

'You've seen what happens when he loses his temper,' Téa said with a distant look in her eyes. 'He beat my husband to death. Vince and I were then complicit in the murder of a mega-corp exec, a capital crime against the State. It didn't matter that he used to beat me, or that he'd caused the death of my unborn child. I knew from that moment on, Vince and I would always be fugitives in the Caldari State. Jonas offered to help us . . . we didn't have anyone else to turn to.'

'I remember the day Jonas brought him to me,' Gable remarked. 'I had no idea . . .'

'I caught a glimpse of you before Jonas told me to stay aboard the *Retford*,' Téa said, sitting back against the corridor bulkhead, opposite a tangled mess of cables and circuitry. 'He said he couldn't be sure you wouldn't exchange us both for the bounty on our heads.'

'He said that, did he?' Gable fumed.

'Jonas has been threatening us with our past ever since we boarded this ship,' Téa said. 'That's how he rules. So, welcome aboard – what's his bounty over you?'

'We used to sleep together,' Gable said matter-of-factly.

'Oh,' Téa said, looking away. '*That* kind of bounty . . .'

'I'm not proud of it at all,' Gable admitted. 'But then, I'm not proud of a lot of things in my past . . .'

WITHOUT EVER TAKING his eyes off the ship's hull, Vince welded the final coupling into place. The segments of damaged armor plating that once covered it were tumbling away into the void behind him. A direct hit here would certainly puncture the hull as well, but given the circumstances, this was the least of their concerns.

A sensor in Vince's engineering kit told him that current was flowing through the newly installed cables.

'Fire it up,' he announced to Jonas. 'Passive strength only, please.'

'Standby,' his earpiece replied.

Moments later, the uppermost array on the mast began to rotate, and the navigation hazard beacon at its top started to blink on and off.

'I'm done out here,' Vince said, packing up his gear.

'Great work,' Jonas said. 'See you inside.'

Vince didn't have to look up to know exactly what path he needed to reach the cargo bay. He knew the *Retford*'s corrugated exterior as well as its labyrinth of passageways inside; by keeping his eyes locked on the hull's surface, he was able to keep his spatial orientation intact. The only visual indication that he was spinning came from the regular brightening and dimming of the hull surface, and the alternating tint on his gloved hands from blue to white as he pulled himself along.

Somewhere along the way, it dawned on him that he was still carrying the severed finger of the assassin who tried to kill him.

Working his way back into the cargo bay, he decided that every other repair task on his list could wait for a while.

Jonas, meanwhile, was studying the trove of data returning from the passive scan, of which most – but not all – was bad news.

TÉA WAS SHAKING her head.

'Lai Dai fired you for treating patients?'

'No, they fired me because I refused to bump executives up in the line,' Gable answered. 'I took patients by illness severity first, then the order they came in. I didn't care what the rules were, and I especially didn't care that they favored treating a manager with a headache over a roid' tunneller with a severed arm. Well, one day I picked the wrong manager to piss off, and that was it.'

'I can't believe you were there at the same time I was,' Téa said. 'Dealing with the same corruption . . . the same bullshit . . . unbelievable.'

'I was replaced before security finished escorting me off that facility,' Gable grumbled. 'Then they blacklisted me. It was the same as taking away my license to practice medicine – who would let me treat them if a mega-corp barred me from treating their own? So I did the only thing I could do . . .'

'You ran,' Téa said. 'Just like us.'

'I was messed up for a long time,' Gable said. 'I had money saved, the means to travel . . . but I was feeling so sorry for myself that I ended up trying every drug there was, slept with more guys while cranked out of my mind than I can even remember . . . I couldn't stand the sight of myself after a while. I was *that* close to just . . . ending it, being done with existence. You know how I wound up on Lorado Station?'

Téa shook her head.

'I'd hit rock bottom. I wanted to go to sleep and never wake up. So I spent everything I had left on enough soothsayer boosters to kill me and hired a ride to Lorado to pick the stuff up,' she said. 'And then, right as I got off the shuttle there, literally as soon as I passed through the airlock, *bam*, two guys get shot right in front of me.'

'Are you serious?' Téa breathed. 'Did you panic?'

'I was high,' Gable said ashamedly. 'So I just went numb. Everyone behind me screamed, ran, hit the floor. Not me. I just stood there, marvelling at it all. But when I saw those two guys lying there with their guts turned inside out, it was like clarity . . . like I'd come home, in some sick way. I knew exactly how to help them, and I didn't care who they were. So I just went to work trying to save their lives.'

'Did you?'

'Yeah, I did,' Gable said with a weak smile. 'Both of them. Turns out one was the station owner. He gave me a job in his little kingdom there, free lodging, armed transport when I needed it, the works. After nearly getting blown away, he spent a fortune on upgrading station security, but that benefited me as well.'

She brought her knees up to her chest, resting her arms over them.

'I became the regional physician for anyone running from Empire law. I dabbled a little in creating new chemical concoctions for some shady cartel-types. It wasn't the life I'd planned, but at least it was a *life*. And I felt wanted for a change, like I'd finally become important to someone for once. Vince came bleeding into my office about a year later. I took him in only because I knew Jonas from Lai Dai. He couldn't afford what the station owner was charging for my services.'

Téa was fascinated with her story. 'It's the high you get from helping people, isn't it?' she asked. 'You're a doctor at heart.'

'No drug *ever* gave me that kind of high,' Gable said. 'I've cleaned up since, but all the resentment is still there. Even if Lai Dai offered to take me back in, I'd never do it. Never. I've met more decent people out here than I ever did in Empire space anyway.'

'Jonas being the perfect example of that,' Téa said.

'Yup,' Gable acknowledged, turning to face her. 'I'm really sorry about your loss.'

'Thank you,' Téa answered truthfully. 'I'm sorry you wound up on the *Retford*.'

'Better here than dead, right?' Gable remarked, standing up slowly. 'That reminds me, I better check on our capsuleer.'

Téa became anxious suddenly. 'Is he . . . safe? I mean, Gear is spending all this time with him . . .'

'He's harmless,' Gable reassured. 'His old personality, whatever it was, is gone. He's almost as much of a kid as Gear now, which is why they're getting along so well. His new worldview is being shaped by his experience here, for better or worse.'

'Worse,' Téa muttered. 'Definitely worse.'

'One thing you should know, though,' Gable warned. 'I don't think he knows about the difference between his race and Gear's, or even ours for that matter. Eventually, he'll have to find out. If we ever get out of here, that could be a problem someday – for him, and for us.'

Téa was considering that when the intercom blared with the deep rumble of Jonas's voice:

'All crew to the galley, right away. Guests may be seen but not heard.'

Both women shook their heads as Gable helped Téa up.

'Let's see what the asshole wants,' she said.

'So here it is,' Jonas started, with his entire crew assembled before him. 'Through pure blind luck, our errant hyperspace jump placed us very close to an acceleration gate, one that's not on the starmap. For those of you who don't know, these gates lead to deadspace pockets, which is where all sorts of illegals and other entities tend to build things that they don't want anyone to find, including shipyards and other structures that we could use to make repairs.'

A combination of angry, disgusted, and terrified looks bounced between each person in the galley. For Jonas, this reaction was hardly unexpected.

'Passive scans reveal the signatures of a dozen or more warships, presumably Blood Raider, parked around the only stargates that we can say for certain will get us out of this system. They also show random warship signatures in different locations surrounding this ship, which means they're actively hunting for us. And if we stay put long enough, they *will* find us.

'There are no habitable planets here, no natural structures we can hide in, and not enough rations or supplies to last us more than a couple of weeks at most. I have no idea what's on the other side of that acceleration gate; for all I know, it could be a Blood Raider wellness spa, or some capsuleer orgy—'

'—or it could be a rogue drone nest,' Vince growled.

'Yes, or that,' Jonas said. 'Or maybe, just fucking maybe, it's someplace where we have a chance of finding refuge.'

'Right,' Téa grumbled.

'This gate is the closest thing to a lucky break we're going to get,' Jonas explained. 'Now, thanks to all of your fine efforts, we can run on impulse without blowing the ship up, but there's nothing we can do about our capacitor without a shipyard. That means we can only do short jumps. And even if we had a deep cap, I'll bet my mother that there are warp bubbles at all the stargates. We get caught in one, and it's over. I know this isn't the best of times, but this acceleration gate is the only option we have.'

'So why bring us in here to tell us?' Vince asked. 'You've already made up your mind on it.'

'Why, Vince, you almost say that as if you have another idea,' Jonas growled. 'So then let's hear it, smartass.'

Vince shot out of his seat. *'Talk to the Blood Raiders,'* he bellowed. 'Trade this fucking capsuleer for our safe passage out of here!'

'Oh, Vince, for fuck's sake, stop with this already!' Téa shouted, to an eruption of disagreements from Gable and Jonas. Gear jumped out front and mimicked someone being electrocuted, then pointed angrily at Vince. Accusations were hurled back and forth, then insults, and then when it all seemed ready to get violent, Marius spoke.

'I support the idea,' he said.

The mob stopped their ramblings mid-sentence.

'I support whatever will spare your lives,' he continued. 'Even if it means giving up my own.'

Jonas folded his arms; Gear appeared desperate.

Marius continued, speaking while gazing out of the galley's sole viewport. 'I've been mistreated from the moment I awakened in your custody, and I'm saying to all of you that I would gladly trade my life to save yours, because of what you mean to Gear, who is my friend, and has been decent and kind.'

'What the hell do you know about friends or decency, slaver?' Vince growled. 'Why don't you just admit that you want to eat him for dinner?'

The capsuleer glared at Vince, rising slowly out of his seat with the aid of the cane that Gear forged for him.

'My name is Marius, *Vince*. Every time you speak, you prove that you're closer to becoming something more despicable than I ever was.'

Vince ignored the insult. 'See Jonas? Give the man up, and we get our shitty lives back.'

'I was born with knowledge of things,' Marius continued. 'I may not remember my personal past, but I know this: only a fool believes they can negotiate with Blood Raiders. Look at your face . . . look at *me*. Both of us can speak to their methods personally.'

'So what do you suggest?' Gable asked. 'Going into this acceleration gate?'

'The captain is right,' Marius answered, drawing an approving nod from Jonas. 'The odds of us finding sanctuary on the other side are infinitely better than our odds of running a blockade. The gate's construction might give us a clue of what to expect when we cross; there are hundreds, if not thousands, of abandoned structures in deadspace pockets that could still be habitable, and possibly harboring automated services where we can repair the ship.'

'See? Capsuleers really are smart,' Jonas said. 'So wrap up whatever you were working on. We're going to short-hop to this gate. It should take three jumps – we'll rest for an hour between each to recover.'

'But what about these rogue drones?' Téa asked. 'What if those are over there?'

Marius turned to face her.

'Then facing the Blood Raiders would be the better choice.'

Muttering a slew of profanities, Vince stormed from the galley, toward the confines of his own cabin.

36

So instructed the Queen to her champion,
'Beware the righteous who seek truth in spirit alone;
The weak of mind are quick to judge with slightest
tempt;
Thus fools go forth to spread false word,
Great misery follows those who heed what only the
weak have heard.
Heed me well for only you shall know;
Within the blue ring of fire lies the final key of revelation.
Find this ring, my champion, and both mind and spirit
shall be strong once more.'

As with every other word of the Scriptures, this verse was permanently etched into Victor's memory, and would persist even if the cybernetic implants augmenting his brain were removed. Told from the Book of Trials (2:13–2:21), this was the story about a quest to understand the truth of a tyrant's reign over an ancient kingdom. The source of the evil king's strength was believed to be a ring imbued with the spirit of demons, which granted its wearer dark, powerful abilities. The paradox, as the story unveils, was that the ring was just a legend; a ruse which made the tyrant powerful only because people allowed themselves to be convinced of its mystical strength.

Sarum said, 'Find the blue ring of fire,' Victor thought, *'for therein lies one last key of revelation.'* According to the Book's passages, the queen was a wise ruler who betrayed her husband because she knew the truth: he had been irreversibly corrupted by the vice of power, and she didn't want the people of her kingdom to live under such hollow rule ever again.

As the camera drones of Victor's bomber gazed at the brilliant bluish-white radiance of T-IPZB system sun, he considered the parallels between the reality of today with the one described in a holy book that was thousands of years old.

The 'blue ring of fire' in the Scriptures was a metaphor, Victor thought. *A metaphor representing the corruption of power and the collapse of those bound to it . . .*

Bound . . . he repeated to himself, bringing the warship's bow about towards the sun. *Out here . . . the ring is the literal description of . . .*

It hit him like a bolt of lightning.

. . . a solar eclipse . . . the star's corona!

The capsuleer's mind worked with the ship's astrometric and navigational processors, performing calculations on the locations of celestial bodies in the system, their orbital paths, speeds, and orientation relative to each other and the star to *which they were all bound to . . . by gravity.*

There were eleven planets and more than fifty moons in the T-IPZB system, and thus dozens of unique vantage points where an eclipse could be underway relative to that specific position in space. There were transitory events currently in progress on several planets to hypothetical observers in fixed locations on the surface. Yet none of the planets were habitable, nor were there any known settlements nearby. But an eclipse could also be 'permanent', if observed from a geosynchronous position far enough from the planet to block just enough of the sun's light . . .

On a hunch, Victor willed his ship to warp toward the planet closest to the sun. Within moments, a cratered, hellish world appeared before him; the planet's surface, devoid of atmosphere, was hot enough to melt lead. He allowed the ship's sensors to scan passively, and within seconds, the signature of an uncharted acceleration gate registered.

This time, he didn't marvel at the miracle; he wouldn't dare to make that mistake again.

Warping to the gate, his instruments warned that several warships were within 10 AU's of his position. Most, he knew, were hunting him.

But one, he knew in his heart, was harboring Falek Grange.

The acceleration gate was ancient; its design was unlike any he had ever seen, unrecognizable even to the computers onboard his ship.

'. . . *for it contains one key of revelation . . .*'

Victor instructed his ship to link with the gate's automated navigation system. As expected, it pointed to a location that his onboard instruments couldn't lock down or detect, a telltale sign that a deadspace complex was on the other side. There, it was shielded from detection by the leftover clouds of plasma particles and charged microscopic dust, the final remnants of an ancient, cataclysmic event such as the collision of planets or a supernova.

But he wouldn't have cared if it was a portal leading to oblivion. This was what Jamyl Sarum demanded of him, and her word would never be questioned again.

Activating the gate, his ship was hurled along a trajectory that kept the scorched world to his left; the planet moved gradually across the face of the sun like a stone rolling over the entrance to a tomb.

When the drives cut out moments later, Victor was staring at an epic blue-star solar eclipse, and there before him was the glistening metallic hulk of a station whose origin was just as alien as the gate which had brought him there. Larger than any man-made structure he had ever seen, his instruments could tell him nothing about its origins or capabilities. But his instincts suggested that this was once a manufacturing facility that had long since been abandoned. Lights were visible on some sections of the station, but the vast majority of it was blackened.

Breathtaking and beautiful, the blue ring of fire was a captivating spectacle; the corona surrounding the black disc took up almost a fifth of the total view provided by his camera drones. If not for the protection offered by the ship's shields, they would begin to wilt from the intense heat in the void.

But he again refused to allow himself to be awed, clearing his mind before calling the master of his existence.

'Your Majesty,' he said. 'I am at the location you spoke of.'

'The test does not end here, Paladin,' she replied immediately. 'You're in danger. Stay hidden, and you will live. When the time is right, you will know what action to take.'

Activating the ship's cloaking technology, the line dropped before he could respond. Settling into a high orbit around the station, he set all of his scanning equipment to passive, and made himself as invisible as the ship allowed.

Settling his thoughts, he looked forward to what she would ask of him next, no matter what the danger. He felt emboldened; strong; even powerful in the face of such incomprehensible forces, daring to allow himself to feel more than insignificant in the face of such overwhelming odds.

But his confidence evaporated when the ship's cameras detected movement inside one of the station's hangars. Magnifying for a closer look, he finally understood the reason for Sarum's warning.

Rogue drones – the only non-natural, self-aware intelligence in the universe that humankind knew of – emerged from the structure; lethal, mechanical creatures that resembled insects with their multitude of appendages and arrays of sensors.

Several of them scoured and skittered along the outside of the hangar entrance, as if to scout the area for intruders. Then, satisfied with the conditions, hundreds – if not thousands – emerged in a vast swarm so thick that it blotted out a section of the eclipse's deadly corona, swirling like a cloud of locusts before inexplicably speeding away toward the intense blue sun behind the planet.

Swallowing his fear, Victor turned his invisible ship away from the hive, quietly putting as much distance between him and the infestation as possible.

37

There was calm, finally.

Mopping up the detritus of rebellion and riot, drones and civil servants combed the streets of one Caldari metropolis after the next, each utterly indistinguishable from another despite the huge distances between them. Damage was assessed, police shifts were relieved, and apprehended criminals were charged with crimes against the State. Incapacitated by stun cuffs and null crowns, they awaited brief, prejudged corporation-run trials that were more of a formality than an actual procedure used to determine guilt or innocence.

A new, introspective reality had settled upon a Caldari society still transfixed with Tibus Heth and the aftermath of his fiery national address. Many among the proletariat, shocked and ashamed at the ease with which they were driven to such violence, found some comfort in his words, if not outright vindication. They returned to daily routines that seemed more shallow and pointless than ever before. Other than those who were punished, most had lost nothing, although the question of what exactly had been gained was still unclear.

On the other hand, the elite knew exactly what they had lost: prestige. It was, they realized, the only real asset that held their place in the universe. No longer revered or aspired to, and increasingly wary of their vulnerability, they felt more isolated than ever before. The reality of these uncertain times begged the question that no elite Caldarian wanted to face:

What if Tibus Heth was right?

To be fair, his economic comparisons with the Gallente Federation were accurate and, legal or not, the Caldari State was forced to accept the legitimacy of his executive status. So, what now? If his point was to scrutinize the excesses of executive compensation and the rift between rich and poor, then what common ground was there to reaffirm a national identity? Wasn't everyone, rich and poor, worse off now because of all this? With such divisions among them, how could they possibly unite in cause and spirit?

Tibus Heth was about to show them how.

Lonetrek Region – Minnen Constellation
The Piak System – Planet III, Moon 5
Caldari Constructions Headquarters Station

Bristling with construction activity, Tibus was directing the dismantling of Mr. Shutsu's private quarters. Amidst the racket of cutting torches and power tools, he was debating plans with a Constructions engineer on how to convert it into a proper 'war room', a nerve center from which his executive team would run the operations of the corporation.

'I don't want any distractions in here,' he growled, referring to the wall-less pool in the middle of the floor. 'Take it out!'

'Sir, I humbly suggest leaving it for now,' the engineer pleaded. 'Removing it will take months, will cost more than its components, and will deny you use of the entire area until we're finished.'

'An underwater ops center,' he grumbled, reaching for his buzzing datapad. 'How are people supposed to concentrate in here with this?' he said, gesturing to the vibrantly colored schools of fish inside the huge tanks circling the floor.

'They say it's relaxing,' the engineer muttered. 'We can build around them, sir.'

'Fine,' he said, holding the device to his mouth. 'What?'

'You've drawn the attention of the elites,' the Broker said. 'Their discussions are amusing. They don't know whether to attack you or offer an alliance.'

Noticing that video was disabled from the Broker's side, Tibus's mood soured even more. He distrusted anyone who didn't have the steel to look him in the eyes.

'Why don't you play some of those conversations back for me?' he growled, supervising as workers hauled away

the former CEO's personal effects. 'I'd love to hear them.
I mean, is there anything out there that you *can't* listen to?'

'I've devoted many lifetimes to the pursuit of information, Tibus. Perhaps someday I'll disclose the full extent
of my reach, but this isn't the time. Right now, we must
focus on expanding your power of rule as quickly as possible.'

'I thought we'd already covered that. We have an executive team, Janus is redistributing assets, the production
lines are rolling again . . .'

'Tibus,' the Broker interrupted, sounding amused. 'I
meant expanding your power of rule over the Caldari
State.'

'What?'

'I think that what you'll find,' the Broker continued,
ignoring Heth's confusion, 'is that most of your countrymen resent the elite, but resent attacking their own kind
even more. Caldarians are, for the most part, content with
their rank in life and tolerant of others who deservedly
achieve more than they do. It's just a matter of managing
expectations, of specifying what they demand in terms
of national pride. This is a blue-collar nation, after all,
and—'

'*Hey,*' Tibus shouted, drawing the attention of some of
the workers. 'What the hell are you talking about? We have
a corporation to run, and you're rambling about bullshit!'

'I'll spell this out for you,' the Broker hissed. 'You
won't last unless you learn to make people depend on
you. What do you think is happening here? Do you think
you're safe now? If these workers – or the rioters sitting in
jails – suspect that you've led them on the wrong path . . .
if you make them suspect for even a moment that what
happened at the Armor Forge was unnecessary, or worse,
that it made their lives more unbearable, they'll drag you

out onto the streets and cut your throat with all the same malice as a traitor.'

'*I know that!*' Tibus roared, then made an effort to lower his voice. 'I'm trying to lead this corporation by example, and I hate having to depend on you for advice on how to do it!'

'Then what exactly *are* you good at?' the Broker asked casually. 'You've established that you can handle yourself in a fight and that you're a competent public speaker. What other qualifications do you bring to the table?'

Tibus was fuming, and the datapad was about to crack from the strength of his hands.

'You're a battlefield veteran,' the Broker continued. 'Did you ever halt your advance when momentum was on your side?'

'No,' Tibus growled. 'What are you suggesting?'

'I'm suggesting – so long as I'm allowed to finish speaking this time – that we continue to grow the seeds you planted in your speech. Blaming the elite for Caldari incompetence will only get you so far, because the truth is that you *need* them right now. And they'd be willing to help if you can divert resentment away from them.'

Tibus picked it up immediately. 'Gallenteans . . .'

'There are, by last count, some two hundred million of them living on Caldari Prime, surrounded by relics of Caldari origin. There are almost as many Caldarians living among them, with tempers just as volatile as yours.'

'What are you getting at?'

'Sometimes, Tibus, a little sacrilege goes a long way to stir the pot.'

'Sacrilege?'

'There are Caldari holy sites, historical landmarks, even supply depots that have significant potential as *statements* . . .'

Tibus's mind was churning with the idea. '. . . and you want to make it look like Gallenteans are making those statements.'

'Precisely. Remember, not all Caldari citizens are suffering as much as those living under Constructions or Lai Dai. You need something more to help bring the rest of the population in line with your ideas.'

'I'm intrigued by this,' Tibus admitted. 'How do we do it?'

'Watch,' the Broker said, as video began to stream on the datapad. Tibus ducked out of sight from the workers.

The screen showed a sedated Caldarian male, seated in an inclined surgery chair, as tentacle-like surgical drone arms descended around him.

'Meet Specialist Davins, a member of the Templis Dragonaurs. You do remember them, don't you Tibus?'

Tibus gasped, recognizing the tattoo on the soldier's forearm, which was identical to his own. 'What are you doing to him?'

'Specialist Davins is comfortable, healthy, and has agreed to this procedure,' the Broker said. 'After all, he's just as passionately hateful of Gallenteans as you are, and fanatically driven by the cause for Caldari purity.'

As he spoke, the tentacles went to work on the man's face, making incisions along the cheekbone, below the eyes, jaws, and forehead.

'What the hell are you doing to him?'

'To become effective at battling the enemy, you must become the enemy,' the Broker answered. 'One hour ago, Specialist Davins donated samples of his bone, muscle tissue, and blood, all of which were used to hyper-grow replacement items to be used right now. This procedure will transform his physical appearance into a Gallentean, straight down to the genetic characteristics of his blood.'

It looked, from Tibus's view, like the machines were butchering him. 'Does it work?'

'I should know best,' the Broker said. 'I use it all the time.'

Fragments of bone were used to raise his cheekbones; facial muscles were augmented to fill the space beneath the excess chin and jawbone that was cut away, nanomechanical arms and lasers were used to reroute and extend nerves and blood vessels around the new facial construction.

'The process is reversible,' he continued. 'We know exactly how to restore Specialist Davins to his former self. The recovery time is quite fast, due in part to the fact we're using his own native tissue, and of course, bionanological sealants to close the wounds as quickly as we open them.'

It was true; what initially appeared like a bloodbath was now transforming into something of a work of art. Specialist Davin's new face looked like a puzzle, with lines and seams denoting where the major incisions were made, but they appeared to be disappearing as the tentacles worked their magic.

'Specialist Davins will be awake within the hour, with minimal discomfort, and be completely recovered within a day,' the Broker said. 'He's quite the expert on Gallentean customs and mannerisms, not to mention that he has intimate knowledge of the streets surrounding various Caldari points of interest.'

Tibus's heart rate was rising quickly. 'You want me to plan an op . . .'

'Several of them,' the Broker said. 'Your speech inspired the Dragonaurs, Tibus. It made them proud to see one of their own reach these heights. They would follow you, if you would only reaffirm your dedication to their principles by following through with your word – the unspoken intent in your speech.'

God, Tibus thought. *If the Dragonaurs are loyal to me . . .*

'You've just been sent a list of names,' the Broker continued. 'With accompanying information on their skills and specialties. All of them are about to undergo the same transformation as Specialist Davins.'

The soldier was, for all appearances, a flesh and blood Gallentean now. Gone were the crisp, sharp cheekbones and rigid jawline of a pureblood Caldari Deteis male; he now had the much softer features of a Gallentean, with a darker complexion and a shorter forehead, a fuller face and thicker, unsightly lips. The resemblance made Tibus shudder in disgust; it was sacriligeous to see a Caldarian defiled like this. Still unconscious, the soldier was gently transferred to a hover stretcher by drones and taken away.

'I have another list for you,' the Broker said, now sounding very serious. 'A list of targets I consider visible enough to induce the sort of rage we're looking for. You'll have to reconcile that with the tactical realities and resources we have available. But that's what you do best – or at least used to. So here's your chance: plan ways to stir the pot, Mr. Heth. Make sure the people of this nation understand what you've been trying to tell them.'

UNDER THE COVER of darkness, the Dragonaurs worked in groups of three. Targeting the most sensitive landmarks on the Broker's list, they launched their undercover mission of mayhem, sometimes even with the help of local Gallentean hoodlums, who were out for trouble anyway and happy to join along with fellow 'extremists.'

Incapacitated by subtle, untraceable amounts of a potent sleeping drug, Federation police units were uncharacteristically inept in responding to the acts of vandalism being reported across numerous cities on Caldari Prime throughout the night. It was thought that the police force was well equipped and well trained; no one could understand why they were unable to stop a pack of Gallentean brigands from nearly beating a young Caldarian couple to death in a public park.

Or why they failed to prevent the spray painting of slogans like 'Exterminate Caldari' and 'The Right Answer' across the remnants of a memorial dedicated to Caldarians killed during the Federation bombardment of that exact location hundreds of years earlier.

Or how they missed catching the criminals who deposited bacterial agents and excrement into the supply silos of Gallentean food production facilities, specifically those that supplied the Caldarian population.

Or how they failed to stop them from setting the last surviving Tikiona State archeological site ablaze in a towering inferno that could be seen for miles in every direction.

In every instance, the Dragonaurs made sure they worked in plain view of security cameras as they committed their acts of depravity.

When daylight finally broke, and Caldarians emerged from homes – whether a work site hab-module or a palatial estate owned by an executive – they found virulent examples of Gallentean treachery everywhere they looked, and most prominently in places regarded as cherished irrespective of class or status. For the Templis Dragonaurs, the mission was accomplished. There were no casualties, no compromises, and the soldiers each disappeared into the population once more, waiting for their next orders.

The Caldari reaction was predictably furious, especially once news drones began descending upon the vandalized areas to bring these disturbing images to the rest of the State. Tibus, watching from his command center, was torn between the satisfaction of having orchestrated a success-ful operation and the guilt of achieving that success at the expense of destroying that which any true Caldarian would hold dear to his heart.

'Are you watching this?' he announced into his datapad.

'I am,' the Broker answered, again without revealing imagery of himself. 'You continue to make the most of the opportunities I grant. Well done.'

'Thanks,' Tibus answered. 'Now what?'

'Now,' the Broker said. 'It's time for me to do my part.'

38

One of the largest cities on Caldari Prime, the city of Tovil was named after the heroic admiral remembered for protecting fleeing Caldarians as Federation armadas embarked on their invasion of the planet. Located near the equator, the densest population centers are encased in climate-controlled domes shielding inhabitants from the bitter cold engulfing most of the planet year round. But the city's suburbs were not afforded such luxuries, and were exposed to an icy winter whose thaw was still months away. Rings of geothermal vents marked the land-scape with towering columns of steam visible for miles along Tovil's outer perimeter, but did little to ease the chill; except for the great rivers on either side of the me-tropolis, most of the city was glistening in ice.

Of the city's sixty million residents, more than half are Caldarian; the rest are first and second-generation Gallen-tean settlers who immigrated there after the war. Living side by side, the two ethnicities never fully integrated, instead preferring isolated, racially homogenous communities. Although most of the planet was inhospitable tundra, the air of Caldari Prime was breathable, and the equatorial regions were temperate during the summer months. Like most cities on the planet, Tovil was built on the coastline, where its vast seas were accessible for recreation and industry.

But mining remained Tovil's primary source of income, with valuable ores and metals buried beneath thick ice sheets along the outskirts of the city. And the Gallenteans, ever since becoming the landlords of Caldari Prime, resolutely shut the Caldarians out from deriving any wealth from them. In fact, there was no Caldarian on the planet with ownership rights to any part of their own ancestral lands, to say nothing of its riches.

It was thus only fitting that the bloodshed would start in the mines of Tovil, where the contrasts between appearance, status, history, and hearts were most vivid.

Upon seeing their monuments defiled by Gallenteans and the memory of their past insulted, Caldari workers at the mines turned their equipment against any and all things – living or otherwise – that were affiliated with the Federation. The scene was the same in many places at once, even beyond the mines and factories: isolated Gallenteans, irrespective of personal prejudice, were indiscriminately confronted by one Caldarian at first; then two; and then by an entire mob.

Racially charged mayhem spread like a pandemic, tearing into the thickest population centers with merciless effect. From the snowdrift-covered roads of the suburbs to the fortified steps of Federation government buildings, all Gallentean institutions in the city of Tovil were under siege by young Caldari males. Fiercely protective of their property, many Gallenteans defended themselves with everything they had, including firearms. But for most, the harder they fought, the more gruesome their deaths when the mobs inevitably overwhelmed them.

Federation police moved in to quell the violence with purposeful vengeance. Caldari rioters were beaten and electrocuted, with the fallen left injured or crippled in the streets like discarded trash. In turn, this induced more violence, and convinced more people on both sides to make hasty judgments of guilt or innocence based on ethnicity alone.

Then someone, somewhere, fired a shot, and a Gallentean police officer fell to the pavement in a bloody spray of convulsions, becoming still within seconds. Here, even the rationale of good men evaporated, and with it, any remaining semblance of restraint. The return fire fusillade dropped several dozen Caldari rioters where they stood, all in plain view of media cameras broadcasting the atrocity as it happened.

Within minutes, the violence had spread to the other cities on Caldari Prime as well.

As word of renewed unrest spread throughout the State, Gallentean expatriates everywhere within Caldari territories realized their lives were in danger. Mega-corporate riot control police on other planets were deployed to stop the violence, but deliberately placed where they could protect Caldari interests only. Most were strangely absent from Gallentean property or assets, all but inviting any harm that would come to them.

'NO!' OTRO GARIUSHI screamed. 'Stop doing this!'

Violence – uncensored, barbaric, and primal – was saturating the news feeds, and it was more than Otro could stand.

'Commander Reppola!' he shouted, jamming his fist onto the desk console's commlink. 'Commander, I need you right now!'

The Ishukone Watch Commander appeared onscreen. 'Yes sir, go ahead . . .'

'I want you to post armed guards at every Gallentean business and residence on Ishukone property,' he frothed. 'Do you understand me? Use drones and armor if you have to, but I mean *all* of them, every single one!'

'I'm already on it, sir—'

'Then do it faster!' Otro raged. He immediately regretted raising his voice to such a trusted friend.

'Yes, sir. If it's any consolation, all's quiet on our worlds.'

'I'm sorry, Mens, I'm just . . .'

'It's hard on us as well,' the commander said, rubbing his temple. Normally dressed in a crisp, spotless uniform, he appeared more haggard than usual. 'The Watch will protect Gallenteans on Ishukone soil, and provide sanctuary for any who seek it. And by the way: we think we know how our "friend" got to the broadcast feeds. I'll let you know when I know for sure.'

'Thanks, Mens . . .'

'Yes, sir.' The line went dead. When Otro looked up, his sister was standing beside him.

'I heard you shouting outside,' she said. 'He's right, you know. It's quiet out there . . .'

'But look at what's happening everywhere else,' Otro growled, pointing at his screens. 'This is all the Broker's work . . . look at how far he's willing to go for this goddamn vaccine. I can't do anything to stop it and it's just killing me.'

'Not yet, you can't,' Mila reassured. 'Mens is close to finding out how he sabotaged us. You'll get your chance.'

Otro looked at his sister with a wild look in his eye. 'Do you trust him?'

'Who?' Mila said, surprised. 'Mens? Are you kidding?'

'The Broker could be anyone,' Otro said. 'Look at these surveillance clips from Caldari Prime – all the vandals are Gallentean. He could have been any one of them. Hell, he could have been all of them!'

'Relax,' Mila said. 'Mens is like a brother to both of us. And he's good at what he does. Trust the people who have carried you here, Otro. They'll get you through this.'

'Try telling that to *them*,' he said, frowning as the bloodshed continued. 'I'm no fan of Gallenteans, Mila, but this . . .'

Transfixed by the savage imagery, she shook her head. 'Every time I think I've seen the worst that men are capable of, inevitably, I end up being surprised again. Every single time.'

'I'll tell you what,' he warned. 'Every option is on the table right now. Whatever it takes to stop this is fair game . . .'

As ONE OF several thoroughfares to the bustling market system of Jita, the Perimeter stargate is among the most travelled bottlenecks in New Eden. Long lines of starships lumbering outside its enormous metallic spires are always expected by the traders and merchants familiar with the system. Because of its heavy traffic, the gate was manned by technicians around the clock, ready to deal with the frequent maintenance failures that occurred there. Starships entering the system relied on the gates for navigation and communications, and these techs were always the first to know whenever one arrived.

But the same didn't hold true for dropships, especially those equipped with cloaking technology.

Two Lima-class variants were making their final approach to the Perimeter stargate, each one ferrying a squad of Ishukone Watch Special Forces commandos. The technicians, distracted by the volume of starship traffic, wouldn't have paid any attention to the comparatively tiny vessels even if they approached uncloaked – unless they got close enough to sound the collision alarm.

When both dropships closed to within 500 meters, they fired braking thrusters, revealing their presence and triggering a shrill alarm inside the gate's control center. In a perfectly executed maneuver, both ships descended quickly onto separate docking collars on the stargate's structure. An airtight seal formed around both hatches, and powerful jolts of electricity coaxed the seals open.

Just under eleven seconds since the collision alarm first sounded, twenty commandos brandishing assault weapons converged on the stargate's control center, catching all of the techs completely off guard.

The soldiers, counting one less technician than they expected to find, demanded to know where the last man was in menacing fashion.

'A leak,' one tech managed to say. 'He got up to piss five minutes ago.'

In a flash, half of the soldiers disappeared, searching the empty bathrooms first and then indiscriminately tearing apart the first floor to find him. Then another commando produced a technician's kit of his own, ripped the instrument panel off the control center's main console, and hurriedly plugged cables and eavesdropping equipment into the circuitry inside.

'Fifth floor, aft section grid junction,' the tech commando

announced, fully tapped into the stargate's internal camera system. 'Move!'

When the commandos stormed the floor, they were greeted with the stench of a decomposing corpse.

'IT WAS A virus,' Commander Reppola reported. 'Our techs are still reconstructing what happened, but they think it's been dormant here for years. The dead gate technician's name and ID all check out; he was hired three years ago, but just rotated to this assignment last week. We're interrogating everyone that was on shift with him, but I doubt it'll help. They're all saying he didn't talk much, and this isn't a very social bunch to begin with.'

Otro glared at Mila. *I told you, he could be anyone*, his look said.

'How long until we get our broadcast feeds back?' he asked.

'It'll be a while,' Mens admitted. 'We have to keep the network quarantined until we can determine how extensive the damage is. If it goes beyond Ishukone, we need to let people know. But, if you'll pardon my overzealousness, I took the liberty of contacting the State Media Outlet. Without giving them any details, I expressed your interest in making a public statement as soon as possible.'

'What'd they say?'

The commander smiled. 'They agreed to a direct national feed, as soon as you want it, and for as long as you need it.'

'All right,' Otro said, clapping his hands together. 'Outstanding work, as always.'

'Thank you, sir. We'll be monitoring everything closely—'

His voice trailed off, apparently distracted by something off-screen. 'Excuse me for a minute, I have to get this . . .'

'Go ahead,' Otro said, turning to Mila. 'Tell the mega-corps I'm going live on the Outlet feed, and that if they know what's good for them, they'll protect Gallentean interests just like we are.'

'That's going to be a tough sell,' she said, moving toward the door. 'But I'll try . . .'

Commander Reppola returned to the screen.

'Sir,' he said. 'I just heard back from the coroner. He says the technician's cause of death was suicide by poisoning. But here's the interesting part: he had about a week to live at most.'

Again, Otro's eyes met Mila's.

'Now, his co-workers all said that he'd been gone for five, maybe ten minutes at most. But the soldiers who found him reported that he looked like someone who was rotting there for weeks. I saw the images, Otro. It looked as if the guy's face was melting off. I have people investigating this closely, but it looks like his tissue was breaking down prematurely, even before he died. It's up to you, but I think that's more than enough evidence to implicate you-know-who.'

'Don't I know it,' Otro growled. 'Please let your Outlet contact know that I'll be on in ten minutes.'

'Ten?' Mila interrupted. 'Don't you want more time?'

'There isn't any left,' Otro said. 'So this one has to be from the heart.'

ONCE AGAIN, THERE was universal pause as the scarred face of Otro Gariushi was electronically transported to every facet of Caldari society. But this was no stranger to the nation, and cheers erupted everywhere. A hero in the eyes of the proletariat, they welcomed the familiar skull and crossbones tattoo on his cheek, praising it as an endorsement of their hatred for Gallenteans and an inspiration to the nationalist fervor gripping the cities of Caldari Prime. Except for the sane among them, they were unprepared for what he was about to say.

'Caldarians,' Otro started. 'I have come before you to deliver this message: those of you who are attacking Gallenteans right now . . . *you are enemies of this State.*'

There was shock, followed by boos and hisses, as more people looked away from the carnage and up toward their icon.

'I take no pride in having to ask you this, but please . . . stop what you're doing . . . take a step back . . . and remember your humanity. You have anger – so do I. We've been reminded of our failure, as a nation, to live up to the expectation of the Caldari ideal. We've made mistakes – ones that we can correct – but this is not the way.

'Our problems come from within. Not from outside of our borders, and not in the past that we're ashamed of. Tibus Heth—'

Otro's voice was drowned out in some places as cheers rang out at the sound of Heth's name.

'—showed you the extent of executive greed in our system of governance. He demonstrated that the elites of this nation have failed to create wealth in a way that benefits those who have labored the most to produce it. In the Caldari State, opportunities are created through the work of good men and women. *Good* people. *Not* animals. *Good* human beings. *Not* savages. We are people who take responsibility for our actions, and we are people who believe that others should be held accountable for theirs.

'But Tibus Heth is wrong. He wants a scapegoat. He wants change through hate. He revealed just how fragile this . . . this concept we call "civilization" is when you test the limits of people's patience. It's true that some people did some horrible things last night . . . evil people who purposely sought to insult us right at our core, to strike directly into our hearts. But to you on Caldari Prime, or anywhere else in this State, *don't let yourself play into the hands of a tyrant*. Don't let him lead you down this path, because I promise you, it will lead to disaster.

'You know my past. You know I've never backed down from a fight. But for the sake of this generation, don't confuse patriotism with cowardice. Heth's appeal to hatred is unnecessary, selfish, and unspeakably dangerous. Now, I'm promising all of you that we will find those responsible for these malicious acts on Caldari Prime and prosecute them to the full extent of the law. And then we'll find those who misled the finances of the mega-corporations for personal gain, and they will be held to account for their greed.

'From the moment I took this post, I have governed Ishukone with the interests of its workers ahead of my own. I commend Tibus Heth for exposing the flaws of mega-corporate governance. But I condemn him for inciting us into anarchy. We are destined for greater things than this. Our path should have never led us here. There is a better way. But you *must* step back from what you're doing now, or else we'll lose everything that we have left of ourselves.

'I'm asking each of you – in fact, I'm demanding it, in the name of this State . . . to be calm. Return to work, to school, to the tasks that we chose on our own accord. You looked to me for guidance once before; now I'm imploring you to trust me again. Follow *me*. Follow the example of Ishukone. We can make this State stronger . . . we can be united in purpose . . . but we will never, ever be united in hate.'

A subtle hand movement signalled the camera to cease recording.

'You just took the biggest risk of your life,' Mila commented. 'I hope this works.'

'Let's just hope Shakor's money is good,' Otro grumbled, reaching for a flask of water and downing most of it in a single gulp. 'Are the mega-corps onboard with us?'

'Insofar as protecting Gallentean assets, yes. But the public reaction to your speech will ultimately dictate how they align.'

'Right . . .' he said, rubbing his chin. 'So remember I said that every option was on the table?'

Mila watched Otro's hands dance over his console. 'Yeah?'

A woman's voice sounded a moment later.

'This is the office of the Gallente Federation Presidency. President Foiritan will speak with you now.'

THE TWO MEN studied each other through screens that were physically separated by hundreds of light years. Until now, they had always been ideologically separated by the same distance.

'Mr. President,' Otro started, with a nod.

'Mr. Gariushi,' President Foiritan replied. 'How much did it pain you to make this call?'

'It was no pain at all,' the Ishukone CEO replied. 'We're doing everything we can to keep your citizens safe.'

'And I'm doing everything I can to avoid using lethal force to stop these riots on Caldari Prime,' President Foiritan said. His face was calm, revealing nothing of what he really thought of his enemy counterpart.

'Then I guess we understand each other,' Otro said.

'I wouldn't be speaking with you otherwise,' the president answered. 'Your efforts to restore peace are commendable. But I'm concerned that the situation is reaching unmanageable proportions.'

'I'm trying really hard to rein Tibus Heth in,' Otro said. 'His rise to power caught the mega-corporations by surprise—'

'Are *you* surprised, Mr. Gariushi?'

'About which part? Heth's ascension, or the fact the mega-corps are surprised? The answer is "no" on both counts. I've been warning them for years that something like this could happen. No one listened to me.'

'Do you think they're listening to you now?'

Otro shook his head. 'To be honest, I don't know.'

President Foiritan took a breath without altering his glare.

'What would you do if you were in my position?' he asked. 'Tibus Heth declares open season on ethnic Gallenteans, and the people of your nation seem more than happy to oblige. Or is it even a nation? Are you speaking on behalf of the Caldari State? Or just Ishukone?'

'Look,' Otro growled. 'I don't have time to list the reasons we have to despise you. It's not relevant right now. What does matter is that you and I are accountable for what happens if we fail to stop this. Our nations are on a collision course, and we need to find a way to work together quickly.'

The president studied him for a few seconds. 'On that point, we both agree. The question is how.'

Now it was Otro who took a deep breath. 'I have reason to believe that Tibus Heth is deliberately inciting these riots, and I don't think – in fact, I *know* – that Gallenteans didn't pull those stunts on Caldari Prime.'

'Obviously, you have proof of this . . .'

'No, I don't . . . not yet. Heth has access to immense wealth and resources—'

'Where does his funding come from?' President Foiritan asked. 'If it's a mega-corporation, you could help by telling us which one . . .'

'It's not a mega-corp. It's an individual.'

'The Broker,' President Foiritan said. 'What does he want?'

Fuck, Otro thought. 'I don't know.'

'Then why do you suspect he's involved?'

Otro's mind scrambled to find the right lie. 'Behavioral patterns and forensic evidence collected from riot sites around the State.'

Foiritan's eyes narrowed. 'We know how the Broker operates. We know how he thinks, we know how he works, and we *usually* know his demands. The trouble is, we can't catch him, and neither can you. So I'm going to ask you a question, and I hope you answer it honestly: have you been in recent contact with him?'

'No.'

'Mr. Gariushi, if we're to avoid a collision, then I need to know that you're serious about averting one.'

'Goddamnit, I said no!'

President Foiritan stared back impassively. 'If it turns out that he's demanding something that we could have provided – if only you'd been honest – then the consequences rest on your conscience, not mine.'

Summoning additional powers of deceit, Otro answered the accusation. 'The Broker hasn't contacted me,' he said. 'And you're a fool if you think you can understand the way a psychopath like him thinks. You're wasting time now, Mr. President. Time that your expatriates don't have. I haven't heard any solutions from you yet – just accusations, which aren't helping anyone.'

'Fine,' President Foiritan said. 'Then what are *your* suggestions?'

'We need to find a way to diffuse Tibus Heth,' Otro said. 'Anything to discredit his claims, something to reaffirm your nation's good intentions. We have to shift blame for economic issues on the corporate missteps of the Caldari State, not Gallentean mistreatment.'

'Do you think that's true?'

'It doesn't matter what I think,' Otro nearly shouted. 'But for the record, *yes*, that's exactly the case. This mess is *our* fault, not yours. All right? Do you feel vindicated now?'

'I will once my expatriates are safe.'

'I can't do anything about that without your help!' Otro snapped. 'You know what? Fine! Let them be butchered! I'm sticking my neck out to keep your people from getting killed! Right now you're living up to the stereotype, and it's playing right into Heth's hands!'

The president stared thoughtfully at him.

'I admire people who take risks,' he started. 'Especially those that do so in the name of decency. I don't claim to know what burdens you, Mr. Gariushi. But in this instance, our interests are aligned, at least on the surface, for the right reasons.'

A file appeared on Otro's console.

'I've taken many risks in my time,' the president continued. 'By God, yes I have. And to be fair, many have worked out quite well for the Federation. But what I'm offering to you now represents the biggest risk I've taken by far. It's an economic package that essentially gives your working men and women a free lunch, which I strongly suggest you encourage them to eat.'

Otro forwarded the file to Mila, who began to scour its contents immediately.

'You'll see that it takes competition away from your workforce,' the president continued. 'Thus making it numerically impossible to blame Federation trade policies for any more . . . "economic missteps." Your industries will only have themselves to do business with. There won't be any interference from us. The blame for failure then falls directly on your so-called "elites", which, based on this conversation, is where I suspect you want it placed.'

Otro could tell from the look on Mila's face that the president wasn't lying.

'We should announce this with haste. I'm recommending a large, high-profile delegation to present it formally,' the president said.

'We can do it here,' Otro suggested. 'Ishukone Headquarters in Malkalen. It doesn't get any more visible than that. Send someone important—'

'My Economic Minister, Wadis Chene, will be leading the delegation. Given my reputation amongst the Caldari people, my advisers think it's best if I sit this one out.'

'Considering the circumstances, Mr. President, I concur,' Otro said. 'Perhaps this meeting will set the stage for a personal visit.'

'Perhaps,' he answered. 'Admiral Alexander Noir will fly the delegates to you. He is popular among your Navy officials and as docile a man that I can find for the occasion. But he'll arrive in much grander fashion than you probably have in mind. That . . . is my sole imposition to this deal. We have an interest in appearing benevolent, but strong.'

'You can send a titan for all I care,' Otro said. 'This is . . . very generous of you.'

Narrowing his eyes, the president studied him for a moment. Otro could tell that it was circumstance which compelled him, not genuine trust. Considering the history between both nations, he didn't blame him at all.

'I respect you, Mr. Gariushi. Again, I see our interests as being aligned. And while this delegation may appear ceremonial in nature, I assure you, its intent and substance are real. There's no room here for negotiation – those terms are as favorable to Caldari interests as they can possibly get.'

'I understand, Mr. President. Thank you.'

'We won't be praised for these decisions. You could have taken the easy way out and given in to the mobs. But you didn't. And by rewarding you with this deal in return, in effect I've allowed the safety of my people to be ransomed by Tibus Heth. That won't go over well with *my* mobs.'

'We're both taking some big chances here,' Otro conceded.

'One great risk deserves another. Meanwhile, let's start preparing a joint announcement. A word of advice: the populace is responding to you. Seize advantage of it while you still can.'

'Will do, Mr. President.'

'Tomorrow, then. Your corporate headquarters in Malkalen.'

'Tomorrow it is, Mr. President. We'll make history for the right reasons.'

39

Tibus Heth was furious.

As much as the sight of burning cities and Gallentean bloodletting would have otherwise delighted him, he was instead pacing back and forth in the tattered construction zone of his command center, wishing that he could crush Otro Gariushi's skull. He didn't take well to being disagreed with – not in a military setting, and certainly not on a national stage.

Wanting desperately to unleash his rage, he punched an equipment locker, leaving it dented and unhinged, and ripping open swaths of flesh on his knuckles in the process. Cursing bitterly, he plunged his fist into the vertical pool. Wisps of his blood floated to its surface, drawing the attention of the fish inside. By the time the Broker finally contacted him, Tibus was about to explode.

'Where the hell have you been?' he demanded. 'I've been trying to get ahold of you for hours!'

'Either compose yourself,' the Broker hissed, 'or cease talking.'

'Otro *fucking* Gariushi just humiliated me in front of the entire Caldari State!' Heth roared, not caring who heard him.

'Yes, and now I want you to embrace him publicly,' the Broker ordered. 'Specify that you're willing to work with him and that you admire his principles.'

'*What?* I'm not going to do that! Have you lost your mind?'

'Yes, Tibus, I have lost my mind,' the Broker answered, without raising his voice even slightly. 'I've lost a lot of minds for deals worth considerably more than lending my services to you. If you ever speak that way to me again, I'll destroy you as quickly as I made you. Learn to embrace respect, Tibus, and you'll live longer. I told you before to wait until I do my part. Now I'm instructing you to swallow your pride and play the peacemaker. I expect you to comply, because everything I tell you is for good reason, and you never, ever have cause to question it.'

Heth was as stunned as he was livid, staring at the blank datapad with his mouth half open.

'Now stop punching things and acting like a fool,' the Broker added. 'You'll have plenty more blood on your hands soon enough.'

Sinq Laison Region – Algintal Constellation
The Parchanier System – Planet IV: 'Jessena'
Sovereignty of the Gallente Federation

Admiral Alexander Noir lived with his wife on the planet of Jessena, on secluded land that included spectacular mountains covered with thick forests and rolling rivers. A single moon was visible in the sky, its white-gray crescent hanging over the valley outside like a gentle spirit, enchanting the land. Although most of Jessena was still pristine, owning such a large part of it was a still a privilege that only the affluent could afford, but Admiral Noir had spent more than a hundred years perfecting the art of investing. It was here that he intended to live out the rest of his days with the woman he had adored unconditionally for the last century.

Yet there was always the Navy, the other woman in his life. For as long as he had known Gail, he had been in the service of the Federation's fleet. Beginning his career as a lowly yeoman, he would eventually become one of the oldest men to ever reach capsuleer status in history, and was awarded the rank of admiral for his accomplishment. Facing retirement, his love of the Navy was more for the majestic ships of her fleet than anything else. His combat days were behind him, and having served on vessels that faced the guns of Caldari warships long before becoming a capsuleer, he abhorred conflict. An ardent believer in the pursuit of peace no matter how bitter the memory of history, he considered his actions today as part of a greater crusade, one as great as humanity itself.

'The president says it's time,' he said to his wife. 'I guess this old man still has one last voyage in him.'

'It better not be your last, Alex,' Gail answered, reaching out to take his wrinkled hands.

'Oh, I didn't mean it that way!' he chuckled, easing himself into the seat beside her. 'I meant that my days of being a pod jockey are coming to a close, I think. It's time for me to learn something else . . . something that maybe both of us could learn together.'

She smiled gently, nudging against him. 'What'd you have in mind?'

'Hover skiing,' he said, drawing an immediate laugh from her. 'I've always wanted to try that.'

'You're silly,' she reminded him, turning serious. 'So where is the Navy whisking my husband off to now?'

'Malkalen,' he answered. 'It's in Caldari space. I just have to fly the delegation there and back. The brass really wants to put on a show, so they're letting me pilot a Nyx for the occasion.'

'A Nyx?'

'She's a supercarrier, and in my eyes, the finest ship in the fleet . . . she's huge, almost five kilometers from bow to stern,' he said, a distant look in his eyes. 'She's just majestic . . . awesome . . . pure, raw beauty. They named this one the *Wandering Saint*, you know.'

'That's certainly a fitting name if you're flying it,' Gail said. 'When will you be back?'

'As soon as these boys and gals sign some paperwork, shake hands, and have their pictures taken. Shouldn't be back any later than tomorrow night.'

'It's horrible what's happening on Caldari Prime,' she said. 'The violence is awful . . . do you think we can trust them?'

'The Caldarians?' His look turned grave. 'When I was young, I would have said no. But one thing I've learned is that if we're to call ourselves "parents" . . . if the obligation to our kids is to leave this universe a better place than the one we inherited, then the worst we can do is pass our conflicts onto them. I don't want the next generation of Gallenteans to despise Caldarians. I want the differences between our two races to go to our graves with us. That said . . . yes, Gail. We can trust them. As parents, we're compelled to give this a chance. And truth be told . . . I'm just proud as all heck to be a part of it.'

'I know you are,' she said, smiling broadly and rubbing his shoulder. 'I love you, Alex. Go make history . . . and then come home quick. I'd like for us to meet the Lears afterward. Then you can tell us all how it went.'

'You got it.' He gave her a kiss on the cheek, and struggled to lift himself from the seat. 'The Navy's sending a courier to bring me topside soon. I have to get a few things together.'

'Need any help?' she asked. 'I left your travel case on the bed, and your uniforms are hanging in the closet.'

'Thanks sweetie, but that's all right,' he said, shuffling across the marble floor toward the master bedroom. 'I'll only be a few minutes.'

Admiral Alexander Noir took his last steps entering the doorway to his spacious room, wondering why the bay windows overlooking the valley were left open. A gentle breeze was blowing inside, bringing in a waft of humidity and the smell of flora outside. Moving forward to reach the control that would close it, he was startled to see a man walk purposefully out from around the corner, where the doors leading to an outdoor deck were.

Alex was at first confused, and then utterly disoriented as he found himself face to face with a perfect image of himself. It was as though he was standing before a mirror, except this man before him was barely dressed, and wearing gloves and sleeves made from a reflective material.

Before he could speak, the impostor waved his hand as

a magician would; a grayish-black mist streamed outward from a canister, catching Alex fully in the face and neck, and then spreading like a shadow over every inch of his body.

Millions of nanolysins – microscopic butchers designed to obliterate the cell membranes of every organic object in its path – began flooding his pulmonary system, spreading internally to every part of his body in seconds. Unable to breathe or make a sound, Noir was suffering unspeakable agony as the invisible predators began to eat him alive, inside and out.

Knowing the end was near, he threw himself on the floor, hoping the sound of his crash would warn his beloved Gail to flee. But this diabolical murderer was there to hold him, and ease his decaying carcass gently to the ground as the life departed his frail body for good.

Tearing apart cells with an insatiable appetite, the nanolysins continued to feast on Noir's corpse, leaving in their wake a sickening ooze of cellular detritus. Tracking the number of seconds since his demise, the Broker knelt beside the mess and inserted an electronic device into the jelly-like puddle beneath Noir's clothes.

In a muted *poof*, a stream of electrical current flashed into the carcass, uniformly aligning the microscopic bots in the current's field with such force that they behaved like flechettes, shredding the ruined tissue and vaporizing the water that remained. All that remained of Noir's corpse was dust, stench, dead nanolysins, cybernetic implants, and a golden wedding band. The Broker worked quickly to clean the remnants off the floor, dumping them into the travel case that Gail Noir had left for her husband.

'Honey! The Navy vehicles are here!' she called out.

The Broker quickly reached inside the case for the wedding band and slid it onto his finger.

'Be right out, dear,' he said, slipping on a pair of trousers from the Admiral's dress uniforms.

'What's that horrible smell?' she asked, appearing in the doorway.

'Just something the wind blew in,' he said with a smile. 'Nothing more.'

She stared at him quizzically. 'Are you all right?'

'I'm fine,' he answered. 'I just need another minute, and I'll be right out.'

Gail took a few steps toward her 'husband' while he continued to get dressed. 'Are you sure? You seem—'

'I said I'm fine,' her husband growled, quickly closing up the front of his shirt. Then he grabbed several uniforms off the rack, tossed them into the case, activated the seals, and heaved it onto the floor.

'Time to go.'

He walked right past her without so much as a glance, the travel case obediently following behind his heels. If she wasn't so shocked by his abrupt departure, or the fact that he had never left without kissing her good-bye in the entirety of their lives, she might have noticed the sliver of Alex's stained shirt sticking out from the case, the same one he was wearing just ten minutes earlier.

'Admiral Alexander Noir' returned the salute of the Navy officers waiting for him outside, and then slipped into the vehicle without ever looking back.

40

Standing before a panel of Federation military officers, Lieutenant Korvin Lears was enduring the administrative equivalent of torture. While most mission debriefings were short, fact-gathering and performance-assessing sessions, this one had erupted into a spectacle involving dozens of personnel in the Navy bureaucracy. A fellow pilot – namely his wingman and captain – had been 'killed' during this mission, and although Captain Yana Marakova was already reanimated and recovering from her ordeal, the fallout of her 'podding' had reached the highest echelons of Navy Command. All of the questioners were skeptical of the events that Korvin had already described, in meticulous detail, for the better part of the last two hours. In particular, they remained unconvinced of who exactly it was that had attacked them in the DE71-9 System shortly after leaving Skarkon. Korvin was well aware of the violence transpiring on Caldari Prime, and knew the panel was hoping that his testimony would differ from the truth.

'Lieutenant, I'd like to re-verify the composition of the attackers,' said lead questioner Vice Admiral Elan Jacobsen. 'You say they were combined Thukker and Republic Fleet ships?'

'For the second time, sir, yes,' Korvin repeated, allowing his frustration to show. 'When the task force ignored our hail, Captain Marakova closed range to get a better look. When she reached—'

'When you say "task force", how exactly do you define that?' Jacobsen interrupted.

'A fleet composed of four dreadnoughts, with supporting assault frigates and heavy cruisers defines a "task force" to me, sir.'

'And how do you know that those were Thukker warships?'

'I was in the Great Wildlands Region for one, and because no one else in New Eden flies ships like those.'

'Ships like *what*, Lieutenant?'

'Minmatar-classes with modified hull structures? Unqualified hull designs somehow fulfilling combat roles?' Korvin answered, trying his best to keep his cool. 'More importantly, "Thukker" is what registered on my ship's threat indicators. I saw them, plus Republic fleet warships.'

Jacobsen unleashed an obnoxious-sounding cough into the microphone, but didn't bother to excuse himself. 'You are aware that your flight recorder information was inconclusive . . .'

'Sir, I crossed back into empire space with less than five percent of my *hull* intact. I was lucky to survive the trip. There weren't many systems left functioning on my Taranis at all when it docked.'

Murmurs spread out among the panel as Jacobsen covered his microphone for a moment before resuming.

'Did it ever occur to you that these so-called "Republic" ships were capsuleers?' he asked.

'It's quite possible that they were, sir, yes.'

'Did you notice the race or names of any of the ship captains you faced?'

'No sir, I did not.'

Jacobsen's eyes narrowed. 'Are you sure?'

'Yes, sir, I'm sure that I didn't,' Korvin snapped. 'When we encountered the Republic ships, my instruments registered the group as "friendly", so there was no need to check pilot metrics on any of them, and there sure as hell wasn't time after they shot at us.'

'So what you're saying is that you cannot confirm that the pilots were *not* Caldarian?'

Korvin lost control.

'No *sir, I cannot confirm nor deny that any Caldari pilots were involved in the attack!* Have you listened to anything I've said?'

'Lieutenant, you're out of order—'

'And *you're* missing the point! I saw Republic Fleet ships working with Thukker warships, escorting a capital ship group that we've never seen before, and you missed the significance of that entirely! You want me to implicate the Caldari in this and I'm not going to do it!'

'*Lieutenant!*' Jacobsen roared. 'That's enough!'

Korvin straightened his posture. 'Yes, *sir.*'

The vice admiral coughed again, filling the room with a disgusting wheeze before continuing.

'This is a fact-finding inquiry, and as you well know, our relations with the Caldari have turned for the worst. Prudence requires us to be wary of *all* instances of aggression – by anyone – toward our pilots. I should remind you that your wingman was *podded* during this mission – a black mark on an otherwise unremarkable flight record, suggestive of the possibility that you abandoned her to die in combat circumstances.'

Korvin was enraged past the point of trying to remain civil. 'Bullshit! You heard her testimony, there wasn't anything I could do! She recognized that and specifically ordered me to retreat!'

Jacobsen ignored him, and some panel members shook their heads.

'Your implications about possible Republic-Thukker collaboration in deep-space operations are noted, but the absence of conclusive flight recorder data and the apparent memory loss suffered by yourself and Captain Marakova requires us to consider *every* possibility, including that you didn't see what you thought you did, and that what you missed could have drastic consequences for the rest of us.'

Resisting the urge to tell the entire panel to fuck off, Korvin instead muttered the canned flight academy response of 'Yes sir.'

Jacobsen leaned forward, his pudgy face wrinkled with a stern look that almost looked like a smirk.

'Given the highly unusual circumstances of the encounter, this panel cannot find any fault with the way you handled yourself. In our judgment, your performance, and that of Captain Marakova's, was adequate. Your flight status will therefore remain active.'

In one of his trademark verbal gaffes, Korvin spoke without thinking.

'I wasn't aware that it was ever in jeopardy of becoming *in*active. Sir.'

Jacobsen's smirk was replaced with a harsh scowl.

'I'll say this much, Lieutenant. Your family connections are the only reason why I haven't bounced your pampered ass right out of this debriefing and into the brig for insolence. And speaking of connections, you'll be part of Admiral Noir's escort contingent to Malkalen. It's a harmless assignment for someone as reluctant to enter combat as you are. Connection or no connection, Lieutenant – if you screw this up, I'll see to it personally that you never fly a ship for this Navy again. Are we clear?'

His face as red as a setting sun, he conceded. 'Yes sir.'

'Now get out of my sight.'

FOR THE TIME being, President Foiritan was amused, almost to the point of laughing.

'You have *got* to be kidding me,' he told his Intelligence Chief.

'There's more,' Ariel said, suppressing the urge to chuckle. She was reading from a statement released by Tibus Heth in response to the announcement of the Gariushi-Foiritan trade deal. 'He said, and I quote, "I welcome Otro Gariushi's initiative to calm the situation on Caldari Prime, and praise his peaceful approach to managing our relationship with the Gallente Federation. I look forward to hearing the details of this agreement, and wish to contribute to the diplomatic process any way that I can to provide the best possible outcome for the Caldari people." *Wow*,' she exclaimed, tossing the datapad onto Foiritan's desk. 'Talk about a reversal on policy!'

'What a snake,' the president scoffed, reaching for the device and twirling it about with his fingers. 'He's getting good advice from someone, that's for sure.' His expression turned serious. 'I suppose you think I should interpret this as welcome news.'

'It buys us more time to get our expatriates out,' Ariel conceded. 'Then we have to deal with the aftermath of these riots. That won't be easy.'

Foiritan grunted, turning away from her. His office overlooked the station hangar, where enclosed highways filled with shuttle speeders and trams crisscrossed a thriving metropolis far below. 'I don't like this. Heth's about-face bothers me. I feel like we're missing something big here.'

'We're not seeing anything that suggests this isn't what it seems, namely that Heth is conceding that there are limits to his power,' Ariel said. 'Otro Gariushi is still the most influential figure in the Caldari State, and Heth's actions haven't changed that.'

'Maybe we should invite him to the conference,' the president mocked, then shook his head. 'No. This deal should make people think twice about all the nonsense that spews from his mouth. At least, it should for rational Caldarians. If there is such a thing.'

'Mr. President, your plan is working. There's going to be political hell to pay, but no matter what, this accomplishes the mission of stopping Heth's momentum and stabilizing the situation enough to *peacefully* move Gallenteans out of harm's way.'

'It's still a costly way to do it,' Foiritan admitted. 'Unwinding from this agreement will be an economic fiasco.'

'We'll cross that bridge when we have to.'

'Yeah,' he said, studying her pointed, intellectual features. 'You know, Ariel, I really get the sense it's me that should be going on this trip.'

She shook her head. 'We talked about this – you know it's way too risky. And not for safety reasons – I actually trust Gariushi – but for public relations. To the extent that Heth succeeded in vilifying you, it's really best to keep volatile factors out of this. Leave it to Wadis and her economic team to manage. They'll do fine.'

'Right,' he conceded, getting up to stretch. 'In a few hours, when this is over, I'll have to deal with Senator Blaque and all the other firebrands who think I'm being too soft on the Caldarians. They'd go to war if they had their way.'

Ariel blinked thoughtfully at him. He never could figure out her expressions, let alone what she was thinking.

'If I may ask a hypothetical question, Mr. President . . . Do *you* think we should go to war? I know what our armed forces are capable of, and the enemy we would face on a battlefield. But it would help me to know what your thoughts are.'

'Fair enough,' he admitted. 'I'll say this: if I knew I could shut the capsuleers out of a conflict, I'd definitely consider war as an option. Their potential involvement makes this a lot more . . . complicated. For one, we couldn't win a war without their support. And two, we have more to lose than anyone else if they decide to stand against us. So, my answer to your question is a resounding *no*. It's easy to want a war when you're living a privileged life, like most of us here in the Federation are. But all the visions of glory and ideological rah-rah go away as soon as someone gets killed. I don't know why it is that so many of us keep forgetting that.'

'HEY,' KORVIN SAID, standing in the doorway. 'How are you holding up?'

Yana was wearing a robe, and there was a steaming mug on the kitchen table in her quarters. Her face was radiant and youthful; the few blemishes that he remembered in intimate detail were no longer there. Her auburn hair, previously long and thick, was gone; but her scalp was now covered with new, growing hair follicles to replace it. While still athletic, her figure was different, clearly not as robust as before. It was difficult for him to accept that the woman – at least, the physical specimen – that he'd made love to before this mess ever happened was dead, and that this person, while every bit as similar as the original, was not *exactly* the same.

'I just made tea,' she said, turning her back to him and moving inside. 'Would you like some?'

'Sure,' he said, trying his best not to stare. Her living quarters were spacious, sterile, and well accommodated, but there was a distinct coldness to it as well. 'How do you feel?'

'I feel fine, Lieutenant,' she said, pouring the cup. 'How did the debriefing go?'

Korvin wasn't sure if he should keep pushing her. But he was intently curious to find out how much she remembered. 'The panel seemed more interested in getting me to agree with who they *wish* had shot at us.'

Yana placed the cup before him. 'What did you tell them?'

'Thanks, Captain,' he said. 'I told them the truth.' The tea was way too hot to sip. 'I told them what happened out there, exactly as I remembered it. How about you?'

'Well, I'm no longer your "Captain" for now,' she said, taking a seat across from him. Even with a shaved head, her face was beautiful. But he missed the mane of hair that flowed wildly in the zero-G compartment. 'There was an error in my clone management.'

Korvin felt his stomach turn over. 'Don't tell me . . .'

'I can't fly interceptors,' she said, straight-faced. 'Even though I have memories of flying my Taranis right up until the point I was killed, I have no idea how I was controlling it.'

'Your clone couldn't handle a full cortex upload?' Korvin asked, astounded. 'The Navy's supposed to make sure that never happens!'

'Someone screwed up.' She shrugged, taking a sip. 'It's as much my own fault for not checking it myself.'

'Yana, I am so sorry . . .' he said earnestly.

'Don't be. It's all part of the job. Besides,' she tapped the metal socket in the back of her neck. 'I'm relearning how to fly one as we speak. In a few days my flight status will be upgraded, and then I get to boss you around some more.'

'Yana, I have to ask,' he said, unable to contain his curiosity any longer. 'What was it like? What do you remember?'

Her face morphed into anger and frustration.

'I remember the helplessness of it all . . . watching those cannon shells punch holes into my ship and not being able to do anything about it. I remember telling you to save yourself, which you obviously did. I remember being furious that I couldn't fight back, watching the ship fall apart around me . . . and then I felt myself being pulled away, like being thrown backward. It hit me what was happening, thinking, "this is where I find out if I'm really immortal or not." There was a bright flash, and this feeling like . . . I had the distinct sensation that I was being watched. I was sure of it . . . but it didn't last. Then, there was blackness, and a voice asking if I knew what my name was. When I opened my eyes, I was inside a CRU, and I had this bad haircut.'

Fascinating, Korvin thought. 'Watched? By what?'

'I don't know,' she said, appearing vulnerable finally, but only for as long as it took for her to regain strength from another sip of her tea. 'Whatever, I'm alive now, aren't I? The immortality part of being a capsuleer apparently works.'

'Was there any pain?' he asked, remembering her scream.

'Besides waking up with a bruised ego, none that I can remember. I wouldn't exactly call the experience pleasant, but I'll live to fight another day. And I want payback on the bastards who did this to me.'

'Captain,' he said, leaning forward to take her hand. She was startled, but Korvin didn't let go of his grip. 'What we saw out there . . . Republic ships, unmarked dreadnoughts, Thukker warships . . . something big is happen-

ing, something that no one's seen before, and the right decision makers here need to find out!'

Yana pulled her hand away. 'None of that matters here,
Lieutenant. We've done more than enough to help the Minmatar Republic, and whatever's happening there has to be
allowed to take its course. We have real problems *here* –
they're estimating the number of Gallentean dead since
Heth took power to be in the *thousands*. This is serious
business, and as Navy personnel, that makes it *our* business. When do you leave for Malkalen?'

Korvin bolted upright. 'How did you know about that?'

'Word travels quickly. Besides, you've got a reputation
around here as a momma's boy.'

Ouch, he thought. 'Is that what you think of me?'

She stared into his eyes with all the tenacity of a pit
viper. 'You haven't proven anything to me, except that
you know how to crawl beneath the ruckus in a bar fight.'

Korvin stood up. 'That's not fair!'

'That's *reality*,' she snapped. 'And just so you know the
truth, your connections are only part of the reason why
you were picked for this mission. They specifically pro-
filed pilots with no aggressive tendencies in their flight
records. The Caldari won't be too welcoming of a peace
delegation composed of pilots with itchy trigger fingers,
would they? The flip side of that coin is that every admiral
in this Navy north *and* south of Alexander Noir thinks
you're a pussy, and the fact I'm not talking to a clone right
now proves it.'

Korvin's jaw dangled like it was weighed down with
cement.

'Get your head out of your ass, Lieutenant,' she growled,
showing him the door. 'Peace delegation or not, they're
sending you into the lion's den. Don't make any mistakes.'

Korvin about-faced for the door without saluting.

'Thanks for the tea,' he mumbled, not knowing what else to say.

UNDER DIFFERENT CIRCUMSTANCES, Korvin might have sought a woman unaffiliated with the Navy, or Federation politics, or anything to do with this lifestyle just to relish in the joy of being admired by someone. But he knew such an effort would be a waste of time, serving to buoy his spirits for just as long as the orgasm lasted. In this high-profile, competitive world of capsuleers and Federation officers, he was nothing; someone undeserving of the crested Navy seal on his sleeve because his family's wealth and influence invalidated it.

Walking deliberately toward his assigned pod gantry, he noticed that other pilots and deck ensigns were avoiding his stare; in some cases, he'd catch them exchange a quick word that was undoubtedly about him and then make an effort not to snicker. He tried to rationalize it, as he always did, by putting all of this in the context of the bigger picture. *This Navy hasn't been tested in a long time*, he reasoned, stepping into an elevator that would take him to the boarding levels. *To earn any respect around here, you have to get a kill under your belt, or get blown to bits by cannon fire. That's fine, I can appreciate that, so long as it's for the right reasons.*

But then his thoughts drifted back to his encounter, to the ships he swore were Republic. Keitan Yun's warning still haunted his memory, so did the news of the Skarkon System's loss to pirates. And now the Federation was looking the other way, in the direction of its ancient nemesis, while these events escaped their attention. *We will pay a price*, he thought, *if we don't make an effort to understand what's happening to the only ally we have left in New Eden.*

When the lift stopped, he was startled to see a contingent of armed Navy guards arrayed in the hall.

Approaching him from the direction of the arrival ports was Admiral Alexander Noir.

'Attention on deck!' Korvin blurted, snapping a salute and standing aside to allow the admiral – whom he once thought of as a grandfather – to pass. The pod gantries for capital ships were dozens of levels overhead, and the admiral was clearly on his way to board the Nyx-class super carrier docked high above them.

As the other non-coms and ensigns in the area snapped to attention, Admiral Noir walked slowly toward the elevator without glancing at anyone or even allowing the group to stand at ease. Normally a jovial, friendly man who shook hands with people everywhere he went, his demeanor was cold, angry, and anxious. His contingent of escorts walked cautiously behind him, careful not to upset the admiral's unusually harsh mood.

Besides the ambient hangar noise, this deck was silent. As the admiral's procession marched toward him, Korvin strained his eyes to seek out Noir's. When it appeared that he would pass without saying hello, Korvin couldn't contain his eagerness any longer.

'Gramps,' he whispered. 'Gramps, it's me!'

The admiral stopped in his tracks and turned toward him with a wicked, sinister look that Korvin never knew he was capable of.

'Is there a problem, Lieutenant?'

It was like being stabbed in the heart. 'Sir, it's me . . . Korvin Lears . . .'

'I can read, thank you,' he snarled, motioning with his chin toward the name tag on his chest. 'Now what's your *problem?*'

Humiliated, Korvin could feel dozens of stares burning

holes into him. Avoiding Noir's glare, he instead focused on the air above him.

'There is no problem, sir . . . none at all.'

Snorting in apparent disgust, the admiral entered the elevator, and the door shut behind him.

41

Derelik Region – Oraron Constellation
The Jarizza System – Planet VI: 'Halturzhan'
Sovereignty of the Ammatar Consulate

Rows upon rows of tall, greenish-golden stalks known as 'tsula' – an edible, genetically engineered multigrain plant used in various industrial processes – were worked over by thousands of slaves every day on the agricultural world of Halturzhan. Despite the availability of drone technology that could cultivate and harvest the crop with much greater efficiency, these vast plantations were run entirely with human labor, namely Minmatar slaves. In a social arrangement unchanged for hundreds of years, the people who tilled these fields were given homes in semi-autonomous communities; food that was abundant so long as they were productive; an education whose curriculum was primarily agriculture, the Scriptures, and Amarr's version of history; and most importantly, a steady supply of the highly addictive drug Vitoc to keep them artificially complacent and blissful.

Completely sheltered from the modern world, the slaves

on Halturzhan believed that a life of servitude was the only existence in the universe. Living in a virtual stone age, most had never heard the term 'New Eden' before; many were so institutionalized that they never even considered the possibility that life existed beyond the fields they tilled. Because of the Vitoc, absolute isolation, meticulous world planning, and advanced behavioral conditioning techniques, this generation of slaves was joyously content to live their entire lives within the boundaries of a single plantation.

Sectioned into swaths of up to hundreds of square kilometers, individual parcels of land were owned by Ammatar overlords who resided in modern, racially homogenous cities far away from the farmlands occupied by slaves. At harvest time, massive land transports would arrive to collect the spoils in exchange for a worthless currency that had value only in the slave community. The symbolic value of the money was used to create meager incentives: funds to build a new church, renovations for the town square, a new set of homes for young slaves coming of age and hoping to start families of their own. The notion of actually following these transports once they left never crossed their minds; they loved where they lived too much to care about where it went. As for the harvests, the unrefined crop was sold to corporate buyers within the Empire, and its proceeds taxed by regional Amarrian governors.

A former Minmatar home world, Halturzhan was the primary settlement of the Nefantar tribe almost nine hundred years earlier. When the Amarrians launched their crusade to conquer the Minmatar, history records that the Nefantar readily surrendered, offering to betray the remaining six tribes in exchange for mercy. The emperor at the time, Damius III, was so impressed with the willingness of the Nefantar to abandon their heritage and embrace Amarr customs that he renamed them 'Ammatars.' Because of their subsequent adoption of the Amarrian religion, they were encouraged to take Minmatar slaves of their own, to which they readily agreed.

Comparatively speaking, the slave populations on Halturzhan and other Ammatar worlds are treated more humanely than those who labor on lands controlled by the five royal Amarrian heirs. But these remote, self-contained communities were not without problems, complicated further by the absence of modern technology at the sites. Outbreaks of disease among man and livestock were common, typical of the risks inherent with placing concentrations of people in communal living areas. As such, when epidemics struck they spread quickly, restricting the productive potential of the land and forcing overlords to intervene on their behalf.

Unlike the slaves on other worlds, the tsula farmers of Halturzhan were irreplaceable because of the isolation system used to control them. Anywhere else, the existing 'problematic' population would be culled and new slaves purchased. This was not an option for the Ammatar, since introducing outsiders to these plantations would yield catastrophic results. But even with this limitation, Ammatar agricultural worlds were more productive than Amarr's, making it difficult to dispute the practice of absorbing the costs necessary to cure slaves of their ailments.

As such, several Ammatar overlords – all of whom were unable to control a particularly nasty strain of virus that had recently surfaced in several plantation communities at once – agreed to enlist the humanitarian services offered by the Sisters of EVE.

The Sisters are a charitable order that offers selfless assistance wherever the human condition is failing. A mutual respect for their work is shared by all the empires, and their transit near or around places beset by tragedy is usually welcome. When contacted by the overlords regarding the deteriorating health situation on Halturzhan, the Sisters welcomed the opportunity to send help and, as always, did so without questioning the reasons why.

Well versed in the science of combating epidemics, the Sisters relied on their extensive experience in pharmacogenetics to determine which treatment would be most effective based on the race and genetic constitution of afflicted populations. Human resistances to physical ailments, various strains of bacteria, and the occasional virus varied across individuals but correlated strongly within ethnicities, and the Sisters knew best how to derive, manufacture, and prescribe cures accordingly. But in this instance, their remedy had failed – not once, but twice, which was unheard of, given their expertise.

According to the overlords, this group of ailing slaves was mostly Sebiestor tribesmen. The Sisters produced a vaccine that was specifically designed for their genetic makeup, but more than half of the population's condition was worsening. Under pressure to deliver a cure faster, the Sisters were left with two possibilities: either their strategy for treating this specific strain was fundamentally flawed; or the population composition was not what the overlords said it was. In both cases, the only way to find out for certain was to draw blood samples from the population for genetic testing. The overlords, faced with the prospect of an inferior harvest, reluctantly agreed.

When the analysis was completed, the Sisters not only discovered that two distinct genetic ethnicities were present, but that more than half belonged to an ethnicity that they had never seen before.

Humanitarians at heart, the Sisters were not blind to the

implications of such a discovery within the confines of a slave camp. And as a neutral, non-political goodwill charity, their loyalties served humanity first, regardless of who it was that demanded their assistance, and irrespective of the circumstances under which it was asked. Rather than reporting their findings directly back to the overlords, they instead submitted the blood samples to Eifyr & Company, the largest biotechnology firm of the Minmatar Republic.

Within an hour of that communication, the corporation announced that the Sisters had discovered a pristine population of Minmatar Starkmanir tribesmen, living right under the noses of the Amarrian conquerors who were certain they had exterminated them two hundred years ago.

Metropolis Region – Gedur Constellation
The Illuin System – Planet III
Republic Parliament Bureau Station

Prime Minister Karin Midular was trying her best to keep control of her government.

As far as the issue of sovereignty was concerned, the Skarkon System had vanished from the Minmatar Republic. Upon entering the system through the Ennur or Mimiror stargates, travelers found their ships completely surrounded by an intimidating Archangel fleet. Ignoring the presence of CONCORD patrols nearby, cartel warships were provoking any pilots who stood in good favor with the Republic. Enterprising capsuleers attempting to take control of the situation discovered that the extent of the Archangel presence in the system was much more formidable than previously thought, locating and destroying several installations in deadspace pockets throughout.

With the situation drawing unwanted media attention to the Republic's problems, the more vociferous members of Parliament were publicly calling for Midular's head. They roared – to practically anyone who would listen – that her incompetence could no longer be tolerated since the Republic was literally losing ground because of it. For their part, the Archangels remained defiant regardless of the threats issued by capsuleers or Midular.

To make matters even worse, the local population was supportive of the cartel. Most of the Archangel warships located in the main shipping lanes were escorted by civilian transports, who were celebrating their newfound 'independence' from the Republic just meters away from weapons that could obliterate them with a single volley. If anyone was going to unsettle the Archangel grip on this system by force, they would have to fire directly through barges loaded with native Minmatars first.

Surrounded by government advisers, politicians, and military officers, Karin Midular was under as much pressure to see through all the different personal agendas as she was to find the right solution to the crisis.

'Options, people,' she demanded, slamming both hands onto the table. 'Not accusations. I want solutions!'

'For the tenth time, resign,' Maleatu Shakor said. 'Why prolong this mess by delaying the inevitable—'

'Oh, shut up, Shakor,' she snapped, raising the eyebrows of everyone else. But she kept on going without a moment's hesitation. 'Admiral Neko! What military options do we have?'

'Tell me to shut up, will you . . .' the old Brutor growled as veins raised along his temples.

'Miss Prime Minister, we can't call this a hostage situation,' announced the Republic Fleet Commander, Admiral Kasora Neko. 'The Archangels aren't forcing civilians to do anything that they don't want to, nor have they harmed anyone. As much as it pains me to say it, there have been ongoing celebrations on the planet itself, with no reports of violence at all.'

'Karin,' interrupted Keitan Yun, drawing a sharp glare from the admiral. Probably more so than anyone else, Admiral Neko empathized with the prime minister not just because she was the commander in chief, but because she believed that the cause of this debacle was for reasons completely beyond her control.

'In the absence of clear solutions, I do think you should issue a statement at least acknowledging what's happening as soon as possible, or else there's going to be a riot in *there*,' he said, motioning in the direction of the Parliament chamber hall, which was currently hosting an emergency session organized by Karin's political enemies. The session was a public relations ploy to demonstrate that Parliament was ready to act, but couldn't because the power to do so was in the hands of the wrong person. 'All you have to do is state that *all* options for resolving the situation peacefully are on the table, but you have to reiterate that the Republic does not negotiate with criminal organizations—'

Seeing another opportunity to reassert her strength, Karin wouldn't even let him finish.

'Thank you, Mr Ambassador, that will be all from you for today.'

Flustered, he began to stutter. 'I'm . . . I'm trying to look out for your . . . your government,' he pleaded. 'Inaction is the worst. . . . worst possible message you can send—'

'*Leave*,' she shouted. 'Your assistance here is no longer needed!'

Keitan flushed red with humiliation, but nodded his head in defeat. 'Yes, Prime Min . . . Minister.' Leaving the room with the weight of everyone's stare on his back, Ameline quietly followed him outside.

'What of the capsuleers?' Karin asked, moving along. Her fatigue was apparent, but the determined look in her eyes revealed nothing but strength and composure. 'Can we appeal to them for more direct assistance?'

'They're engaging the Archangels in every instance where CONCORD won't get involved – at least most of the time,' Admiral Neko reported. 'They've uncovered significant cartel assets, but there are more than forty moons in that system. There's bound to be much more there than we've seen, and thus far we've been lucky in that civilian casualties have been minimal during these battles.'

'And you're saying that we can't engage them directly without hitting civilian ships at the gates?'

'That's correct. It's exactly what they want us to do: put an artillery shell through a civ barge and broadcast the massacre all over the news. My captains are good, but we'd be asking too much of them in this case. It's a tactical nightmare, and mistakes are inevitable.'

'We can't use special operations? Covert ops? The Valklears?' Midular said desperately.

'Too many variables, too many unknowns, a lot of casualties on both sides . . . very high risk, very low returns.'

'Then what do you recommend?'

The admiral spoke with confidence, as if she had already thought every possibility through.

'I think we should bring in a show of force and tempt them to take the first shot. Then we're acting in self-defense when we fire back. Plus, my commanders are drafting plans to draw the noncombatants away from the Archangel warships. Then we can then minimize – but *not* eliminate – civilian casualties . . .'

Completely unannounced, a young Vherokior page

suddenly barged into the room, with a burly security guard close behind him.

'The news!' he shouted in an almost comical, squeaky voice. He darted around the conference room where the guard couldn't reach him. 'Put it on! Quick!'

Karin reached for the control on the table. The breaking story broadcast was already underway:

'. . . *Eifyr corporation officials have confirmed the existence of a Starkmanir tribe living in Ammatar space whose numbers are believed – and this is not yet confirmed – to number in the tens of thousands. The existence of this tribe, long believed to be extinct, living within the confines of what were once Nefantar-controlled worlds is, quite frankly, nothing short of astonishing. To quote the Eifyr official, "our tests are 99 percent accurate in identifying ethnic-specific genetic traits, and no one is more stunned than we are." No official word has yet been released by Midular's government, who has yet to take action on the deteriorating situation in the Skarkon System, which lost communication with the Republic government ever since the Archangels claimed sovereignty there . . .'*

The room erupted into an explosive cacophony of shouts and insults with such ferocity that the guards posted outside peered in to check if any violence was about to ensue.

Amid the roar of demands for action, accusations, and hastily proposed policies, Maleatu Shakor slipped out of the room and moved past the puzzled guards without saying a word, with his Khuumak drawn and hanging menacingly from his hand.

42

Domain Region – Throne Worlds Constellation
The Amarr System – Planet Oris: Emperor Family
Academy Station
Saint Kuria the Prophet Cathedral

Chamberlain Karsoth, fresh from a productive meeting with the Privy Council, was unable to stop the hideous grin from stretching his jowls across the thick cheekbones of his face. Escorted by a contingent of Royal Paladin Guards, he was unabashedly delighted in the extreme power of his position. With the snap of a finger he could destroy worlds, command riches that exceeded the wealth of legendary kings, or have any physical possession that his wicked heart desired.

Such a simple thing to rule an empire, he thought, letting the implants in his legs do most of the work in hauling his girth down the marble stairs. *Pitting the Heirs against each another, stringing the Reformists along, crushing the influence of the Theology Council, preserving my image as a pious traditionalist* – he nearly laughed – *such simple things indeed*. Managing any one of these tasks – from its strategy to the visualization of every conceivable outcome that could emerge – was unfathomably complex for most, but for him it came easily. Such was his only genetic gift: a razor-sharp intellect, which more than compensated for his physical deformities and made him such a deadly foe to cross.

As one leg heaved after the next, the Amarr Court Chamberlain was daydreaming about which deviance would satisfy his indulgence for the evening when the news finally reached him. His Chief Adviser, Lady Camoul Hinda, was waiting for him at the bottom of the steps. She wasn't intimidated by the sheer bulk of the man in person, and crisply brought him up to speed with the events that had transpired in the Minmatar Republic.

'Starkmanir?' he asked, as the implants in his joints hissed from the strain of supporting the weight of his 180 kilo frame. 'Are you certain?'

'The Eifyr corporation is, my lord,' she answered. 'I won't believe it myself until our scientists confirm their findings.'

'How *interesting*,' he mused. 'Old Damius must have turned over in his grave. Has the Ammatar Consulate contacted you yet?'

'No, my lord.'

'Summon them . . . bring them here to answer in person,' he said, rubbing his jowls. 'On second thought, wait. How did the Minmatars react?'

'My lord, the Republic is nearly insolvent. They've released no formal acknowledgement of this development or the Archangel blockade in Skarkon, and our spies report disunity at every level of government right up to Midular's cabinet.'

Karsoth grinned. 'Does she have any supporters left?'

'Admiral Neko and the Republic Fleet remain steadfast in their loyalty. Beside them, there is only one other – the ambassador who made a fool of himself before the CONCORD Assembly.'

'Ah yes, Ambassador Yun. He entertains me, that one,' Karsoth thought for a moment. 'Get rid of him, Camoul. In fact, let all the dogs loose . . . any targets of opportunity are fair game now.'

He eyed her longingly, resisting the urge to penetrate her right here on the steps of the cathedral.

'Before you summon the Consulate,' he continued, salivating at the thought of flesh beneath her black and gold tunic, 'release an official Court statement. Specify that the Amarr Empire will investigate these claims further, and do all we can to preserve the Starkmanir. Do this as quickly as you can.'

'Such would almost certainly ruin Midular if we were to speak to this matter before her.'

'Observant, Camoul! Then I want you to coordinate with Lady Callor at the Ministry of Internal Order . . . formulate an efficient pogrom for getting rid of the Starkmanir *permanently*. Don't let cost be a factor – you'll get everything you need. By the time the Ammatar Consulate gets back, I want the preliminary outline for this in place. Be candid with them about your extermination plans, and watch how they react very closely. If they attempt to stall you, *I want to know about it*. In fact, I may join you for this occasion myself.'

'As you wish, my lord,' she said, turning to obey his command.

'Oh, and Camoul,' he said with a hideous smile. 'You look absolutely succulent when you agree to genocide.'

'Thank you . . . my lord.'

Metropolis Region – Gedur Constellation
The Illuin System – Planet III
Republic Parliament Bureau Station

Keitan Yun could hear Ameline's footsteps behind him as he walked angrily toward the shelter of his office. The roar of hundreds of shouting men and women in Parliament was reverberating through the rustic, dark hallways, much the same way that Keitan's frustrations were pounding on his ego.

'Get away from me,' he growled, without looking behind him. The door to his office was several meters ahead. I'm not in the mood for your shadowing—'

He felt a hand clamp heavily on his shoulder and whirl him around, pushing him gently against the corridor wall. A second hand clamped over his mouth.

Keitan snapped, unleashing a tantrum of flailing kicks and punches like a toddler. They struck her arms and shins harmlessly, doing nothing to dislodge Ameline's grip. She wasn't fazed in the slightest, except now she held a finger over her own mouth, and flashed her mesmerizing eyes in the direction of his office.

'Shhh . . .'

Angrily, Keitan glanced to his right, and after a moment, finally understood her concern: the entry pad was activated, indicating that someone was inside his office.

'Wait here,' she said quietly. Keitan's pulse began to race; there was no one else in the hall, but the sound of distant conversations and ambient station noise seemed much louder than usual.

She moved stealthily toward the office, took one last look up and down the corridor, and then entered. Terrified for a moment as the door hissed shut behind her, Keitan suddenly felt silly. It was gullible of him to fall for her suspicions of peril lurking everywhere, and even more foolish of him to believe that danger could even exist in the main government station of the Minmatar Republic. Glitches in wiring were hardly infrequent here; maintenance and security personnel had the means to access anywhere they wished, including his office. With his anger returning even stronger than before, he decided to hell with Ameline's instructions, and barged inside with his head up—

—just in time to see a human body fly laterally across his view. The man slammed headfirst into one of his bookcases with such force that it fell over in a crash, spilling tomes and shelves with a racket that resounded deep into the hallway where Keitan was standing.

'What in the name of—'

In a blur, Ameline – bleeding from her lip and nose – yanked Keitan inside the office; he felt a rush of air behind his neck as he was pushed to the floor. It was there, on his way down, that he realized a second attacker had nearly struck him from behind. Fuelled with a burst of adrenaline, he scampered on his hands and knees to take refuge behind an antique table. Meanwhile, his assailant calmly made sure that the office door was shut behind him before parrying a leaping kick attack from Ameline.

Keitan saw that the two attackers were Minmatar, and looked as if they had every right to be here. The one lying next to the toppled bookcase was a Veherokior maintenance tech; his station pass was still dangling from his waist. The other was a Brutor guard, one of at least hundreds on this station alone. A staccato of thuds, strikes, and screeches filled the air as an incredulous Keitan watched Ameline fight this attacker – who was at least twelve kilos heavier – in hand-to-hand combat at speeds that were difficult to comprehend.

The crumpling sound of books and broken furniture drew his attention; he saw the technician rise from the debris and rip a dagger from his arm, ignoring the blood that erupted behind it and the pain he had to be enduring. Making eye contact with Keitan, the tech flicked his wrist, sending the knife hurling toward him.

Keitan shrieked and shut his eyes; then he heard a *thunk* as the blade buried itself in the table leg beside him. A crash followed as Ameline tumbled to the floor, felled by the Brutor's powerful forearm strike. But she rolled and exploded out of a tuck immediately, using the momentum to propel herself toward the other assailant.

Unable to defend himself with the wound in his arm, the tech was stunned as Ameline snap-punched his temple. Whirling around, she then pivoted and shot a powerful sidekick upward that planted the heel of her white boot into the pursuing Brutor's mouth, dislodging several of his teeth and sending him reeling toward the door.

In a flash, she returned to the stunned tech and palm-struck him in the nose. As his chin flew upward and exposed his neck, her right elbow streaked forward and crushed his windpipe in a sickening crunch. Unable to breathe, he collapsed to the floor, but the enraged Brutor landed a *thwap-thwap-thwap* blur of jabs to the small of her back; she shrieked in pain, and wildly threw her fist behind to counter.

He ducked beneath her blind strike easily, then unloaded both fists into her solar plexus as she turned. As the air in her lungs exploded out of her mouth, he leapt upward and planted his own boot into her chest with a potent kick that sent her hurling backward through the air. Crashing violently into a collection of Keitan's scale model Republic warships, she didn't move once she finally settled.

The Brutor assailant, spitting out a wad of blood mixed with fragments of his own teeth, began moving in to finish her off.

Driven by a rage and courage that he never knew he had, Keitan ripped the knife out of the table leg and jumped to his feet. Summoning as much physical strength as he could, he charged the Brutor's back like a madman, howling at the top of his lungs, his arm raised over his head grasping the weapon that had nearly killed him.

The Brutor turned – slowly – giving him a look of disgust; Keitan never knew what hit him as the man's fist darted forward and smashed into his forehead. Reduced to a numbed stupor, Keitan's knees buckled beneath him and the knife fell from his hand. The Brutor grabbed his throat and began to squeeze; Keitan saw only a tunnel-vision image of his killer's Minmatar face swirling about as the life started to leave his body.

Ironic, he thought, *that I should perish while staring at the race I tried to save.*

But then he saw the Brutor's head inexplicably split in half, and the sweet taste of air began rushing back into his lungs as the clamp around his neck released. Keitan fell onto his knees, coughing happily since such meant that he was still alive.

Ameline knelt in front of him; somewhere behind her the assailant collapsed. Her lovely face was bruised and bleeding, but she spoke as if there was nothing extraordinary about the circumstances.

'I told you to wait outside,' she said, examining the swelling knuckle impressions on his forehead.

'I'd be dead had I listened to you,' he wheezed.

She placed both of her bloodied hands onto his shoulders. 'Me, too,' she admitted, with an appreciative smile. 'That was brave, Keitan. Thank you.'

Still woozy, he was in too much discomfort to appreciate the comment. 'Never mind that. I think getting . . . socked in the head might have fixed my stutter.' He noticed how bad the damage was to her face and winced.

'Maleatu Shakor was right. Looks like we're both worse for wear thanks to my ignorance.'

'Let's get you to your feet,' she said, helping him up. 'I think you're ready to start asserting yourself.'

'Yes, I . . . oh my,' he gasped, finally noticing what had caused the Brutor's death: Ameline had taken the metal scale-model of a Tempest-class battleship and cleaved it into his head; the ship's communications and power sail structure was sticking out from in between his eyes.

Minmatars killing Minmatars, he thought. *It speaks mountains of the Republic.* 'Who were these people?'

'These two were on Karsoth's payroll,' she said, stepping around the growing puddle of blood beneath the dead assassin. 'And there are more of them here.'

Keitan raised his eyebrow. 'You knew who they were before this?'

'I have every one of their names and faces committed to memory,' she said. 'It's why the Elders assigned me to protect you.'

Keitan rubbed his neck. 'I don't suppose it makes any sense to go after them all in one sweep.'

'That is precisely the plan, but not yet. The Elders will decide when the time is right.'

Scanning the shattered remnants of his office, Keitan swore to himself that his days at this station were finished.

'What were they doing in here?'

Ameline pointed toward the door. The control panel covering the servo mechanism was removed, with wires cleanly disconnected from it. A technician's satchel filled with electronic equipment and tools was on the floor beneath it.

'There's a bomb in there. The tech was installing it when I entered. He would have probably told you he was

here to upgrade the security mechanism on the door. Then
the next time you tried to leave this office . . .'

'I see,' Keitan said. Slumped over a pile of books, the
dead tech's face was a bluish-pale, and his arm and sleeve
were matted dark red.

'The Brutor guard was his shadow,' Ameline continued,
glancing toward the other corpse. 'A backup to make sure
the job was completed without incident. When you opened
the door, he heard the ruckus . . .'

'Right,' Keitan grumbled, walking to the satchel and removing a suspicious item from it. 'Is this the explosive?'

Ameline nodded.

'Why didn't the security sensors detect it?'

Ameline answered with a question: 'Why didn't anyone else come to help us?'

Keitan looked down at the bomb in his hand. *It's over*,
he thought. *The Elders were right.*

He held out his elbow, playfully beckoning her to take
it. 'Care to escort me back to the prime minister's office?'

Ameline smiled, even as a drop of blood rolled off her
chin.

'Don't mind if I do.'

SPANNING JUST OVER two hundred meters in diameter,
the Parliament chamber hall resembled a vast amphitheater, except this one was treated more like a gladiator's
arena than a statesman's assembly room. Sections of
benches were designated for the various political parties of
the Republic; the four largest – each of which held roughly
the same number of district seats – were the Brutors, Sebiestors, Krusuals, and the Vherokiors. In addition to these
democratized tribes, there were dozens of recognized
'movements' or 'people's fronts', sometimes with only a

single seat, that also had representation in the government. As head of the current ruling party Sebiestors, Karin Midular was the prime minister. By default, the post of speaker was held by the head of the defeated party in the last general election. That distinction belonged to Maleatu Shakor, the firebrand leader of the Brutors.

While originally founded on the rigid ethnic majorities of the Minmatar race, the modern political landscape depicting each tribe was much more diluted, especially in the densest population centers of the Republic where the outcome of national elections were mostly decided. Although the Sebiestors were the ruling party, many within its numerous districts belonged to different ethnicities. The party name, while tribal in origin, was now more representative of political ideals and philosophies. That such ideals often clashed with each other was an inevitable consequence of democracy. Midular's 'progressive-moderate' agenda was popular enough to win an election once, but opinions change with fortunes, and the crumbling state of the Republic gave Shakor's 'right-wing conservatism' more appeal to citizens now than ever before.

At center stage of the Parliament chamber hall was the area known as the 'pit', distinctive for its four elevated and distinctly ornate podium stands. As prime minister, Karin Midular's place was in the center; the others were to the side and slightly below. Beneath the stands were benches for panel speakers, witnesses, and the media. A camera system projected volumetric images of all pit speakers into the space above their heads, filling the chamber so that representatives in the highest seats could see the Republic's leaders 'face to face.'

Heeding a Krusual party call for 'solidarity' during this emergency session, the hall was packed to capacity because many representatives, correctly anticipating the session to be volatile, doubled the amount of protection they usually brought with them. The added security, plus the station guards and the media personnel falling over each other to cover the event, made for one of the largest crowds to ever convene in the hall. But neither the prime minister nor Parliament speaker were present, leaving the other two party leads clamoring for the opportunity to speak. Inevitably, voices were raised and tempers flared during the open forum of heckles and shouts.

When the mayhem was dangerously close to reaching violence, Maleatu Shakor finally appeared in the pit, his Khuumak in hand and a string of bodyguards surrounding him.

'How strong is Minmatar now?' he roared. The chamber erupted with an explosion of mixed shouts and applause; Maleatu allowed the audience its frenzy for a moment before continuing.

'How strong are we, who have followed Midular and her Republic into this nightmare, when we have cartels laying claim to our lands, and our people prefer the rule of criminals to ours? How does that reflect on the merit of *this* government? *Incompetence! Inexcusable debacle!'*

The chamber seemed to be shaking from the chorus of boos and whistles.

'And now we find that our precious Starkmanir have survived; that against all odds they have found a way to live; a way to overcome the genocide programs enacted against them by the cursed Amarrians. The Minmatar spirit still burns within them! Their hearts still beat within their chests! And how will our government heed their call for help? *Appeasement?'*

Objects were now being hurled from the stands toward the Sebiestor representatives of Midular's party, who responded in kind with insults. Security guards were already

moving between the rows and threatening to remove people from the hall.

'My conscience won't allow this to continue. We have
failed to act in the name of Minmatar; we are failing our
cause, our people, and our history by abiding to this flawed
system. But for this one last time, since the Sebiestor party
won't acknowledge the realities that exist beyond the legislation for this baseless government, I hereby invoke my
right as Speaker to submit to all of you, *right now*, a vote of
no confidence for the government of Karin Midular!'

Maleatu couldn't hear himself finish speaking as the
chamber roar deafened him; the representatives seemed to
surge toward the pit, screaming 'yes' to vote for Midular's
ouster, banging on the electronic controls that would register their vote.

THE TWO BRUTOR station guards posted shoulder to
shoulder outside the executive cabinet room were adamantly
opposed to allowing the battered-looking couple to enter, although the shouting from inside could be heard from where
Keitan was standing.

'Look,' one of the guards said, noting the bloody condition of the duo. 'I don't know what kind of kinky mating
rituals you guys are into, but you're not getting in here.
Midular's orders, sorry.'

'You're sorry, are you?' Keitan demanded. 'Then I'm
afraid you'll have to speak with my associate.'

As he stepped aside, Ameline stepped up to the two
towering guards and, before they could react, grabbed both
men's testicles and squeezed them so hard that they were
unable to speak, let alone defend themselves.

'That looks like it hurts,' Keitan observed. 'Don't
worry, we'll send for help.'

When their weapons fell to the floor, he threw open the

cabinet room doors. Inside, the shouting match stopped abruptly and the room's occupants stared at him in disbelief. Karin Midular was still at the table's head, ready to explode.

'Ambassador Yun!' she bellowed. 'How many times do I—'

Keitan tossed the bomb onto the table. As it slid along its length, anyone who was still seated rose out of their chairs. The contraption came to a rest right below Karin's open mouth.

'A Minmatar technician was just caught installing that in my office,' Keitan said calmly. 'Do you know what it is?' he asked, walking slowly into the room. His anger was welling up like a tectonic fissure. 'It's a bomb, Karin. *A bomb . . . in my office! Here, in the main government station of this Republic!*'

'Well, is the thing live now?' Admiral Neko exclaimed, backing against the wall.

Keitan ignored her. '*Minmatar assassins just tried to kill us,*' he raged, shaking his fists at the group. 'Feel free to inspect the two corpses in my office – check the surveillance video, assuming it hasn't been confiscated by traitors. The indecision of this government is begging more deaths *right now*! There are probably dozens of assassins here, trying to sow as much discord as possible—'

'The fucking bomb!' Admiral Neko shrieked. 'Is it live or not!'

'No,' Ameline said, entering the room and drawing gasps with her bloodied appearance. 'They didn't have time to arm it.'

'Both of you, into my office, *now*,' Midular ordered, jumping up from her seat. 'The rest of you know what to do – move it!'

Keitan grabbed the explosive device off the table and

stormed after her, with Ameline following close on his heels. Everyone cleared a path as they hurried by; upon entering Midular's office, the door closed behind them.

Karin ran her quivering hands over her scalp. 'All right . . . explain to me, exactly, what happened?'

'I told you,' Keitan growled. 'Flesh and blood Minmatar tribesmen of *your government* just tried to murder us, and they were on Karsoth's payroll. He's sending assassins into the heart of *this Republic* right now, brazenly trying to kill us in the open and daring us to do something about it!'

'Are you certain they were spies?' Karin asked, in a futile attempt to find reason in the midst of this madness. 'Are you sure they weren't just political dissidents—'

Keitan smashed his fist onto her desk. 'Karin! Every part of your government is saturated with spies! Everything we've ever done or planned was compromised from the start! There's hardly anyone left you can actually trust! What do you think is happening? This is the *valley*—' he pointed to the bomb. 'It does not go any lower than here!'

'It doesn't?' she said, giving him a crazed look. 'Maleatu Shakor forced a vote of no confidence while you were away! *Now* he does this, when the only solutions I have left require the use of force! *Now he does this*, when I must have absolute control over the Republic Fleet, the *last fucking semblance of democratic power that I had left, he just took away from me!*'

Keitan knew that she was right: the Republic constitution forbade a prime minister from using executive powers to authorize any use of force when the conduct of her rule was in question, as expressed by a parliamentary vote of no confidence. Karin Midular was now literally powerless. She was trembling; her eyes were a bottomless pit devoid of any hope. As strong as she was, this was too much for anyone to bear.

Feeling genuine compassion for her, Keitan calmed himself as best he could.

'Karin,' he started. 'I've followed your entire political career, and I've always admired your tenacity and the boldness of your convictions. Your heart was always in the right place. You did everything you could with what little you had to work with.'

Her bottom lip was quivering; she was losing the battle to stay composed.

'There is a way out of this, but you have to trust me. I need you to believe in *me*, believe that I love this Republic as much as you do, and that what I'm about to prescribe is all that remains for us to salvage the legacy of your premiership.'

He took a breath, bracing for what would come after he spoke.

'Endorse my demand to CONCORD that we be lawfully allowed to retaliate against slavery. *Please*. It will rejuvenate support for you, and—'

'Oh, another one!' Karin snapped, the fire returning to her eyes. 'Another singular agenda that I have to see through! You're really the same as all the other leeches in government . . . you son of a *bitch!* To think that I was starting to believe you for a moment . . .'

Keitan was horrified, but Ameline never so much as flinched.

'Get out,' Karin hissed, standing up and storming toward him. 'For the third and last time, get out of my fucking sight!'

'Karin, please think about this—'

'*Get out!*' she roared, as Brutor guards stormed into

the room. 'Security, see to it that these people are removed!'

'Enough,' Keitan said, stepping in front of Ameline. 'We were leaving anyway.'

He spoke over his shoulder while walking out.

'The valley is a dangerous place to walk alone, Karin.'

43

Having sown as much political turmoil as he could, Maleatu Shakor left the raucous chamber hall with a heavy heart. He took no pleasure in destroying Karin Midular; although he disdained her politics, as a person he considered her someone to be admired – a weakness that he would admit to no one. But fate had placed her squarely in the crosshairs of history, and there was nothing he could do but watch her, and her failed government, fall in the name of saving the Minmatar race. Guided by the strong hands of security guards provided by the Elders, he was escorted back to his own private quarters – one that was inaccessible to all but himself. When the door closed behind him, the room's sensors recognized his presence and announced that he was being summoned.

A hover chair positioned itself against a nondescript section of his spartan living space. Locking into place, the wall behind it transformed into a communications array; then a neuro-interface probe emerged and settled beneath the headrest.

Feeling his way into the seat, his torso reclined gently as the probe inserted into the socket in his skull. For a moment, his sight flickered back, viewing his living quarters through the sensors in the room. Then he was transported to a vision of complete darkness, in which the only light was the seven apparitions of the Elders.

'How close are you to securing the Insorum vaccine?' one asked.

'Gariushi gave me his word that he was committed to selling his existing stock to me,' Maleatu answered. 'But we never agreed on a specific time frame.'

'Will he be receptive to more money if he delivers sooner?'

'With the developments in the Caldari State, I regret to say that I cannot reach him, or his CFO. They are now center stage of the escalating national crisis there – he is to host a Gallentean diplomatic mission in Malkalen very soon.'

'Do you think he will go against his word?'

'It's difficult to say,' Maleatu conceded. 'In my heart, I don't believe he wants to. But it would be a mistake to question his dedication to the State. If he believes the Caldari will benefit more by forfeiting this deal . . .'

There was silence, and then the brightness of the Elders intensified.

'Then we must launch our attack sooner than planned.'

While not unexpected, Maleatu was nevertheless shocked to hear them say it.

'The Starkmanir development . . .' he started.

'Unexpected, and unfortunate. It places them in immediate danger . . . we already know that Karsoth plans to exterminate them.'

Maleatu's stomach turned. 'I can double my efforts to close with Gariushi faster, but—'

'Every moment that we do nothing places them in greater peril; time is no longer on our side. We must proceed immediately.'

'But what of their Vitoc addictions? If you pull those slaves out now—'

'We will place them in cryonic stasis, or supply them with Vitoc until we recover the vaccine or develop our own. These are unpleasant alternatives, but we have no choice. The Sanctuaries are prepared, the fleet is almost ready, and our titans are operational. The countdown begins now. It's time to give CONCORD our final warning.'

MINMATAR HISTORY, ESPECIALLY the history of the Republic, was now dead to Keitan Yun. There were new horizons ahead for him; a new history to write; and he had no desire to ever look back. His head was still throbbing viciously from the attack, but he was undeterred by the pain as he followed Ameline toward the ship hangar. The Wolf-class assault frigate that had taken them to the Sanctuaries had returned.

'We'll be safe in here' she said, leading him inside. As the airlock depressurized behind them, he hurriedly sought a medical station on board – not for his own wounds, but for Ameline's.

'I have to do something about those cuts,' he said, poking his head in and out of cabins as he searched. 'I suppose I miss your magnificent, unblemished Starkmanir beauty.'

'Don't worry about me,' she said, catching up with him. Looking directly into his eyes, she spoke for the first time without authority; instead, her voice was almost a plea for help.

'Keitan – the Elders want to speak with you. The plans they spoke of . . . they're moving sooner than anyone anticipated.'

'I welcome whatever it is they have to say,' he said boldly. 'I belong to them now.'

Keitan felt the ship decouple from its docking gantry. It dawned on him that any communications that took place would be through the ship's arrays, and not the station's.

'They'll be pleased to hear that,' she said. 'You're going to need that kind of confidence for what they're about to ask of you.'

Genesis Region – Sanctum Constellation
The Yulai System – Planet IX
CONCORD Bureau Station

'Chair Speaker Pauksuo,' the drone announced. 'Ambassador Yun is trying to reach you. He expressed urgency, and requests an immediate meeting to discuss a pending state of emergency in the Minmatar Republic. Do you wish to speak with him?'

She considered the discredited ambassador's request for a moment. CONCORD avoids meddling in the political affairs of nation states; this policy was the cornerstone of the agency's directive and essential to maintaining its impartial neutrality. But with the situation worsening in Skarkon, and now with this latest Starkmanir fiasco, a declared state of emergency in the Republic could have profound implications on how CONCORD enforced the law. The danger of an escalating conflict was real, and *that* was cause for serious concern. Regardless of his antics on the Assembly floor, she was compelled to take his call.

'All right.'

The volumetric image of Keitan Yun appeared before her.

'Good heavens,' she exclaimed, noticing the bruising on his face. 'What happened to you?'

'Thank you for accepting this meeting in such short order, your honor. As you can see, these are troubling times for the Republic.'

'So I've heard, but what kind of trouble put that bruise on your forehead?'

'Someone tried to kill me in my own office, right here in the capital of the Republic,' he answered casually.

Satisfied to see her bottom lip fall, he continued before she could get in another word.

'But that isn't the reason why I've contacted you. My government is about to declare a state of emergency, and I've been asked to discuss our "official" diplomatic *and* military options in advance, if any. Thus, I am formally exercising our option for DED representation as well.'

'DED representation?' The chair speaker raised her eyebrows. 'Are you certain?'

'I am. The circumstances demand it.'

'Very well,' she answered, conferencing in a direct line with the Commander of CONCORD'S military branch, DED Admiral Kjersidur Elladall. After a few moments, his uniformed hulk appeared beside Keitan's diminutive frame. 'Admiral, this is Ambassador Yun of the Minmatar Republic. He has invoked his right to DED counsel for this session.'

The admiral straightened up and clasped his hands behind his back. 'Very well Ambassador, how can we help you?'

Keitan's image turned so that his bony shoulders were roughly square with his. 'Are your advisers and law agents participating on this conference?'

The admiral frowned. 'The necessary personnel are on the line, Ambassador. Do we have time for introductions? Your request sounds urgent.'

'Admiral, the more people that listen from your organization, the better. We want as . . . *objective* . . . an evaluation of our situation as possible.'

'Mr. Ambassador, I'm waiting patiently for the facts of your emergency, so that I may prescribe how, if at all, the assets of the DED and CONCORD can be of assistance.'

Keitan matched the admiral's defiant pose, clasping his own hands behind his back and puffing his scrawny chest out. 'Very well, then. My invocation of the Minmatar Republic's sovereign right to this meeting, as defined by the laws of CONCORD, is to serve you, and the entirety of your organization, a warning.'

Chair Speaker Pauksuo flinched, but the DED commander misinterpreted him. 'Warning regarding which scenario, the Archangel lockdown, or the Starkmanir discovery?'

Keitan shook his head. 'Neither, Admiral. I meant that I'm issuing a warning directly to you, and every uniformed serviceman and woman of the DED and CONCORD. Either you heed it, or some of you will end up paying with your lives. That fate rests on your conscience, not mine.'

It was Admiral Elladall's turn to flinch. 'Did I just hear you correctly? Speaker Pauksuo? What did this man just say to me?'

The chair speaker was brilliantly livid. 'Ambassador Yun, what the hell do you think—'

But Keitan was resolved now, empowered with a sense of duty that was greater than any he'd ever known. For the first time, CONCORD really meant nothing to him, and these two were going to listen to what he had to say, no matter what respect they thought themselves entitled to, and no matter what the rules of diplomacy were.

'*Chamberlain Karsoth ordered an assassination attempt on my life,*' Keitan roared. 'So sorry to disappoint both of you, but I survived. Not long ago I returned from your Assembly, humiliated and disgraced for having asked for the mere right to defend ourselves from Amarrian subjugation—'

'*Ambassador,*' they both started to say. But Keitan outscreamed them both.

'*May we do so when they sponsor assassinations against members of our government?*' he screamed, silencing both CONCORD officials. Savoring their shocked expressions, he continued, speaking through clenched teeth, and broiling with anger.

'A courtesy to ask, since I already know the answer. But I want to hear it again from *you*, Admiral, and *you*, Chair Speaker, for my own conscience, so that I may rest knowing *I did everything I could* to spare you from what is to come, I'm going to ask you *for the last time:* will CONCORD interfere with the justice that is rightfully ours to take against the Amarr Empire?'

Admiral Elladall was a large, intimidating man who could reduce people to puddles with the intensity of his stare alone, and right now he was glaring at Keitan with as much contempt as he was capable of.

'Ambassador Yun, I don't take kindly to being threatened, and there is no way that Karin Midular sanctioned this. Your audacity *baffles* me. You're in more trouble than you can possibly fathom. In fact, I—'

The admiral was suddenly interrupted by a barrage of alerts originating from CONCORD commanders stationed in Yulai; repeated messages with FLASH priorities assaulted his datapad with requests for orders.

Caught off guard, his eyes widened in disbelief; he wasn't aware of the words that slipped from his mouth as he absorbed the information before him.

'Here?' he breathed, as Speaker Pauksuo helplessly looked on. 'That's impossible!'

'No,' Keitan said, folding his arms in triumph. 'It isn't.'

WHILE KEITAN YUN held his furious gaze at the two hapless CONCORD officials, personnel aboard the CON-CORD Bureau Station in Yulai reported the emergence of a dazzling 'celestial phenomena' just twenty kilometers away. Very few people in New Eden, even among the cap-suleer population, had ever seen a cynosural field in per-son before; fewer still recognized them for what they were. The sustained explosion of purple and white fire, with its swirling, luminescent vortex of time and space, was visi-ble to everyone in the vicinity. Hundreds of people inside the station crowded next to viewports to witness the spec-tacle; barely a handful of them even knew what they were looking at.

But when the Naglfar-class dreadnoughts – fifteen in all – emerged from the vortex and approached with their siege turrets trained on the station, the people backed away from the windows, sensing that these visitors had death on their agenda. One by one, the dreadnoughts – each a towering be-hemoth of destruction more than four kilometers high – surrounded the station in a perfect circle. Inside those capi-tal ships were crews that numbered in the thousands, mili-tary hangars that sheltered dropships, and barracks that held several armored divisions.

Then the cavalry arrived.

Dozens of Minmatar-designed battleships, cruisers, and assault frigates emerged from the vortex, quickly taking up defensive positions around each dreadnought, their gun turrets rotating in their nacelles searching for targets to devour.

An army was amassed outside the most powerful law enforcement agency in New Eden, and the alarm Klaxons blaring throughout were inciting panic because it was the first time they had ever been sounded. CONCORD warships were pouring into the system by the dozens, but couldn't attack the intruders because their own rules of engagement forbade them unless attacked first. This was a nightmare for the DED commanders; all it would take was a few salvoes from the dreadnoughts' massive siege cannons to obliterate the station's defenses and then start pulverizing the hull.

More ominous still, every ship bore Thukker or Republic insignia markings – despite the common belief that these two were bitter foes – and were completely unidentifiable to the friend-or-foe sensors of CONCORD'S instruments. Not a single shot had been fired – yet – as the CONCORD warships nervously orbited the intruders, which did nothing but stay motionless, intently focused on the five-spindled station before them.

'WILL YOU TAKE my warning seriously now, Admiral?' Keitan asked.

Both CONCORD officials were clearly distressed; neither was prepared to deal with such extraordinary circumstances. But the anger boiled through regardless.

'Ambassador,' Admiral Elladall growled. 'I don't know what game you think you're playing, but you better tell them to back off—'

'You're still not listening to me, Admiral,' Keitan interrupted. 'My exact advice to you, and to CONCORD, is exactly that: *back off.* You have *thirty days* to reconsider your hypocrisy in blocking Minmatar's right to defend itself. If you attempt to interfere with us after this period, we will no longer recognize the CONCORD Assembly as a governing authority of the Minmatar people, *and we will defend ourselves accordingly.* Speaker Pauksuo? Do you understand me? Thirty days. Make sure your Inner Circle *masters* understand that.'

Both officials were speechless as the mysterious fleet, ignoring the CONCORD warships that were practically brushing against them, began to retreat back into the cynosural field.

'Farewell for now,' Keitan said. 'I pray that you both come to your senses.'

Keitan's image vanished as the communication terminated and the last of the mighty dreadnoughts disappeared; the black void swallowed up the spectacular cynosural field, leaving no trace of its existence behind. All that remained was the CONCORD reaction fleet, whose captains were relieved but utterly terrified of the havoc which had almost come to pass. Skimming over an analysis of the invader's attack force composition, Admiral Elladall doubted there was enough defensive firepower on hand to prevent that fleet – whoever they were – from inflicting monstrous casualties on the station. No matter what they did, had these intruders decided to open fire, the resulting loss of life would be catastrophic.

One thing was certain, though, and it shone through all of the questions and uncertainty of the day's events: someone at the Republic, if not Keitan Yun himself, was going to pay for this. *No one*, the admiral thought, *not even God Himself, threatens CONCORD on its own jurisdiction and gets away with it.*

'Midular,' Chair Speaker Pauksuo growled to her drone. 'Get me Karin Midular. Now.'

AGAIN, INTERNATIONAL NEWS feeds were the source of an unending nightmare for the Republic's prime minister:

video of the CONCORD Bureau Station in Yulai, the epicenter of international diplomacy, held under siege by what appeared to be a Minmatar fleet. Admiral Neko, disguising her immense stress much better than Karin Midular, was calmly taking reports from Republic Fleet commanders in the vicinity of Yulai, each of whom reported the same thing: those ships, while 'Republic' in appearance, were nothing of the kind, nor was there any reason for the Fleet to ever cooperate with the Thukkers. Moreover, the entirety of the Republic fleet was accounted for down to the last ship, either in space or docked.

Such was emphatically explained, in exhaustive detail, to the CONCORD officials hammering Karin Midular for an explanation.

'So, you didn't authorize that fleet to threaten our assets in Yulai?'

'Speaker Pauksuo, those were *not* Republic ships,' Karin insisted. 'More obviously, we simply don't have the capability to generate jump portals or cynosural fields within secure space. You know that!'

'I can assure you that we're investigating exactly how they were able to do that,' she said, just as Admiral Elladall joined the conversation. 'But let me ask you a question that you better be able to answer: why was that fleet cooperating with Keitan Yun?'

Karin Midular blinked.

'I beg your pardon?'

'You mean you don't know?' Both CONCORD officials exchanged grave looks.

Karin was now pale. 'Know . . . what?' she asked weakly.

'Prime Minister,' Admiral Elladall said. 'Keitan Yun threatened the entire CONCORD organization with an ultimatum, warning us not to interfere with acts of aggression between Minmatar and the Amarr Empire.'

It can't be, she thought. *He wouldn't dare.* 'What?'

Admiral Elladall's eyes were unwavering. 'He also said that he was speaking on your behalf.'

That insane bastard. 'He said that?'

'On behalf of Minmatar, to be exact,' Speaker Pauksuo added.

Karin was trembling visibly now.

'I did *not authorize* that son of a *bitch* to do any of this!'

Neither official appeared convinced. 'Premier Midular, we don't tolerate threats to CONCORD, period. We're aware of the issues with the Republic right now, and I'd be remiss if I didn't share our own concerns for both your personal safety and the integrity of your nation state. But you have to rein your people in, Karin.'

'Please, you have to understand that—'

Admiral Elladall waved her off. 'Your answers are making our confidence in you even worse. We're extremely concerned that you're losing control of your armed forces—'

'My fleet commander is standing right beside me, and she assures that—'

'There are *no* assurances when your Assembly ambassador threatens our organization and then backs it up with an armada at our front door,' the admiral barked. 'I repeat: get a hold of your people. For your own sake.'

'Can we at least prevent the media from discovering Keitan Yun's role in this debacle?'

The admiral gave her a surprised look.

'We're far past that, Karin. Someone already leaked it.'

The communication dropped off before she could respond. Karin paused for a moment, slammed her fist onto the desk, and unleashed a blood-curling scream as Admiral Neko closed the door.

44

Thirteen Gallentean starships sliced across the void of pearl-strewn blackness in a glorious spectacle of power more reminiscent of a royal gala than a fighting force. Among its ranks were four Federation Navy Megathron-class battleships, each one almost a thousand meters in length; these were escorted by eight Taranis-class inter-ceptors, one of which was piloted by Lieutenant Korvin Lears. All of these vessels flew in a symmetric formation around its majestic flagship: a Nyx-class supercarrier, the *FNS Wandering Saint*, whose presence was so breathtak-ing that its immense destructive power was lost in the vis-age of its beauty.

With a centerline nearly five kilometers long, the Nyx was a triumph of Gallentean engineering. Designed to project power in the deep-space battlegrounds contested by capsuleers, she carried squadrons of fighters – single-manned spacecraft with deceptively potent firepower for their tiny size – that could eviscerate opposing frigates, cruisers, and even battleships in the right conditions. As a capital ship, the Nyx was equipped with a jump drive that could carry it across the ether between the stars in an in-stant; she was far too large to fit into stargates anyway. But she had to follow a path of cynosural beacons set ahead by reconnaissance ships; only then could she lock onto a target destination and navigate through. As the Nyx jumped from one system to the next, she waited for her es-corts to arrive through the stargate network behind her.

Gliding beside the majestic supercarrier in military parade formation, the procession of starships and fighters were taking a highly visible route to the Malkalen System through Federation space. Upon entering the cluster of stars known as the Caldari Border Zone, a contingent of Ishukone warships joined the formation, escorting them into sovereign territory of the Caldari State. Several smaller Caldari Navy warships joined as well, taking positions high above the Nyx, so that its crews could see – and quietly admire – the epic starship below.

To some, the sight of these two fleets flying side by side was a vision of hope, but many more remained sceptical. Although they were participants in a peace accord, the wounds opened by the rioting, bigotry, and nationalism were still too fresh. This was no goodwill delegation; it was a truce that had been forced by the extreme animosity between two civilizations. The hatred was bad for everyone, people reasoned, and the sooner it could be placed behind them, the better.

For Lieutenant Lears, the sight was nothing short of terrifying.

Flying in formation with three other interceptors, he rotated his drone cameras to view the underside of a Megathron, looking nervously at the blaster turrets locked in their forward, non-aggressive positions – the naval equivalent of a sidearm with the safety on. Towering behind its sleek, cyan-black armor was the huge cross section of the Nyx, with its myriad of viewports, navigation beacons, and electronics arrays. *A literal city of Federation personnel and equipment was right there*, he thought, *in the lion's den with the rest of us, and I can't say for certain who or what is flying that ship.*

Korvin was rife with trepidation; he could sense danger everywhere around him, but was unable explain why to anyone. His rational side couldn't accept why Admiral Noir would be so cold to him on the eve of such a momentous occasion. This was a peace mission, the very focus of his own personal endeavors, and he should have been elated and boisterous with joy, joking playfully with the Navy crewmembers he loved; and, at the least, offering him a strong handshake during their encounter at the pod gantries.

It was so utterly uncharacteristic of him that no explanation could account for his behavior, and that led Korvin to the irrational conclusion that *it therefore just couldn't have been him*, and his heart and soul was certain that had to be the case, regardless of the fact that it was impossible . . .

. . . *wasn't it?*

While one part of his mind wrestled with these anxieties, the rest operated the ship, keeping it in formation with the other interceptors, surveying the Caldari vessels nearby and the dozens of random starships they passed along the way. But as much responsibility as this mission demanded of him, his irresistible urge to know what was happening elsewhere in New Eden remained. For Korvin Lears, the greatest concern was that his ability to see the big picture was compromised by his anxieties. Part of his consciousness tapped into the Scope news feeds broadcasting on subspace channels . . .

. . . and there was Keitan Yun again, a humble man inexplicably making a huge spectacle of himself before an international audience for the second time, only now there was a fleet of warships surrounding the CONCORD Assembly station in Yulai – *and they appeared to be the same Republic and Thukker attackers that had nearly succeeded in killing him outside Skarkon.*

What the hell is happening? he wanted to scream. Unable to restrain himself, he willed his communications arrays to reach out to the beleaguered – or empowered,

Korvin couldn't tell which – ambassador and friend. Escort duties or not, he had questions that demanded answers right this instant.

KEITAN WAS GENTLY dabbing biofoam into Ameline's wounds when she bolted upright suddenly, startling him.

'Skarkon,' she said, settling into a trance. 'The Archangels have lifted their blockade and are pulling out of the system.'

'Really . . .' Somehow, Keitan knew, she was in communication with the Elders. 'Why?'

Closing her eyes, she appeared completely tranquil. 'Mutiny.'

Keitan was astounded. 'Are you certain?'

'News of the Starkmanir's survival has split their loyalties,' she said with a smile. 'Some want to take matters into their own hands.'

'Unbelievable,' he breathed, looking away for a moment before gazing back. Her face, partially coated in the biological nano-sealant, was already healing much faster than normal. He marvelled at the mystery of her, and of the forgotten race that she was a part of.

'How do they do that?' he asked. 'Contact you wherever you are . . .'

Taking a seat across from him, her slim but muscular arms contracted in dark ripples as she reached for her bloodstained white coat.

'A cybernetic chip was implanted in my ocular lobe. It's a subspace transceiver . . . I see their instructions in front of me like printed words hanging in the air. They know where I am at all times.'

'Good heavens,' he said, nearly horrified at the prospect of someone having that kind of power over her. 'Isn't that . . . a violation of your privacy?'

'I knew the risks,' she said, smiling at him. 'I volunteered for this.'

'To protect me?'

'To *guide you.*'

Keitan leaned back into his seat, shaking his head. 'I don't know if I should be flattered or concerned, to be quite honest.'

Ameline leaned forward, dazzling him with her brilliant green eyes.

'I would be *honored*, Keitan. The Elders picked you for who you are, for what you believe in, and for what you can do to help us restore Minmatar. You have a gift, and you can use it to help more people than you could ever dream of in the Sanctuaries. As wise and powerful as the Elders are, they have immense respect for individual talents and strengths. They never stop learning from people, as they will one day learn from *you.*'

Stunned, Keitan looked at the biofoam tube in his hand, reflecting momentarily on how lucky he was to still be alive.

'Then why did you volunteer?'

Pulling the coat over her shoulders, she stood up.

'Because I think you're a great man, and your humility is what will make you a king among us.'

The frail Sebiestor couldn't find the words to answer her with, but the sound of the Wolf re-coupling with the station's gantry broke his spell.

'Why did we dock?'

Her expression turned sad. 'Prime Minister Midular is trying to reach you, perhaps for the last time.'

So, this where I part ways with the Republic for good, he thought. 'I see.'

'The same with Maleatu Shakor. She has summoned both of you.'

As soon as the mechanical rumbling ceased, his data-pad started to buzz.

'Is that her?'

'No,' he said, suddenly remiss. 'It's an old friend.'

'PROFESSOR YUN,' KORVIN said, just as his interceptor arrived in the New Caldari system, where the Nyx and her fighter escorts were patiently waiting. The Malkalen System was one jump away. 'I mean, Ambassador . . . sorry to trouble you, but do you have time to answer some questions?'

'For you, of course,' Keitan said. 'What's troubling you?'

'That's exactly what I wanted to ask *you*, sir,' Korvin said, scanning the increasing number of Caldari ships within sensor range. 'I saw what happened in Yulai . . . they're saying that you were responsible for it.'

There was a pause. 'I told you before that drastic changes were imminent, Korvin. I—'

'*Please* don't be cryptic!' he pleaded. 'What *aren't* you telling me? Why did you threaten CONCORD, of all things? I would say that you've gone crazy except for this phantom fleet that backed you up!'

'You know the history of the Republic, Korvin. I taught it to you. It's time for change—'

'You taught me to respect the democratic institutions of law and order!' he shouted. 'Why won't you give me a direct answer? Who are you working for?'

'I work for the Minmatar people—'

'*Don't . . . patronize me,*' Korvin fumed. 'I need straight answers here! One moment you're telling me to "stay out of harm's way", the next I'm nearly killed by a mixed Republic-Thukker task force, and *then* they're showing up in Yulai on the heels of *your* threats to CONCORD! For fuck's sake, Keitan! What are you running behind Midular's back?'

'You saw the fleet before today?' Keitan breathed. 'When did this happen?'

'What does it matter when?' Korvin screamed. 'They attacked us! They killed my wingman! She's a capsuleer, but a Federation Navy pilot! An *ally*! Why, Keitan? Tell me what's happening!'

'Oh, Korvin . . . You were lucky to survive. Where are you now?'

Korvin was so angry that he was having trouble keeping his Taranis flying straight and level.

'On my way to Malkalen, with the rest of the Gallentean peace initiative!'

'And still, with such awesome responsibilities, you concern yourself with Minmatar affairs. You are a monument to the spirit of your race, Korvin. You are selfless, and I will never forget you.'

'What?'

'Focus on what you're doing,' Keitan said before cutting himself off. 'Events have already been set into motion for Minmatar that cannot be undone, even if I could tell you the truth. But you must be prepared for what is to come. Above all else, trust your instincts. They serve you well – you wouldn't be speaking with me otherwise. *Keep listening to them*, and someday we shall speak again!'

'*Goddamnit*, Keitan! You're not telling me anything that I need to hear!'

'Take care of yourself, Korvin. Good-bye.'

The line went dead just as the fleet jumped into the Malkalen System.

45

Lonetrek Region – Sela Constellation
The Malkalen System – Planet V, Moon 1
Ishukone Corporate Headquarters

Shifting uncomfortably from one foot to the other before a full-length mirror, Otro Gariushi called for his sister. He had two surprises for her, one of which was sure to disappoint.

Approaching his office moments later, Mila was dressed in a sleeveless dark top with a v-cut that exposed a subtle amount of cleavage, tapering tightly around her slim waist and then extending into an elegant dress that covered her feet, with several trains dancing behind her as she walked. It was evening attire that she reserved exclusively for diplomatic affairs, and as always, she looked absolutely resplendent for a woman her age; strong, sleek, and quietly sensual.

She was, however, completely unprepared for Otro's choice of clothing.

'Hey,' he said, straightening out – Mila couldn't believe it – the *tie* on his dress suit. 'How does this look?'

'I've never seen you in a suit before,' she stammered, staring at him as if he had two heads.

'Shit . . .' Otro looked squeamish. 'No good?'

'It's surprisingly good, actually,' she said, brushing a spec of lint off his shoulder. 'Very . . . uncharacteristic of you.'

'I'm told this would be more appropriate than the usual maverick look.'

Mila wouldn't have been able to stop the grin on her lips even if she tried.

'A suit . . . with a skull and crossbones tattoo on your face. It works, I think. Very cosmopolitan.'

Otro stamped his foot like a little kid.

'Do I look ridiculous in this or not?'

'No,' she said, shaking her head. 'Quite the contrary. You look like a national leader, a statesman who can show us the way out of these dangerous times.'

She marvelled at her younger brother, silently asking and then answering the question of why he had never married or raised children. The reason was tragically simple for both siblings: they were ashamed of who they were before the Ishukone chapter of their lives began. In their own way, both were guilty of destroying relationships, families, and lives; they could never allow themselves the privilege of companionship, lest their many enemies exploit their weakness by striking those closest to them.

'You look your usual, stellar self,' Otro admitted, checking his datapad. 'Makes me uncomfortable when you dress like that, though.'

'Thanks,' she answered, allowing a weak smile. 'Nice to see you're still protective after all these years.'

'The Federation reps are on their way,' Otro said, turning serious. 'Minister Chene and her party are boarding the shuttle now.'

'Then we'd better get going,' Mila said. 'Try to relax – you look great. Trust me.'

'Actually . . . I need you to sit this one out for an hour or so.'

'Really?'

'Mens and his team have been working around the clock to trace the origins of the virus that the Broker used to sabotage our broadcast nets. They found a few things along the way that I'd like you to have a look at, if it's all right with you.'

It wasn't and Otro knew it wouldn't be. But this was the Broker, and finding him took precedence over everything else.

'Fine,' she said dejectedly. 'I'll get changed—'

'No, no . . .' Otro said, putting a hand on her shoulder. 'You'll be back in time for when they start dinner. It's just for an hour – the purpose of this initial meeting is only to get our handshakes on camera. The real negotiations won't begin until tomorrow, so, please . . . stay dressed just the way you are. You're going to knock 'em out when they meet you later on.'

'All right,' Mila said. 'Where is he?'

'At the helm of his Raven in the main hangar.'

'I'll do what I can,' she said, turning away, 'Good luck out there, Otro.'

'Thanks . . . you too.'

Essence Region – Vieres Constellation
The Ladistier System – Planet IV, Moon 4
Presidential Bureau Station

After watching international newsfeed commentaries debating the merit of the pending 'Malkalen Economic Summit', President Foiritan had turned uncharacteristically nervous, and decided to contact his away team.

'Wadis, are you sure you're up for this?' he asked.

The Federation Economic Minister sounded resolved and steadfast. 'Mr. President, your plan is in good hands,' she answered. 'We're as ready as we're going to get.'

'Do you think we've forgotten anything?'

'Not at all,' she laughed. 'This is the best we can do – in

fact, it's everything we can do, and it will have to be enough. This mission is the very essence of a goodwill peace initiative, right, Admiral?'

The response from Noir was delayed. 'As the minister said, we are ready.'

The president was absorbed in thought, alternating his glance between the newsfeeds and the stellar view of space outside of his quarters. 'They'll remember you for this, Wadis.'

'It's your policy,' she said, blinking at him with her enormous blue eyes. 'I'm just the messenger.'

'You know, my run here as president will be over soon. Someday, I hope a candidate like you succeeds me.'

'Why, thank you, Mr. President. I'll remember you said that during the next elections.'

He smiled. 'I bet you will.'

'It's time,' she said, looking off-screen. 'I'll give you a status in a couple of hours.'

'Until then, I'll be watching on the news. Godspeed, Wadis.'

As the line terminated, President Foiritan felt a strange, powerful sensation that it was he that should be making this journey, no matter what the consensus of his cabinet, and regardless of the valid reasons why they opposed it.

Lonetrek Region – Sela Constellation
The Malkalen System – Planet V, Moon I
Ishukone Corporate Headquarters

From his vantage, Korvin was able to watch the supercarrier's enormous bay doors slowly open, exposing a bevy of smaller warships stowed inside. The delegation shuttle, a tiny speck of dust next to the monstrosity, emerged and turned gracefully toward the station; it entered the hangar several minutes later without incident.

Korvin breathed a little easier, but not by much.

Besides the occasional, brief order on the command channel, Noir hadn't spoken a word to anyone, nor was there any chatter among the Federation pilots in the battle group.

The waiting game had begun, and Korvin knew his anxiety wouldn't lift until they were on their way back home.

A THOUSAND CAMERA drone flashes commemorated the arrival of the Gallentean delegation to Ishukone Headquarters, where its iconic CEO was captured embracing the Federation Economic Minister as if she were an old friend. Strong, two-handed handshakes were exchanged between the members of both delegations, where much fuss was made over Otro's uncharacteristic choice of attire – to which Wadis playfully referred as mounting evidence of Otro's aging. The Ishukone event planners had gone to great lengths to make sure their guests felt comfortable, which included a host of special invitations to 'moderately' aligned State personnel ranging from assembly line workers to political figures, all of whom were eager for the opportunity to meet the Gallenteans.

Following the photo op was a question and answer session with the media, during which both Otro and Wadis expressed deep regret at the recent escalations in ethnic violence, conceded mutual blame for its origins, and accepted responsibility in taking the necessary steps to prevent it from happening again. When asked directly if he was attempting to supersede Tibus Heth's aggressive 'power play' entrance into Caldari politics, Otro answered

that he wasn't aware of *any* power contests in this part of
the State, drawing a chuckle from the audience that quickly
evolved into full-blown cheering from the Ishukone crowd.
More seriously, he added that he planned to hold Tibus at
his word to give the peace process a chance.

The Ishukone reception hall's main attraction was an
enormous, hangar-sized viewport constructed of transparent nanoalloy, offering a spectacular panorama of the
heavens and the fleet parked outside. The Nyx was the centerpiece of the frame, its long broadside parallel to the
station, blinking and shimmering with thousands of lights
in the distance. Among the mingling and networking taking place between Ishukone personnel and the delegation,
Otro and Wadis found each other in the crowd.

'History is such a fragile thing,' the Federation Economic Minister said, sipping from her glass. 'Do you think
we were delicate enough this evening?'

'I do,' Otro concluded. 'They say making the right decision is difficult, but that wasn't the case here at all. I
can't emphasize enough just how impressed I am with
President Foiritan's efforts to bridge the gap between us, I
really can't.'

'I'll be sure to pass that along,' Wadis said, nodding her
approval. 'When I was young, I remember being told of
the horrors of Nouvelle Rouvenor and was convinced that
Caldarians were soulless creatures who knew only how to
inflict pain on others. When I became old enough to think
for myself, I learned about how our imperialist forefathers
attempted to take control of sovereign Caldari lands, dismissing your own culture as too primitive for their tastes,
or too unworthy a cause for true democracy . . .'

She turned to face him, speaking deliberately.

'And then I read about the war for Caldari Prime, and
of those who fought and died on both sides . . . of the two

million alone who lost their lives at Hueromont, versus the loss of your own home world . . . one vicious cycle of barbarism after the next, repeating endlessly until we find the courage to stop it. You speak of hope today just as the last two generations have for decades. And yet I sense that this time is different. I believe that our consciences can rest, content in the knowledge that we – you and I – did everything we could to keep hope alive. This is just the first step.'

'The first of many steps,' Otro said, admiring the eccentric woman for her sincerity. He raised his glass. 'To hope. It's an honor to be working with you, Minister Chene.'

'Cheers, Otro,' she answered, happily clinking her glass against his. 'To the greatest of hopes indeed. Now, where is your lovely CFO? I was very much looking forward to meeting her!'

Otro grinned. 'She should be joining us shortly, and will definitely be attending all of our closed-door sessions tomorrow.'

'Excellent, I've prepared a few items for her to review whenever she can spare—'

Otro's datapad started to buzz wildly. 'I'll bet this is her. Please excuse me.'

The incoming call wasn't Mila at all.

'Nice suit,' the Broker said. 'You look like someone who wants to make a deal.'

Otro's stomach turned upside down as he turned away from the puzzled Wadis, moving quickly toward secluded space in the gala hall.

'Not now, you selfish—'

'You know I prefer to negotiate in person,' the Broker interrupted. 'I'm practically looking right at you. But where is your sister? I should think she wouldn't want to miss such a grand affair.'

Otro spun around, scanning every guest in view, cursing quietly through his teeth.

'Show yourself,' he growled. 'And I'll share what I think of you in person.'

'Manners, Otro,' the Broker scoffed. 'You dressed for a civil discussion, and I dressed . . . to dictate my final terms to you.'

His eyes darted wildly from person to person. 'Tell me where, you son of a bitch—'

'Just look for the "wandering saint" in the crowd.'

'"Saint"? What the fuck are you—'

Otro's head snapped toward the window, at the Federation supercarrier beyond.

No, he thought. *Impossible.*

'Peekaboo,' the Broker taunted.

'Bullshit,' Otro said. 'I'm calling your bluff—'

'Don't you like it?' the Broker hissed. 'Let me show you my better side.'

An aspect change on the Nyx drew a wondrous gasp from the guests as the capital ship started a lazy turn to port, pointing its bow directly toward the station while its escorts scurried out of the way, hastily realigning themselves in formation.

Anyone with naval flight experience would have noticed that the escorts weren't ready for the turn. That excluded everyone at the gala except Otro, whose keen perception also detected that the capital ship was accelerating.

Then his capsuleer intelligence calculated that there wasn't enough time to evacuate people if . . .

It can't be, Otro thought, as his heart started to race. *For the love of everything good . . . it can't be possible!*

'I'm told that the kinetic energy of this Nyx alone is approximately four kilotons,' the Broker continued. 'I'm new at flying supercarriers, Otro. I'm not sure I'll be able to stop this one in time. Unless, of course—'

'I told you, I can't do it!' Otro nearly screamed, as numbers started rolling through his head. *Approximate crew strength of a Nyx: 2,600 people. Approximate number of station crew and maintenance personnel: 55,000 people. Approximate resident population of this station . . . 250,000 people!*

Mother of God!

'Listen to me. It's impossible! You have to understand that, the money is already—'

'Nothing is impossible. I'm telling you that I'll cover the costs of you cancelling the deal with the *other* party, and I'll even raise my bid for the Insorum. I'm a man of my word, Otro. Call off your deal, and I'll stop this catastrophe from happening.'

'You'll never get through the shields,' Otro said, his mind racing. 'This station's shield's can withstand—'

The lights inside the gala room inexplicably dimmed for a moment and then restored back to normal, causing a stir among the crowd. Some were starting to take notice of the Nyx's growing aspect ratio in the window.

'I've never said this to anyone before,' the Broker said, as Otro's datapad lit up with a flurry of emergency messages. 'But you're starting to make me angry.'

KORVIN WASN'T SURE if he was the only one who saw it: a tiny flash coming from the station itself, on a linear plane extending directly in front of the Nyx. Moments earlier, its unannounced vector change nearly caused several of the escort warships to collide with each other. This was the last straw, and he could sense other pilots finally starting to question the circumstances as well. Something had to be done, and the anxiety compelled him to make an announcement publicly, on the command channel where everyone in the fleet would hear it.

'Super Saint One, this is Echo-Six, requesting an updated flight directive and escort instructions, over.'

Admiral Noir's reprimand was a loud, wicked hiss:

'Echo-Six, you will maintain your flight attitude and stay off this command channel!'

Korvin saw the formation loosen up as additional Caldari warships arrived. Doing a quick count, he figured that the Federation fleet was outnumbered by as much as three to one. Without question, the adversaries were thinking the same thing he was.

'Yes, sir,' he answered, watching a Caldari Navy assault frigate take position alongside of him. Its gun turrets were already pointing in his direction.

'IT WAS A goddamn EMP burst,' Mens reported from inside his Raven-class battleship as it approached the station. 'A shaped charge right over the shield emitters in the southwest quadrant. How the hell it got there without anyone noticing, I have no idea. The flash everyone else saw was from electrostatic arcs that jumped when the switchover failed. Everything in the decks above you is running on backup power . . . Otro, that entire side of the station is *exposed.*'

Mila, who was listening from inside her passenger cabin onboard, was resisting the urge to panic.

'It's him, isn't it? The Broker?'

'Yes,' Otro answered. 'I have to start getting people out of here—'

'Just give it to him,' Mila suddenly pleaded. 'Give him the damn vaccine and be done with it!'

'Otro, that Nyx is picking up speed,' Mens warned, bringing his warship alongside a pair of Ishukone Scorpion-class battleships facing the Federation fleet. Streams of civilian shuttles, barges, and warships were already pouring out of the station's cavernous hangar as they cruised past. 'Harbor control just told me that its captain – this Noir guy – is ignoring their requests to change course. I'm calling in reinforcements, but we don't have the time or firepower to neutralize that thing, not at this range.'

Mila wasn't thinking about anyone else's life but her brother's.

'Get the hell out of there!' she shouted. 'Just board a ship and go!'

'Mila, there isn't time,' he said. 'And I'm not leaving before I get everyone else out—'

'Otro, wait a minute,' she stammered, realizing an awful truth. 'Where are your clones stored?'

'Here,' he answered.

THE EVACUATION ALARMS inside the station were deafening.

'Ladies and gentlemen, please follow the security personnel, thcy'll lead you to safety,' Otro shouted as loudly as he could without sounding desperate. Ishukone guards were everywhere, herding people to the exits. Trams were waiting outside to take them to the hangar bay, or to the nearest available jettison pods – whichever would get them off the station fastest. 'This is no drill! It is time for everyone to leave!'

'This is your last chance,' the Broker whispered into his ear. 'Sell the Insorum to *me*.'

'I won't let you have it,' Otro said, his bottom lip quivering as he surveyed the panic and confusion. 'Never.'

'What a price you'll pay for this. Ishukone and the Caldari State will burn because of your decision! Pity that you won't live long enough to regret your decision. I'd love to see you suffer for it!'

'You can't hide from me forever,' Otro swore, making a pact with the devil. 'Not even in hell.'

Wadis ran up to him in the midst of the confusion. 'Is *that*' – she pointed toward the window with the looming Nyx dead-center of it – 'the reason for this evacuation?'

'Yes,' Otro admitted, taking the earpiece out. 'Admiral Noir is either ignoring our requests for him to change course, or he's no longer in command of that ship.'

'Nonsense,' she scoffed, raising a datapad of her own. 'Alex, old chap, what in heaven's name are you doing with that grand toy of yours? You've got everyone in here all excited for no reason—'

'Heaven,' Admiral Noir said. 'I see its golden gates are opening before me, here on the dawn of my greatest contribution yet to the Gallentean race . . .'

'Admiral, you're not making any . . . sense . . .'

Her voice trailed off when she realized that Admiral Noir was broadcasting their conversation locally, where everyone in the system – and well beyond, with the media there as well – could hear it.

The ancient 'admiral' was now addressing all of New Eden on the final voyage of 'his' life.

'I have . . . an obligation to my beloved Federation to settle accounts with this hateful race, these cursed Caldarians. For my entire life, I have mourned for Hueromont, wishing, praying, *willing* for the day when I could strike back on behalf of those souls who perished. Fate has bestowed upon me this grand opportunity, this great day, to take vengeance for all those who gave their lives for the

Federation, the true guardian of our precious Gallentean race . . . may you rest in peace now, brave souls of Hueromont, and you, kindred spirits of Nouvelle Rouvenor, knowing that I will take back what was stolen from you . . . Curse you, Caldari . . . may I take as many of you with me that I can!'

Trembling, Otro Gariushi reached for his datapad.

ALTHOUGH KORVIN COULD neither accept what he was witnessing nor believe what he had just heard, his survival instincts began to take control of his actions, and he began easing his interceptor away from the doomed Nyx as it hurled toward imminent cataclysm. As if to follow his lead, the other Federation ships began doing the same. Ahead, he could see squadrons of fighters launching from the supercarrier's forward runway, immediately pulling upward to arc back over the vessel's rear to avoid the collision.

The command line erupted with more evil from Admiral Noir.

'We're trapped! Attack them, you fools! Fight for your lives while you still can!'

'MILA, LISTEN TO me,' Otro pleaded. 'Are you with me, sis? I need you to listen carefully to me . . .'

She was a torrent of tears, fear, regret, and anger, trying to find the composure to listen to her brother's final words.

'I'm going to recite coordinates for the UBX-CC System,' Otro said, trying to stay calm. 'That's where the Insorum facility is – no one else knows this . . . that was to protect you, but now you have to carry this burden. Are you listening to me? Mila!'

'Yes,' she whispered.

Otro spoke three sets of nine numbers: a stellar grid co-ordinate.

'There's an acceleration gate there,' he said. 'You'll be interrogated by drones, they'll ask you questions about me, personal stuff that only you can answer. It's the only way they'll know for sure it's you and not some imposter. Please say something, I'm almost out of time . . .'

'Yes . . .' she quivered through tears. Mens himself, immersed in the Raven's pod capsule dozens of meters above her, could feel his own tears mixing with the neuro-embryonic fluid surrounding him.

'Mila listen . . . give Maleatu Shakor the Insorum. Don't take any payment for it, not one single credit. This might not make up for all the bad things I've done, but I won't trade any more lives for money. Okay? Promise?'

The Nyx's silhoutte was almost the entire width of the viewport.

'Otro, please don't go, please don't—'

'I want you and Mens to disappear,' Otro said, finally losing his own composure. 'Stay away from Heth . . . the drones will look after you. Wait the storm out . . . do some good with the time you have. You gotta be strong, I know you're strong . . . it's why this happened . . . I . . .'

Otto was scared to die, but thankful for the chance to feel like a human being again.

'I love you, Mila. I'm your brother, so I'm gonna go first . . .'

The angel of death was staring Otro right in the eyes. *I'll go quietly*, he thought. *Just don't come for her for a long time. Please.*

THE FNS *WANDERING Saint* glided silently, as all things did in space; unwavering and unstoppable; with terrible purpose and magnificent beauty; and slammed into the station with apocalyptic force. The leading edge of the Nyx bashed through the unshielded armor and hull with horrific ease, pulverizing deck after deck, penetrating deeper and deeper inside until striking one of the station's main support structures. The abrupt halt in momentum caused the aft remnants of the Nyx to collapse forward into the expanding cavity of molten metal before it, breaching and then ripping its reactors apart in dual, inefficient nuclear explosions that vaporized several cubic kilometers of metal and flesh in an instant.

The concussion waves split through the station with invincible cruelty, collapsing bulkheads and shattering reinforced composite alloy like brittle rust as its explosive force extended violently throughout the entire structure.

As billions of horrified people watched throughout New Eden, a fireball dozens of kilometers in diameter lit the space of Malkalen in a brilliant flash, marking the deaths of more than three hundred thousand Caldari souls, and with them, the only man who could stop them all from falling into the abyss.

The wails and screams of Mila Gariushi could be heard from every deck aboard the Raven.

Elsewhere, the howls of a triumphant Tibus Heth rang just as loudly.

46

As the space surrounding the burning station erupted into a light show of cannon fire and missile contrails, Korvin's attention was divided evenly between his threat indicators and the system readings of his Taranis. The question of who shot who first was irrelevant; no captain was going to wait for an interpretation of the rules of engagement. There was an expanding disc of nuclear fire radiating from the corporate headquarters of the Ishukone Corporation, a wicked bow wave upon which the souls of thousands had perished. Those pilots and captains who witnessed the cataclysm firsthand were now being directed by a deadly mix of survival instincts and rage.

For the Gallenteans, escape was impossible. Multiple Caldari Navy interdictors appeared moments before the collision, and their warp inhibitor fields were now overlapping the entire sphere of engagement for the Federation ships. Command and control was in shambles; Admiral Noir had been in charge of the entire battlegroup, and every ship within it depended on the Nyx for both firepower and defenses. No captain would be able to take effective charge of a scenario like this; for most of the crewmen aboard the Federation ships in Malkalen, this battle would be their last.

The first casualties were the squadrons of orphaned fighters aimlessly orbiting the ruined station; without the carrier's telemetry feeds and targeting information, they could do little to coordinate any kind of strategy and were mercilessly obliterated by sentry gun batteries defending the remnants of Ishukone Headquarters. In groups of up to three at a time, the nimble crafts vanished in puffs of light, their pilots vaporized instantly.

Missiles were tracking Korvin's ship; it was impossible to evade them completely, but if he kept his speed up, he could perhaps survive long enough to give one or more of his comrades time to escape. Locking onto the nearest Caldari interdictor, he used the Taranis's speed to close range quickly and activated the stasis webifiers, crippling the enemy craft's momentum. Angling sharply to avoid a collision, Korvin opened fire with each of his rail guns as he streaked past, peppering his target with antimatter slugs that impacted against its shields and armor plating in violent bursts of coruscation.

Unable to maneuver, the interdictor returned fire with a barrage of missiles; but it couldn't withstand the sustained punishment of the Taranis's guns. In a brilliant flash that Korvin would never forget, the interdictor exploded, taking its single warp inhibitor field down with it. But his elation vanished as his Taranis was buffeted by a series of armor-shredding explosions; Condor-class Caldari Navy interceptors were now descending upon him like a swarm of angry wasps. When one cut across the nose of his ship, he instinctively turned after it and fired.

Surprisingly, the Caldari interceptor exploded immediately; the craft was already heavily damaged when Korvin attacked it. But the next missile wave had arrived; just milliseconds before their impact, the Taranis's disaster management CPU jettisoned his pod. Korvin could feel the tiny craft slipping out through an ejection port in the hull while the rest of his ship was torn to scrap in a series of explosions.

Korvin knew his hunters wouldn't stop there.

Before he could escape, his pod was immobilized, first

by a warp scrambler, and then by a stasis web. All he could do now was wait for his real capsuleer legacy to begin; to cheat death as the body he was born in was executed.

He absorbed every detail of his surroundings as the missiles came for him: the burning station, listing to one side with a grievous wound in her midsection; he wondered how many people, if any, were still alive inside. He saw the spine of a Federation Navy Megathron crack in half as rail gun fire eviscerated its hull; amazingly, its heavy neutron blasters kept firing for a few moments until the cabin lights inside went dark for good.

More death, he thought, as the first explosion rocked his pod. *How many crew on a Megathron . . . six, maybe seven hundred people blotted out of existence just like that . . .*

The pod started to break apart, venting his flesh to the void; but Korvin felt nothing except the distinct sensation of being pulled away from reality. He saw a corpse floating in space – his own – and then a glimpse of the Malkalen System's sun. He was suddenly thrust toward its orange-yellow fire . . .

. . . and then there was a tranquil blackness followed with the crisp, smooth, female voice of a computer:

'Good morning, pilot. How do you feel?'

Korvin opened his cloned eyes for the first time, light years away from the spot where he had perished. Safely within the boundaries of Federation space, he was certain that other capsuleers from the same battle were awakening nearby as well.

Metropolis Region – Gedur Constellation
The Illuin System – Planet III
Republic Parliament Bureau Station

Approaching from opposite directions, both men were surprised to see each other as they neared the door to Karin
Midular's office.

'I doubt we were both summoned here by accident,' Keitan Yun remarked, noting the four guards behind Maleatu
Shakor. Unlike Ameline, these were Brutors, and each of
them seemed more than capable of tearing people's limbs
off.

'We've been called to the discipliner's office,' Maleatu
said with a wry smile. 'Separately, but for all the same reasons.' He marched forward, enthusiastically placing a hand
on Keitan's shoulder, looking toward him with his clouded
eyes. 'Well done, man! I wish I could have seen the look
on the faces of those CONCORD bastards when the fleet
showed up.'

'I'd be lying if I said I didn't enjoy it,' Keitan replied. 'I
wish I could do it again, to be honest.'

Maleatu laughed. 'Let's see what the lady wants, then,'
he said, turning to face Ameline. 'You'll stay here with the
others, won't you, dear?'

'Of course, sir,' she answered with a slight bow, taking
her place alongside the other bodyguards while intimidated station personnel kept their distance.

'"Sir"?' Keitan joked. 'Well . . . she never calls *me*
that—'

'Neither will anyone else in this government,' Karin

Midular scolded as the doors were thrown open. 'Not in any official capacity. Inside, both of you.'

They complied, knowing full well what awaited them. Out of respect – at least from Keitan's point of view – they were going to let her have her moment.

'You're both relieved of your posts, effective immediately,' Karin growled. 'Your clearance passes and credentials will only get you off this station. Don't even bother attempting to get back into your government offices or any Parliament chamber to retrieve your things – we'll ship it to you, wherever you wind up. I could care less, personally.'

'Ouch,' Maleatu mocked.

The embattled prime minister spoke from the heart, glaring at the old Brutor with malice.

'I've given you every measure of decency . . . respected every chance to work with you, to at least debate in civilized fashion the policies which could have actually done some good for people, but no, you had to choose the hard road, this . . . nonsensical Brutor machismo, this . . . this neo-conservative, testosterone-laden, pigheaded stubbornness that kicks your tribe everywhere but earns them nothing, as if a blind man was leading it—'

'That was low,' Maleatu coughed. 'Unprofessional by your own standards—'

Karin snapped at him with fury in her eyes.

'*A vote of no confidence?* You selfish *bastard*! When the nation is already in panic, *you*, a so-called *patriot* of Minmatar, exploit the situation to advance your own *political* agenda? You always claimed to be above such things, but your hypocrisy astounds me!'

She turned a fierce scowl toward Keitan.

'And you . . . you *traitor*!'

Keitan straightened his posture, now feeling her pain, and with it, a significant measure of guilt.

'I saw in you the chance for such remarkable accomplishments,' she said. 'A man who loved the Republic and sought to mend the history that we can never change, but endeavor mightily to never repeat. I gave you the opportunity of a lifetime! Why did you turn against me? What have I done, personally, to betray you?'

Her question was sincere, and as such, Keitan found himself wholly unprepared to answer it.

'Is there nothing that you can say for yourself? Nothing at all to restore the faith I once had in you?'

Keitan looked down. He desperately wanted to tell her the truth, but his new purpose in life forbade it.

Karin shook her head sadly at him.

'I'm going to build this Republic by myself, since neither of you have the courage to build it with me. I'm going to fight with everything I've got to make this government work. You're both spineless quitters and the sight of you disgusts me.'

'You'd do well to listen to his warnings,' Maleatu muttered, motioning toward Keitan. 'I sincerely mean that.'

'Those "warnings" have earned him a prison sentence,' she snapped. 'I'll admit I don't understand what that was at Yulai, but I can say this: nothing can protect him from the wrath of CONCORD. And now, after having the chance to glimpse his soul . . . I hope that wrath is without a shred of pity.'

That was hurtful to Keitan, and Karin could see that.

'I've nothing more to say to either of you,' she snarled, holding her glare at both of them. 'Get out of my sight . . . get out of my *Republic*!'

Keitan couldn't bring himself to look at her, and Maleatu, being his usual self, just grunted. They left without saying anything more.

When then doors closed, Karin collapsed into her chair.

The stress was taking a physical toll on her; it was becoming a challenge just for her to move. But as difficult as these times were, she knew this was only the beginning.

Leaning forward, she reached for two oversized documents lying on her desk. Ironically, they had been right under the nose of Maleatu Shakor just a moment earlier.

With an aching hand, Karin Midular lifted a pen to sign an official decree to dissolve the Republic Parliament and call for new elections.

KEITAN AND MALEATU emerged from Karin Midular's office into a station that was now a maelstrom of activity. They saw crowds of people gathering around holovids and news feed screens everywhere, gasping and pointing as if something terrible had happened. Ameline approached them with a grave look on her face.

'Keitan, you said your friend was on his way to Malkalen?' she asked. 'Was he part of the Gallentean delegation?'

The former Republic ambassador's stomach froze, and Maleatu's head perked up.

'Yes,' he answered. 'Why do you ask?'

MENTALLY DRAINED, MALEATU leaned back against the door to his personal quarters. Two hours had passed since he was officially ousted from the Republic government, but he couldn't have cared less.

Mercy!

He had no love for the Caldarians, but a tremor rippled through the bulk of his frame as he contemplated the horror of what had taken place in Malkalen. Stations were supposed to be indestructible; the notion that the sure, solid ground beneath his feet right now could be vulnerable to such calamity was inconceivable.

For that reason, it was the reports of trapped survivors which disturbed Maleatu the most. Armadas of emergency ships were arriving at Ishukone Headquarters; search and rescue MTACs were descending onto the station's vast surface, cutting away metallic carnage, and installing forced-entry docking collars to reach the people inside. As the damage continued to spread, several smaller explosions had rocked the station since the initial strike, and more than one datapad communication of someone saying good-bye to a loved one had been recorded.

Without question, Otro Garuishi was dead. Of the hundreds of thousands of people whose lives were already taken, his loss was devastating to *every* Caldarian. In the name of achieving peace, the national hero had opened his arms to embrace a Gallentean foe, and it had cost him his life. That was the most unforgivable treachery of all; there would be no doves left in the State after this. War was an inevitable prospect, and Tibus Heth was perfectly poised to take power because of it.

But Maleatu's grieving was not for Gariushi's life, but for the paramount secret that had perished with him. Although the Elders were prepared to move without it, Insorum was the key to making the transition from imprisonment to freedom as painless for the slaves as possible. Now, that prospect had gone up in flames, and with it any chance of the invasion going smoothly . . .

His datapad started to buzz, and the device's vibration signature injected waves of dread into his veins: It was Kinachi Hepimeki, the Ishukone CFO.

Her voice was tired, defeated, and unspeakably sad.

'Maleatu . . .'

'I'm relieved to hear that you're all right,' he said, hoping she would interpret his concern in the right context. 'At least, physically—'

'Otro asked me to give you a message.'

'Is he . . . ?'

'Take these numbers down. I'm only going to say them once.'

She recited the stellar coordinates from memory while he typed them into his datapad. He knew what they represented.

'For your safety?' he asked, implying the question of why she didn't just send the location electronically.

'For the deal's safety,' she answered.

That raised an alarm with him, but now wasn't the time to press her.

'Which system?' he asked.

'UBX-CC.'

Outstanding, he thought. *Right in between Caldari and Minmatar space. Clever fellow, that Otro was.*

'You'll have to use dead reckoning to reach that location,' she added. 'It's hidden in a deadspace pocket. There's an acceleration gate there – the Insorum facility is on the other side. There are drones guarding it, and they know you're coming.'

So that's how he was able to do it, he thought. Otro only mentioned that the facility was fully automated, but he never said anything about having to deal with drones. Maleatu became annoyed.

'What kind of protection will we need to bring with us—'

'Do *not* open fire on them. These drones were loyal to Otro, and now they're loyal to me. But they'll defend themselves if provoked. You have to go in person – they won't give the vaccine to anyone else.'

'All right,' he muttered. 'Then we're free to bring containers with us to transport—'

'Don't attempt to approach the facility or you'll be attacked. And if the drones sense they won't survive, they'll destroy the factory.'

Of course, he thought. *Otro was always one to hedge his bets.*

'I don't mean this to come across as personal,' Maleatu said cautiously. 'But what assurances do I have that you've given me your word?'

'My word . . .' she answered weakly. 'My real name isn't Kinachi Hepimeki.'

Maleatu stood upright. 'It isn't?'

'No,' she answered. 'It's Mila. Mila Gariushi. Otro was my brother.'

Stunned, he backed into the door behind him again.

'There's maybe five other people in New Eden who know that,' she said, nearly breaking up. 'So that's just going to have to do.'

'Very well,' he swallowed. 'We'll make payment upon receipt of the merchandise—'

'No payment is necessary,' she said.

Maleatu was certain he didn't hear that right. 'I . . . beg your pardon?'

'I said . . .' she started painfully. '*Otro* said . . . that he refused to take any money for saving lives. Those were his last words.'

It wasn't often when a Brutor's soul was touched by an outsider, but Maleatu hadn't known such respect and admiration for a man like this in a long time.

'With everything that's happened, there has to be concern for your safety,' he started. 'I think it might be best if you . . . disappeared. We can protect you . . .'

'I don't need your protection,' she snapped.

Maleatu didn't know what else to say.

'I'm truly sorry for your loss, Mila.'
There was a pause before she answered.
'Someday you'll really mean that.'

Geminate Region – F-ZNNG Constellation
System UBX-CC – The Mjolnir Nebula
Insorum Production Facility

Following the coordinates that Mila had provided, Maleatu Shakor and an Elder war fleet following him were led on a journey to the fringes of the Mjolnir Nebula. Otro Gariushi had not only selected a deadspace pocket to hide his facility, but he also chose one of the most unforgiving environments of space to work in. It was no wonder he used drones for construction: in addition to being buried in a thick dust cloud that reduced the visibility of camera drones to just a few hundred meters, the ambient temperature of the surrounding space was a blistering 3,000 Kelvin – enough heat to gradually decay the shields of every ship in the fleet.

A human effort to build facilities in such lethal conditions would have been disastrous; unshielded construction vehicles such as MTACs or survival suits would be incinerated by the high temperatures, and occasional pockets of turbulence pushing gas and dust at dozens of kilometers per second could pulverize unfinished structures. Yet sitting before them was a fully functional acceleration gate, right at the exact spot where Mila Gariushi said it would be.

Maleatu appreciated the lengths that Otro had gone to protect their investment.

Flying an unarmed Vigil-class frigate, he willed the

tiny craft forward and activated the gate as dozens of Elder warships waited behind him. It was the smallest ship he'd piloted in decades, and the only time in his life that he had ever flown without weapons.

Propelled deeper into the nebula, an alien world emerged that made his skin crawl.

The drone complex that Mila had described was actually a massive hive constructed of salvaged metal; Maleatu could only imagine where the scrap had come from. Slithering with mechanical creatures, the structure was distinctly organic in appearance, reminding him of the deadly insect nests native to his home planet of Matar. Spanning as much view as the reduced camera drone visibility would allow, he could see other structures partially obscured by the swirling wisps of stellar cloud dust – hundreds of them. There was a collective awareness here that Maleatu could sense, as if a million alien eyes were staring at him; there was no doubt that his ship was passively targeted the moment he arrived.

A menacing drone with an elongated thorax and tentacles that extended into pincers approached his ship; the creature was easily twice the size of the Vigil. Then two smaller drones detached from the creature's underside; one was emitting a red beam of light.

Maleatu was hailed by an entity that identified itself as VILAMO.

'State your business here.'

The smaller drones were much more animated than the larger guardian; both were expressing a keen curiosity in the Vigil.

'My name is Maleatu Shakor, and I represent—'

'Who sent you?'

'Kinachi Hepimeki.'

Threat indicators began screeching as multiple drones targeted the Vigil. The guardian drone moved closer and began curling its tentacles toward the ship.

VILAMO repeated his question:

'Who sent you?'

'Mila did,' he panicked. 'Mila Gariushi!'

The two curious drones began to probe his ship as the tentacles backed off.

'Master Gariushi is well, then?'

Oh no, Maleatu thought. 'You mean, Otro?'

'Master Gariushi.'

One of the drones appeared to be trying to find its way inside his ship. *These things are testing me*, Maleatu screamed to himself. *Tell the goddamn truth!*

'Master Gariushi is dead,' he said, holding his breath for a moment. Then he quickly added: 'He left his sister in charge before he passed on.'

'Just until Master Gariushi returns.'

'Yes, fine,' Maleatu breathed. *Whatever, you dumb drone.* 'Just until he comes back.'

'Do you know when that will be?'

'Probably not for a long time.'

The curious drones moved back toward the guardian. Maleatu wondered if VILAMO was the one with the red eye, or if it was the collective name for every single drone that was here.

'You have come for the Insorum. What will you do with it?'

What fucking business is it of yours? Maleatu fumed. 'I'm going to use it to treat people that are addicted to Vitoc,' he answered.

'You don't plan to sell the vaccine to anyone else, do you?'

Great Matar! How protective are these monsters?

'No, I don't plan on selling it to anyone! That Insorum is going to free Minmatar slaves – nothing else!'

An unnerving silence followed. Maleatu sensed that this artificial VILAMO entity was quantifiably sizing him up, running AI algorithms designed to evaluate the merit of his answers based on the information they could derive from his ship, the Elder fleet waiting back at the acceleration gate, and whatever Mila disclosed. He had no idea what hold Otro had over these pesky creatures, but the protective intelligence built into them was downright disturbing. These creatures were capable of learning and evolving just like their rogue counterparts, only these had a clear agenda that pressed beyond just giving him the Insorum.

No, Maleatu thought. *These drones are looking for something specific; they are tireless; and they have all of eternity to pursue their ambitions.*

'Maleatu Shakor, I don't trust you. But this is what Master Gariushi wanted, so I will comply. Send only your freighters through the gate. We will fill them with as much supply as they can accommodate. We will include various vaccine delivery apparatus to assist with your invasion—'

What the fuck!

'—syringes, tablets, liquids, barometric delivery systems for both localized and planetary operations; gaseous variants for use in compromising hardened structures, along with various projectile-based warheads that can be fired from Minmatar weapons of all calibers.'

Maleatu was stunned. 'Are you including the vaccine's formula as well?'

'Master Gariushi said no one can ever have that. No exceptions.'

'So every time we need more . . .'

'You see me. If any harm befalls Master Gariushi's sister, regardless of how the damage is inflicted, I will destroy the vaccine first, and then I will determine if the destruction of additional objects is necessary.'

An icy lead ball formed in Maleatu's stomach. 'I understand.'

'Start bringing your ships through. Minmatar slaves are waiting.'

47

Contrasting sharply with the aerial highways and tiers of city buildings were billions of tiny points of light; simple candles and torches that adorned every metropolis in the Caldari State. Lining every avenue and causeway, they were bolted into streetlamps and buildings; packs of Caldarians walked solemnly to vigils, gathering around shrines and laying flowers beneath effigies of Otro Gariushi.

Nearby each of these makeshift memorials, dramatic images of Tibus Heth's trials at the Armor Forge flickered in the light from the dancing flames.

Universal mourning encompassed Caldari society; the old and the young, the rich and the poor, the liberal and the militant; all were devastated – and enraged – by this crushing loss. For all its industrial might, the Ishukone Corporation had ceased operations, its millions of workers too numbed with grief and uncertainty to focus. In every colony, city, shanty, and station of Caldari space, adults spoke openly of war, while children – ripe with aspirations of becoming heroes like Otro Gariushi and Tibus Heth – swooshed toy Caldari Navy ships through their homes and playgrounds, imagining the glory of shooting down Federation Navy ships; or ran down streets with toy rifles pretending to gun down Gallentean foes.

Many Caldari parents encouraged this behavior, themselves eager to participate for real in the fantasies gripping the imaginations of their children. The mandatory basic military training of this culture meant that every adult knew how to handle a rifle, and now most were eager to put that skill to good use. Abetting this sentiment were the 'Provists', the nickname for the legions of followers spreading the political gospel of Tibus Heth.

While officially employees of the Caldari Constructions Corporation, these men and women – dressed in dark blue military uniforms accented with the Caldari State emblem – were the agents in charge of running Heth's propaganda machine. It was they who provided the torches and candles for the mourning of Gariushi; they who made certain that the image of Tibus Heth was never far from view anywhere in the State; they who used all the technology available to them to spam datapads with footage of the Malkalen disaster; they who purchased huge blocks of advertising space to display graphic images of the mutilated bodies pulled from the wreckage; and it was they who established a strong presence in fringe Caldari settlements, among the poor, working-class denizens far from the densest cities, to provide children with toys to enact their fantasies of heroically butchering Gallenteans.

Orchestrating this meticulous, perfectly executed strategy of psychological warfare were the Templis Dragonaurs, now serving as officers within Heth's newly commissioned

Caldari Providence Directorate, the official name of the Provists. The highly visible, charitable side of their actions, or the public face of Heth's patriotic ideology, was a mask for much darker affairs. Behind the scenes, the Dragonaurs were acting as the non-negotiable muscle through which the real forces of change were being driven.

Embedded in Caldari society for centuries while keeping their cult affiliation with the organization secret, the Dragonaurs were now asserting themselves publicly, but under the Caldari Providence Directorate name. Every member was a steadfast, devout believer in Heth's cause for Caldari purity. No longer would they stay in the shadows to plan their attacks on Federation property or to plot assassinations of left-leaning Caldari officials; they were now sanctioned weapons of Tibus Heth, backed by the immense wealth of the Broker, and supported by the overwhelming majority of citizens in the Caldari State.

Every Provist that engaged the public on Heth's behalf was a physical specimen of Caldari perfection; attractive looks with athletic builds and a magnetic, inspiring charisma that made them astonishingly capable sellers of ideas. With the Broker's vast resources available to them, their intelligence services amassed personal information about key individuals in the State; the less-visible figures who served on corporate boards and regional political forums, whose collective decisions determined the balance of power within mega-corporations, regional governments, and ultimately the entire nation.

Those individuals who welcomed the 'suggestions' offered by Provists without questioning the motives behind them found a powerful ally in Tibus Heth. Within seventy-two hours of the attack in Malkalen, the CEO of the Ytiri Warehousing Corporation – a freight and shipping subsidiary of mighty Kaalakiota – resigned from his position specifically to award full control of company assets and strategic operations to Tibus Heth himself, as described in his own words to the media:

'By taking this step, we are embodying the ideal that will always be the legacy of Otro Gariushi: that the State's needs are greater than ourselves. We are a nation in crisis; the acquisition of wealth or political gain no longer has any virtue in this corporation. As a Caldarian and Chief Executive Officer, my actions are a patriotic imperative. The atrocity committed by the Federation has demonstrated just how vulnerable we are, and the depths to which we have fallen. Mr. Heth, the men and women of the Ytiri Corporation are at your command.'

Ytiri was a small corporation, but the enthusiastic willingness of its leadership to relinquish control of operations was symbolically paramount, garnering instant popularity among the masses. Provists were standing nearby when the CEO announced his decision; they took the podium immediately afterward, explaining the working relationship between the two merged corporations, and eloquently detailing the financial arrangement to appease the markets. Answering difficult technical questions with articulate, dulcet candor, they were impressive even to the sceptics among the media and corporate executives watching nationwide.

Anti-Gallentean ideals were implicit with every speaking point, as were subtle tributes to Tibus Heth's leadership. It was profitable to detest the Federation, they explained; what better way to revitalize a struggling economy than by beating the war drums with as much vigor as the State could provide. The entire presentation was placed in the context of what happened at Malkalen. Among the proletariat masses, there were no dissenters to the autocracy taking shape in the Caldari State, and the

Provist's power-consolidation overtures were a welcome measure of leadership and solidarity during very dangerous times.

Those that took exception to the aggressive political changes taking place in the Caldari State experienced a different side of Heth's ideals altogether.

The Forge Region – Kimotoro Constellation
The New Caldari System – Planet II: Matias
Sovereignty of the Caldari State

Rocks, spires, and forests rose from a harsh landscape covered in snow as the Home Guard dropship descended through layers of clouds on its approach to the sprawling metropolis of Khyyrth. Buffeted by strong wind gusts, the craft soared between a pair of mountain peaks and settled gently into the city's northernmost spaceport.

Every disaster brings hidden opportunities, Haatakan Oiritsuu thought, watching the final moments of the Ytiri press conference from the privacy of her armored limousine. *I wonder how many other weaklings are getting ready to throw themselves at Heth's feet.* Several military escort vehicles were idling beside the dropship's landing skids as her driver eased the vehicle down the craft's exit ramp. Home Guard soldiers cleared the crowded streets ahead of the convoy as they moved north toward open space, where a sudden demarcation line separated the dense urban sprawl of Khyyrth's outer limits with the private land owned by Haatakan. At the cost of billions of credits – partially her own money, but mostly Kaalakiota's – she had hundreds of square kilometers of land adjacent to the thriving metropolis cleared of all man-made objects, converting the property into her own personal wilderness sanctuary.

Under different circumstances, she might have laughed openly at the Ytiri CEO for his cowardice. *A pathetic man completely unfit for managing difficult situations*, she thought, watching the throngs of people looking curiously into the windows of her car as they passed. But there was nothing funny about this, not with the possible implications to her own power. Tibus Heth was a monster of her own creation, a direct consequence of her decision to use force to retake the space elevators at the Constructions Armor Forge. In the aftermath of Malkalen, there was only one national hero left, and the bloodthirsty masses held her accountable for ordering his death. She cursed quietly as the convoy sped across the gated threshold into her lands, contemplating how to neutralize Heth's nauseating exploitation of Ishukone's tragedy to bolster his own power.

Trees zipped past the window as they entered the thickly wooded area of her personal retreat. The interlocking causeways and buildings of Khyyrth were many kilometers behind, although its huge metal towers were still visible from clearings.

Unexpectedly, the convoy slowed to a complete halt.

She keyed the car's intercom control immediately. 'Why arc we stopping?'

Neither the driver nor the bodyguard sitting in front answered. Instead, both men stepped outside.

'What the hell?' she muttered, getting out of the car herself.

'Hey!' she yelled. 'Where do you think you're going?'

Without acknowledging her, the men stepped into the open hatch of a Home Guard APC. When it closed, the entire convoy continued down the road, leaving her and the limousine behind. Infuriated, she rushed forward to the driver's seat, only to discover that the controls had been locked down. Although the engine was still idling, the vehicle was useless to everyone except the driver or a trained electronics technician.

A light sleet started to fall, and the intensifying wind was starting to howl, carving its way through the needles of the trees on either side of the road. Having made this journey many times, she knew that she was about midway between her estate and city limits, surrounded on all sides by wilderness and harsh terrain that stretched for dozens of kilometers in every direction.

Furious, she reached for her datapad, vowing to punish the individuals responsible for this. But the device – which was working perfectly well at the spaceport – reported that no comm signal was available for use. That, she knew, was possible only if it was being actively jammed.

Haatakan was more afraid than angry by now.

She was startled by the muted whine of a hovercar's engine as it approached from the direction of the city. Squinting through the freezing sleet, she could see that it bore the markings of Home Guard. Scrambling out of the way to avoid being hit, the car stopped abruptly within inches of her hips.

Four Provists stepped out.

'You'd better have a good explanation for this,' Haatakan growled.

They said nothing, casually surrounding her. The 'lead' Provist was a much taller woman than she was, clearly Caldarian, and seemed unbothered by the cold.

'I'll wait inside while you get this limo moving again,' Haatakan demanded, moving toward the car door. But one of the Provists thrust a strong arm in front to keep her from passing.

'All right,' Haatakan said, turning away from the car to face them. 'What do you want?'

A buzzing datapad broke the uncomfortable silence.

The lead Provist withdrew the device from her coat, holding it to her ear.

Then she extended it toward Haatakan.

'It's for you,' the Provist growled.

The driving sleet storm was worsening, stinging her exposed face and hands. Reluctantly, Haatakan took the device. It was Jaan Omura, Chairperson of the Kaalakiota Board of Directors.

'Good day!' Jaan asked cheerfully. 'Is this a bad time?'

Haatakan glanced at the lead Provist, who shook her head imperceptibly.

'Not at all,' she muttered. 'What can I do for you?'

'Well, I'm the bearer of good and bad news,' Jaan said. 'The bad news is that we've voted unanimously to grant emergency powers of Kaalakiota's operations to Tibus Heth, including those of our subsidiaries. You'll have to step down from your post as soon as possible – voluntarily, of course.'

Haatakan was twice as vexed as before. 'You can't do that without shareholder approval,' she snapped. 'You'll have to float that proposal in a proxy—'

'We know how the process works,' Jaan interrupted. 'But we also understand the distinction between processes that were appropriate for different times – times certainly less extenuating than what we face now. Malkalen has compelled us to reevaluate what's best for this corporation, within the greater context of what's best for the Caldari State.'

'Naturally,' Haatakan said dryly. 'Of course, the simplest explanation for your rationale is that you've been brainwashed by Tibus Heth and the legion of misfits touting him as the salvation to human suffering.'

Jaan spoke solemnly.

'I'm very sorry to hear you say that, Haatakan. The

good news I was about to tell you is that we were ready to vote on whether or not to keep you with the company in a lesser role. But after hearing your biased opinions, coupled with the fact that the entire board is listening, I believe you may have jeopardized your chances for a favorable resolution.'

Haatakan knew what was happening; she understood that her power was lost the moment that Federation Nyx slammed into Ishukone's headquarters. Only she never fully acknowledged it until now, when the new reality was thrust upon her. Yet she still remained composed.

'I see; so then we've established that you've *all* lost your minds,' she hissed through chattering teeth. 'Mr. Heth's self-righteous declarations have won your hearts. How inspiring. Really, what chance did I stand for "favorable" resolution in light of such rampant idiocy?'

'You're making this easy for us,' Jaan said matter-of-factly. 'But despite your arrogance, we think it's only fair to leave at least one option with you. My associate will explain what that is. I look forward to hearing your decision . . . or not at all.'

The communication ended, and the limousine's door opened.

'You look cold, Ms. Oiritsuu,' the lead Provist said. 'Won't you please step inside?'

Haatakan hurriedly complied, rubbing her hands together and savoring the vehicle's interior warmth. The Provist took a seat across from her.

'Tell me something,' she started, unbuttoning her trench coat. 'Why do you use an armed convoy to take you to your palace? Is it your ego? Or is it that you're aware of just how loathed you really are?'

Haatakan said nothing, glaring at the sharp features of

this Provist's face and memorizing every feature. *Someday*, she thought, *I'm going to kill you.*

'Let me tell you about this road you're on,' the Provist said, taking her leather gloves off. 'In one direction, you'll find relative peace and comfort . . .'

The Provist reached into her coat, causing Haatakan to instinctively flinch backward in her seat. But instead of a gun, she pulled out a bundle of paper instead.

'In the other direction,' the Provist continued, unfurling the documents. 'The road leads back to the misery you created. We'll put you back on the streets that you were supposed to nurture, maybe introduce you to the workers you forced to live in shanties, so that you might appreciate the full extent of your legacy as the State's most powerful CEO.'

Leaning forward, the Provist placed the papers next to Haatakan, who gave them an expressionless glance.

'What's this?' she asked.

The Provist leaned back, folding her hands on her lap.

'Your single option. By signing those documents, you are confirming your resignation from Kaalakiota, and transferring the bulk of your . . . considerable . . . possessions to the Caldari State. We'll make sure that your charity gets the attention it deserves – consider it our way of casting your tarnished reputation in a positive light. You'll be permitted to keep this land and the palace, plus provisions that should last for the duration of your exile.'

'Duration?' Haatakan asked.

'Meaning, the rest of your life,' the Provist said. 'You can never leave these grounds again.'

Haatakan Oiritsuu was a strong woman, and remained defiant even when on the brink of losing everything.

'And if I refuse?'

'Well, Ms. Oiritsuu, these woods are vast,' the Provist

said, looking out of the limousine's window. The sound of sleet pounding the vehicle seemed louder than before as she turned her gray eyes back toward her.

'It's very easy to lose your way in them.'

For reasons that would qualify as insane for most people, the challenge of starting over was wildly enticing to Haatakan. She had survived worse things. Only this time, her motivation wasn't money, nor was it a desire to reach the top of the corporate world yet again.

Her charge was to destroy Tibus Heth. She would make him regret not killing her now – assuming she lived through the rest of this day.

The Provist extended a pen toward her, and Haatakan took it boldly.

'The Caldari people know what's best for them,' the former CEO said, signing away control of half the State's industrial base to Tibus Heth. She knew that with Kaalakiota in his grip, it was just a matter of time before the other mega-corporations followed.

'If this is what they truly want . . . then who am I to dispute that?'

THERE WAS NO corpse to bury, no remains to cremate; not even the possibility that the scattered dust surrounding the station could have once been the body of Otro Gariushi. Officially a recovery operation, search teams continued to scour the disaster site aboard Ishukone Headquarters, unable to find any trace of the reception area where Otro was last believed to have been standing at the time of impact.

Lost in the chaos was the fact that it was not just Caldari civilians alone that Admiral Noir had murdered. In addition to killing his own crew and the entire Federation delegation, not the least of which included his nation's economic minister, he had wiped out the starship crews using the station as temporary housing between deployments. For this reason, the casualty figures were much, much worse than originally feared.

The official count placed the number of confirmed dead at approximately 385,000 people; most of these victims were permanent residents who perished immediately from the collision and nuclear blasts that followed. But more than 600,000 remained missing, of which a third were anonymous crews of all races who were unintentionally placed in harm's way by the ship captains and capsuleers who used the station's hangar facilities. Of the mere 5,000 who had miraculously survived, none were unscathed; their horrific trauma injuries ranged from pulverized bones to radiation burns and its accompanying sickness. Malkalen was an unmitigated catastrophe of biblical proportions; if Noir's intent was to amass a body count greater than what terrorists had accomplished at Nouvelle Rouvenor decades earlier, then he had succeeded.

The Federation's passionate insistence that Noir's actions were just as unexpected to them as to the rest of New Eden was dismissed by Caldari officials, reflecting the sentiment of the people they represented. President Foiritan's pleas for calm and restraint until the facts could be sorted fuelled the conspiracy theory that his personal selection of Admiral Noir was a calculated decision made with full awareness of his deep rooted hate for the Caldari State. The more adamant his denouncements of the event were, the more convinced sceptics were that the Gallentean president secretly endorsed Noir's hideous actions.

The station itself, deformed but intact, finally had auxiliary power restored by engineers as repair MTACs and drones continued their work within the mountain-sized cavities carved out by the destruction, giving it a ghostly appearance in the greenish hue of Malkalen space. This live scene was the backdrop for Tibus Heth as he stood before a broadcast audience of billions, now about to make a live national address to the Caldari State for the first time since the disaster occurred.

Once again, he held New Eden captive with his presence; he appeared solemn, as if his heart was heavy with loss.

'Friends . . . patriots . . . to all Caldarians . . . please join me for a moment of silence in honor of all those whose lives were taken in Malkalen, and especially for the loss of a true Caldari hero: Otro Gariushi.'

Alone at the podium, Tibus Heth bowed his head, while before him thousands of Provists stood in sectioned formations, each of their heads bowed in reverence. Caldari State regalia was everywhere, arranged perfectly in banners, pendants, and fanions. For a full sixty seconds, the nation ceased all activity; from the financial markets to the factories, there was not a single soul who dared to make a sound.

Then Tibus Heth looked up with fire in his eyes.

'Rarely in the course of history has a civilization so blatantly abused the tenets of human decency. What should have been an occasion for celebration has instead become an atrocity of such profound evil that it defies comprehension. Never before have I known such pain; never before have I been pushed to the very limits of what I can stand; of what my heart can bear as I grieve for all those who were murdered right before my eyes, no less by those who came here in the name of peace, using an olive branch to conceal the blade of a dagger.

'But now my patriots, it is time for us to stand up, take this knife from our back, and point it in the direction from whence it came. Haatakan Oiritsuu has graciously stepped down as Chief Executive Officer, and the Kaalakiota board has appointed me as the corporation's acting director. Along with our comrades from Ytiri, we have united to form a brotherhood of Provists – those who are devoted to the rebuilding of our great nation, to restoring Caldari pre-eminence in New Eden, to protecting our borders from Federation treachery, and strengthening our culture in the image of our ancestor's spirit.

'As part of the Provist vow to this State, I am realigning the resources of our nation to address the isolation we face in the wake of this barbaric attack. We will build ships, and we will train crews to fly them. We will educate engineers and scientists, and we will use their innovations to build the technology we need to outsmart the enemy. We will man assembly lines and factories; there will be no idle hands among us. We will work in unison as one nation, just as our ancestors before us. We will persevere in the face of evil, and we will never again make the same mistakes twice.

'Brothers and sisters, we have failed to understand that Gallentean treachery is without bounds; it is an endless cycle of deceit, and hundreds of thousands of Caldari souls are dead because of it. There are enemies within our midst, and I will *not* allow Malkalen to happen again! By virtue of the emergency powers vested in me by the Caldari people, all Gallentean expatriates living within the boundaries of this State are hereby considered enemies of Caldari. As a security precaution, they will be quarantined and held for questioning until their innocence is proven. I implore all those of Gallentean descent to comply peacefully with the Provists, who are executing these orders by my decree. Those who do not resist will be treated well, and I urge you to pacify those who do – for their sake and yours.

'To you mighty Caldarians, I say this: we will rise from

these ashes! You are all part of a greater purpose; you are all part of a single Caldari spirit. Let us bury our dead and honor their memory by returning to the work that must now be done. Perform your role with passion and urgency; we know not when or where the enemy will strike next. In the name of all those who were taken from us, in the name of Otro Gariushi, and in the name of the Caldari State, the restoration of our national greatness begins now!'

As the audience erupted into uproarious applause and cheers, Tibus stood proud, admiring the brigades of uniformed men and women gazing upon him with hope and adulation, seeing him as the leader who was destined to take them to greatness.

A rising crescendo of delirious praise reverberated across the State, while Heth's Provists began their sanctioned mission to completely remove Gallenteans from Caldari space by any means necessary.

But on Caldari Prime, it was the Gallenteans – enraged by Heth's words – who sought the eradication of native Caldarians. Smoke began to rise over the planet's cities as fierce, merciless rioting began to rip the civilization there apart.

PART IV

Event Horizon

48

Lord Aulus Gord hurtled through space within the confines of a pod capsule, the miniscule command craft that was once the heart of a mighty battlecruiser; it seemed as though an eternity had passed since its majestic hull was reduced to slag by the Bhaalgorn's cannons. Sustained by the neuro-embryonic fluid of his pod, Aulus roamed the cosmos, taking every precaution to avoid the patrols of warlords and faction pirates who claimed sovereignty to these forbidden stars.

With his clones destroyed and no safe port of harbor to return to, he wandered helplessly from system to system. He had received no instructions from Lord Victor, nor could he risk contacting him for fear of jeopardizing his life – if he was even still alive. Years ago both men swore to Falek Grange that to the end, they would remain devoted allies to his cause. If it was true that Chamberlain Karsoth – the most powerful man in Amarr – was indeed hunting them, then it was all just a matter of time before they paid the ultimate price for their loyalty.

The pod would keep him alive for months, perhaps even

years. But Aulus knew that one way or the other, this craft would be his tomb.

Too proud a man to feel sorry for himself, he instead marvelled at the hopelessness of his fate. Here he was, one of mankind's elite warriors, an 'immortal' trapped inside the very device which made him so, damned to roam the depths of space while all that separated him from the icy void was a few dozen centimeters of nanomorphic alloy. Appreciative of the irony, he prepared for his fate with pride and calm, believing that his memory was worthy of respect and honor to those who mattered most to him.

Lord Aulus Gord, the Paladin warrior, whose strength was as great as the stars even in the face of death, became completely undone at the sound of a woman's whisper directly into his submerged ear:

Go to New Eden, Jamyl Sarum instructed him. *Marcus Jror awaits you there.*

Impossible, Aulus thought. *A figment of a deranged imagination, a psychosis induced by the circumstances and perfectly explainable within the bounds of science—*

Her Majesty spoke to him again:

Lord Falek is alive, and Victor will bring him to me. You are a loyal servant, Aulus. Your devotion will be rewarded.

Aulus had never met Jamyl Sarum; he only worshiped the legend of who she was, before and after her death at the Succession Trials. But he was certain that he had just encountered the divine, and set his course for the New Eden System with resurrected purpose.

Genesis Region – EVE Constellation
The New Eden System – 3.1 Light Years from Point Genesis
Sovereignty of the Amarr Empire

Marcus Jror was alarmed that the news arrived by conventional means, and not telepathically – by far the most sinister ability that she had acquired since awakening.

So Aulus Gord is coming, he thought. *Why is she sending him here . . . for his safety, or her own?*

He turned his gaze toward the pulsing white glow outside. The outer boundary of the EVE gate – *the collapsed natural wormhole that was the birth of us all* – was more than three light years away, and yet it filled most of the visible void from his platform aboard the *Significance.* To his back was New Eden's sun, a lonely Type-K2 V star, a nondescript point of light on a cloak of darkness. Beside the sole planet which orbited that sun, this entire region of space was strangely devoid of celestial objects, as if the EVE gate forbade the existence of all else in her presence.

Perhaps the gate limits Sarum's power, he mused. The scientist in him craved to learn the truth, and there was only one dangerous way to test his hypothesis.

'*Your father was a wretched disgrace, and your God is dead to me!*' he bellowed, bracing himself for a response. Hearing none, he blasphemed Jamyl Sarum and the Faith in a frenzied, frothing tirade that prompted the ship's medical AI to question his sanity. Marcus paused again, waiting for threats of damnation to whisper in his ear.

But there was only silence.

It wasn't complete proof, he knew. Death could be awaiting his return, but his instincts – which had yet to fail him – told him that her paranormal abilities were limited here—

Limited, no doubt, by the presence of EVE.

Bristling with salvage equipment and deep-space scanning arrays, the *Significance* was the only ship of its kind in the Amarr military. At more than twice the cost of a carrier, it was a 'cross-capsule variant' starship: although captained by a pod pilot, the ship was equipped with an internal pod gantry, allowing the pilot to be extracted and leaving him free to roam about its structure.

Despite being nearly a kilometer in length, the research vessel had a crew of exactly one – Marcus – who was assisted by drones and the ship's AI. Not a fighting ship by any means, she was constructed for the explicit purpose of locating and recovering Terran equipment. Every system and device onboard the *Significance* was a state-of-the-art innovation in starship technology; she could travel farther, faster, and more efficiently than any other ship in New Eden; she could pinpoint the location of every ship around her for thousands of AUs; and it was almost impossible to approach her undetected.

Until the construction of this ship – a project funded by Jamyl Sarum before her death, run by Falek Grange, and executed by Marcus in complete secrecy – hunting for relics of the Old World was all but impossible. Knowledge that a place called 'Terra' ever existed, or that the origin of New Eden's trillions of inhabitants came from worlds on the other side of EVE, was considered legend or fable by many. The governments of nation states were content to keep it that way, perhaps because the truth was too painful for humankind to accept.

Far beyond the range of any sensors in Empire space, the *Significance* was closer to the collapsed wormhole's singularity – known as 'Point Genesis' – than any capsuleer had ever travelled before. At last, the fruits of decades of research and massive sums of money were reaped: intact samples of Terran artifacts were floating just 100 meters in front of where Marcus was standing.

But it was neither technology, nor money, nor even science as Marcus understood it which had finally brought the *Significance* to this exact spot in the universe. It was the word of Jamyl Sarum – or, he thought, *the word of something that purports to be her*, which had led him here.

Marcus was staring at Point Genesis when the ship's sensors detected the helpless pod of Aulus Gord enter the New Eden system.

I don't believe in miracles, Marcus thought, de-cloaking the *Significance* and sending the commander location coordinates. *I hope for Jamyl's sake that Aulus Gord doesn't either.*

IT TOOK NEARLY twenty hours for the pod to reach the *Significance*.

'Commander Gord,' Marcus said, snapping a quick salute. 'Welcome aboard. It doesn't surprise me at all that you survived.'

'So did Victor,' Aulus replied, soaking wet from the pod fluid. He looked delirious, as if beholding an oasis following months in a desert. 'And Falek Grange as well!'

Marcus was cautious. *This man thinks he has seen the Light.*

'He did? How do you know?'

Aulus turned his eyes toward the heavens. 'Her Majesty told me,' he said, muttering a prayer beneath his trembling lips. '*Jamyl Sarum* told me! Do you know what this means?'

'I know of Sarum's awakening,' Marcus said. 'Tell me something . . . what did Victor say of her?'

The commander's eyes were crazed. 'That she was *resurrected* . . . that our faith was well placed . . . that she is now truly divine!'

'I see,' Marcus said, taking slow steps toward the deranged man. 'She spoke to you, didn't she . . . whispered into your ear?'

Aulus swallowed and turned pale, his eyes darting everywhere as if searching for spirits.

'You fear that she can hear you now?' Marcus pressed.

'Don't speak that way!' Aulus said, feigning strength.
'Don't test her!'

'She can't hear us,' Marcus said. 'Not from here . . .'
He pointed toward EVE.

'We're damned for speaking of this,' Aulus panicked.
'You should take care with her name!'

'Jamyl Sarum depends on us as much as we're counting
on her,' Marcus said. 'She needs something that's here, and
this ship is the only means she has to recover it.'

'Blasphemy!' Aulus cried. 'You're going to get us both
killed! Even if what you're saying is true, she can read our
souls! Our faith must be pure!'

Marcus lost his patience.

'Don't you *ever* question my faith!' he bellowed. 'I believe in her more than you'll ever know. The Amarr throne
belongs to her, and I'm willing to die for my conviction to
that belief. But . . . I'm not convinced that the woman who
spoke to you is the Jamyl Sarum that we remember.'

Aulus was trembling; he appeared lost and angry. 'You
are an unbeliever,' he stammered, clenching his fists. 'I
should strike you down where you stand . . .'

But Marcus snapped his arm forward, striking him in the
face with the back of his hand. Security drones quickly
moved forward to prevent Aulus from retaliating.

'You swore an oath to protect her!' Marcus seethed. 'That
means you *must* ask the difficult questions! How could she
have powers now where there were none before?'

'Divinity!' Aulus screamed, even as drones pointed
weapons at the man's chest. 'Miracles! The Faith that we
cherish!'

'Commander, I am a *scientist!* She kept me at her side

for that reason! I have an obligation to question that which I don't understand!'

Marcus stepped in between the drones.

'Do you know what happened to her?' he asked, staring intently at the commander's eyes. 'I was there, Aulus . . . right at Falek's side when it happened. I remember every detail . . . When her ship self-destructed, everything went precisely according to plan. Her toxin injection was painless; the transneural scan, flawless; the transmission of brain state data, *perfect* . . . she should have awakened in her clone immediately, as any other capsuleer would have.

'But when the data arrived, the cortex constructors didn't begin uploading information to her clone. Instead, they paused, as if unsure of the data they received. We thought the system froze because of some error, but it turns out that . . . it was rewriting itself.'

Aulus took a step back. '*What* was rewriting itself?'

'The code that assimilates brain state information and instructs the cortex constructors what neural pathways to create. The only way to stop it was by shutting the entire array down. We had copies of older state data we could have used to restore her, but . . . we just couldn't rule out that doing so would kill her. It's never been done before, interrupting the reanimation process. It was Falek's decision to let it continue.'

'Marcus, I don't believe you—'

'We knew *exactly* how much data should have come from her pod,' Marcus said, now pacing back and forth. 'Checksum figures always arrive first. And what left her pod just before breach was precisely, to the last bit, accurate to our prediction. But what we received was . . . thousands of times greater . . . volumes of information more than what we expected. We checked, and triple-checked every sequence in the logs . . .'

Marcus drifted off for a moment. 'It's as if the information was tampered with in mid-flight.'

'That's impossible!' Aulus scoffed. 'Subspace is instantaneous; there isn't *time* to intercept data transmissions!'

Marcus stopped in mid-stride to glare at him. 'Time, relative to *what*? Or *whom*?'

'If you're implying the Almighty,' Aulus said, folding his arms. 'Then you're only proving my point that you're blind to the work of God.'

'Oh, faith always explains what man cannot comprehend,' Marcus mocked. 'You know, Aulus, it wasn't just state information that arrived. Keys to unlocking every layer of encryption we have to prevent someone from tampering with the cortex constructors arrived . . . then instructions on how to process the unexpected data – how to actually burn information into parts of the brain that we've never touched before!

'For three years Falek and I stood by helplessly as this machine began changing her brain in ways we never thought possible. It was as if we were watching the evolution of our race, but accelerated thousands of times over. You're a rational man, Aulus. Or at least you were. Ask yourself: how could she have possibly acquired the power of telepathy? It shouldn't even exist. And yet with her, it does.'

'How many times do I have to say it,' Aulus said. 'Some things are better left to faith!'

'My devotion to her forbids me from accepting that!' Marcus erupted. 'That's precisely how evil takes root in this universe, can't you see that? When we stop asking questions, we begin to destroy ourselves!'

Aulus refused to yield the high ground. 'But there will always be mysteries that we can never understand!'

'She is not what she used to be!' Marcus shouted. 'You

haven't witnessed her spells, nor heard when she speaks in tongues, how she knows things that she can't possibly know . . . personal things, painful things, memories you wish you could abandon—'

'It's called divinity!' Aulus shouted. 'Accept it!'

'Not when she uses that power against you!' Marcus countered. 'The God I believe in, the God that our Faith proclaims does *not* do such things! She is manipulative, arrogant, and deceitful in that form . . . she has the strength of ten men and the anger to use it for destructive purpose! We didn't do that to her! And I am determined to find out what did!'

'Marcus, part of your faith is finding the courage to acknowledge when science reaches its end!' Aulus said, pacing as he spoke. 'Listen to your heart; what has happened to her is beyond thought, well outside the capacity of our pathetic minds to comprehend. This is a miracle, and you should accept it as such!'

The scientist glared at him with searing intensity.

'You're wrong, Aulus. If anything, her change inspired me to believe with absolute certainty that we are nowhere near the "end of science." The Jamyl Sarum that I know still lives – you should hear her cry out for Falek, her pleas for him to be at her side. She's begging for help, and to be rid of this thing that's invaded her. That doesn't sound like divinity to me, and I won't leave it to faith to find out!'

A drone's voice spoke:

'Captain, confidence scanning algorithms are complete. Targeted artifacts are weapon components. The equipment is damaged, but intact. We can reverse-engineer it. Proceed with recovery operations?'

'Weapons . . .' Marcus breathed, turning briskly for the bridge. 'Yes, as quickly as you can.'

'What recovery operation?' Aulus asked.

'More *divinity* at work,' Marcus mocked. 'Or more precisely, Terran artifacts – the technologies we lost during the Dark Ages. The new Jamyl Sarum directed me to this exact spot in a search grid more than six light years across.' Marcus shook his head. 'Those—' he pointed toward the dark silhouette of an unfamiliar starship hulk on the ship's main view-finder '—are the remnants of Terran freighters.'

Aulus blinked his eyes at the wreck, trying to grasp that he was beholding equipment built more than thirty thousand years ago. He could see scavenger drones operating nearby, carefully removing a modular shipping container from the mainline of the freighter wreck. Dozens of other tumbling wrecks were nearby.

'We're close to Point Genesis,' Marcus said. 'Yet this wreckage is moving away from it, on a trajectory that aligns directly with its center. Do you know what that means?'

'That it came from there,' Aulus answered. 'Somehow.'

Marcus frowned. 'We don't know if it came through before, during, or after EVE collapsed. There are hidden wreckages of Terran origin scattered everywhere here, and most of them are invisible – cloaked by the Jovians, as it turns out. They went to great lengths to keep us from finding it, yet they made no attempt to stop me after I discovered these.'

'Jovians?' Aulus asked. 'Stopping you from finding what, exactly?'

'Components that I suspect are for constructing a starship weapon – something that cannot be defended against, not with New Eden technology. It's fuelled by a rare mineral that we call isogen-5, and we *think* it can only be found near blue stars. The material is impossibly unstable to work with, but we've recovered samples from debris fields surrounding EVE – all inside specialized canisters constructed by Terrans.'

'Why did she send you for this weapon?'

'Why else, Aulus, but to be the wrath of God when she returns to claim her Empire?'

49

Delve Region – D5-S0W Constellation
System T-IPZB

Vince was haunted by the same nightmare again: the bulkhead disappeared just meters from where he was standing, and the instant pressure differential siphoned the air out of his lungs in a suffocating blast. A crewmember – he couldn't tell which one – was thrown into the void as he himself tumbled toward the jagged gash in the ship's hull, gasping for air and trying to grab hold of something, anything, to keep him away from a cruel, savage death outside . . .

He awakened to the sound of his own scream, drenched in sweat, clutching the sides of his own bunk so hard that the dry skin on his knuckles was splitting apart; small droplets of blood coursed between the crevices of his fingers. Sitting up too quickly, Vince felt a wave of nausea overtake him as the room lagged behind his vision; he hunched over and sprayed vomit onto the floor.

Close to the limits of his sanity, Vince struggled to get his bearings as the effects of cynosis began to dissipate. The *Retford* had just completed its third and final hyperspace jump before reaching the acceleration gate; as soon as Jonas and Téa awakened – and recovered from symptoms they had to be enduring by now – the *Retford* would go through to face whatever horrors awaited them on the other side.

Burying his head in his hands, Vince fought against the desperation threatening to tear him apart. The stink of bile and sweat was so putrid that he thought he might throw up again; he ran his trembling fingers through his hair, pulling it so hard that his scalp began to stretch. He hated the *Retford* and despised its crew; as protective as he was of his own sister, she had sided with Jonas too many times, and his patience with her was exhausted.

The assassin's datapad, still resting on his workbench, snapped him out of his craze. Vince no longer lived for the hope of stepping off the *Retford* alive; he had accepted that was impossible now. He lived only to expose this Amarrian capsuleer – 'Marius', or whatever he called himself – for the monster that he *had* to be, just to make Jonas regret his arrogance before he died as well.

Slumping over the inert device, he tried to pry open its cover using his hands. When it wouldn't move, he wedged a micro-spanner between the seams as a fulcrum, bolted the device onto the bench with a clamp, and smashed down on the makeshift lever. The cover flew off . . .

. . . and a small explosive charge popped out, falling to the floor and coming to rest between his legs. He'd seen them before during his corporate days: a paper-thin wafer of explosives used near data storage devices to destroy the contents should they fall into the wrong hands.

By pure luck, this one didn't detonate. Perhaps it was defective; more likely was that it had been disabled when Vince had beaten the life out of its owner. Kicking it aside, he removed the device's battery and installed a power cable of his own. Then he reached for the drug tin; the assassin's finger was mottled gray and ripe with decomposition.

Removing the digit, Vince brushed off the dried blood from the tip and pressed it against the screen.

The datapad sprang to life immediately.

Vince began scouring through its files, skimming past instructions on how to perform Covenant rituals on victims; past technical specifications of Blood Raider scout ships; and then found instructions from a colonel instructing 'Kasha' – the apparent name of the woman who tried to kill him – to 'seek and destroy Lord Falek Grange of the Theology Council.'

Theology Council?

The immediate recognition made his blood pressure rise.

'Lord' Falek Grange?

He swore that he remembered hearing that name before.

There were recorded audio conversations stored on the device; he played the most recent one first. He recognized the voice of the assassin:

'. . . Falek Grange is here somewhere, I'm certain.'

So that's where I heard it.

Inspired, Vince scoured the device for anything else he could learn about the man, but there was nothing except for a physical description, a list of known acquaintances, and personal habits. He instructed the datapad to retrieve the man's biographical history.

A subspace connection is required for NEOCOM lookup, it reported.

Vince set the device down and ripped open the bulkhead panelling of his cabin. A cable hub with open ports connecting to the *Retford*'s comm masts was inside.

MARIUS FELT SOMETHING change with the *Retford*. Placing a hand on the bulkhead beside his bunk, he 'listened' to what the ship's hull was telling his instincts. It wasn't as powerful as when he sensed the engine problems before; this was much more subtle.

But something had just changed. Of that, he was certain.

LORD VICTOR COULDN'T believe what his own NEO-COM was telling him.

The *Retford* had just broadcast its presence to every capsuleer in the system, appearing on the local comm channel and giving every nearby starship and rogue drone a strong signal to track. Still orbiting the alien station, Victor could detect more Covenant warships entering the system, no doubt alerted by the hundreds already hunting the *Retford* and reinforcing the blockades at all the stargates.

He flailed a clenched fist forward within his pod of his bomber, wishing that it would strike something.

What the hell are they doing?

FIGHTING THROUGH HIS own cynosis-induced haze, Jonas was mumbling something about a lap dance when he felt a slap to his temple.

'We made it,' Téa said nervously. 'Look.'

Shaking his head to rid himself of the dizziness, he squinted at the forward view. An acceleration gate was shimmering against the void, less than twenty kilometers away.

'Is everyone else up?' he grunted, shifting his frame in the captain's chair.

'Who cares?' Téa said, scanning her instruments with a scowl. 'Let's just get this over with.'

Jonas raised an eyebrow. 'Easy . . . everyone needs to be alert when we go through. Go check up on everyone—'

'Just use the damn intercom and ask them yourself,'

she said angrily. 'What difference does it make if they're awake? Let them sleep through it, so they don't have to see what kills them.'

'Hey!' Jonas snapped, but quickly calmed himself. 'We can get through this. Don't think about the outcome, just focus on your job.'

'Save the inspirational bullshit for someone else,' she muttered, unbuckling her straps as she prepared to leave the bridge. 'I think it's safe to say that we've all heard enough of it—'

His hand darted forward and clamped onto her wrist.

'Sit down,' he growled. 'And listen carefully.'

She did so reluctantly, with nothing but hatred in her eyes.

'Do you know what the key to survival is? Not just here, in this shit predicament we're in, but in general?'

'Enlighten me.'

'Risk,' he said, shaking a fist at her. 'You have to take a risk! That's the only way to improve your life. You and Vince accuse me of taking advantage of your past, but guess what: I'm an accomplice. An accessory to murder. I'm sheltering fugitives of the Caldari State. I'm just as fucked as the both of you.'

'Oh, cry me a river, Jonas!' she exclaimed, rolling her eyes in disgust and yanking her arm free. 'Trying to turn this around, you make me so *sick* to my stomach!'

Jonas held his gaze, unmoved by her outburst.

'You can look at this one of two ways: either I took you both onboard because – God forbid – I genuinely *cared* about you guys and wanted to help, *or*, our interests were aligned. You needed to escape, I needed a crew, and here we all are – still alive, and not wearing a null crown in prison waiting to be executed. We all took a risk, and we're all still breathing because of it!'

Téa was furious. 'So that gives you the right to risk our lives with complete abandon, to chase whatever pipe dreams you see fit at our expense?'

'We did what was necessary to get by—'

'*Not "we", you!*' she shouted. '*You* took that capsuleer aboard despite our protests against it! Oh, you're a magnificent captain, all right. It wasn't enough to just be wanted for murder, now we're human traffickers as well. *Great* play, Skipper. Thanks for gambling away our humanity as well!'

Again, Jonas was defiant.

'That capsuleer took his own risks and lost. Humanity's got nothing to do with it. This is nature, Téa. It's a dog eat dog universe, and we have to fight for our scraps. Whether he's killed or saved thousands of people doesn't matter worth a damn. The fact is, he'd be dead for sure if we hadn't picked him up. But instead of doing it for "humanity", I did it for money. For *our* survival.'

'Go to hell,' she snapped, standing up. But Jonas grabbed her wrist again and pulled her back into the seat.

'I want us all to have a better life,' he said. 'I want us to not have to worry about money. I want us to not have to run anymore. Now I have no idea what's waiting for us on the other side of that gate, but whatever it is, it's not going to fucking care if we like each other or not. Understand? *If we don't work together, we are going to die for sure.* Can you at least comprehend that?'

She turned toward him.

'You're a strong woman,' he continued. 'You have to be because *we* need you to be, to get through this alive. Now please . . . go check on the others. When you come back, I'll have the ship right on top of that acceleration gate for you.'

They stared at each other for a few moments, and then Téa left the bridge without saying a word.

Genesis Region – EVE Constellation
The New Eden System: 3.1 Light Years from Point Genesis

Marcus, struggling to suppress his exhilaration, reported his success to Jamyl Sarum through a keyed subspace transmission. His message read:

Terran weapons have been recovered and reverse-engineering processes are underway. What are your orders?

'How long will it take?' Aulus asked, peering over his shoulder as drones hovered nearby. 'Do you think you can build it?'

'There are only so many ways these components can be manufactured,' Marcus said. 'Assuming they were fabricated using engineering methods we've already seen, we could have one built within hours.'

'Hours?' Aulus was astonished. 'That soon?'

'This is all the result of Falek Grange's efforts,' Marcus said, his eyes shimmering with the output data of the reverse-engineering algorithms. 'The man loved science as much as I; he gave me enough resources to pursue this for decades if necessary.' Deep within the hull of the *Significance*, arrays of scanning equipment and nanobots were scouring, penetrating, and exploring the device, feeding petabytes of information to powerful computers as it discovered how the component worked. 'We've been productive with the time and money, all in preparation for this moment . . . and what is to come.'

Aulus was beaming. 'All for Her Majesty's glory . . .'

'Yes,' Marcus muttered, struggling to hide his disgust for Aulus's piety. 'You know, Falek loved her like a daughter – and perhaps even more. As for Jamyl, well . . . let's just say that the affection was . . . *reciprocated*.'

Aulus turned crimson. 'Whatever it is that you're implying, Marcus, you need to hold your tongue. These matters—'

Whirling around to face him, Marcus interrupted '— are matters that you need to know, for your own sake. Jamyl Sarum is still human, Aulus, and don't you forget that!'

A comm link's chime interrupted the exchange; a message from Her Majesty had arrived.

Return to the Matriarch Citadel as quickly as you can. The life of Falek Grange depends on it.

Marius knew that he was staring at something that even his old self wouldn't have recognized. The acceleration gate that the *Retford* was approaching was unfamiliar; his pre-programmed knowledge of these structures was of no help in determining the gate's origins. Mesmerized by its alien design, he had this strange feeling that he was nearing something sacred.

'So what is it?' Téa said from behind him. 'What's on the other side of that?'

'I don't know,' he answered, keeping his eyes fixated on the gate. 'To be perfectly honest, I don't think that New Eden technology constructed it.'

'Great,' Téa muttered from the doorway. 'Still think we should go through?'

'Yes,' Marius answered. 'We don't have any choice.'

Vince suddenly appeared in the doorway; Téa put her hand across to keep him from entering.

'Stop,' she said. 'Don't be a pain in the ass. We have to get to our stations, we're about to go through that thing.'

'I just want a word with him,' Vince said, leaning over her arm. Gear was standing in the hallway with a frown on his face. 'In private.'

'Just fucking say it already,' she snarled.

'Sure,' he said, staring at Marius with a deranged smile. 'I know who you are, *Falek*.'

50

There will be neither compassion nor mercy;
Nor peace, nor solace
For those who bear witness to these Signs
And still do not believe.
                              —*Book of Reclaiming, 25:10*

Victor had seen enough.

Where God spoke to the whole of Amarr through the Scriptures, right now, at this moment, the Almighty was speaking directly to him alone. Holding his invisible orbit around the alien station, Victor swore that he would become the strongest Paladin in the Empire; the surest sword in God's army among the living; adored by the righteous and feared by the wicked. *For I have witnessed these Signs*, Victor thought, *and I am forever a part of the history that will record the afflictions of Lord Falek Grange and the glorious redemption of his good name in an empire ruled by Jamyl Sarum.* No man would have faith stronger than his; and for Jamyl Sarum, she would have no greater servant.

A sudden streak of light made Victor's heart skip a beat; a plasma contrail deposited a tiny ship against the backdrop of the cosmos. The bomber's passive targeting sensors acquired the vessel immediately:

The Retford! *Here, at the ring of fire!*

Heavily damaged, with evidence of makeshift repairs all over its ravaged hull, the craft could have only reached this point by entering the acceleration gate; Victor prayed that they weren't followed. Remaining motionless for a few moments, as if to verify that it was still in one piece, the *Retford* turned – slowly, like the crippled ship she was – toward the station.

Falek Grange was right there, he thought, willing his bomber to follow them. *So tantalizingly close . . . but how to get him off the ship?* There was no way to coerce the crew – however many there were – to release him without jeopardizing his life; and opening fire, even as a warning shot, was out of the question given the fragile condition of the ship. And the rogue drones, once they returned . . .

Patience, Jamyl Sarum whispered to him from across the cosmos. *The time will come . . .*

EXCEPT FOR THEIR shallow breathing, there wasn't a sound to be heard on the *Retford*. Almost everyone onboard was crammed against any viewport they could find, staring through the ship's transparent nanoalloy at the blue-white solar eclipse and the ominous structure beyond.

Jonas broke the silence first.

'All right!' he said approvingly. 'Téa, is anything else out there?'

She was as pale as a ghost, staring with an open jaw at

the spectacle. 'Have . . . you ever seen anything like this before?'

'C'mon Téa, concentrate! Tell me what's out there!' he demanded.

'Nothing,' she muttered, reverting back to her console. 'It's just us . . . and that . . . station.'

'You see? We're going to be all right!' Jonas exclaimed, slapping her thigh. He adjusted the ship's heading, setting a course directly toward the epic structure. 'Scan it to see if there's a hangar or something.'

'Oh, there's a hangar all right,' she said nervously. 'But it's bigger than any I've ever seen, including the corporate shipyards in Caldari space.'

'Does it have power?'

'Yes . . . but not throughout the entire structure.'

'Good enough for me,' he answered, opening up the throttle to gain more speed.

'MARIUS, ARE YOU all right?' Gable asked.

The capsuleer was terrified, gasping as he stared through the galley window; the blue-white beams from the sun's corona were bathing everything inside with an eerie tint. Gear sat beside him with a concerned look on his face.

Marius swallowed before speaking. 'I know this is impossible,' he muttered. 'But . . . I swear I've been here before.'

'It could well be that you once were,' Gable said, placing her fingers on his wrist and frowning. 'But if you're sensing familiarity now, it's not because of any retained memories . . .'

'I think this station is Terran,' he said, quivering sharply.

Gable stiffened. 'Are you sure?'

The station was absolutely massive; a huge chasm filled

the view as the *Retford* moved toward the entrance of what looked like a hangar; an engraving with letters as big as the ship itself spelled out words that Gable could discern:

EUROPA YARDS CONSORTIUM

'Europa Yards?' she muttered. 'I've never heard of them . . .'

'No one has,' Marius said, backing away from the viewport as the hangar loomed even larger. 'We shouldn't be this close . . .'

'Wait . . .' Gable was stunned, feeling a sharp tug on her sleeve. Gear appeared to be demanding an explanation. 'What makes you think that it's Terran?'

'I don't know . . .' He backed into a chair and sat down, breathing even harder. 'Instincts.'

'Well, I hope you're wrong,' she said, turning toward Gear. 'You haven't heard the story of EVE yet?'

The boy emphatically shook his head.

'"EVE" is the name of an ancient wormhole in the New Eden System,' she explained. 'It collapsed thousands of years ago, but not before our ancestors had already gone through. They were trapped here . . . cut off from their origins, a place we think they called "Terra." Whether that was one system or a cluster, nobody can say. Whatever it was, it's someplace unfathomably far from here, perhaps even across the universe. The pioneers stranded here after the collapse nearly perished . . . we wouldn't return to the stars for many millennia, after a long dark age in which we started over, relearning everything that brought us here in the first place.'

The capsuleer's hands were shaking as Gable spoke.

'If Marius is right, then these ruins aren't just ghosts of our past,' she continued, as the boy listened eagerly, mesmerized by the tale. 'You see, EVE is . . . the womb through which humanity was born, and whatever lies on the other side . . . it's who we once were. We're *all* descendants of that time . . . every single one of us.'

She marvelled at the ancient structure, awed by its enormity. 'Apparently, what we've become isn't nearly as great as how we once were.'

Marius suddenly felt a powerful presence within him, as foreign and alien as the station outside.

We shall be great once again, my love, a female voice whispered into his ear. *With you by my side.*

He shrieked, clutching his head so violently that it sent his cane hurling to the floor.

'Marius!' Gable shouted, dropping to his side; Gear appeared ready to panic.

Your trials will be over soon, the voice spoke. *We will rule together, with God as our beacon.*

As if in great pain, Marius clenched his teeth and rose to his feet.

'We have to leave here,' he warned. 'None of us is safe . . . Gear especially! Tell Jonas to warp out!'

'What are you talking about?' Gable asked, grabbing his shoulders. Sedating him was becoming a serious option. 'What do you see?'

Marius lunged for his cane, and began hobbling toward the bridge as fast as he could.

'COME ON, SOME of these have to be working,' Jonas muttered, gently guiding the ship through the colossal hangar. Except for the strobe of the *Retford*'s searchlights, the entirety of the structure was dark; collision lights spaced

every 500 meters along the inner cityscape of walls, platforms, towers, and spires formed a latticework that seemed
to extend into eternity.

'Those gantries were built to accommodate ships much
larger than this,' Téa said, her eyes as wide as saucers. 'Battleships, at least. More likely dreads and carriers. Those
collars are way too big for our hookups.'

'You're so negative all the time,' Jonas mocked, moving
the ship away from the platforms and deeper inside the
structure. 'There have to be storage hangars here, adjacent
to these docks,' he said, pointing. 'Scan these walls for
cavities behind them, there's bound to be equipment here
that we can use—'

'You won't be able to use anything that you find,' Marius breathed, standing in the doorway of the bridge. 'We
should leave this place immediately.'

'Wait, wait, wait,' Jonas said. 'Settle down. We just found
an abandoned station, and there's nothing guarding it. Relax.'

'This station is *Terran*,' Marius warned. 'And there are
dangers here that cannot be seen nor understood!'

'Dangers?' Téa asked. 'What kind of dangers?'

'The kind that can see us before we see them,' Marius
answered.

'Who's "them"?' Jonas asked.

'I don't know, damnit!' Marius exploded. 'The technology that built this place is infinitely more robust than our
own! For the boy's sake especially, we have to go!'

As Jonas and Téa both turned in their seats to face him,
Marius was yanked forcefully backward from the doorway, his cane clanging to a rest on the corridor grating.
Springing out of the captain's chair amid a slew of profanities, Jonas reached the corridor just in time to see the capsuleer being dragged toward the engine room by Vince.

Containment hatch seals descended and locked into place behind him, blocking the frothing Jonas from catching up.

VICTOR WOULD HAVE choked the *Retford* captain with his bare hands if he could.

The salvage frigate had entered the hangar – a catastrophically foolish idea, given its unknown origins and evidence of rogue drone activity nearby. Victor couldn't approach them without giving his presence away, which carried the risk of spooking them into doing something rash that would get someone killed. Stealth technology was defeated by proximity; if the bomber approached within 2,500 meters of any object, the light-bending cloak mechanisms would fail, and his ship would be detectable to anything nearby.

Following them into the hangar, let alone keeping visual contact with the *Retford*, was therefore impossible.

THE VOICE OF Vince was carried throughout the *Retford* by the intercom system.

'Did you guys know we have a "lord" among us?' he started, tying the last knot to bind the capsuleer's hands behind his back. 'I feel so . . . violated, having been so close to royalty all this time without being introduced.'

Falek looked up at his deranged captor. 'Vince . . . the cynosis, it's getting the better of you. You need synaptic modulators to control the—'

The back of Vince's hand cracked across his face, temporarily blinding him with a rush of pain.

'I'd like for everyone to meet . . . *Lord . . . Falek . . . Grange, the Immortal!* Falek Grange, the Amarrian Holder! Falek Grange, the Theology Council Justice!'

Grinning ferociously, Vince was shouting over the

clang of spanners and wrenches onto the hatch as the *Retford* crew tried to get inside.

'Did you know that Lord Falek Grange is the proud owner of more than two *thousand* Minmatar slaves? You hear that, Gear? Two thousand men, women, and children. He once had half of his stock culled – slaughtered like livestock. And why? Because one of them forgot to kneel before the Holy Sign in his own private cathedral. He even had all the bodies vaporized – and I quote – "to fully rid his home of the unclean spectacle." That's right, little champ . . . your hero is an overlord, the worst kind of bastard there is, and he'd kill you without thinking twice about it. But that's not even the best part!'

A line of sparks erupted over the doorway as someone on the other side began cutting through with a blowtorch. But neither man cared; to Vince's delight and Falek's horror, both were transfixed with the truth.

'As if this slave-culling, holy-rolling, lord-skunking motherfucker didn't have enough blood on his hands . . .'

With the line of molten metal and sparks reaching halfway around the hatch, Vince hoisted a spanner over his shoulder and swung it down onto Falek's knee. The capsuleer's scream was excruciating, but Vince kept right on talking.

'Lordy Falek here decided to aim a little higher – so high, in fact, that he became *the* number one public enemy of the Amarr Empire today. I gotta hand it to you, Jonas. You didn't pick up just any pod jockey. You picked up someone charged with attempted murder on – and I just love this – the Amarr Court Chamberlain, the highest official in their entire fucking Empire! What a perfect fit for this boat, right? The more murderers on board, the merrier!'

Vince delivered another bone-crushing blow to the same knee as before. But the mental anguish for Falek was far worse than the explosion of pain in his leg. For every rejection of what Vince was saying, there was an opposite anguish that acknowledged its despicable truth. Regardless of this new life, he was responsible for the actions of his former self – and had to accept the consequences whether he believed he was capable of such atrocities or not.

Do not fear your faith, Falek, the woman's voice whispered. *Embrace it.*

He gnashed his teeth and shut his eyes; whoever this was speaking to him had all the makings of the worst evil that he had ever known – except for perhaps himself.

'Vince,' Falek breathed through short breaths. 'There's only one way you could have found this out about me—'

A crushing punch sent spittle and blood flying out of his mouth.

'No more talking, overlord,' Vince growled.

'NEOCOM broadcasts are system-wide,' Falek warned, spitting. 'You're telling everything out there where we are!'

'Yeah,' Vince said, raising the spanner and taking aim at his head. 'You're not going to have to worry about that anymore . . .'

A shrill, deafening alarm roared through the engine room. As the sparks around the door abruptly stopped, the spanner dropped out of Vince's hand; he knew what the alarm was, and that it couldn't be tripped manually. Scared out of his mind, he ran to the door and began unscrewing the hatch, working at it with as much strength as he had. The sparks suddenly resumed, showering the man in biting sparks; within seconds, the entire frame crashed to the grating.

It was Gear who stood there, wearing a welder's mask that was too big and holding a live cutting torch. He ignored Vince, and ran straight toward the wounded Falek.

Still seated at the bridge, Téa was looking at the reddish glow of a rogue drone's engine contrails, just a few hundred meters in front of her. Her wavering voice rang through the *Retford*'s intercom, drowning out the wailing urgency of the alarm:

'Battle stations, you assholes!'

51

The swarm returned just as Victor made his decision to act.

From 500 kilometers away, the horde of rogue drones resembled a blue aurora; a wispy cloud of effervescent dust rolling through the depths of space. Magnifying the image, Victor saw that their tentacles were laden with a glowing blue crystalline material. They were returning from a harvest of some kind, and the extra mass was slowing them down. But the timing of their return was no coincidence; there was an intruder in their hive, and they intended to dispatch it.

Scanning through the walls of the station, the *Retford* and a single drone were spaced less than a kilometer apart from each other in the cavernous hangar, facing each other down as if about to duel. This was the moment of truth; the final test of faith, and Victor did not hesitate.

Leaving the *Retford*'s fate to God, he turned his ship toward the swarm, accelerating to the highest velocity possible while cloaked. The bomber was armed with a single

AOE (area-of-effect) weapon, and he knew he would have only one chance to use it.

'YOU CAN STILL facc me?' Falek asked incredulously, as Gear cut the bonds loose. 'I've done all these horrible things, and yet you can still—'

Gear leapt in front of him, signing frantically with his hands.

You're not that person anymore, he motioned, heaving a rucksack off his shoulders onto the floor. Pulling out an injector gun, he loaded a drug cylinder into its breach before setting it down again.

This is for your pain. We're really going to need your help to get out of this mess!

Falek winced as the boy placed the gun's nozzle against his neck with one hand. He heard a short, loud *hiss* as painkillers and adrenaline flooded his veins; the burning pain in his smashed knee disappeared instantly, but he was still unable to bend it.

Gear handed his walking cane to him.

This is who you are, he signed, pointing to the engraving. *Marius*.

A rapid succcssion of loud, metallic strikes reverbated throughout the hull, startling both of them.

'What's firing at us?' the capsuleer asked, reaching up with his good hand. As Gear helped him up, he noticed that the engineer's station was abandoned, and that Vince was nowhere to be found.

'WATCH OUT!' TÉA screamed, pointing toward an overpass structure rushing at them from the darkness. Jonas barely reacted in time, pushing *Retford*'s bow down just a few degrees to avoid a collision; cannon rounds streaked past the bridge from behind them, impacting in bright flashes against the hangar walls ahead.

'She's handling like shit,' Jonas swore. Sweat trickled down into his eyes as he wrenched the controls over, alternating his concentration between the radar imagery on the console and the bridge viewport. 'Where the fuck is Vince?'

Another set of strikes followed by a loud bang rattled the hull; red warnings appeared all over the controls.

'That last one hit armor,' Téa muttered. 'Shields are gone, recharge rates are half of what they used to be—'

A much louder shot shook them both in their seats, and the ship suddenly began yawing to one side. Alarm Klaxons filled the bridge with collision warnings as Jonas slammed his hand onto the intercom.

'*Vince!* Where the fuck are you!'

Spiralling toward the hangar surface, Jonas fought desperately to regain control of the *Retford*. Relentless in its pursuit, the rogue drone weaved through the structures, coming at them with startling agility and speed. Téa began to moan; the *Retford*'s graviton compensators couldn't keep up with G-forces induced by the spin. As more cannon fire coruscated around them, Jonas began to sense that the end was near.

But the ship suddenly corrected on its own, its lateral thrusters firing in precise sequences that Jonas realized were being directed from the engine room. Still moving at hundreds of meters per second, the frigate glided away from catastrophe.

'Plasma breach, portside dorsal thruster,' the capsuleer's calm voice reported over the intercom. 'Increasing thrust output on the ventral twin to compensate. Maximum centerline velocity reduced by six percent.'

Téa was panting so hard that Jonas wondered if she was hyperventilating.

'Jonas,' Marius continued. 'Set your heading for the hangar entrance. Hold it straight and level – you can't out-maneuver the drone. We'll buy you as much time as we can.'

'Who's *we*?' Téa asked.

'Vince is symptomatic of acute cynosis,' Marius warned. 'He is a danger to this ship and its crew, and his present whereabouts are unknown.'

They were thrown forward into the restraints as more cannon rounds lanced the hull.

As Jonas steered the bow toward the hangar entrance, the mechanical beast positioned itself between them and freedom. But before he could do anything about it, the *Retford*'s single railgun opened fire, landing a direct hit on the drone and scattering its cannon fire off the mark.

'*Yes!*' Jonas shouted. 'Who's the gunner back there?'

A second salvo erupted from the gun, illuminating the hangar as its white streak slammed into the drone, blasting several of its appendages to bits.

'Gear is,' Marius announced proudly. 'Now, *go!*'

Jonas demanded as much thrust from the *Retford* as she could muster.

VICTOR ESTIMATED THERE were over three hundred drones in the swarm, and that he was right at the fringe of their gun range.

Setting the weapon's flight range to zero, Victor willed the AOE weapon to drop out of the launcher and reverse-thrust until it was completely stopped in space.

Uncloaking, the entire swarm targeted him while he pushed the bomber as fast as its engines would allow, trying to get as far away from the predicted blast radius as possible.

* * *

GABLE UNDERSTOOD HER role in the fight for the *Retford*'s survival.

Stumbling down the corridor, she braced herself against the jolts and bangs as the ship catapulted forward under fire. Seeking her target and finding it, she crouched low, careful to make as little noise as possible, waiting for the right chance to strike.

Vince was waiting to die inside his bunk, curled into a ball on the floor, whimpering in a deranged, hysterical stupor.

Seizing the distraction of another terrifying crash, she lunged forward with an injector gun, driving the nozzle into his back and forcing enough tranquilizers into him to sedate several men at once.

JUST AS THE last section of armor plating was blasted off the *Retford*, the rogue drone, now behind them, exploded in a brilliant fireworks display. Jonas howled in delight; the hangar entrance was less than a kilometer away.

'*Yeeeaaah!*' he screamed, looking over at Téa. 'That's why we fly, baby! *Wooo!*'

'Jonas!' she shouted. 'Look out!'

His eyes returned to the forward view just in time to see a much larger Predator-type drone emerge near the hangar entrance and open fire with its cannons.

THE *RETFORD* WAS hit with such force that it knocked the vessel perpendicular to its trajectory. Engulfed in flames for a moment, the ship's inertia carried it out of the hangar amidst a hail of its own fragments. Three large-bore cannon shells had exploded on or near the aft quadrant of the ship, ripping the engine pylons off completely and venting the capacitor array to space; errant bursts of plasma and sparks leaked through holes in the hull as it tumbled forward.

Without power, propulsion, or capacitor reserves, the *Retford* ceased being a ship; she was instead as worthless as scrap. The Predator quickly caught up and stabilized the vessel with its own tractor beam, eager to strip it down for precious parts and capture any human specimens still alive inside.

Just as the beast's tentacles lashed out at the *Retford*'s hull, a salvo of missiles slammed into its thorax, knocking it away from the wreckage before being blown apart as the warheads exploded.

Reloading the bomber's launchers, Victor maneuvered as close to the *Retford* wreck as he could.

Then he began to pray.

. . . wheeze . . . wheeze . . . wheeze . . .

Weightless, Marius kicked himself free of a tangled web of alloy and cables; he didn't notice the globules of blood emerge from a deep gash in his leg. He could hear the echoes of shouts; Jonas at least was still alive; he could hear a woman's panicked voice as well. But his ears were drawing him toward an awful sound, so terrible that it invoked the greatest dread he had ever known, far greater than any of the horrors experienced on this ship.

. . . wheeze . . . wheeze . . . wheeze . . .

The sound was coming from the direction of the gunnery station.

Pulling himself out of the engine room, he swatted aside debris floating before him, then collided with globules of blood that weren't his own. The temperature had risen sharply, something nearby was extremely hot, and there was a danger of fire.

. . . wheeze . . .

He looked up, and shrieked in horror.

Gear was still buckled into the gunnery chair, which was

now facedown across the hatchway access to the compartment; a tangled mess of metal was pinning the chair in
place. The boy's arms and legs were without movement,
floating free of the straps. His eyes were wide and scared;
his mouth opening and closing in convulsive gasps.

Marius could see that his neck was broken.

Kicking upward to reach him, intense heat met his face
on the way up. Something had already caught fire above
the debris.

He reached out to the boy's hand, cupping it with his
own as an orange flame darted across the compartment.

. . . *wheeze* . . .

Determined to free him, Marius lodged his good leg
into the ladder rung, then reached out with his arm to push
against a flat section of the debris pinning the chair in
place. It was scalding hot; he reflexively pulled away.

Then he took one look at Gear and found all the strength
and desperation he needed.

Screaming, he placed his hand onto the surface and
pushed as hard as he could; even as his flesh sizzled and
burned, he drove with his leg harder and harder until his
blackened palm was without pain.

The debris wouldn't move, and more orange streaks
joined the fiery dance behind it.

. . . *wheeze* . . .

Marius erupted into a fit of bereaving agony, tears swelled
out of his eyes as he pressed his head gently against the
boy's forehead.

'You were all the best of my life . . .' he started to say,
when something latched onto his ankle and pulled him violently away.

'He's gone, let him go!' Jonas shouted, wrapping his
arms around him. 'Abandon ship!'

'No!' Marius screamed, as the fire danced around the

chair, leaping across to the tiny limbs floating beside it. He fought against the grip of Jonas, kicking hard against the bulkhead. 'Let me go! Let me go! I want to stay with him! I want to stay—'

'You can't help him!' Jonas shouted, tightening his grip. 'The ship's gonna explode!'

Marius screamed away the last of his sanity as the fire engulfed Gear.

VICTOR SAW A cargo container jettison from the remnants of the *Retford*.

Without a moment's doubt about its contents, the ship's recovery system had it safely onboard in seconds; he turned his attention back to the attacking drones. He realized that the bomb would detonate further behind the bulk of the swarm than he planned; it was a miscalculation with potentially lethal implications. Opening the ship's thruster to full power, his targeting computer locked up the nearest drone, and he prepared himself for a fight against enormous odds.

A crimson-purple cataclysm blossomed in space; a perfect sphere of nuclear death engulfed half of the swarm. But then, for no reason that Victor could discern at first, the remaining drones – all, he realized, which bore the mysterious blue substance on their appendages – detonated as well, each one obliterated in spectacular blue-white explosions.

As the shockwaves passed harmlessly over his shields, the threat sensor went blank; no hostiles were targeting him any longer. Re-cloaking just as more angry drones emerged from the hangar, he turned the ship away from the station and checked the cargo bay for the first time.

Lord Falek Grange was aboard – badly wounded, but alive. Four Caldarians were with him; two were unconscious.

Victor never doubted that Falek would be inside, and his faith was affirmed for good.

JONAS PRESSED HIS face against the viewport, struggling to catch a glimpse of his beloved *Retford* one last time. She was there, dying slowly; the bridge and galley viewports were both flickering red and orange from the inside. It struck him how fragile the ship looked from here, yet how powerful he felt at her controls. The *Retford* exploded before his eyes, leaving behind a twisted, deformed wreck; it was all that remained of his life's work and ambitions.

'Medical kit,' Gable said, frantically searching the seamless walls of the enclosure. 'Jonas! Help me find a goddamn medical kit!'

A powerful voice spoke from the intercom.

'This is Lord Victor Eliade, the commander of this vessel. Be calm; medical provisions are located *here*—'

Unfolding from the room's walls was a series of containers, each one clearly labelled.

'Food supplements and water supplies are there. It should be enough to sustain you until we reach safety.'

Jonas looked around for a camera, but could find none. Gable frantically grabbed armfuls of medical equipment and brought it to Falek, who was drifting away. Téa was already unconscious, lying at his side and bleeding from wounds to her face and head.

'Thank you for rescuing us,' Jonas said, looking at the ceiling. 'I don't know how we can repay you for this—'

'You saved Lord Falek's life,' Victor said, his heart filled with joy. 'And for that, we are in your debt.'

52

Delve Region – YX-LYK Constellation
System MJXW-P: The Matriarch Citadel

Guided to its berth by harbor tugs, the *Significance*
docked as gantries extended across from the hangar platform, linking the starship with the station. Built to offload
large battleship crews, the airlock corridors seemed oversized for the two men who emerged from the mammoth
research vessel. Aulus walked in a trance, closing his eyes
occasionally and murmuring passages from the Scriptures.
Marcus ignored him, focusing only on the welfare of Jamyl
Sarum and the precious information locked away in the
databanks of the *Significance*.

Neither man was prepared for the reception waiting for
them at the hangar platform.

Jamyl Sarum, dressed in a gown that revealed the full
extent of her robustness, was already at the door's entrance.
At least a dozen armed Paladins were arrayed across the
concourse entrance behind her.

Aulus fell to his knees; Marcus followed suit more deliberately.

'Merciful Lady, I am humbled to be in your presence!'
Aulus said, facing the ground.

'Your Majesty,' Marcus said, bowing his head.

'My faithful servant,' Jamyl said, guiding Aulus to his
feet. 'You have sacrificed everything for me. Rest now, for
you will be one of my captains in the battle for Amarr.'

Aulus was struggling to control his emotions; a single
tear of joy fell down his cheek. Succumbing to her presence, he was hypnotized by her unnatural radiance, which
stirred both spiritual and carnal desires within him.

'Your Majesty,' he said, bowing. She returned his mesmerized gaze with the smile of an angel when he marched past; the Paladin guards performed an honorary salute as he entered the concourse.

Marcus witnessed the exchange and frowned.

'Now *you*,' she hissed, whirling around and snapping her hand around his throat. 'Your schemes have incurred my wrath.'

Marcus *felt* her furor vibrate within his heart, but he remained defiant. 'I serve Jamyl Sarum, not you,' he gasped. 'And my work serves the interests of Amarr, not yours.'

'Your *work* is all that keeps you alive,' she said, releasing her grip. 'Upload your schematics to the industrial complex. When the prototype is complete, it is to be installed on my ship—'

'No!' Marcus shouted, rising to his feet. 'It hasn't been tested yet! Reverse-engineering Terran technology has never been done before—'

He was suddenly struck with an overwhelming desire to kneel; it crashed against his own willpower, leaving him clutching at his temples. Enraged, he fought against this rape of his mind, but a terrible high-pitched wail within his skull tormented his psyche, ceasing only when he dropped to his knees.

'Kneel there until you bleed,' she growled. 'Kneel there until you *suffer*—'

She gasped once; then her eyes bulged as she convulsed with seizure. Marcus felt her mental grip on him release, and lunged forward to brace her. When the guards began charging toward them, she turned and waved them off.

'Stay where you are!' she gasped. 'Not one step further!'

They halted immediately.

'My lady,' Marcus said. She was drenched in sweat, and her face had turned sickly pale. 'Is that you?'

'I don't know anymore,' she gasped. 'Thank God you're here! Marcus, I can see things now, things that I shouldn't be able to at all!'

'I'm going to get to the bottom of this,' he said, looking up at the guards. 'Water! She needs water now!'

'No!' she said, panting. 'Not yet . . . the longer I stay weakened, the longer I have *myself*.'

'But at such cost,' Marcus cursed, suddenly thinking of a parasite. He would return to that thought when circumstances allowed. 'Your Majesty, I have to warn you about this weapon—'

'There's no time to test it,' she said, as slaves moved past the guards with flasks. 'Leave it there!' she ordered. They set them down and scurried away as frightened children would.

'That weapon turns a ship's defenses against itself,' Marcus pleaded. 'Your shields will vaporize your own armor and anything else in its path!'

'Victor and Falek are both trapped in a Blood Raider blockade, and this weapon is the only way we can break them out,' she gasped. 'I have no choice.'

'If it even works at all!' Marcus implored. 'Even I can't say what it's fully capable of! Please, for the sake of the throne, just give me some more time!'

'Marcus, I miss him so much, I . . . I *need* to see him, I *must* find a way to restore him to what he was! That goal is all I share with this beast within me . . .'

'But I only recovered five charges,' Marcus insisted. 'That's not enough to break a blockade!'

'Five will be more than enough,' she said. 'There's

more to that weapon than you know, and Victor discovered where isogen-5 can be harvested.'

'He did?' Marcus's eyes bulged at what she already knew. 'Where?'

'It's in the T-IPZB system,' where he is now, and where you must eventually go.'

'I can't believe it,' Marcus said. 'How can it even possibly be mined?'

'That is what you must discover – how the Terran containment canisters work. Only rogue drones can harvest the material without them, and I don't know what they're using it for. No matter what, this weapon is the key to our success! We cannot take the throne without it! When *she* is distracted, you must travel to that system to begin more research—'

Her sleek, muscular arms were wrapped around his shoulders. 'But first you must return to New Eden as quickly as you can. I can't say why, but . . . I know you'll be safe there—'

Marcus was astonished. 'I can't leave you to this creature's device—'

'This creature wants to hurt you, and I need you to find out what it is before that can happen! You are all I can trust now, Marcus . . . the clues you need must be near the EVE gate!'

'It will be done, my lady,' Marcus breathed. 'Can you control these abilities in your other state?'

'Fighting its influence is exhausting,' she said, beginning to fade, her mouth as dry as cotton. 'Perhaps in time, I will . . . but for now *go*, Marcus. Get away from here. Get far away from me! Learn what you can . . . please . . .'

Marcus waved the slaves over as she slipped back into tremors; she desperately needed water.

By the time she drank the flasks, he was already back

aboard the *Significance*, raising the ship's reactor output in preparation for departure, and wondering if he would ever be able to leave its confines again.

FALEK OPENED HIS eyes and found a familiar sight: Gable frantically working on his battered body, doing what she could to make his miserable existence bearable.

'Don't bother,' he said weakly. 'No painkillers, no comfort . . . just let me die.'

'I can't help it,' she answered, biting her bottom lip. Her hair was matted down from blood and sweat. 'Maybe I'm selfish, but I think I'm doing this just to keep sane.'

'You were right to hate me,' he whispered.

'No, I wasn't,' she said, speaking through tears. 'I couldn't have been more wrong about you, Marius. I am so, so sorry about Gear . . .'

'I could have saved him.' The capsuleer looked away from her, his eyes glazing over. 'But, Vince . . . he took away my leg, and Jonas . . . he took away my arm.'

He turned his eyes back to hers. '*I could have saved him.*'

She saw anger in him for the first time, and found it reassuring. This capsuleer was more of a man than any of the *Retford* crew.

Falek felt a loving calm descend over him; a falsely reassuring aura that he knew came from something else; something sinister; something from his past. There was no compassion in this 'love', or sympathy for his loss.

'What should I do?' he asked, ignoring the aura. 'Vow vengeance? Swear retribution?' He turned his head toward Vince, who lay unconscious besides him. 'Or should I just forgive?'

Gable looked up toward Jonas, who stood against the bulkhead with his arms folded.

'Whichever you decide,' she said, 'I support you.'

* * *

TWELVE APOCALYPSE-CLASS BATTLESHIPS waited outside the Matriarch Citadel, each one piloted by a capsuleer who had spent his entire life in complete isolation from the rest of New Eden. None had ever left the T-IPZB System, or fired a weapon in live combat. Bred from the genes of great warriors present and past, they were raised for a singular purpose: To be the eternal Arch Guardians of Jamyl Sarum whenever she took to the heavens.

These were elite Paladin pilots, sworn upholders of the Faith, beholden only to the resurgence of the true empress and her seat at the center of all Empires.

The thirteenth battleship – an Abaddon – broke the hangar's plane. It was piloted by Her Majesty the Queen, the first voyage since her Divine Resurrection.

History would one day record this moment as the birth of the Reclaiming.

53

Marius awakened from a nightmare of Gear begging him for help.

As the ceiling of the bomber's cargo bay emerged from the horrible dream, he realized that he was alone. *The nightmare was real*, he thought, shutting his eyes in misery. *The* Retford *is gone; and Gear is dead*. With his leg and arm encased in nanosplints, Marius couldn't move without inducing unbearable pain.

Be still, my love, her voice whispered. *You are safe now.*

Whoever she was, she wanted him to forget his ordeals

and instead focus on her warming presence. But Marius wasn't fooled.

Resolved to shut the voice out as best he could, his free hand rested against a bulkhead. This was a pod capsule ship; it was strong, powerful, and well equipped; and in stark contradiction to the *Retford*, functioning perfectly.

'I separated you from the others,' a voice boomed. 'I am Victor, the pilot of this ship. You don't remember me at all, do you?'

'No,' Marius answered. 'The people you separated me from are my friends—'

'They won't be harmed,' Victor said. *At least not by me*, he thought. 'What did they tell you about your past?'

Marius felt the pain in his knee flare up as the memory of Vince's discovery returned.

'That my name is Falek Grange,' he answered weakly. 'That I am Amarrian, that I am a murderer, and that I am guilty of high treason against the Amarr Empire.'

'Lord Falek,' Victor said. 'You are no murderer . . . you are a champion among men, and it strengthens my heart to see you again.'

'You're misguided.' Marius shook his head. 'Any who describe Falek Grange in good terms is a bastard as well.'

'Falek, you've been close to divinity for most of your life! Jamyl Sarum herself seeks to be reunited with you!'

'Is that her name?' Marius asked. 'The one I hear whispering to me? Oh, I can hear your reverence for her in the sound of your voice, and still, that name means absolutely *nothing* to me.'

'She's to become the Empress of Amarr, thanks to *your* efforts. You have no idea of the awe that men have for what you've accomplished!'

'And what is that, exactly? The butchering of women

and children for their lack of reverence? What praise has "Falek Grange" earned for being a traitorous assassin?'

'*You did no such thing!*' Victor shouted. 'The Chamberlain placed a bounty on your head once he learned of your efforts to place Sarum in power, and you'll be loved by Amarr once the truth is known!'

'If the man I used to be is loved,' Marius scoffed, 'then Amarr is as vile to me as my former name.'

'You're mistaken,' Victor said. 'You need only place your faith in the Scriptures—'

'To hell with your religion,' Marius growled. 'I'll stand trial for whatever crimes Falek Grange has committed, but I won't be addressed by that name ever again.'

HE IS FAR worse than I imagined, Victor thought. *And it poses a dilemma for others to decide; here was a man who once stood at the pinnacle of Amarrian glory; there was no greater Paladin than Falek Grange. He was willing to die for the convictions that once defined him, and now, he rejects them. Should he be granted leniency for blaspheming that which is – or was – most sacred to him? Or must he relearn the Faith through other means – even by force, if necessary?*

But to treat this man as a slave . . . he was like a brother to me!

A surge of doubt and compassion passed through him.

This is the paradox of immortality . . . if we treat the living as just future memories – mere passing entities to be cherished only when it suits us – then should we treat each clone as an independent life, discounting the merit of past deeds as irrelevant from one copy to the next?

Victor stared at the battered, helpless carcass lying in his cargo hold.

Only the legendary Falek Grange could beg such ques-

tions. If he were any lesser man, it would be far easier to just hold onto the memory of what he once was.

SENSING THAT HE was more of a prisoner than a rescued passenger, Jonas paced back and forth in front of the boundary that dropped between them and Marius. Vince, fully immobilized in a null crown that Gable placed on him, had just awakened.

'Hey Jonas, did you get your reward?' he taunted. 'Did you win your prize?'

'Go back to sleep,' Jonas muttered. 'You're more useful that way.'

Despite being completely paralyzed from the neck down, Vince unleashed a maniacal laugh. 'Guess what, Joney-boy? You're not the captain of this boat! You're not the captain of *any* boat. You're a fuckin' *zero*, man. You're *nothing*!'

'Guys, *please*,' Gable, who was kneeling beside the unconscious Téa, pleaded.

'Hey Vince – where are you gonna run now?' Jonas sneered. 'You got anyplace to go? Huh? How are you gonna get there? Or did you forget that you're a piss-broke fugitive?'

'You know what, Joney-boy?' Vince giggled. 'You're the biggest pussy I've ever met. Seriously, I should have taken that gun of yours and bashed your head in with it years ago.'

'I wasn't the one crying like a baby back there when it hit the fan!' Jonas shouted. 'If you'd been at your fucking post, we wouldn't be in this jam!'

'*Guys!*' Gable half-yelled, half-whispered. 'For your sister's sake, Vince, shut the fuck up!'

'Take off the null crown,' Vince sneered, through a series of laughs. 'You're worthless without a ship. Now I want to get some. I'm salivating for a shot at the title here, Joney-boy. Take it off! I want a little *pussy*!'

Incensed to the point of madness, Jonas had heard enough. Before Gable could react, he lunged forward, kicking the null crown off Vince's head.

'C'mon, you piece of shit,' Jonas growled, raising his fists.

As Gable rushed forward with an injector gun, Vince jumped to his feet; he parried her attack and pushed her to the floor.

With a deranged grin on his face, Vince charged at Jonas like a stampeding bull. But instead of dodging his charge, Jonas raised his knee as high as he could at the last possible moment before they collided. On contact, he pulled Vince toward him as they both fell backward. With his full body weight crashing upon the knee jammed into his chest, the right side of Vince's ribcage was crushed on impact.

The force of the blow would have left any other man gasping for air; but instead, in a fit of superhuman willpower, Vince used the momentum of his own bounce to wrench himself forward into a dominant position over Jonas. Despite being incapacitated on one side, Vince pinned Jonas down and began raining haymakers onto his head with psychotic abandon. Unable to wrestle free, Jonas did his best to fend off the fury; one, then two punches got through cleanly, opening gashes beneath his eyes. He was astounded at Vince's strength, and wondered how much longer he would last until . . .

For the first time since the *Retford*'s demise, Téa spoke: 'Where's Gear?'

Vince halted his bloodied fist in mid-strike.

'Is Gear all right? I want to see him.'

Gable scrambled across the floor to check on her vital

signs. Téa's face was badly burned; her side of the bridge had taken the brunt of the force in the final drone attack. Jonas, despite being seated right next to her, had miraculously avoided similar injury.

'Téa, please rest,' Gable said. 'You're safe now.'

'Gear? Where are you, sweetie?' Téa pleaded. Vince pulled himself off of Jonas and rolled onto his bottom, leaning his back against the bulkhead. A blank expression was on his face.

Jonas, woozy from the pummelling, did the same.

'I'm going to give you something to help you sleep,' Gable said, rummaging through the med kit.

'He'd be here by now,' Téa whispered, her eyes closing again. 'Let me go . . .'

Her blood pressure dropped abruptly; the chest monitor blared a warning as Téa's heart stopped beating. Gable's actions went into overdrive; as she worked frantically to revive her, the two men just sat against the wall and stared.

THE SENSATION OF Jamyl Sarum's voice speaking within his own mind distracted Victor from the curious debacle unfolding within the cargo hold of his bomber.

It is done, she told him. *The heathen blockade at the T-M0FA gate has been turned to dust. Warp to the LUA5-L gate, Paladin, but at maximum range. Make sure your passengers witness what unfolds.*

Victor willed himself to remain calm. There were at least a hundred Blood Raider ships on that side of the blockade alone; Jamyl Sarum had to be commanding a fleet at least twice that size to break through so easily.

STILL UNCONSCIOUS, TÉA'S heart was beating again, but her blood pressure remained dangerously low. Satisfied that she was stable for the time being, Gable was overwhelmed with fatigue as the adrenaline rush wore off. Slumping down in exhaustion, she stole a glance at the two men seated across from her. That was the longest she could stand looking at them; she was wholly disgusted with herself for ever having desired either one.

The cause of Gear's death could be placed right at their feet, and they both knew it.

A wave of disorientation passed over them; the ship had just gone into warp unannounced. But the sensation didn't last, nor was the effect as profound as it usually was on the *Retford*. When the ship exited hyperspace, the pilot's voice boomed through the bay.

'Look,' Victor said, as a volumetric image of the space outside formed before them. 'See for yourself the miracle of why you're still alive, and the power behind the Faith.'

SURROUNDED BY THE translucent shimmer of a warp inhibitor bubble, the space surrounding the LUA5-L stargate was awash in the plasma contrails of dozens of Blood Raider warships. But Victor saw they were in disarray, unsure or unbelieving of what had happened to the rest of their fleet as the gate suddenly became active.

When its brilliant flash subsided, the imposing silhouettes of thirteen Amarrian battleships remained. Victor couldn't believe what he was seeing; surely more help would come through. But the gate remained dark, and the Abaddon piloted by Jamyl Sarum moved to the front of a perfect line formation of Apocalypse battleships.

Then she turned her warship's bow toward the thickest concentration of the Covenant fleet.

Perhaps it was the sight of a resurrected Sarum that gave the Blood Raiders pause; or it was their incredulous disbelief that such a small contingent of enemy ships dared to face them. However perceived, this sight would be their last.

A blue-white sphere of fire projected in front of the Abaddon; intensifying electrostatic arcs began leaping outside it. The battleship changed from its golden-hued color to radiant white; Victor thought the ship was about to turn into molten slag when, as in a scene of God's wrath described in the Scriptures, the ball of energy erupted into a cataclysmic arc-charge dozens of kilometers long.

Cutting through space like lightning, the bolt slammed into the lead Bhaalgorn-class battleship and then branched out, spreading from ship to ship. Every Covenant hull coruscated in electrostatic charges; and then, as if all infected by the same disease, Victor saw the shield bubbles surrounding each ship implode violently all at once.

Dozens of explosions and overlapping shockwaves rippled through space; no sooner had the bolt dissipated when the Apocalypse battleships behind Sarum opened fire in unison, walking their combined firepower across each defenseless, maimed Blood Raider ship; explosions blossomed against everything that the searing white beams touched.

Marius was watching all this, horrified by the display of unbridled death and destruction, as Victor's voice called out again.

'Isn't it beautiful?' he whispered. 'She is the hand of God now; Amarr is hers to rule, and you helped show her the path.'

'This isn't the work of God,' Marius breathed, wondering how many thousands of lives had just perished in front of him. 'This is the work of a tyrant.'

* * *

WHEN THE GUNS of the Arch Guardians ceased, only the charred, smoldering ruins of the Blood Raider fleet remained, floating through space like so many ashes drifting in a breeze. Filled with pride and purpose, Victor uncloaked the bomber and approached the triumphant line of Amarrian warships. But he was alarmed to see that Sarum's Abaddon was adrift; its bow was pointed downward relative to the other ships, and the lights inside seemed to flicker in unison throughout.

Marius was observing the same when her voice returned, but she was not the arrogant, self-loving being of before. This time, her voice was very human.

Falek, she begged. *Help me, please!*

54

The Forge Region – Kimotoro Constellation
The Perimeter System – Planet II, Moon I
Caldari Navy Headquarters Station

Enthusiastic fanfare accompanied the arrival of Tibus Heth to Caldari Navy Headquarters, all of which occurred within sight of press cameras nearby. Surrounded by his entourage of Provists, he worked his way through the halls of the station like a seasoned politician, shaking the hands of every serviceman or woman who asked, and posing for pictures with crewmembers and captains alike.

All such enthusiasm ceased after his brief introduction

to Fleet Admiral Morda Engsten, who allowed a long, uncomfortable period of silence to follow.

As the head of the Caldari Navy, she was unaccustomed to making time to meet with non-military personnel, especially now that tensions with the Federation were the highest in decades. Nor did she care for his dramatic entrance, or for his insistence that their meeting be held at the Navy's war center, or for the Provist thugs standing behind him.

Content to just study him, Admiral Engsten held her stare at the Caldari State's most powerful man, sceptical of both his character, and his intentions.

'Are you going to ask me to have a seat?' Tibus finally asked, with a polite smile.

She nodded her head. 'Please.'

As Tibus slowly lowered himself into his chair, Morda remained standing, staring at the Provists.

'Is there a problem?' Tibus asked pleasantly. 'They're just advisers.'

'Mr. Heth, your stature as a mega-corporate executive earned you the privilege of arranging this meeting on short notice,' she said sternly. 'But it was *not* an open invitation to bring guests. Access to this center requires the highest security clearance in the Navy, and we will follow procedure accordingly. Kindly ask them to leave.'

Tibus's smile evaporated; he held the admiral's gaze for a moment before looking over his shoulder. The Provists left without a word.

'Now,' she said, finally taking her seat. 'Before we begin, you should know that my interests serve the Caldari State. My responsibility is the patrol of its borders and the protection of all assets within them, irrespective of corporation politics, and whether I personally agree with them or not. *My* agenda is as clear as the stars on this uniform, Mr. Heth. On the other hand, your agenda is a bit of a mystery. Your rise to power is alarming and your speeches have directly endangered Caldari citizens, which, quite frankly, I take personal exception to. All that said,' she leaned back, never taking her eyes off of his. 'What can I do for you?'

'First,' Tibus said solemnly, 'I wish to extend my personal condolences to you on the loss of Otro Gariushi. I know that he was a close friend.'

'Yes, he was,' she answered curtly. *And you've conveniently managed to turn his death to your advantage*, she wanted to say. 'Surely you didn't travel all this way just to say that.'

'Admiral,' Tibus started, folding his hands on the table, 'you may not think so, but we share the same interests. We *both* want what's best for the Caldari State. I asked for this meeting to share my plans for pursuing that ambition, and how you can help.'

'I'm not a politician,' she said, also folding her hands. 'There's absolutely nothing I can help you with in that regard.'

'Yes, and that's precisely why I decided to share this with you privately, before going to the other State executives with it – which, incidentally, will place a spotlight of sorts on yourself, depending on whether or not you decide to cooperate.'

She leaned forward. 'Is that a threat, Mr. Heth?'

'That depends on who you ask,' he answered with a smile. 'You see, some of us are of the opinion that a war will revitalize the State's economy. In light of recent tragic events, I've come here to seek your reputable expertise on the subject.'

Admiral Engsten stood up. 'Mr. Heth, you're wrong to

assume that our interests are aligned if it's more blood-shed you seek. This meeting is adjourned—'

'Not long ago worker riots were tearing the State apart,' Tibus said calmly. 'Caldarians killing Caldarians, most of them underemployed, underprivileged, undercompensated factory workers. Now, whether you choose to admit this or not, here's the reality . . .'

Tibus leaned forward.

'. . . with or without me – or even Otro Gariushi – blood-shed was inevitable. The question you should be asking is not how it can be *stopped*, but how it can be made *productive*. Wars can accomplish that.'

She slammed her hand on the table. 'War is exactly what Gariushi spent a lifetime trying to avoid!'

'Yes, and look what that accomplished.' He shrugged. 'Admiral, it's plainly evident that a war with the Federation is staring you right in the face, and I don't need your support to convince others of that. We both know that this table is tilted in *my* direction. I can easily have your stars placed on someone else. But that's not what I want. Your reputation as both a commander and battlefield tactician is exemplary, and most importantly, the troops trust you. This is your chance to lead them in a fight for something we *all* believe in.'

He extended his hand, gesturing for her to sit back down.

'As I said, our interests are aligned,' he continued. 'We just differ on how best to proceed.'

She hated him.

She despised his arrogance and his contempt for her. He didn't respect her, or the sacred military institution she was charged to lead. Yet the State loved him, worshipped him, *wanted* to follow him toward whatever hell he sought. His rise to power was bitter proof that the foundation of their society – the mega-corporation – had rotted to the point of collapse, and the Federation – the arrogant, self-righteous bastards that they are – had all but encouraged it.

Morda's responsibility, as both a warrioress and a leader of warriors, was to avoid conflict, not seek it. These decisions – the ones that place the people of entire nations in peril – are always a last resort, to be considered only when all other preventive measures had failed. Yet the Caldari people were behaving in a manner that suggested they believed no other option remained.

Tibus Heth was right, she thought. The megacorporations had failed, and his proposal – launching a war to avert a wider collapse – was socioeconomic triage. But a war uniting the nation under what banner, exactly? Gallentean hatred? Or was this really a matter of survival, as so many of the hawks suggested?

Was this the moment? she asked herself, again staring at the creature seated across from her. *If the exact moment when the Caldari State failed could be captured in time, would this be it?*

'Very well, Mr. Heth,' she said, leaving the answer of that question to fate. 'What do you propose?'

Tibus's eyes flashed with eagerness, and his pleasant smile returned.

'How many active divisions do we have available,' he began, 'to execute a surface invasion of Caldari Prime?'

55

Lonetrek Region – Minnen Constellation
The Piak System – Planet III, Moon 5
Caldari Providence Directorate Headquarters
(formerly Caldari Constructions Headquarters
Station)

Amazing, Tibus thought to himself, *that something so despicable could become so beautiful.* Once a corporate symbol of everything that was wrong with the State, the former Caldari Constructions station was now a national icon of hope and inspiration. As the enormous outer boundaries of the hangar passed overhead, Tibus caught glimpses of Caldari supremacy at work: Navy starships glistening in berths below; boarding platforms filled with rows of Provist recruits preparing for training exercises; and dozens of industrial ships offloading arms and equipment. Beaming with pride, Tibus rested his hands on the viewport's edge, taking in the majestic scenery as the ship navigated through the docking bay.

Without question, the Caldari war machine was in motion.

A stagnant military searching for an identity now found themselves inundated with civilian students eager to build on what they already knew. The Templis Dragonaurs, masquerading as Provists, had prepared for this scenario for decades; they masterfully coordinated with the Navy on the logistical effort of supplying recruits with the training and provisions they needed to become instruments of war. What would take months or even years for other nations took mere weeks for the Caldari, who combined the power of patriotic devotion with biotechnology to quickly convert civilians into the fighting soldiers they aspired to be. This was a culture established on conflict; what had been a distracting zeal for industrial strength was now a societal lust for military might.

All of this was set into motion because one man – Tibus Heth – had the courage to fight for what he believed in, which in turn had inspired an entire nation to do the same. The Broker, for all his power and conceit, had been true to his word. Tibus no longer suspected that his intent was anything other than what he claimed it to be: the absolute establishment of Caldari preeminence in New Eden. While the Broker's massive contribution of money and resources supported this effort, Tibus Heth was the face of it, driving forth the national effort for supremacy.

As the command ship locked into place, Tibus scanned the stream of reports filing into his datapad. The nation-wide roundup of Gallenteans was going well; several instances of resistance had been dealt with harshly, just as he ordered. Those attempting to leave the State peacefully were, for the most part, unmolested and allowed to continue – provided that they 'donated' all personal assets and property to the Protectorate as a matter of 'goodwill.'

Caldari Prime was the real problem. Fierce sectarian fighting had erupted in many cities, most notably in Arcurio and Tovil; open hostilities between the two ethnicities had caused much destruction to both life and property. But Tibus didn't so much as flinch at the casualty figures. Violence was to be expected, which served the intended purpose of reinforcing the urgency to take the planet back from the Federation, despite the seemingly impossible odds of success.

War planning for the invasion was going well; it was now more a procurement issue than anything else. The mega-corporations were fully cooperative; in addition to ramp-ing up production schedules for ships and equipment, each was conscripting underutilized workers for ship crew or infantry training. Keeping true to the principles outlined in his fiery national address after Otro Gariushi's death, there were no idle hands in Caldari society.

The Protectorate Directors – the highest officers under Heth's command – were proving themselves to be exceptional leaders. In particular, the performance of Janus had been outstanding. He met every challenge that Tibus – and in some cases the Broker – had asked of him. In addition to coordinating the massive industrial shift underway with the mega-corporations, he was working closely with the secretive Dragonaurs to assemble, train, and deploy additional Provists, moving them to wherever they were needed and spreading Heth's ideology far and wide throughout the State.

It was going perfectly, Tibus thought, as the airlock door opened to a row of saluting Provists. *Not too bad for a lowly MTAC operator.*

Geminate Region – F-ZNNG Constellation
System UBX-CC – The Mjolnir Nebula
Insorum Production Facility

She still wore her evening gown, now creased and tattered, for it had been in her brother's presence in the final moments of his life.

For Mila Gariushi, shock was the prevailing misery of her grieving.

As strong as she was, nothing in her tumultuous past prepared her for the utter cruelty of this change. A maelstrom of emotions assaulted her, exacerbated by the extreme variance in her outlook of life and the question of its purpose. Sadness and anger, switching radically from one to the other, decimated her spirit; the Federation Nyx crashed into the station over and over; Otro's spoke his last words to her again and again; and the passage of time was failing to make either memory any more bearable.

So surreal was this departure from the life she recognized; from the eve of a wonderful, hopeful occasion, to here, this hell, a drone hive surrounded by the broiling dust of a nebula; her only protection from the monster that was the Broker. The drones watching over her, insect-like and menacing in appearance yet devoted to her unconditionally, were hardly any consolation. Mens Reppola, the Ishukone Watch commander who brought her to this place on Otro's orders, had long since returned to Malkalen to deal with the crisis at home – namely Tibus Heth and his insane Gallentean pogrom, and his intent to fuel the demand for vengeance among the Ishukone territories.

Tragedy is always more cruel to leaders, whose public burden precludes them from mourning in private. While the world didn't know that she was Otro's sister, she was nevertheless the Ishukone CFO, and had always been authorized to make executive decisions on his behalf. Thousands of messages had queued for her, ranging from condolences to financial reports; factory output quotas to personnel changes; all of them seeking her leadership; and all of it equally worthless to her now. Some requests were dated, leaving senders to their own conclusions, forcing them to take their own initiative – and usually with a Provist standing nearby.

Reports of Protectorate harassment had been documented by every manager in the corporation. The Provists were aggressively soliciting Ishukone employees, most of whom embraced them as the only suitable means to honor – and avenge – the memory of Otro Gariushi. Even worse, the Board sought her counsel on whether to award Heth with an operating share in the corporation, just as all the other mega-corporations had.

From her perspective, the decision was already made. Whether she wanted to or not, *Ishukone* wanted to follow Tibus Heth. Even her most trusted colleagues were suggesting the same; the corporation just couldn't afford to take the high ground anymore. Serving him was the only way to stave off a complete financial collapse.

Mila knew that they were right. Insorum was supposed to be their savior, and not a single credit would ever be collected for it.

Tears welled up in her eyes. The hardest part about grieving was learning to let go.

Essence Region – Crux Constellation
The Luminaire System – Caldari Prime
Sovereignty of the Gallente Federation
City of Tovil

Rows of Federation riot police and sentry drones stood with their backs to the makeshift borders separating Gallentean districts from Caldari slums. For now, the streets were empty, but littered with the blood and ruin of rampant mayhem. Throughout the layers of elevated highways and spires of Tovil, armed transports were shuttling more police toward the densest concentrations of the city.

The radical shift in forces left sensitive military installations such as space elevator complexes, spaceports, and power stations relatively unguarded. But most were located in remote areas that only Gallenteans were allowed near. Anxious to crush the uprising, Federation commanders pulled troops from these sites to assist in dispatching the

Caldari brigands whose only goal was to wreak as much destruction as possible.

Only sentry drones, low-ranking officers, and inexperienced municipal police were left behind. The duty was frustrating and tedious; they spoke openly of Caldari racism, incensed at their barbarism and the trouble they had caused. They wanted to be part of the action, eager to defend Gallenteans and rid the planet of Caldarians for good.

Their chance to do just that was announced with the arrival of Federation troops, who produced Navy Command orders to relieve them. They were getting their wish to be reassigned to the heart of the violence in the central districts of Tovil.

Ecstatic to be leaving their boring posts behind, none of them ever considered the possibility that these Gallentean-looking men were actually Templis Dragonaur Special Forces, several of whom wished them the best of luck in 'bashing as many Caldari skulls as they could find.'

'WITH THE EXCEPTION of Ishukone, all the other executives are in,' Janus said, scanning the notes in his datapad. 'They've agreed to supply the Navy with additional ships, troops, and equipment in exchange for future options on the spoils of war.'

Tibus grunted. 'You didn't promise them anything, did you?'

'Of course not. Their contributions will bring the total number of active divisions up to 1100, of which less than a quarter are mechanized.'

Tibus considered that for a moment. 'It'll be enough. They agreed to Navy control?'

'Yes. But these numbers represent the entire bulk of our terrestrial attack forces right now. Until we bring recruits fully up to speed, we won't be able to replace losses, our flanks will be exposed, and then there's the issue of a likely CONCORD response—'

'I understand the risks,' he said, keeping a watchful eye on the corps of officers scurrying about the floor beneath him in his command center. 'What's Ishukone's story? Are we leaning on them hard enough?'

'Any harder and they'll fall over,' Janus muttered. 'Control rests with Kinachi Hepimeki, who's rumored to have gone into hiding—'

A Provist comm technician announced that the Ishukone Chief Financial Officer was on the line. Both men looked at each other.

'Nice timing,' Tibus remarked.

'Should I leave?' Janus asked.

Tibus shook his head, but waved him to where he wouldn't be seen. Then he keyed his console.

'I was just about to reach out to you, Ms. Hepimeki.'

There was pain etched all over her face, and Tibus was surprised to find himself feeling a touch of sympathy for her.

'The Ishukone board has voted to participate with the other mega-corporations in granting you strategic control over all industrial assets,' she said, notably without returning his greeting. 'You'll also receive our full corporate disclosure, including operating schemas for each of our business lines.'

Tibus smiled. 'You almost sound like it hurts you to tell me that.'

She continued as if she didn't hear him.

'That disclosure details a very precarious financial position. Until now, Ishukone employees have been sheltered from the State's economic problems, but we cannot sustain this model for much longer.'

'Of course not,' Tibus scoffed. 'You're hardly telling me anything that's surprising.'

'The board is searching for a new CEO,' she said. 'I advised them that I will *not* be seeking to fill that post and in fact that I am resigning. I have refused their offers of compensation to stay, and have surrendered my entire stake in the corporation to them.'

Tibus nodded his approval. 'That's admirable of you, Ms. Hepimeki. You know, Otro's death was tragic, but I'm a man who tries to see the good in things. Perhaps his death marked the beginning of something illustrious, something that he was unable to create himself. The workers of Ishukone are mobilized now, more inspired by the memory of his loss than that of when he was alive . . .'

Mila snapped.

'You fucking *pig*,' she snarled. 'Only a sick bastard would say that!'

For Tibus, the room turned red.

'Mind your tongue,' he growled. 'Resignation or not, I can find you no matter where you are—'

'You don't fool me, Heth,' she shouted. 'Leader, please! A *coward* is what you are!'

Tibus laughed at her.

'Have a look at the banners proclaiming my greatness throughout the State,' he roared. 'My leadership speaks for itself. What's your excuse?'

'The Broker is all your strength,' she hissed. 'Only you're too stupid to realize that he's going to destroy you after he gets what he wants.'

'The Broker?' Tibus folded his arms. 'Who's he?'

Mila shook her head, her eyes ablaze, her spirit infused with the purest hatred of all.

'You're going to burn, Heth,' she snarled. 'Just you wait.'

56

Domain Region – Throne Worlds Constellation
The Amarr System – Planet Oris
Emperor Family Academy Station

Ever since arriving in the Throne Worlds, the Ammatar
Consulate Ambassador found it more and more difficult to
maintain a calm appearance. Denied permission to approach the royalty concourse, his pilot was instead directed
to a shipping platform; and instead of being greeted by
royal servants or the Amarr Chancellor, he was met by several armed Paladins, who forbade his entourage from following.

Ignoring his protests, the guards confiscated his datapad and escorted him to the grimy office of a storage ware-
house buried deep within the station. As a foreign dignitary,
he had every right to be outraged at this reception. But instead, a dreadful anxiety prevailed, and was amplified tenfold when he saw that Chamberlain Karsoth himself was
waiting inside.

Accompanied by his adviser Camoul Hinda, the overwhelming presence of the Chamberlain was enough to stir
the pits of his stomach in disgust, but the industrial bland-
ness of the room, absent of the ornate decorations that
usually lavished the halls of diplomatic affairs, was as un-
settling to him as the four Paladins guarding its only exit.

The Chamberlain's boyishly blue eyes were already
recording every feature on his guest's face.

'Do I make you uncomfortable, Ambassador?'

Clearing his throat, the ambassador observed that

Camoul was partially focused on her datapad, alternating attention between the device and him.

'If by "uncomfortable" you mean "disappointed with my surroundings", then yes,' he said. 'I've been a guest here many times, and this is the first that I've seen of this place.'

'Oh? I rather like it,' the Chamberlain answered, holding his glare. 'I find that an ambience of minimalism is appropriate whenever I'm searching for the truth. I think it will help us both to . . . *focus*.'

'You don't have to search for the truth,' the ambassador said. 'You need only ask, and you shall have it.'

'Very well then, I'll start with two questions . . . Why are there Starkmanirs living on Halturzhan, and where else are they residing within the Ammatar Consulate?'

The ambassador swallowed to keep the bile from going all the way up his throat.

'I'm sorry to say I don't know the answer to either question, but can assure you that we're doing our best to find out.'

Chamberlain Karsoth smacked his lips. 'Ah, but you are failing to convince me, Ambassador. That's a concern for both of us.'

With a subtle hand gesture, the guards stepped aside as a large slaver – a carnivorous, canine beast used by Amarrian overlords to guard the slaves on plantations – trotted into the room, its tongue dangling through oversized fangs, brushing against the ambassador's quivering legs as it passed.

The obcdient animal sat beside Karsoth, who ran his fingers through its cropped mane.

'You know that I've repeatedly summoned the Consulate *Governor* for this meeting,' he said. 'Why did she send you instead?'

The ambassador stared nervously at the beast, which

growled softly beneath the enormous hand of the Chamberlain.

'She sent me in her stead so that she can continue her focus on finding answers to the very questions you ask,' he answered. 'All of the plantation owners have been brought before district investigators; transaction records are being scrutinized; it's literally an immense pool of data to sift through to find out how this happened, and who – if anyone – is responsible for abetting it. It could take months to produce results – these plantations have been in place for generations, and we can't risk endangering the isolation program that makes them so productive.'

Karsoth smiled. 'Whose interests does that strategy serve?'

'Why, it serves both Amarr *and* Ammatar!' the ambassador reasoned. 'We cannot jeopardize production output, it would be far too costly for the Empire's coffers.'

'You presume to know Amarr's best interests, then?' Karsoth asked. 'As the representative of a nation that is subservient to it?'

'I know only how to act on what is best for the throne, my lord.'

A diabolical frown stretched across the Chamberlain's face.

'I alone speak for such things, Ambassador.'

In a flash of brute force and speed, the slaver suddenly sprang forward, knocking the ambassador onto his back and pinning him to the floor, flashing its dripping wet fangs just inches away from his face.

'Stop!' the ambassador pleaded, unable to defend himself. 'Have you gone mad? What are you doing?'

Chamberlain Karsoth now seemed relaxed.

'My interests – and thus the interests of the Amarr Empire – are best served by moving this matter to an expeditious close. The mere existence of even a single Starkmanir speaks of treason, and in the numbers that were found in Ammatar, a *collaborative* effort of treason. I don't take well to being slighted, or ignored, and your death benefits me by making those points absolutely clear to the Consulate Governor.'

'We had nothing to do with it!' the ambassador breathed, terrified out of his mind. 'I'm telling you the truth, I swear it!'

Karsoth appeared sympathetic.

'Regrettably, the person that should have delivered the truth is not here, and thus you will pay the price for her misjudgment. Be at peace, Ambassador. Take solace in the fact that your remnants will be buried honorably.'

The ambassador's scream was cut short with a wet, gurgling noise as the meat of his neck was torn away by the slaver's jaws. As the voracious beast feasted, the man's face was ripped apart to the delight of Chamberlain Karsoth, who watched with eager fascination.

Camoul, who was hardened to such acts of depravity but no less resentful of them, used a pause in the carnage to deliver some disturbing news.

'My lord, Imperial Navy ELINT outposts have sent word of a surprising development with the Blood Raiders—'

'Oh Camoul, shush!' he muttered. 'Can't this wait until after the show? And don't you have a pogrom to organize?'

'The first vessels of the Ammatar Reprogramming Initiative are ready,' she commented. 'But we're waiting for hard data on which plantations to exterminate—'

'Just exterminate them all,' he said, leaning forward to glimpse a better view of the carnage. 'Why wait?'

'Because it would be much more efficient to isolate the

most concentrated pockets, to minimize the operational costs and economic impact to the Empire.'

Karsoth looked at her incredulously. 'My, you're being bold! If memory serves, the man with the missing throat over there just told me the same thing.'

'Yes, and I was here when he did,' she said, which made his eyes widen more. 'Chamberlain Karsoth, the Blood Raiders are broadcasting a distress signal of sorts across local subspace channels in the Delve Region, plus every military channel of theirs that we know of.'

'So *what*, Camoul?' he said, agitated. 'What's wrong with you today?'

She raised a thoughtful eyebrow at him. 'It says "Abandon Karsoth's mandate to destroy Falek Grange; Sarum the Unholy has returned."'

Camoul looked up from her datapad to study his reaction, which she swore revealed the slightest hint of surprise.

'The message keeps repeating over and over,' she continued, as the sound of the slaver's growls and gnawing teeth filled the air. 'Do you have any idea what it means?'

Lonetrek Region – Minnen Constellation
The Piak System – Planet III, Moon 5
Caldari Providence Directorate Headquarters

'Sir,' the Provist technician announced. 'It's the Federation President.'

Tibus looked up from his display, upon which were the

draft schematics and battle plans for the invasion of Caldari Prime. The technician was looking at him earnestly, and the entire command center paused from their work to listen.

'He asked to speak with you specifically – and there are others listening on his side.'

'All right,' Tibus said, resting his forearms on the desk.

For the first time, the two national leaders stared at images of each other.

From the journey that began in the mud of the Caldari Constructions Armor Forge complex to this moment, Tibus was now face to face with Federation President Souro Foiritan, one of the most powerful men in New Eden; his supreme arch nemesis, and the incarnation of all the evil and abomination that had been the source of his hateful passion for most of his life.

President Foiritan, staring back at the grainy picture, didn't see a man who could be reasoned with. He recognized the hate in his eyes and the utter contempt that he made no effort to hide. This was someone who dealt in absolutes; traditional channels of diplomacy and political reasoning would be of no use here.

Tibus spoke first.

'Well,' he growled, 'to what do I owe this occasion?'

'Mr. Heth,' President Foiritan said. 'Every corporate executive in our diplomatic channels keeps referring me to your so-called "Providence Directorate." Is this the provincial government of the Caldari State? And if so, are you prepared to speak for it?'

'The answer is "yes" on both counts,' Tibus snarled, only peripherally aware that he had just officially seized power of an empire. 'Now, what can I do for you?'

The furious president charged to the offensive.

'I'm going to declare martial law on Caldari Prime,' he said. 'To be strictly enforced, with no exceptions, unless you make a public appeal for calm.'

Tibus leaned forward. 'What did you just say to me?'

'Your actions have purposely incited the population into violence,' the president growled. 'And real people – both Caldari and Gallenteans – are getting killed because of it! You used a tragedy to invoke a crusade of extremist ideology against not just us, but all of humanity! Where is your sense of decency and compassion—'

The Caldari dictator jumped to his feet.

'Half a million people are dead because of your compassion!' he roared, as spittle flew out of his mouth. '"Humanity', spare me your delusional self-righteousness! You sent no peace delegation to us! You sent a bomb, a bigot, a *bastard* to illustrate in the clearest terms the very reasons why I *despise* you to the Caldari people! And you dare accuse me of inciting violence, you *hypocrite*!'

President Foiritan exhaled forcefully, his face flushed red with anger and embarrassment.

'The Malkalen catastrophe has no words or explanation that will give either of us solace,' he started deliberately. 'We simply do not understand it; we've investigated every possibility trying to find an answer to why Admiral Noir did what he did . . . and every single time, our efforts turn up nothing. But the awful truth is that this was the act of *one man* – a madman to be sure, but one man alone! I have grieved every passing moment since that horrible day! We've all lost someone dear to us, and steering our countries toward deeper crisis is *not* the way to make—'

'Stop right there,' Tibus interrupted. 'I've no *reason* to believe you. The Caldari people don't trust you. Even your own Gallenteans doubt your honesty. And no words, not even my own, can change that. They've drawn their own conclusions, and you will bear the consequences of that.'

'Listen to me, *please*,' the president implored. 'Do you really believe us capable of such a thing? Is your vision of Gallenteans so warped that you would seriously entertain the notion that this was *deliberate*? You saw what we were offering . . . we had every intention of helping you! The trade agreement just needed a signature, for God's sake! I've had time to dwell on this, and I can say with resolute conviction that there is nothing, nothing at all that I could have done differently! This was the act of *one man*, a deranged madman who had us all fooled, someone who snapped at the perfect time, and his actions can never be undone . . . but we have a responsibility as the leaders of nations to stem this tide and move on!'

Tibus glared back at him, and slowly lowered himself back into his seat. Everyone in the command center was hanging onto every word of the exchange.

'You've been a leader for longer than I have,' he said, clasping his hands. 'We have to do what's right for us *all* . . . something to put people's minds at ease, to assure them of their place in this new reality.'

President Foiritan was holding his breath.

'I'll make an appeal for calm,' Tibus announced. 'On my own terms, within the next twenty-four hours.'

The president nodded his head. 'You've restored my faith that our relationship can improve.'

Tibus smiled. 'And you've lived up to every expectation I had of you.'

57

Sinq Liason Region – Gallente Border
Zone Constellation
The Ambeke System – Tripwire Outpost 39
Sovereignty of the Gallente Federation

Just outside the heliosphere of the Ambeke System, a Federation Navy support cruiser approached one of dozens of listening outposts arrayed in a region of space collectively known as the Border Zone.

A constellation separating the Gallente Federation from the Caldari State, this celestial border was monitored by a series of deep space sensor arrays. From the safety of these hidden locations, stealthy eavesdropping 'scout buoys' were routinely launched into the stargates bridging border systems, where they emerged in enemy territory and travelled undetected to their assigned 'points of interest.' Once positioned, telemetry was relayed through specialized 'fluid routers' – communication devices that use quantum communication technology to instantaneously link the buoys to outposts irrespective of physical distance.

An accepted consequence of the tense relationship between the two nations, thousands of these costly probes were launched through the gates each year by both sides, often with decoys to distract the sweep operations by opposing navies to hunt down and destroy them. Known as the Borden Zone Defense Matrix – or 'Tripwire' – these probes and outposts formed the front lines of an early warning detection system that both sides relied on to track the movement of ships across the border – especially large numbers of them at once.

No treaty or armistice regulated the use of these automated incursions. Spying, as it were, was a known pursuit whose rewards outweighed the risks. Neither nation would insult the other by claiming the probes didn't exist, let alone sign documents that promised to refrain from using them.

The super-secret Tripwire Outposts arrayed on the Gallentean side of the matrix linked directly with weapon emplacements surrounding the stargates and the command structure of the Federation Navy. Patrolled by warships at all times, additional rapid-response forces were on constant standby, ready to thwart a Caldari push through the Border Zone – an absolute strategic necessity if the State was crazy enough to attempt an invasion of Federation space.

As the cruiser locked into place with the docking gantry, a squad of Navy tech engineers assembled in the boarding area. This was a routine maintenance dispatch; four more outposts were scheduled after this one. As the airlock door opened behind him, the chief technician reviewed his task docket.

'All right people, listen up!' he announced. 'Nilsson! Launch tubes one through five, mechanical and electronic fittings, and take some rep droids with you.'

'Aye!'

'Rhaegar! Comm arrays, scopes and gyros!'

'Aye, Chief.'

'Jenkinson! Fluid routers and log banks, take a rep droid with—'

Loud, desperate coughing interrupted the assignment process; the crowd of techs parted and turned toward the distraction. Specialist Ames Jenkinson, an eight-year veteran of this battalion's engineering company, was doubled over.

'Jenks?' the chief looked annoyed. 'You alright?'

'Just some hyperspace sickness,' the man wheezed, aided by fellow colleagues. His skin was pale, and beads of sweat were forming all along his forehead, 'I'll be fine.'

'Medic!' the chief shouted. 'Please tend to Mr. Jenkinson—'

'That's not necessary,' Ames insisted, straightening up. 'Sorry for holding everything up. I'll be fine, sir. Fluid routers and log banks. Let's keep moving.'

As medical personnel began approaching, the chief looked him over suspiciously. The man was right – there was a tight schedule to keep, with more urgency than usual because of all the commotion in the Caldari State. Jenkinson was also the most talented engineer here by far; fluid router diagnostics required specialized expertise. Getting another specialist out here on short notice would ruin this maintenance cycle, and damned if that was going to happen on his watch.

This is the Navy, the chief concluded. *Anyone who can still stand is well enough to work in my book.*

'Carry on, then,' he said, waving off the medics. 'But as soon as you're done, check yourself into sick bay.'

Ames Jenkinson reached for his maintenance satchel. 'Aye, sir.'

IN THE BARRACKS of a Navy station several systems away, the remnants of the real Ames Jenkinson were washing down a shower drain, along with the billions of nanolysins that had sucked the life from him. The technician had died where he stood, and the Broker, as he had done so many times before, assumed the man's life and identity with ruthless precision.

But there was more urgency in his actions now than ever before.

Maintaining his composure long enough to move out of sight from the rest of the group, the Broker entered a service elevator and shut the door before his assigned rep drone could follow. He collapsed in a fit of convulsions, and could barely conjure the motor skills to select the level where the fluid routers were located. Writhing so violently that his limbs were banging against the cage of the lift, he grabbed the injector gun in his breast pocket but dropped it; cursing viciously, he reached again, thrust it into his gyrating thigh, and squeezed the trigger. A stream of steroids, pain killers, and . . .

. . . *Vitoc* . . .

. . . flooded his synthetic bloodstream, easing his physical symptoms – but by no means eliminating them completely. Wracked with pain everywhere in his body – pain that was now constant in his every incarnation – he flew into a psychotic fit of rage, spitting vehement oaths in every breath, and directing them all at Otro Gariushi.

The value of Insorum to the Broker was not that it could free millions of Minmatar slaves – he could care less about them, or the vaccine's immense blackmail worth to the Amarr Empire.

Far from it.

Insorum held the key to fighting the mutating disease that was slowly killing the Broker and every copy of himself. And Otro Gariushi, goddamn him, had refused to sell it.

Even the master digital copy of the genetic data which formed the core of the Broker's cloning technology was infectcd, thus preserving the mysterious biochemical intelligence that eluded his desperate attempts to understand how and why it responded only to the RNA sequences present in Vitoc.

Until he discovered a cure, every copy of himself would expire faster than the one before it. Soon, there would be no essence left to animate, and the Broker would exist only as a set of memories and flawed genetic code stored in the memory of a computer.

Calming himself just enough to focus on the task at hand, he brushed his hand over his forehead, expecting sweat but instead finding blood smeared on his palm. He was hemorrhaging through his pores – a warning that this copy of himself was close to expiring.

Rage forced him through the agony.

Death never concerned the Broker before. Every copy of himself was subservient to his higher will; every consciousness installed in every clone accepted the knowledge that this existence was temporary, and served a unique purpose that benefited the Original: the one who had fathered the illustrious technology that made him all but invincible.

Yet despite all of his power, his wealth, his intelligence, and his willpower, the Broker was dying.

He threw open the lift door, dragging his satchel toward the rows of numbered fluid routers ahead. An automated security checkpoint confirmed the identity of Navy Specialist Ames Jenkinson, and the door retracted to allow him inside.

Until now, playing God with his own life had been simple. How he had become infected with this disease, and whether it was intentional – he doubted this – or more likely an unforeseen consequence or error in the cloning process that he himself had engineered, he didn't know. But the only compound in existence that could treat a mutating viral strain was Insorum, and with that bastard Gariushi dead, its secrets were lost.

And so the Broker pushed himself on, solely for the purpose of smearing Gariushi's memory, to follow through on his promise to destroy everything that was sacred to him.

Tibus Heth, imbecile that he was, had served his purpose, and was now a failed investment that he cared nothing about.

Mad, toxic hatred consumed the Broker's decaying essence. As blood dripped off his brow, he lifted open the seal leading to the solid state memory banks behind the first fluid router. All the while cursing the thought of Otro Gariushi, the Broker set about the impossibly complicated and dangerous task of disabling the Federation side of the Border Zone Matrix.

He knew exactly how, thanks to Federation Navy Grand Admiral Anvent Eturrer, who had dutifully sent him detailed specifications in exchange for triple his usual compensation.

58

Essence Region – Vieres Constellation
The Ladistier System – Planet VI, Moon 4
Federation Presidential Headquarters Station

A close-up of a younger man's face, nervous and urgent, filled the grainy transmission.

'This will be my last report,' he said. 'I've done everything I could to avoid this, but I'm out of time.'

A sharp noise sounded in the background, drawing his nervous glare away momentarily before staring back into the camera.

'The production level at this Lai Dai shipyard is the highest it's been since I started this assignment – six Phoenix-class dreadnoughts have been completed in the past week alone, plus dozens of battlecruisers . . . the logistics pipeline needed to support this kind of output is just astonishing . . .'

A burst of static paused the transmission.

'. . . it's hard to believe that the motivation for this is genuine, unremitting hatred . . . you can't put it into words until you see the look in their eyes, until you hear the conversations on the streets, until you see what's happening in the assembly plants and classrooms for yourself . . . it's surreal in its wickedness, what they're capable of now that they've all committed to this creed . . .'

Another burst, much louder than the first, interrupted his report. Other voices could be heard in the background now.

'Heth's Provists have turned the State inside out . . . I've lost contact with every other cell, and I don't know how they've been able to find us all so quickly . . . all reports are that everything leaving the shipyards here is heading to staging areas somewhere in the Border Zone, including enough troops and equipment to execute a surface invasion. The Caldari Navy has tripled its probe sweep operations and seems to be directing the production outflows of every industrial project in the State. I've included all the data I could find with this transmission . . .'

Frantic shouts of a nearby companion could be heard:

'They're inside! They're inside the build—'

The man stared back into the camera. 'What's happened here cannot be undone. War is coming to our nations . . .'

Gunfire erupted nearby; the man flinched.

'I've done what I believed was right . . . please tell my family that I love them . . .'

A single gunshot ended the transmission for good.

Despite the presence of the entire presidential cabinet, silence endured in the Situation Room. The empty seat left for Wadis Chene was a grim reminder of what was at stake.

'We haven't heard from the agent since,' Intelligence Chief Ariel Orviegnoure said. 'Just about overnight we've lost contact with every field officer we have in the Caldari State. They've disappeared without a trace . . . we don't even know if it's because they've turned or just been executed—'

'How the hell are they doing this?' President Foiritan demanded. Normally a vibrant man, the stress of late was carving deep lines into his face. 'They must have contacts here, and you have to find them!'

'We've doubled our counter-intelligence efforts, and all of it's turned out nothing,' she answered. 'I'm doing everything I can.'

'Then you need to do more, Ariel!' the president snarled, leaning forward. 'You have unlimited funds, resources, whatever it takes. Find out what the hell is causing it!'

'Yes, sir. Before we lost contact, we confirmed that the Provists are under the explicit supervision, and in some cases, direct command, of the Templis Dragonaurs.'

'It's too fucking late to do anything about that now,' the president fumed. Ariel's comment drew widening eyes, many of whom couldn't believe that a notorious terrorist organization had gained so much power in the State. But the president was focusing on matters he believed could still be controlled.

'Tell me what's happening at the border!'

'The Border Zone itself is quiet, but we're seeing a wartime buildup in forces elsewhere,' she answered. 'We're talking ship and manpower levels not seen since the last Gallente–Caldari war.'

'But that's complete insanity!' he shouted, slamming his hand down on the table. 'Does Heth have any idea what he's up against? We out-man and out-gun him by at least four to one! Wasn't running them out of Luminaire humil-

iating enough? Or do we have to rout them again to prove
our point?'

Rising out of his seat in frustration, word suddenly arrived that Tibus Heth was about to address the nation. As
the lights in the room dimmed, a volumetric image formed
above the cabinet room table; the dictator was seated behind a desk adorned with Providence Directorate regalia,
and behind him was the national seal of the Caldari State.

'This bastard better keep his word and ask for calm,'
the president growled.

'PATRIOTS OF THE Caldari State,' Tibus Heth started.
'Since my last address, you have inspired me with your
dedication of cause and spirit. You heeded the nation's call;
you believe in its urgency, and your commitment would
make our forefathers proud.

'But it wasn't until I reflected upon your noble actions
that I fully understood the spirit of these times. Your urgency is predicated on fear. You that reside on stations in
Caldari Space: you fear Malkalen. You that live in the ghet-
tos and shanties of Caldari Prime: you fear the Federation.
You aren't alone, because we *all* live in the shadow cast
over us by an Empire that we cannot control, and we do so
day after day, year after year, with fear and apprehension.
Oh, I see your motivation. Your actions are *reactive* to
fear. Instead of forging the future of our race with dignity
and enlightenment, we recoil deeper into our shells, en-
trenching ourselves behind the walls protecting what little
remains of our pride.

'The Federation president contacted me, all but demanding that I petition you for calm, both within our sovereign
borders and on Caldari Prime. If I refused, he threatened
to impose martial law – in essence, a threat to silence all
those who raise their voice to the Federation. He said that

I have a responsibility to, and I quote, *"stem this tide."* To that, I said only that my responsibility is to place the minds of our people at ease.

'We Caldarians know only one way to act when threatened. Your minds will be placed at ease only with the knowledge that you are acting not just to defend yourselves *temporarily.* Your minds will be at ease only with the knowledge that the culture of Caldari generations past will persevere in the face of *today's* treachery and malice, of *today's* deceit and misgivings. Your actions *today* are for time immortal: that fear will be no more, that we will be rid of the shadow plaguing our existence, and that tomorrow we forge a new future for ourselves, *on our terms,* for the might and glory of the Caldari State that belongs only to *us*!

'Beloved patriots, let it be known that on this day, all men and women of age shall be considered eligible for *mandatory conscription to active military service* on behalf of the Caldari Providence Directorate.

'The citizens of this State must bear responsibility for its survival equally; we must *all* shoulder the burden of providing freedom for the generations that follow us. We must be prepared for selfless sacrifice in the dark days ahead; we must stop at nothing to protect our right to exist from the evil regime that would take everything from us.

'Reporting instructions are forthcoming from your corporation leads and regional government heads. Let us never live in fear again.'

'SON OF A *bitch!*' President Foiritan shouted. He was furious, and unable to calm himself down. 'I petition him for peace, and he initiates a national *draft* instead?'

Running both hands through his hair, he turned to face his beleaguered cabinet.

'Is this really the end of diplomacy?' he asked. 'Can anyone here propose *anything* to stop me from what I have to do next?'

The grim resignation on the faces of the people seated before him answered his questions.

Dear God, he thought. *How did it come to this?*

'Then our worst fears have become reality,' he said solemnly. 'Ariel . . . contact the banks. Tell them to freeze all Caldari money and assets, and that I'm authorizing it by executive decree. Inform the police and military commanders on Caldari Prime that martial law is now in full effect. Enough is enough . . . tell them to curfew the Caldari neighborhoods, and that if anyone gets out of line . . . they're free to use their own discretion to deal with the matter swiftly.'

Ariel gave him a determined nod of approval. 'Yes sir.'

President Foiritan turned toward the commander of all Federation armed forces.

'Admiral Eturrer, raise the alert status of the Navy. Double the Tripwire incursions and start moving warships to the border. Issue a nationwide warning that Caldari citizens won't be permitted to reenter the Federation once they leave.'

'Right away,' the admiral acknowledged. 'Don't worry about the Border Zone. Tripwire will prevent any Caldari surprises.'

'I hope for all our sakes that you're right,' the president warned.

WITH SKIN SLOUGHING off his face and arms, the Broker agonized through the last changes to sabotage the fluid routers. The Tripwire probes, once launched, would transmit randomized, pre-recorded telemetry of normal peacetime shipping traffic along the border no matter how many

Caldari warships were arrayed there. Admiral Eturrer was candid in his report that the Federation Navy relied too heavily on Tripwire for intelligence, and that the Templis Dragonaurs had successfully purged the Federation spies operating on the Caldari side of the stargates.

The Broker's work was flawless; no one would ever detect that anything was wrong until it was too late.

Inspired by vengeance, he struggled to enter the last notes into his datapad. Before the life left his clone, he sent one message to Tibus Heth:

'Destiny is yours for the taking.'

59

Metropolis Region – Gedur Constellation
The Illuin System – Planet III
Republic Parliament Bureau Station

Karin Midular was moments away from making the most crucial announcement of her political career when the Republic Fleet Grand Admiral appeared before her.

'Are you sure you want to do this?' Admiral Neko asked. 'There's going to be hell to pay . . .'

'We're in hell already,' Karin Midular said. 'This government is beyond repair . . . starting over is the only way.'

'Then we'll be standing by to assist,' Admiral Neko said. 'The fleet is fully deployed along stargates and population centers close to Empire hubs. The Archangels have disappeared, but we'll be ready for them if they return.'

'You're a loyal friend,' Karin said. 'Thank you.'

'No thanks necessary,' Admiral Neko said. 'I'll always be loyal to the Republic, and my job is to protect it at all costs.'

'Then tell me something,' Karin asked. 'What are your thoughts about Keitan Yun, and his hostility to CONCORD?'

'Well . . . if you're asking for my honest opinion, then I hope you're ready for an honest answer.'

'Of course, by all means please,' Karin insisted. 'I want your honesty. What do you think about what he's done?'

The admiral took a deep breath. 'My heart agrees with him. But my responsibility to the Republic takes precedence over my passion.'

Karin considered that carefully. 'And with news of the Starkmanirs' survival, he seems all the more justified in his assertions, doesn't he?'

'The news of their survival gives me more hope than I've had for our race in a long time,' the admiral admitted.

'But we had hope here, in the Republic!' Karin said angrily. 'How the hell could he stand up to CONCORD like that? And what the hell were those ships in Yulai?'

'I think they were the Elders,' the admiral said matter-of-factly. 'Only they could earn the loyalty of the Thukker Tribe . . . and only they could sneak that kind of firepower into Empire space.'

'The Elders are mystical entities!' Karin insisted. 'Mere fables, bedtime stories for children!'

'Maybe, maybe not,' Admiral Neko confessed. 'The problem with miracles is that you can either refuse to believe what your eyes tell you, or you can choose to see things that don't exist. The truth hangs somewhere in between. When Keitan's ultimatum is up, we'll finally know the truth. And then we'll all have to decide how to see it.'

'And how will you?' Karin demanded. 'If those ships – the "Elders", as you say – return and attack CONCORD, what will you believe? That it's a miracle?'

Admiral Neko looked her straight in the eyes when answering.

'I believe that I would see it as the first real chance we've ever had to liberate our race.'

'Well, you really are loyal then,' Karin muttered, discouraged that even Admiral Neko had disagreed with her policies all this time as well. 'Look at where we are today, and what the war drums have done for us. Votes of no confidence, dissolved governments. . . . this is what happens when societies follow their hearts, and not the law!'

'In our heritage, the two were never exclusive,' the admiral answered. 'Your bid to separate them is why the Republic has failed.'

Karin stared at her last ally in disbelief.

'Godspeed in your assignment, Admiral,' she said curtly.

THE PARLIAMENT HALL was a rambunctious cacophony of heckling and jeers, shouts and insults as Karin Midular stepped up to the podium to confront the democratically elected Minmatar government. As the hapless session moderator filling in for Maleatu Shakor demanded order, the hall's roar lowered just enough so Karin's voice, accompanied by the image of her face filling the vast amphitheater, could be heard.

'We are in crisis, and no consensus is forthcoming,' she began. 'This government is paralyzed by an inability to reach compromise on even the most basic precepts of democracy. Shame on us all for failing to set aside our differences! The people of this Republic deserve better, and they were misinformed with the promise of sweeping reform! With rare exception, you have instead delivered to them the selfish, singular agendas advanced by corruption and bribes, betraying the very conscience of this nation!'

A roar of insults followed; more security guards were gathering at the base of the amphitheater as enraged politicians rushed forward.

Karin Midular held the signed decree over her head.

'Your vote of no confidence is symbolic only; it holds no sway over my legal authority in this hall, nor will I be intimidated by your consistent determination to undermine me. Your failure to uphold your duty as servants to the people of this nation leaves me no choice. By the laws written into the constitution of this Republic, I have signed the motion to dissolve this government, with immediate effect, and to call for new elections within two months . . .'

The barrier of guards was overrun; anything not bolted down was hurled through the air; Brutor and Sebiestor representatives accusing each other of treason engaged in fistfights; and members from all parties were charging the podium trying to reach Karin Midular.

Before she fully understood what was happening, she was whisked away from the podium by security guards struggling to protect her from the angry mob.

SETTLED INTO THE uncomfortable environ of the station's military barracks, Karin Midular contemplated the next steps as the fury raged on in Parliament. From this location she would be safe; preparations were already underway to transport her to a secluded retreat, where she would plan the next elections, rearrange her cabinet, seek new allies . . . and with any luck, deal forcibly with the rampant corruption plaguing her government.

Gathering her bearings as guards scurried back and forth, her datapad began to buzz: Maleatu Shakor was trying to reach her. Reluctantly, she accepted the transmission.

'What do you want?' she snarled. 'I don't take calls from non-members of government.'

'To express my admiration for your courage,' he said. 'In all sincerity, you make me proud.'

'I don't need your praise, ridicule, or sarcasm, Maleatu. Good-bye.'

'Wait,' he said. 'You're in danger. The guard unit charged with your protection is infiltrated with agents of Chamberlain Karsoth. We may be political enemies, but Karin, I would *never* joke of such things. I can offer you refuge – complete sanctuary from this, where you can plan your government and take time to regroup as you see fit . . .'

'No,' she stubbornly said. 'Your chivalry is flattering, but I refuse to associate myself with you any longer. You turned your back on this government, and now I've turned mine to you.'

In a rush of self-affirming liberation, she ended the link before he could continue. She never felt so proud to have taken a stand for what she believed in, and although such emotions were altruistic in essence, it was nevertheless true that she was the Minmatar people's voice, as decided by an election that they participated in on their own volition.

Activating the news link, her outlook abruptly changed as footage of the chaotic scene in Parliament was broadcast. The networks, no doubt influenced by Karsoth's money or even collaborators within her own government, were sensationalizing the event as the end of Midular's 'reign', and possibly the end of the Republic in its current form as well.

Watching herself being dragged away from the podium by security guards made her confidence disappear. The urgency of Maleatu's warning began to take root in her anxiety.

* * *

THE RIOTING BEGAN in the most impoverished cities of the Minmatar Republic first.

Encouraged by rival gangs seeking to fill the vacuum left by Midular's dissolved government, desperate people seeking the bare necessities of life, both on planets and on settlements throughout Minmatar space, turned against the political parties that they voted into power. In some regions, they rebelled directly against the cartels controlling their puppets in public office. They raided government buildings, raided food silos and merchandise outposts, and attacked every symbol of wealth and affluence – most of which were controlled by criminals themselves. Private property was defended with lethal force; where civilians prevailed, looters rampaged over anything they could find, outrunning and outsmarting the police who tried to stop them.

Karin Midular had unwittingly started a rebellion against the Republic – not just against its figureheads, but against the principles behind it, and perhaps against democracy itself.

For those who could afford to do so, the spaceports were quickly flooding with civilians trying to escape from the madness, and the space lanes were clogged with transports filled with Minmatar refugees attempting to flee toward Federation space. Belligerent gangs immediately moved to block the entry points, threatening the hordes of civilians with deadly force if they didn't turn back.

Admiral Neko, patrolling near the Federation-Republic border herself, gave the order to open fire on anyone preventing the refugees from leaving.

As Karin Midular looked on, the first fireballs erupted in space around the stargates. Minmatars were killing Minmatars again, in space that was their own, while more than a third of them remained enslaved by the Amarr Empire.

60

Metropolis Region – Gedur Constellation
The Illuin System – Planet III
Republic Parliament Bureau Station

Within several hours of Karin Midular's last conversation with Maleatu Shakor, a Mammoth-class industrial registered with the Republic fleet approached Parliament Bureau Station, following the same clearance ritual with harbor control personnel as any other ship attempting to dock.

'Your docking request has been accepted,' the controller said. 'Just in time, too – we're about to lock this facility down.'

'Oh?' the pilot said. 'What's going on?'

'Don't you watch the news?' the controller accused. 'Midular dissolved her government, and the defunct parliament is ripping the place apart.'

'Is that bad?' the pilot asked. 'I don't want any trouble. We'll be extra quick to offload and be on our way.'

'Okay, terrific,' the controller muttered as harbor tugs nestled alongside the lumbering industrial ship. *Clueless asshole*, he thought, shaking his head. *Idiots like him are all part of the problem around here.*

Meanwhile, the industrial pilot keyed his own intercom.

'Egress in three,' he announced to the elite troops arranged in the cargo bay. 'Check weapon safeties, verify KOS data in your TACNETs. Knockdown rules only for non-targets. Rendezvous with Keitan Yun at Deck Level Six-Sigma.'

'Copy,' the squad captain replied, making sure his own Republic Guard uniform looked crisp before inspecting the appearance of his troops one last time.

* * *

BLISSFULLY SLUMBERING THROUGH a sound sleep, Keitan was suddenly awakened to the sound of Ameline's unannounced entrance into the cabin.

'Get up,' she ordered, throwing fresh clothes at him. 'The Elders have instructed us to bring Karin Midular to the Sanctuaries.'

Stifling a disoriented yawn, he stretched himself out. 'As comfortable as this Wolf is, I'm almost glad for the change of scenery,' he muttered. 'When do we leave?'

'Now,' she said, as the ship reattached itself to the station's airlock. 'And I won't be accompanying you.'

Keitan was fully awake now. 'Why not?'

'To draw less attention,' she said. 'We're both to be apprehended on sight anywhere near Parliament, unless you're in escorted custody. Republic Guards will meet you at the gate in a few minutes.'

'But aren't they mostly infiltrated with traitors—'

'Not the *Republic's* Guards,' she said with a smile. '*Our* guards. Plead your case to Karin – you're there to reassure her, but don't take "no" for an answer. This is for her own safety – the window to get her out will shut very quickly once the shooting starts.'

'Shooting?'

WORKING FURIOUSLY IN her temporary barracks office, Karin Midular kept one eye on the situation with Parliament – her best source of information was the press, of all things – and the other on the worsening developments throughout the Republic. In near constant communication with Admiral Neko, she was working with regional governors to manage the national emergency when the churlish voice of a Republic Guard broke her concentration.

'So where will you go after this?' he asked.

Annoyed, she looked up from her console. The interruption was abrupt and contemptible – she was so focused that she didn't even hear him come in.

'I'm not sure yet,' she answered half-honestly. 'There are several options, but no matter what, I intend on coming back here, where the Republic government belongs.'

'Mmhmm,' the guard mused. A middle-aged Vherokior tribesman, his eyes were shifting back and forth, alternating between the door and her chest. Karin noticed a second guard standing outside, peering into the office with a strange grin on his face. Both struck her as being repulsive, both in appearance and mannerism.

'You know, a lot of people don't care for you,' the guard said, approaching her desk. 'But I care about you a lot. I'm a . . . big admirer.'

Deviance was in his eyes; Karin sensed danger as the second guard shut the door and stood outside with his back against it.

'That's kind, but you shouldn't be in here,' she said forcefully. 'And I'm sure your sergeant will want to have a word with you about it.'

'Oh, the sarge? He's standing right outside,' the guard said, approaching around the desk. 'You know, you're an attractive woman. Powerful, too – "Premier Midular"; I like that.'

Karin leapt out of her chair as he reached out to touch her face.

'Guard, you're out of line!' she said. 'Get away from me or else—'

'Or else what?' he smiled, shutting down her console as he walked past. 'You'll call for help? Scream for the guards? Don't worry, more of them will be along once I'm finished.'

He lunged forward, humored by her frantic attempt to defend herself. She screamed as he pushed her on top of the desk; then felt an explosion of pain as his fist crashed into her face.

'Don't you get it?' he said, ripping away the bottom half of her robe. 'You're under a lot of stress; you *need* what I'm about to give you.'

Coughing out the blood pooling in her sinuses, she muttered weakly: 'You'll never get away with this . . .'

His utility belt crashed to the floor along with his pants. 'Oh yeah, scold me,' he said, running his hands along the inside of her thighs; then grabbing and tearing off her undergarments. 'I *love* being scolded . . .'

She kicked with all her might, but he was too strong; she tried to scream but he only hit her harder. Taking pleasure in her cries of desperation and pain, he grabbed hold of both her legs before thrusting himself inside. Karin struggled with what little strength she had left; the thought of being violated by this animal was too much to bear when all of a sudden, an intense flash blinded her; then a loud bang made her feel like her eardrums had collapsed.

A wailing, pitched tone filled her ears; her sight was a tangle of green splotches and sparks. The distant sound of many pairs of boots charging into the room reached through to her; the sound of a brief struggle followed next.

'Dear God!' she heard a familiar voice say, like someone speaking through a cushion. 'Do you have a medic with you?'

The frantic face of Keitan Yun appeared over her. 'Karin!' she saw him mouth. 'Are you all right?'

He stepped aside as another guard – a Brutor, but with the gentlest eyes she'd ever seen – placed a pair of electronic devices over her ears. Within seconds, the ringing subsided, and more sounds became audible.

'Better?' he asked.

'Yes,' she mumbled. 'But my nose—'

'It's broken,' he continued, giving her nanogauze wrap. 'Hold this beneath it. When I lift you up, it's going to hurt a little.'

She felt a strong set of hands slide underneath her back; as she was lifted upright, thick crimson ooze drained from her nose and into the gauze. Then she felt a tingling sensation as the medical nanos followed the blood to its source, trying to bridge the micro-tears in her sinuses.

The medic backed off; Keitan took her by both shoulders.

'Karin . . .' he said.

'What are you . . . how . . .' she whimpered, about ready to burst with emotion.

'Shhh,' he said, tightening his grip. 'There's no time now for tears, Karin . . . the guard who did this to you is part of Karsoth's network. The men I'm with now are here to get you out. Do you understand me?'

She sat there holding the gauze, numb with confusion that was quietly turning into anger.

'Two minutes, sir,' she heard someone say. *Did someone just refer to Keitan Yun as 'sir'?*

'Karin, listen to me,' he said. 'You would have been killed had we not arrived. It's over.'

She felt him help her up to her feet, and the anger grew tenfold with the realization that she was naked from the waist down; the sight of her torn robe on the floor made her furious.

Is this really happening to me?

'Can we get something to cover her up?' Keitan demanded.

'There isn't time,' the medic answered. 'We have to move. Now.'

Karin surveyed an unreal scene before her; the man who

violated her was on his back, also naked from the waist down; Brutor guards were standing on each of his limbs, pinning him to the floor.

'What's going to happen to him?' she asked.

The medic with the gentle eyes unholstered a gun.

'Sir . . .' he said, indicating what was about to happen.

'Karin, let's leave the office,' Keitan warned.

'No,' she said, as every 'guard' in the room turned to look at her. 'I want to watch.'

Great Wildlands Region – T-W4L3 Constellation System H9S-WC

As the hours and systems went by, it became increasingly difficult for Karin Midular to gauge which part of her nightmare was more shocking.

From victimization to vengeance, the experience left her soul just as defiled as her physical self. The simple and damning truth was that witnessing the execution of her rapist was immensely and grotesquely satisfying, which ran counter to every shred of decency in her privileged background.

Then there was the paradox of the medic; his kind words, the compassion in his eyes, and the strange tools of his trade: a medpack and a gun, which he used to both heal and kill without hesitation.

The memory ran through her mind over and over again in intimate detail: the muted *thwap* of the gunshot, the wet, cracking sound of skull and brains dispersing on the floor, and the unique smell of blood. It was horrible and awful; yet strangely sweet and satisfying as well.

Keitan's face lightened and darkened as the ship – this

Wolf-class assault frigate that they had all rushed to – hurtled through system after system to an unknown destination. To this point, he had yet to speak a word.

'You're surprised at yourself, aren't you?' he said finally.

She looked at his small, feeble frame, which suddenly seemed stronger than she remembered it.

'I keep thinking about what would have happened had you not showed up,' she said. 'And of that execution.'

'That bullet was an act of mercy,' Keitan growled. 'He deserved far worse.'

Karin recalled the surreal scene at the barracks: dozens of Republic Guards lying about, paralyzed with null collars; and among them, many dead bodies lying in pools of blood, all of them shot at close range. She remembered that Keitan's men had marked each corpse with a small device.

'What were your soldiers tossing onto the bodies?' she asked.

'Datacores,' Keitan said. 'Documented evidence of their treason . . . more than enough to implicate any of them in a court of law. The Elders don't kill without good reason.'

'Is that really where you're taking me now?'

'Oh, yes,' he said, pointing at the viewport ahead. 'To the Sanctuaries . . .'

Her eyes widened as Thukker warships pulled alongside them.

'How is this possible?' she said, letting all her vulnerabilities show. 'Enemies of the Republic flying side by side with us . . .'

'*Minmatars* flying side by side with us,' Keitan corrected, smiling as he spoke. 'You remind me of when I saw this for the first time . . .'

When the Sanctuaries – their beautiful blue-green

spheres and the immense armada surrounding them – filled the view, she was breathless.

'Are those titans?' she managed, pointing to the largest structures in the fleet.

'Yes,' Keitan said, marveling at the epic display of ships. 'Three in all, one for each task force about to embark on the largest military campaign in the history of our race.'

'This will only bring horrors to the Republic!' she gasped, amazed at the sheer array of firepower before her: thousands of Minmatar warships filled the space ahead, their red-orange plasma contrails lighting the surrounding space like a fiery nebula. 'Everything we've worked for will be lost!'

'Karin,' he said solemnly. 'We've been raped for long enough.'

She gave him the stare of a murderer, but he continued anyway.

'The injustice that you suffered happened once. For millions of others right in Amarr, it happens every *day*. CONCORD allows it to persist, Karin. Those warships you see there will make certain that justice is served – as it was served for you – and with that justice, the empowerment of our race.'

A jump portal opened before one of the titans; its intense, swirling vortex made her squint.

'The Elders will prevail where government has failed. This is our time. Now, if you'll please excuse me,' he said, as the armada began entering the portal. 'I have a promise to fulfill to CONCORD.'

61

Essence Region – Crux Constellation
The Algogille System – Planet XIII
Federation Navy Testing Facilities Station

The debriefings that seemed like they would never end finally closed, and the award ceremony that followed was completed with little enthusiasm.

Lieutenant Korvin Lears was presented with the Wings of Valor for his performance in the Malkalen Battle – a dark spot in the history of Gallente-Caldari relations whose consequences were only beginning to unfold. Awarded for 'outstanding combat performance in the face of overwhelming tactical circumstances,' the platinum emblem was mounted on a plaque with a mold-cut golden signature of Grand Admiral Anvent Eturrer. It was the first time in a generation that the Wings had been awarded to an active serviceman, and as such made Korvin the sole possessor of a trophy that was the envy of every pilot in the Federation Navy.

Priceless as it was, the plaque was currently resting on a bar, with two empty shot glasses covering the admiral's signature.

Resting his cloned hand against his new head, with its young hair follicles covering an unblemished scalp, Korvin used his other hand to slam down another shot of . . . whatever it was that he'd asked the bartender for. Watching his reflection, he still wasn't used to the look of his baby skin; the scar on his square chin was gone, and not a single birthmark or blemish remained of his former self.

In exchange for that scar, two black pins now adorned his uniform, one for each of his confirmed kills during the battle which had claimed the flesh that he was born in. Above them was a 'Rejuvenation Ribbon', presented for having been killed himself – and then successfully reanimated – in the line of duty, an almost equally awe-inspiring insignia to his colleagues in the Navy.

The newfound popularity didn't matter worth a damn to him.

The investigation to learn the motivations behind Admiral Noir's despicable act was going nowhere. Asked about his relationship to the old veteran, Korvin Lears held back nothing, explaining everything about his family's ties with him and reiterating – with emotional difficulty at times – that there was absolutely nothing to hint of what was coming, and no warnings at all about his premeditations. All he could truthfully say was that the admiral was clearly not himself when he boarded that Nyx; indeed, everyone who was close to him – including his poor wife, who was also subject to the humiliation of testifying before the investigation panel – would attest to the exact same observation.

Cleared of any misconduct, Korvin was instead praised for recording the first official kills of Caldari Navy 'aggressors' since the last war, and he couldn't be more ashamed of himself for it.

Raising his hand for another drink, a familiar voice spoke out from behind him.

'Make that two,' Captain Yana Marakova said, taking a seat. 'What are you doing here? There's a private reception in the O-Deck.'

When the bartender brought out the two shot glasses, Korvin eagerly grabbed his.

'I thought I'd test the metabolic capacity of this clone instead,' he mumbled, downing the glass. 'Cheers.'

Narrowing her eyes, she took the drink and tried to drain it – and began choking immediately.

'Looks like you need another clone upgrade,' he muttered, placing the glass facedown on the award plaque. While she tried to regain her composure, he took note of how her hair was growing back in; she looked much more vibrant and healthy than when they last met. But she still was only a fraction of the magnificence that he recalled of their first encounter.

'I miss the old you,' he blurted. 'And you know I'd have to be drunk to confess that.'

'Not necessarily,' she choked. 'Why are you doing this to yourself?'

'I . . . am celebrating my award,' he mumbled. 'But I think I just wanna fly solo for this one.'

'Bullshit,' she muttered, lowering her voice. 'I have firsthand experience of your celebrations, Lieutenant. You don't ever fly solo for long . . .'

'Right.' Korvin looked at her in exasperation. 'Makes you wonder then, exactly, *what* it is that I'm supposed to be celebrating. Perhaps that half a million people are dead. Or that we're about to go to war with the Caldari State. Fucking brilliant, let's all drink till we drop.'

She looked at him incredulously. 'You should be celebrating the Navy's recognition of your bravery against impossible odds . . .'

'Yana, we . . . don't . . . *die*,' he growled through clenched teeth. 'Pretty easy to be brave when you have that quality, isn't it? What about everyone else's "odds"? The poor sods that got burned alive, asphyxiated, or ripped to pieces during that "great" battle, huh? The ones that are considered "lucky" get a decent burial, while I get an award.' He held out an empty glass. 'Down the hatch, Cap'n! Start . . . the celebratin'!'

'What is it with you, anyway?' she asked, shaking her head. 'Korvin, you've become a hero around here! You've cleared your name for good and shed the image of being a pampered pretty boy—'

Korvin slammed his hand down next to the award plaque, knocking the shot glasses off. Several patrons in the bar, most of them Federation officers, turned and stared.

'You once told me about your experience being . . . podded,' he stammered. 'Of being *watched*, of feeling helpless. You know what being podded was like for me? It was *seamless*. I saw my own goddamn corpse floating in space, and then I woke up as if I'd just dreamt the whole thing. And this, this is the afterlife. A continuation of that dream.'

'That's our gift,' she said, almost kindly. 'It's good that the transition was so natural for you—'

'I always wanted to be a part of history,' he interrupted. 'That's why I joined the Navy. But now I want my old life back more than anything. I miss having something to believe in . . . of the mortal urgency to live in the "now" and savor the *moment*. I miss not knowing what happens after all this ends. I'd give all of this up in a heartbeat to have that mystery back!'

'Korvin, learn to embrace your gift,' she said quietly, looking around to see if anyone was taking note of this embarrassment. 'Use it to do some good for those who can't share it with you. And please keep your voice down, and try to remember that you're drunk—'

'Because of these fucking ribbons and awards and medals and all the other hoo-rah and horseshit, we're right on the verge of war!' he bellowed, drawing the full attention of everyone. Yana buried her face in her hand as Korvin roared on. 'Before we were capsuleers, that might have meant something to you! But you've forgotten what war costs to everyone else: *we* measure it with a medal

count, *they* measure it with a fucking *body* count! That's why you and I are so different, Captain, because I understand that, and you don't!'

Thoroughly furious now, Yana took a moment to look him over.

'Did you forget what your obligations are, Lieutenant?' she asked.

'Oh, here we go,' he said, rolling his eyes. 'For king and country, I am thy servant, et cetera, et—'

'You are bound to this Federation whether you agree with its choice of "celebrations" or not,' she scolded. 'Wars are what we do, and when called to battle it's not our place to understand nor question the reasons why we've been led down this path. Oh, you're right, Lieutenant, we *are* different. I don't question my responsibility, let alone ponder my place in the fucking universe every time I'm asked to do my job! You know why? Because if I do, *real* people, the people your sympathies are pouring out to, will die, in wars that we have an obligation to fight in. The Navy praised you for fighting well on their behalf, and here you are bitching that you had a chance to save the very people you signed on to protect!'

Korvin stared miserably at her piercing glare with glassy, unfocused eyes.

'Do you even know that tomorrow is the thirtieth day of Keitan Yun's ultimatum to CONCORD?'

'Oh, for fuck's sake,' she said, getting out of her seat. 'That comment alone makes what I came here to tell you all the more ridiculous. In fact, I can't even believe that I'm going to tell you at all.'

'Captain, you're my CO,' he said through his drunken haze, lowering his voice as if about to tell her a secret. 'But it's still okay to want me.'

She stared at him with complete disgust.

'You've been assigned to the Border Zone,' she said crisply. 'You report at 04:00 tomorrow.'

Korvin's heart froze.

'They want our best pilots patrolling the edge,' she said. 'Of all people, you apparently fit that description now.'

She stormed away shaking her head.

'Sober up, you pathetic jerkoff.'

Essence Region – Vieres Constellation
The Ladistier System – Planet IV, Moon 4
Presidential Bureau Station
Sovereignty of the Gallente Federation

A volumetric starmap of the New Eden cluster hung in the space above President Foiritan and his assembled cabinet members, plus representatives from the Federation Senate. Admiral Eturrer, with his entire command staff present, was at the head of the room directing the national security briefing underway. Standing beside the admiral was Agen Goisin, the Federation Secretary of State.

'Travel advisories for citizens have been established at every stargate in the Zone,' the admiral continued. 'We're still getting a trickle of expats returning from the Caldari side. Of everyone that we've interviewed, none have reported seeing any more warships than normal at these chokepoints, which is consistent with what Tripwire is telling us.'

'And yet that contradicts our HUMINT,' Ariel interrupted, drawing a glare from the admiral. 'We know for certain that Heth is building up Caldari forces to wartime levels, but not where.'

'How many expats are still left in Caldari space?' the president asked.

'Officially, about five million,' she answered. 'Of those, we've only heard from a third of them. The rest have disappeared. Could be hiding, could be dead . . . we just don't know.'

'Do we know where the ones we've heard from are?' the president asked.

'We only know where they *were*, which makes an active incursion to get them out impossible,' the admiral said. 'Not to mention an act of war that plays into Heth's hand. Until we get better *intel*—' He paused to shoot a glance at Ariel. 'Our strategy right now is to be especially diligent where we have to be no matter what: at the Border. No offensive against the Federation is possible without crossing into *here*—'

The map zoomed into the Border Zone constellation; the approximate locations of Navy task force fleets were indicated with green triangles.

'—and we own this side of the fence. Additionally, we can strike just about anywhere in Caldari space from these points, *if* that ever becomes an option. Sir, between our defensive placements, our increased patrols, and Tripwire, we're prepared for anything. That's a promise. Even without advanced warning of an invasion, we can crush any Caldari advance on a purely reactive basis alone.'

'If you say so,' President Foiritan grunted. 'What's the status with Caldari Prime?'

'The largest cities are completely isolated and locked down,' Ariel said. 'Federation police have corralled all Caldari expatriates and civilians back into their respective districts, sealed them in with makeshift barriers, and are enforcing curfews with armed patrols.'

'Any casualties?'

'I'm ashamed to report that spilling blood on both sides

was unavoidable,' she admitted. 'It took brute force to put down those riots.'

'I understand,' he acknowledged, noting that there would be hell to pay for this later on. 'What about elsewhere in the Federation? Do we know where the Caldari expats are?'

'We do, and in many cases, we actually have their support,' she said. 'Some of them have even participated in rallies *against* Tibus Heth, which surprised us. But that also placed us at odds with them because of the asset lockdown order. While not as widespread as Caldari Prime, there have been several hundred arrests of Caldari civilians who are understandably pissed off that they can't get to their own money.'

'Too bad,' the president said. 'Is that the best we can do with Caldari now?'

Admiral Eturrer spoke with confidence. 'Militarily, yes,' he said. 'We're prepared.'

Ariel was hesitant. 'The sooner we can find a diplomatic solution, the better,' she admitted. 'We've imposed totalitarian measures against a fraction of the people that live here. This is the Federation; a great majority of the population views our policy as violating the most basic democratic principles of this nation, and they're ready to hold us accountable.'

'Diplomatic measures will be forthcoming once Heth stops acting like an asshole,' the president growled. 'If that's even possible.'

'I'm afraid to announce that this is all comparatively good news,' Agen interrupted. 'To get right to the point, we've lost all diplomatic contact with the Minmatar Republic.'

The president leaned forward. 'Excuse me?'

'Every single channel to the Republic has been unresponsive since the dissolution of Midular's government. As for the premier herself, she's vanished. We have no information at all on her whereabouts. We don't know if she's in hiding, or if she was possibly even kidnapped.'

'Kidnapped!' the president exclaimed.

Ariel confirmed the news. 'She was last seen in the military barracks of the Republic Parliament Station. Reports are still coming in, but there were shots fired, a number of guards were killed or incapacitated, and then she was gone.'

'More importantly, we don't know if this is a coup,' Agen said. 'Maleatu Shakor hasn't been seen since leading a vote of no confidence against Midular. With all the infighting among the other tribes, there are no frontrunner strongmen left in their government, and thus no *legal* candidates to vie for power. The cartels, on the other hand . . .'

'I understand the implications of a power vacuum there,' the president snapped. 'Who the hell can we help?'

'There's widespread panic in the Republic,' Ariel said. 'Anyone who can leave is doing just that. The crossings are all overwhelmed with fleeing refugees. We don't know where to take them, and the number has doubled several times over in the past forty-eight hours. Following them through are the occasional Archangel patrols, who for some reason are directing their wrath at those leaving the Republic.'

The president looked like he was about to lose his temper. 'Are we defending the refugees?'

'The amount of civilian Federation traffic in the area makes that a difficult prospect,' Admiral Eturrer said. 'But if you issued a travel advisory . . .'

'A *second* advisory?' the president exclaimed. 'On two different Federation borders?'

'And an advisory to our expatriates in Republic space, who now have good reason to be concerned for their own safety,' Agen warned, clearing his throat. 'I know it's politically damaging, but there isn't—'

'*Politically damaging?*' the president exclaimed. 'Fuck the ratings, I'm worried about starting a civilian panic!'

'The news feeds are certainly fueling that sentiment,' Ariel said. 'Coverage of Minmatar events have been nonstop since the Starkmanir discovery, and cameras are at all the border crossings, capturing all the panic in real time and our apparent disorganization in dealing with it. Between the conspiracy theories about our so called "motives" at Malkalen, and the unanswered butchering of Federation civilians in Caldari space, people are speculating that if nothing else, this is the beginning of the end for this administration.'

'Well, do you think it is?' the president asked. 'Most of us have been working together for years now, and we haven't faced adversity like this before. Are we up to the challenge?'

Some half-hearted nods went around the room.

'*Are we up to the goddamn challenge!*' the president bellowed, rising out of his seat.

A series of affirmations went around to an approximate unison of 'Yes, sir!'

'Good,' he said, straightening out his suit. 'Admiral, keep up with those Border Zone patrols and report back to me every two hours from now on. Step them up if you have to – don't bet the ranch on Tripwire. We've been fooled by technology before.'

'Yes, sir.'

'Agen, you do whatever you have to to find out who's in charge of the Republic, and I want *everyone* in here to do what you can to find shelter for those refugees. I'll order these travel advisories, but so help me, Admiral, if you see Archangels attacking civilians on this side of the border, you'd better let 'em have it!'

'With pleasure, sir.'

'Ariel, do what you can to find some fresh eyes and ears outside our borders so we can see what's happening out there. Priority number one is finding Karin Midular, we need to help her if we can. Give Agen whatever he needs to do it.'

'On it, sir.'

'The rest of you, keep your cool and *do your jobs*. We're in some thick woods here, but we didn't become the best nation in New Eden by acting complacent and hoping someone else steps up. We do this together and we'll be fine. Dismissed!'

As the crowd moved toward the exits, President Foiritan tapped Ariel's shoulder.

'Hang around a minute,' he said, making sure everyone else was on their way out. When they were alone, he still spoke quietly.

'Any word on our rat yet?' he asked dryly.

'None,' she said, clearly frustrated. 'But the Broker is involved, and so is someone way up high, possibly even in your own cabinet.'

'How do you know?'

'Because another technician turned into a puddle, this time at one of the Border Zone outposts.'

The president shook his head. 'Ariel, don't tell me that, please . . .'

'We think that he died before he could do any damage,' she answered, rubbing her eyes. 'Dozens of our best people are at the site now running tests – everything is green.'

'I've heard that before,' he answered.

'I know. But it still doesn't change anything about what we're doing. Our entire strategy, whether we can see what's happening on the other side or not, is to protect the Border Zone, and we're doing that. What concerns me more is how the hell the Broker got to that technician.'

'What do you mean?'

'Mr. President, there are only a handful of people who even know who those techs are. Tripwire is one of the most classified programs we have in the Vault, and those engineers all consented to around-the-clock Federation surveillance of their personal lives. They can't do *anything* without us knowing it, and we pay them a fortune for that and their technical expertise. Only someone with access to the Vault could find out who they were, and more importantly, learn how to sabotage Tripwire.'

'So who do you suspect on my cabinet?' he asked, folding his arms.

She took a deep breath. 'Sir, in general, only Navy personnel have the technical know-how to even understand something as sophisticated as Tripwire.'

The president's face turned pale, matching Ariel's natural skin tone. *If it was Grand Admiral Eturrer . . .*

'We have no proof, Mr. President. Only suspicions.'

'Oh, Ariel, I hope you're wrong,' he muttered. 'Honestly, that scares me more than anything else I've heard today.'

She paused a moment, and the glow of her intellectual features seemed to fade away with fatigue.

'There are fears you can conquer, and fears that exist for good reason,' she said. 'This one is worse than the sum of them all.'

PART V

Hell Born

62

A searing wind howled through the blistering dream-scape; its scorching heat set the golden fields in which Jamyl Sarum stood ablaze. Enraged as the inferno engulfed everything in its path, she looked upon her lands with furious resolve as they burned, determined to find the cause of this wickedness. Carried by the anger in her heart, she pushed through the fire toward the great cliffs of her kingdom.

Reaching the summit, she saw in the distance that the gates of hell were opening above Amarr; a swirling maelstrom of darkness from which the screams of the damned sounded far and wide. Her people were fleeing, running as fast as they could toward the base of the cliff, looking up to her and begging for salvation.

Seven beasts leapt down from the gates, brandishing horns from which the impaled corpses of the righteous hung; they each set their serpent eyes upon her with a savage hunger. Familiar, hideous beasts they were to Jamyl Sarum, who reached behind her neck to unsheathe her sword. Its blade glowed white from the heat, and she held it ready, for this evil was the greatest danger she had ever faced. Unleashing a roar, the beasts sprang forward to attack . . .

. . . and then her vision transformed, reaching across space and time; she saw thousands of Minmatar ships approaching the Empire border, and the Elders were among them.

She awakened with a start, her chest heaving.

'Victor!' she screamed, drawing in the servants and guards outside her chambers. *'Ready my ship!'*

Genesis Region – Sanctum Constellation
The Yulai System – Planet IX
CONCORD Bureau Station

Arriving at the command center earlier than usual, Chair Speaker Pauksuo wanted to believe that there was nothing special about this day. Strange dreams had plagued her the night before, so much so that she found herself feeling anxious as she prowled the hallways of the CONCORD Bureau station.

It could have been the sudden deterioration of Caldari-Gallente relations, she thought. Or perhaps the fact that all contact with the Minmatar Republic had been lost, and that its prime minister had vanished.

But she refused to admit that the cause of her anxiety was that today was the thirtieth day since Keitan Yun's warning.

It was foolish to allow such a thing to haunt her, she knew, watching the uniformed personnel of CONCORD carry about their responsibilities, scurrying about the center and performing the tasks of great men and women, each one doing their part to maintain law and order in New Eden. They were the peacekeepers of civilization, and as such they were the heroes of the empires, not their enemy. And together, they were protected under the unbreakable bastion of CONCORD military strength; no foe had ever confronted such power and survived.

Looking through the great viewports, she recalled when Minmatar warships were right outside, ready to deal death. That moment was just thirty days ago. It was impossible to think that could happen again.

Wasn't it?

MARIUS HEARD THE cargo door open; a blinding light shone inside. Squinting, he saw two shadows appear; big, armored men rushed inside.

'Lord Falek,' they breathed, bowing before him. A hover stretcher was brought inside; the Paladins lifted him gently onto it. Marius became unsettled at this deference in treatment; only Gear had ever treated him with such respect.

'You there,' he croaked. 'Who are you? Where are you taking me?'

'My liege, we are your Paladins,' the man said, looking down at him. 'Her Majesty wishes to see you.'

Puzzled, Marius raised his head to see where the stretcher was leading. To his immense surprise, he saw rows of these soldiers lining the corridor through which he was carried; they performed a salute in unison as he passed.

Sickened at the display of cult pageantry, he rested his head back upon the gurney, watching the long strobes of light arcing high above him. *No man should ever pay me homage*, he thought.

A door opened, and he was flooded with a surge of the same powerful presence he felt in space. This time, it was both love and anger; compassion and spite; the way a mother would scorn a son for disappearing without notice; the way a thief would gaze upon a priceless stone.

'Falek . . .'

When she appeared over him, he was overwhelmed. There was gentleness in her eyes that a man could confess his every sin to. But Marius knew better as the memory of her sinister whispers returned. *No*, he thought, *this is no angel*, and his soul felt nothing but fear and contempt for her. He thought immediately of Gear, and was wracked with anguish at the thought of his horrible fate.

'You miss that boy more than you do me?' she asked, as her expression changed to sadness. 'Does my presence do nothing to reassure you?'

Marius became furious.

'Are you asking me how I can mourn the loss of a child?'

Rage flashed across her face for a moment; Marius felt it scrape against the inside of his skull. Composing herself, she appeared disappointed.

'I can restore you to the man you once were,' she said. 'We can find a way, Falek, to recondition you—'

Stopping in mid-sentence, she suddenly appeared disoriented; the blood rushed away from her face as she collapsed to her knees and began to weep at his side.

'Falek, I missed you,' she sobbed, pale as a ghost. 'Tell me that you remember something, anything . . .'

Sensing the humanity in her, Marius recognized that this was an authentic plea for help.

'I'm sorry, but I don't know you,' he admitted. 'Nor how I can help you . . .'

Lord Victor entered the room, accompanied by servants. They quickly helped Jamyl to her feet, and gave her water.

'My lady, your ship is ready,' he said solemnly.

Ignoring Victor, she made a final plea to Marius. 'It's not just me begging for your help,' she breathed, right on the brink of losing consciousness. 'All of New Eden cries out for what you once knew . . .'

Marius stared at her with confusion, not knowing what to say; the servants hurried her off before he could answer.

'I was once your apprentice,' Victor said, resting his hand on the gurney. 'You taught me more about our Faith than a lifetime of teachings from the Church. No one was closer to her than you.'

'Who is she?' Marius asked. 'Is my association with her the reason for this . . . reverence?'

'She is Jamyl Sarum, reigning heir to one of five royal houses that rule Amarr,' Victor answered. 'There is a prophecy which speaks to the rise of a queen who will lead the Reclamation of New Eden under Amarr rule, and we – you, Lord Falek – believe that she is the one.'

' "Prophecy?" "Reclamation of New Eden?" ' Marius spat. 'Your faith has crippled your intelligence. You say I was close to this woman?'

Victor suppressed his urge to lash out.

'You were her guardian and teacher,' he said calmly. 'She is the people's queen – the heir that they would choose over their own sovereigns to claim the Amarr throne. Your privileged standing with her earned you many powerful enemies, including none other than Chamberlain Karsoth himself – the acting ruler of Amarr. Once he suspected there was a chance she could have survived, he launched a campaign to murder her former allies. He nearly succeeded.'

Marius grunted at the notion of being even mildly associated with the Amarr Empire at all.

'When she disappeared, she left behind a kingdom in its own right,' Victor continued. 'She holds title to her own system, with entire worlds and legions of Paladins loyal to her alone. They would *all* die for her, Falek. They held fast to their belief that she would one day return, and for your role in helping her, you will be a king among them.'

'I want no part of it,' Marius struggled, wincing from the pain shooting across his battered carcass. 'What trick is this that allows her to whisper across the stars, to see what we think and believe!'

'Divinity, Lord Falek. She is the embodiment of what we believe in. Our place as the masters of all living things in this universe is secured through her.'

'Complete arrogance,' Marius said. 'No divine entity would allow such things.'

'To you, maybe,' Victor said. 'But not to your old self.'

He leaned in close to Marius, staring the frightened capsuleer right in the eyes.

'I would follow her to the edge of the universe and beyond if she asked,' he growled. 'I will gladly lay down my life for hers. So would every Paladin in this garrison, and all those in Amarr. There was a time when you would have as well. If Her Majesty wishes to restore you, then you'll remember none of this blasphemy you speak. But until then, Falek . . . don't test my patience.'

'She doesn't have that right,' Marius cried. 'This is who I am now . . . Falek Grange is dead, and to hell with his allegiances!'

Victor waved in the medics waiting outside. They were under instructions to repair his injuries – including the destroyed neural interface socket in his skull, but only if it wouldn't kill him.

'No, you will be as you once were, if she wishes it,' Victor said. 'Now, rest . . . the universe is about to change, and there will be a role for you in the new world order whether you believe in it or not.'

They hauled him away despite his protests; within moments he was drugged asleep. Victor had to focus as hard as he could to keep his thoughts clear. Keeping Falek Grange as he was now was temptingly advantageous to his own personal ambitions.

Domain Region – Maddam Constellation
The Sarum Prime System – Planet III: Mekhios
City of Xerah

The first brilliant rays of sunlight broke through the veil of night, and the crescent moons Kala and Alia were still shining brightly in the sky when House Steward Pomik Haromi arose for morning prayers. Perched on a balcony high above the planet's capital city of Xerah, he knelt before the rising sun as its orange radiance spread across the thick metropolis below. As the acting regional governor and overseer of House Sarum, he was the effective ruler of these lands, although he never once considered them as his own.

Kneeling, he shut his eyes and murmured his favorite passages from the Scriptures, welcoming the cool morning breeze and the spiritual solitude of this great height. But as always, he did so with great sadness in his heart. Life had become bearable in the years since Jamyl Sarum's death, but only insofar as he became accustomed to a new normalcy, ruling the land as he thought she might have, and holding fast to the prophecy of her return.

Every session ended with a prayer for her and the reverence of her memory. And when he arose to go back indoors, her volumetric image was standing before him, projected from the datacomm console that he always kept turned off during prayers.

Pomik Haromi collapsed to his knees, quivering with fear.

'My loyal servant,' Jamyl said. 'You've done well, Pomik.'

'Am I dreaming this?' he breathed. 'Is that really you?'

'This is no dream.' She smiled. 'I stand before you now as I once did years ago, my friend. But now, I am risen, and with me, the Reclaiming is about to begin anew.'

'Praise be to God,' he stammered. 'Your visage brings me such strength, I have no words . . .'

'Rise to your feet quickly, Paladin,' she warned. 'The seven beasts are upon us. Ring every bell in the land; send a call to arms to every Paladin in my House; hide the slaves from the skies. We will be tested as never before.'

'The seven beasts of Minmatar?' he exclaimed. 'How can this be?'

'We all knew this day would come,' she said. 'This is our test, and now is our time!'

His pulse accelerated. 'Should I warn the other heirs?'

'No,' she said sternly. 'Hold the line until my return.'

'When will this be? How will we know?'

Her image disappeared, leaving him awash in wonder, unsure if what he had witnessed was real. Staggering to the console, he wanted to replay the message. But for him, it was enough just to see that some length of video had been recorded.

The Reclaiming is upon us, he thought. *And the return of Jamyl Sarum is real!*

With as much haste as he could bring to bear, he sent frantic calls to every commander under the banner of House Sarum. Soon, every cathedral on the planet was bristling with activity; rumors of a miracle from God began circulating among the people.

The next Amarrian to receive Jamyl Sarum's presence was the Grand Admiral of the Imperial Navy.

63

'Hey!' Jonas shouted, trying to get some kind of reaction out of the guard. 'Have we done something wrong?'

Upon arriving at this strange outpost, the *Retford* crew who could walk under their own power were escorted to what Jonas would describe as holding cells. Téa and Vince were whisked away on stretchers by Amarrian medics; or at least, they appeared to be medical personnel to him. The culture here was far more orthodox and extreme than any he had ever experienced; everyone he saw, no matter what their role, could pass as a priest or cleric to him. As far as he knew, Gable was also restricted to a private cell like his own; religious ornaments were inscribed everywhere inside, and both hardcover and electronic versions of the Amarrian Scriptures were inside.

It all made Jonas patently uncomfortable, and the guard kept ignoring him.

'Can you at least tell me what's going on?' Jonas asked. An invisible barrier kept him from getting any closer. 'Is my crew all right?'

'They are recovering,' a woman's voice boomed from beyond the cell; Jonas staggered backward from the source of the words, which felt like they nearly burst his eardrums. A radiant Amarrian woman emerged; she immediately struck Jonas as a queen, and he instinctively withdrew from his own belligerence. The pilot of the craft which had rescued the *Retford* crew, 'Lord Victor', was beside her.

'I am Jamyl Sarum, heiress to the Amarr Empire,' she said, shutting down the electric barrier to his cell. 'I will be the caretaker of your crew, for now.'

'My name is Jonas Varitec, captain of the—'

'—*Retford*, yes. You risked everything to save someone precious to *me*,' she said, stepping closer to him. 'To do so noble a thing, without knowing what I know, is an act of our Merciful Lord.'

He was mesmerized by her presence, and enchanted with her beauty. But for reasons he would never understand, he knew better than to lie.

'When we found his wreck, I alone made the decision to pick him up because of what he could be worth,' he admitted. 'I wish I could say that I did it for . . . altruistic purposes.'

He looked directly into her gentle eyes. 'I also want to apologize for his treatment aboard my ship. I wish I could have done more to protect him from the . . . animosity that some of my crew harbored toward him.'

'You are wise to speak the truth,' she said with a smile. 'Walk with me . . .'

She took him by the shoulder, leading him outside the cell and into the promenade. 'Your actions were an act of survival to save yourself, your crew, and Lord Falek.'

They stepped through an archway onto a vast platform. 'You wanted a reward, Captain. And so I shall grant you one . . .'

When he walked to the platform's edge, he realized that they were inside the station's massive hangar; the glimmering hulk of a Drake-class battlecruiser, a fearsome warship of Caldari design, was perched in a docking gantry high above them.

'Your heart wants to command men, to lead them across the heavens,' she said, amused by the Caldarian's reaction. 'So I will give you a new ship, with a crew, to do with as you please.'

Jonas was speechless; the Drake was hundreds of meters in length, and bristling with missile bays that each rivalled the entire *Retford* in size.

'I can't . . . I can't handle a ship like this,' he confessed. 'I don't even have the know-how to command—'

'Your crimes prevent you from returning to Caldari space,' she said, stepping beside him. 'So you will learn among the Khanids. There, you will find allies – fellow Caldarians just like yourself – who are versed in both of our cultures. They will teach you the skills you need to command this ship.'

Jonas wanted to embrace this moment and cherish the realization of a lifelong dream, but the notion that Jamyl Sarum even knew what that was invoked his suspicion.

'What about the rest of the *Retford* crew?' he asked. 'They deserve this more than I . . .'

'Your care isn't welcome,' she laughed. 'Neither woman wishes to see you again, and the man "Vince" wants you dead. Would you reject my offer to satisfy your promises to them?'

There was no hesitation.

'Yes, I would,' he said. 'I've done some bad things, but . . .'

'You seek reprieve from the torment of your own conscience,' she said, smiling. 'Learn to embrace our faith, Jonas Varitec, and you will never know guilt again. You will keep your reward, as your crew will keep theirs. Gable is also welcome by the Khanids; after we supplement her medical talents with our own, she will join us as a sanctioned practitioner of medicine. Twice, she saved Falek's life, and as such, she is close to my heart.'

'What about Téa and Vince?'

'To Téa, I granted the gift of a new womb . . . the means for her to birth a child of her own . . . and to Vince . . .'

She paused and smiled.

'What about him?'

'To him I gave the gift of immortality,' she said, almost wickedly. 'He will no longer fear death.'

Jonas was stunned. 'You made him a capsuleer?'

'He has a new destiny,' she said, turning toward him. 'You do as well.'

He looked up at his precious reward. The ship was worth tens of millions of credits; he could sell it and start a new life, never having to worry about money again. Or, he could venture back to the stars, and go wherever adventure took him. But without the *Retford* crew, he felt very alone.

'Farewell, Jonas,' she said, turning away. 'Remember, redemption is found only through my faith. Embrace it, and you will become invincible.'

Joined by a group of armed guards, Jamyl Sarum left the *Retford* captain, certain that she would never see him again.

The Forge Region – Kimotoro Constellation
The Perimeter System
Caldari Protectorate Deadspace Staging Ground
Six-November

The Caldari Navy was ready.

Metal behemoths commanded by both man and machine awaited their orders, hidden in their secret staging areas in the Tannolen and Perimeter Systems of the Border

Zone. The Provist officers among them spoke of vigilance, duty, honor, and above all else, retribution. They preached that although they knew not the minute or hour, their participation in a historic undertaking to restore the dignity of their race was inevitable.

But Tibus Heth, standing at the doorstep of the moment that he promised to Caldarians, was indecisive.

'Why haven't you struck them yet?' the Broker demanded. 'Don't you dare falter on me, not now!'

The Caldari dictator was uncharacteristically nervous, pacing back and forth in the privacy of his personal office. 'Because the plan is imperfect,' he explained. 'Our rearguard is completely exposed, and our strategy depends too much on how CONCORD reacts to both our strikes and a Federation counteroffensive. The corporations want time to train more troops, build more defenses—'

'I don't care about them . . .' the Broker garbled, his voice trailing off into a guttural gurgle before continuing. 'I gave you an empire, Heth. I demand something back in return! I won't let you become weak at the moment of truth!'

'This isn't the moment!' Tibus shouted. 'We can take Caldari Prime, but we can't hold it and fight off a CONCORD response at the same time—'

'You have the element of surprise, you have the loyalty of your troops, you have everything you need – except for courage!' the Broker hissed.

'Goddamn you, listen to me,' Tibus growled. 'It's the corporations that lack the spine for this, and for good reason. They've committed everything to the staging areas in the Border Zone. Do you understand? There's nothing left to defend against a Federation counterattack! I can't hold Caldari Prime, defend against CONCORD, and protect my flanks at the same time. We could lose everything—'

The Broker was somewhere between insanity and psychosis.

'But you had nothing! *Nothing!* You hear me? You told them that a life of indignity isn't worth living, and now you can change that! Don't you cower away from destiny now! Don't you let them down!'

'This isn't a fucking game!' Tibus screamed. 'We're not ready!'

Sinq Laison Region – Gallente Border Zone Constellation
The Iyen-Oursta System
Sovereignty of the Gallente Federation

Korvin Lears weaved his Taranis through a pack of Federation Navy dreadnoughts, lost in his own daze of anxieties. Monitoring the command channel as he patrolled the Border Zone, he paid little mind to the squadron of interceptors flying on either side of him. He instead focused on the stargates leading into Caldari space, and worried more about what he couldn't see. He thought about his enemy counterparts flying on the far side of that gate; his equals, young ambitious cadets with their entire lives ahead of them, with enormous amounts of responsibility resting on their shoulders and no idea of how to make sense of the events that brought them there.

Or maybe this made perfect sense to them, he thought. *After all, we killed hundreds of thousands of Caldarians. In cold blood, we murdered their national hero. They've every right to despise us, to justify our destruction for all the wrongs we've inflicted on them.*

Korvin wrenched his ship away from the Federation capital ships; his wingmen stayed in perfect formation, eager to impress him.

Or maybe there's nothing on the other side of those gates at all, just like Tripwire is telling us.

We see what we want to see, he thought, setting course for the Synchelle System, careful to stay within Federation borders. *No matter what race or creed we are.*

Genesis Region – Sanctum Constellation
The Yulai System – Planet IX
CONCORD Bureau Station

The station's defenses went into a state of elevated alert just as Chair Speaker Pauksuo was becoming comfortable with the idea that nothing would happen today.

She raised DED Admiral Kjersidur Elladall on the commlink.

'Several ships with civilian tags in Yulai just disappeared,' he reported. 'But they haven't left the system, nor are there any indications they've been destroyed.'

'You think they *cloaked*?' she asked nervously.

'We're looking for them,' he assured her. 'Don't panic, it's nothing extraordinary.'

'I'll stop panicking when this bloody day ends,' she said. 'Is there anything else out there?'

Before he could answer, the lights inside the comm facility dimmed. As technicians scurried about the control center trying to find the cause of the defect, an image formed before the main viewports, exactly where the Minmatar ambassador appeared the first time.

'That's not us,' a tech shouted. 'We don't know who's doing it—'

It was Keitan Yun. He stood dressed in Republic parliamentary robes, his hands resting on his hips.

'Your decision, Chair Speaker,' he said.

The image transformed from a full body apparition to a close-up of Keitan's face. She knew exactly what she was going to say; she had rehearsed it a thousand times already.

'Mr. Yun, by the power vested in me through the sanctioned articles of CONCORD, and in direct accordance with the laws of the sovereign nation members of this council, I hereby declare you an enemy of this organization, and have issued a warrant for your immediate arrest on multiple violations of CONCORD statute. The court will consider your immediate surrender favorably in the determination of your sentence after trail.'

Keitan Yun said nothing; his expression remained unchanged. But a single tear formed in his eye; everyone in the command center took pause as it rolled slowly past the man's nose, veering off toward the worn lines in his cheek.

'May your God have mercy on you all,' he said, his image fading.

Chair Speaker Pauksuo found herself mesmerized by the teardrop; it vanished to reveal a cynosural beacon forming in the space beyond the viewports.

64

The Fall of CONCORD/The Elders' War

Zero Hour

Genesis Region – Sanctum Constellation
The Yulai System – Planet IX
CONCORD Bureau Station

DED Admiral Kjersidur Elladall, commander of the most prestigious and powerful law enforcement agency in New Eden, fired the first shot of the war.

The intentions of hundreds of Minmatar warships pouring through the celestial vortex were obvious; in the unanimous interest of survival, there was an obvious need to abort the engagement rules of CONCORD law. Dozens of Naglfar-class dreadnoughts emerged; then squadron after squadron of heavy assault cruisers and battleships arrived through the Kemerk and Tourier stargates, each escorted by hordes of nimble, vicious assault frigates and interceptors.

All bore the mysterious combination of Republic Fleet and Thukker Tribe markings.

Joined by hundreds of fellow CONCORD and DED warships, Admiral Elladall watched as his missiles and cannon shells found their mark, blossoming into a fiery explosion upon the hull of his target.

Then he braced himself for the wrath of this hell-born enemy's return fire.

As his ship shuddered from the impact of artillery fire, he

watched the enemy dreadnoughts surround the spindle-shaped CONCORD Bureau Station. From his vantage, the Naglfars appeared as massive blades closing to butcher a defenseless creature; the sentry gun batteries surrounding the station were already disabled as sheets of armor-piercing projectiles rained destruction upon them.

The two opposing fleets clashed in the space combat equivalent of a knife fight; warships of unimaginable size were maneuvering within hundreds of meters of each other, exchanging missiles, cannon fire, and death as countless smaller craft weaved in between.

Spotting still more enemy warships warping into the field of engagement, Admiral Elladall – managing the chaos of this epic battle as only a capsuleer-trained mind could – issued the unprecedented order to shut down every stargate leading into the Yulai System. He wanted to contain the enemy here, even if it meant preventing more CONCORD reinforcements from entering. This was where they would make their stand, and if it was to be their last, so be it.

But he could do nothing about the swirling jump portal, and whatever hell was waiting on the other side for the right opportunity to enter.

A POWERFUL JOLT knocked Chair Speaker Pauksuo off her feet; the dreaded battle station Klaxons were wailing throughout the chaos of the station's control center. Picking herself off the floor, she called out to a nearby technician.

'What the hell was that?' she shouted.

'Artillery shells hitting the station's armor,' he shouted back, reaching back up to his terminal. 'I can't believe how fast they took down our shields—'

Another loud bang made them both jump; general warning messages were blaring through the center's intercom.

'How much longer will our defenses hold?' she asked, now thoroughly panicked.

'There aren't any defenses left,' he exclaimed. 'The sentry guns are gone and they're hitting the comm towers with everything they have!'

'Why the towers?' she demanded, steadying herself against some railing.

The technician gave her an incredulous look.

'Because without those towers, CONCORD stops working, that's why!'

IT MUST HAVE been the deadspace pockets, Admiral Elladall thought, as explosions dotted the space surrounding his battleship; he was now directing all of his firepower against the dreadnoughts pounding away at the CONCORD station. *They could hide anything in those . . . ships, stations, maybe even an entire stargate network we know nothing about . . .*

He winced as the first comm tower exploded; one of the station's spindle-structures broke apart in a series of secondary detonations from the inside. He couldn't fathom the number of people who were just murdered; the raging battle at hand forbade him from wasting a single moment dwelling on it. Instead, he fought that much harder, redirecting the ships around him to concentrate their fire on the remaining dreadnoughts. The station was all but lost anyway; plasma and fireball bursts were shooting through gashes in its hull; the sheer amount of firepower that these monsters had brought to bear against them was absolutely devastating.

But CONCORD was still fighting the good fight, having destroyed or crippled dozens of the smaller escorts protecting the dreadnought fleet; the wreckage of battered ships from both sides was littering the battlefield, along with entire clouds of corpses from the crew who died within their hulls. Admiral Elladall estimated that at least four hundred ships remained in-system, of which less than half were now part of the Minmatar adversary.

All hope of winning the war of attrition evaporated when the silhouette of a Ragnarok-class titan appeared in the jump portal; this was the monster that had wrought most of the firepower arrayed against them, and she was coming here to finish what her voracious minions had begun.

CHAIR SPEAKER PAUKSUO gasped when the warning to abandon station was sounded. Between the horror of the destruction around her and the remorse of her personal failure to avert this catastrophe, the final moments of her life would be hell for both body and soul.

Running for dear life toward the nearest lifeboat batteries, a violent explosion ripped the concourse hallway behind her to pieces; a desperate crewman diving to make it across the containment barrier was crushed as unforgiving breach seals closed down upon him. Aghast at the gruesome scene for a moment, she turned forward and found herself staring through a viewport in the concourse bulkhead. There, just beyond the nanoalloy plating, was the towering hulk of a grievously damaged Naglfar, listing to one side and absorbing cannon fire from dozens of CONCORD battleships.

How deep is their contempt for us guardians of peace, she wondered, *when they would sacrifice their own lives just to take ours . . .*

A flash erupted from the dreadnought's siege cannons, ending her life painlessly.

AS THE RAGNAROK – all twenty-four kilometers of it – emerged fully from the portal, Admiral Elladall would witness a surreal spectacle from the Minmatar fleet: a general retreat, in which every warship disengaged CONCORD vessels and headed straight for the titan's hangar bays; streams of lifeboats and pods were already ejecting from the remaining dreadnoughts, even as their guns continued firing into the station.

He had vastly underestimated the lengths that these Minmatars would go to destroy them.

The colossal titan, armed with an area-effect superweapon, was about to break the spine of every ship – friend or foe – in the area.

Admiral Elladall refused to call a retreat, and instead ordered his remaining ships to attack the titan. If his crew, and the tens of thousands of other DED and CONCORD personnel fighting for their lives right this instant were worth anything, it was spending the last moments of their existence fighting for the cause of justice, and not savagery.

As the last lifeboat disappeared, he could see tens of thousands of missiles emerging from the titan, growing like a cloud of white-hot flechettes, until the entire battlefield was saturated with them.

They all detonated at once. His last thought before awakening in a clone was to wonder what havoc was about to descend upon New Eden.

+ 00:17:01

Essence Region – Vieres Constellation
The Ladistier System – Planet IV, Moon 4
Presidential Bureau Station

'Mr. President, we have an emergency,' Grand Admiral Anvent Eturrer announced. 'CONCORD just went offline.'

'Excuse me?'

'CONCORD is gone,' the admiral replied. 'And the Yulai System has been shut down – no traffic permitted, not even for Empire police forces. We have pictures from someone trapped there, sir.'

'What the hell do you mean, trapped?'

'See for yourself,' the admiral muttered, as imagery of the ship graveyard in Yulai formed before him.

'Mother of God . . .' the president gasped, and was then silenced as the image panned to the remnants of the CONCORD Bureau Station.

'Who did this?' he asked quietly.

'The Minmatars,' Admiral Eturrer answered. 'The same rogue composite fleet that Keitan Yun warned would do this.'

President Foiritan took a step backward. 'Pull some of your assets off the Border Zone,' he said. 'Keep your most experienced units there, but send the rest to the Republic border. Come to think of it,' he paused, taking a breath. 'Put some on the Amarr border as well.'

'Sir, are you sure that's wise?'

'Do I have a fucking choice, Admiral?'

Domain Region – Throne Worlds Constellation
The Amarr System – Planet Oris
Emperor Family Academy Station

'Madam Adviser, the Chamberlain is . . . indisposed,' the Paladin announced, doing his best to avoid revealing his own personal loathing of the man. 'He left orders not to be disturbed.'

'Of course he did,' Camoul Hinda scowled. 'You're going to let me pass anyway.'

'I can't let you do that,' he said, placing his burly arm before her. 'He made a point of mentioning to keep you out especially.'

'Well then,' she said, inching closer. 'Would *you* feel comfortable delivering news that concerns the safety of all Amarr yourself? Or would you rather that *I* interrupt whoever it is he's fucking?'

'Madam, *please*,' the guard whispered. 'I have a duty to uphold to him—'

'Duty?' she laughed. 'You really are a fool, aren't you!'

Looking the young soldier over, she actually pitied him. Karsoth would have him disgraced – if he was lucky – no matter which choice he made.

'I'll leave this bit of news with you to do as you please,' she said. 'CONCORD is offline. I don't expect you to know what that means. But suffice it to say that this nation has never been more vulnerable to an attack in its entire history!'

The Chief Adviser to Chamberlain Karsoth began walking away.

'Now we'll see just how sincere your Paladin convictions really are.'

+ 00:17:42

The Forge Region – Kimotoro Constellation
The Perimeter System
Caldari Protectorate Deadspace Staging Ground Six-November

Janus barged into Tibus's personal field office unannounced.

'CONCORD was just attacked!' he exclaimed.

Still furious from his argument with the Broker, the dictator glared at him.

'What?'

'Turn on your vid link,' he said, pointing his datapad toward the desk. 'CONCORD ships are leaving their posts at every gate from here to Torrinos!'

The carnage from Yulai was apparent in the imagery; Tibus's expression changed from anger to amazement.

'Who did this?'

'The Minmatars!' Janus said, excitedly. 'They knocked the CONCORD comm arrays offline – they can't talk to each other or coordinate their fire teams . . . this may be temporary, but for now, they are *gone*!'

Beneath his hand, the datapad of Tibus Heth began to vibrate. Without looking, he knew it was the Broker. But he needed no more persuasion. There would never be a better time than now.

'Here we go,' he said, getting up. 'I'm on my way to my dropship. I'll coordinate—'

'Whoa, wait a minute,' Janus interruptcd. 'You're not going planetside during this thing, are you?'

'The hell I'm not,' Tibus scoffed, pulling an old Pithum-2 blaster from his desk drawer. Inspecting the nostalgic weapon, he looked forward to firing it again. 'I've waited a lifetime for this, and I plan to see it up close and personal.'

'But—' Janus protested, before being waved off.

'I'll coordinate strikes from my dropship,' Tibus repeated, putting his hand on the man's shoulder. 'I'm flying with the 5th Dragonaurs, so you know which TACNET channel to follow the action on.'

A surge of adrenaline rushed through both men as they realized what was about to happen.

'Blue Phoenix is a *go*,' Tibus announced into his datapad. 'It's time to go home, Caldarians.'

65

The Liberation of Halturzhan/The Rape of Ammatar

+ 00:18:59

Derelik Region – Oraron Constellation
The Jarizza System – Asghatil Stargate
Sovereignty of the Ammatar Consulate

A routine patrol was, as usual, the primary task on the day's mission docket for the war vessels of the Ammatar Fleet. Long gone was the excitement of taking command of a battleship in anticipation of peril and adventure. Between the 'fathering' presence of Amarr and the governance of space lanes by CONCORD, there were few challenges for what little there was of the Ammatar armed forces. These days, patrols were as tedious as any chore, and the sheer boredom of it all was wearing heavily into a young Ammatar captain's patience.

The fleet advisory warning that CONCORD was offline was thus blessed news for him. His enthusiasm renewed, he dutifully marched up and down the bridge of his Armageddon-class battleship, barking superfluous orders and prompting discreet eye rolls from the officers seated in the trenches below. They were patrolling in Jarizza, a system located near the heart of the Consulate territories and thus far from the border systems where trouble, if it was to come at all, would be. *The captain is just leaping at the chance to prove himself*, they thought. Still, duty required them to match the rigor of his enthusiasm, even when it seemed unfounded.

But when sixty Minmatar warships suddenly appeared from behind them, apathy switched to confusion; when the invading marauders immediately opened fire, confusion became pure despair.

'We're under attack!' the captain screamed into the comm channel. 'Republic Fleet ships and . . . the Thukker tribe, at the Asghatil gate in—'

An explosion on the bridge cut him off; when he came to, there was a numbing ring in his ears, and his vision was clouded. Sensing panic around him, he had the presence of mind to raise himself from the deck to restore order.

But he was feeling overwhelmingly lethargic, which was odd given the urgency of his surroundings. For some reason, he just couldn't find the means or the will to stand back up.

There wouldn't be time for him to realize that both of his legs had been severed in the blast. Before he expired, it occurred to him that these attackers had come from the direction of the planet Halturzhan, which was just so strange . . .

Planet Halturzhan – Northeast Continental Provence Abanar Coast Plantations – Plot 64

Harim awakened to the sound of fluttering curtains in the morning breeze; he hopped off the straw mattress, careful not to wake his younger sister sleeping across from him. Peering outside the brick-mortar structure, he knew the day would be glorious; perhaps a little windy, but not overly so. The cool air would make for excellent working conditions in the mill; he hoped to learn how to cast metals in time for the harvest season, when tools were always wearing down or breaking during the effort to cut down the thick tsula stalks.

Tiptoeing around the snoring members of his family, he noticed that the breeze blowing through the house had a different smell to it; something sweet was in the air. Scurrying to the front entrance, he pushed the heavy wooden door open just enough to let himself outside . . .

. . . and just in time to see a great metallic falcon screech overhead; it was the most wondrous creature he had ever seen. Soaring low over the village, it then ascended straight upward with surreal speed and effortless grace. Wandering out farther into the courtyard, he couldn't help but think this was a messenger from God. Who else could construct such a thing? Flight was forbidden to the living . . . only spirits and the birds of the skies could do that.

By now his family was awake; his aunt was screaming for him to come back indoors, but his curiosity was just too great. He wandered farther outside, into the square, where others from the village were also craning their necks to follow the metal falcon; then everyone gasped as a canister of some kind dropped from beneath its wings, descending into the wind toward the waving, golden tsula fields nearby.

Long before hitting the ground, the canister exploded; everyone turned to flee as a mysterious gray smoke blew toward them. Harim tripped as he tried to run back indoors; the sweet smell from earlier was much stronger this time, and now it was absolutely overpowering. He felt pacified, even as his aunt collapsed, herself inundated with the sweet vapor, just as everyone else in the village now was.

Somewhere through his euphoric haze, he caught a glimpse of a great flying citadel descending from the sky, flattening dozens and dozens of rows of the precious tsula crops as it landed. He was amazed that he didn't care; normally, the wanton destruction of sacred tsula would invoke the wrath of the entire village.

Unknown to young Harim, slaves on every other plantation village on Halturzhan were bearing witness to the same miraculous spectacles: metallic falcons, sweet vapor, flying citadels, and the distinct sensation that Vitoc was no longer the master of their lives.

IN THE PLANET'S capital city of Sandruez, Ammatar Consulate Governor Ana Utulf sat at her desk, rereading the statement that she was about to release to the public. Glancing at the time, she circled her finger around the transmit control of her console, calmly waiting for the seconds to tick down.

Beneath the desk, her other hand was wrapped tightly around the grip of a blaster.

At any moment, her security adviser would rush inside to relay news of the destruction of Ammatar security patrols in space, and the surface invasion of hundreds of thousands of Minmatar troops. She despised the man; he intervened with her every policy, address, and anything else remotely associated with governing Ammatar. Most stinging of all, he believed that he was entitled to everything in her personal life as well. Appointed directly by Chamberlain Karsoth in a so-called 'advisory' role to Ammatar affairs years ago, he was more like the proxy ruler of the land, acting with the 'Chamberlain's grace' wherever he saw fit.

Keeping the ancient secret of both the Elders' resurgence and the existence of Starkmanir plantations was all the more difficult because of him.

Pathetic Amarr loyalist that he was, he would demand that she order a counterattack; to rally the people into a religious fervor on the Chamberlain's behalf; to rise to some spiritual, nonsensical 'test of faith' and throw themselves at the guns of the aggressors until help from the Imperial Navy arrived.

Not today, she thought angrily. *No more of this subservient, lesser-creature grovelling to Amarr and their phoney Chamberlain.*

A thunderous boom shook her chambers; alarms were triggered all over the palace. She checked the time again; just as the Elders had promised, the troops were right on schedule.

No more pretending to submit to the subjugation of my ancestral brothers and sisters.

The door to her chambers flew open; as always, this pig of a man never bothered to knock for anything.

'How could you just sit there?' he demanded. 'We're under attack! Summon the Imperial Guard to secure my protection, you incompetent bitch!'

Rage pulled the weapon above the desk; she paused to savor the look of surprise on his ugly Amarrian face.

'No,' she said, squeezing the trigger once.

As the bolt melted a hole in his chest, she sprang up from her chair, teeth clenched.

'This is for the Starkmanir,' she growled, firing a second time as he fell; then she kept firing until there was no charge left in the weapon, and all that remained of her Amarr-appointed adviser was a smoldering heap of cauterized flesh.

'Pig . . .' she muttered, spitting onto the corpse just as ten heavily armed commandos sprinted into the chamber, weapons levelled at her. Their rust-brown, jagged armor and full face masks made them unmistakably Minmatar.

She tossed her weapon at their feet.

'Ana Utulf?' one asked.

'Yes,' she answered proudly.

The man lowered his rifle; the others followed suit.

'Dropship's idling on the roof,' he said. 'Did you send the word?'

She looked down at the console, then pressed the transmit control.

'The word is given,' she said, moving toward them.

Domain Region – Throne Worlds Constellation
The Amarr System – Planet Oris
Emperor Family Academy Station

Chamberlain Karsoth heaved his bulk toward the command center, partially dressed and cursing vehemently as his mechanical implants announced his passage through the corridors; his entourage of guards, clerics, and slaves werc in close tow.

Camoul was already waiting for him when he arrived, making sure to stand where everyone – Paladins, officers, and technicians alike – could hear them.

'I presume you received the memo about CONCORD,' she said wryly. 'While you were busy, a Minmatar invasion force moved virtually uncontested into Ammatar space. Thousands of dropships have landed on the surface of Halturzhan, and enemy troops have neutralized all of the defenses surrounding Sandruez.'

'Thank you, Camoul,' he snarled. 'Let's take this to the situation room.'

'Did I mention that they have Insorum?' she said, holding her ground. The rest of the control center was so quiet that only the whir of machines and circulation of air through the vents overhead could be heard. 'Airburst canisters were detonated over every plantation in the northern hemisphere of the planet. There are probably, oh, several million slaves across those continents?'

Karsoth, his face red with fury, pointed toward the situation room.

'*Now*, Ms. Hinda!'

'One last item, Chamberlain. The Ammatar Consulate Governor just released a statement to the Ammatar populace,' she announced, reading from her datapad. 'Shall I read it aloud?'

'No, damn you!' Karsoth cursed.

'Citizens of Ammatar, do not be alarmed. The warriors descending upon your lands are your brothers. Do not attack them, and you will not be harmed. They are here to return the Starkmanir to the Elders – the true spiritual and tribal leaders of the Minmatar race. I assure you that the

Elders are no legend; they are real, and they have returned to bring unity to our people once again.'

'*Camoul!*'

'History records that we – the Nefantar – betrayed the Minmatar tribes centuries ago to appease our Amarrian overlords. That is what the emperors want you to believe. But the truth is this: your ancestors collaborated with Amarr to protect what remained of the Starkmanir tribe. The only way to save them from Paladin butchers was to take them in as slaves. This desperate act, designed by the Elders, was to preserve the whole of what we really are.'

'Guards, seize her!' Karsoth shouted. 'Muzzle that woman's mouth!'

Looking up for the briefest of moments, she still appeared unfazed, even as some Paladins reluctantly began moving toward her.

Defiantly, she raised her voice and continued reading.

'Now they are offering you an invitation to join them, but not as an *Ammatar:* an Amarrian pet, never to reach their divine stature or so-called purity, to be always looked down upon as just barely more human than the slaves they demand we keep. They ask instead that you join them as *Nefantars*, one of the seven original Minmatar tribes – the race that flows in your blood.'

'You are *disappointing* me, Camoul!' Karsoth frothed, taking some steps toward her.

'The Elders offer a world of paradise, of beauty, of the restoration of our souls. You will be safe there. You will not be treated as an enemy. You will be equals among all others. I can never offer you those things here, nor can Amarr. Leave your worldly possessions behind, find the nearest Minmatar soldier, and follow him, for he is your *brother.* If you do not . . . remember always that this world –

indeed, all the worlds of Amarr – will never be the same again.'

'You've just signed your death warrant,' Karsoth growled, as the guards reached her.

'As have you,' she said, folding her arms. 'A Ragnorak-class titan was just reported jumping into the Kor-Azor Region. We've just been invaded, Chamberlain Karsoth, and it happened on *your* watch!'

'BUT I'M HAPPY here,' Harim pleaded, as his younger sister's frightened cries haunted him. 'This place is our home . . . I don't know anything else!'

'There's a better home for your family up there,' the soldier said, looking toward the sky. 'Where we can show you how to forge better tools . . . to learn how to build one of those—'

He pointed at the dropship idling in the tsula fields.

'And then, you'll learn to fly it yourself,' he continued.

'Really?' the boy asked, his eyes full of hope. His aunt, holding the hand of his terrified sister, came forward. The square was filled with armed soldiers, hurrying bewildered – and at times, deranged – slaves, all of whom were suddenly released from their Vitoc addiction, toward the dropship.

'Where will you take us?' she asked. 'Did God send you?'

A distant blast boomed from above, startling the villagers; everyone looked up and pointed toward the sky. High above them, streaks of wreckage were scorching across the clouds, trailing flames and smoke contrails as the larger pieces flew apart, hurtling toward the surface. Somewhere in the space above them, a battle was raging, and time was running out.

'We're not gods, we're your family,' he said, placing a heavy arm on her shoulder. 'You are a Starkmanir, and you will never call another man "master" ever again.'

66

Kor-Azor's Deception

+ 00:19:59

Domain Region – Norgoh Constellation
The Safizon System – Planet II, Moon I
Imperial Navy Headquarter Station

There is good news in all this, Imperial Grand Admiral Kezti Sundara thought.

Staring down at the display of icons depicting where the attacks were taking place, several aides hovered nearby, waiting nervously for him to acknowledge the Chamberlain's demand for an explanation.

For what little comfort it was, the Minmatars were not invading to conquer territory. If their assault on the Ammatar Consulate territories was any example, this was merely a spirited quest to take back their own kind – a great heist of sorts. They were using their numerical advantage in ships and manpower to expedite the removal of slaves from installations and cities as quickly as possible, pausing only to destroy what was absolutely necessary to accomplish that. All of their momentum to this point – supplemented with these damned Insorum blitzes – was being driven solely by the element of surprise.

Nothing in the intelligence archives suggested that these

so called Minmatar 'Elders' were anything more than a legend. Their appearance now, after all these years, was a mystery – to say nothing of how they managed to build such a massive army in secrecy. This was a monolithic failure on Amarr's part, and one that would be examined closely once the fighting stopped.

But even still, it was no wonder that Minmatar remained enslaved all this time. Their strategic blunder spoke volumes for why they were destined to remain inferior creatures: they were making it obvious that this was all just a large-scale hostage rescue operation. And there was an easy way to make certain that rescue failed, with minimum investment on Amarr's part.

We'll let them have their damn slaves, he thought, grunting slightly. *And then we'll kill them all in space.*

'What's that, Admiral?' Chamberlain Karsoth demanded. 'Speak up, damnit!'

It took all of the willpower that the admiral could summon to remain composed. As much as he wanted to squeeze his hands around the Chamberlain's neck, duty compelled him to listen politely to his tirade.

'Why haven't you moved to counter them in Ammatar?' Karsoth continued. 'Where is this legendary competence that precedes your reputation?'

'Ammatar was lost before this invasion ever started,' Grand Admiral Sundara answered calmly. 'It was never worth defending to begin with.'

Karsoth's eyes opened wide. 'I *beg* your pardon?'

'The Ammatars aren't resisting,' the admiral said. 'Populations of the Irshah, Arnola, and Jayneleb systems alone have all gone willingly. More systems are likely preparing to do the same now. The protection offered by the Imperial Navy extends only to those who are sincere to our faith, and to whom the bonds of our allegiance are unbreakable. I will defend Amarr, Chamberlain. Not the half-breed neighbors of this Empire.'

'You should be taking the fight to those worlds to defend *ours*!' Karsoth shouted. 'Bloody *their* lands to keep the invaders from entering the space of True Amarr!'

'My lord, if you believe you can lead the Paladins of Amarr better than I, then by all means, say the word,' the admiral said, narrowing his eyes at the Chamberlain. 'Otherwise, I think you should leave the art of waging war to me.'

'Oh, I'll deal with your conduct another time,' Karsoth growled. 'Now tell me, what exactly are you doing to defend *my* Empire?'

'We're going to make our first stand in the Kor-Azor Region,' the admiral answered patiently. 'Then we're going to let them in even further.'

'Further? I see why you're hailed as being so brilliant—'

'Their numbers exceed those that we used against them in the first invasions centuries ago, my lord. Our generation has never seen a fleet this large. Their spearheads are strong, they are led by able field commanders, and they have at least three titans operating within our borders. Our static defenses were never designed to repel such an attack. The only way to defeat them is to concede some ground, close the gaps behind them, and kill them here, on our terms, in our territory.'

'And how is that plan going?'

'The Battle for Kor-Azor has already begun, my lord.'

'So has the test for your survival,' Karsoth growled. 'My expectations for you are very high, Admiral. Don't disappoint me.'

The transmission ended. Grand Admiral Sundara took a deep breath before standing up. He hadn't issued any orders to defend the Kor-Azor worlds at all. Instead, he had lied to the Court Chamberlain and thus committed an act of high treason, and his subordinates knew it.

'Ready my ship,' he said. 'Order the fleet commanders to converge on Sarum Prime.'

The young Paladin was shocked. '*All* of them, sir?'

'Yes.'

'But, my lord,' the subordinate put his datapad down in disbelief. 'We're going to give up that much ground?'

'I'm doing this for two reasons,' the admiral said, raising his voice so everyone nearby could hear him. 'One is that the Sarum Worlds are where the Minmatars will strike next. They're targeting the heirs who are harshest to slaves. The second reason is that Jamyl Sarum is alive.'

The subordinate's eyes opened as wide as saucers.

'There isn't a man in here who doesn't know about the prophecy of her return,' the admiral said. 'Nor is there anyone here who can stand the Chamberlain's illegitimacy any longer. We have been invaded, Paladins. For the first time in our history, an enemy treads upon holy land. This is our greatest test of faith yet. How will you respond?'

He studied the expressions of the men arrayed before him, and liked what he saw.

'Now, ready my ship,' the admiral repeated. 'Give word to the fleet. We'll face these animals down with an empress leading us into battle.'

Kor-Azor Region – Geben Constellation
The Kor-Azor Prime System – Planet 'Eclipticum'
Kor-Azor Family Bureau Headquarter Station

'Thirty seconds!' the master sergeant announced.

Deep within the siege bay of a Naglfar-class dreadnought, a young Sebiestor lieutenant checked the systems of his combat MTAC one last time. Taped to the electronics console was a print of his girlfriend, lovely Tasha, who was still back in Sanctuaries, no doubt praying for his safe return. A scientist by trade, she – like many others, male and female alike – was chosen by the Elders to remain behind for this colossal operation, in which every role, no matter how big or small, was honorable and just. If he survived, they would marry upon his return. If not, the spirit of Minmatar would carry on, as would she – in time, after the heartbreak was gone.

This war is greater than any two Minmatars, he thought. *The inevitable loss, the sacrifice, the pain; these things are universally understood as necessary for the betterment of the generations after us.*

Looking away from her picture, he inspected the other MTAC walkers in the bay. Dozens of them were racked in groups of four, attached to rocket sleds that would propel them across the void to the station's immense surface. Their mission was straightforward: inject Insorum into the station's air circulation system. The second engineering battalion would take the station hangar and pave the way for the boarding infantry, but not until Insorum was flowing throughout its halls, bringing the slaves onboard to their senses. Right now, this dreadnought's cannons were hammering away at the station's armor; as soon as enough plating was disintegrated, the MTACs – equipped with cutting devices powerful enough to penetrate the station's hull – would launch into action.

A battle of gigantic dimensions was raging outside, yet he was practically in his own universe within the belly of the dreadnought. The siege bay was already depressurized; no sounds could reach him. It was actually serene here, except for the reddish glow of the hangar and the dark, imposing silhouettes of the clustered MTAC walkers hanging from their gantries like pods of insects.

'Bay doors opening, stand by!'

His daydreaming ceased as the hangar doors pulled apart like great curtains, unveiling the hellish stage beyond. The golden-tinted station was straight ahead; his instruments showed that its surface was still more than ten kilometers away, yet it filled the ever-widening view like a planet. Intermittent flashes of light meant trouble; the dreadnought captain was ejecting them into a hot zone, where space combat between warships was happening nearby.

'For Minmatar, lads!' the master sergeant announced. 'Go, go, go!'

He felt himself accelerated to breakneck speed as the rockets suddenly fired; the siege bay flashed by in an instant. But once clear of the doors, time seemed to slow down as the navigation systems took control of the brief flight toward the surface. Turning in his harness to see what was happening around him, he spotted other rocket sleds beside him in formation; some were already veering off toward separate locations on the station. Another flash caught his eye; a damaged Apocalypse-class battleship was several kilometers below him, losing a close-range fight with a Minmatar Tempest. Gaping, flaming holes were in the Amarrian warship's hull, but instead of firing back toward its attacker, the gun turrets were tracking something else . . .

Seven beams of white fire lanced out, blinding him. Wincing, he could hear the computer's proximity warning; the sled's braking thrusters were already firing. Blinking his eyes through the phosphenes, he looked to where he last saw the other sleds, unsurprised that many were no longer there.

A loud *ka-chunk-hiss* marked the impact of the walker's

legs onto the station surface; his instruments were already probing beneath the battered station surface for the air circulation system. As schematic diagrams superimposed onto his view, he set off immediately, marching along the surface and trying to forget about the comrades who had just perished. The other three MTACs in his squad were marching beside him, rotating their torsos back and forth in gentle sweeps, keeping watch for danger.

Their metallic hulks cast long shadows on the surface as the Apocalypse detonated in a brilliant flash, just as the lieutenant found the structural 'vein' they were looking for. Activating the vehicle's cutting torches, he began removing sections of the station's hull, careful not to hurl debris toward his colleagues.

+ 00:24:37

Covering his mouth with one hand while choking through the sweet-smelling smog pouring through the vents, the Paladin raised the datapad close to his face.

TERMINATE ALL SLAVES WITH IMMEDIATE EFFECT.

That was the official word from STATCOM. The Minmatar attackers had successfully landed several armored MTAC battalions onto the station and compromised the air circulation system. The corridors were now saturated with an airborne variant of Insorum, and the effect would make the slaves temporarily lethargic. But once they came to . . .

The sound of a gunshot made him jump.

'C'mon, you!' a voice shouted. 'You have orders, Paladin!'

Stepping clear of the smoke, he saw the deck officer levelling his pistol at a group of incapacitated slaves bound by stun cuffs and ankle chains. This crew had been on its way to receive Vitoc injections before a scheduled delivery for planetside labor. The brains of at least one of them was scattered on the officer's boots.

'They're inside the hangar now, you know,' he said, squeezing off another round with gruesome effect. 'Trying to mount a rescue of their fellow roaches. Can you imagine?'

A third shot made the Paladin flinch. Some of the other slaves were finally stirring.

'You know what's going to happen when these things wake up,' the deck officer warned. 'So take that weapon of yours and start defending yourself.'

The Paladin felt nauseous; he couldn't tell if it was from the sweet gas lingering in his nostrils, or the sight of exposed gray matter, bone, and blood.

'It's okay to be a little hesitant,' the deck officer said. 'But, you do know that the only way off this station is in a life pod, right?'

Bam. A fourth execution.

'And you're going to have to fight your way to one if you don't start acting with a little more haste.'

It was true, the Paladin realized. Every slave on this station – and there were thousands here at any given moment, considering that this was a processing facility for them – would be a potential assassin once this dreaded Insorum worked its biochemical evil upon them. Amarr was at war now. *Our stations, our homes, and our worlds are under attack*, he reasoned. There was only one way to respond if he was to survive.

Slowly, the Paladin unholstered his weapon.

'That's it,' the deck officer smiled. 'Go ahead now. The first one's always the hardest, but after that, it gets easier.'

Pressing the gun's barrel against the nearest slave's head, he startled when he realized that she – it was a she! – was fully awake now.

'Do it,' the deck officer taunted. 'For the emperor.'

Amazed at how little fear she displayed while staring into the barrel of a gun, he paused again, entranced by the contempt in her eyes.

Then two shots rang out in quick succession.

Unsure if he had pulled the trigger himself, he found himself lying on the floor and staring into the open mouth of the deck officer, who now had a hole in the middle of his forehead.

Aware that the life was slipping out of his body, the Paladin made no attempt to resist the warmness filling his chest. The question of who had shot him was unimportant. As a True Amarr, his soul was pure, and the gates of paradise were just beyond. Besides, which emperor was the deck officer referring to?

His primary mission completed, the lieutenant led his MTAC squad toward the station hangar. The second engineering battalion had already secured access points to the docking gantries, which were now filled with Minmatar transports. As his MTAC climbed through the hangar's outer threshold, the lieutenant found himself staring at a triumphant sight that made tears well up in his eyes: lines and lines of slaves, with Minmatar soldiers nearby, boarding ships that would take them back to the Sanctuaries.

Looking back out toward space, he could see little else except for patrolling Minmatar warships and the clear skies of Eclipticum. Thousands of dropships were already descending to the surface amid long black streams of smoke caused by the surface bombardment minutes before. Insorum was soaking the atmosphere, carried by jet streams across the planet, wreaking havoc among an Amarrian population ill prepared to deal with the sudden freedom of millions of slaves.

It's a shame we can't rescue them all, the lieutenant thought, urging his mechanical machine forward. His squad, just like all the others returning from their assignments, needed to be evacuated. Personnel took precedence over equipment; what couldn't be transported would be scuttled. Reports were filtering in about how well the Ammatar invasions were progressing; word was that nearly all of the Starkmanirs were on their way back to the Sanctuaries.

The young Sebiestor stole one more glance toward Eclipticum. *We'll be back for these worlds someday*, he thought. *But so far, it's a good start.*

67

Pride of Sarum

+ 00:23:55

Domain Region – Maddam Constellation
The Sarum Prime System – Planet III: Mekhios
City of Xerah

With church bells ringing long before the Elder warships arrived in the Domain Region, the people of Xerah were ready for the worst.

Led by the divinely inspired charge of House Steward Pomik Haromi, planetary defenses were manned to full capacity for the first time in decades. Under the guidance of Paladins, citizens fortified their homes with weapons and supplies; streets, causeways, and transit platforms were all blockaded; tanks, artillery pieces, combat MTACs, assault aircraft, and anti-aircraft weapons were removed from armories and assigned to hastily called-up reserves. These were a war-loving people; their devotion to God and to their legendary queen made them all but invincible in both heart and spirit. Nowhere else in Amarr did people act with such courage or conviction; nowhere else was Chamberlain Karsoth's irrelevance more evident than here.

On the nineteenth minute of the Elders' strike, Pomik was contacted directly by Grand Admiral Sundara. He reiterated what the House Steward knew already from Sarum's warning: to hide the heathens from the skies. Slaves were rushed underground and sealed inside reinforced structures at a panicked pace; *use any means necessary*, the House Steward warned. *Get them off the streets, get them out of the open, give them masks to breathe in*, he proclaimed. *Short of those measures, execute them. You'll understand why soon enough.*

No sooner had the people of Xerah complied when the first Insorum-delivering drones appeared over the city; the Paladins immediately filled the air with laser fire to shoot them down. But Pomik screamed for them to stop.

'Don't hit them!' he pleaded. 'Let them explode . . . let the infidels fill the sky with Insorum. Let them fill our lungs with it! *Let them think our slaves are free!*'

GRAND ADMIRAL SUNDARA was already charging at full speed when they arrived.

A thousand Minmatar ships, led by their cursed Ragnorak flagship, warped into the space above Mekhios, not fifty kilometers from the hulls of the Righteous.

That was exactly where he wanted them, and precisely where his instincts expected them to be.

Leading the fleet from an Avatar-class titan – a colossal warship every bit as powerful as the Ragnorak in both size and firepower – he could sense confusion amongst the enemy:

We weren't supposed to have this much firepower ready for them. We weren't supposed to be prepared for their attack.

Surveying the thick formation ahead, he thought back to the wars of the ancients; to the days when warriors clad in mail and steel faced each other down on grassy fields; when entire armies would bravely stare across the very soil upon which men were about to fall; to the courage that soldiers would find in the comrades standing at their shoulders. In a primal roar, they would charge and clash with the enemy, face to face with clubs and swords and hell incarnate.

Here, in the void, they would do the same.

I want to stare into the eyes of the men I kill tonight, he thought.

Boundless furor consumed his heart as the outlines of Thukker and Minmatar ships grew larger.

You dare to show yourselves at these worlds? You dare to defile this holy ground? Then by God, I shall have your blood!

It didn't matter that Jamyl Sarum was alive, or that she was preparing to join this battle right now. It didn't matter that Amarr was being tested – not just her military, but the very faith that had carried their civilization for millennia. Grand Admiral Sundara would be here to give his life regardless of duty or prophecy.

He watched as the enemy unleashed their surface drones and fired their Insorum warheads toward his beloved planet, filling the space beneath them with a swarm of filth. Yet his fleet, closing range ever faster, still refrained from opening fire, further puzzling the enemy.

They would fire only when the Minmatars completed their Insorum bombardment, and not one moment sooner.

IT WAS TAKING too long, the Thukker infantryman thought. *Way too long.*

Locked inside the rocket pod of a jump magazine, the soldier monitored the data scrolling across his TACNET. They were more than six minutes past the zero mark, which meant they had lost the element of surprise. Unable to see anything except for mission data, he had been isolated from the outside world since boarding the dropship. As part of the airborne division, these 'fast-egress' surface operation troop transports carried up to fifty soldiers grouped in five separate ten-man, honeycomb-shaped 'magazines' held beneath the craft's wings. The magazines were loaded with maglev-assisted rocket pods designed to quickly transport soldiers to the ground, minimizing the time spent in the air and thus making them less vulnerable to ground fire.

A launch warning suddenly flashed across the soldier's vision; the ground assault was on.

He felt the dropship emerge from the dreadnought's hangar bay; his stomach lifted as the gravity disappeared, then was pressed back into his harness as the craft accelerated. A counter ticked off the seconds until he would be on the surface; his mission specs were updating dynamically to compensate for the delayed launch. Insorum canisters had saturated the city of Xerah, but preliminary reconnaissance data revealed none of the panic and confusion that the same tactics had generated on other Amarrian worlds.

In fact, the streets were completely devoid of citizens and slaves alike. That was cause for alarm.

While their dropship was en route, the fixed-emplacement defenses ringing the city were being pounded from orbit by the fleet's siege weapons. The mission of his airborne division was to secure several large Sarum Palace buildings surrounding a spaceport; in addition to housing large concentrations of slaves, they would serve as rally points from which liberated slaves elsewhere in the city could be brought for evacuation.

As the dropship entered the atmosphere of Mekhios, the soldier thought about his brother, who was assigned to an armored MTAC division in the Kor-Azor theater. Before parting ways in the Sanctuaries, they embraced, reassuring each other that if they had to die, they would do so knowing that others would live to taste the freedom that their own lives had provided.

He hadn't heard from him since the invasion began.

And here, this very world upon which he was descending, was the defining essence of why so many Minmatars would die today, for nowhere else in Amarr were slaves treated with more cruelty. The decision to launch, regardless of the city's apparent preparations for their attack, was impelled by this fact. There was no turning back now, for it was better for those slaves to die than to live on in such indignity – or with the knowledge that there were brothers and sisters who could have helped them, but chose not to.

A sharp, powerful jolt shook the ship; he felt the impact vibrate through the hull and into the structure of the protective cage around him. Encased in body armor, video of the outside world was now online; his helmet and mask were ringed with cameras that projected imagery directly onto his retina. The scene from the surface was hellish: torrents of anti-aircraft fire were rising from the cityscape below, and flaming craters marked the spots where other dropships had met their fate.

A second jolt caused a burst of static in his vision; he felt the craft yaw wildly to one side, prompting ejection warnings. Smoke clouded the image; his dropship had been hit, and was now spiralling out of control.

The jump magazines fired, detaching from the ship's undercarriage on their own power; four were struck immediately by directed ground fire and exploded. To save himself, the soldier fired the engines in his rocket pod; he was slammed hard into the harness as the tiny craft propelled away from danger. Programmed for this specific emergency, the pod automatically sought an alleyway between two low-rise structures, controlling its descent with thrusters and maglevs. When it struck the ground, his harness detached as the pod broke apart into segments. Snapping up his weapon, he searched for a target.

He was alone. The ground shook beneath his feet and the early morning sky flashed brightly; a heavy explosion detonated nearby, perhaps from the crash impact of his own dropship. The air was thick with Insorum; its sweet smell was fouled with the acrid taste of smoke.

New orders appeared on his TACNET: destroy the surface-to-air defenses in this city block. No mention at all was given to freeing slaves. The surface bombardment had only destroyed fixed emplacement weapons, and the dropships were getting murdered by mobile defenses. Clamping down on the sensor diodes attached to his tongue, he moved into the shadows and began working his way northeast, toward the nearest mobile AA battery; several other fellow soldiers were already doing the same. It was located on the roof of a nearby building; those that couldn't join them were assisting others pinned down by Paladins tracking the drop locations of pods.

The invasion had turned into an unmitigated disaster. Running out into the open, tracer fire lanced toward him; there was a gun nest in the balcony of a nearby building. The ground in front of him burst into a hail of debris and dirt as he sprinted for dear life; then motion sensor cameras attached to the back of his helmet detected movement on his flank. Diving over the hood of a parked hovercar, he found refuge from the balcony's line of fire; he heaved a plasma grenade back in the direction he had come from. As it sailed through the air, he could hear the staccato of gun-fire, shouts, and screams echoing through the streets. At least one MTAC was nearby; he could feel the rhythmic vi-brations of its heavy legs impacting the ground as it moved from street to street.

As soon as the grenade detonated, he broke into a sprint toward the entrance of his objective; he could hear the gun battery blasting away at dropships in the sky. His comrades were already inside, warning him that Amarrian troops were defending all the access points to the roof. Staying low, he moved past marble columns near the entrance; two plain-clothes Amarrians were erecting a barrier across the hall-way. Squeezing the trigger twice, he downed both of them with deadly marksmanship. Then he detected more move-ment behind him: he dropped to a knee as he whirled around.

He found himself face to face with a Minmatar slave: a little girl no more than ten years old.

'Are you here to take us away?' she asked.

The soldier leapt up, grabbed the child with one arm, and moved her back into the corridor.

'A vapor passed through here,' she said. 'I feel lost . . .'

'Are you here with anyone else?' he asked.

'They were forcing us into the basement when the gas came,' she said. 'I fell asleep, and when I woke up, I was alone . . .'

A huge blast outside shook the building and collapsed some of the ceiling inside the lobby. Unfazed by the terror, he reached out to cusp the child's mouth to muzzle her scream.

'Listen,' he said, removing his hand slowly. Schematics of the building were displayed in his TACNET, and there were several options for going upward. 'What's the fastest way to get to the roof?'

Breathing in short, shallow gasps, the young girl was too scared to answer.

'Be strong now,' the soldier said. 'I'm going to take you to a safe place, but I need to get to the roof first.'

'I . . . I don't remember . . .'

He sought out the soldiers near the roof through the TACNET.

'Which ingress route topside, over.'

A static-laced response came back amidst the sound of gunfire.

'Southeast stairwell, watch for traps.'

'Copy,' he said, taking the girl gently by the shoulders. 'I'm going to the other side, there are stairs there. Stay here – I promise I'll come back for you.'

'No! It's not safe,' she pleaded, snapping out of her daze and latching onto his arm. 'I saw bad people with guns go that way before you arrived. Use this side. The elevators have their own power. It's faster . . . hurry! This way!'

It was the sincerity in her eyes that convinced him.

'All right, but stay out of sight,' he said, moving toward the lifts. 'I'll be right back.'

The concourse hallway was large, but there was good cover behind all the ornate pillars and statues. *Maybe not enough to stop munitions*, he thought, *but enough to stay out of sight.* Sunlight was pouring through holes in the far side of the wall; the sound of more rocket pods landing nearby filled the air.

Good, he thought. *At least we're not completely alone in here . . .*

As soon as he rounded the corner to where the lifts were, he froze. At least a dozen Paladins were waiting for him with their weapons drawn.

His heart was crushed as their barrels erupted; falling to the floor, he realized that he wouldn't be able to help the little girl.

In writhing, agonizing pain, he could still sense movement behind him. *It was her*, he thought, *poor thing . . .*

With all the strength he could muster, he tried to warn her.

'Get out of here!' he stammered, as the Paladins gathered over him. 'Run!'

Then she stood over him as well, holding a blank, soulless stare; she was just one Minmatar child, surrounded by Amarrian overlords. It was emotionally overwhelming for him, even more than the burning agony in his chest and abdomen.

'Run from them!' he said. 'Get away!'

Instead she turned toward the guard, who produced a Vitoc syringe. Her eyes widened, and she reached out eagerly. But he pulled it away.

'No,' the guard said. 'Earn it.'

He extended his pistol toward her – grip first. She took it with her tiny hands; she was barely able to hold its weight. But she didn't need to be able to – not for long.

As she clumsily pointed the barrel down toward him, he remembered the promise to his brother.

'I'm sorry,' he whispered to her, a single tear falling from his eye. 'I'm so very sorry . . .'

68

+ 00:29:01

Essence Region – Crux Constellation
The Algogille System – Kassigainen Stargate
Sovereignty of the Gallente Federation

Korvin Lears wasn't paying attention to the loose formation of interceptors on his wing, let alone the space surrounding the Kassigainen Stargate. Instead, he was doing everything possible to find information about what was happening light years from here in the Amarr Empire.

Short of asking fleet command directly – which would certainly earn him a harsh reprimand – that task was proving next to impossible. From what little data he could gather, he inferred that the 'Minmatar' attack on CONCORD was a precursor to an invasion of the Amarr Empire. But there was no sovereign identity to the attackers. The Republic Fleet Grand Admiral – the highest official who was even reachable in their government – had emphatically denied that the attackers were in any way affiliated with the Republic, which was technically defunct and lawless without a prime minister or government to speak of.

Regardless of the invader's sovereignty, there was no question about their ethnicity. Down to the last man, they were all Minmatars, and acting with a conformity of purpose the likes of which humankind had never seen.

Who was guiding them? Korvin wondered. *Under what banner were these people fighting? They just launched a preemptive strike on Amarr, an act completely unprecedented in history, and put troops on the surface of their capital worlds, no less! This was what Keitan knew was going to happen!*

Korvin's musings distracted him from the seemingly harmless industrial sitting near the gate, which was now projecting a cynosural field off its bow; his wingmen noticed the anomaly a full second before he did.

'Cyno spike!' the pilot warned. 'Coming from the industrial!'

The beacon exploded into a swirling vortex nearly on top of the small interceptor; Korvin willed his ship to steer away from its deadly plane.

'Get out of there!' he shouted. 'Use your burners, man!'

But the younger, inexperienced pilot reacted too late; an enormous hulk was already coming through the vortex. The resulting collision bashed the interceptor into thousands of pieces, its fragments rumbling aside like so much scrap; the rest of Korvin's wing barely cleared the towering vessel in time.

That vessel was a Caldari Navy Phoenix-class dreadnought.

'What the *fuck*!' Korvin shouted, just as two more dreadnoughts emerged – and then a third and fourth. Then the Kassigainen stargate became active; in just a few seconds, dozens of Rokh-class battleships were deposited within kilometers of their position as capital ships continued to emerge from the jump portal.

'Command, this is Lieutenant Lears at checkpoint Algogille, where the hell are you?' he screamed, looping his ship over the stream of enemy warships.

'Lears, Command. What's the problem?' the annoyed voice responded.

'My problem?' he shouted. 'A goddamn Caldari task force just jumped into Algogille, that's my problem!'

'Lears, Tripwire scopes are all blank, are your systems functioning—'

'My wingman just got run over by a dreadnought!' he bellowed. There were over forty capital ships in-system now, but none of them were targeting him or his remaining wings. 'Tripwire is fucked! Send the Customs ships on the Luminaire gate – *oh my God . . .*'

The Caldari battleship group suddenly warped toward Luminaire; no sooner had they vanished when Scorpion-class warships emerged from the Kassigainen stargate to replace them.

Then the silhouette of a Leviathan-class titan appeared in the jump portal.

A mayday distress call went out on the Federation command channel: the Customs ships near the Luminaire gate were already under attack.

Korvin couldn't believe it.

'Command, Tripwire is sabotaged, a major Caldari incursion is underway in Algogille—'

The titan opened a second jump portal, and capital ships – numbering in the hundreds and still growing – began entering.

Korvin knew exactly where they were heading.

'Warp to the Luminaire gate,' he ordered his wingmen,

wrenching his ship around the jump portal. 'Go directly in and split up into two groups – one of you warp to Caldari Prime, the other to the capital. *Go!*'

There wasn't time for protocol anymore.

'Attention all Federation ships, this is Lieutenant Korvin Lears at checkpoint Algogille,' he announced on the command channel. 'A Caldari invasion of Federation space is underway, repeat, an invasion of Federation space is underway . . . the enemy fleet target destination is Luminaire, we are en route to confirm.'

His Taranis was already hurling through the warp tunnel when Admiral Eturrer spoke up on the command channel.

'Lieutenant, you're not authorized to give fleet orders on this channel—'

'Fuck authorization! Your whole goddamn plan depended on Tripwire, and it failed!'

'Lieutenant!'

The Luminaire stargate emerged before him; the wreckage of at least three Federation Customs ships was floating nearby. Three dozen Caldari Navy Rokh warships were already in sniping positions some two hundred kilometers off the gate.

'Tell the president that we've been invaded by the Caldari State and we're already taking casualties,' he shouted, activating the stargate just as another wingman was vaporized by the Rokh's railguns. 'And that at least one titan-backed fleet is converging on Luminaire!'

The Day of Knives

+ 00:29:01

Metropolis Region – Barvigrard Constellation
The Bei System – Colelie Stargate
Minmatar Republic – Gallente Federation Border

There was a stir amongst the hordes of refugees leaving Minmatar space.

While most of them were too simple to understand the significance of CONCORD's disappearance, they all understood the significance of the word 'invasion' – and that it was happening to the Amarr Empire. But for them, it only added more urgency to escape the beleaguered, chaotic worlds of the Minmatar Republic.

For Grand Admiral Kasora Neko, the sudden disappearance of the Archangel gangs and thugs harassing the refugees was a welcome development, but deeply alarming just the same. She knew firsthand that the invaders – she assumed they were the Elders – had accomplished the dual-impossible feats of shattering CONCORD and launching a multi-front offensive on Amarrian space. The problem was that she couldn't keep the rest of the Republic Fleet under her command from learning that as well, and it was already a tenuous command at best. Her vice admirals were reporting numerous cases of abandonment in their ranks; several captains had already disobeyed deployment orders to go join the strike against Amarr.

If the invaders were the Elders, and if they were allegedly fighting on behalf of Minmatar, they made absolutely no attempt to communicate with the Republic government at all. That was just as well; there was still no information on where Karin Midular was or what exactly had happened to her. As if the responsibility for controlling the violence at the Republic's borders wasn't enough pressure, foreign governments were already relying on Admiral Neko to make statements on behalf of a nation that was literally decapitated.

As her Maelstrom-class battleship idled beside the Colelie Stargate, she was aware of her physical self shaking her head through the viscous fluid of her pod. *The surreal contradiction of Minmatar affairs is sickening*, she thought. *What a sad, sad scene . . . Republic Fleet warships protecting fleeing refugees – those whom had given up hope for the Republic – while the battle to free their own kind raged elsewhere.*

For the third time in less than twenty minutes, she found her attention drawn to a civilian transport arriving from the stargate, heading back *into* the Republic rather than leaving it. The Mammoth-class industrial slowly turned past the lines of ships waiting for clearance to leave. With CONCORD gone and the NEOCOM offline, there was no way to investigate the vessel's captain or gauge his intentions – not without physically intercepting the ship.

Then she was contacted by Keitan Yun.

'Greetings, Admiral,' he said. 'I see the border situation has stabilized.'

'You,' she snarled. 'I'd arrest you myself if you were here.'

'I think I may have won an executive pardon,' he said,

as Karin Midular joined the conversation. 'But I understand your concern.'

'Karin!' Admiral Neko exclaimed. 'Where have you been?'

The prime minister, appearing haggard and angry, said nothing as Keitan looked on with concern. While the admiral waited for them to say something, another Mammoth materialized outside the stargate, and just like all the others, headed in the opposite direction of traffic.

'Tell her the truth,' Keitan urged.

The prime minister took a deep breath.

'My bodyguards attacked me at Parliament,' Karin admitted. 'And then . . . I was raped.'

'Raped?' Admiral Neko's vision turned red, but she remained calm. 'Are you safe now?'

'I owe Keitan Yun my life,' Karin continued. 'They would have killed me for sure had he not arrived with . . .'

The admiral couldn't help herself; she willed her battleship to follow the mysterious freighter, leaving her escorts to stay on patrol at the stargate.

'With what?' she asked.

'With the Elders,' Karin admitted. 'Men sent by the Elders to protect me. You were right about them . . .'

The freighter was turning to warp; Admiral Neko aligned herself behind it.

'So they take responsibility for attacking CONCORD?' she asked. 'And for the Amarr invasion?'

'Yes,' Karin nodded. 'They're behind all of it.'

'I have to ask,' Admiral Neko said. 'Was justice served to the man who violated you?'

'It was,' Karin said, struggling to hold her voice steady. 'And justice continues to be served right now, as we speak.'

'In Amarr?' The Mammoth emerged from hyperspace outside the Uttindar stargate; she targeted the vessel and ordered it to stop its engines. The pilot complied without saying a word.

'And the Republic,' Karin said.

She brought the Maelstrom alongside the industrial, training its cannons on its hull.

'You may have noticed some industrial ships passing through the Gallentean borders,' Karin said. 'Mammoths travelling against the tide . . .'

Alarmed, Admiral Neko said nothing as she studied one of those exact ships now.

'They were sent by the Elders as well,' Karin continued. 'Their holds are filled with assassins, and together they are carrying out the largest series of murders in the history of the Republic.'

Admiral Neko hailed the ship in her gunsights.

'Mammoth transport Nine-Alpha Tango, this is a warship of the Republic Fleet performing a customs inspection. Identify, over.'

There was no response, except for the blinking collision lights on the vessel's long, blocky hull.

'They're purging the government of corruption,' Karin said. 'It's happening on stations, on planets . . . to guards, members of parliament, regional governors . . . the Elders know *everything* about how we've been sabotaged to the point of insolvency . . .'

'Karin, I'm not sure that I'm understanding you correctly,' she growled, focusing on the industrial.

'Every corpse will be accompanied with a datacore containing detailed information about their crimes. The evidence, and thus the justification for these . . . measures, is compelling.'

'You're willing to bet the integrity of our system of law on that?' Admiral Neko said. 'Take their word for it that these people deserve to be murdered in cold blood? What are we doing defending the border then? What's left to protect at this point?'

'A new beginning for the Republic,' she answered. 'I believe the Elders now, just as you did. I finally see just how hopeless this government was . . . how paralyzed we were.'

'Karin, what's going to happen if the Elders' invasion fails, and the Amarrians counterattack our own borders?' Admiral Neko demanded. 'Who's going to be left to defend it?'

'The Elders won't let us down,' Karin assured. 'When this purge is complete, I'll return to office and start the process of installing a new government, including a prime minister to replace *me*. And I'll rely on you, as I always have, to defend our right to do that.'

Admiral Neko glared at the industrial hovering just meters off her bow.

'Nine-Alpha Tango, carry on,' she said, releasing her target lock. 'Resume your course and Godspeed.'

As the ship moved silently toward the Uttindar stargate, Admiral Neko wondered just how much blood had been spilled by these assassins already, and how much more was to come.

If Minmatars want to kill each other, so be it, she thought angrily, selecting a fleet-wide broadcast for her next orders. *But I'll be damned if I'm going to allow it to be spilled by Amarrians. Not in the Republic, anyway.*

'Attention all Republic Fleet warships,' she announced. 'This is Grand Admiral Kasora Neko. You have new command orders: group at the crossings to Amarr space and prepare for a possible Amarrian attack. These orders apply to every ship in every territory of the Minmatar Republic, to every man and woman in active service *and* the reserves. If you call one of the Seven Tribes your own, then you have a personal stake in the outcome of these times, and your actions now will define how future generations of our race survive – or not at all.'

69

+ 00:31:23

Essence Region – Crux Constellation
The Luminaire System – Caldari Prime
City of Tovil – Dengmar Power Generation Plant
Sovereignty of the Gallente Federation

After a long, tiresome day of mind-numbing boredom and wasted time, the sun was finally setting.

Assigned guard duty at one of the city's power generation plants, an older Federation police officer grumbled about the need to stay for the full length of his shift. Sitting alone in the confines of a police speeder, he cursed the desk captain and berated the reasoning for his assignment. Granted, there was relative safety here, for which he was grateful. Most of the fighting and rioting was happening near the Caldari districts, which, at his age, he could do without. Those types of engagements were best left to the younger, fitter, eager troopers anxious to throw themselves into the fray to showcase their patriotism and commitment to duty.

But then what was the point of guarding the employee entrance to a power generation facility? The streets were controlled, Federation businesses were open, Gallenteans were openly carrying on with their lives, and the Caldari vermin responsible for all this mess was corralled behind electric fencing and barricades. Why assign him – an officer with just a few more years until retirement – to babysit a fortified door entrance?

Of course, the urgency for wanting to leave early was to get home in time for a birthday celebration dinner with his oldest son, who was leaving soon for the engineering academy. They grow up fast, he explained to his captain. When the realization hits that you don't have forever to spend time with them, you seize every chance you get to make up for that. It's only a few minutes early, for crying out loud!

No, it's *thirty* minutes early, the captain told him. We're short on manpower, so you have to stay for the entire shift. Sorry.

Slamming the console, he daydreamed of family memories while watching the hustle and bustle of the streets below. He singled out a young couple holding hands; a trio of chattering businessmen; a pack of kids hoverboarding through the sculptures and gardens. It was a brisk evening, and already the brightest stars in the sky were shining through the twilight above. The breeze carried the sound of street musicians and the din of a thousand conversations; the air smelled of everything from gourmet cooking to the rich mineral scent of the glacier-fed river nearby.

What a perfect night to be sitting in a patrol speeder, he thought miserably. But then his hopes were raised as a Federation police transport pulled up to the curb at the base of the marble stairs below. Leaning forward in his seat to peer over the console, he thought he might be relieved early after all . . .

An earsplitting crack of thunder rattled his rib cage; it was so powerful that the vehicle shook as the sound passed overhead and reverberated through the skyscrapers. Startled, he instinctively checked himself for damage – there was none, nor was there any that he could see to the car, or to the structures outside; people on the street were helping frightened, upset pedestrians off the ground and scurrying to get indoors.

Then he realized that the speeder had lost power. As he tried to restart it, a second blast of thunder shook him down to the bone; his hands began shaking when he realized that the vehicle was completely dead.

An employee ran out from the building behind him, banging on the car door to get his attention.

'EMP strike!' the man yelled frantically. 'We were just hit with a double surge of – what the hell is *that*?'

The roar of a ramjet startled the police officer as both men looked upward. A military drone flew low overhead, banking sharply in between two buildings farther down the street. Toggling the commlink on his uniform, the officer tried to contact the command desk, but all he heard was static.

Before it disappeared, the officer swore he saw the Caldari State seal painted on the underside of the drone.

'Get back inside and barricade yourself behind something!' he screamed at the employee. 'Run!'

As the terrified man turned away, there was a sharp *crack* as his back exploded in a reddish-white mist; he tumbled to the ground in an awkward heap. The officer hesitated, partly in shock from the warm spray of blood across his face, partly from hearing gunfire for the first time outside of a training range. Looking ahead, he saw Federation police officers advancing toward him, confused by the fact that each was brandishing a Minmatar assault rifle.

In a harsh moment of reckoning, it occurred to him that those weapons were completely devoid of electronic parts.

Ripping a plasma rifle off the console rack, he found that the charge-fired, magnetic-bottle guidance weapon couldn't be fired. The battery and electronics had been fried, just like the speeder he was sitting in.

Three bullets lodged themselves in the windshield directly in front of the officer's face. The man who had fired them looked like an ethnic Gallentean, and he was cursing that the rounds failed to penetrate the material.

'We're on the same side!' the officer screamed as the man approached the side of the vehicle. 'What the hell are you doing?'

'Believe me,' the 'Gallentean' said, taking aim. 'It's better for you this way.'

The Federation police officer would never know that he was the second casualty of Tibus Heth's invasion of Caldari Prime, or that his wasn't the only skull being collapsed by Templis Dragonaur special forces at strategic installations all over the planet.

KORVIN'S SHIP WAS in the Luminaire system for less than a second before coming under attack by Caldari warships.

Beset by a sensor-jamming electromagnetic onslaught, the space surrounding the Algogille stargate was awash in pulsing strobes of effulgence from the sheer amount of radiation generated by Caldari Navy EW ships orbiting nearby. Nothing could withstand such a concentrated electronic bombardment; every ship jumping into the system through this gate would be blind and helpless, unable to lock targets or fire their weapons. The only way to beat the barrage was through brute force, literally by bringing more ships through than the Caldari already had camped there – a price that the Caldari Navy was betting the Federation wasn't willing to pay.

Korvin was able to escape only because his was the first ship to land in the blockade before its full lethality could be brought to bear, warping mere nanoseconds before dozens of drive-crippling interdictor bubbles were cast over the gate. As his Taranis began hurtling toward Caldari Prime, there was just enough time to see his remaining wingmen – hopelessly immobilized the instant they arrived – annihilated by the rail fire of a hundred ships.

This has to be a nightmare, he thought, his veins flooded with adrenaline. As his Taranis passed through the serene tranquility of the warp core, temporarily detached from the universe and impervious to the horrors awaiting him on the other side, he asked himself one last question:

How did we fail to stop this?

When the warp tunnel dissipated and the metropolis-strewn ice planet filled his view, he saw just how real the nightmare was.

The iconic scene was sure to inspire the soul of every Provist in New Eden: the Leviathan was already in orbit above Caldari Prime, anchored above the ruins of a Caldari station built long before the Gallenteans drove them away in the last war. The same fleet he saw amassing in Algogille was here now as well, assuming siege positions above the planet; the flickering wrecks of at least thirty Federation Navy warships were nearby.

Korvin doubted they ever knew what hit them.

Like the downpour beneath a distant tempest, the space between the Caldari dreadnought fleet and the planet's atmosphere below was tinted darker than the rest; a quick zoom with his camera drones revealed tens of thousands of dropships and support drones descending to the surface. Federation orbital defenses were already in ruins, and there was no planet-based anti-spacecraft fire lancing up through the clouds at the attackers.

The Caldari Navy had succeeded in establishing absolute space-superiority over a planet right in the capital system of the Gallente Federation.

Nearby, the Dragonfly fighter squadron of a Chimera-class supercarrier was already targeting Korvin's interceptor and accelerating to attack speed.

There was only one option available to him. Keying both the command channel and the local, he began to speak.

'Attention all Gallenteans, this is Lieutenant Korvin Lears of the Federation Navy . . .'

He pointed the nose of his ship toward the cloud of dropships and ignited his microwarp drive.

'The Caldari State has just launched a surface invasion of Caldari Prime,' he continued, just as the fighters opened fire on him. 'My wingmen are all dead, the reinforcements in this system are already destroyed, and in a few moments, I'll be killed and reanimated in a cloning bay far away from here . . .'

Sensing what he was about to do, the fighter pilots became more urgent in their attack, trying in vain to close the distance with his speedy Taranis.

'As a capsuleer, I have the privilege of immortality, but the rest of you . . . you brave citizens on the surface, whom we were charged to protect, do not. We have failed you, and for that, we can only beg for your forgiveness . . .'

Aiming his ship toward the densest cluster of dropships he could find, he activated the self-destruct sequence on the Taranis.

'Your legacy will inspire me in every life I have to fight for your liberation,' he said, releasing his mental grip on the spacecraft's controls. 'Fight these invaders with all your heart and soul; show no remorse and take no prisoners, for these aren't humans that descend upon your homes . . .'

Korvin's last realization before the Taranis's nuclear power plant detonated was that his ship was less than 300 miles from the surface of Caldari Prime, and almost directly over the city of Tovil.

For the Caldari Navy dropship crews and troops near the blast radius of Korvin's ship, life simply ceased to exist.

The explosion was visible from the ground as a brilliant white flash that would hang in the sky for several minutes; concentric cirrus-like rings emanated from the blast point marking the exact spot where Korvin Lears died for the second time.

The electromagnetic pulse of the blast overwhelmed the electronics of dozens of dropships immediately, compromising their atmospheric entry angles and causing them to break apart in long streaks of fiery debris; many of their charred carcasses took the tops off of buildings as they crashed to the surface, touching off explosions at impact sites that claimed both Caldari and Gallentean life alike.

Thousands of troops and untold pieces of Caldari equipment ranging from rifles to MTACs, tanks and APCs were lost by the actions of Korvin Lears. The Dragonaurs on the ground, pausing their murderous strikes for a moment to look up at the sky, prayed that one very special dropship – one flying with the 5th Dragonaurs Armored Division – was still intact.

Then they resumed their deadly work, proceeding with the invasion plan as only devoted servants of Caldari ultra-nationalism could.

Until the dropships landed, they were the only men in the densest cities of Caldari Prime with functioning weapons. When they weren't murdering the guards of military installations, they used their deceiving appearance to spread panic and disinformation, encouraging the masses to emerge from their city blocks into the open.

Because of the Federation imposition of martial law, the local Caldarians were still quarantined in isolated segments of the city. Heth's invasion planners were going to exploit that convenience, especially now that so much equipment was just lost in the skies over Tovil. Destructive brute force would substitute for what the lost dropship teams were supposed to take intact with surgical precision. The surface bombardment began immediately; chunks of white-hot plasma hurled down from space, incinerating buildings, collapsing overpasses, and leaving craters several meters deep as native Gallenteans fled in terror.

The weapon officers directing the siege guns on Caldari dreadnoughts knew exactly where the Caldari civilian concentrations were located, and were thus free to attack any unassigned target of military value – all except for the Gallentean residential sectors of the city.

Tibus Heth needed those for something else.

70

00:40:03

Essence Region – Crux Constellation
The Luminaire System – Caldari Prime
City of Arcurio: Federation Municipal Governance
District

Descending toward the surface of Caldari Prime aboard a
heavy transport dropship, Tibus Heth cursed the lingering
flash in the sky as it disappeared beneath the horizon. It
was pure luck that his group missed the blast radius of that
Federation interceptor; a few seconds earlier in their approach and they would all be atoms now. But that was war,
and in his mind, an appropriate metaphor for life: timing
was everything, but it was luck that determined the fate of
moments in between.

Strapped into the armored cockpit of a combat MTAC,
torrents of information were passing before his eyes, re-
laying casualty estimates and the adjustment of battle plans
accordingly. As testament to the competency of the Provist chain of command and Caldari military efficiency, the
Tovil theater of operations had regrouped – but not without
a cost.

'We lost about thirty seconds,' Admiral Morda Engsten
reported. 'The damage was spread across the units assigned
to the northern sections of Tovil. They'll have to do more
with less, but it's still doable.'

'Did any more starships make it through your blockade?'

Heth asked casually. 'Or do I have assurances that it won't happen again?'

'The only assurance is that we have to hold off a Federation counterattack for thirty seconds longer than we planned, and that you have thirty seconds *less* to fulfill your mission,' she snapped. 'We've pushed our entire fleet through the Algogille stargate and managed to get a second Leviathan into the system. Blockades are holding at the Mies and Pettinck stargates – we've destroyed dozens of Federation ships attempting to break through. But we're completely fenced into Luminaire – there's nothing standing between the Gallenteans and Caldari space.'

'Admiral, civilian casualties are no concern,' Tibus reminded her. 'Tovil's units have unrestricted firing orders – make sure they understand that.'

The dropship's pilot interrupted: 'Sixty seconds!'

'The troops know they're free to engage,' she said. 'But what they need to hear now is that their inspirational leader wasn't incinerated during that blast!'

'Of course, Admiral,' Tibus smiled. 'You should encourage your captains to hold their blockade for just a little while longer.'

'Good luck then, Commander Heth . . . but for God's sake, hurry!'

+ 00:40:09

Caldari Prime
City of Tovil: Valley Norge Shopping District
Federation Armory 62B

A wild-eyed Federation private sprinted through the main floor of a swank women's department store, avoiding the huddled groups of mortified shoppers cowering beneath merchandise stands and blocks of rubble. He ignored their cries for help; there was absolutely nothing he could do for them. With each stride, the burn in his legs intensified; blood was trickling from the nicks and scratches in his face. That was the full extent of his injuries thus far; he was the sole survivor of a group of soldiers who fell victim to a Caldari gunship's strafing run outside the armory. There was enough time to hear the roar of its engines, but not much else. As the building facade in front of him broke apart in a flash, he was driven into the pavement; when he picked himself back up, his comrades were no longer there.

Their loss did nothing to lessen his desperate urge to keep on living.

A rhythmic rumble persisted beneath his boots as they impacted against the floor; he knew it was from the convoy of MTACs and tanks in the streets outside as they rushed away from the armory. *They should have been destroyed*, he thought. *The Caldarians must have planned to take the vehicles intact, but the explosion in the sky – whatever it was – changed their plans*. That bought the Federation Marines 62-Bravo Company of Valley Norge some time – *at least until the orbital bombardment hits us, as it has every other military installation in the city*. By rushing to save as many fighting vehicles as possible, there was some hope that an effective counterattack could be mounted, for all the good it would do at this point.

The Caldarians had achieved absolute space superiority, which gave Federation ground forces no chance of defending themselves with any degree of success.

'Help us!' a woman screamed, throwing herself in the soldier's path and latching on to him. 'What are we supposed to do?'

Wresting the woman's arms off of him, he kept running.

'Just go home!' he panted over his shoulder, dodging more collapsing debris from the ceiling. 'Stay there until it's safe!'

'Safe?' she screamed. 'How are we even supposed to *get* home? Goddamn you, help us!'

She doesn't matter anymore, he told himself, pushing himself past the point of exhaustion to continue on. *No one here does.* This building was located directly next to the armory, and would likely be obliterated along with everything else nearby when the bombardment came. Cutting through here to reach the rally point was the only 'safe' way to stay beyond the crosshairs of Caldari gunships outside; to have even a remote chance of surviving, these people would have to follow him there within the next sixty seconds.

Given that they were mostly affluent women who happened to be shopping for exotic underwear when the sky began to fall, the soldier wrote off their chances completely.

Bolting past malfunctioning ad platforms and shattered crystal displays, he cursed at the static on his commlink. Intermittent jamming from the EW drones flying overhead was making communications next to impossible; they were lucky to get the word out about the rally point. Clutching his rifle as he rounded past the entrance to what was once a lush arboretum, he spotted more victims crushed beneath the felled support archways of the structure's roof.

The Navy failed us, he thought, scurrying through a hole carved through the building walls by pulse fire. *An invasion force this big should have never made it into Lu-*

minaire. The mechanical leg of a Federation MTAC stomped by; its tri-pedalled foot was pulverizing the rubble beneath its weight as it marched down the street. Citizens wandered about dazed and confused; many bleeding from injuries as other random Samaritans assisted them, screaming for help. Incapacitated medical drones and police equipment lay in ruins amongst the smoke and debris that was everywhere; it was inconceivable that just one hour earlier, this hellish war zone was a posh shopping district in the bustling downtown area.

The air reeked of death and suffering, and still his lungs couldn't gulp enough of it down as he battled fatigue to reach the rally point just ahead. Other exhausted, terrified Federation infantrymen emerged from the smoke, struggling to get as far away from the armory as possible. As his commlink suddenly sprang to life, the CO shouted for the men to hurry; a Caldari Navy dreadnought had reached firing position some three hundred miles above them.

With only two hundred meters to go, the private considered that the most probable reason why the jamming stopped was because enemy troops were already on the ground.

+ 00:41:15

City of Arcurio: Federation Municipal Governance District

'Thirty seconds, look alive back there!' the dropship pilot announced, drawing a broad grin beneath Tibus Heth's visored mask. Linked to the Caldari Navy's TACNET, he was able to watch the ship break through the cloud cover over the familiar Arcurio metropolis – the very city in which he was born. It was nightfall, and with the advance team firmly in control of the power stations, only the Caldari districts of the city were lighted. The rest – where millions of Gallenteans were cowering in terror right now – was pitch black.

Columns of smoke rose from fiery craters where AA batteries and armories once stood; if not for the Dragonaurs superb work, the sky would be filled with missiles and plasma, stopping this glorious invasion in mid-flight.

Not today, he thought, watching the dropship's pulse turrets spit fire toward a group of targets on the ground. *And not ever again.*

Toggling the global command channel, he addressed the men and women of his army.

'Welcome home, Caldarians!' he thundered, keeping a close eye on the altimeter. 'Have courage, soldiers! Those who have fallen, and those who *will* fall on this day of days, join the indomitable Tikkonian quest to restore the greatness of our civilization! The warrior spirits of your ancestors demand that you liberate your brothers and sisters! Heed the call and you are *invincible*! There is no greater honor, no greater glory than this moment . . . Seize it! Do you see the hallowed ground before your eyes? Do you see your lands defiled by Gallentean filth? Take it back from them! It's yours!'

A powerful jolt announced the dropship's touchdown on the paved streets of Arcurio.

'Hot zone!' the pilot shouted. 'Egress now, now, *now*!'

As the ramp lowered, small arms fire began smacking the ship's interior immediately. Escorted by two other Rhykevance-class MTACs, Tibus throttled his walker forward at full speed. Red targets were all over the TACNET; plasma fire coming from the edges of buildings and the tiered city rooftops above was already lancing into his armor. Behind him, the dropship took to the air, kicking up dust while its pulse turrets returned fire down the street. The target objective was dead ahead: the Arcurio Provincial Government Headquarters. The few Federation forces that survived the orbital bombardment had set up a defensive perimeter around the complex.

'Five hundred meters to glory!' he shouted, finding a Federation infantryman and opening fire with the MTAC's shoulder-mounted heavy machine guns. The soldier disintegrated as the rounds found their mark, pumping adrenaline through the veins of the Caldari dictator and filling his soul with a primal urge that made him want to kill even more. This machine was a far cry from the one he'd piloted at the Armor Forge. Equipped with an array of anti-armor and anti-air weapons, the Rhykevance was strong enough to withstand at least one direct hit from a tank round, and agile enough to operate effectively within the narrow, three-dimensional terrain of modern, multi-level urban cityscapes. With cannons blasting away, Tibus stepped the vehicle over barriers designed to stop tanks with ease, mowing down every Gallentean combatant he could find.

A virtually uncontested slaughter such as this would be impossible without the Navy's gunship dominance of the skies and the other mechanized squadrons converging on the government complex from every side. Provist infantry divisions were already erecting barriers surrounding the Gallentean districts; in a short time, no one inside would be able to leave them without permission from the Caldari Providence Directorate.

+ 00:42:24

Caldari Prime
City of Tovil – Valley Norge Shopping District
2400 meters from Armory 62B

The Federation private had just thrown himself over a plex-isteel barricade when the skies behind him turned from night to day.

A pillar of fire descended from the clouds directly over the armory; the plasma bolt's uniform charge generated current with the surrounding air mass and engulfed the area in lightning. The searing heat and electricity shattered the hardened structure and vaporized everything within, burning straight through the main city block tier and into the sublevels beneath it. Building materials superheated by the blast exploded; the weapons and ordnance stores remaining behind contributed that much more force to the carnage. The expanding shockwave carved a sphere of destruction for hundreds of meters in every direction; hovercars, MTACs, and even tanks within line of sight of the blast were thrown into the air like so much rubble.

As the concussive wave passed over the barrier, both of the private's eardrums were collapsed, and with them, his bearing of the reality surrounding him. Disoriented, he stood straight up, oblivious to how foolish an act that was. Glancing back at the direction from which he came, he saw the destruction wrought by the bombardment: the building that he had run through minutes earlier was now smoldering ruins, and charred corpses littered the streets surrounding it. An MTAC marched directly over his head; its cannons and blasters were raining streams of fire toward a Caldari tank that emerged from the block opposite where the arboretum once stood.

Mesmerized as the tank exploded, he was startled as the MTAC's leg was blown off; only a well-aimed shell fired from a second tank was capable of such a feat. Unmitigated violence was happening at speeds that seemed all the more surreal since he was deaf to it all; the ground beneath him shook as the massive walker crashed into the ground. A comrade grabbed him by the shoulders and began to scream, probably telling him to get protection, even as the pavement behind him began exploding in parallel lines of molten slag.

He was on his back, staring at the nighttime sky. A gunship was orbiting high overhead; he could see the illuminated Caldari State logo on its underside.

Before departing this life, the private realized that the city of Tovil was lost, and that what would follow was not something worth living through at all.

+ 00:42:29

City of Arcurio: Federation Municipal Governance District

'They're putting up a fight, men!' Tibus roared with glee, murdering everything he could find. 'This is where they're going to make their stand! For Malkalen! Keeping pushing forward!'

A staggered convoy of tanks roared past his MTAC squad as they reached the main square, their turrets firing indiscriminately at buildings and infrastructure even when no target was in their sights; it was enough to just wreck anything and everything in their path. The Municipal Government Headquarters building was just ahead; a towering pole with a shredded, hole-ridden Federation flag fluttering high in the wind marked the only target objective still left standing – and that was no accident at all.

Following the entire scene from beginning to end were military camera drones, recording Tibus Heth's MTAC from several different angles at once as it marched across the square toward victory.

Somewhere overhead, a Gallentean air transport was shot out of the sky by Caldari Navy gunships; its fiery plumes streaked to the ground in a violent crash. The shattered carcasses of Federation MTACs and tanks littered the streets surrounding the government complex; the distant sound of orbital strikes carried like thunder across the battlefield; the skies flickered like a lightning storm as the tops of buildings burned into the night. Hundreds of Provist troops surged into the building as Tibus walked his MTAC straight up the steps, through the great pillars and onto the base of the flag mast.

Tibus Heth climbed out of the cockpit, down the ladder rungs along the vehicle's legs and jumped to the ground. As Federation troops were marched outside with their hands on their heads, he limped purposely toward the flagpole and grabbed hold of its cables, wrenching them downward as fast as he could. Provist troops cheered him on, several reaching up to assist him as he ripped the Federation flag off. With Caldari Navy MTACs flooding the area with searchlights, Tibus Heth – surrounded by fellow comrades of the 5th Dragonaur Armored Division – raised the flag of the Caldari State over the city of Arcurio.

After nearly two hundred years of Federation occupation, Tibus Heth and the Caldari Navy had retaken the planet of Caldari Prime.

He ripped the datapad off his utility belt.

'Admiral! Are we ready?'

She responded immediately.

'The city barriers are in place, and all orbital siege guns have their targets locked. Now is the time, Tibus!'

The blood in the dictator's veins turned to fire.

'Then get me President Foiritan right away!'

71

+ 00:42:40

Essence Region – Vieres Constellation
The Ladistier System – Planet IV, Moon 4
Presidential Bureau Station

Federation Navy Grand Admiral Anvent Eturrer spoke calmly, without betraying any indication that he was pressured, or that he was even concerned about what had just transpired in Luminaire.

'What do you mean, "closed off"?' President Foiritan demanded. 'How the fuck does the capital system of the Gallente Federation get "closed off"? I'm not following you.'

'It appears the Caldari have moved the *entirety* of their armed forces into the system,' the admiral answered. 'The far sides of the stargates leading to Luminaire are completely locked down by EW platforms and surrounded by mines. All of our attempts to send ships through have failed, but we may try other tactics to break their lock on the system.'

'Other *tactics*?' the president fumed. 'How many Caldari ships are over there, exactly?'

'Two Leviathan-class titans, at least one of which is in orbit over Caldari Prime; about five thousand starships of various classes; more than one hundred thousand dropships and gunships; and we estimate about 1100 divisions, or more than twenty million troops, on the surface—'

'Twenty *million*?'

'Yes, all of which are operating with complete impunity on the planet; the cities of Tovil and Arcurio are both completely surrounded. The only good news is that Gallente Prime is untouched; no Caldari ships are orbiting it, which is just as well because there aren't any Federation ships left to defend it.'

The president, surrounded by most of his cabinet members, glared at the screen projection of the nonchalant Grand Admiral.

'How many ships did you say attempted to get through that blockade so far?'

'Thirty-nine, to be exact.'

'Did you inflict any casualties at all on Caldari forces?'

'We caught the tail end of the convoys jumping into Luminaire, shooting down or crippling ten enemy ships,' the admiral said proudly.

'Ten ships.' The president shook his head. 'So what happened to Tripwire?'

'We're going to investigate causes for a possible failure—'

'You're relieved, Admiral,' the president snarled. 'Vice Admiral Ranchel is the new acting commander of Federation armed forces.'

A portrait of the vice admiral appeared next to Anvent Eturrer; full video wasn't possible because, unlike his commanding officer, he was inside the pod capsule of a Nyx-class supercarrier in the Algogille system.

The admiral smirked. 'Mr. President, we're at *war*. Relieving your commander during ongoing military operations—'

'—is something I should have done a long time ago, thank you, now piss off!'

The image disappeared, and President Foiritan banged his fist on the table.

'Ariel, make goddamn sure he does *not* leave Federation space, understood?'

'Yes, sir,' the intelligence chief replied, typing furiously into her datapad. She was paler than usual, but her demeanor was both sad and furious all at once.

'How bad are the casualties on Caldari Prime?' the president asked.

'Worse than any of us can bear,' she said. 'We estimate civilian toll is in the millions . . .'

'There are hundreds of thousands of police, troops, and reservists down there,' he growled. 'What about them? Couldn't they do anything to curb these losses at all?'

'Not when they're outnumbered twenty to one,' General Borgier, the Federation Joint Chief of Staff, grumbled. 'Sir, the total peacetime number of troops and police officers on Caldari Prime is about one million, and most of them were desk jockeys in riot control gear when the landings started. They were also completely exposed to the orbital bombardment. To make matters worse, inside jobs disabled planetary defenses, allowing the Caldarians to compromise hardened targets in both cities.'

'Inside jobs?'

'Advanced commando teams on the ground long before the invasion started. But that's beside the point. To be blunt, planetary defenses just wouldn't have mattered. What good are a few megapulse rails and missile batteries against an armada that large? In the end, the result would be the same. No shield generator could absorb a barrage that intense.'

'All right,' the president said. 'Vice Admiral Ranchel, how can we defeat this blockade?'

'Only with brute force, sir,' the carrier pilot said. 'Covert ops can't break through because the Luminaire side is completely saturated with proximity mines. The Caldarians have locked themselves in tight, and the only way to drive them out is by sacrificing hundreds, if not thousands of ships. We would pay the largest space-faring price in human life by far in Federation Navy history. And after all that, even if we can reach Caldari Prime, I really don't know how much good it will do, or how many people we'll save down there.'

'Then what do you suggest?' the president nearly shouted. 'That we do nothing? We have the best-equipped, highest paid military in New Eden, and you're telling me that it never occurred to the war planners here that a full scale Caldari invasion was possible?'

'Mr. President, too much of our strategy counted on early warning intelligence,' the vice admiral admitted, his voice steady. 'Tibus Heth shut down our HUMINT networks, and now Tripwire has failed us. To say we were unprepared is the understatement of the millennium. In my opinion, there's only one option, and it's an incomplete one at best.'

'An incomplete option,' the president scoffed. 'Great, let's hear it.'

'Ariel can confirm this, but judging from the numbers they've committed to Caldari Prime, there's *at most* a skeleton defense from Luminaire all the way to New Caldari, sir. The road to their capital system is clear, but . . .'

'But what?'

'A full scale retaliatory strike on the order of what the Caldarians have accomplished is impossible now.'

'And that's because—'

'—of the peacetime readiness level of our corps. We can bombard their worlds into a dark age, but we can't take their planets. Our troop levels have never been lower – besides high pay, there's no incentive for citizens to join the armed forces; our reliance on drones is defeated by Caldari EW prowess; and our military is focused almost exclusively on ship power.'

'Bomb them back to the dark ages then! Give me something to take back from those bastards, Admiral!'

'Then the Tierijev System is where we can start,' he said. 'It's completely surrounded by Federation systems, and enough Navy assets are already in place to mount a strike. Give the word, and well send those teams to immobilize defences inside Tierijev. We'll take casualties, but the rational bet is that there can't possibly be a force there equivalent to the one we engaged in Algogille.'

'Do it,' the president ordered. 'Destroy every military installation in that system.'

A drone's voice interrupted the session: 'Sir, Tibus Heth has contacted us, and wishes to speak with you.'

All eyes fell on the president, whose face was as red as a sunset. Signalling his consent to accept the message, the image of Tibus Heth – clad in his military fatigues and body armor – formed at the head of the room.

'President Foiritan,' Tibus announced. 'Before you say

even a single word, allow me to show you the new reality of Caldari Prime . . .'

His image faded to the sight of a Leviathan floating against the backdrop of the planet; the city lights that once shone from its surface all the way to space were now an irregular series of bright orange points, each one an inferno left by Heth's army as it swept across the former Federation world. As the image zoomed closer, perfect squares of city lights surrounded by darkness emerged from the picture.

'This world is ours,' Tibus continued. 'It was taken from us exactly one hundred and ninety years ago by the Gallente Federation. We have returned to take it back.'

The imagery faded to the view of a waving Caldari State flag; then panned back to reveal that it was flying over the city of Arcurio. For as far as the eye could see, Provist soldiers and armored vehicles were patrolling the streets nearby.

'Many Gallenteans died today for the heinous crimes of their great-grandparents,' Tibus continued. 'And while it's true that I was less than cautious in the pursuit of my ambitions, I am not without mercy. Your advisers must have informed you of the strength of my forces here in Luminaire. Gallente Prime – the birth world of your race – is still *untouched*. I could burn that world to ashes, and yet I want no such thing. All I want is our home world – the one you evicted us from. I'm a man of my word: acknowledge the Caldari sovereignty of Caldari Prime, and the killing stops now.'

President Foiritan was visibly trembling.

'What kind of general do you think you are, exposing your flanks for all to see?' he growled. 'You threaten me here, now, after what you've done, and expect me to heed your demands? You have that little faith in what we're capable of, and no respect at all for the restraint we've shown in attempting to deal with you honorably? No, Heth, I think not. You really are a madman. I will not negotiate with a criminal. You've thrown down this gauntlet, and you'd better expect to have it thrown back!'

Tibus was unmoved.

'It's true that Caldari space is open for you to rape, just as Caldari Prime was for you so long ago. You plan to start with Tierijev, because that's easiest for you. Let me show you why you're not going to do that.'

The camera view changed back to an aerial view of the city and the patchwork of light and dark below, then it focused in on a darkened segment. The scene was total darkness at first, but then the greenish-white hue of light amplification equipment revealed what the night was really concealing.

Unremitting panic was evident in the streets. Magnifying to street level, Gallenteans roamed the dark trying to get help and finding none; trams, hovercars, anything that had been moving was stopped dead in its tracks; absolutely none of the luxuries and dire necessities made possible by electricity were available.

Without power, the underpinning of modern civilization itself was absent.

'Look at them all,' Tibus said. 'So many people, young and old, good and evil, rich and poor, all sharing one thing in common: their ethnicity.'

The video suddenly played back recordings of orbital plasma strikes against military targets on the planet; the horrible columns of fire descending from the sky obliterating everything they touched drew gasps from people in the room.

The image zoomed back out to the Caldari dreadnought armada in space.

'Note the damage to *hardened* targets,' Tibus continued. 'Now imagine what those strikes could do to *people*. Every Gallentean in the cities of Tovil and Arcurio has a siege cannon pointing down at them. It's ironic, don't you think? They're all trapped within the districts imposed by your very own declaration of martial law.'

Now the president was staring at a close-up of the dictator, and the cold, unyielding look in his gray eyes.

'Contrary to what you may know of me, I don't care for war, or unnecessary killing,' Tibus said. 'So I'll state this in the clearest possible terms: turn your ships away from my borders, and the bloodshed stops. But so help me, if you so much as undock a starship near Caldari space, I'll rid my home world of every Gallentean on its soil.'

So this is how it ends for us, President Foiritan thought. *The absolute ruination of peace and prosperity; the end of my administration and the enlightened prosperity I worked tirelessly to provide; everything we've accomplished will forever be shadowed by the bane of one Tibus Heth.*

'Do you understand, Mr. President?' he asked, glaring at him. 'We have an agreement?'

This is a war I cannot fight, the president thought. *This is a war that will be won or lost by our capsuleers.*

Unable to voice his agreement, he nodded imperceptibly.

'Good,' Tibus continued. 'Then one more item remains before I deliver this glorious news to the Caldari State. My fleet will begin returning to their ports, as they are not all needed to enforce our agreement here. They *will*, of course, be permitted to transit back the way they came, *unchallenged* by your forces.'

Gallenteans will speak of this humiliation for generations to come, the president thought. *Mine will be a legacy of despair; for time immemorial, I am the fool who lost Caldari Prime.*

'Vice Admiral Ranchel,' he said, staring at his cabinet members one by one as if to cast blame on each of them for this catastrophe. 'Stand down your ships. The Caldari fleet will be allowed to pass.'

There was a long pause before the Federation Navy commander answered.

'If this is how it has to be . . . then yes, sir. Standing down.'

72

+ 00:45:01

Domain Region – Maddam Constellation
The Sarum Prime System – Planet III: Mekhios
300 miles above Xerah

Grand Admiral Sundara knew in his heart that the outcome of this battle would herald a crucial turning point in Amarr's history – one that would redefine the nation after its ancient failure at Vak'Atioth. Cataclysmic fighting was underway over the skies of Mekhios; the two fleets were entangled in brutal close-range slugfests of artillery and laser cannon fire. As frigates, drones, and fighters weaved in and out of the fray, massive warships exchanged blows from such proximity that weapon impacts against enemy hulls were just as damaging to the vessel that fired them; the twisted wrecks and debris of hundreds of ships littered the battlefield, creating lethal collision hazards for the crews and pilots embroiled in combat.

They fought not for their lives, but for their impassioned desire to kill as many of the opposite race as possible. From a great distance, the battle appeared as a nebulous cloud flickering from within as thousands of explosions blossomed throughout the chaos. Towering columns of smoke rising from hellish red blemishes on the planet's surface marked where several warships met their end; their great hulls, even as they broke apart during their fiery descent through the atmosphere, were many times more devastating than orbital bombardments.

Directing his Imperial fleet with deadly precision, the admiral wasn't nearly through filling his cup with Minmatar blood when the miraculous visage of Jamyl Sarum appeared before him.

It was time.

Without hesitation, he ordered his commanders to leave the battlefield at once. Loyal, fervent believers to a man, they did so immediately, knowing that the ascendancy of their queen was about to begin.

As the Amarrian ships disengaged, Admiral Sundara could sense the relief and triumph of his Minmatar adversary. They made no attempt to follow the packs of damaged Imperial vessels deserting the fight; they sought only to resume surface operations to retrieve slaves as quickly as possible.

That strategy was about to cost them dearly.

+ 00:46:59

Genesis Region – Sanctum Constellation
The Yulai System – Inner Circle Tribunal Station

Glaring at his work through the facemask of a survival suit, the CONCORD technician muttered a curse at the screens, cables, and open electronics panels before him. Glancing around the depressurized maintenance corridor near the station's upper tier for a moment, he exhaled forcibly, wishing he had more time to think this through.

'All right, throw 'em on three,' he grumbled, shaking his head. 'One . . . two . . . three!'

The lights inside the corridor dimmed, and the warning meters on his instruments spiked to red.

'Turn it off!' he shouted. 'Off!'

He grimaced as the readings dropped back to normal. But the lights flickered for a few more seconds before stabilizing.

'Fuck me,' he growled, punching the console. 'It's still not enough. Not by a long shot.'

'You have to be kidding,' his earpiece barked back. 'There's nothing left to power off down here!'

The drone AI in his terminal produced figures indicating they were short by almost a terawatt.

'You said the hangar's offline?' he asked, hoping the answer would be different this time.

'Yes! What's next? Life support?' the head foreman asked sarcastically. 'And don't ask us to overload the reactor, because we're not doing it – not without evacuating the station first.'

Rebuilding what the Minmatars had destroyed at CONCORD Bureau Station was impossible, but DED and Inner

Circle engineers hoped that its core functionality – the communication hub supporting the NEOCOM and all the isolated comm channels used exclusively by CONCORD strike forces – could be replaced. The Bureau Station was built to support the array's vast power needs, but the Inner Circle Tribunal Station's power output – now the largest in the system with equipment capable of delivering the proper signal strength – still wasn't enough.

'Then it can't be done,' the technician admitted. 'It's just not possible from here.'

'That's unacceptable,' the head foreman growled. 'Inner Circle people are standing on my shoulders to see how we're doing with this, and they're not going to accept the answer that "it can't be done"!'

'Well, what the hell do you want, for me to melt the whole goddamn station into slag?'

'If you have to, yes!' the head foreman shouted. 'I told you, if we have to kick everyone out of here to get our fleet back in working order, say so! There's a ship graveyard where the Bureau used to be, and speaking on behalf of CONCORD, I'm looking for a little payback!'

The idea hit the technician like a sandbag filled with cement.

'Ships,' he mumbled. 'You said, "ship" . . .'

'Yeah, so what?'

'Well,' the technician mumbled, typing away at the drone AI's terminal. 'A ship generates a *lot* of power . . .'

+ 00:48:20

City of Xerah – Industrial District
Carthum Conglomerate Warehouse Facility

'We're in!' the soldier screamed over the intercom. 'Go!'

The dropship pilot pushed the throttle all the way forward; the craft shuddered as the engines unleashed maximum thrust. Flight indicators on his display turned to green; the master sergeant had secured the ramp doors, and the inner seals were locked for space flight. As the cumbersome craft lifted off the ground, a volley of rockets streaked across his field of view; a moment later, nearby explosions lit up the skies above.

'Thukker Talon Three-Six, go to ballistic pronto,' a gunship escort warned. 'Airborne hostiles inbound, over.'

'Copy,' the pilot acknowledged, toggling the ship's active countermeasures. His two gunship escorts, flying low to mask their position from enemy search radars, disappeared as the spacecraft rose over the Xerah skyline; bright white streaks of anti-aircraft fire were spitting at the sky from different locations all over the city.

What a disaster, the pilot thought, keeping an eye on his altimeter as they soared away from the industrial complex. *It was supposed to be over by now.* Instead, the operation disintegrated into a prolonged, costly fight on the ground, the air, and in space. Listening to the chatter of gunship pilots as they hunted for targets, he glanced at the inventory of his craft's hold: twenty Thukker commandos and almost two hundred slaves recovered from a raid executed through purely improvised means.

Fighting their way into a deceased drop team's objective, they discovered the slaves locked inside an ore transport, caked in soot and begging for Vitoc. Instead, they received a neck injection of Insorum and were all hauled – one by one – outside the facility, where he'd landed his ship under fire to pick them up.

It was one small victory in a campaign that was rampant with defeat. If there was time – and he actually made it back to a dreadnought or carrier intact – he would return to recover more troops – and what few slaves they managed to liberate during this debacle.

Expecting to see more hardships as the dropship broke through the Mekhios atmosphere into space, he instead witnessed a miracle: the Amarrian fleet was retreating. Leaving mangled hulls in its wake, he could see the behemoth Amarrian titan drifting away from the Elder force; the plasma contrails of thousands of thrusters lingered briefly as enemy ships disappeared one by one. As news of the change in fortune spread throughout the comm channels, he accelerated his craft to maximum speed, eager to drop off his cargo and return to the surface.

When the last enemy ship escaped into warp, thirteen Amarrian battleships arrived.

+ 00:49:00

Jamyl Sarum came to her senses within the synthetic reality of the Abbadon's pod capsule.

Vaguely aware that she had suffered another episode, the pod fluid was refreshingly nourishing, lessening the drastic effects of emerging from her alter ego. But now, staring through camera drones at hordes of Minmatar warships looming in the murky haze beyond, the terrifying hopelessness of her plight became apparent.

When the voice spoke, the memory of how she got there returned.

Your adversary awaits, the Other said. *Do you have the courage to smite them? The will to become the Queen of Destiny? The Empress of the Ages? The Goddess of Amarr?*

Fighting to deny its evil existence, she spun her cameras to see who was with her. The twelve Arch Guardians of the Citadel were there, all piloting Apocalypse-class battleships. She could sense that the Minmatar fleet was stunned; that they recognized her return from death and gave pause, astonished that she would appear now, so lightly armed, so alone, so tempting for them to lash out and destroy in the name of avenging untold numbers of the damned in one swift blow . . .

Such weakness. Still not ready to rule an empire.

Jamyl suddenly remembered what her ship was capable of, and of the great danger it posed.

So little faith, even when your immortality is assured! You weak, pathetic coward! Have you learned nothing of your powers?

'Shut up!' she screamed, convulsing in her pod as threat sensors announced that her ship was being targeted by the Minmatar armada. 'Get away from me!'

End yourself, Jamyl, and let me live!

Her anger was supreme; her madness was elemental fury.

'Shut up, goddamn you! *Goddamn you!*'

Yes, feel the rage, and the power and the might and the glory of God! Release me, Jamyl! Release me unto my prey!

No longer in conscious control of her actions, the firing sequence for the Terran superweapon was primed.

+ 00:49:05

'Kill her!'

The dropship pilot was barely aware he said the words aloud. But his sentiment was felt by every other Minmatar witnessing the event. The entire operation had ceased in its tracks; ships returning with holds full of liberated slaves delayed entering the hangar bays of dreadnoughts as the queen of darkness showed herself on the battlefield; Jamyl Sarum had returned from the grave.

'*Kill her!*' he shouted this time, beholding the source of Minmatar misery and wanting desperately, with near uncontrollable malice, to act on his hatred.

But then her ship began to glow in an eerie whitish hue; bolts of lightning encircled the entire vessel from bow to stern as it erupted into a blinding light.

The pilot swore he heard the shrieking laughter of a woman.

A blue-white lightning lashed out from the radiance, striking the Ragnarok titan and then arcing like a spreading plague to every other ship in the fleet. Blinded by the brilliant flash, the pilot wrenched the control stick backward, pulling his craft away from the towering capital ship ahead. Horrified to the core of his soul, he watched the bolt as it leapt from ship to ship; he saw the bubble auras of shields coruscate from white to fiery red as their defenses turned inward, directing their repulsive force toward the very hulls they were designed to protect; most shattered instantly while others were left hopelessly crippled.

Before the pilot's eyes, the great Ragnarok began to break apart; the cries of a million Minmatars filled the comm channels as panic, despair, and death brought doom to the Elder task force. Sarum's fleet raked their deadly beams of fire from ship to ship like soulless executioners, systematically destroying everything that survived the apocalyptic attack.

As the bolt lashed out toward him, the pilot cursed at God with every shred of hate in his soul.

+ 00:49:12

All across the burning city of Xerah, the fighting ceased as a brilliant flash illuminated the sky. A great aurora spread across the heavens, and the Thukker infantrymen lost all hope as their commlinks went dead and the TACNET dropped offline.

In that moment, each man understood that they were doomed.

These soldiers, wielding weapons that until now were aimed at the enemy, looked at one another in horror while the triumphant cheers of the Amarrian city filled the air. They knew what had to be done.

The few slaves in their midst, waiting for dropships that would never return, would die to Minmatar bullets first. If there was any justice left in the universe, rounds fired after that would end the lives of some Paladins next.

But every soldier would make sure to leave one bullet for himself.

73

The Kor-Azor Region – Geben Constellation

Across the hundreds of battlefields strewn over the cityscapes, mines, and fields of the Kor-Azor worlds, Minmatar soldiers fighting for the Elder Task Force received emergency orders which made them all feel as if they were stabbed in the heart.

Displayed prominently on the TACNET of every combatant, a five-minute timer began counting backward. Once it reached zero, the fleet was going to withdraw from Amarrian space in a full-fledged retreat back to the Sanctuaries. It was just enough time – assuming everyone was where they were supposed to be – to stop what they were doing and get onboard a jump-capable ship.

The instructions were clear in pointing out that there would be no exceptions once time ran out.

Nowhere was this more urgent than to those fighting amidst the rubble on countless battlegrounds as bewildered slaves were herded onto idling dropships. The soldiers had trained for this contingency, specifically to abandon all current objectives at a moment's notice, no matter how close they were to completing them. But in many cases, the human touch – the inherent compassion evident in the bond between Minmatars and the liberation of fellow Minmatars from oppression – was a powerful deterrent.

The orders brought home the grim realization that there just wasn't enough time to rescue them all. Although they may have saved millions, for those left behind, life would become far worse than before.

As Elder dropships began rising over the worlds of Doriam Kor-Azor, dread began filling the hearts of every Minmatar in the fleet, especially as they watched the ground fade away and become obscured with clouds.

None of them knew why the order was given, or that the entirety of the Sarum Theater Task Force had been erased from existence.

Domain Region – Maddam Constellation
The Sarum Prime System – Planet III: Mekhios
300 miles above Xerah

The voice of Grand Admiral Sundara called out from the distance, from the blackness, from the hell that had become her life.

'My lady, all you all right?'

The inky haze of the space outside her ship – adrift and glimmering with bursts of electrostatic energy along its grievously damaged hull – flickered back into view.

'Please, say something!'

Unlike the attack on the Blood Raiders, this detonation had damaged both her physical self and the ship. Without looking, she could already sense that every crewmember onboard was dead.

'If you can hear me, eject!' he pleaded. 'Eject now, and we'll bring you in!'

Across from her ship was a wasteland of death; smoldering, tumbling wrecks of a thousand ships surrounded by the great tombs of gutted capital ships and the black, charred mausoleum of the Ragnarok.

My God, did I do this? she asked, bracing for the Other

to answer. But she heard only silence, and then became aware of the Imperial fleet arranged behind her, and of the approaching repair ships.

Pain wracked every fiber of her body.

'No,' she stammered, barely able to concentrate. 'Keep your ships away.'

'We can't leave you like this!' the admiral pleaded. 'At least let us take you aboard, and you can lead from here!'

Nearly every system on the Abbadon was inoperable. Only the propulsion systems remained intact, and she wished that it would explode and end her cursed existence.

'Set course for Kor-Azor Region, Admiral,' she whispered, aligning her battered vessel for warp. 'The enemy is not yet vanquished . . .'

Great Wildlands Region – T-W4L3 Constellation System H9S-WC: The Elder Sanctuaries

'Karin . . .'

The Republic prime minister looked up from reading and saw her long-time political archenemy standing in the doorway.

'Are you all right?' Maleatu asked, finding his way into a seat.

She glared at his clouded gray eyes and found herself numb to the hostile relationship they had before. There was nothing left for her to say, and she was certain he understood that.

'I am deeply sorry about what happened,' he said. 'I wish we could have acted sooner.'

The memory of being violated rushed back, but she didn't try to push it away. Instead, she embraced it, accepting that she was no longer the woman she was before.

'I never thanked you for looking after me,' she said coldly.

The old man turned his unfocused stare toward the ground.

'I may have been unkind to you, Karin, but I'm no savage.'

'Of course you're not,' she said. 'No savage that I know wears a Khumaak on his back.'

With a grunt, he nodded, accepting the jab from her. 'It's finished now, Karin. The Elder's purge of the Republic is complete.'

'Is it?' she asked. 'Then I suppose I'll mop the blood of my adversaries from the halls of Parliament when I return.'

Ameline and Keitan Yun appeared in the doorway; both appeared grave.

'The Elders invasion just suffered a huge setback,' Maleatu continued. 'Jamyl Sarum has returned.'

'What?'

'She is armed with a weapon that . . .'

He stopped himself before continuing.

'It's something we cannot defend against. Our forces at Sarum Prime suffered unspeakable casualties.'

'Cannot defend against?' Anger began to bubble in her heart. 'What does that mean for the others?'

'They're returning from the battlefield.'

Karin stood up. 'Have they completed their mission?'

'They fell short of the numbers they had hoped to liberate, but—'

'Was it worth it, Maleatu?' she demanded. 'All those people killed during this . . .'

Maleatu slammed the butt of his walking cane on the floor. 'Why don't you ask the ones they saved?'

'No,' she fumed. 'I'll ask the ones they left *behind*.'

'Those are the risks we took—'

'You *assumed* risks that weren't yours to take,' she frothed. 'That was always the burden of *elected* leaders, in which a populace confers authority to make such decisions on their behalf!'

'The Elders have the bloodlines of all seven tribes in their midst now, Karin. That alone justified the risks and the cost,' Maleatu said. 'It restores the hope that we can return to what we once were. Every Minmatar aspires to that.'

'Oh?' she mocked. 'What did the Elders plan to do with all those lacking such aspirations? Tell me, Maleatu: what happens if Sarum turns that weapon on us? Will the Elders defend the Minmatars who can't accompany them to their hidden Utopia?'

'Karin, it's time,' Keitan interrupted. 'There's a ship waiting to take you back.'

'Take me back to what?' she growled. 'My smoldering Republic? Very well, Ambassador – or should I say, *Adviser* Yun. Ameline will be accompanying us?'

'Yes,' Keitan answered. 'She'll be heading your security detail, which will follow you everywhere you go for as long as you live.'

'As long as I live?' she laughed. 'How long will that be with Jamyl Sarum lurking at the gates?'

'The capsuleers will guard the gates from now on,' Maleatu said. 'They won't let the Republic fall.'

'That's a bold assumption,' she hissed. 'So what exactly are your plans now? Where will you be when the wrath of Sarum reaches all the way to Matar?'

'I'm staying here,' he answered, handing her a signed document. 'You sacked me, but here's a resignation letter anyway. There will be elections among the Brutors for someone to replace me.'

'Fine,' she said, reaching out and taking the document. 'Then I guess this is good-bye, Maleatu.'

He rose to his feet, offering a hand. 'If you ever need anything—'

She walked past him, ignoring his outstretched hand.

'—I know I never will, Maleatu. And I certainly wouldn't ask you if I did.'

+ 00:55:46

The Kor-Azor Region – Gebem Constellation
The Kor-Azor Prime System

Now numbering in the thousands, the Imperial Navy fleet reached the Kor-Azor Prime System with Jamyl Sarum and Admiral Sundara leading their triumphant charge. News was spreading throughout the Empire of her miraculous return and the deliverance of Mekhios from evil; the halls of cathedrals were packed with worshippers, even in cities ravaged by the Minmatar attack. As bell towers rang and congregations praised the glory of the Almighty, the Amarrian fleet reached the battlefield just as the Elder Task Force had committed to leaving.

With their hulls turned away, the Amarrians shot them in the backs as they fled, and those Minmatar soldiers who allowed their humanity to stand in the way of the Elder's orders to retreat were now perishing within sight of their only way home.

To preserve everything that had been gained, and to justify the sacrifices made by so many, escaping the wrath of Sarum's deadly super-weapon was all that mattered.

Genesis Region – Sanctum Constellation
The Yulai System – Inner Circle Tribunal Station

'Wow,' the technician admitted. 'That was quick.'

Surrounding the station were several dozen CONCORD and DED warships; more than a hundred had already entered the hangar bay. They represented just a fraction of the total that were available to resume the work of restoring New Eden to order.

'Those battleships are good for over ten thousand megawatts each,' the head foreman announced. 'Transfer lines are already tapped into the mains. You'll be drawing from all of them at once, so make sure you know what you're fucking doing.'

'Thanks,' the technician muttered, moving away from the viewport back toward his instruments. The AI was already scanning the new connections into its algorithms, concluding that a full powerup was possible, but not assured.

'I can't promise anything,' he warned, tapping away. 'This has never been done before.'

'We never imagined we'd need to,' the foreman conceded. 'But no matter – it's in your hands now. Make it work!'

They had enough power for the startup – the question was whether or not they could sustain it. If nothing else, he hoped they had enough to carry the absolute minimum broadcast strength needed to coordinate CONCORD warships in the field.

'All right,' the tech said, rubbing his gloved hands together. 'On three, okay—'

'To hell with three,' the foreman said. 'I'm throwing it right *now* . . .'

+ 01:07:20

Heimatar Region – Hed Constellation
The Vard System – Ezzara Stargate

The border was disturbingly quiet.

It had been eerie – if not nerve-wracking – to be sitting beside a stargate that bordered an Empire whose fanatical minions could come crashing through at any moment. Even worse, there was profound guilt that right now, at this very moment, fellow Minmatars were making the ultimate sacrifice in the name of freeing themselves from those very same zealots.

But at what cost, she lamented. *What terrible cost.*

As much as the spiritual warrior in her wanted desperately to be part of what the Elders were trying to accomplish, her rational side was furious with them. Whether compelled for noble reasons or not, this undertaking was something that should have been for all Minmatars to decide. By not including the Republic in their plans, the Elders had placed the lives of countless more people in jeopardy than they hoped to save.

But then she realized the lunacy of her reasoning. Even now, with thousands of Republic warships amassed along the border of their bitter adversary, she couldn't be certain of how they'd respond to her orders. She questioned their loyalty to the point where it wouldn't surprise her if they abandoned their assignments the moment the fighting began.

That was emblematic of the Republic's failure. Even if Karin Midular was the hawk that so many wished she would become, someone would still object to her ambitions. We would never convince ourselves or agree on anything to the scale that demanded a feat so impossible as invading an Empire to recover the pride of our race.

And besides, what difference would it have made had their fumbling Republic even reached consensus? she thought. *CONCORD would stand in the way regardless.*

It was unity that separated the Elders from the Republic – unity of cause, spirit, and mind. But the risk of unity was when it was forged for the wrong purpose. It was usually only in hindsight, when the damage was already done, that its dangers became clear enough for all to see. Admiral Neko had no doubt that when Amarr unleashed the full extent of its retaliatory wrath against the Republic, the fault of Minmatar unity and the selfishness of the Elder's actions would be apparent.

Suddenly, the instruments projected in her vision flickered; the startup sequence of the NEOCOM scrolled past her view. Every ship captain in the fleet was seeing the same broadcast, including a priority notification from CONCORD:

TO THE MILITARY FORCES OF ALL NATION-STATE MEMBERS OF THE CONCORD BUREAU ASSEMBLY:
CEASE ALL NON-SANCTIONED COMBAT OPERATIONS IMMEDIATELY. FAILURE TO COMPLY WITH THIS MANDATE IS PUNISHABLE WITH DEADLY FORCE. DED AND CONCORD COUNTERTHREAT DEPLOYMENT CAPABILITIES HAVE BEEN RESTORED. REPEAT: CEASE ALL COMBAT OPERATIONS AND FALL BACK TO RECOGNIZED TERRITORIAL BOUNDARIES.

TRAVEL ADVISORY – THREAT LEVEL CRITICAL:
MERCENARIES POSING AS MINMATAR REPUBLIC AND/OR THUKKER WARSHIPS HAVE BEEN SPOTTED NEAR THE MINMATAR/AMMATAR AND MINMATAR/AMARR BORDERS. THIS GROUP IS EXTREMELY DANGEROUS AND WILL ATTACK WITHOUT PROVOCATION. CAPABLE FORCES ARE ENCOURAGED TO ENGAGE WITH EXTREME PREJUDICE. THESE MERCENARIES ARE CHARGED WITH CRIMES AGAINST HU-

MANITY. EACH CONFIRMED KILL WILL BE COMPENSATED BY UP TO 10 MILLION CREDITS EACH, AND 100 MILLION IF CAPTAINS ARE BROUGHT IN ALIVE.

The stargate suddenly became active, drawing her attention away from the CONCORD message. Bracing herself for combat, she focused on the threat sensors of her display.

A Hurricane-class battlecruiser emerged. It was battered and scarred; as it turned away from the gate, a stream of debris trailed off its hull. Within seconds, another Elder warship appeared; and then a third.

The three Elder ships, all badly damaged, paused before the Minmatar fleet assembled before them, as if begging them to pass.

A Republic Fleet commander patrolling alongside her spoke first.

'Admiral . . . should we engage?'

Staring at the Elder vessels, her heart filled with pride, sadness, anger, and hope.

'No,' she said. 'Let them pass. All of them.'

'Yes, Admiral,' the commander said approvingly. More ships arrived through the gate; soon cynosural fields formed around them, and the mighty capital ships of the fleet emerged.

As they warped away, Admiral Neko prayed that their holds were filled with liberated slaves, and that Jamyl Sarum would heed CONCORD's warning not to cross the line.

Domain Region – Throne Worlds Constellation
The Amarr System – Planet Oris
Emperor Family Academy Station

Options, Chamberlain Karsoth thought. *It's always important to have options.*

No longer clothed in holy garments, he was now dressed as an overlord: a dark cloak was draped over his massive frame, and a pronounced hood covered half of his face as he lumbered down the long, dark concourse. Far from the cathedral where he presided over the Empire, this was the 'Merchants and Appropriations' level, and unlike the hangar approach he was accustomed to, this route had neither religious pageantry nor breathtaking views of the station's vast promenades.

Instead, these commerce chambers were the auction grounds for Amarrian goods and services, the centerpiece of which was slaves. Traders haggled over the drugged specimens like cattle, testing for both muscle and mental competence for whatever task it was they sought them for. Vitoc canisters and slave-control merchandise lined the shops of merchants; glaive collars, stun cuffs, Z-sticks, labor implants, reconditioning software, and every other means of facilitating human incarceration were for sale amongst the vendors. Huddled groups of Minmatar slaves with blank expressions followed overlords from one recruitment desk to the next, behind which were lines of prospectors seeking slaves for various labor projects across the Empire.

A seamless merge into this stratum of Amarrian society was complicated only by his great stature; he was much taller than everyone around him. Yet even with the audible strain of his implants carrying most of his weight, he was fairly unremarkable in this group. This crowd was rife with cybernetically augmented individuals of all kinds, and his own modifications weren't nearly as exotic or masochistic as the others he saw milling around him.

The truth was that he felt more at home here, amongst the scoundrels and villains and junkies than he ever would presiding over Paladins and priests. Because, he knew, this was the real face of humanity, and not the hypocrisy of organized religion which, until now, he had benefited handsomely from.

Murmurs of Sarum's return dominated the conversations around him, but her name wasn't spoken of in enthusiastic terms. These denizens of commerce weren't the most pious of individuals, and with Sarum renowned for her zealotry, her return would likely bring about reform that could undo the welcome changes brought by Chamberlain Karsoth. He had heard his name mentioned numerous times already, and in favorable terms for the most part – except for the usual jabs about his ridiculous weight and fiery sermons.

Surrounded by two dozen of his favorite 'pets' – slaves that he intended to take with him – he made his way to the courier desks. Pilots of all backgrounds resided there, among them some capsuleers. Vendors and suppliers were bidding on transport contracts, negotiating fees based on shipping routes and cargo. Karsoth knew who the more popular pilots were; they were the ones who bragged about dodging customs checkpoints with laughable ease, or boasted of their ability to run through the most dangerous regions of space with regular success.

He made a point of avoiding them, and instead found exactly what he was looking for in a nondescript loner: a bright-eyed but inexperienced capsuleer having a difficult time securing a contract for any kind of work.

Karsoth marched his entire entourage up to him. Looking up, the pilot was obviously startled by his size, but elated that anyone had bothered talking to him at all.

'How much would you charge to transport me and my property here to the Kulu System?'

'Really?' The pilot's eyes lit up. 'Great! Umm, let's see, that's eight jumps . . .' He counted all the slaves standing around him. 'Twenty-five passengers . . . any other cargo?'

'Besides the clothes on my back and a fair supply of Vitoc, no.'

'Good, then space shouldn't be too much of a problem,' he said, grabbing his datapad. 'How about one hundred thousand?'

'I'll tell you what,' Karsoth said. 'If we can leave within the next five minutes, I'll give you twice that.'

'*Two* hundred thousand! Well yes sir, I believe we can do that!' the pilot exclaimed, jumping up to extend his hand. Karsoth, of course, wouldn't touch it. 'It's an Impairor-class frigate . . . might be a little cramped in there.'

'Not at all.' Karsoth smiled, pulling one of his slaves closer to him. 'That's how I prefer it.'

'Right,' the pilot muttered. 'Well, it's in docking bay 29-Gamma, this level. Ship's called the *Glory Lore*!'

'Very well,' Karsoth said. 'We're on our way.'

As the pilot hurried away to the pod gantries, Karsoth squeezed the pet in his grasp. Like him, all the slaves were dressed in cloaks that obscured their faces, and obediently followed his orders in a Vitoc-induced state of bliss.

But his newest favorite wasn't Minmatar at all.

Camoul Hinda, drugged out of her mind, could only do exactly what her new master demanded. And Karsoth would demand much in the next days and weeks, or however long it took for him to lose interest in violating her again and again. For now at least, she would help him pass the time as he escaped from the Amarr Empire one jump at a time – anonymously, and forever hunted.

Devoid Region – Semou Constellation
The Ezzara System – Vard Stargate

'Should we follow them, my lady?'

Vaguely aware of the CONCORD warships now standing between Amarr and the Minmatar Republic, the voice of Grand Admiral Sundara seemed even more distant than before, and the vigor in his voice was lost to the despair corrupting her body and soul.

For her, the battle that routed Minmatar forces as they fled across the border was as opaque to her as a dream; she played no active role in its execution, yet her presence alone was the source of majestic inspiration to the Imperial Navy. The sheer reverence and devotion of these strangers amazed her; thousands of ships, crewed by thousands of people, and every single one of them ready to lay down their life for her. With a path of destruction following her from the moment she returned to the Amarr Empire, Jamyl Sarum finally understood the magnitude of her responsibility.

If Falek Grange had coached her to expect such loyalty from the Empire before her death, she felt no such obsession now. In the minds of devout Amarrians, she was back from the dead to lead them to a promised land, to a cultural and spiritual pinnacle that she herself was wholly unfamiliar with and absolutely loath to pursue, if for no other reason than she felt no such passion in her own heart, and because the Other – that despicable, malignant creature that infested her life – did.

Those souls manning the CONCORD warships before her were defiantly the opposite of those inside the gold-tinted hulls of the Imperial Navy, and every bit as committed to their own duties. Silently, she welcomed them as saviors preventing an apocalyptic conflict from escalating. The Other wanted to lash out and destroy them, as she would every other obstacle in their path to the Republic's home worlds. But for now, Jamyl could control her. She realized now that it was the weakened physical state of her own body which kept the Other away, which was bound to the reality that it needed Jamyl to survive.

And so the answer to the question posed by Grand Admiral Sundara – in whom she saw, with her newfound abilities, a devout, gifted, and loyal man – was clear to her.

'No,' she answered, turning her damaged ship slowly away from the Vard Stargate. 'Let them escape with their bounty. When the time is right, we shall return.'

'As you wish,' the admiral said. 'To where then, Your Majesty?'

'To the Amarr System,' she said weakly. 'So that I may claim what you and your Paladins have given me.'

Domain Region – Sosarir Constellation
The Nererut System – Chemal Tech Station

With the exception of Jamyl Sarum and Aritcio Kor-Azor, the royal heirs to the Amarrian throne sat before each other for the first time in years, and their uncomfortable demeanors reflected the ancient rivalry between their families and the perilous nature of these extraordinary times.

Yoshin Ardishapur glared at the religious adviser sitting in place of Kor-Azor.

'Are you authorized to speak for your crippled master?' he hissed.

'I am,' the adviser said. 'I'll be sure to pass along your well wishes.'

'And I'm sure he's sane enough to understand them, just as he's capable of understanding that half of his worlds have been overrun by slaves!'

'Enough!' Uriam Kador snapped. 'We're here because Jamyl Sarum is back, and she's driven the Minmatars from our space. Needless to say, we all have a stake in whether or not she makes a bid for power!'

'Her presence defiles our culture,' Yonis scoffed. 'Clearly, she is cloned, and has forsaken her right to the throne, let alone an honorable existence.'

'She is beloved by the people,' Catiz Tash-Murkon warned. 'And not just in her own House. Amarrians everywhere see her return as the fulfilment of a prophecy.'

'She also has the loyalty of the Imperial Navy,' Uriam added. 'There isn't a Paladin in all Amarr who wouldn't die for her.'

'Unholy sacrilege,' Yonis scoffed. 'If anything, her return renews calls for Succession Trials to select a proper emperor immediately, just as the Scriptures demand!'

'Since when have you renewed such interest in killing yourself?' Catiz mocked. 'Is it divine imperative that makes you willing to play dice with your own life? Or is it more *worldly* ambitions that fuel your devotion?'

'Careful, Catiz,' Uriam said, noting the look of fury on the face of Yonis. 'If we have trials, he could be emperor one day. As could I, or you, or even the deranged invalid that is Aritcio Kor-Azor. None of us can know for sure – unless we make assurances ourselves.'

'What in God's name are you talking about?' Yonis growled.

'Since you asked,' Uriam smiled, 'I propose that we renounce the Chamberlain's right to call for Trials, and declare absolute loyalty to Jamyl Sarum,' he said, glaring at Kor-Azor's adviser, who didn't make a sound.

'No!' Yonis shouted. 'If we do that, we forfeit our right to ever lay claim to the throne again! We would be abolishing a tradition that has been fundamental to our heritage since—'

'—since the days when we were hunting animals with sharp sticks,' Catiz quipped. 'This is a new age, one that will be ruled by empyreans. The capsuleers and their gift of immortality govern the physical world now, not the primitive traditions of the ancients.'

'You blaspheme!' Yonis exclaimed. 'It isn't your place to—'

'Spare us the religious arguments,' Uriam said. 'You're not exactly a convincing Paladin. We each have our own kingdoms to rule, and as such, a great deal to lose. Just the same, it hasn't exactly been *beneficial* to be emperor of late, has it?'

'I won't tolerate departure from tradition,' Yonis growled, standing up. 'And I certainly won't declare loyalty to Jamyl Sarum!'

'Then I will,' Catiz said.

'As will I,' said Uriam. Everyone stared at Kor-Azor's adviser, who remained quiet.

'Well?' Yonis demanded. 'What say you, woman?'

The religious adviser turned her piercing eyes toward the much older heir.

'Before he was justly mutilated as punishment for his many indiscretions,' she started, 'he was a man who would go to great lengths to protect his rule. His greed was insatiable, and his egotistical desire to preserve his prestige as an heir knew no bounds whatsoever. I see much of him in all of you. If I ruled on how he once was – before he was deprived of his flesh and sanity – he would agree to this, despite my emphatic warning that he treasons against God himself by doing so.'

'Then we'll proceed by virtue of a three to one majority,' Uriam said proudly. 'Yonis, your sanctimonious views disappoint me. I expected more honesty from you.'

'You'll live to regret those words,' Yonis growled.

'Will I?' Uriam sneered. 'Not if Jamyl learns of your objections to her rule.'

That shut the man up and drew a glare.

'Then our loyalty to Sarum is unanimous,' Catiz said. '*If* she sees fit to rewrite tradition in the ways of the new order, then we will – including you, Yonis – concede to her rule over our worlds. Besides . . . with the support of all Amarr behind her now, for God's sake, we would look all the worse if she had to demand our loyalty *or* the throne.'

'Yes, better to offer it now, and be accepted by the masses that rule over *us*,' Uriam agreed. He glanced at the religious adviser, who returned his stare with fire in her eyes.

'May the esteemed Kor-Azor heir remind you of what happens when you fail to recognize that, Yonis.'

Domain Region – Throne Worlds Constellation
The Amarr System – Planet Oris
Emperor Family Academy Station

Illuminated by the radiance of Amarr's orange-gold sun, Marius sat alone in the private cabin of an Imperial warship as it approached the Emperor Station. Resting across from him were the garments he was expected to wear upon his reintroduction to the royal lifestyle of his past: the tunic of a prestigious Holder in Amarrian society and as a Justice of the Theology Council.

The sight of them made him hate himself even more.

He preferred the miserable life aboard the *Retford*, even if the bulk of his memories were more vicious than kind. On that tiny vessel there persisted rays of hope; subtle clues that meaning could be wrought from this new existence. For one, there was Gable's innate compassion and desire to heal others. Then there was Jonas; whatever his motives for overruling the wishes of his crew to rescue him, he had in truth saved his life. For the first time, determining if that life was worth living was up to him alone.

He owed it to Gear, whom he missed with all his heart, to make the most of this chance.

The irony of his memory was that the boy was like a father figure to him. Where Marius could have preached endlessly about starships and technology, it was Gear who had demonstrated the human tenets of courage, kindness, and perseverance.

Marius knew what kind of man he wanted to be because of a Minmatar child. Yet from this point on, he would be immersed in a culture that saw fit to persecute and enslave his kind.

His was a heavy burden to bear: a past that he abhorred, a place in a society that wasn't his own, and a reality in which he was a fallen angel amongst a legion of empyreans whose age was only now beginning.

It was during this revelation when her voice found him again:

Falek . . .

Composing himself, he glanced up and saw the great station's hangar approaching; Jamyl Sarum's wounded Abbadon was just ahead, surrounded by a great procession of Imperial warships. But he could sense her pain; he could feel the burns and lacerations in her skin, and even more chillingly, the agonizing torment in her soul.

'Claiming your destiny now, are you?' he breathed.

Like yours, not the one of my choosing.

'Please,' he said. 'Leave me be. I'm not the person you remember, and I don't know who you are.'

Falek . . . the monster that you once were is inside of me now . . . you're the one who put it there.

Marius buried his head in his hands.

Without you, there will be only the believers of a spiteful god that know only Amarr supremacy. Please, Falek, stand by my side, and we'll find our way through this darkness together.

'You will be an empress, adored by trillions, and you can keep me at your side against my will,' Marius breathed, squinting through tears at the irradiance of golden hulls shining into the room. 'But from now until your end, you will always, always be alone.'

75

Genesis Region – EVE Constellation
The New Eden System
30 Light Years from Point Genesis

Far from the battlefields where the last cries of conquerors and the vanquished carried across the Empires, a Jovian scientist was breathing his last.

He was the last living creature aboard a ship that was hurled through Point Genesis, which – contrary to Empire lore – was not at all what it seemed. If the Jovians could feel hope the way Marius did – indeed, the way all humans should – then the hope of an entire race was dying along with him.

His final mission complete, he crawled past the corpses of those who anguished until the end, laboring toward the pulsing light streaming through a corridor viewport illuminating the macabre tomb within. Gasping in agony against the base of its frame, the scientist ran his pale, wet hands over the smooth, glass-like texture of his face, staring into the black orbs of those Joves who had perished before him.

The Eidolon-class battleship upon which he suffered – an enigmatic vessel universally feared for its great power – was little more than a mutilated carcass. Drifting helplessly in the currents of space, great chasms were gashed into her hull; the ribs of her structure were exposed in several places throughout. She was as dismembered as the vessel could structurally withstand without breaking apart.

It was as if the Eidolon had been tortured to death.

Struggling to raise himself above the frame, the scientist wanted to feel despair. But instead, he felt nothing – except for physical pain. Emotions, weeded out of the Jove's genetics through countless generations of progressive bio-engineering, would have given meaning to the sacrifice that this particular ship had made.

It would have signified that the Jovians still possessed their humanity.

The stream of light intensified; its pulsing rhythm accelerated, alternating from light to dark so quickly that motion inside the corridor passed by in strobes.

Turning to face the swirling magnificence of EVE, the scientist saw that she had grown angry; deadly bolts of energy that had been travelling for years soared from her womb, warning that the end of his life was near.

The radiation was searing, the brightness overwhelming; the Jovian tried to shield his eyes as EVE lashed out and engulfed the Eidolon in a violent fury.

ABOUT THE AUTHOR

Tony Gonzales was born in Jersey City, New Jersey, in 1973. He graduated from the Richard Stockton College of New Jersey in 1995 with a B.A. in political science and has an M.B.A. from Rutgers University. He is an intellectual property development manager for CCP Games in Reykjavik, Iceland, and is the author of two EVE Online novellas, "Ruthless" and "Theodicy." This is his first published work.